IN LOVE. . . .

Madelaina was in love as she'd never before experienced it. Tolomeo slowly removed her clothing, which she permitted without protest, without shame. When she was completely naked, he picked up her sun-kissed body in his powerful arms and walked with her into the crystal pool, where he kissed her, gently at first, then with increasing fervor. . . .

Her head fell back; her dark hair fanned on the water's surface like wisps of black lace; her neck, a graceful curve of ivory satin, reflected in the moonlight. Her body grew electric, sparking at every pulse point, and she clung to him breathlessly. "I love you," she said almost against her will. "I love you. Sweet, sweet Jesus!" she exclaimed. "Never have I experienced such emotion, such love! Speak the word, Tolomeo, and I shall remain with you until my last dying breath."

Tolomeo heaved her up out of the water and carried her to the mossy embankment, where he lay her clinging body on a slightly rounded knoll. He kissed her lightly with open, wet, inviting lips. His hands artfully caressed her body until it quivered like a field of heather in a light wind. . . .

Time had no meaning. She couldn't begin to estimate how long they'd been together, making love, fulfilling the other's _____ *until she saw a rosy hue i* _____ *predawn lights.*

Madelaina

by
Michaela Morgan

PINNACLE BOOKS   LOS ANGELES

For
Jim and Roz Schiros
With *Love* and *Devotion*

MADELAINA

Copyright © 1977 by Gloria Vitanza Basile

An original Pinnacle Books edition, published for the first time anywhere.

ISBN: 0-523-40151-5

First printing, October 1977

Cover illustration by Lou Marchetti

Printed in the United States of America

PINNACLE BOOKS, INC.
One Century Plaza
2029 Century Park East
Los Angeles, California 90067

Book One

The Mozambique

Chapter 1

Spain, 1909

Madelaina Obregon awakened this morning prepared for what she expected would be the most exciting day of her young life. Never did she dream that by nightfall she'd be a changed woman ... or that she might never learn of the circumstances that brought about the changes.

A burst of bright sunshine spread vast cheer over the hills of Sanlucar de Barramedas. The Spanish countryside had never looked as colorful and appealing to her. Throngs of gaily dressed people had milled excitedly in and about the ancient city for days, having traveled from the nearby villages and hill country to this mecca just to witness the skilled perfection of Joselito Barrancas, the finest matador in all Spain.

Time passed swiftly on this day, and Madelaina had hardly enough time to see all that her eager, impressionable eyes wanted to devour. She'd arrived the day before in the company of her uncle, Don Diego Obregon, Don Felipe Cortez, and his son Armando Cortez, her truest friend.

Now, finally, they were at the Plaza de Toros, seated in their private box witnessing the colorful pageantry of the *corrida*. Leaning forward in her seat, her eyes feasting on the spectacular pomp and ceremony, Madelaina felt as if her heart would burst with excitement. Then, suddenly, the arena was cleared as the rumbling sounds of kettledrums echoed throughout the ring and a lone trumpeter held up his horn to sound the prelude of the contest between man and beast. All heads turned expectantly, their voices subdued as the sound of thun-

3

dering hooves seemed to shatter the earth around them. Two thousand pounds of black dynamite came sliding down the shoot and crashing through the gate only to come to a full halt when the glaring sun blinded the bull. Clouds of gray dust swirled all around him at the sudden stop, and el toro tossed his powerful head to the right and left until he caught sight of his enemy. A short distance away, in a glittering suit of gold embroidery, Joselito Barrancas, stood in a formidable pose, eyeing *his* enemy before he moved in to divert the beast.

Then—like all exciting things must—the *corrida* came to an end. Madelaina, a true *aficionada* still saturated with youth's exuberance, glanced about the dispersing crowd eager to locate the young man responsible for this most marvelous day in her life—Manuelito Perez.

She craned her neck and stretched her small, lithe form to see over the heads of the endless hordes. Don Diego and Don Cortez, both dressed in the elegant black suits of wealthy *hacendados*, were engaged in animated conversation with ring officials. She could hear them reconstruct the *corrida* play by play, raving over the merits of Joselito Barrancas. She laughed when they appeared more ebullient over the performances of the fierce and brave bulls, for these had been the bulls from their ranches. Both *gachupíns* were breeders of the formidable Concha bulls from Las Marismas, not far from Sanlucar.

Observing Madelaina from a short distance, with a frown of annoyance on his handsome face, Armando Cortez simultaneously gave passing *señoritas* a careful once-over with roving eyes as he fingered the lapels of his well-cut suit with its flared trousers, bolero jacket, and white silk ruffled shirt. He stood braced in the posture of the proud, haughty *gachupín*, unmistakably the mark of a Spanish *hacendado*. He removed a heavy gold watch from his vest pocket, glanced at it briefly, and slipped it back into place. Tapping the toe of his left boot impatiently against the plank floor, he lit a

4

thin, brown *cigarro* with a *diablo* struck against the wooden seat nearby. He could feel the rising excitement as visions of the next several hours filled him with eager anticipation.

Madelaina wouldn't back out now—not now. She'd promised. She wasn't the kind to break a promise, he told himself. By the look on her pretty but anxious face, he supposed she was looking for Manuelito. Damn! If that *peón* wasn't such a good friend he'd have put him in his place long ago. Going around with calf eyes, lovesick over Madelaina! But without Manuelito's help this day might have never come to pass—at least not so soon. Madelaina, such a child in matters of the heart, hadn't sat still long enough for him to make overtures to her.

Once again Armando's attention was taken by the pretty young girls descending from an upper level in the Plaza. With a flourishing sweep, he whipped off his black, flat-crowned sombrero and bowed to them in the manner of a gallant. For a few moments he attended to the social amenities of his class.

Madelaina, still glancing about in all directions, tossed her head jauntily and shrugged impatiently. Where could Manuelito have gone to? Why hadn't he remained as he'd promised? She paused to straighten the jacket of her fitted traveling suit and reluctantly removed the bloodred rose from behind her ear where she'd tucked it when Manuelito gave it to her earlier. She began to twirl the blossom in her fingers as her vibrant brown eyes flickered in rising annoyance. She tapped the toe of her right slipper in total vexation. Manuelito was nowhere. He had vanished. *Very well, Señor Matador, spoil the best day of my life by being petulant and surly. See if I care!*

She felt uncomfortable in this new hair style which made her look so grown-up. Even Armando's eyes had widened with desire when he caught sight of her dressed like this. Her thick, coal black hair, waist length and usually hanging free, had been lifted off her neck and dressed into two satiny coils. Even the suit to

5

her was a farce. She'd have been more content to wear her *matadora* suit: men's trousers, shirt and bolero, boots, and a flat-crowned sombrero.

Madelaina, not about to jeopardize this very special day in her life by getting into a skirmish with her aunt Doña Louisa over suitable wearing apparel for a young woman of her social stature, had submitted to the older woman's overbearing manner without contest.

It wasn't easy for Madelaina to submit to maternal supervision, and she was constantly at odds with her aunt. Her formative years had been spent under the haphazard guidance of her father, General Alvaro Obregon, who'd allowed her to roam the forts of Mexico where he was stationed, under the casual supervision of countless *dueñas* unable to cope with her headstrong, tomboy attitudes. The motherless girl child had become an army brat very early in her young life, right under the nose of her father.

Obregon was unable to handle the tedious ritual of raising such a defiant child, who emulated the men of authority she saw each day. Frustrated and bewildered at his lot in life, he was unable to cope with the constant trials and tribulations of a growing daughter's needs. And when complaints reached him from the various wives and mothers in the military compounds that he was too permissive, too lax, and too easily won over by this tomboy, he was forced to take some remedial action: He sent her packing off to Spain to become a lady.

But that was four years ago. A lot had happened to Madelaina, and although at first she thought she'd die if she had to remain in Spain without seeing her father, she'd grown accustomed to her new life. Not that she'd taken to the life of a *gachupín* and the refined ways of a lady. No, not that at all. It's just that a freedom of spirit and a profound love for all things in nature pervaded the soul of this naïve child growing into womanhood. What she came to love and marvel at were the bulls at the Obregon and Cortez haciendas.

"Madelaina!" The sound of her name being called

6

interrupted her reverie. *"Vamenos, querida.* Let's go, my dear." It was Armando Cortez. Sweet, handsome, patient Armando, her dearest friend in the whole world.

Madelaina nodded and stepped down from the wooden seats which she'd climbed to gain a better view of the area in her search of Manuelito. *Very well, Manuelito, go off by yourself and sulk,* she told herself stormily. *It isn't my fault that things got so mixed up today!* Even as she thought these words and pouted petulantly, she grew more dismayed at her inability to locate Manuelito Perez. Worse, she didn't understand the strange feeling of consternation gripping her, nor did she comprehend the feeling of attachment she suddenly experienced for Manuelito. Emotions shot through Madelaina, emotions she had never been faced with before. Her stomach felt fluttery, she was chilled with a rising excitement, then, experienced a glow of perspiration on her forehead. She fanned herself with a lace handkerchief. *Perhaps it's the scorching sun.* The smell of the spicy, aromatic foods eaten by the *peóns,* mixed with the odors of the bull ring and the excrement of horses and bulls, hung heavy over the Plaza and wafted up to her nostrils, increasing her discomfort.

"I'm coming, Armando," she called, glancing soulfully at the blood rose before wistfully tossing it into the bull ring below. She forced a light smile as she gazed up into Armando's suggestive eyes. Damn! Why had she made him that stupid promise? She'd much rather have gone to meet Joselito Barrancas as Manuelito had suggested. For some unearthly reason, she'd promised Armando the rest of the afternoon. And he in turn had promised her the most glorious surprise of her young life. Now she focused her attention on what that might possibly be.

Madelaina's curiosity had been aroused by the mystery and suspense Armando projected. He refused to speak of the surprise except to say it was the one way she could pay him back for providing her with many glorious hours spent in learning the art of bullfighting.

7

After all, it *was* Armando who had persuaded Manuelito to teach Madelaina the art of the *corrida*. She owed him something, didn't she?

"Tell me, *querida*, did you enjoy the *corrida*?" asked Armando patiently.

"You have to ask?" she retorted, still glancing anxiously about for some sign of Manuelito. "Where is he, Armando?" she queried. "I don't understand why he couldn't have been seated with us. After all, it was due to his cleverness that we came by the tickets for this day. And it was through him that Barrancas dedicated the bull to me. I know."

"Madelaina, dear, you *know* why he couldn't be seated with us. Why must you try my patience with such questions? Our people frown on associating with the peasants. It is not the custom. Please don't persist in this attitude."

"Ah, Armando, if Doña Sofia could hear you talk like this, her avante-garde mentality would rebel. To the devil with customs. Manuelito is my friend. I presumed he was yours also. I think we should go and look for him." Her eyes were everywhere, nodding to a few and smiling at others who passed.

"Listen—did you forget the promise you made me?" he whispered suggestively.

Madelaina turned sharply in his direction. A flicker of annoyance passed over her face, then she smiled. "No. Of course I didn't. I made you a solemn promise. An Obregon never breaks a promise."

Watching the young couple meet with their friends, Don Diego Obregon and Don Felipe Cortez beamed with approval. Both grandees laughed tolerantly and were reminded of their own spirited youth, as the gay couple took off with three other young couples on the pretext of attending a gala held by Doña Sofia. Doña Sofia Marabella was a free-spirited, free-thinking woman, who believed in creating her own world by rebelling against all authority and accepting responsibility for her own actions, no matter what the dictates of society, traditional morality, or religious faith.

8

Neither Don Diego nor Don Cortez ever bothered to consider the implications or complications of a relationship between Madelaina and Armando; both men had had many serious talks about this young couple who seemed so devoted for so long. Both *hacendados* were pleased with the idea of an alliance between two such powerful families; they would become a formidable power in both business and politics in their country.

Look how they'd taken to each other! Armando, reared in the proper virtues, could be trusted not to besmirch her name. In two years when he finished military training, they could be married. And Madelaina, that innocent trusting child with immense affection in her heart, could be trusted not to bring disgrace or dishonor upon the name of Obregon—couldn't she?

Recalling their own tempestuous, lust-filled youth, neither man dared reveal his thoughts. They smiled enigmatically.

Don Diego watched them depart with a merry twinkle in his eyes. He'd already written to his brother, General Obregon, in Cuernavaca, hinting at such a marriage, and received what could be considered sanction of the possible betrothal. Only if Madelaina is fully willing, wrote her father. But in any case, before such an event took place, he wanted Madelaina to return to Mexico when her schooling was completed in two years. She'd be eighteen then and mature enough to accept the responsibilities of womanhood and the rigors of running a household. If the marriage took place, it would be in Mexico.

Don Diego sighed as he lit a cigar. He waved as the young couples climbed into the cabriolets. He took more pleasure in Madelaina than he did in either of his own two daughters. She had a bright, inquisitive mind; in fact, at times she drove him to distraction with her countless questions. Nonetheless she was the apple of his eye.

Madelaina Obregon had turned sixteen on this fifteenth day of May, 1909, so her excitement was tenfold since she'd been able to spend it in the manner most pleasing to her.

Now, two hours after the *corrida*, scintillating thoughts of what had transpired earlier were temporarily dimmed by the magnificent splendor and opulence that greeted her when she and Armando entered the old palace. Purported to have been the country estate of Queen Isabella, one of her ancestors, the sprawling estate stood high in the hills overlooking Sanlucar de Barramedas and the open sea of sapphire waters in majestic dignity. From this very port Columbus had set sail for the New World! Imagine, she thought as she passed through the elegant foyer.

She allowed her dark, impressionable eyes to roam in every direction. Wherever she looked something unique and astonishing commanded her attention. She followed Armando to the top of the spiral staircase with its graceful rail of gilded wood, and turned left through a corridor on the second floor into a very special room.

Armando closed the door behind them, and taking her hand, he ushered her through the unusual salon. The walls and ceiling were painted in a continuous fresco depicting a bawdy life in the ancient Greek and Roman eras, the likes of which she'd never seen or heard of before. Men and women—in some cases gods and goddesses, and in others only men—were engaged in what was described to her as forbidden sexual pleasures.

Madelaina had no intention of appearing stupid, or ignorant, or less worldly than Armando, two years her senior, a man to whom she'd been devoted these past four years. Sent to Spain from Mexico by her father to learn the social graces of refinement and womanhood and complete her education so she could eventually assume the duties of running her father's hacienda in Cuernavaca, Mexico, Madelaina had made few friends. Only Armando Cortez, son of a grandee, and his servant, Manuelito Perez, understood her passion for bulls and her love for the glorious pageantry of the *corrida*.

10

It was Armando who had first encouraged her. He'd actually bullied Manuelito into teaching her to make expert passes with a cape—*verónicas magnifica*—for Manuelito was preparing to be the greatest of all matadors in Spain.

It was at the Cortez hacienda that Manuelito persisted daily, for hours on end, to teach her the art of bullfighting. And all this in conspiracy against her uncle Don Diego Obregon and her aunt Doña Louisa. *Dios mios*! If they ever learned what she was doing—off would come her head!

It was true, sighed Madelaina. Armando and Manuelito were the only true friends she'd made since her arrival in Las Marismas. It was because Armando had been instrumental in bringing her such happiness that Madelaina was about to return the favor by keeping her promise to the son of Don Felipe Cortez.

She had no real conception of what was about to happen, although Armando continued to pique her interest with hints of something so marvelous that it was beyond description. Even on the ride to the palace he remained enigmatic and would only roll his eyes skyward when she eagerly questioned him about the surprise. Now, as she gazed about her at the explicit scenes in this grand old palace, her curiosity was heightened.

"What are they all doing?" she asked Armando, her eyes fixed on the countless frescoes.

"Making love, silly goose." He helped her remove her garnet-red velvet jacket. "Exactly what we intend doing today."

"It seems so complicated." She took off her feathered bonnet and shook out her raven-black hair until it cascaded over the shoulders of her flesh-colored Alençon lace camisole. She expressed her naïveté glibly. "Do we have to get undressed as they are?" Observing the erotica, she smiled at the seeming foolishness of it all. Even the bedposts were carved into male and female figures doing what to Madelaina seemed the most foolish things she'd ever seen in her entire

11

life. At the top of the four-poster bed, at each of the upper corners, the bent figure of a female trailed down to the figure of a male with his head upturned, accepting flowing liquid into his mouth. Madelaina giggled openly and moved on to the next scene and the next. Her eyes widened like saucers and her face turned berry red.

With a certain measure of pretended worldliness, Armando laughed at her discomfort. "This, *querida*, is called Forbidden Love. You see? Already progress has been made. Notice in this picture there are no little demons, no little devils lurking in the background of the painting. Only cupids wait to descend upon the lovers. Not Satan with his fiery red tongs."

Madelaina examined the highly erotic pictures and scenes in her stride, certainly with no overbearing desire to emulate their contents and not in the least titillated by their explicit frankness. Still, there was a queasy feeling in her stomach, a feeling of fluttering birds which made her feel uneasy. She hoped Armando would hurry up and do what it was he was dying to do and be done with it. His preamble, for goodness' sake, had been long enough and drawn out over a period of three months. He kept playing games with her, innocent games bent on provoking her curiosity. It seemed so pointless to her. Why couldn't he have asked her straight out?

One day, not long ago, following an exhilarating two-hour workout with Manuelito and the bulls, she had mastered a somewhat difficult *verónica*. She had been so thrilled by the praise from both Manuelito and the men who stood watching her that she ran to Armando's side and hugged him dearly. "Oh, thank you, *querido*, Armando," she gushed at him. "Thank you for making all this possible."

Flushed with excitement and inflated with pride, she smiled dazzlingly at the spectators who clapped their hands and shouted "*olé*" to her. She hadn't seen the dark-eyed scowl of her sullen teacher Manuelito. What she noticed was that Armando held her in a manner

12

totally different than ever before. He hugged her tighter than usual, with a marked degree of possessiveness. Their eyes met in a tender, affectionate moment, bringing a blush to her cheeks. She hadn't fully understood the flush of pleasure she experienced, only that when it happened, she moved instinctively out of his embrace and busied herself brushing imaginary dust and dirt from her shirt and trousers.

Armando had moved in closer to her that day and whispered softly, "Do you really appreciate all I've done to coax Manuelito to tutor you in bullfighting?"

"Of course," she'd replied. "How many times must I tell you how happy you've made me?"

"Then, you'll do me a favor—as I've done for you?"

Madelaina had chided him. "You have to ask?"

That's how all this had begun—as a reciprocal favor.

Now, Armando devoured her with his eyes as they lay side by side on the four-poster bed in total nudity. What a beautiful man Armando is, Madelaina thought. She loved the feel of his thick, curly brown hair as she ran her fingers through it. His eyes, the color of a turbulent green sea, had a hypnotic effect on her. Though he was a bit overly impassioned at times and inclined toward the melodramatic, she listened politely as he spouted verse and sweet nonsensical tidbits in her ear.

"Oh, my sweet, I am enchanted with you," he whispered seductively. "I need you desperately. My heart swells in your presence. Can't you see how consumed I am with your very being—your body—your soul? If we don't express our love the way a man does with a woman, my heart will wither and die."

Madelaina suppressed a desire to laugh. Deep inside her, she felt all this was a bit naughty and wicked, but how in all sense of decency and love could she permit Armando's heart to wither and die? How? He was her very best friend. He was.

As she lay back on the feather mattress thinking of all that happened to her on this special day, Armando's heated body covered her and he made several motions

13

to penetrate her body. Very well, she thought, do what you must, Armando, dear. I have better things to think about.

What a day! Her sixteenth birthday. An exquisite ring with two perfectly matched ten-carat diamonds which had been handed down from Queen Isabella had arrived two days before as a gift from her father. The ring, too overpowering for her small hands, had been placed in her jewel case along with the letter from her loving Papa.

Armando groaned and moaned over her, and she tried to accommodate his movements as he whispered what she must do.

Her thoughts wandered back to a far more exciting and rapturous event—the *corrida* earlier that afternoon. Joselito Barrancas! The greatest matador in all Spain! *Dios mios*, such excitement. At four o'clock in the afternoon she'd seen the splendor of a contest between man and beast. Imagine, Barrancas had dedicated the bull to her. And all because he was friend to Manuelito Perez. It had all been too much—a day of firsts for her. Her first diamond ring, her first *corrida*, and her first—her first—?

"Armando," she whispered as she pulled back from him and searched his eyes questioningly. His face hovered over hers with swollen features, an odd expression etched on his face. She almost giggled at his intense expression. "What do they call this?" she asked easily.

"What do they call what?" he muttered incoherently with a peculiar breathlessness.

"What we're doing, of course."

"Making love, you silly goose. I'm seducing you," he said with exaggerated and sinister tones, evoking a giggling response from her.

"That's what this is called—making love?" She felt his body with less discomfort for several moments, then suddenly she felt a stab of pain penetrate her body. She gasped aloud and moaned, "You hurt me, Armando. You hurt me."

14

"Only for a moment, *querida*," he replied apologetically. "Then you will feel marvelous."

For goodness' sake, thought Madelaina. It wasn't that bad. She could stand the momentary discomfort to appease a friend. She'd been gored twice in the upper left thigh, seriously enough for a doctor to have to stitch it together, and hadn't complained over the pain and discomfort. Why complain over something as minor as this?

For the next several moments Armando didn't talk. His face screwed up tightly into an expression of what she considered total agony. For an instant she grew alarmed, and when she heard little animal noises emanating from his throat, she tensed. The momentum of his pelvic thrusts made him appear frenzied and out of control. Then, it ended. He fell on her body, sweating, panting, breathing heavily and erratically, but fully spent. He appeared exhausted, and in the dim light coming from the colored lamps on the wall overhead, his face seemed peaceful. She understood very little of this and Armando hadn't explained much to her. There has to be something more pleasurable in all this, she told herself.

When Armando felt his strength returning, he sat up in bed, pushed his tousled hair back off his face, and pulled Madelaina closer to him. He lit up a small *cigarrillo* and inhaled several times. Then he explained.

"It's called many things by many people, *querida*. Intercourse, coupling, seduction—you know. At the hacienda we call it breeding."

She gazed up at the ceiling and walls. "Is that what they're doing—all those people?" She waved her hands about. "Breeding!" She gave a start.

He laughed. "At least you took notice of them. I was beginning to think you were made of ice."

"How could I not have seen them? I've been staring at them all the time you've done what you've wanted to do. *Breeding*?" She sat up. "Oh, Armando, does that mean I will be in foal?" she asked in alarm.

"Madelaina! Bite your tongue! We'd be skinned

alive if such a thing happened. Surely you'll know what to do—won't you?"

"Oh, sure," she said, trying to appear worldly. "What do you mean you thought I was made of ice?"

"Only that you didn't seem to delight in our experience. But, I see I was wrong. All the time you were fantasizing about those wicked pictures overhead."

Madelaina lowered her eyes and turned from him in a gesture he interpreted as coquettishness. It was nothing like that at all. She had felt nothing but keen disappointment. She'd never tell Armando, of course. Nothing had happened the way he had hinted it would with all his poetic rhetoric. Where was the blissful paradise he'd described so many times? Her eager, inquisitive eyes trailed back to the ceiling. Why had so much been made about this business of lovemaking? True, the pictures had stirred a response in her—more than Armando had been capable of doing. Even his words had moved her to a strange and breathless excitement. She almost wished she hadn't experienced anything else, since she found the actual physical act lacking.

In all the pictures swirling overhead, the couples seemed to be having so much fun. Engaged in various acts of sexual pleasure in a variety of sexual positions, they did indeed make it look like fun and games. There was a healthy frankness to the woman who sat astride her male companion holding his penis in her hand, apparently guiding it into more pleasurable channels. And in the next fresco, where a man held the woman in his arms apparently doing several things at once. Madelaina concluded he must have been a gymnast, an acrobat, or a contortionist of some sort.

Madelaina felt terribly let down. She'd felt more excitement at the bullfights than she had with Armando in their acts of forbidden pleasure.

Armando's voice began purring once again in that impassioned tone. She turned her head toward him and watched as his hand stole upward toward her fully rounded breasts. She felt a strange tingling, a murmur,

16

something she hadn't felt earlier, and she tried with difficulty to understand what was happening.

"A woman," whispered Armando, "a woman. There's nothing like a woman. The passion of a woman is like a rare, exotic fruit. Gather her beauty while you can, release the passion in her many treasures, for in it is the power of Eros, greater than the power of Zeus. Eros, the creator of flowers and trees, is the power that makes rivers flow and winds blow. Nothing in man is greater, more divine than the strapping powers of Eros."

"How beautiful, Armando," she whispered. "Did you write this?" She loved his voice. It thrilled her more to hear him speak than it did for him to go through these outlandish gyrations.

He continued, spurred on by her compliments. "You who are beautiful of face shall lie on your back where I can feast upon you. If your back is a thing of divine beauty, then let my eyes devour you. Ride me, you small thing of perfection, as lover rides lover in unbroken rhythm and let me devour you in all your splendor."

Madelaina listened dutifully to all he told her. It all seemed so very important to him, how could she let him know how truly disappointed she was? She wouldn't hurt Armando Cortez for anything in the whole world. She closed her eyes and listened as Armando again worked himself up into a state of frenzy.

There were many things Madelaina, having led a sheltered life, knew little of. To begin with, she didn't know that this former palace had, over the centuries, become a high-class bordello, where the young rogues and wealthy *hacendados* could either entertain their own young ladies or participate in sexual pleasures with the many talented girls the *madama* supplied.

She considered all Armando's machinations a bit much and concluded he was a lovesick, calf-eyed Lothario. His words, beautiful and inspiring, although a bit foolish at times, affected her deeply. Nonetheless, he was her best friend, her truest. She made a solemn

17

vow that whenever he wanted to exchange his love with her, she'd let him take his pleasure, but never would she tell him she felt none of the enjoyment he seemed to get from coupling. Why she didn't enjoy it was something she didn't give much thought to until later, much later.

She lay a cool hand on his upper arm. Armando was sound asleep. She lay back against the pillows, and glancing at the locket around her neck, a birthday gift from Armando, her mind suddenly became overwhelmed with thoughts of Manuelito. She hadn't been able to shut him from her mind all afternoon.

Madelaina had been comparing the cape passes of Barrancas with her own when the face of Manuelito Perez imposed itself on her thoughts. She blinked her eyes several times trying to recall the image of the matador, but only Manuelito's face persisted, with a stern, disapproving look on his dark, craggy features.

The sound of hushed laughter from the next room interrupted Madelaina's reverie. Armando was still asleep. Soundlessly, Madelaina slipped off the bed, curious to learn if Armando's friends and their girl friends were faring well and enjoying themselves. She simply had to talk to some of the girls to learn more about this enigmatic sex that possessed Armando's every waking moment. Perhaps she had much to learn before she could enjoy herself. Damn! Armando wouldn't build something up in her mind only to permit it to turn into such a letdown for her—would he?

She carefully pulled the bolt on the door and turned the handle. The door, only slightly ajar, gave her a tunneled view of the next room's interior. It was furnished somewhat like the room she and Armando shared, and on a large four-poster bed were sprawled three girls engaged in sexual pleasures.

Madelaina's eyes opened wide and she stared in open-mouthed astonishment when the door suddenly opened, her arm was grasped firmly, and she was dragged into the room.

"For Christ's sake! Close the damned door!"

18

shouted a tall, muscular man with the most atrocious accent she'd ever heard. She glanced up into a pair of sapphire blue eyes dancing with merriment. "It's about time they sent you!" He appraised her. "A little young, aren'tcha? They tell me young is best. Ya can train 'em yore own way." It was the twang to the bad Spanish he spoke that made him difficult to understand. A half-smile played on his face.

Madelaina struggled to free herself. "Yore a little devil, ain'tcha?" he purred.

The girls on the bed paused in their pleasures, laughing hilariously at him. "Pierre, that's not Teresina!" they shouted, exploding in merriment.

"Let me go!" shouted Madelaina, with fire in her eyes. She gave him a swift kick, but it was ineffective since she was barefoot. She bit him deeply.

He held her at arm's length and searched her face. "Not Teresina? Then who the hell are you?" He frowned, no longer amused by her protests.

"My fiancé is in the next room and if you don't let me go, I'll scream!"

"Yer fiancé?" The stranger laughed loudly and with considerable humor. "Yer fiancé! What kind of a man would bring his fiancée to a place like this?" Now they were all laughing. The naked girls on the bed, raised on their knees, had paused to stare at this interloper and, finding her predicament humorous, laughed heartily. Shaky and distraught, Madelaina took advantage of the moment and disappeared through the door, bolting it shut tight and leaning heavily against it.

She was perspiring. Her face paled with humiliation and tears sprang to her eyes. She glanced at Armando, still in repose, and she began to dress hastily. She'd never been so terrified, humiliated, and filled with fierce resentment as she had in these past few moments. Her heart beat furiously.

Something about the stranger's words, his actions, and his attitude toward her made her feel dirty and slimy. He treated her like the *putas* she'd seen in Mexico City's red-light district, like the *putas* and *cam-*

19

pesinas who hovered around the forts commanded by her father, who were treated with disrespect. His words cut her deeply. What kind of a man would bring his fiancée to such a place? What kind of a place was this? Her thoughts ran rampant. She finished dressing, and glancing at Armando, she felt a tinge of concern at leaving him.

Well, wherever it was he had brought her, he had certainly been here before, of that she was positive. And he certainly hadn't been concerned with her virtue if this was the kind of a place she began to think it was.

"Madelaina!" Armando had awakened. He slipped off the bed and rushed to her side just as she was about to slip out the door. "Where are you going?"

"I have to leave," she said with a note of urgency to her voice.

"Why? It's still early. Besides, I have another surprise for you."

Madelaina's face fell. "You do?" she said with noticeable dismay. Sounds of laughter from the next room made her start.

"Don't act so enthusiastic," said Armando dryly. "Look, if you don't want to fulfill our bargain—"

"It's not that. Well—well, just what kind of a place is this?" she asked hotly.

"Now what brought that on?"

She told him what she'd seen in the next room. "I don't understand any of this." She didn't tell him about the tall, blue-eyed stranger who mistook her for someone called Teresina. She was afraid Armando might challenge the stranger to a duel or some such foolishness. Such was the nature of his Spanish arrogance.

"I'm very confused. Why does a man have three women to make love with? None of this makes any sense at all—not after what you've told me about love between a man and a woman. You said you make love with someone you admire, a true friend, someone you love. How can a man make love to three women?" she blurted finally, totally disorganized.

20

"Well," said Armando in that insufferable worldly manner, "men are different than women. They have more vigor, many more needs to fill than a woman." He began to remove her velvet jacket again. She shrugged against him and pulled it into place.

"No, Armando! I am leaving. I want to go home. Besides, I've got to find Manuelito. I think it's shabby the way we treated him today. I've thought of nothing else this past hour. I must apologize to him—that is if he'll accept my apology. After all, it was he who bought the tickets for my birthday!"

"Very well then, I'll leave with you. Wait until I dress and make myself presentable," he told her with a hint of irritation in his voice.

"It's not necessary. I'll hire a carriage to take me to Doña Sofia's *casa*. "Stay and enjoy yourself—I understand there are plenty of *putas* available!"

Armando's green eyes cut sharply in her direction, surprised at her candor.

"And—and don't bother to deny this place is a—a—bordello!" She ran out the door and descended the magnificent spiral staircase. Just as she was about to skirt past a large salon filled to capacity with gaily chatting men and women, Madelaina stopped short. She was thunderstruck. Grateful for the dimly lit foyer, she slipped behind the cascading drapes at one side of the archway to shield her from the eyes of her uncle, Don Diego Obregon, and Armando's father, Don Felipe Cortez, who brushed past her on the arms of two outrageously bawdy women.

She wanted the floor to open up and swallow her. Why? Why? Why, she asked herself, were they here with such women? Both were married men, happily, she thought—and why were they in the company of such women? *Dios mios.* She simply didn't understand much at all. She couldn't wait for them to climb the stairs so she could slip out the door unnoticed.

Outside the sun was setting, covering the shabby seaport town with a coppery glow as if it were being showered with topaz crystals.

21

Confusion swirled around her like a room full of massive spider webs. She almost missed hailing a passing carriage. At her instruction the driver drove maniacally to the estate of Doña Sofia Marabella. All the way back she tried to hold back a hailstorm of tears, self-doubt, recrimination, and humiliation. Through it all she kept seeing the face of Manuelito Perez. "Oh, Manuelito," she cried passionately. "Where are you now that I need you?"

Manuelito Perez, indeed! If Madelaina knew just what part her skilled instructor had played in all this, she might not have called out to him in desperation.

Two years before, Manuelito, one of Spain's future matadors, had been hired by the grandee's son, Armando, to humor the girl, the foolish child whose greatest passion was to learn the art of bullfighting.

"Teach her all you can, Manuelito," had been Armando's instructions, accompanied by a broad wink. Perez turned to the fourteen-year-old girl. She was slim, built like a boy with *tetas* like mosquito bites. He shook his head with marked irritation. Teach a girl to match wits with a bull? Hah! At sixteen, Perez, an *aficionado* since age seven, looked upon the wide-eyed, enthusiastic girl with contempt. Women! Bah! Didn't they know their place in this world of men? Despite his scornful reluctance to do Armando's bidding, he was still a peasant, a servant, who had to respect his master's wishes.

Embarrassment flooded his sharp, dark features daily when the girl appeared like clockwork at the hacienda of Don Cortez. She rode her black stallion, Don Quixote, ten kilometers back and forth from the hacienda of Don Obregon each day after classes for nearly two years and had never been late. She had taken to bullfighting as if she were born to it. Onlookers—ranch hands, breeders, and peasant laborers—wondered what possessed the girl to learn such an art. Those who once scoffed and made snide remarks behind her back began to observe her patient, talented work with the cape in astonished silence. Suddenly they became her most devout boosters. Hadn't they told Manuelito how exceptional she was? Hadn't they encouraged her from the first? It was simply amazing how many supporters she'd attracted since Manuelito determined to turn this pupil into an artist. Everyday he made her repeat the artful passes with more precision and tenacity until she performed *verónicas* that hypnotized the bulls and lured them into doing her bidding.

Manuelito Perez had fallen in love almost against his will. It was amazing how in two years a young beanstalk had suddenly transformed into a seductress, a woman of desire. She'd grown into a fiery-eyed beauty whose dark, almond-shaped eyes, bordered by double-fringed lashes, resembled the wings of a black *mariposa*—a butterfly. Her long hair, the color of anthracite and iridescent in the bright sunlight, was twisted into a pigtail when she worked the bulls. Her sweet fragrance of roses intoxicated his senses. Manuelito constantly fought the overwhelming desire to gather her into his arms, smother her with kisses, and satisfy his fully aroused manliness. He dreamt each night of making wild, passionate love to her. But the dark-skinned, well-muscled young man, who strutted with animal sensuality, convinced himself he had no chance with this elusive young *princesa*.

In addition to the social stigma and upper class taboos, which were obstacles in themselves, Madelaina had eyes only for the bulls. He admitted this on more than one occasion to his many friends. This fascination between girl and bulls was something most unusual. The animals, hundreds of pounds of dynamite and sharp, lethal horns, seemed to bend to her every whim. Even the fiercest of bulls became obedient. True, she'd never fought the full-grown bulls. Those she had fought, however, were formidable enough for any man, let alone a woman. It was uncanny. More incredible than anything Manuelito had ever experienced. When he described this mysterious rapport to some of the mata-

23

dors and their managers at the Plaza de Toros in Sanlucar, they laughed at him and called him *muy loco*, very crazy.

"Your imagination is distorted by the love you feel for the wench," they'd tell him, while plying him with more drinks to loosen his tongue. And Manuelito would drink—and drink—and drink more than he ever had in his life because of the seeming futility of his love for Madelaina Obregon.

He was well aware that, next to the bulls, Madelaina's heart was caught up in Armando Cortez. They'd been inseparable, especially since she'd bloomed into womanhood. Their devotion to one another stirred rumors of a future betrothal. What hopes did Manuelito have—except to allow his thoughts to evaporate into vain imaginings? Something manly within him wouldn't accept this fate.

As her sixteenth birthday approached, Manuelito racked his brain to think of something special for her, something no one else would think to give her. No jewelry or costly baubles. The bastard son of a lowly peasant could afford neither the gifts nor such thoughts of grandeur.

One month before the *corrida*, Manuelito cut Madelaina's instruction time to one hour a day instead of three. His excuse was he had to ride the distance from Las Marismas to Sanlucar to work at the Plaza de Toros. He didn't mention he had accepted a menial job preparing the stalls and bull runs and shoots for the arrival of the Miuras, Salamancas, and Conchas from the various breeding ranches. All this he did to earn the price of the box tickets to the bullfights starring the great Joselito Barrancas, the exhilarating matador all Spain had taken to their hearts.

The day he showed the tickets to Madelaina—before he had a chance to explain they were his birthday present to her so they could attend the *corrida* together—Madelaina thoughtlessly turned to Armando and explained the wonderful gesture. For the young instructor, her reaction put him in his proper place.

"What an absolutely splendid gesture, Manuelito," said Armando, accepting the tickets as if they'd been donated to him as a gift. Tall, well-muscled, wearing long sideburns and a moustache of the dons, Armando smiled through his dazzling white teeth and slapped his friend affectionately on the shoulders. He was the same age as Manuelito. He was a man, like him, with the same fiery passions, the same emotions of love and hate, but here the resemblance ended.

Don Armando Cortez was highborn, the son of a grandee. Manuelito was a bastard, the son of a peasant, a lowborn tiller of the earth, a herder of animal manure. That was the difference. And what a difference in the eyes of Manuelito Perez! Of what use was it being born a man in such a life, without hope?

Disillusioned, heartbroken, filled with countless frustrations, Manuelito returned to Sanlucar de Barramedas to do the last day's work at the Plaza de Toros. He walked slowly, without heart, through the tortuous, narrow streets filled with low, ramshackle buildings. He didn't know how long he walked or where he was going. Very few lights illuminated his way. A pale moon formed grotesque shadows between hunched buildings. It was a background for dark and mysterious purposes, covered in silence and the intangible presence of danger. He barely recognized an old familiar section of town.

A voice, hoarse with age and filled with a measure of premonition, came at him from the shadows. "What evil brings you to this part of town?"

"Who's there?" he cried out, trying to pierce the darkness with his eyes.

"Don't you know me?"

He glanced cautiously at the dark form hunched over in a shadowy doorway. It was the village *bruja*, a sorceress, the aged sister of his dead mother. "Oh," he said dully. "It's you. I want no truck with you. Begone!"

"Ah, but you do. You've already sent for me."

25

"Are you some crazy woman? I've not thought about you since I was a boy, before my mother died."

"Therein lies your problem. Come in, Manuelito. You need me as I need you. I have already prepared the potion."

Almost against his will he followed the sister of his dead mother into the filthy hovel. A dirty curtain served as a door. Inside, candles burned, casting oblique shadows over the walls and ceiling. The stench of pungent herbs clung to the air, the odors of marijuana and dried mushrooms. His dark, electric eyes and his high-boned cheeks took on the prominence of his ancestors, spotlighting for an instant a remarkable classic profile of stubborn arrogance and princely forebearance. There was unquestionable beauty in this young man, descended from the Moors and bitterly resentful of his lot in life.

The *bruja* handed him a small white chamois sack. "Give this to her, either in wine or water. It's tasteless. Then, my nephew, she'll not be able to resist you."

"How do you know what's in my heart? Do I wear my feelings on my shirtsleeves for the world to see? I've said nothing to any one," he retorted both with astonishment and indignation.

As the *bruja* rocked to and fro, seated cross-legged upon the hearth, she nodded her head. "Listen, my nephew, between us has always been a mysterious bond, stronger than any I've known. The time has come, young stallion, for me to impart certain secrets. Your mother and I were once great beauties. In our day we were sought by the most elegant of men. Devils tempted us to love men who abandoned us. The man who abandoned your mother and made you his bastard was the brother of Don Felipe Cortez, Federico, the uncle of Armando Cortez who makes you his lackey. The man who abandoned me—and I thank God I was not with child—was Don Diego Obregon. Need I tell you more? Now, at long last, through you, the burning desires of retribution shall be realized. You understand?"

26

The fire in her eyes lit the embers in Manuelito's soul. Was it truly possible his own father was a *gachupín*, a highborn Spaniard? Armando and he were first cousins? It's not possible! He, Manuelito Perez, a bastard, had the blood of *gachupíns*, noble blood. He was a Cortez! He had been four years old the day a courier came from Don Felipe Cortez requesting that they live at the hacienda near Las Marismas where the *hacendado* raised bulls for breeding purposes. Mother and son would always have a roof over their heads, they'd been assured by Don Cortez. Because Manuelito's father had been distantly related to him, the grandee felt a certain familial responsibility. Manuelito had never been told this story. Imagine. He was a Cortez! An incredible surge of happiness swept through him, shaking him to the core with a breathlessness he'd never before experienced—except in the bull ring when he triumphed over a bull and the ranch hands told him one day he'd be the best matador in all Spain.

Dios mios! Now he could take his proper place. He might even ask Madelaina to marry him!

As if she could read his thoughts, the *bruja* cautioned him. "You must not reveal what I have told you, my nephew. You must say nothing to any one. Do nothing except what I instruct you to do. Else you'll not be able to take your proper place. These highstruttin' nobles have been known to dispose of obstacles in their path. When it comes to money, they are a different breed of men. Listen to me, my nephew, and let us be in full accord."

Her words pierced his daydreams, rupturing them for several moments. He found himself listening and nodding despite himself, even as confusion stirred in him. "But Madelaina is not the *daughter* of Don Diego Obregon. What has she to do with your revenge?"

"He loves his niece more than he loves his own children. To Don Diego she is the sun, the moon, and the stars. You must make her fall in love with you until she declares her love—which she'll do readily if you

27

administer the potion. Then the Cortez family will do right by you; they will see you get your rightful share, for the union with the Obregon family means a powerful one for all involved. Then we shall both have what we want. You, Don Matador, will be more appreciated. Through this potion will come all you've ever desired."

"And you, *bruja*, are one of those people who can ruin everything if your magic fails."

"I ask you, Manuelito—what else do you have at this moment? You strolled down the street moments ago ready to plunge a knife into your breast, filled to overflowing with despair and disillusionment."

He nodded. "That's true." She spoke with such conviction, he sensed something stirring deeply within him. He hadn't had time to fully digest all he'd learned, and for a few moments he inclined his head in ultimate despair.

"Look, witch, a bull's horn in my breast can kill or else is cured and forgotten. But a wound to the heart will bleed as long as I live." For an instant he hung his head between his hands as he sat on the chair facing the sister of his dead mother. Too many things soared through his mind, too many slights, hurts, and emotional scars. "All right," he said at last, stiffening perceptibly. "Tell me what I have to do. But mark my words—if through your efforts I lose the only things worth loving in my life, I shall return to cut out your heart."

On the day of the *corrida*, Manuelito cut a handsome figure in his finest suit: black fitted trousers with flared bottoms, short jacket and white silk shirt, and a flat-crowned don's hat. He was beautiful!

"What a fine figure of a man you are, Manuelito," exclaimed Madelaina, coming to the door of her apartment at the mansion of Doña Sofia Marabella. The Obregon and Cortez entourage stayed here during the festivities of the *corrida*. The wealthy society matron entertained lavishly during the bullfight season. Madelaina, it seemed, was seeing Manuelito for the first time as a handsome young man. As he stood before her, the *dueña* questioned his presence.

"Would the *señorita* enjoy watching the selection of the bulls at twelve o'clock?" he asked respectfully, feeling an excitement at the expression of delight in her eyes.

"Oh, Manuelito, I'd love it. I doubt if Armando has awakened yet. He stayed up quite late at the party last night." She shouted to him over a screen partition, placed between them by her *dueña*, a sober-eyed, dried-up old fig of a woman who eyed all of Madelaina's male friends with suspicious eyes.

Manuelito had entered the luxurious suite of rooms and took his place exactly where the *dueña*, Doña Ines, indicated.

Madelaina dressed hurriedly into her *matadora* pants and jacket, against the stern admonishment of Doña Ines. "I'll not be seen in public with one dressed so shamefully!" exclaimed the horrified older woman. "You dare dress like that here in Sanlucar? You'll scandalize the name of Obregon!"

"Then don't come, you old crocodile! Who asked you anyway? I'll have protection enough from Manuelito! He's ten times stronger than you, and much more fun!" She grabbed her hat, dashed to the other side of the screen, and grabbed Manuelito's hand. "Let's go before she fully understands what I've said!"

"I understand, you unspeakable hussy. Who'll protect you against Manuelito, eh? He's a man! A real man, and don't you forget it! He's not like those other dandies you surround yourself with!" Doña Ines nodded in approval.

"I won't forget it, crocodile. And you'd better sharpen your teeth to prepare for the battle you'll encounter when you explain my absence to Don Diego!"

She slammed the door behind them, and they both raced breathlessly down the steps into the courtyard where Manuelito had readied two horses for them.

"I've never seen you so beautiful, Manuelito," she exclaimed.

29

They arrived at the Plaza de Toros feeling like mischievous children. For many engrossing moments, they watched the matador's entourage select and match the bulls to fight that afternoon. And when Manuelito offered Madelaina a refreshing lemon ice laced with the magic potion, she was totally unaware of his intent. He watched her as a cagey lion might stalk his prey, but was unable to detect any marked difference in her attitude toward him.

Perhaps he expected miracles. He had forgotten to ask the *bruja* how long before such a potion took effect. They returned to the mansion of Doña Sofia. Madelaina thanked him with her usual affectionate gusto and returned to her quarters where she had to dress up like a lady for the *corrida*. Manuelito retired to his quarters until it was time to leave, brooding, bewildered, and upset by all that happened.

Sanlucar de Barramedas was in festival. The sun shone brightly in azure blue skies. Cafés filled to capacity with frolicking people. Through the narrow cobbled streets, carriages, filled to overflowing with youth and beauty, trundled on noisily. Crowds poured into the Plaza de Toros. Flirtations, toasts from wine bottles and goatskins, the aroma of spicy sausages, the fragrance of flowers peddled by poor peasants in large straw baskets, the gay costumes of elegant women, coquettish glances, and the somber formality of the high-strutting, proud gentlemen provided an exciting backdrop—like a pulse-throbbing scenario of life teeming with boundless excitement. None of this moved Manuelito Perez.

At four o'clock in the afternoon the trumpets blasted loud and clear. The procession of matadors marched across the sands in their spectacular, glittering finery. All the while Manuelito, seated some distance away from the private box he had worked so hard for, kept his eyes on Madelaina, waiting for some sign to indicate she was succumbing to his charms. Nothing! He saw nothing unusual. Manuelito had felt better when he had no hope than he did now, filled with false hope.

The *corrida* ended. He had hardly seen it at all. He had barely heard the wild acclaim of the crowd, the wild, deafening *"olés."* Even the hurricane of applause had failed to stir him. His own hero—the greatest of matadors in all Spain—had failed to evoke more than a fleeting emotion. He had seen Madelaina hold tightly to Armando's arm and it felt as if a sharp stiletto had pierced his heart.

Lurking the background of the festivities, Manuelito's black thoughts grew more volatile. That vile *bruja*! What did she know? He was a fool to listen to her. He saw the grandees and their parties swarm together where he should have been welcome and wasn't. The excitement on Madelaina's face at seeing her first professional bullfights, which he, Manuelito, had made possible and for which he'd received a mere thank you from Don Armando, left him sullen, sulky, and more determined than ever to become the greatest of all matadors. Then he'd come back and demand his birthright. He'd have to assert himself from a loftier position than any of them, before he could look down his nose at them! That would be a day to end all days! Then Madelaina would cling to him as she clung to that dandy, Armando Cortez.

No more teaching young thankless pupils, girls included, who hadn't the sense to recognize the tremendous depth of his love. *Oh, Madelaina! If only you had allowed me, I would have shown you the earth, the moon, and the stars!*

He went back into Sanlucar and began drinking heavily at the tavern where the greatest of bullfighters always came after victory to be revered by their people. There was no question, on this day a new hero had been born to the bullring, a madman who would one day frighten the Miuras and when the time would come for the kill, he would effect it with such skill, the crowd would go mad hailing this bright new matador. Manuelito would be the master of all masters. He would become the greatest. Manuelito Perez vowed never again to be cast aside by anyone like Madelaina

Obregon. He saw all this in his mind as clearly as if it were happening to him at that moment.

What Manuelito didn't know, and would probably never learn, was how the love potion had affected Madelaina. If he only knew that Madelaina had looked for him in every face in the crowd and had later become apathetic to Armando's advances to the point of driving the grandee's son to utter distraction, Manuelito might have remained in Las Marismas and fallen heir to the love of this strange girl who excited his emotions and stirred his heart.

Six months later all hell was about to erupt at the hacienda of Don Diego Obregon, much of it due to the mysterious disappearance of Manuelito Perez. No one had seen him since Madelaina's birthday. At Madelaina's urgings, Armando had combed the city for him; the jails had been searched, even the morgue in case he'd been done in. It was as if Manuelito Perez never existed. Brokenhearted, Madelaina missed him bitterly. She hadn't even gone to the hacienda of Don Cortez to contest the bulls.

Then one day, she received a letter from Manuelito. She ran to her quarters and pulled a chair up before the fire and read: "*Querida* Señorita Obregon." It began with such formality she cringed. "I am writing to tell you of my wickedness. My conscience tears me apart because I permitted a *bruja* to bewitch you. Forgive me. My heart bled with the pain of loving you because I could do nothing to convey my love. When I saw you leaving the bordello of Madama Tarragona so distraught, I realized how low and base and vile I'd become to stoop to the lengths I did to cause your deflowerment. May the Holy Virgin forgive me. I am shamed forever. Your obedient servant, Manuelito Perez."

Studying the childish scrawl of his signature, Madelaina realized Manuelito had probably hired the services of a professional letter writer. Perhaps through such a person they might learn more of his whereabouts. Tears stung her eyes as she read and reread the

32

letter. She couldn't believe her eyes. He had bewitched her. He'd been in love with her all this time? How cruel of her not to have noticed or encouraged him. She glanced at the postmark. Madrid. So far away. So, he'd seen her leave Madama Tarragona's—it was a *bordello* after all. She flushed hotly in embarrassment that he'd have seen her leave such a place. What must he have thought seeing her flee such a place? Bewitched, eh? Is that why she'd felt nothing with Armando? Questions coursed through her brain helterskelter.

She'd seen little of Armando. He'd gone on bivouac with his regiment. There was talk of war with Morocco. She'd coupled with Armando a few times after Madama Tarragona's, but never amid such luxurious trappings. She was growing bored with the entire thing and began to detest those stolen hours in a stable or tack room, especially when she felt the workers on the hacienda suspected their love tryst. They looked upon her with new, all-knowing eyes that made her uncomfortable.

Madelaina flung Manuelito's letter aside and paced the room as myriad thoughts filled her with confusion. Finally, without consciously thinking, she dressed in her *matadora* pants and jacket and went to seek solace among the truest of all her friends—the bulls. It was the first time she'd handled a bull on the hacienda of her uncle Don Diego. Well, customs be damned! She needed to feel closer to Manuelito. Perhaps in this way she could erase the guilt she felt for the indecent manner she'd treated him.

33

Chapter 2

Don Diego Obregon stood on the balcony of the upper portico of the sprawling hacienda overlooking Las Marismas, the swamp lands where he raised the finest bulls in all of Spain—the Concha bulls. When his forefathers first received the land in a grant from Queen Isabella, they considered themselves in the queen's disfavor, for the land was marshy and in the winter fit for no man. It was an animal and bird paradise, a primitive tideland where birds from all over Europe and Africa arrived in unbelievable numbers to breed. This land, situated on the Río Guadalquivir close to Sevilla, was utterly desolate in winter and magnificent in summer.

When Don Diego's forefathers made note of the wild bulls in the vicinity and learned how they thrived and what magnificent specimens they produced, they saw a fortune in their future and rightly so. An erratic nature and improbable elements all combined to produce the finest of animals, many of which had gone down in history as the bravest of all bulls.

However, it wasn't to reminisce on the shrewd foresight of his ancestors that Don Diego had been commanded to the upper balcony by his hysterical wife, Doña Louisa, who quickly escaped inside to hide her eyes from the terrible and disgraceful sight going on the small bullring next to the stables. He stood there staring at the trim figure in the slim black pants, white shirt, and bolero jacket of a matador. A black, flat-crowned hat sat squarely on the *torero*'s head, making it impossible for Don Diego to recognize the face. So many young men came during the *tienta* to test the bulls. He studied the stance and form of the figure

34

making expert passes with a red and gold cape as the young bulls charged.

"So!" He grunted aloud. "For this you remove me bodily from my study where an important conference was in progress with my fellow *hacendados*? To show me the antics of some young *torero*?" Don Diego saw nothing he hadn't seen countless times before, many young, brave lads were grimly determined to rise above the stature of Joselito Barrancas. Why was this one any different? Drawing his dark brows together in a scowl, his usual taciturn expression faded.

"Doña Louisa!" he called loudly to his wife. "Doña Louisa! Come here at once and tell me the meaning of this charade."

His wife, once a stunning beauty with patrician features, was now in her fifties, with age lines and wrinkles creasing her brow. She reappeared behind him, her emotions pitched at a high key. She had raised four sons and two daughters and for the past few years had been given the duty of raising the daughter of her husband's brother, General Alvaro Obregon, a duty which had become most difficult of late and had contributed to her increasing anxiety and worry.

Catching her husband's sullen stare, her eyes traveled past him beyond the courtyard until they rested on the slim-hipped figure, still engrossed in making passes at the young bulls. She pointed a slender finger toward the center of the ring and stepped closer to her husband.

"There! Out there! Do you not see her?"

"Her?" Don Diego's eyes darted about the area. He saw no woman. "Well, speak up, woman. Who is this *her* you refer to?"

Doña Louisa pushed the black lace mantilla off her face revealing her dark hair, tinged with gray, severely parted in the center, and pulled back tightly into a bun. She drew herself up proudly, a regal figure in black silk with a high-necked choker of pearls. She had an "I told you so" look on her face.

"Madelaina Obregon. Your niece—that's who!"

Don Diego's head turned sharply in a double take.

35

Astonished and wide-eyed with a mixture of shock and secret pride, he stared intently at his niece, who looked like a young man in the attire she wore. A mixed expression of bafflement and pride crossed his aristocratic face, his eyebrows arched sharply.

"Didn't I tell you she was hopeless, my husband? Completely unmanageable. For five years I have endured every rebellious act. I can take no more. You must send her back to her father at once!" Her voice rose in hysterical cadence. "Why can't she be like other young ladies—like our girls, so lovely and feminine and already eyeing prospective husbands," she said with vain pride. "Madelaina is incorrigible! At school, her tutors whisper she's a radical, a rebel. It's not enough the war with America has just ended—she has to mouth off about the Republic. I tell you, my husband, this is the end. You must send her back to Mexico to her own father. Let him concern himself with her behavior. Mexico is just the place for this wildcat—this *charra*!"

Don Diego listened halfheartedly. His eyes were trained on his favorite niece, who had had the bad misfortune to be born a woman. She was, after all, the image of her father. The handsome, well-educated General Alvaro Obregon was among the brightest, most promising militarists in the army of Presidente Porfirio Diaz. A man of immense dignity, he had graduated with honor from the University at Madrid and from the Berlin Military Academy and later married the daughter of Marquis Francesco Alvarez, an exorbitantly wealthy nobleman from Cordoba. He had taken his beautiful wife to Mexico to live, to the hacienda of the Obregon family, a land grant bestowed upon Don Diego's father who fought alongside General Diaz against Maximilian. Five years following the birth of Madelaina, her mother contracted a mysterious disease and died, leaving the child in the care of her father, a devoted army man with no time to raise a daughter properly. The fact that Madelaina's formative years were spent as an army brat surrounded only by men

36

disturbed her father. When she became a woman at twelve years of age, her father knew it was time to send her to Spain. In the care of his brother and sister-in-law, she would be educated with her cousins in fine finishing schools and learn the ways of a woman who must eventually assume the responsibility of running the Obregon hacienda and adapt herself to the presidential court.

Madelaina had experienced no burning desire to go to Spain, but because she loved her father infinitely and desired only to please him, she had done as he wished. In Spain, at the don's hacienda, she had gone through all the motions, doing what was expected of her, but every free moment would bring about a change in her. She'd shed all the female accouterments, don a pair of trousers and a man's *camisa* and go into the barns where the bulls were bred. She was filled with such fascination for the bulls and all the wildlife in the marshes that nothing else impressed her.

Don Diego sighed deeply. She'd been a rebel all right, he thought as he studied the activity in the bullring. "Ahhhh!" he exclaimed suddenly. "Look at that, Doña Louisa! She puts a professional matador to shame with such passes!"

His spouse threw her hands into the air, fully exasperated with him. "You are worse than she to encourage her! I tell you, my husband, she must go back to Mexico! I'll not permit her to put crazy ideas into the heads of Maria Luisa and Maria Theresa! Do you understand? This time my word is final. Else you shall be banging against a locked bedroom door." She picked up her skirts, spun on her heels, and tossed her head haughtily as she disappeared inside.

Don Diego shrugged perceptibly. Ah, the life of a don here in the wilderness is bound by his wife's bedroom manners. He felt dismayed. He recalled last spring when he took his young niece to the *corrida* in Sanlucar de Barramedas; how flushed her face was when she saw the colorful pageant of glittering matadors in their bravery against the bulls. He vaguely remembered that she had expressed a desire to perform such feats. Now, as he saw the agility, the well-practiced passes, the perfectly coordinated stance of a matador, he realized that she must have been learning the art.

Dark, cloudy skies overhead reflected his mood. The wind had risen.

All I need is to send back a matador instead of a refined lady to her father! Alvaro would never speak with me again. I'd be an outcast!

Don Diego could no longer delay the inevitable and keep peace with his wife. He had no concubines here in Las Marismas, no little *casitas* with one or two mistresses to run to. He missed Madrid passionately for this very reason. Soon it would be winter and travel would be difficult. He had to keep peace with his wife at any cost.

Twenty minutes later, Madelaina Obregon stood before her uncle in his study, dusty, sweating, and flushed with excitement, unable to believe her ears. In a little over a month she'd be back in Mexico with her father and all she loved. Her period of confinement was over. She barely heard the words of apology flow from Don Diego's lips, and she hardly cared.

"You understand, my child, this is not my doing. I shall miss you with all my heart. You've been the only breath of spring in my life for five years, but, in all conscience, I cannot permit you to remain here where you persist in pursuing such dangerous and risky exploits—which, I might add, cause your Tia Louisa's heart to palpitate with fear for your life."

"Yes, Tio Diego, I understand. And thank you. Thank you so much for everything!" She hugged him and beamed with happiness.

She ran upstairs to her room filled with a joy she hadn't known in nearly five years. She felt as if the heavens had opened up and drenched her in a torrent of love and happiness. She only wished Manuelito were here to share her joy.

Outside the heavens erupted in all their madness; the

storm clouds exploded into a fury of a torrential down-pour. The sound of rain against the trees and buildings reached her ears, and she dashed to the balcony doors, flung them open, and stood at the balustrade looking at the sky, rain falling on her face. She flung off the flat-brimmed matador hat, loosened her dark thick hair, shook it out, and allowed the rain to beat against her upturned face. She looked beyond the hacienda proper toward the gray mist hanging low over the marshlands she loved; they had been her sanctuary when she missed her father and Mexico most.

Winter was upon Las Marismas. Soon the ranch would be half under water. But that was all right. It was perfect for the bulls. Oh, how she'd miss these fine, fierce animals. She'd miss them most of all. She promised herself that before she left she would go out among them to bid them farewell.

As Manuelito attested, the effect Madelaina had on the bulls, and they on her, was incredible. When she first arrived at the hacienda, she rode out to see them. She had been severely warned to keep her distance, for bulls were at best unpredictable and so quick you could never tell if one charged you until it was over and too late. The bulls had remained immobile, eyeing her from a distance through some mystical lenses that permitted them to know she was no enemy of theirs. It was almost as if they felt the love she had for them. They never charged her although she came very close to them, a phenomenon even Don Diego found unbelievable and perplexing. If only he knew the half of it.

Besides the bulls, Madelaina would miss the exotic birds, especially those who chose to remain in the marshes year round: goldfinches, thick as bees in a hive, swallows, griffon vultures, partridge, magpies, crested coots, a wide variety of owls and, of course, the purple gallinules. But the bird that fascinated Madelaina the most was the snowy white cattle egret, a bird of year-round residence which not only feeds from cattle but rides on them. In silhouette, with its yellow

39

legs and long saffron bill, it resembles a miniature stork.

Drenched to the skin, Madelaina went back into her room and moved toward the cages of the many injured birds she had found and nursed back to health. A sudden surge of sadness come over her. She could take none of these birds with her and this pained her deeply. She slowly took down the cages, and one at a time she carried them to the balcony, opened them, and released all the birds. The pair of exquisite goldfinch eyed her skeptically; one flew out, then the other, circled about, returning for a moment, and finally disappeared into the mist. The coot was next to leave, then the screechy-voiced snow white owl.

The egret would be next. She called him Pancho Villa for no reason other than his obvious rebellion during the early stages of confinement and later for his expertise at banditry. She had trained him to move about the room uncaged, and he was always stealing something shiny and glittery from her dressing table. *"Bandido!"* she'd storm at him. "Pancho Villa!" She was forever looking for her earrings, or jeweled hairpins, or some such bauble.

Her father's letters came from various areas of Mexico—wherever his duties took him. Often there was mention of an outlaw, a *bandido* who was becoming as popular as another southern *bandido*, whose name she couldn't recall. But the name Pancho Villa remained in her memory, and now, because of the egret, she'd never forget the name. The young beauty didn't know it at that moment, but there would soon be countless reasons why the name Pancho Villa would forever be engrained in her memory.

"Go! Go, Pancho!" she coaxed the bird. The egret remained in his cage, not interested in the freedom she was giving him. She took him from the cage and tossed him into the air. He flapped his wings, dropped a few feet, and circled back, landing on the balcony. "Go, you fool!" she urged. "I'm giving you your freedom." He cocked his head from side to side, eyed her as if

40

she had lost her senses, shook the water from his plumage, and walked the railing toward her. Dismayed, she cried, "Oh, dear, Pancho, why don't you leave? I can't take you with me, and Tia Louisa would never allow you to stay here; you're too much of a nuisance."

The bird stood firm, ruffled his plumage once or twice, and blinked. He was no fool. He flew back into the bedroom and alighted on her dressing table. Madelaina followed him back into the room totally dismayed, yet secretly happy that he loved her enough to refuse his freedom.

As she quickly slipped out of her wet clothes and hung them over the back of a high chair to dry near the fire, she tried her best to appeal to Pancho's intelligence.

"I have too much to do to worry about you. I've got to dress and pack and say good-bye to Armando." She paused. *Madre de Dios*—Armando! She hadn't seen him at the *tienta* that day. Certainly she couldn't leave without saying good-bye to Armando Cortez! She rushed to the door and pulled a damask cord, summoning one of the servants. She pulled a simple cotton dress over her head, an olive green dress, one she felt certain would please her aunt. It was the least she could do in these her final days at the hacienda. She buttoned it at the neck when a knock sounded at her door.

"Ah, Paco," she addressed herself to the stable boy. "Did Señor Cortez come to the *tienta* today?"

The boy shook his head. He had not seen Señor Cortez. With all his duties, he had seen no one. Besides, he told her in his Spanish dialect, this weather would have kept God from making an appearance. Suddenly his eyes brightened. "*Señorita*, it was rumored around the stable that Señor Cortez has volunteered for duty with the army—bound for Morocco." He scratched his head. "*Si*, I am sure that is. what I heard."

But she had heard nothing. At least Armando hadn't

41

mentioned anything about joining the army one way or another. "Go," she said. "Leave me. If I need you, I'll call."

She paced the floor for several moments. He wouldn't have left without saying good-bye, she reassured herself. Finally, unable to endure the suspense, she grabbed a cloak, ran down the steps, crossed the muddied courtyard, and once inside the deserted stables, she saddled her stallion herself. In the pouring rain she rode Don Quixote five kilometers to the Cortez hacienda, searching everywhere for Armando. No one had seen him since early morning. He was in Sevilla on business and expected later. Wouldn't the *señorita* take refuge from the storm? The wrath of Boreas was upon them.

Disappointed at not finding him, she returned to Don Diego's estate muddied and soaked to the skin. In her room, she disrobed, washed, dressed in warmer clothing, and sat before the fire. Drawing her escritoire closer to the fires to keep warm, she wrote Armando a letter. There was so much to do—clothes to be packed, a suitable companion to be found—how was it possible it could all be accomplished in four days? Four days? That would mean her departure was scheduled for Monday, December 1, 1909.

She began to write in her delicate hand:

"Querido Armando:

It is with a mixture of sadness and exquisite happiness that I write this to you. On Monday, God willing, I shall depart for my home in Mexico to reside with and keep house for my father, one of the duties to which a woman is resigned. It happened quite by a strange coincidence and quite hastily, I might add. I received a letter from Manuelito today! Thank the blessed Virgin he is fine—and in Madrid someplace, although he didn't elaborate on what he was doing. Feeling somewhat despondent over the revelation of his love for me contained in the letter, I felt the urge to handle the bulls.

Well, need I tell you what happened? My *tia* saw

42

me—she was very upset that I had disgraced myself to do such a terrible thing as fight the bulls. One thing led to another, and I have been given permission to return to my country.

As exuberant as I am to be leaving, I entertain mixed feelings of despair to be leaving you. Truly, *querido*, you've been more than just a friend and superb lover—" Madelaina hesitated over this word, then shrugged and wrote it anyway. "The many moments we shared together are imprinted upon my heart and soul until I die. In your heart I'll know you'll cherish me more than any other, since it was you who plucked my virginity. I wished I loved you as you claim to love me. One day you'll find true love, and I shall become the faded dream of your youth. *Querido*, you will always be welcome at the hacienda of my father and should you need further enticement, the most desirous of maidens reside in Mexico. The idea should titillate your senses and prompt a speedy visit to our shores."

Before she sealed the letter, she added a postscript. "Please, Armando, if ever you find Manuelito Perez, tell him for me how terribly disappointed I was that he should have left us without a farewell. Tell him that I will always love him as I've loved you, and that I wish him happiness and peace wherever he is. I know one day, if he dedicates himself to his art, he will be better than any matador in all of Spain. Tell him how miserable we've all felt that he should have disappeared from our lives without thinking how much he'd hurt us. But it's all in the past and I only have good thoughts for him. More important, tell him all is forgiven. He'll understand. Madelaina Obregon."

She sealed the beige parchment envelope, scented it with floral sachets, and stamped her father's crest upon it with sealing wax. Then she ran hastily down the back steps toward the kitchen and butter rooms, where she found young Paco doing errands for the cook in preparation for the evening meal.

"Paco! Paco!" she called to him and guided him outside into the rear portico. "Ride swiftly to the hacienda

43

of Don Felipe Cortez and place this letter personally into the hands of Don Armando. Into no one else's hands, understand?"

The alert brown-skinned ten-year-old nodded dutifully and craftily eyed the few coins she pressed into his hands, with another eye on the brooding elements. "All right, you little thief," she scolded, giving him a few more coins.

"*Si, matadora! Al punto,*" he said with a broad wink. He glanced apprehensively at the darkening sky and the pouring rain which had already formed large puddles. He jingled the coins in his trousers and shrugged. "*Hasta luego!*" he cried bravely and disappeared into the stables.

Dinner that evening was filled with a strained silence. Madelaina noticed that everyone avoided talking, and moreover, they avoided her eyes. Immediately afterward, she was summoned to the private study of her uncle Don Diego. Doña Louisa, standing like a frozen statue before the fireplace, remained immobile while Madelaina shuffled self-consciously before them, glancing from one to the other. When she saw the familiar beige envelope in her uncle's hands, she tensed. *Madre de Dios!* Mother of God! They know.

They both, uncle and aunt, began speaking simultaneously. She was unable to make out a word either of them said in the highly emotional confusion. Her aunt screamed hysterically, calling her vile names and insisting that Don Felipe's son be made to do the honorable thing. Hadn't she know all along that Madelaina was no good? Whom had she taken after? Whose indecent genes had she inherited? How had she permitted herself to be seduced like a common *puta*, a whore? What would she tell the general? How could they explain her deflowerment? That she'd been to a bordello—a whorehouse?

Don Diego insisted the right thing be done. Armando would have to marry her and make an honest woman of her. He would confer with Don Cortez. After all, it would be a good marriage, one which would insure an ample dowry. If they had coupled together in the first place, there must have been some attraction between them. Yes, it was settled. There would be a quick marriage, one that could be arranged before her ship sailed.

Despite Madelaina's protestations, her anger, her displeasure, and all the arguments she could offer against marrying someone she didn't love, her words met deaf ears. How could *she* know what she wanted, when she wasn't responsible for her actions? She had just turned sixteen in May. She was still a child. *They* knew what must be done. And it had to be done in a hurry. It was the only way they could explain to her father the fact that she hadn't taken to her studies as well as expected. Madelaina was no virgin—no lady—but by God, they would turn her into one through marriage.

For an hour she listened to their stormy rantings and ravings, to their curses, their embarrassment, and she vowed right then and there she'd leave the hacienda. There would be no marriage between her and Armando Cortez, despite what her aunt and uncle commanded. She wasn't about to marry a man she didn't love. What's more, she wouldn't demean Armando by having him coerced into doing something he had no mind to do. Never once had she confronted her uncle with the fact she'd seen him at the bordello. Why was it so terrible?

"No! No!" she cried out. "Never! Never will I marry Armando Cortez! Nothing you both do will make me change my mind!" She ran from the study and raced up the stairs, two at a time. She slammed her door and bolted it. Frenzied and erratic, she glanced about the room, uncertain of what to do first. Being of sound mind, she went immediately for her cash box. Her father had sent her money for which she had little use, since she didn't splurge on costly wardrobes or jewels and other costly baubles in which young women often indulged. Now, as she searched through her box and

45

frantically counted the money, she realized that, although a tidy sum had accumulated, there wasn't nearly enough to book passage back to Mexico. The black *torero*'s suit she'd worn earlier that day was dry. She quickly slipped into it. She pulled her thick black hair atop her head, pinned it flat, then put on her *camisa*. Dismayed by her protruding breasts, she reached for a band of linen in the drawer of a chest and bound her upper torso. She folded the *pesetas* into a makeshift moneybelt and put on her shirt and jacket. At least with the jacket, her breasts weren't as prominent. She took hope. She placed the round, flat-crowned hat squarely on her head and studied her reflection in the mirror. Without makeup, she might pass for a young man. Might, she told herself, realizing she would have to be on guard every moment. She could take no clothing, no luggage, at least not from this house. She would have to follow the Guadalquivir to the coast to either Sanlucar or Cadiz. From there, she would travel to Lisbon to get a commercial boat to Cuba, then on to Vera Cruz and then Mexico City.

But would her money take her that far? What would she do? What?

She searched frantically through her jewelry for anything she could convert to cash. The moneylenders would give little for her possessions, but anything would help her reach her destination. The double diamond ring, a costly necklace of diamonds and rubies which had belonged to her mother, and four rings were stuffed into a linen handkerchief and shoved into her inner jacket pocket. She glanced about the room and in a final gesture walked back to the escritoire. Taking pen in hand, she wrote a note to her aunt and uncle: "Thank you for all you've done. I cannot be responsible for ruining two lives, my own and that of Armando Cortez. God bless you both, Madelaina Obregon, your loving niece."

All the while her pet egret continued to eye her askance in a nearly human manner. She refrained from conversing with him for fear she'd relent and take him

46

with her. She propped the note up in clear view, next to a photograph of her father in full dress uniform astride his white stallion, where her aunt and uncle would be certain to find it when they came looking for her.

About ready to slip the bolt and open the door, she took one last glance about the room she'd occupied for so long. Her eyes fell on Pancho Villa. He looked so forlorn, her heart melted. Quickly she reached for a small wooden cage she used to confine a sick bird. "All right, you *bribón*—you rascal—you win," she whispered to him. She placed him inside and firmly secured the latch. She grasped the cage in her hand, slipped the door bolt with the other, and let herself out into the gleaming tiled corridor where she cautiously moved toward the back steps, which yawned before her like an endless black pit.

It wasn't until she reached the last step that she realized she hadn't said good-bye to her cousins, Maria Theresa and Maria Luisa. She wasn't about to take time now for fear they'd try to change her mind. She'd write them from Lisbon as soon as her passage had been secured and express her affection for them both. They really had little in common, but they had been the closest thing to family she'd ever known and deserved a soft place in her heart.

Thank God the servants had retired. She cursed at the sound of her leather boots clicking on the tiles and walked on her toes to the rear door. Outside, the downpour was steady and unrelenting. She grabbed a cape from a wooden peg on the wall, wrapped herself in it, and shielding Pancho Villa, made her way across the courtyard, grateful for the rain which covered up any noise she might have made. She hoped the stable boys had retired. Once in a while they'd remain awake playing cards and drinking wine. But on such a night, they'd retire to their cabins, drink hot thick coffee or chocolate, and get into bed with their *putas* or wives to keep the chill from their bones.

She resaddled Don Quixote, calming the stallion

47

with soothing words. In no time, she was braving the elements, following the precarious route along the Guadalquivir, and giving thanks to God she knew the route with her eyes closed. It wasn't until dawn broke that she first saw faint signs of Sanlucar de Barramedas. For an instant she felt a tinge of regret. She glanced back over her shoulder. The rain had turned into a faint drizzle. She would miss Las Marismas, her uncle, and life at the hacienda, for in her heart had been stored a wealth of fond memories of Armando Cortez and Manuelito Perez.

Madelaina disliked Sanlucar de Barramedas; it was a dirty, low-lying seaport town at the mouth of the Guadalquivir. About the only favorable mention ever made of Sanlucar was that Manzanilla, one of Spain's noblest wines, was made there, and of course the fact that Christopher Columbus set sail from this dreary port on his third voyage to the New World. Also, Magellan had set sail from here to circumnavigate the globe. Madelaina had learned all this from her tutor in history, but it was not for these that she'd remembered Sanlucar. It was for the ancient Moorish-style bullring where Manuelito had sacrificed so much to get her box seats for the *corrida*. It was for the fond memories of Doña Sofia's mansion on her birthday and of course that palace up on the hill where Armando made love to her and deflowered her. Those were memories. But she had no time to think about this. Not now. She headed her horse along the waterfront. She had to get a ship which would transport her to Lisbon. This was her primary concern and she had no time to dawdle.

At the waterfront, which had just begun to yawn awake, she listened to the water lapping against the stone walls of the basin and swirling in eddies around the steps leading below to the dinghies and fishing boats. Somewhere a chain clanked heavily. Madelaina tethered her horse to a hitching post and walked in bold strides up and down the dock. At one end, the gates were closed. How would she get through them and past the custom officials? Her money wouldn't furnish the bribe they'd demand for allowing her through without a passport. Suddenly she realized she had left her old passport at the hacienda. What a fool. Why hadn't she thought of it? Now, more complications!

As she swaggered along the cobblestones, in as masculine a manner as could be affected, and tried to ward off the cold, damp chill, she saw a sailor emerge from an old building at the opposite side of the shipping basin. She slipped back alongside a siding that stored line. The sailor approached unsteadily along the water side, singing an untranslatable French folk song. He was evidently returning from an all-night carousal in the warm bed of a woman; he had an unmistakable look of content on his face. No one else was within sight. Madelaina, growing bolder, stepped out before him, barring his path. The sailor broke off in his song and, with a look of astonishment, stopped short and instinctively felt for his knife sheath.

"*Por favor,*" she began, affecting a deep husky voice. "I wish to ask you a few questions. Do you understand my Spanish?"

He shook his head, replying in a most unusual accented French that he was a Frenchman and didn't understand a word of Spanish.

She relaxed. Her French was excellent. In his language she asked him for a moment of his time to reply to some questions.

"Are you armed?" he asked suspiciously, his hand still on his sheath.

"No. I only wish your help." She regretted instantly telling him she carried no weapons. She had to make a quick decision. "I must get away from here. I must get passage to Vera Cruz."

"A stowaway? Is that it? You wish to be a stowaway?"

She hadn't considered that, but it sounded as if it might solve her financial worries. She didn't catch the appraising looks he gave her.

"Are you running from the police?"

"No. From a shotgun wedding."

"Ahhh!" He laughed with jocular contempt. "They'll get ya every time if you let 'em!" He spoke atrocious French, with a peculiar, unfamiliar twang.

"Which vessel are you with?"

"An oil tanker to Brazil. Shipping oil one way and munitions the other. With all these blasted wars in every other nation, a man can make money no other way."

Madelaina tried to bargain with him. "All I have is my horse and saddle." She pointed to the handsome stallion and the silver-studded saddle.

"Are you sure it's yours to begin with? I don't intend being nabbed for stealing horses," he replied, appraising both the stallion and this unusual stranger.

"I assure you it's mine!" she said, forgetting herself by letting a touch of arrogance creep into her natural voice.

Alerted by the change in her voice, the sailor, Pierre, grabbed her by the arm and with his free hand whipped off her hat in a sudden quick movement.

"*Mon Dieu*! You are a woman! No, no, no, no, I want no part of this. I will not take it upon my conscience to stowaway a woman among a hundred rape-happy lusty men. No, no, no, no!" He wagged a finger at her.

"Then tell me, please, what am I to do? I left my passport at home. I have no money, but I must get to Vera Cruz. Once I get to Mexico City, my father will reimburse you what money I owe."

It was difficult making herself understood, and more difficult understanding him. But in any language, she recognized a stern no and a firm disapproval. "You will have to go to Lisbon and board a commercial ship, m'amselle," he insisted. "But without a passport—there is no hope. Unless—"

"Unless what?"

He rubbed his fingers together. "For a certain price, there are those artists who will perform services of procuring passports for people in your circumstances." He gazed at the horse and slowly they approached it. "It is your horse—for certain?" he asked. "*Mon Dieu*, such a beauty!"

"He's a thoroughbred," she said proudly. "I wish only that I could take him with me to Mexico. My father would be more than happy to pay for his transportation. He is called Don Quixote—my horse, not my father."

The Frenchman studied her through new eyes. "Just who is your father that he is so able to pay for such costly expenses? Why did he not send you the money to come home properly as befits a m'amselle?" he asked suspiciously.

Somehow, she knew she could trust him. She had to. There was no other way. In his eyes, she saw a gentleness, nothing cold and calculating or lecherous. "I am the daughter of General Alvaro Obregon, Premier Chief of the Army of Presidente Diaz in Mexico," she said with a marked tinge of pride.

Pierre Duprez glanced sharply in her direction. His expression changed noticeably. He pulled himself up, and before her eyes he became another person. She noticed his powerful physique, his muscular forearms, the impressive upper torso, narrow waist and muscular thighs bulging through his faded denim trousers. His blue eyes, remarkably blue, seemed familiar to Madelaina. She had the feeling she knew this man from someplace. The ragged sailor suit seemed out of place on him, and she determined that under his bearded stubble he might be quite handsome.

In that atrocious French accent he asked her if she spoke English.

"Yes," she replied. "Not as well as I speak French, Italian, and Spanish, but I do comprehend the gringo talk and speak it moderately." Madelaina paused a moment. Where did she know this man from? "Why?" she asked.

"Because, m'am, ah am an American. Ah'm presently en route to Texas, mahself. Being a freedom fighter, ah intend ta join the people's revolution against that there President Diaz and men like yer father." His speech became brittle, his manner curt.

"There's a revolution in my country?" she asked in astonishment.

"If it hasn't already begun, it's damned near set ta explode. How long ya been away from Mexico?"

She detected his gringo drawl and suddenly it came to her. He'd been the man in the room next to the one she shared with Armando on her birthday—at that fancy bordello high in the hills. *Dios mios*! She felt the heat of embarrassment flood her body and rise to her face. She turned from him so he wouldn't recognize her. "Five years," she said dully.

"Pretty doggone good fer ya. Y'all 've been kept on a shelf while that dictator Diaz has been splittin' up the pie pretty good. He's become a dangblasted millionaire while the pore *peóns* hafta grub fer their breakfast like dirt scratchin' chickens."

"What do you know of the *peóns* in Mexico?"

"M'am, ah know plenty about 'em. It's the same everywhere. *Peóns* are the poor people in every land cheated by the rich. They don't have a chance unless men like me and this here Pancho Villa of yours take up the banner and help 'em get up a grub stake to help 'em along in life. The way ah hear it, this here *El Presidente* of yours has been squeezing them pore Indians right off their lands, and there ain't a damned thing they can do about it. It's a damn shame. Ah guess, m'am, it's about as bad a thing as the white man did ta the Indians in my country. They been castrated, turned into eunuchs, stripped of all respect for themselves and their tribes. The way ah see it, someone's gotta fight for the rights of them poor bastards—or else they're gonna die off and become extinct. Ain't nobody gonna know who he is or what he is no more."

"Are you declaring me your enemy?" she asked, listening intently.

He pondered this a moment. "Well, if this here General Obreygon is yore fathah—an' ah'm about ta be fightin' right along side of Pancho Villa—yeah, ya

52

might say that's the short of it." His Texas drawl grew more obvious.

"You won't help me get home so I can see what's happening in my land?"

"Ain't much a li'l thing like you can do anyway. So ya might figure you should stay heah an' marry the man—shotgun or not."

"No! Never!" she retorted hotly. "I'll die first. Mexico is my country. I must return to see what I can do to help matters. If what you say is true—I am certain my father knows nothing of such terrible goings on. He would never condon *El Presidente*'s robbing the poor of their lands.

"Listen, ain't General Obreygon the one that's been giving Zapata a few stickeroonies?"

"I do not undetstand—*stickeroonies*?"

"You know—a few blasts. A peppering with a few rounds of buckshot. Raising a small war," he explained.

"I have no idea of what you speak. I've never heard of the name Zapata."

The gringo studied her with a smile of amusement on his lips. "You know somethin', li'l lady? Ah think you and me is gonna have us a few long talks. Ah can see yer education needs a little boost or two, ya hear?"

Madelaina didn't like his attitude or his insolence. He had been frank and polite up to a certain point. Could she help it if she didn't know about the revolution? He made her feel as if the unfortunate mess was her fault. But, she had no choice, and he did seem to be knowledgeable and worldly.

As it turned out, Madelaina's education needed more of a boost, but it wasn't until they were aboard the Portugese liner *Mozambique*, where they were registered as Mr. and Mrs. Peter Duprez, that they were able to exchange views on the revolution in Mexico and other vital matters.

Before that, Duprez had attempted every way he knew possible to get a forged passport for Madelaina Obregon. It was not a lack of money that forced the

53

forgers to decline his offer—it's just that the authorities had cracked down. Every decent forger had closed shop temporarily and fled Lisbon. An old friend of his, Madama Julia Bolivar, the proprietress of a bordello on the waterfront, had greeted the dejected young American with openhearted warmth and plied him with drinks on the house, when he sought her out.

"I cannot believe this is Pierre Duprez so down in the mouth, with such a long face. Are you ready to have a good time, *señor*, like always? Maria is available—even Philomia—to make you laugh—no?"

"Not this time, Portegee," he said with genuine affection in his voice. "This time I have many problems." He could trust Portegee. She was a regular dame—all heart, and right where it counted. She had never skinned him or any of the friends he'd sent to her, and she could always be counted on in scary times—when they were fleeing France or Germany where his freedom fighting had taken him. Her large bedroom eyes always contained secret mirth.

Portegee laughed her lusty, bawdy laugh, grabbed a bottle of wine and two glasses, and pulled him toward the back of the whorehouse into her makeshift office. "Sit down, gringo. Tell Portegee all about it. Sometimes another head can think clearer, no?" She searched his eyes. "Has some worthless, two-timing *puta* carved her heart into yours? Eh?" She poured the wine and they clinked glasses. "To love—eh, gringo?" She patted her frizzed blonde hair.

"Nothing better to drink to than that, Portegee." He drank the contents of the glass and she poured more. "Now, tell Portegee all about it, so I can see a smile return to your face and once more your blue eyes will light up my day."

He told her his problem, omitting only the identity of his passenger.

"*Si*, things are tough here. The authorities are cracking down, since the war—Portugal wishes to remain neutral, and with so many war criminals escaping, they try to keep relations with our neighbors on a friendly basis."

She pondered the situation for several minutes, then a light flared in her dark eyes. "What is so impossible? You are an American citizen, no?"

"Yes."

"Then marry the girl! Under your passport she can go wherever you go." She wiped the corners of her full red lips and smiled at her wisdom.

"But that's impossible! I hardly know her," he stammered.

"So you have it annulled when you get to America. Once she is in her country—and her papers are available to her—she will be in no trouble. You see how easy it is?" She reached over and planted a juicy wet kiss on his lips.

An hour later, after explaining the situation to Madelaina, he grew apologetic. "The only possible way we can get you aboard the *Mozambique* is as Mrs. Peter Duprez, my wife."

Madelaina stared at him. "But this is incredible. No, it is impossible! I am Catholic. I would have to be married by a priest."

"All the more reason to get it annulled when I get you home safely to Mexico."

"This is the only way, Mr. Duprez?"

"Afraid so, li'l girl." He explained the situation. "Besides we can save money on the passage by sharing one cabin."

Her suspicion was piqued. "But," she protested. "But—"

"Don't worry, li'l girl. Ya don't have ta fear me. Ah wouldn't touch a young 'un like ya. Ah don't aim to be put in the brig or face a firing squad. I know Mexican laws, ya hear? Besides, it would be against my grain to molest a young 'un."

That afternoon, Madelaina Obregon and Peter Duprez were married by a magistrate in dismal, shabby surroundings. She told herself not to mind all this, that it was only an expedient to get to her country, that

55

nothing mattered except returning to her father. So she closed her eyes and recited the vows as if by rote. Peter slipped a golden circlet around her third finger and hoped the magistrate hadn't noticed it was a gold earring. Earlier Peter Duprez had bought her a dove gray travel suit with whalebone corsets, the latest in fashion, and a few other travel clothes and accessories. "Ya just can't get hitched in those bullfighter's pants—it jus' ain't decent," he teased her.

The next morning, Mr. and Mrs. Peter Duprez boarded the ship with only a mere alteration of his papers—the inclusion of a wife. After the custom officials saw the delirium of love written on Mrs. Peter Duprez's face, they were ushered to the bridal suite, which Peter had been able to afford by saving the cost of separate fares. Below, stored in the hold with other animals was the satiny beauty Don Quixote, with whom Peter Duprez couldn't part.

Settled in the larger cabin which boasted twin beds and a small sitting room and bath, Madelaina relaxed and tried to devote herself to making their four weeks aboard ship as enjoyable as possible. None of the other passengers thought it strange when Mr. and Mrs. Peter Duprez remained in their cabin most of the trip—they were newlyweds. The captain had readily informed the more inquisitive. At night after dinner in their cabin, when most of the other passengers had retired or remained in the lounge playing cards or socializing, Peter and Madelaina would walk along the promenade deck. Peter was insistent on the exercise. It was in the intimacy of dinner each night that they got to know more about each other.

She expounded on the breeding of bulls and explained how one breed became far superior to another through interbreeding and how the environment contributed to the strength and bravery of the breed. As she talked, Peter Dupez became fascinated with this beautiful creature who talked more like a man than any young woman he'd ever met.

"Ah always thought the Miura bulls were the

bravest," he told her in reflection. He'd seen the runs at Pampalona, and the Miura were fierce and frightening. "They even turned on each other," he told her.

"Only because bulls can't tolerate other bulls whose smells they don't know. They'll duel such intruders to the death," she said. "Many matadors refuse to fight Miuras—they are too unpredictable. You see, the Andalucia bulls, due to the rocky terrain, develop hooves and leg muscles far stronger than the Salamanca bulls who are subjected to a softer soil and find no need to develop such strength. It's a well-known fact, the southern bulls from Las Marismas from the hacienda of my uncle are far superior to any. The effort produced when the bulls lift their legs from the sucking sand develops muscles in their thighs and knees—where it counts."

In Lisbon Peter had purchased an ample wardrobe for the crossing, and she dressed exquisitely for him, knowing how it pleased him. The lights of appreciation in his eyes told enough. She found herself doing more than she felt capable of doing for a stranger. Each day, she saw desire mount in him. He was superb at controlling his emotions and his desire, and he maintained a superb pose of aloofness and detachment. It was Madelaina who began to feel the pangs of desire shoot through her, something unfulfilled with Armando, which demanded attention. The low pains in her stomach, coupled with the anxiety of thinking she didn't appeal to Peter as a woman, left her nervous and high strung. Her body, awakened to pleasure, now craved it.

Her naïveté when she first coupled with Armando had disappeared after she studied a few books in Don Diego's library. Having watched the breeding of bulls and the foaling of horses since the age of fourteen, Madelaina had quickly dismissed any illusion she'd nurtured about storks and cabbage patches. What confused her was the foreplay and the little courtship rites.

She had plenty of time to think about Armando Cortez and how he made his desire for her known. He had told her straight out. She had accepted that. But it was different with Peter Duprez. She sensed it. Because he had had three woman making love to him the first night she saw him, she assumed he'd have to be more worldly than Armando.

The urge for coupling grew stronger by the day. She asked herself why Peter didn't express himself the way Armando had. Didn't he wish to share his feelings of love with her? She attempted to delude herself into thinking Peter felt no such emotions toward her, but her womanly intuition negated this when she clearly saw the desire in his eyes. What then? Are gringos simply men without emotions? Is it only the Spaniard who's fired by his passionate emotions and moved to consummating such feelings in the act of love?

The second week out to sea, Madelaina dressed in an exquisite and revealing black Alençon lace dress. With her black silky hair piled high atop her head, she looked like an artist's masterpiece. She had her father's patrician good looks, her mother's pale complexion, and an earthy quality that belied fragility.

Immeasurably impressed by her appearance, Peter expressed his feelings and brought a pleasurable flush to her cheeks. "Ya shore look gussied up right pretty there, *señorita*," he drawled, pouring champagne for her just before dinner.

On this night she remained quiet and mysterious, her eyes reflecting the burning desire for him which she tried desperately to conceal. She had decided she was going to make a few passes at him, a few *verónicas*, as she did with the bulls. After all, it was like a game, this lovemaking, a contest of wits between two people, just as it was when she matched wits with the animals.

They got through the guinea hens, sautéed in mushrooms and wine sauce, and sat talking over demi-tasse. They had sipped the last of the champagne. Madelaina felt warm inside. She intended to meet him head on, to ask him straight out—the way he talked.

"Peter, why do you not wish to express love with me the way a man does with a woman?"

"What?" His cup to his lips, Peter sputtered over the

hot coffee and quickly reached for his napkin. He wiped his chin, pressing the fabric against his lips, his china blue eyes twinkling with a mixture of mirth and astonishment. "What's that ya say? Dang-blasted hot coffee! Ah—who said ah didn't?"

"But you have not asked me. You have not declared that you need me desperately, that your heart would wither and die if we did not couple."

Peter sat back on the sofa, very still now and searched her eyes deeply. He had made no advances for several reasons. One, she was the daughter of General Obregon, and he didn't cotton to the thought of hanging by his neck in the very near future. Two, she was only sixteen. Gads, he was no cradle snatcher. True, she didn't look sixteen. At least nineteen. And tonight even twenty. No way would he work himself up to even consider bagging the wench under these conditions, even though the thought had crossed his mind countless times. He just kept shoving those reasons into the foreground of his thoughts whenever the thought struck him. Under this pressure—and the sudden seductive posture on her part—he asked the most pertinent question he could think of, under the circumstances.

"Tell me, little one. Have ya been asked by others? Have many declared they needed ya desperately—that their hearts would wither and die if ya didn't couple with them?" A half-amused smile twitched at the corner of his lips.

"But of course. How else would I know of such things?" she asked with an air of worldliness and unabashed honesty.

"Well, ah'll be a dang-blasted, ring-tailed monkey's uncle." He rose to his feet and paced the floor in utter astonishment. He lit a cigar and puffed on it furiously. "Ya mean someone used that line on ya and ya fell for it?" Her hurt reaction brought an instant change of words. "What ah mean is that—uh—er—" Peter couldn't bring himself to speak so frankly of such things. *There's a time and place for everything—but not discussing it like this. The little baggage—and all without a sense of shame!*

"Why are you so embarrassed? Can you not speak easily of such things?"

"No! And you shouldn't either!"

"You gringos are a strange breed. Quite exasperating at times."

"We gringos have more sense than those—uh—Spaniards ya been fooling with! Exasperatin' or not," he added ruefully.

"Fooling with? I don't understand. We were quite sincere, Peter." Madelaina paused, her face cherry pink. "No. That's not quite true, Peter. Armando was sincere, I think. It was I who was insincere. I didn't feel what he told me I'd feel. But I never told him. I wouldn't hurt his feelings. Poor Armando. You see—that's why I wouldn't allow myself to be pushed into marriage. I will not lie to the man I love. To have lied to him was proof enough in my eyes that I didn't love him."

"Ya make it sound so simple, little one, that ah swear ah'm mighty confused." He paced the confines of their cabin in marked agitation. Why was he angry? She didn't mean a damn ta him. She'd given him her horse and saddle—a helluva a bargain. She had plenty of money to have paid for her own passage, only she didn't know it. He'd told her right off that he was joining with Pancho Villa and that her father was his natural enemy. He'd given her the option to back off, but she didn't. Now, here she was, after two weeks at sea, asking him questions to which he had no answers.

Hell's bells! Peter Duprez was no cherry. He'd laid women on every continent: young'uns, old, black and white, even redskins, rich and poor, whores and ladies, but he'd never met the likes o' this Obregon girl. At times she was like one o' the boys. She even asked him to let her smoke a ceegar, them skinny jobs from Cuba—the best. And now, bold as she pleased, she was askin' him to lay her. That's the short o' it, he told

60

himself. Well, he was jus' gonna hafta tell her, like it was.

"There's somethin's a man's gotta do for himself, Little Fox," he told her. "And askin' a lady to bed is one o' 'em." There, that oughta do it, he thought.

"Well, then, Peter, ask me. I'm willing. I'm so willing that I can't bear it much longer," she said in all honesty. "Why do you call me Little Fox?"

Peter Duprez paused in the lighting of his cigar. His mouth hung agape. He had to move quickly to catch the burning stogie before it burned his vest. "Ya know somethin', Little Fox?" he said, ignoring her last question. "You and me is gonna have us a few more long talks. Yer education needs more boostin', ya hear?"

Before she could say anything else, Peter had left to go above deck. Dismayed, Madelaina recalled she hadn't said the things she wanted to tell him. She pulled on a wrap and went on deck to find him. The music of the orchestra wafted out from the salon. The sounds of laughter, of people enjoying themselves echoed from one end of the ship to the other. A gust of wind came at her and she raised her head and gazed up into the sky. The stars hung heavy overhead. It was a clear, balmy night, and the moon on the ocean gave it a tranquil appearance. Madelaina wished she felt as tranquil as the sea. A turbulence churned inside her, one she couldn't control or make subside. She wasn't about to ask Peter to share his love with her again. He had made her feel like a fool.

She stood at the aft rail, not sure of how long she had been there, when a voice called to her. "Don't be startled, Little Fox. It's only me. But ya hadn't better be doing like this—leavin' the cabin all alone. It can be dangerous walkin' around at night on a ship. It's too easy ta fall and go overboard."

She said nothing.

"I had to do me a little thinkin' about all ya said. Ya asked me why I don't want ta express love with ya the way that there Armando Cortez did." He turned her to face him. Her wide dark eyes lifted to meet his.

61

"If ya know what's good fe ya, little one, you'll stop asking for it, 'cause I'm likely ta take ya up on it."

"If Teresina and the other three girls can take you, Peter, I don't see why I can't," she challenged defiantly.

He frowned deeply, his eyes narrowed. She could see the questions in his eyes. Several long moments passed before he asked. "What do ya know of Teresina and three girls?" He acted a bit self-conscious, all the while searching her face for some sign of recognition.

"It's not what you think." She suddenly laughed, giving her some relief from the built-up tension. "You know how difficult it is to sleep at night?"

"Ya don't mean ta be telling me yer falling in love with me."

"I don't know what I'm trying to say. But it's terribly frustrating to be considered a child when you have the body and intelligence of a woman."

"So. Ya think yer a woman? Who put that into yer head—that there Armando fella?" he said with biting sarcasm. He tenderly drew her wrap up around her neck, closer to her face. "It's getting cooler now. Stay bundled up. I don' wancha ta be catching yer death before ah get ya to Mexico."

"Why do you keep speaking of him in such a bad way? Armando was my friend."

"Ah'll jus' betcha he was. Look, ya better get back to the cabin. If ya don't ah'm likely to start teachin' ya what life is really all about."

He was very close to her now. Her small flushed face tilted up to his. Dark fires burned brightly in her eyes and reached out into the depths of his heart, stirring him to high passion. He reached toward her, held her face between his strong hands, and kissed her lightly at first. Her response both startled him and delighted him. She kissed him back the way Armando taught her. "I want to know about life, Peter," she said quietly.

"Whooooa, Little Fox." He backed off. "Yer goin' a mite fast for this old cowhand. Ya hadn't oughta be doing me like that!" He whistled softly. "Let's walk for a spell." He swallowed hard at the increased sweep of passion surging through him. It happened so fast, Peter had no strength left to resist her. Besides, the wench was asking for it like no one he'd ever met. It was a thoroughly new experience for him to play the hunted rather than the hunter in the game of love.

For two weeks he had examined the consequences and the implications of messing around with the daughter of a respected Mexican general. One thing was certain: the kind of thoughts he was thinking now would not be recommended for the promotion of friendly relations between gringos and *latinos*. Ten minutes later, nestled in each other's arms, Peter Duprez shouted aloud, "To hell with promoting relations between the gringos and *latinos*." He fairly startled Madelaina by such a declaration.

She lay naked next to his warm, strong body and inhaled the very presence of him in her arms. And Peter, inhaling the scent of rose petals, found his passion increasing.

For a time he just held her, doing nothing, just feeling her. He told her to do the same. After a few awkward moments, she began to feel the difference. With Armando Cortez' bumbling sexual exertions, she had felt nothing. Now she was confronted with so many new sensations, she didn't know which to record first.

"What shall I do? What do you want me to do first?" she asked in innocence.

"Just lie there quiet like, Little Fox. Just feel me. Let yer own feelings take hold. Mother Nature will step in right after that ta tell ya what ta do."

He kissed her again. Madelaina let herself go. Here was a master craftsman, not a bumbling apprentice. In moments the warmth of his body fused into hers and she felt a rising excitement, a tingling sensation from head to toe. He lifted her raven tresses and fanned them out on the pillow and buried his face next to her neck. She could feel the warmth, the shivering sensation of his hot breath on her ears and neck. Her skin tingled, the tiny hairs on her body stood on end.

His warm passionate kisses began on her lips and traveled the side of her face to her ears and throat. Then, he kissed her breasts and began to nibble at them. How tender, how gentle he was, she thought. Yet he's setting me on fire with all these light kisses and almost imperceptible movements. She wanted to speak, to tell him what she felt, but she felt certain he knew, so she concentrated on the feeling, which to her was the most exquisite, intoxicating sensation she'd ever experienced.

His expert hands, soft and sensuous, moved slowly down her body caressing every curve, every soft, graceful line, over her hips and down her thigh. With his mouth over her lips, he placed her hand over his manhood and felt her reaction. Her eyes fluttered open in amazement. He was built like some of the seed bulls on the *rancho*. Under her touch it seemed to expand and tremble with anticipation. She began to manipulate it in fast jerking movements as Armando had requested her to do. Instantly his hand clasped over hers and he slowed her down to a caressing touch. Slowly and sensuously, up and down and around. "Easy, now, Li'l Fox, slow and gentle, that's it."

Madelaina had wanted this, never knowing she'd feel such exquisite delight. Peter placed his hand gently between her thighs, stroking her lightly until he reached the velvety lips. She moved sensuously under his touch. So many new sensations crashed through her body and mind, she was unable to distinguish them or feel them individually. She wanted all—at once. It was all too pleasurable—too scintillating.

If this was the coupling men and women did together, God, how beautiful!

Oh, she had so much to write Armando about. After all, he was only a boy. Peter Duprez was a man. *Madre de Dios!* What a man! She knew the difference between men, now. With a man one doesn't think— one feels—feels—feels.

Peter swung her arms around his neck and whispered, "Cling to me, hold me tight, little one. Ya see jus' how ready ya are? The honey's jus' dripping from ya." He sighed heavily. "Ya can't know how much ah've been wantin' ya. From the moment ah first realized ya were a woman, like any red-blooded man, ah desired ya. When ah learned who ya were, ah jus' pushed myself away from ya. Not 'cause ah didn't hanker after ya, ya sweet li'l thing."

"I'm glad for that, Peter," she whispered huskily.

"Ah don't want ya to be afraid, now. Yer almost like a li'l ole virgin, ya know. Ah'll not frighten ya. Ya hear?" He spoke softly to her, telling her sweet endearing things to make her feel she was his only concern in the world. She felt such a strong pull toward him. Their bodies clung in such a magnetic pull, it left them breathless and quivering until both their bodies trembled with ecstasy.

"How much a fool you must have thought me," she said.

He cut her off sharply. "Shhh, sweet li'l thing. If yer mind's working like that ah haven't performed well enough. Just lay back and feel, let me communicate— let us both communicate what we feel."

Her hand slid down his back, feeling the strength of his muscles, the smoothness of his back, and its amazing warmth. Her hands moved around to his powerful chest and down his shoulders to the rippling biceps. She found her inexperienced hands gliding along with no thought as to what they should be doing. And when he groaned excitedly with little small animal sounds as she touched certain sensitive areas, she found herself making mental notes and repeating the strokes. Again she got the desired response. It was a powerful feeling knowing that by her touch she could make a man respond to her, an exciting one, one which thrilled her and made her more receptive. She hadn't time to think. All she could do was feel.

"I've never felt so deliriously happy."

"On another night I shall lead ya further into the

65

chambers of love, sweet Little Fox. But everything in moderation. First things first," he teased.

"You mean there's more than this?" She groaned. "I don't think I could take much more. I'm hurting right now," she whispered. "Inside my stomach are a thousand little hummingbirds fluttering their wings, dying to escape."

Peter chuckled. "Ah know the feeling. It's like having yer guts bust wide open."

He slipped over her body, spreading her legs apart, and began to enter her, slowly. She sighed with intense pleasure. He lifted her buttocks to meet him and began a series of slow, sensual thrusts. Madelaina felt a quiver shoot through her; tiny explosions burst inside her. Her eyes opened in frenzy. She looked up at him in the shaft of moonlight coming through the open porthole. His blue eyes were liquid fire; his body was like a lightning rod touching hers and making it do his bidding. Suddenly she exploded internally, time and again.

She must have had a half-dozen orgasms, something she hadn't experienced before and couldn't identify until later when Peter explained them to her. Only after she experienced these pleasures did Peter begin to make his thrusts deeper and even more sensual. Feeling him swollen inside her, she felt certain he had penetrated her up to her breasts. He leaned over her and began to kiss and suck her breasts with long clinging kisses that once again drove her to the pinnacle of sensation. Finally, she saw his eyes take on a half-crazed expression. He seemed to be in agony. He uttered soft animal growls in his throat. When it seemed neither he nor she could endure the agony any longer, it suddenly turned into ecstasy for them both. Peter spilled his juices into her and continued to experience such excitement, it took a while before either of them could move.

Off in the distance the sound of water lapping up against the boat returned them to the world of reality. Music from the ship's orchestra drifted faintly down to them. The sounds of their heartbeats, somewhat diffused, and a perceptible awareness made them shiver involuntarily and reach out for one another. Peter rose first. He went to the small bathroom and returned with a small bowl of water, soap, and a cloth. He placed them next to the bed, rinsed out the cloth, soaped it well, and spoke softly.

"Ah never stopped to think—this is the way a li'l fox gets baby foxes, ya hear? Now, ah'm not certain this'll do it, sweet thing, but ya'll bear down, hear?"

"I don't understand you. What does bear down mean?"

"Well, push—like ya was going to have a baby."

"But I've never had a baby. I still don't know what you mean."

"Ya sure make it hard on a guy. Didn't them *dueñas* teach ya nothin'?" He grew frustrated. "Give me your hand," he instructed. That done he placed it over his midriff. "See how relaxed it is?"

She nodded.

He tightened his muscles as he might bear down in a bowel movement. Instantly she felt it and her face reddened. "Why didn't you tell me it's like performing a bodily function?" It was the daintiest way she could put it without embarrassing both of them. "That's what you desire of me?"

He nodded.

Madelaina responded and felt a warm flow flush from her vagina as his semen was expelled. "Like ah said, ah don't know what good this does, but some of them little Frenchies do this right away, then wash like I'm washing ya now." He cleaned her off and wiped the perspiration from her body.

"Cleanliness is next ta Godliness, I was taught as a child, and honey, ya know it always stayed with me." He dried her off with a soft towel.

"Now, it's your turn," she said pulling him down on the bed next to her. She moved the bedside lamp, so she could see better. She sponged him off and heard him sigh contentedly. Her manipulations didn't stop. In

67

less than a few seconds, Peter Duprez was hard again and fully excited. "Listen, Little Fox, ya know yer in trouble already—"

"Good," she cooed. "Trouble never frightened me off."

Peter cocked an eye toward her. He gave a start. "Well, I be a dang-blasted, ring-tailed monkey's uncle! It's you!" He sat up in bed and grabbed her shoulders and studied her under the light, taking in her total nudity. "It's you! The little girl at the *madama's* in Sanlucar. No wonder you knew about Teresina and the three girls!" He fell back on the bed in an overexaggerated gesture of a small boy being caught in a naughty act. Then he broke into laughter.

"Whoooeeee. What in tarnation were ya doing there?"

"You ridiculed me long enough, don't you remember? 'What kind of a fiancé brings ya to a place like this?'" she said mocking him.

He slapped his forehead with his hand. "Oh, woe is me. Was it the first time fer ya?"

"It was my sixteenth birthday. I'll never forget it."

"Will ya ever forget this night?" he said softly, nuzzling her neck.

"Never."

"Promise?"

"Will there be more nights like this before we get to Mexico?"

"Ya jus' try and stop me."

"Then I'll never forget. Oh, *querido*—you know I won't."

68

Chapter 3

Two weeks after that rapturous night, and the many more exciting and thrilling nights they shared together, the *Mozambique* docked in Vera Cruz. Madelaina Obregon and her gringo husband descended the gangplank arm in arm. She had never looked more radiant, more vibrant and teeming with life. As they passed through customs, with very little delay, heads turned in their direction admiring the handsome young couple whose every pore oozed with love.

She inhaled the tropical air of her country and felt instantly at home. Madelaina was no longer the naïve young girl who left Mexico five years before, nor the deflowered virgin who left Las Marismas a month ago. She had been talked to, loved, educated, and brainwashed into an acute awareness of the world around her, by this strange, unusual man, this freedom fighter who hated injustices to mankind with a passion. Peter Duprez had opened her eyes to many things besides love and the sexual lust between man and woman. Thanks to him she knew the difference. She had grown up over these past two weeks as she'd never dared dream she would.

He'd opened her eyes to the needs of her people, and she learned of the terrible injustices meted out under the Diaz dictatorship: mass starvation, lack of education, and all the grave inequities foisted upon people when a government favors the wealthy class over the poor. The spirit of revolt screaming from the very bowels of the earth came alive for her through Peter's words. Even though she'd been indoctrinated to Doña Sofia Marabella's progressive ideas, she never took them as seriously as when Peter spoke. Countless times

69

she said, "I can't believe my father would be a part of such inhuman practices. I'm certain he's unaware of such atrocious practices."

Peter Duprez listened to her words but said nothing in defense of Obregon.

Now they were on the final leg of their journey. Madelaina hadn't prepared herself for a future without Peter; on the other hand, she hadn't primed herself for a life including him. She just hadn't allowed thoughts of separation to come into her mind. She wanted to enjoy every second spent with him.

Peter had booked adjoining suites at the Reforma Hotel in Vera Cruz. The port was overcrowded and accommodations very limited. Peter had had to bribe the room clerk in order to get the rooms. The hot and humid climate prostrated nearly every tourist in sight, and the Duprez couple were no different. They took refuge in their hotel suite, drew the blinds, and removed most of their damp clothing to relax until the sun set. Peter ordered champagne and ice delivered to their suite.

While the exuberant couple relaxed and planned their last few hours together, the nosey desk clerk, who'd seen the size of Peter's bankroll, entertained second thoughts. Earlier when he examined the passports and entry papers, he paused at the name: Madelaina Obregon—*Duprez*? Her papers claimed she was the daughter of General Alvaro Obregon. Why then had the *gachupín* married a gringo? That in itself wasn't enough to stir his curiosity, but *this* gringo? The name Peter Duprez was familiar to him. In the past five days, strange, brooding men had been making inquiries about a certain Peter Duprez. All these men wore the clothing of gringo cowboys—*charros*! Ugh! And these men had been seen in the company of recognized revolutionists—radicals who threatened to overthrow the government of Diaz.

Earlier, sensing that the man's interest was more than idle curiosity, Peter had drawn him aside, and stuffing a thick wad of bills into the clerk's vest pocket, he whispered conspiratorially, "The general don't know

70

we got ourselves hitched up, *amigo*. We want it to be a surprise. Got it?" He held a lean, tanned forefinger to his lips. "Understand?"

"*Si, señor*, perfectly," stammered the clerk glancing at the bills. "Not a word shall escape these lips. Enjoy your stay, *señor*."

"There ya go, atta boy," said Peter. Stepping aside, he allowed Madelaina to swish by him in the smart traveling suit he had purchased for her in the finest shop in Lisbon. It was dove gray, worn over a very tight corset with whaleboning that drew her in at the waist until she could hardly breathe. It pushed up her bosoms and thrust them forward, accentuating her hour-glass figure. No matter where she walked, roving male eyes, with obvious desire written in them, followed her.

Once in their suite of rooms, Madelaina could hardly wait to shed the cumbersome fashions which the modiste assured them were fresh from Paris. For all she cared they could remain on the dummies in store windows; they seemed to be made for inanimate objects, not real living, breathing people.

Her sheer silk blouse, a see-through worn over a camisole slip trimmed in light blue ribbons, with its high neck and leg o' mutton sleeves was almost naughty. Peter liked it and she enjoyed pleasing him. She had grown extremely fond of him, but Madelaina, without a barometer to measure, never figured she had fallen head over heels in love with him.

He had planned to go out for approximately an hour, but the heat had been so intense, he hadn't minded in the least when they both shed their clothing and relaxed in the suite, taking themselves a siesta with the rest of Vera Cruz' inhabitants.

They bathed and relaxed luxuriously, sipping champagne. Lying naked on the bed, Madelaina studied Peter with affectionate eyes. Something about the way he walked, all his mannerisms, endeared him more to her each day. His well-muscled legs, standing firm and strong, the languid way he walked, so sure of himself,

71

so easy and nonchalant, made her heart reach out to him.

She giggled as she recollected what he'd thought about her egret when she insisted on taking the bird with her. He burst into riotous laughter when she told Peter the bird's name was Pancho Villa.

"Ya jus don't know how humorous that is," he exclaimed slapping his knee. "Jus' be sure ya remember one thing, Li'l Fox. Between the real Pancho Villa and that there li'l bird o' yers, they ain't no resemblance. An' don'cha forget it, ya hear?"

He had teased her about the intended shotgun wedding to Armando countless times. "Nowadays girls woulda jumped at the chance to marry someone like him, so's they wouldn't tarnish their good name."

"Well, I won't be forced into such a ridiculous union, unless we both love each other beyond all else. Marriage is a sacred commitment, Peter. A one-sided marriage is detestable. It has no chance for survival."

"Honey, ya gotta know that most marriages are lopsided. In some places children are betrothed before they're born. Is it not the custom among Castilians?"

"It won't be in *my* marriage," she had told him with fierce determination.

The last night aboard the *Mozambique*, they had shared tender moments.

"Yer a strange li'l maverick, ya know. Ah've got a feeling yer life's gonna be full of ups and downs." He had moved closer to her, kissed her tenderly, and for a time lay next to her, his arms holding her firmly next to his lean, hard body.

"When I first saw ya on the waterfront, ya had me bamboozled. Ya were so gussied up in them pants and bandages, I couldn't detect the woman in ya. When I learned the truth, ya sure stirred up a mess of pigeons in my stomach." He held her tighter, and Madelaina had clung to him as if she was drowning.

And now, Peter Duprez sipped his champagne and let his eyes devour her. Damn! He hadn't meant to get himself all involved with this little baggage. He moved

72

across the floor, lay next to her on the bed, and in silence he began to kiss her over and over and over. He couldn't keep from her any longer, and when he entered her, she sighed in ecstasy. Peter was a marvelous lover, so well practiced, so worldly—all manliness. He made no move to satisfy himself until she first was pleasured, not once, but many times. Then, he'd arouse her passion once again and take his own pleasure with her.

All thoughts of Armando and his bungling lovemaking had faded into oblivion. To begin with, there had been nothing between them except a brother-sister relationship, a true affection—certainly nothing that could be confused with love—or the love she felt with Peter.

Madelaina became quiet and introverted. "I'll never be the same, Peter," she said at long last. "I'm not sure how I'll fare without you. You've left a tremendous imprint on my life. I'll never forget you. You have done something to me to make me special. What it is I can't put into words. But, when we part, a part of me will always be with you."

"If ya keep talkin' like that, Li'l Fox, it's gonna be hard on the both o' us."

Madelaina turned to look into his misty blue eyes. She stroked his face tenderly and brushed his curls off his face. A small sigh escaped her lips and Peter moved down to kiss her and clung to her tighter than usual. She'd seen something else in his eyes. Perhaps he wasn't as tough, as impervious to emotions as he liked to pretend. His eyes had the faint trace of tears in them. She swallowed hard.

"Ah'm gonna hate when tomorrow comes," he whispered, blinking his eyes.

"We'll see each other again," she said with bravado.

He smiled reluctantly. "If ya think ah'll be welcome in Mexico City when it's learned ah'm a *Villista*, Li'l Fox. . . ." He tilted his head and glanced at her through amused eyes.

"I shall try to convince my father he'd be a fool to

73

fight for *El Presidente* if what you say is true. It's possible the army knows nothing of the Diaz deception."

He laughed at her naïveté. "The *Rurales* are loyal to Diaz. You think they aren't aware of what they do to their own flesh and blood—their own people?"

"Then why do they not simply lay down their arms—stop fighting?"

"My, Li'l Fox, how naïve ya are. Ya don't know the greed and avarice of politicians. Power is a deadly addictive, worse than a case o' syphilis. Once ya get it, ya can't get rid of it an' it stays on ta distort yer mind and warp yer soul."

"How is it you've been inspired to fight another man's cause? Is there some ulterior motive which I haven't detected?" she asked him at last.

"Ah've got me a friend—name o' Tracy Richards. He's a fat ole cat who fought in more Latin American revolutions than anyone ah know. He caught up ta me, jus' as ah was aiming to go to Morocco to fight against Spain. In his letter he wrote, 'Any man with a horse, a weapon, and the balls ta fight is welcome to come and join Pancho Villa. Well, honey, ah bought me a horse in Sanlucar by the name o' Don Quixote, remember?"

They both laughed in amusement. "An' ah got me plenty o' weapons—"

Madelaina interrupted. "And, *querido*, I can attest to the size of your balls."

Peter leaned in and hugged her dearly, even though he found it humorous, the way she spoke those words said more than "I love you." Peter was suddenly struck with a premonition. He moved a few inches away from her, cupped her chin in his hand, and looked intently into her eyes. "Listen to me, darlin'. Don'cha be saying nothin' about them guns ah transported, ya hear? Ah'll be skinned an' fried an' left out for bear bait if the *Federales* know ah've been supplyin' 'em."

"After all you've done for me, Peter, do you think you need to caution me?"

Peter Duprez felt terribly uneasy. He lit a cigarette and puffed on it thoughtfully. He'd already told her too

74

much and he knew it. It wasn't like him. Damn! The moonlight and romance and the ocean voyage had got to him. Now he was back in enemy territory where he had to live by his wits, to feel and sense danger at every turn. He *had* changed. Women to him were to be used and cast aside, not to grow soft and mushy over.

He whipped himself mentally. Here perhaps was the one woman who could prove to be his deadliest enemy. Sonovabitch! Whatever had possessed him to be so talkative? Well, one thing's for sure, she didn't know the location of the arms being shipped to ole Tracy Richards. If that information should leak out, he'd be a goner.

Madelaina watched him change into another person. He had risen from the bed, consumed with his thoughts, so preoccupied he hardly noticed her presence. He quickly began to dress, his face creased in frowns.

"Like ah said before, honey, ah've got business ta take care of. Ah've gotta be moving mah tail before the sun sets. Now, ya get yoreself gussied up like before, an' tonight when ah return, we'll have ourselves a rip-roaring good time. Ah've gotta make sure Don Quixote got off the boat an' is stabled down for the night, so ah can leave first thing in the morning. Ya be ready in two hours, ya hear?"

Madelaina stretched out her arms to him and puckered her lips.

He glanced at her with a half-smile and retraced his steps. He leaned down and planted a passionate kiss on her moist, ready lips. She clung to him tightly. "Ya gonna start all that over again? Ah'll be back, baby— an' maybe tonight ah'll tell ya what all went on in the palace at Sanlucar with three women."

Madelaina beamed. "You promise?"

"I promise." He kissed her again and started out the door. He turned back to her with second thoughts. He went into the adjoining room where his luggage had been placed, rifled through a bag and returned with a black velvet box.

75

"Wear it tonight."

Madelaina opened the box. The twin diamond ring, the heirloom of her ancestors glistened brightly at her. "You didn't sell it? How did you get the money," she asked wondrously, waving her hands about the room, "for all this?"

"There was enough with what we had. Ah jus' couldn't part with that ring, honey, 'cause it'll look jus' grand on the hand of Peter Duprez' wife." He disappeared through the door.

Madelaina lay back and fell asleep. When she awakened, she bathed again, and with Peter's words flooding her consciousness, she carefully selected her dinner dress. She decided on wearing the same Alençon lace gown she wore the first night Peter seduced her—or had she seduced him?

She piled her thick hair atop her head and managed to twist it into coils at the back that hung in five curls. She applied Peter's favorite perfume and stood back to admire her reflection. She looked radiant and divinely in love, thanks to Peter.

It was nearly six o'clock by the small antique watch she'd worn pinned to her traveling costume. Peter should have been back by now. "What's keeping him?" she asked Pancho, the egret. The bird, getting used to new surroundings, cocked his head and ignored her in favor of Peter's key chain on the bureau top. Madelaina paced back and forth in the room. She opened the shutters and glanced down at the collection of squat adobe buildings with their red tiled roofs which had been the same for countless years. Beyond a few scrubby palm trees that probably had been divine in the days of Cortez, she glanced toward the waterfront, out at the countless ships in the sea, and wondered why nearly every nation had fought to control this dirty, smelly, squalid city.

Unable to concentrate, she let the shutter fall back into place. She couldn't dismiss from her mind the feeling of impending doom. It was nothing she could clearly define in her mind, but she had the feeling that

76

something was about to happen. She paced the floor in nervous agitation till she felt suddenly compelled to change into her dove gray traveling suit, complete with the whalebone corset she detested.

She was buttoning the last button when a knock sounded briskly on the door.

Heaving a sigh of relief, she ran swiftly across the room and flung open the door expecting to see Peter. She stopped dead still, a startled look of astonishment on her face when four *Federales* dressed in their German tunics and snap-brim caps saluted her smartly.

"Señorita Madelaina Obregon?" One of the officers addressed her in English.

"*Si*, I am Madelaina Obregon. What is it you wish?" She saw no reason to perpetuate the farce of the marriage now that she was safe in her own country. She would explain it all to her father. He'd understand.

"Ah, then you are not Madam Duprez as it states on your hotel registration?" He gave her no time to reply. "You are to come with us at once. Your father requests you to be under full military escort to Mexico City. We got here in time!"

"In time for what? I am perfectly safe. I am returning to the capital in the morning. Please thank my father for his concern, Lieutenant."

Lieutenant Guiterrez introduced himself. "I am attached to your father's command in Zacatecas." He hesitated for only a brief moment, then braced himself stiffly. "With your permission, *señorita*, we are under orders. You must return with us at once."

"That's impossible! You see—well, you don't understand. I am and I'm not married—in one sense of the word." She stopped, afraid she'd get Peter and herself into deeper waters since she entered the country falsely. "Well, damnit, Guiterrez, I'm telling you I don't wish your services at this time. I'll be prepared to leave with you in the morning." She made use of the cuss words she'd picked up from Peter.

"I am sorry, *señorita*," apologized Lieutenant Guiterrez. Being the dedicated soldier he was, he assumed command of the situation. "Are these your belongings?" He indicated the small trunk and some other baggage in the room. He noticed the rumpled bed, the champagne and glasses and smiled tightly. The soldier with him opened the door to the adjoining room where Peter's belongings lay open, strewn about the floor.

Madelaina was stunned. Someone had gone through Peter's things, and she hadn't heard a sound. A third soldier moved in, packed her things, tossing them quickly and efficiently into her satchel and trunk.

Her protests met deaf ears. She was furious, but there wasn't anything she could do about it. Finally, she lost her temper and cussed them all out in Spanish. "I insist I can't leave until my friend returns!"

"You told me you weren't married, so I take it you mean Peter Duprez. I am certain he shan't be returning. Now then—shall we go?"

"What? What's that you say? Speak up, Guiterrez, or I'll have you reduced to cleaning out jackass dung!" she exploded angrily. "Now where's Señor Duprez?"

"I regret, Señorita Obregon, the gringo has been placed under arrest—your father's orders."

"My father's orders? Why? What on earth for, you blithering idiot!" she screamed at him. "Why?"

At this point Lieutenant Guiterrez seemed totally bewildered. He reached into his tunic and pulled out an impressive-looking document. "Conspiracy to kidnap the daughter of an Mexican patriot and hold her for ransom."

Madelaina's anger turned into wide-eyed disbelief, then she burst into laughter at the incredible stupidity. "My dear Lieutenant Guiterrez, for your information, Mr. Duprez has been my escort, my guardian, the only protection I had to transport me safely to these shores. I might add, for goodness' sake, without his grave concern over my safety, I might never have reached Vera Cruz.

"Now, if you have any sense, you'll leave me and make certain no harm comes to Mr. Duprez, whom I'll

78

confide to you is a very important gringo in his country. We do not wish to offend our Yankee neighbors, do we?" Not once did Madelaina refer to Peter Duprez as her husband or think to insist on this fact. Perhaps it was because it was all so new, or because she had never had to defend her actions.

"I regret, *señorita*, and can only repeat, I am under full military orders to deliver you personally to Mexico City. There is no way I can disobey without being court-martialed. Now, if you're ready, I shall escort you to the Federal Building to prepare to embark for the capital." He bowed stiffly.

It was useless to argue. She grabbed her purse and walked out the door fuming with anger. In the lobby she saw four additional *Federales* flanking Peter Duprez. She ran to his side and recoiled when she saw the cold, hard contempt in his eyes for her as he studied her traveling costume. Seeing her prepared for travel rather than dining gave him the answer he wanted. He turned from her, as if she didn't exist.

When she saw the handcuffs on Peter's wrists, she turned to Lieutenant Guiterrez. "What is the meaning of this?" she demanded hotly. When she heard the sound of paced applause coming from Peter's hands, she turned swiftly from Guiterrez and stared at Peter with disbelief in her eyes. "You—don't—Peter, you can't think I had anything to do with this? You can't believe I betrayed you."

He stared long and hard at her for several moments, then, turning to the officers, said, *"Vamenos, amigos.* Let's go, ya heah? Ah've seen mah wife now and ah know the truth." He turned his back on her and moved ahead of Lieutenant Guiterrez's party with full military escort as if he'd been a vile, contemptible murderer.

"Peter," she called after him. "I didn't betray you! Believe me I had nothing to do with all this!" But again she was speaking to deaf ears.

Dismayed, hurt to the quick, and feeling as if she'd been stabbed through the heart, she dragged herself to the waiting carriage, boarded it, and sat back against the black leather cushions, tears streaming down her face. She felt a terrible sinking sensation at the pit of her stomach knowing that Peter Duprez would forever be her enemy. Between Vera Cruz and Mexico City, Madelaina would tell herself over and again that he should have known she wouldn't betray him. He should have known. But he hadn't.

It wasn't difficult to piece it together in the way Peter Duprez might. She was the daughter of Alvaro Obregon, General Supreme in Diaz' army. It wasn't inconceivable that she had been planted in Sanlucar, that she might have known he was transporting weapons to this Captain Richards and had joined the rebel Pancho Villa in fighting against the dictatorship. Peter Duprez was a complicated man. His work was sacred to him. Hadn't he told her so many times? But, this soldier of fortune, this freedom fighter who boasted he knew women, didn't know Madelaina Obregon, the woman he called Little Fox.

He may have wooed women on every continent, but he didn't know her or the stuff of which she was made. Very well, they had loved and consoled each other, they had poured out their frustrations to one another, confided their hopes and dreams for the future, and in some of those moments Madelaina had felt a tinge of resentment that he'd known so many women. In those four weeks aboard the *Mozambique*, she came to respect him and depend on him for so much. Now he was gone. She felt an enormous emptiness. She thought of many things, including the long list of faceless women he'd loved and left. She had fallen in love with Peter Duprez. She hadn't known it an hour ago, but she knew it now.

Because he turned on her in those last few moments, because he believed she'd betrayed him, she began to imagine things. Was it possible he really intended holding her for ransom? He'd known from the start who she was. What caused him to change his mind and personally escort the daughter of General Obregon to Vera Cruz. He'd told her he was joining with Pancho

Villa's revolutionary army. What more proof did she need that he considered her an enemy. God! What frightening and confusing thoughts. She hadn't betrayed Peter. Who did? Somehow she was going to discover the culprit if it took all her life.

Pale and tired, Madelaina didn't sleep a wink all night. In the early morning, when her escorts departed from the Federal Building with her in the coach, her face wore a pensive, withdrawn appearance. Wherever she looked, she thought of Peter. The bright azure sky brought his eyes into focus, the golden wheat fields reminded her of his sun-streaked hair. She had to shut him from her memory if she expected to think straight. She forced herself to contemplate her father and grew flushed with anger. How had he learned of her presence in Vera Cruz? It was impossible for news to have reached him from Spain before she arrived. The *Mozambique* was one of the fastest ships sailing the Atlantic. How then? Had someone communicated with him in reference to a ransom? Try as she did she couldn't accept the fact that Peter had done such a thing.

They stopped in Puebla to change horses and eat. She wasn't hungry and barely tasted a morsel. Glancing out beyond the plains up to the twin volcanoes, she thought, *They still look the same as they did five years ago. But I am not the same and I never will be.*

Once again they were on the road to Mexico City, where they stopped to change horses, then she was escorted to the hacienda of her father in Cuernavaca.

General Obregon wasn't at home when his daughter arrived. Doña Paola, her *dueña*, greeted her with tears streaming down her old, withered cheeks and exclaimed over the many changes in Madelaina. It was only yesterday she had left the hacienda. Five years? Incredible! Five years had evaporated leaving no traces of the child. After a few amenities necessary to appease the countless servants who stood in line waiting to be greeted and embraced, Madelaina begged to be excused. Quickly climbing the stairs of the grand villa, she slipped behind the door of her old quarters.

The silent rooms were filled with countless memories, but the daughter of General Obregon, no longer interested in faded memories and unfullfilled dreams, was teeming with life, her interest only in the present. Placing Pancho's cage on the railing of the balcony leading off the bedroom, she gazed about the verdant, rolling countryside of luxurious Cuernavaca.

"Breathe the air in deeply, Pancho," she told the egret. "Out there are many people who, like us, want to be free. Why you prefer remaining cooped up in your cage baffles me. If only we could talk, I might understand you more. Oh, Pancho, I'm so confused. What I've seen of the world and of people is a terrible puzzlement to me. You think one day I'll learn to unravel the puzzle?"

The egret cocked his head from side to side. The pity of it was he couldn't console his mistress.

In the coming days she missed Peter Duprez as if a part of her were gone forever and she'd need him to make her whole again. She took to glancing at her wardrobe—the one Peter bought for her—holding her clothes close in her arms, trying to recall every moment of happiness they'd shared together. She even wore the double diamond ring daily, refusing to remove it, because he had given it to her as a token of love—even if it was hers to begin with. She cherished everything, every thought and memory of him, until it began to affect her health.

And then one day she made a decision.

Book Two

Zorrita—
Little Fox

Chapter 4

February, 1911

The cumbersome wagon trundled noisily along the rutted road toward the sprawling fortification at the outskirts of Zacatecas, some 500 kilometers north of Mexico City, a redoubt commanded by General Alvaro Obregon.

A gray dawn had broken a half-hour before; a few sleepy-eyed sentries guarded the ramparts. Yawning, stretching soldiers, rubbing the sleep from their eyes, moved sluggishly about the outskirts of the encampment, while *campesinas*, camp followers, moved about preparing fires, making coffee, and grinding meal for breakfast. A few domestic animals straggled through the clearing: a goat with neck bells clanging, a cud-chewing cow staring empty-eyed in forlorn contentment, a flurry of squawking chickens pecking about for food.

Seated hunched over in the wagon, silent, introverted, and straining at the heavy shackles on her feet and wrists, Madelaina Obregon stared sullenly at the encampment below the ridge. Soon the fort appeared over the ridge. She was shabbily dressed in the attire of a *campesina*—a *soldadera*—with a black *rebozo* covering her head. Her grimy, dirt-stained face was sunkissed to a tawny copper after many months spent in the desert of Sonora close to the man she'd sworn to follow. Madelaina bit her lips, grimly determined to run from her father again. The closer they drew to the fort, the angrier and sicker she felt. She'd been through ten nightmares of hell since her father's spies had caught up with her. She would have to obliterate them all from mind as she had done in the past.

Madelaina knew what to expect and she dreaded the outcome, yet she stubbornly vowed that no one would deter her from keeping her solemn oath—to join the revolution. The general, her father, could scream, yell, excoriate her all he wished; he could call her vile names or call her a foolish, romantic adolescent, a simpering idealist who at eighteen knew nothing of life. Let him. She could care less. In the past twelve months she'd become more of a woman than she'd be for the rest of her life, living the prim, proper life of a dandy—a chocolate drinker's wife.

En route to the fort, Madelaina tired to imagine what her arrival would be like, but even her worst fears were nothing compared to the actual confrontation with her father. For ten full minutes after she alit from the wagon and stood facing him in his private office, he raged and ranted, and stormed.

"Pancho Villa! Pancho Villa! PANCHO VILLA! Daughter, if you Pancho Villa me once more, I shall have you beaten to within an inch of your life!"

General Obregon, a tall, exceedingly handsome *gachupín*, who strutted like a peacock, was deeply tanned; his black eyes were as bright as coals and filled with a fierceness Madelaina had never witnessed before. He paced the room like an impassioned and enraged Miura bull, fuming with indignation, resentment, and reproach for his stubborn, mule-headed daughter. He tugged nervously at his thick brush moustache from time to time. "For this I sent you to Spain?" He punctuated his words with broad arm movements, pointing to her appearance. "For this? Look at you! I sent you abroad to fine finishing schools in Spain to have you return a rebel—a revolutionist—a *soldadera*? You, the daugher of General Obregon, are a *campesina*—a camp follower of that murderous barbarian!"

The general, fully exasperated and at his wit's end with his daughter, was no longer able to cope with her mood of rebellion or any of her adolescent fervor. But this last was too much. He turned back to her. "What do you suppose *El Presidente* would say if it were known the daughter of his most trusted general has become a devout disciple of that murderous outlaw, that northern *guerrillo*, who is worse even than that pest Emiliano Zapata from Moreles in the south, eh? What?"

"He's no barbarian, Papa. Villa has only the love of Mexico and his people in his heart," she retorted defiantly with a toss of her head that caused the *rebozo* to slip off. Her long, black hair was gray with soot and dust from the long journey. Her father sniffed the air with sufficient distaste for her to know the stench of travel clung to her pungently. But she didn't care. She was glad it annoyed him. Served him right for sending his soldiers to kidnap her and bring her back to a life she rejected. Her voice softened. "Papa, he is like no man I have ever met. If only you would meet him, you'd see what I've been trying to tell you."

The general clenched his fists tightly at his sides. "How dare you? How dare you? I forbid you to mention that barbaric filth in my presence!" He raged and paced the floor angrily, stopping short every now and again as the sight of his daughter in such wild disarray offended his dignity. "Look at you! Just look at you! I am ashamed to claim you as my daughter! Who could tell that under all that filth you were once a fine young lady who smelled of springtime and sweet roses, that your eyes were filled with tenderness and love and the fulfillment of dreams." He stared with revulsion at her coarse peasant clothing: the low-cut, off-the-shoulder, gypsy blouse of bleached cotton, now soiled and scraggly, the dusty cotton skirt, and soiled, run-down mountain boots. She had the scrubby look of a *campesina*. "Oh, the shame of it all! That the daughter of Don Alvaro Obregon, general in Porfirio Diaz' army, whose own father fought against Maximilian, should fall into such utter disrepute is unbearable to me. I'd sooner see you dead, Madelaina! Dead! Do you understand?"

"Then shoot me, Papa." She reached for a rifle from a holster on the wall of the large salon and tossed it to him with the remarkable agility of one used to the handling of such weapons. He caught it, somewhat surprised at both the sudden movement and her familiarity with such weapons. For a moment their eyes met and held like two warriors from opposite camps—hers, defiant and challenging; his, shocked, hurt, and humiliated, yet fired with wrath and punitive thoughts.

The general sighed deeply; his shoulders sagged as if he'd been bested in battle. He carefully placed the rifle on the gleaming mahogany desk and moved behind it to seat himself. "What am I do to with you, child? I am beside myself," he said with a terrible solemnness. "I cannot permit my only daughter, descendant of royal blood, to become a mere *campesina*, a *puta*! A whore—no better than the worst prostitute in the bawdy houses of Mexico City or the gutters of Madrid. What shall I do with you? You do not even hold sacred the honor to your own father!" His sadness was so overwhelming it touched her heart. "*Querida*, you are lost to me. You tell me what I should do. What would you do?"

"I do not know, Papa. All I know is I must follow him. Your soldiers can bring me back time and again. I will escape each chance I get to return to him, just to be near him. How he inspires his people, Papa. He is filled to overflowing with love! If you were to meet him, you'd see."

"Love? Hah! That butcher!"

"And what is Huerta? And Carranza? *AND* Diaz? You think them to be good? They are no better and far worse than Villa. He has compassion, he cares, Papa. He cares for Mexico and what happens to her!" she cried.

"You could be a queen, Madelaina, or at least the president's lady," said her father wistfully. Then he stopped short. "*Querida*! You haven't!" He was aghast. The thought of his own flesh and blood coupling with that vicious outlaw turned his blood cold. "You haven't—" He could not bring himself to utter the words.

"Coupled with Villa, Papa?" She supplied the words

88

for him. "Don't be afraid to say it. No, I have not slept with him. He hardly knows I exist. I sit in the outer circle with the other women just eager to catch a look at him when he rides by on Seven Leagues, his magnificent black stallion. Villa has no eyes for me. He is much too busy preparing a life for his people to be concerned with the likes of me. But that doesn't mean I haven't slept with other men," she said with bold defiance. "As a *campesina*, I must make myself available to whoever chooses me."

General Obregon felt sick. He stared at her in stunned silence. He could not believe his ears. "*Dios mios*, what have I done that my own daughter must revile me? What will I do with such a willful, stubborn wildcat?"

"Oh, Papa, if I were a man, I'd be fighting alongside him, right next to him, as a first-ranking officer!" she cried passionately, hoping to make her father understand.

He was aghast. "You'd fight with my sworn enemy? Against your own father?" If he'd been mortally stabbed, he couldn't have been more wounded than he was in that moment.

"He is not *your* sworn enemy. He is the enemy of Diaz. He's the champion of Mexico. Deep down you both want the same for Mexico—then why do you fight on opposite sides?" she asked incredulously. "Couldn't you join together against the enemies of Mexico?"

"Are you crazy, child?" Obregon's heart hardened in that instant. "I can see I shall have to take measures to protect you from yourself." He rose again, walked to the fireplace, and warmed his hands near the coals, for he was suddenly shot through with icy chills. Malaria never really leaves you. He had already had many a bout with the disease, but it was not the hot and cold chills of malaria plaguing him. He raged against the headstrong, willful stubbornness of his own flesh and blood. Why were they unable to communicate? He paced the floor as their conversation replayed in his mind like a faulty victrola. "I'll not be ridiculed, daughter! I'll not be made a laughingstock, not by my own flesh and blood! I know what is whispered among my own men, and I feel sicker and more traitorous when I walk among them issuing orders knowing my daughter is whoring in the camps of my nation's enemies. Thank God news of your defection hasn't reached *El Presidente*! There'll be hell to pay! All I've worked hard for in my life would go up in smoke if news reached the presidential palace!"

Perhaps this was why he worked harder, fought harder, and sat up nights contemplating his military moves against the rebels, he told himself.

Watching him, Madelaina admitted she hadn't ever seen her father so utterly without composure, so violent that he lost control, so totally disorganized. She entertained second thoughts. Had she gone too far? Had she overstepped the boundaries of his tolerance? She lowered shame-filled eyes because she knew she had hurt the only person she really loved. She stared sullenly at the tips of her dusty, mud-covered boots, wondering why he was so stubborn. Why wouldn't he at least listen to what she had to say? Even as she asked herself these questions, she knew the answers. They were too much alike, these two. She was the image of him: the same proud Spanish beauty, fiercely proud of their heritage, a strong self-identification, a firm belief in themselves and their ideals, and a stubborn conviction that they could do no wrong. Born on the same day of the same month, two decades apart, they were both tempestuous, bull-headed, earthy people who continuously locked horns. Over the years, and through education and duty in the field, the general had mellowed considerably, but he always knew the direction in which his life took him. What had happened to his daughter was intolerable.

Madelaina had felt like a fiercely impassioned man trapped in the body of a woman. She was no homosexual—she was too much a woman. However, the strong identification with her father made her resent being a prisoner in a woman's body. How would the general like it if he suddenly found himself imprisoned in the body of a woman, subjected to the morality, sexuality, bias, and prejudice that accompanied that gender? What General Obregon failed to accept was that his daughter had the mentality of a man, the adventurous, soul-searching spirit that drives men into the world to seek their fortunes. She possessed none of the shyness and resignation to which most woman are trained early in life. He couldn't understand her and he refused to listen when she tried to explain how she felt. They had reached an impasse long before Madelaina decided she had had enough of the woman's role and went in search of Peter Duprez. Somewhere in the camps of Pancho Villa to the north in Sonora she felt certain she would have found him and her old stallion Don Quixote. Peter would understand when he heard she found no solace in keeping house for her father who absented himself ten months out of the year or more. Besides, she wanted to be Peter's wife. She ached for his love.

General Obregon had had enough on this day. He had taken more than a man in his station in life should be forced to take from so rebellious a daughter. He turned again to look at her and grew more disgusted with her appearance. "Very well, it's ended." He asserted himself as he should have a year ago when she returned with such revolutionary thoughts burning in her. "A convent! That's the answer for you! A cloister where you can meditate on your wicked ways. Where in the silence of the soul you will understand how you've wreaked havoc with your father's life as well as your own."

"Corporal Jimenez!" he called, as Madelaina's eyes burned defiantly into his.

Instantly a soldier dressed in a somber uniform, much like the general's except for the distinction of rank, entered the room and braced himself in a stiff salute.

"Si, mi Generale."

"You will escort the *señorita* to her quarters. She is

91

to be kept under strict guard around the clock until further orders, when she'll be sent to the Madrigal de Los Altos at Manzanillo," he snapped brittlely.

"You wouldn't dare!" cried Madelaina losing all sense of decorum. "I'll run away again. I swear!" The thought of that unholy convent shook her.

"To whore and demean yourself? To bring shame and humiliation upon the name of Obregon? Over my dead body, *querida*. Over my dead body."

"If it takes whoring to win the revolution, then I'll whore and demean myself, and if it must be over your dead body—then so be it!" she retorted hotly.

With an impatient wave of his hand, the general dismissed her and the wide-eyed corporal, who stood as one transfixed listening to the hatred exchanged between father and daughter. Anyone else, he was certain, would've been whipped to within an inch of her life. Women! Bah! He stood to one side, allowing the wench to pass. A shapely skirt such as he'd not seen in Zacatecas.

Rumors, of the general's daughter and her strange affection for that savage and uncultured *peón*, that illiterate hillsman, Pancho Villa, had circulated faster than the pox, infecting the entire encampment. But Corporal Jimenez had set aside the tales as being too far-fetched. Never would a *gachupín* permit such disgraceful conduct in his house. Yet, *Dios mios*, here was the culprit in the flesh, and she was an abomination worse than the rumored gossip. Much bad news was this *chiquita*.

They disappeared into the outer villa as General Obregon sank deeply into a soft leather chair before the fire. He struck an attitude of remote contemplation as he thought of his daughter. There wasn't enough for him to do in this war against Pancho Villa and Emiliano Zapata that he had to once again wet nurse his only child to prevent her from becoming a revolutionary. *Damn her mother for dying and leaving her on my hands! Damn my dedication to the military!*

His thoughts rolled back in time to the day when

Madelaina was twelve years old. One day was etched vividly in his mind. Madelaina had rushed into his office, flushed with terror, interrupting a very important staff meeting to tell her father she was bleeding to death. Flushed with embarrassment, he had instructed her to take such trivia to the *dueña*, not him. He had seen the confusion in her eyes, the sudden and startling recoiling at what she presumed to be rebuke and stern disapproval.

He had realized that she faced the onset of her menstrual cycle without previous indoctrination, and she had grown fearful at the onset of painful cramps and the mystifying flow of blood. But, *Dios mios*, such things were the affairs of women, not men. True she had always come to him with all the minor travails that beset children. Right before his eyes he'd been aware that his censure had so baffled Madelaina that from that moment until she departed for Spain, she had retreated into a shell of introversion. The chemical changes in her body forced her into a life totally unacceptable to her immature mind. He recalled that when her firm young breasts began to bud, she would bind herself to appear flat. She even avoided all the physical activities she had previously enjoyed—riding horses, even running about in the courtyard—for they made her too self-conscious of the bulges under her shirtwaist.

The day he announced she must go to Spain for schooling and the attainment of social graces to become a real lady, she had remained silent. They had been enemies for the past several months—what did anything matter? Well, she'd get over this stubborn posture and one day she'd thank him for such advantages.

Hah! General Obregon grunted sullenly. She had thanked him all right! Imagine—all the way to Spain—to an elegant finishing school—to become a fine lady—and what was his reward? A revolutionary! *Dios mios*, the daughter of General Alvaro Obregon— a revolutionary? He shook his head and lit a fat cigar

93

with a *diablo* he struck against a stone before the fire. There'd been many signs along the way. Why had he ignored them? Couched in between the lines of letters from his sister-in-law, Doña Louisa Obregon, were hints at Madelaina's individualism. She'd balked stubbornly at falling into the empty-headed, pampered ways of *gachupín* society which her three cousins emulated to Madelaina's distraction, he'd been told. Even Madelaina herself had written him expressing a disinclination for so superficial a life. "It's not for the likes of Madelaina Obregon," she'd tell her father. "All they know, Papa, is how to trap a man and raise little *niños*."

Then, there'd been more telltale signs, like those letters from her instructors, who suggested perhaps their school wasn't the correct one for Madelaina. She continuously cut classes, much to the consternation of her tutors, and could always be found at the hacienda of Don Felipe Cortez indulging in her penchant for the bulls. Madelaina's own letters to her father were filled to overflowing with bullfighting—how she loved the exhilarating experience of the *corrida*. She pointed out the countless characteristics of the various varieties of bulls bred in Spain and suggested that her father take up the lucrative hobby of breeding bulls. In addition, there had been letters in which she would expound on the unfortunate poverty of the street *peóns*, uneducated with no real chance to exist in a highly competitive world. Always on the side of the downtrodden, the underdog, with an inborn curiosity about nature, Madelaina had confessed to him that many of her schoolmates found her strange and alien to their way of thinking. She had, therefore, kept her own counsel and contained her feelings. She had frequently mentioned Armando Cortez and this—this peasant, Manuelito Perez. And then his brother, Don Diego, had mentioned a proposed betrothal between the Cortez and Obregon families. Now he almost wished he had encouraged the union.

Madelaina's father had never mentioned in his let-

94

ters to her that he thought her interest in the bulls unusual for a woman. He chose to refer to her personal qualities, her beauty and feminine virtues. He reminded her of the coming-out cotillion to be held at the presidential palace on her return to Mexico. He spoke of the countless eligible men, the handsome young bachelors considered to be the season's catch. One in particular, whom the general would delight in addressing as his son-in-law, was Captain Felipe de Cordoba, son of one of his former army compatriots, now retired as a wealthy *hacendado*, owner of vast parcels of land and most of Cuernavaca. His dream for a long time had been to arrange a wedding between Felipe and his daughter.

Not a day had passed after Madelaina's return to Spain, a happy occasion for both father and daughter, that she didn't bubble over with countless questions about the fabled Centaur of the North, Pancho Villa. He recalled her livid indignation over the treatment of the gringo, Peter Duprez, demanding he give her reasons for the shabby treatment given Duprez, when it had been through his kindness and care that she arrived in Mexico safely.

She explained the necessity of posing as his wife but never revealed the intimacies between them; there had never been a closeness with her father to warrant such confidentiality. In those early days, soon after her arrival, there had been a degree of honesty between them. The general revealed the name of the man who contacted the Federal troops about some kidnapping attempt on her person. The name of the man was unfamiliar, until he explained that some room clerk at the Reforma Hotel in Vera Cruz had recognized the name Duprez as the gringo whom several revolutionaries had been waiting for to effect a business deal. He contacted the *Federales* instantly. Rumor had it that this gringo Duprez was supplying weapons to the rebels—Madero's men. The room clerk put two and two together and came up with more than met the eye—including the contrived kidnapping charges.

95

General Obregon received a wire from Vera Cruz, and although he had had no word of Madelaina's intended arrival in Mexico, he took no chances. He ordered her to be detained and had her escorted back to Cuernavaca by his own trusted Lieutenant Guiterrez, who happened to be in Vera Cruz on business for the general. Duprez, of course, was detained. However, and this greatly pleased Madelaina, Peter had escaped the clutches of his jailer. Since there was no real crime, charges against him had been dropped. However, without Madelaina's knowledge, General Obregon had requested a complete dossier on this man Peter Duprez, although he had yet to receive one. Duprez proved more elusive than his daughter had this past year. For a time things went smoothly at the Obregon hacienda, following Madelaina's return from Spain.

One day before the general left the hacienda to take his troops into Moreles, Madelaina had asked him nonchalantly, "Papa, do you know of a certain Don Abraham Gonzalez?"

"Are you referring to that rabble-rousing *fanático*, chief of the Antireelectionists in Chihuahua? But how is it you know of him, *querida*?" The general was more astonished than concerned.

"I heard him speak in the Zocalo, in the square before the presidential palace, declaring it was he who recruited Pancho Villa to support Francesco Madero in the revolution. He spoke with much fire, Papa."

Her father laughed tolerantly, tilted her chin up so her large, questioning eyes met his. "Why does such a beautiful young woman trouble herself with the politics of a fanatic?" He always patronized her, treated her inquiries like the whimsical, passing fancies of a child. "Have you decided on the date to schedule the ball to introduce you to Mexico's society, *querida*?"

"No," she said quietly, feeling let down.

"Then, think about it. Have an answer prepared for my return. I'm most anxious to show you off to Capitán Felipe de Cordoba." He watched her face.

"Yes, Papa," she replied dutifully, not really hearing

him. She walked with him to the edge of the enclosed courtyard where uniformed soldiers on horseback waited for the general to mount, so they could fall into place behind him.

"*Capitán*? Felipe de Cordoba is a *capitán*? *My* Felipe?" Her face broke into a sunshine of smiles. "You mean—" She gestured to a spot about three feet off the ground. "You mean *my* Felipe is a *capitán*?"

General Obregon laughed heartily. He held his hand several inches above his own head. "I mean Felipe de Cordoba—*your* Felipe—is a *capitán!*"

He swung to his saddle, blew her a kiss, raised his hand in a signal, and the mounted soldiers fell into place behind their general and left the grounds of the hacienda. His last glimpse of Madelaina had been when he turned his head to look back. She waved to him from a distance, averting her head as dust swirled around her.

General Obregon's return trip from Moreles brought defeat on two fronts: Emiliano Zapata to the south, and his daughter at home. His daughter had left—gone— no one knew where. It wasn't bad enough to hear such distressing news, but a letter had arrived from his brother, Don Diego, explaining her disappearance from his hacienda and her strange behavior in the past, including her passion for bulls and the fact that she had become a *matadora* of talent. He explained many things and included the letter Madelaina had written to Armando Cortez—"which is self-explanatory, my dear brother," the don had written. After the general had read both letters, it was simply more than he could take at one sitting.

He had to question the servants about his daugher's disappearance and subject himself to the sad laments of hysterical servants, especially those of *dueña*, Doña Paola, who brought him a letter written by Madelaina.

Tugging nervously at his moustache, the general lowered his eyes to the letter and read:

"*Querido* Papa: Do not worry about me. I have gone to do what must be done for Mexico and the

97

revolution. Try to understand that I love you with all my heart, but, like you, I love Mexico more."

It was utterly inconceivable to General Obregon that he should be in possession of such a letter from his only daughter. *I'm dreaming all this*, he told himself. *It isn't happening*. But it was true. The servants told him and his brother's letter told him what he refused to believe about the peculiar nature of his daughter. The *dueña*, Doña Paola—a woman of sixty, wise in her ways, and concerned with the young girl's safety—gave him the most insight into the character of his daughter.

"*Mi Generale*," she began without fear of reprisal or the beating he promised her for her carelessness with the young *señorita*, "your daughter is no usual woman. She is unlike any of the silly, empty-headed young girls I have tutored and chaperoned in my long life. Pardon my boldness, but the child is so much like you it appears that you were cut from the same cloth. Her misery is that she has a real brain in that head of hers and she needs to use it. She thinks, listens, and broods over the dilemma of our people. True, she listens to the rabble-rousers as well as the *politicos* from all the political parties. When we go to Mexico City, it is not to go to the *modista* or to the fancy shops. At times my feet grow weary walking through Chapultepec Park and the Avenida Juarez as we stop and listen to what each of the braying jackals say. One day, just a few days before she departed, we had stopped at Doña Carranza's villa on the Reforma. We sat sipping our chocolate when a reporter for the newspaper in Mexico City arrived to interview her daughters who were making their debut to society at the Fiesta Blanca dos Flores. When he had finished with the interview, Doña Carranza asked the young man to take chocolate with us.

"Immediately, the reporter began to fill us with stories of the mission from which he'd returned only two days before. He'd been to Sonora, to the many camps of Pancho Villa, who has become an integral *jefe* in the revolution—with your permission, *mi Generale*.

98

"Your daughter, *Madre de Dios*, was all ears. How many questions she asked. Much to the consternation of all the women, she monopolized the conversation. The others, tiring of politics, retired to the salon to show me the ornaments, the ball gowns, and all the festoons for the affair. Your daughter, lacking the manners and good graces of our polite society, continued to huddle with this—uh—Miguel Guerra. Each time I attempted to part them, she sternly commanded me to permit her to finish her conversation with the *señor* and cautioned me if I opened my mouth again, she'd have me beaten—whipped—flogged! I was so humiliated, *mi Generale*, but I remained at her side and listened to every word. I've never seen such interest spring into those wide, innocent eyes as I did when this Señor Guerra mentioned Pancho Villa. *Dios mios*! If only I had used my strength and dragged her from the villa, by her hair, if necessary, this terrible tragedy might never have occurred," wailed the *dueña*.

For days General Obregon had paced the floor of his villa, worried sick and filled with a growing anxiety over her whereabouts. He was filled with recriminations. He'd not been the proper father to her. He'd thought more of his career than his growing daughter. He should have insisted sooner on her entrance into society. He should have brought eligible bachelors into the house, prepared galas. The old and staid morals were rapidly disappearing. This was 1911, a new century parting with old customs. He, also, should have changed. He should have listened to her ideas, permitted her to vent her feelings in some way and not let them bottle up inside her until they were ready to burst. If Madelaina were married, she'd have been inundated with responsibilities; there'd be little time left for her to nurture fancy ideas of revolution. It had taken a week of self-torment, anguish, and self-condemnation before General Obregon grew sensible and checked with the newspaper office to learn more about this Miguel Guerra, who had apparently encouraged her to become a rebel. He never knew, of course, that the reporter had only been a means to an end for Madelaina. General Obregon learned only that Guerra had returned to the camps of Villa to report on the progress of the revolution. He also learned that Francesco Madero and his Antireelectionists were planning to meet with the Sonoran cougar and plan for victory.

General Obregon knew then where his daughter could be found and he feared for her life. How would she manage? If Pancho Villa ever learned that the daughter of Alvaro Obregon, general to *El Presidente*'s army was in his vicinity, he could hold her for the highest ransom possible and be assured he'd get every cent requested.

Sick with worry, General Obregon dispatched three of his most trusted spies to infiltrate the camps of Pancho Villa, using as bait the name Miguel Guerro. "Wherever he goes, rest assured my daughter will be close by," he had told them bitterly. With photographs of the Obregon girl concealed on their persons, they had scattered to the north. A year passed before they located her far from any place that Guerra might have been. They had abducted her from Pancho Villa's hideout in the Blue Mountains. Two weeks ago word reached him that his daughter and her captors were en route to Zacatecas, present location of the Obregon encampment.

She was home at last. What to do with her? What to do? She'd changed considerably. Obregon observed her critically and saw that even now, despite her deplorable condition and the raw stink of wilderness emanating from her person, she looked a highly desirable wench. He could imagine just how desirable she might be to that dog Villa. He'd heard the vile rumors about Villa's voracious sexual appetite. His lusty manliness had attracted a large group of *campesinas* who fought over him. They said the fool married all the women with whom he coupled to satisfy some moralistic religious quirk—never mind that bigamy was against the law!

Madre de Dios! Mother of God, he shuddered. That

100

his own daughter might have been the bride of Pancho Villa was something for which he had neither stomach or desire. He'd never live down such a horrendous scandal. Father-in-law to Villa! Oh, that vile, scurrilous dog! That animal!

In a week's time, General Obregon would face Zapata again. Then would come the inevitable battle with Villa. It had to come. Rumors of Pancho Villa's growing strength had poured into his encampment this past year since Diaz was reelected to office in December, 1910. The reelection of Diaz and that audacious speech he made to his constituents (with false humility Diaz stated he longed to retire from public life but felt duty-bound to accept the presidency as long as his people wanted him) had set Villa off on a course of violent revenge. A rigged election insuring Diaz's despotic dictatorship had fired Villa's anger to the point that he immediately allied himself to Francesco Madero, the little Sephardic Jew acknowledged as the head of the popular revolution.

After that alliance, there ensued too many petty court intrigues, too much talk, too little action by the leaders of the Antireelectionist movement to suit Villa. Too many arguments and futuristic plans to attack this city or that never materialized. Worse, there were too many delays in bringing Francesco Madero, who operated out of El Paso, Texas, back into Mexico and immediate power. While they procrastinated, Federal troops and heavy artillery arrived daily from the south. Crack units under highly skilled and expertly trained army regulars, fully experienced in Indian fighting and guerrilla tactics, were quietly building an invisible chain to isolate revolutionary forces and later push them against the Yankee borders. This and much more was being readied for the moment Papa Diaz gave the word.

General Obregon had come to know his enemy well. Pancho Villa, an untrained hot-head outlaw, had learned guerrilla tactics, fought emotionally, and considered the business of war puzzling as hell. This became apparent to Obregon several times when, in the heat of emotionalism, Villa had assaulted falling forts and flimsy garrisons of half-assed Federal soldiers barely able to fight back. Although Villa and his men fought like hell, they were unable to achieve the most minute victory. Obregon felt that Villa would naturally be no match against a full battalion and armored divisions that fought scientifically under the most stringent military discipline.

Neither Obregon nor his countless technically trained associates had counted on Pancho Villa's insatiable curiosity, his eager, open-minded thinking, or, more important, the point he made of never making the same mistake twice. If he couldn't profit from his failures or mistakes, he had told himself long ago, there was no hope for him. Villa's philosophy of learning through trial and error was the lever that would elevate him to supreme power against all odds.

These *Científicos*, as the regular army was called, sold Pancho Villa short every step of the way. Obregon, who was planning an encounter with Villa in the not too distant future, knew not the calibre of man with whom he had to deal. This fact gave him some concern. The man who could entice the daughter of General Alvaro Obregon to defect to his side had to be someone special. Just how special he might be is what kept General Obregon awake nights.

At noon, on this day of his daughter's return, General Obregon decided to enlist the services of one of his most enticing concubines. Dolores Chavez would make him forget his troubles for a time. He lost no time in seeking her out.

"*Querida*, have you missed me, my little one?"

"Is this answer enough, *mi Generale*? Hold me more tight."

"Like this?"

"Is much better. Then Dolores can make your troubles melt."

"All my troubles?"

102

"All, *mi Generale*. Kiss me again and I will show you paradise."

"When I leave this time will you be my *campesina*? Come with me?"

"Whatever you desire, *mi Generale*."

"Little tigress. You are lying to me. You screw everything in pants. Do you never say no?"

"Never, *mi Generale*."

"I could have you beaten for such impudence."

"Then beat me. It will make no difference. I shall be as always, a hot tamale, eager to love."

He laughed heartily at her candor, at her daring. "What a terrible thing to say to me when you know I shall be leaving soon. Perhaps I shall be killed—or shot at least."

"And if you do, *mi Generale*, it will be with at least three *putas* at your side, going down in a great fanfare of glory. *Viva* Obregon!"

He laughed pleasurably. "What a tigress you are. A treat for a saddened heart."

"You grow harder, now, *mi Generale*. You think it's time?"

"Give me more time—it's all too pleasurable—all so needed."

"Today you are a bull, eh?"

"Just a bull? Not a Miura? I am saddened to hear it. I want to be a Miura."

"It isn't possible. Your heart is too heavy."

"*Querida—mi querida—*"

"*Si mi Generale?*"

"You talk too much. Lie back. Relax and be still."

"With pleasure, *mi Generale*."

Halfway through his second passionate dalliance with Dolores, General Obregon stopped short, struck suddenly with inspiration. He sat up in the four-poster bed and pushed the dark-eyed, naked woman from him. When she questioned him with a silent, puzzled look, he arose from the bed and walked about in his long johns, preoccupied with thought. "Go," he told her. "You can go now."

103

She began to pout and protest that she hadn't received her share of the pleasure, but certain he hadn't heard her protests and wouldn't, she submissively slipped into her cotton Indian dress and removed herself from the bed chamber, having no desire to interfere in his thoughts. In Dolores' eyes shined the reflection of her lover, Corporal Jimenez, whom she ran to search for the moment she left the general's quarters.

In those next few moments after Dolores absented herself, General Obregon was planning the most important military coup in his impressive military career. How? In this house, under this very roof, less than 500 feet from this very room was the only person who could tell him the truth of Pancho Villa's strength, the tactics he employed, the number of men he commanded, the quantity of the weapons at his disposal—*his daughter!*

How to cultivate her? How to draw her out? After all he'd said to her, threatened her with, how would he exact the needed information? He dressed hastily as one in fever. At first, plaguing self-recriminations made him flush shamefully that he'd consider using his own daughter as a spy. But his daughter, by her own admission, was a *puta*—a whore! His own brother attested to it! Very well, then, if she insisted on being a *puta*, he was going to make it count. Alvaro Obregon was no fool. He knew exactly what victory for him against Villa would mean to his career. He was young, not yet forty. He was virile, shrewd, the most talented tactician in *El Presidente*'s army. One day Alvaro Obregon would be president of Mexico. It was so written: the finger of destiny had always pointed to this.

As for Madelaina, she'd grow out of this crazy school girl talk of revolution, just as he and countless university students in each generation had done.

He returned to his office to plan his strategy. He would buy Dolores a small bauble since it was she who, in a way, inspired this stroke of genius. Obregon patted his moustache into place, as he stood facing the mirror in the cramped quarters he used in this old fortress. He admired the handsome reflection staring back at him and wondered if Dolores had already found Corporal Jimenez to satisfy her heated sexual passions. Then, quickly dismissing her from mind, he planned the strategy he intended for his daughter. It would begin with dinner that night. Considering that Madelaina had concealed her love for Peter Duprez from her father, it wasn't odd that he hadn't given the man much thought. Once or twice, he had wondered about their relationship, but, because she didn't moon about like a love-struck woman, he had dismissed Duprez from his mind. He had completely forgotten that he'd once ordered a dossier on the man which had never been delivered to him. Now he wondered about Duprez, his eyes lighting up with inspiration.

Chapter 5

Madelaina sat soaking in the wooden tub in her spartan, plank-floored room, which boasted only the barest necessities: a sturdy bed, a commode with a pitcher and basin in white, cracked crockery, a bureau, and a chair. And, of course, for the next few moments, the luxury of this wooden bathtub, provided by her new *dueña*, a gargantuan woman named Concepción Montoya, who watched her sternly with a look of disapproval in her eyes. Her black hair, parted Indian style down the center, was braided at each side of her fat face, and her dark eyes were everywhere. She had just finished washing Madelaina's hair and scrubbing her with a coarse cloth and plenty of soap.

Breathing heavily, she said, "Finish yourself."

More than a year had passed since Madelaina had bathed like this with perfumed bath salts and the attentive assistance of another woman. Her wet satiny hair sat atop her head like black squiggly ribbons, coiled damply and speared through with bone hairpins. Candles and oil lamps provided illumination since the barracklike building had only a solitary window across which bars had been fitted years ago, making it every inch a jail. Scrubbed clean of the grime and filth, Madelaina emerged a vision of loveliness. Her olive complexion had tanned to a tawny, coppery glow. Her high cheekbones were punctuated with sunken hollows that gave a woman the gaunt yet highly desirable expression of a mysterious madonna. The boyish qualities she had returned to Mexico with over a year ago had disappeared. An overly starchy diet of tortillas and corn had put a little flesh on in the right places, and her body had matured beautifully into womanhood. Her lips, full and provocative, formed a perpetual pout which enticed any man who glanced at her.

Madelaina Obregon, known in other circles as "Zorrita"—little fox—had never given her real name in the many camps she had traveled in her search for Peter Duprez. After she had left the hacienda of her father in the company of Miguel Guerra, she realized how much she had missed a man's companionship and the love he could provide. For two months after she left Peter in Vera Cruz, she had tried to be all her father wished her to be, but each day she felt more discontented. She had met her father's friends, the women of their world, and she found them terribly empty, infinitely lacking in intelligence, and so wrapped up in their small, petty biases and social intrigues that she felt suffocated. She would have enjoyed the company of the courtesans more, certain that they could discuss far more interesting subjects than the cost of food, the insolence of servants, or the limited quantity of fabrics available for *modistas* to create gowns.

Tired of pouring tea and chocolate for these supercilious, rattle-brained, empty-headed, waddling ducks, Madelaina took to reading the newspapers and listening to the laments of her people. Besides, Peter Duprez had turned a light on in her brain, one that could never be extinguished, and created in her an insatiable thirst for more knowledge of her people and country.

As she lay back against the wooden head-rest provided by Concepción, she sighed heavily, reflecting morbidly on what had brought her to this end. She tried to blot out the memories of this past year. She had more immediate things to reflect upon. The Madrigal, for example. Her father couldn't possibly mean to send her to a convent where the girls were kept virtual prisoners! She thought these practices had gone out with the Inquisition.

It stood to reason however, if there were more young women who shared her ideals, they might have to be imprisoned so as not to bring disgrace upon the heads of their class-conscious, socially oriented

107

families. Madrigal de Los Altos wasn't what it appeared to be to the uninitiated. Rumors of the fortresslike citadel overlooking the Bay of Monzanillo on the Gulf of California had reached her long ago, but she shoved them aside as mere foolish prattle by superstitious gossip mongers. Now she was determined to learn more about the place before foolishly causing her own imprisonment. She had learned much this past year, particularly the art of survival. Madelaina had grown cunning and deceptive; she knew how to use many artful female ploys. At first, she was grossly displeased that she could resort to such falseness, but she later learned that any tool was vital in the art of survival, that it didn't matter how false you were to yourself or anyone else as long as you got what you wanted. Peasant women, she learned, were far more vicious than she had imagined, not bird-brains like the sheltered women of Mexico and Madrid.

Campesinas, putas, whores, followers of the rebels as well as those of the *soldados* were a strange breed. No clinging vines, no timid violets, or blushing virgins, these. They were well-seasoned, hardened women whose very existence on earth was a nightmare. They took life as they found it—without illusion. And they took lovers one after another as they might pluck berries from a bush. Tall or short, fat, or skinny, ugly or comely, when the guitars started up around the campfires each night and romance filled the air, heavy with the earthy smells of men, wine, and animals; each woman turned into a queen, prancing her wares about in a sort of provocative, ritualistic dance aimed clearly at some poor slob couldn't escape once a *campesina* tagged him for her own.

Each woman, a sorceress in her own right, was ready to spring into a jealous rage when her lover's eyes strayed. Many a time Madelaina had witnessed a blazing stream of bullets empty into a man who strayed from his little *gatitta*, his little cat. Consequently, Madelaina, with more things to concern herself with than the mercurial temperaments of these wild, untamed women, kept to herself, never trespassing on the territory of another.

She had made one friend, Antonetta Maripoza, a woman who was not so caressingly lovely as the most beautiful woman in camp nor as hardened as the ugliest. Fascinating, with countless stories to tell, she kept Madelaina at her side and taught her to make her own meal on a *metate*, how to cook excellent tamales, enchiladas, and tortillas with frijoles or meat. What amazed Madelaina was the incongruity of the woman's past. She had lived in San Francisco and El Paso before coming to Mexico to join Villa. She once owned fandango houses and gambling palaces, wore lacy and beribboned finery with gorgeous silk mantillas draped carelessly over one shoulder. She had been a fancy coquette with flashy, monied dandies of the gambling palaces and sporty saloons. Her fling at the mad gaieties of life had given her remarkable poise and the worldly stature of a woman who knew her way around in a world of men. It was no secret that Antonetta was the woman of Pancho Villa, special to him in a way no other had been, with the exception of his beloved wife, Lucita, whom he kept out of his world of conflict, war, and strife.

Antonetta promised to tell Madelaina about their love affair. Hopeless as it might seem at the moment, it had survived and remained as magnificent as ever; it was "something she'd do all over again," the red-haired lady with the blue green eyes had told her.

Madelaina stirred in her bath. Her father's spies had tracked her down shortly after that night, and she hadn't seen Antonetta again. Why didn't her father understand? Why couldn't she make the general realize she wasn't the same girl she was a year ago. She was a woman now. Had been for a long time, but not in the same way she'd been in this past year. She had grown wise to the ways of men. She knew the power she held over them—that is, all except General Villa. Even the fact that he hadn't shown any interest in her didn't bother her, because she knew she could have enticed him if she tried. But then what would she have been? A *puta*, another whore? Another woman who like Antonetta lost her identity? Another lowly peasant with whom he'd violate religious sacraments, then make a sham of the whole thing by permitting some priest to recite vows of marriage, only to be left alone later?

No, this was not what Madelaina Obregon would settle for. Although Pancho Villa was thirty-four years old, he was quite appealing, more handsome than had been rumored. His appeal was enormous. How many fights would break out among the women in camp to see who vied first for his favor? His aloofness to most women baffled her until she learned he was hopelessly in love with his own wife, whom he kept safely out of his camps and out of public life. He would go to her periodically when things were at their worst, when he, like all leaders, needed inspiration and encouragement. He had coupled with the women only to satisfy his masculine needs. More important than anything else was victory for Francesco Madero and Mexico.

The love he had for this Sephardic Jew was nothing short of adulation. It was clear that Madero's victory would be possible only through Pancho Villa, who became Madero's strength. And to Madelaina Obregon, it became even clearer that only through the love and respect she held in her heart for Pancho Villa could she one day be elevated to the position of adviser to him. This is what she wanted—to be Villa's second in command, a *soldadera* with respect. Anyone would have laughed himself silly if he had heard of this dream of hers. But it was not silly to the daughter of General Obregon. If her father was the right arm of Presidente Diaz, could she not be Pancho Villa's right arm?

In the year of following Villa's army, she had found no trace of her husband, Peter Duprez, or of her old horse, Don Quixote. There were times she lusted after Duprez. She relived those days aboard the *Mozambique* until the images began to wear thin and she decided there was no time for memories. The time had come to create new images, fresh pictures. She could

110

no longer exist or sustain her emotional nature on fading memories.

Her father hadn't minced words this morning. He had made it perfectly clear that he'd been horrified to learn of the fashion she had chosen to live. A *campesina* of Pancho Villa's—indeed! Living worse than a land *peón* by her wits and her body. It was unthinkable that the daughter of General Alvaro Obregon had fallen into such degradation. She belonged to the upper class of a sophisticated society and should be wearing the finest gowns and the most exquisite jewels and married to a wealthy *hacendado* or royalty—a man who would keep her on a pedestal.

How many times Madelaina pondered these very thoughts herself. Living like the lowest of the poverty-stricken peasants, searching every face for that of Peter Duprez, fighting off the drunken soldiers when they became too obnoxious and demanding. She had lied, telling them she was diseased so they'd leave her alone. It wasn't a bad alibi—only word spread quickly in each camp and she'd have to move on to the next. She had no desire to consort with any man. Even though she told her father she'd be honored to be Villa's woman, it was not the truth. She only said these things to taunt him.

The image of Peter Duprez appeared before her constantly, and she began to think herself hopelessly in love with this man who had been her husband for two weeks. Why hadn't she been able to find him? She knew he had escaped the calaboose; her father wouldn't have lied about that. She had asked about him carefully, dropping the name Tracy Richards once or twice, but none of it did any good. No one had heard anything. Antonetta had heard the name Richards near Juarez from a few scraggly mercenaries, but not the name Duprez. She was careful not to mention more than she should about anything. The constant loneliness of her self-inflicted isolation began to wear on her. She was getting no place. She hadn't found Peter Duprez, and this fact seemed to possess her and drive her

111

to look harder for her husband. Even the word "husband" grew important in her mind, and at times she relished the fact that she was married. But it had become too great a burden to bear, and when she was overtaken by those two brutes who worked for her father, Madelaina Obergon had secretly felt glad to have been found. To return to civilization for a while—gain a new perspective—this is what she needed for a while. What had happened after her capture before her arrival, had been grotesque. She wiggled her toes and sank deeper in the tub to blot out the terrifying memories when suddenly a sharp rap on the door jarred her back to reality.

"Enter," she called. Looking about for Concepción, she was astonished to find she had been left alone sometime during her reflections. She arose from the tub just as Corporal Jimenez entered. He gazed at her nudity with an expression of astonishment. His lips moved, but no words formed. He tried to apologize for his intrusion. Her shameless audacity, the provocative expression in her dark alluring eyes froze the words and expression on his face.

"Well, what is it, *soldado*?" she asked. "Hand me the towel."

Flustered, he looked about the room for the towel and saw it hanging on the wooden stand not three feet from him. Unable to take his eyes from her voluptuous body, he reached for and handed it to her with trembling hands, uncertain of the message he read in her eyes.

"You act as if you've never seen a woman before. Is it true?"

He puffed up with importance. "I am a man, *señorita*. I have been a man for a long time. More of a man than anyone you've met."

"Ahhh," she said coyly, rubbing her body suggestively. "I see." Madelaina saw even more. She saw in Corporal Jiminez a means of escape. He was young, impressionable, and completely vulnerable. "What is it

112

you came for?" She led him back to the reason for his appearance in her room.

He braced himself instantly. "Your father, General Obregon, requests your presence in his office immediately."

"Tell my father, the general, to go straight to hell," she said nicely.

"But—but—" he sputtered. "That I cannot do, *señorita*. He'd strike me down." The thought of such insubordination tickled his fancy for a moment.

"*My father, the general,* would *do* such a thing? My, my. I thought only Pancho Villa and Emiliano Zapata were animals," she remarked sarcastically.

"No, *señorita*, the animals are the *Rurales*," he whispered confidentially.

"*Rurales*, eh?" She raised a subtle eyebrow. She had seen their ruthlessness, their brutality, cruelty, and despicable violence. "*Si*, it's true. The *Rurales* are no hummingbirds." She tossed aside her towel and slipped into a cotton dressing gown while the pop-eyed corporal swallowed hard and turned the other way. If only she wasn't the general's daughter, he told himself.

"The Mexican Rural Police are loyal to Diaz, *señorita*. They are necessary to maintain the law, especially in the territory of Moreles where Zapata and his *bandidos* crawl."

"The *Rurales* are Cossacks!" she said bitingly. "They are hard-riding, hard-fighting butchers of men," she spat. "I have seen the results of their vicious hunting sprees."

"Do they compare with Villa's *fruit trees*?" Corporal Paco Jimenez referred to the name given to the many trees from which Villa hung Federal soldiers after the capture of a town. The Centaur of the North wasted neither rope nor bullets on his enemies. Stringing their bodies together by their necks in a continuous coil, he often managed to dispose of six men with one line.

While Madelaina reflected on this, the corporal grew momentarily bolder. He continued to assess her

113

womanly virtues. "With your permission, *señorita*, is it true you were Villa's *puta*—his whore?"

She spun around, her face burning with anger. In that instant, Corporal Jimenez shook in his boots and clearly would have liked nothing better than for the ground to open up and swallow him, for he'd seen this same expression on the face of General Obregon many times.

In a second she regained control of herself. Holding back her wrath, she turned on the womanly wiles. "And if I was, Corporal—what is it to you? Is the corporal thinking he might fill Villa's shoes?"

He squirmed, flushed hotly, and glanced about the room uneasily. Then he leaned in closer and spoke conspiratorially. "Does the *señorita* wish to learn for herself that my shoes are far more impressive than Pancho Villa's?"

"You are my captor, Corporal, and I your prisoner. How can I speak of *my* desire?" She smiled so irrepressibly that he forgot everything but his passion, an oversight for which he could be shot. But no such thought entered his head.

He stepped closer to her, unaware that through the open-grilled window a pair of black eyes were silently observing the goings on. Dolores Chavez had found her lover, Paco Jimenez. She fastened her intent tigress eyes on the couple.

Corporal Jimenez kissed the general's daughter roughly, like a bumbling schoolboy in a candystore wanting everything in sight. Nervous and highly agitated, afraid of being discovered and excited at kissing the woman of Pancho Villa, he practically raped her.

Outside, the fates were moving things into place. As Dolores, boiling over with jealous rage, continued to observe her lover in the act of fornication, the fleshy Concepción, with rolls of flab on her arms and broad hips bouncing as she walked along the dirt path, kicked up swirls of dust with her bare feet. She toted parcels of fresh clothing for the general's daughter. She sent a brood of chickens scattering, playfully slapped the rump of a donkey, and whistled a broken tune. Passing a campfire where a few camp followers prepared the noon meal, she gave them a broad wink. They gestured to her with their eyes and tossed a few barbs her way.

"Has he whipped his lusty daughter yet? Is it true she is Villa's woman? The peacock can no longer preen his feathers now that his daughter is less than us. Will the *generale* pass the grand *puta* off in a white gown to display her purity when he arranges for her marriage? Concepción, ask her if Villa is the bull they say he is with women."

"*Cuidado, putas*! Careful, whores!" growled Concepción. "Get back to work. Mind your business or the general will scatter you into the desert and feed you to the coyotes!" She continued to walk past them, turned the corner, and stopped, arrested by the sight of Dolores raised up on her toes peering into the window, obviously up to no good. Alert to trouble brewing the moment she saw Dolores eagerly fingering a knife in a sheath at her waist, the obese *dueña* tossed aside her parcels, lifted her red cotton Indian dress, and removed a bull whip from her leather boots. She snapped her wrist expertly in a swift flicking motion and caught the girl around the torso, pinning her arms to her waist.

Wincing at the pain, Dolores turned, her face inflamed with indignation, just as Concepción moved forward, slipping the whip between her hands in a hand-over-hand movement. Displaying remarkable agility for the enormous weight she carried, she pulled the girl toward her, out of range of the open window. Glancing over her shoulder, she noticed the feverish movements on the bed by the couple sprawled rakishly upon it.

"What crazy ideas are brewing inside that foolish head of yours?" she hissed at the younger girl in her throaty voice.

"I'll kill him. I'll cut off his *culjiones*! Then he'll see how it is to make love to another *puta*! Villa's woman! Bah!" She spat angrily.

"Silence, you fool! Who are you to talk? Are you

115

not Obregon's *puta*? Then why do you complain, woman? Perhaps Paco knows nothing of Raoul and Pepe, or Tomassino, eh? You think I should advise him of such things?" Sullenly, Dolores backed away, rubbing her wrists where the whip had cut her. She filled with black wrath, both for Concepción and Paco Jimenez. The unusual light in her eyes arrested the larger woman, who read them instantly.

"If you're thinking to inform General Obregon about this sordid affair, it is best to remember that I, Concepción Montoya, can also speak out. There is a matter of the murder of Rosita Munoz who made eyes with Paco and was found dead by the creek."

Dolores' eyes narrowed to slits. She collected herself, knowing she'd come face to face with a deadly enemy. Saying nothing, she backed away and finally took off into the shadows.

Watching her until she was out of sight, the Indian woman folded her bull whip, lifted her skirts, and puffing laboriously, she slipped the whip back into the oversized red leather boots of which she was extremely proud. Picking up her parcels, she braced herself, and with grim determination written on her face, she kicked in the door with a loud banging noise. Corporal Paco Jimenez leapt into the air with a look of terror on his face.

"Stupid son of a pig's whore!" she cursed at him in her Indian dialect. "Out! Out! Out!" She picked up his rifle, which he had carelessly dropped on the floor in the heat of his passion to get to Madelaina. She fired it into the air! "Out before I blast off your worthless ass! *Mentecato! Burro!*"

Corporal Jimenez, trousers falling around his ankles, tried desperately to run away and avoid the wrath and wild shooting of that crazy Indian—that mad woman Concepción. A firing squad—prison—anything was better than this hard-hearted, pistol-packing mama.

"And you—" She leveled her scornful black eyes on Madelaina. "*Puta!* Yes, *PUTA!* Have you no shame? No sense of decency? No thought to honor the name of

116

your father? *Puta*—whore! If you were the seed of my loins I'd thrash you to within an inch of your life—to teach you the manners of a high-born *gachupín!*" The woman tossed the rifle on the table and moved toward the girl, her high cheek bones rigid, her mouth curling in contempt at the odious scene she had witnessed. For an instant their eyes met, silently challenging, each silently threatening the other.

Madelaina's laughter echoed through the thin-walled room. "You know, Concepción, you'd make a true *soldadera* for Villa's army. If you ever tire of playing warden for my father, let me know. I'll take you to where your people are fighting for Mexico and not that pig Diaz!" She laughed even harder when Concepción thrust the parcels at her, a glowering look in her dark, brooding eyes.

"Dress yourself, *puta!* Your father, the general, wishes to see you at once."

"*Si, alcaide!* But only because *you* order me to. Not my father." She saluted the large woman mockingly.

"There are no suitable *tiendas* here in Zacatecas for the clothing one of your stature must wear. You will adorn yourself and be satisfied with these peasant cottons until more can be purchased or made, *comprender?*" snapped Concepción acrimoniously, unable to disguise either her contempt or the disrespect in her voice, a fact which annoyed Madelaina intensely.

"Hold your tongue, woman!" she ordered haughtily. "You braying daughter of a castrated ox. How dare you speak in that manner to the daughter of General Alvaro Obregon? Speak with a civil tongue in your head or I shall have you beaten to within an inch of your life." Her Castilian upbringing came to the fore.

Concepción moved her girth about until she faced the girl squarely.

"Act like a lady instead of a whore and you shall be treated as one."

"Take care, woman, you have overstepped the boundaries. I shall have Pancho Villa eat you alive!" she stormed angrily.

117

"And I shall have Doroteo Arango crush you like meal and feed you to the coyotes," countered the enormous woman, watching the girl through cautious eyes.

Madelaina paled. "How, who—how do you know Doroteo Arango?" she asked cagily, on her guard. She faltered, her eyes narrowed to slits as she held the skirt in mid-air ready to pull over her head—frozen, unable to move.

"I am the sister of Doroteo Arango," she said with extreme caution, her eyes searching the room for eavesdroppers. She waddled over to the grilled window and peered outside into the late afternoon shadows.

"You—are the—*sister* of Pancho Villa?" She searched Concepción's face. Quickly she pulled the skirt down over her blouse, hooked it at the side, tucking in the white embroidered blouse at the waist. "But what are you doing here? Why are you not where the fighting takes place?"

"Ayiee! Be silent, girl! Here even the walls have ears." She moved toward her charge. "I go where I can best serve Doroteo. Presently I am needed here." Her contempt for the girl wasn't reduced. "If you insist on being a *puta*, why do you pick on lowly corporals with jealous mistresses skilled in the art of murder? If I'd been detained a moment longer—" She rolled her eyes upward. She explained about Dolores, about the ready knife itching for a target. "If you truly wish to serve the people's revolution in the cause of Pancho Villa for Mexico, you would select your companions with care. You would cooperate with your father, the general, learn of planned attacks, troop trains, military installations! A tiger doesn't engage in battle unless he is certain of victory. He will never select a foe far superior to him."

"Do my ears hear your words? Or are they the words of some prophet?" Wheels turned in Madelaina's mind. "Of course. Join your enemy. Let him think he's superior to you and has convinced you to mend your ways. Let him point out the error of your ways. Mean-

118

while, during his unguarded moments, he will impart to you the most vital of secrets.

"You know the answer to your questions," replied Concepción guilefully.

"Tell my father, the general, that his daughter will come to him as soon as she makes herself presentable," said Madelaina, drawing herself up imperiously. "Meanwhile go out. Find suitable clothing for the daughter of General Obregon! If you must break into a *tienda* to bring what I need, do it! I shall wait for you!"

Concepción's eyes lit up with excitement. "How is it you have not slept with Doroteo yet? Is my brother blind? Is he dead and unable to feel? It is not possible one such as you could have escaped his eyes. Tell me. *Madre de Dios*, and I called you a *puta*? Ayeiii. One day I shall pay for using such abrasive language on you. I am known as Little Fox—my code name to my brother."

"Que va, Little Fox. That is what I am called in the camps of Villa."

Concepción was taken aback. "Then it is a double blessing—a sign, for certain. Two Little Foxes? *Si*, it is a good omen, such a good omen!" She laughed gleefully, slapping her thighs, waddling off, and locking the door behind her. We shall see, the fat woman told herself.

Madelaina moved swiftly to the window, and glancing about the busy compound, she saw the Indian woman talking with two soldiers who saluted her and marched toward the building, posting themselves outside the Little Fox's door. The general's daughter smiled enigmatically.

Concepción outdid herself. Madelaina would never ask any self-respecting *bandida* how she came by such finery and all in the correct size. It was important to her that she dress with meticulous care to bring approval to her father's eyes. The course she had decided upon during those few serious moments spent discoursing with Concepción would mark the turning point in her life.

Scenting herself with the perfume her *dueña* had supplied. Madelaina stiffened imperceptibly at the heavy scent of musk. She usually wore a scent of roses and this seemed a bit heavy for her. But she had no choice. During Concepción's absence, she'd dressed her hair, brushing it thickly atop her head and coiling it into two large buns in back. Then she stepped into the lacy petticoats of beige cotton and slipped on a rust-colored muslin dress, drawn tight at the waist, with a sheer beige lace bib and high collar. Short puffed sleeves were caught with beige and violet ribbons to match the same trim on her petticoats, which showed as she swished her skirts. The dress emphasized her firm breasts and added a touch of dignified class and elegance to her.

Watching her, it was plain to see Concepción admired her appearance. She nodded approvingly. "Now that we are in accord, *chiquita*, you must be on your guard. Do not push too hard, be too buttery or he will suspect ulterior motives, *comprender*? You know what to do?"

"*Si*, Concepción. I know what to do," she said quietly. The knowledge that this woman was sister to Pancho Villa had created a strange reaction in her. Awed by the fact, she was almost obsequious to the *dueña*, something which Concepción warned her about.

"You must not treat me with such respect. Assert yourself, girl, as befits a woman in your class or your father as well as the other *campesinas* will become suspicious."

"It is most difficult for me to command the sister of General Pancho Villa, the idol of the revolution," she said.

"Hush, child! Put more vinegar on your tongue when you speak with me!"

"I'll try. But don't expect miracles."

"You must do better than try," ordered the *dueña*. "Your father, the general, is much, much too smart. It is

120

most unfortunate that he has no Indian blood in him as does my brother Doroteo." She shook her head sadly and her braids went flying. "If he had some Indian in him, *chiquita*, he and Villa would leave a whirlwind in their wake. One day, perhaps you will tell me how it is that a *princesa* like you should shoulder the cause of the Indian."

"One day I shall tell you. Meanwhile you have only to thank one very special gringo," said Madelaina, putting the final touches to her hair and face.

"Ugh—a gringo, eh? Poooeeey," she grunted. "What do they know?"

"Enough, woman, to have convinced the daughter of General Obregon that that chocolate drinker Diaz must die or be dethroned!"

"Hush, child!" cautioned Concepción, placing a fat finger over her lips. She scurried over to the window and peered out at the sunset. The hot Mexican sun had turned the sky into a pulsating orange-gold, illuminating the bleak desert sands into gold dust. The compound was deserted, manned only by a few indolent guards, while the soldiers ate their dinners.

"Not even in my presence are you to speak such dangerous thoughts. There are some things you must discuss only with your maker, *comprender*?"

Madelaina nodded dutifully. She left her quarters en route for her father's study. Concepción couldn't believe the coincidence of the names. "Little Fox," she said over and over in her mind. With two Little Foxes, how can Doroteo lose?

Chapter 6

As Madelaina entered the study, her father stood before the fires warming himself. God, he was beautiful—so handsome, tall, and fine—and so gallant, even in that stiff, unadorned German uniform *El Presidente* permitted his soldiers to wear. One-half the army wore French uniforms, the other half, German. Why they didn't wear one uniform? Something designed for the Mexican army? Was this a sign that President Diaz might be attempting to placate both foreign nations? Politics was certainly confusing at times.

She cleared her throat. "Good evening Father. I'm sorry to have delayed coming to you. I did want to please you, rather than disgrace you as I must have upon my arrival this morning." Her subdued voice startled him.

General Obregon turned slightly, expecting something as bedraggled as he'd seen earlier. An expression of amazement spread through his tired face as he crossed the room toward her. "My dear, you look simply exquisite. I cannot believe these eyes. Is it you? Is it really you?" He reached for her hands, kissed them, and turned her around so he could take in with full appreciation her radiant looks. "You are a beautiful woman, *querida*. I can deny that fact no longer." He led her to a seat before the fire. "Sherry?" His own attitude was so changed that Madelaina was on guard.

"Please, Father. I'd like that very much. I must add that you also look distinguished in your uniform. Although I don't see why you don't wear the French uniforms. They are so much more pleasant to look upon than those plain, unadorned Kaiser tunics."

"The measure of a soldier is not the uniform he

122

wears. You of all people should know this, since you fancy Pancho Villa so much."

"Father," she said rather sharply, "please let us not discuss a subject that might provoke either of us. I want to get to know you, understand you, and determine in my heart whether or not I've been in error these past many months. I've seen a lot—my eyes have been opened to more than I'd ever known. Yet something compels me to examine your feelings. You are doing what you believe in, so it can't be all that wrong. Perhaps if you can encourage me to see things through your eyes, I might learn my views are not the only ones that count. We've been apart for so long. Perhaps there are things you can explain to me—so that I can try to understand."

"*Querida*, am I hearing you correctly? You fill me with joy. If I could only believe you wish to be equitable in your assessment of me and my political views—that you're willing to hear both sides of the question—that you'll not run off at the first emotional turbulence and will think things out." The general eyed his daughter through calculating eyes. What had brought this change in her? The reversal of her temperament struck a note of caution in him. They sipped the sherry in silence.

"I wish to try, Papa. I dislike this estrangement, perhaps more than you. I've been lonely. I've regretted much and in my many hours of wandering through this desolate country of ours, there've been moments when I've missed you so much, I've cried myself sick."

"This is true, *querida*? Oh my child," he exclaimed, drawing her closer to him on the leather sofa. She lay her head on his shoulder. He dabbed at the tears springing in the corner of his eyes. "My heart is filled with a father's love which you've for so long denied me."

Behind them, the shadowy figure of Concepción withdrew, leaving them alone for a reunion. Outside she shuffled her portly frame through the dust toward her own quarters. Concepción Montoya was number one *dueña* here at the fortress of Zacatecas. Whenever the *Federales* moved in new troops, she was there to take care of the girl children of the highest-ranking officer. Obeying only the commanding officer of the fort, she took no guff from anyone and often told off the soldiers. Because she held such special power among the *campesinas* and because of her imposing stature, she was seldom questioned. She did her work exceptionally well; she even procured women for the generals when necessary. And for these favors, she was permitted a small *casita,* where she could retire when necessary. Her husband had been killed two years before fighting with Zapata near Moreles. She had taken a job in Zacatecas, because she was tired of grubbing for her food, tired of being a lowly *peón.* She minded her own business and tended only to her own affairs. A year ago, she had been visited by her brother Doroteo, who had assumed the alias of an old bandit leader, Francisco Pancho Villa, when forced into the hills as a criminal. She thought about this as she entered her house and busily set about completing a few of the important duties she had to perform.

Inside her meager little *casita,* Concepción drew the cotton muslin curtains over the window, bolted the door, sat down at a crude table, and lit a candle. She picked up a pencil and laboriously scribbled a message on paper: *"Take heart. It is beginning. Soon expect the word of Little Fox."*

She rolled the thin paper up very tightly into a pellet and went outside the backyard where she kept pigeons. Behind the larger boxes there was one special cage containing a very special pigeon. She fastened the pellet to his leg, then pushed him up into the air. *"Vaya con Dios,"* she whispered. In the darkening purple-hued twilight she could barely make out the outline of the dove. She went inside, prepared coffee, wrapped herself in a *rebozo,* and lit a fire in the stone fireplace. She sat down in her rocker—the one gringo luxury she allowed herself. Rocking to and fro, turning her thoughts inward, she reflected upon her brother's life.

At age 16, Doroteo Arango, having shot the son of a

wealthy *hacendado* for raping his sister Martine, re-named Concepción, took to the hills as a criminal, hunted by the police and the dreaded *Rurales*. After sixteen years of banditry, living by his wits as a vandal and murderer, and becoming a living legend, he was contacted by the rebel leader, chief of the Antireelectionist movement, Señor Gonzalez to pledge his allegiance to Don Francesco Madero in support of the revolution.

"Can you believe this?" he had asked his sister a year ago when he sneaked into the military outpost disguised as a *Federale*. "They want me—Pancho Villa—to fight like a soldier!" he told his favorite sister, whom he loved with a passion.

"Can you trust them, Doroteo? They are all alike, such men. They want you until they have the needed power and then you become bait for the vultures," she had cautioned him. And then he told her of the meeting between himself and Señor Gonzalez at the Gonzalez house in Chihuahua.

At this unusual meeting, Pancho Villa remained highly suspicious and rightfully so. Such men had brought only despair and frustration into his life. They had forced him into the hills to vandalize and scratch out an existence like some chicken; he was unable to view them without distrust. There was no doubt that Don Gonzalez was as distressed as Pancho Villa. Before him stood the savage, a man who had crushed the *Rurales* so many times they refused to hunt him down. Ambush after ambush had been set for this terrifying *bandido* and always Villa emerged the victor. Pancho Villa's reputation had preceded him. Now his services were greatly needed and desired.

The question was how to entice him over to their side. Don Gonzalez began by spouting democratic ideals, those conceived by Mexican intellectuals and idealists, university students, professors, artists, and all creative nationalists. "But all this is nothing without the support of men like you, the masses of oppressed people close to the soil," he told Villa.

125

"Are you some crazy man—*muy loco*—to think that anyone can change the paternalistic government of Presidente Diaz who has ruled Mexico for 31 years? A man who has brought oppression, starvation, and a spoils system to our lands? A man who favors the rich over the poor?" Pancho had been outraged. "Listen, you fool. You have never tasted the wrath of the *Rurales,* felt the burning sting of their whips as they slashed through clothing to bring blood to a man's back. You've never felt their spurs on your face or a noose around your neck. Have you ever seen the games these devils play with the *peón.* They dream up sweet little games—see? They cut out your tongue if you talk back to a *hacendado*—no matter what grave injustice he may have done you. They shave your feet, then make you 'walk over cactus. Whatever you plant—no matter how many hours of back-breaking sweat it takes—they pull it out faster. And Presidente Diaz encourages such satanic behavior. Diaz and his stinking *Federales* and the *hacendados* can do no wrong. The people are wrong and the unborn child in his mother's womb is wrong—but not the rich man."

Gonzalez agreed. "That's why we are revolting. We want to combat the dictator who has no place in a democracy in a civilized nation. We are willing to risk all we have, but it cannot be accomplished without you. The revolutionary forces need you, Pancho Villa."

"Hah!" declared Pancho with inborn native intelligence. "You need the masses for man power, men who are willing to be shot—men who will not be missed! Is this not so, Don Revolutionary?"

For an hour Don Gonzalez used his most convincing oratorical zeal in hopes of convincing Pancho Villa, but it seemed hopeless until he mentioned that *El Presidente* was usurping too much power.

"Imagine, Diaz tossed Francesco Madero into jail for preaching freedom. The poor man made the mistake of stating publicly that Diaz should encourage free elections, that he shouldn't succeed himself in office."

"For this he was tossed into the *calabozo*?"

126

"It was in all the papers—didn't you read about it?"

Too proud to tell Gonzalez that he was illiterate, Pancho Villa said, "A man who's seen the inside of a Diaz jail cannot be too bad.'

That was as much as her brother would tell her at that time. However, he enlisted her aid in inaugurating one of the slickest espionage circuits ever embraced by an outlaw, or in Mexico, or perhaps in the world.

It was not all peaches and cream for Villa in the beginning. Even though Concepción and those homing pigeons, so expertly trained by her and Pancho, had diligently performed their duties so that Villa and Emiliano Zapata knew in advance of any military plans set against them, the outlaws had encountered many defeats when forced to fight a disciplined army.

When Concepción first heard rumors that the daughter of her new commanding officer, General Obregon, was a *Villista* at heart, she refused to believe it. But rumors like chickens come home to roost, and from each of the general's paramours, most of whom she had supplied herself, she learned of his discontent with his own flesh and blood. She began to believe the rumors and comforted herself with the knowledge that the girl must be quite intelligent to be on the side of the people—and not that pig Diaz.

Concepción had looked forward to encountering this young female rebel, but she never dreamed the rebellious girl hadn't come to the attention of her brother, who always had a roving eye for beauty. Now that she'd met Madelaina and had seen for herself the venom between father and daughter, she saw in the girl a far more valuable tool than she herself had ever been to her brother and their cause. She dozed off in her rocker, conjuring up exaulted plans of success.

General Obregon and his daughter enjoyed their dinner and returned to his study to sip their coffee.

"It must have been a hard life you endured these past twelve months, my child," he said, "one I never would have chosen for you. Now, tell your father about this man Pancho Villa. Tell me what inspires you to

127

follow him—ignoring all you have, disregarding the life to which you've become accustomed, setting aside all your friends and social graces. It would suit me to understand your dedication. Each day I face so many enemies of *El Presidente,* that I, too, have wondered, why he has reaped such dissatisfaction."

"You have, Father?" she questioned, trying to remember he was her enemy. "Perhaps I should enlighten you."

"Very well. I promise to listen without bias until you are finished."

Remembering Concepción's words about not being too easy, she grew guarded. "Why, suddenly, Father, are you willing to listen to me, when in the past you have closed your ears?"

"As I said earlier, each day I face so many enemies, I can no longer bear the cross of knowing my daughter chooses to be my enemy. So, tell me. Why should I embrace the politics of Pancho Villa—and, of course, Francesco Madero? Convince me I've been wrong in supporting Porfirio Diaz."

"Well, Papa, it's just that Diaz is not an honest man. He has lied and cheated his people and made a mockery of them for so long, he must be dethroned, if only to allow Mexico the freedom enjoyed by our North American neighbors. They seem to be prospering under democratic rule—why cannot Mexico enjoy the same better life? There is prosperity for all."

"Did you observe when you were among the people of this hero that he and his people stand no chance against our—*regular*—army. The man is not trained. His men will be pushovers in any contest." He tried to conceal his sardonic contempt.

"*Was not* trained, Papa. *Was not* trained. He is now. For months after his first encounter with the regulars, he suffered defeat after defeat. But he has surprising recuperative powers, Papa. He trains his men on maneuvers, just like the *Científicos*—the regulars. It was at Camargo that General Villa seduced your *Científicos.* I was there, Papa. I saw with my eyes what happened."

128

"And that was—"

"General Villa sat on his stallion Seven Leagues on the small hill overlooking Camargo. He watched his cavalry dismount, extend their skirmish lines, and sweep down the plain to face the Federal trenches. As they ran forward I could see the tiny puffs of smoke escape their rifles. Instantly the *Federales* shot back. The *Villistas* advanced, half-crouching, half-snaking forward, their weapons halfway to their shoulders levering rounds into their rifles and firing. Nearly two hundred men charged the trenches, and once in the range of the *Federales*, the officers brandished their swords. Up they went and forward, the counter-musketry rattling in the wind, obscuring the parapets with smoke. They saw the *Villistas* wavering and at the second fusillade the ranks broke up. The attackers fled like pack rats. Papa, it was the disorderly flight of a defeated troop—"

The general interrupted his daughter. "You see, I told you there is no hope for an untrained army against the regulars."

"Wait, Papa, I haven't finished. The *Científicos*, following usual procedure, arose en masse. Their buglers sounded the call for pursuit. A *degüello*, for sure. They were spirited, those blue coats, as they sprang from their trenches in their eagerness to kill."

The general's eyes lit up as he listened.

"Then from nowhere there arose a cry, a terrifying scream, '*Viva Villa! Viva Villa!*' Suddenly, the main rebel army broke from cover, and charging both flanks with a volley of fire, surprised and surrounded the *Porfiristas*. Cut off from their protective trenches, they milled about in panic. Trapped on all sides, their flanks collapsed, the beaten regulars dropped their rifles begging for quarter."

"You were that close to action, *querida*?" asked her father, surprised by her command of the military jargon. Yet earlier he had seen her handle a rifle expertly; he should have known she had become a *soldadera* in the true sense of the word.

129

"I was that close, Papa. So you see, I can tell you firsthand that Pancho Villa is no longer a bumbling outlaw, a stupid *guerrillo*. He has been trained like a *Científico*."

The general filed that bit of news away quite carefully. Why was it his spies had said nothing to him of such progress? He made a note to recruit new spies. Perhaps they, too, were falling for Villa's mercurial charm, just as his own daughter had done.

"And just who trained the *Villastas* like *Científicos*?"

"Before I tell you that, Papa, I want you to know that at least two-dozen army privates wanted to get on the firing squad to shoot their own officers. I heard Pancho Villa remark that it was something to bear in mind: recruits, already trained *Federales* with their own equipment. Now he remains in Camargo and Santa Rosalia. At least he was there when your *charros* kidnapped me."

General Obregon mulled over this bit of news. These twin cities ranked fourth in population and commerce in the state of Chihuahua and were vital to the Diaz regime due to their close proximity to the United States. Santa Rosalia was an Indian pueblo; Camargo, an important military post and shipping center for cattle and mining. For some reason unknown to him, Pancho Villa withdrew his 500 man force when he learned that a Federal column headed by General Navarro, a formidable militarist, was en route to decimate him. He would in time learn why Villa had done this. His guess at this point was that Villa, lacking military and political experience, couldn't properly evaluate the remarkable military defeat, nor was he sophisticated enough to grasp the importance of holding these twin cities under his command.

"While there I saw him distribute foods to the poor, he kept order, appointed committees of Antireelectionists to government posts. He also executed members of his own army for looting. So you see, Papa, Villa has broken with banditry. It's plain to see that."

"What else did you see of this man they call *Jefe?*"

"Well, Papa, this man Pancho Villa, it appears, laid the foundation for the loyalty of his people during his outlaw days. He had paid off their debts, given them protection against the vile and greedy *hacendados*, and always left the people enough money to buy a pair of shoes. He even passed out candy to the small ones, the *niñitos.* He shared his ups and downs with his people and long ago began to build a single unified force. The people responded to him because in the past he came out of nowhere to champion their cause. He is a man who knows his people, his judgment of horses is uncontested, and he knows Mexico like the lines on his hands. He is their hope, their dream, all their expectations rolled into one powerful man."

Their after-dinner *tête-à-tête* was interrupted when an orderly appeared announcing the arrival of a guest. Captain Felipe de Cordoba swept into the study like a breath of fresh air. The affection between these men was quite obvious.

"Felipe!" cried General Obregon, rising to meet the dashing young officer. "What a sight for sore eyes. What brings you to Zacatecas?"

Madelaina glanced from one to the other politely until her father had the presence of mind to introduce them. "Madelaina, don't tell me you've no recollection of the old friend with whom you played so recklessly as a child in Monterrey? Felipe, is it possible you no longer recollect your childhood sweetheart?"

They stared at one another, hesitant at first, both recalling nearly a decade ago when they played together as children at the military encampment where their fathers were stationed.

"But it's not possible!" exclaimed Felipe. "This is the holy terror who frightened me, drove me to distraction, then broke my heart by leaving for Spain?"

"Felipe?" She stared at the handsome officer with tanned skin against his light brown, almost golden hair, unable to believe her eyes. This man with broad shoulders, muscular thighs straining against tight pant legs,

131

and green eyes sparkling with deviltry was Felipe? She couldn't believe it. The last time she saw him he was skinny, knock-kneed, and his skin was a series of little bumps like a rough contour map. And so uncoordinated he was laughable. Felipe, two years her senior, had always been dominated by the girl. He had matured into a princely, strapping man. A fetching smile with even white teeth glistened against his dark bronzed skin. She ran forward into his arms and embraced him warmly. "Come, sit down by the fire." She pulled on his hands and sat opposite him. General Obregon sat alongside them both and engaged Felipe in small talk as Madelaina poured hot coffee laced with brandy. She listened with polite reserve as the two men spoke and noticed that from time to time Felipe cast sidelong glances of excited appraisal at her.

Madelaina recalled the last day they spent together as if it had happened only yesterday.

She and Felipe often played together, the usual games of children. They had been a bit naughty that day, watching her father and his latest courtesan in the act of love-making through one of the bamboo blinds. After a while they both tired of things they didn't quite understand. They jumped off the tree branch by the side of the small house occupied by the major general and walked along the path in the direction of the tall iron gate that sheltered the small fragrant garden.

"Why must you go to Spain?" he had asked with noticeable sadness.

"To grow up and become a fine lady. To be educated so when I return I shall be as smart as my papa," she had explained.

"I like you as you are. I don't want you to leave. My heart will break if I don't see you," he had told her.

"You should be happy I'm leaving. I shan't bedevil you any longer." Madelaina grabbed his hand and intertwined it in hers, suddenly unable to cope with his words or the rash of emotion he demonstrated in those moments. For so long they'd been the fiercest of rivals; she with her little gang of hangers on, he with his, always playing soldiers against foreign conquerors—often the French, at times the Germans or even the Russians. And always as generals of opposing forces.

They had walked about the inner courtyard under the watchful eyes of a *dueña* nodding and dozing in the shade of the portico, hoping to avoid the intense heat of an August afternoon. For a time they paused at the gate to watch the sentinels on guard duty march at their posts. Spying the two children, the soldiers snapped to attention and saluted them smartly. The youngsters both returned the salute, then they relaxed as if they were indeed of the army of Diaz.

"I won't be here when you return, *querida*," Felipe had told her.

"Why not? Where will you be?" she asked. Her interest had been caught up in the activity beyond the compound. An elegant black carriage, drawn by six perfectly matching black horses, came crashing through the open gates at the entrance to the fortification, kicking up swirls of dust, pulled onto the large cobblestones dividing the military compound from the general barracks, and came to a full stop not far from where they stood.

"*El Presidente!*" hissed Felipe. "See the presidential seal on the doors of the carriage. We must salute!" He held himself in a stiff salute. Out of the corner of his eyes he saw her standing relaxed, showing no interest in the proper decorum. "Why are you not saluting?" he asked her, puffed up with importance. "I shall put you on report for insubordination, for dereliction of duty, for anything else I can think of if you don't show respect to Presidente Diaz," he blurted with youthful zeal.

"Oh, shut up, Felipe. You're such a bore." Her attention centered on the group of men huddled about Diaz, her father and Felipe's father among them. They were talking reservedly with the president.

From across the compound, beyond the stables where the cavalry kept their horses, she'd seen four soldiers escorting a heavily bearded man, a *peón*, dressed in filthy rags, down the walkway. The man's

133

eyes, sensitive to the sun, kept blinking and averting
his eyes from the overhead brightness. He was a mess,
wobbly and uncoordinated; it seemed he couldn't walk
with any strength and his legs looked rubbery.

Felipe caught sight of him. He took Madelaina's arm
and tried to pull her away from the gate. "It's best we
don't see this. Let's go." His frantic gestures had only
increased her stubbornness.

"No. Why is it best we don't see this? What's going
go happen?"

"I want to leave. I don't want to witness this," he
said urgently, knowing what would soon happen. He
attempted to take her hand again, but she resisted. Her
eyes were fixed on the four soldiers and their prisoner
as they squared a corner and appeared to be coming
toward them. About twenty feet away, they made another sharp right turn, walking past the iron gate in the
direction of the supply depot and arsenal and heading
for the isolated area behind Obregon's quarters. Madelaina had never forgotten this scene.

President Diaz and his officers glanced up and
watched the prisoner and the military detail attached to
him in stoical silence, until they were out of their
sights, hidden from view by the high wall to the left of
the patio and garden.

El Presidente and the covey of high-ranking military
officers turned in a body and slowly commenced to
walk in the same direction.

"Come with me," Madelaina had shouted. "I want
to see this."

"No," wailed Felipe. "I'm going home."

"*Vieja*—old woman! No! Worse! You are a baby!"
She had ridiculed him. "If you do not obey my command, it will be the *calabozo* for you!" She had assumed lead position in the game they usually played, in
which she always asserted her power over him by
merely taking command.

Before Felipe could protest further, she had yanked
hard on his hand and pulled him after her. They had
run the length of the garden and climbed the vines that

134

wove a path to the top of the wall, behind the flowering magnolia trees. Finally, in full view of the small dirt enclosure, they saw the prisoner being led to the center of the yard. The poor wretched fool was still sun blind. She'd never seen this courtyard.

"Can he see, Felipe?" she remembered asking.

"He's been in the iron box," the lad said quietly.

Iron box! They both knew of the iron box: a square metal box large enough to hold a man, constructed partially above ground, covering a hole in the ground in which prisoners—very bad prisoners—were confined in solitary. The principle of the box insured it to be hotter than an oven, heated by the broiling sun during the day and at night even hotter, for the iron contained the heat for many hours. Water was given sparingly, and even less food. The poor, dehydrated wretch would also suffer from hallucinations common to malnutrition. The children didn't know all this when they observed the goings on, but they were to learn of it and think on it as they matured over the years.

"What will they do, Felipe?" She hadn't seen this before and was fascinated by the display of pomp and protocol. She sensed something unusual would happen since *El Presidente* had appeared so unexpectedly. The sound of drums were heard.

"Let's go. I don't want to see this," Felipe had wailed, turning green. "I don't feel well. Please, let me go home."

"Felipe! Stop being such a baby!" she taunted him. "How do you think your father, the *coronel*, would feel to see you acting so infantile?"

"I don't care. It makes no difference. I won't witness the execution!"

"What execution?" Her eyes had widened appreciably.

"They don't come into this yard unless they intend to shoot a man. It's the firing squad—don't you know anything?" he said with more courage.

"The *firing squad*?" Her voice wavered slightly. She saw her father enter the small courtyard in the company of *El Presidente* and the others.

135

"But why? Why will they shoot him?"

"You really don't know much, do you? That's *El Tigre*—an enemy of *El Presidente*." He assumed the insufferable air of a know-it-all.

"But what has he done?" She felt the stirring of the drum beats.

"What does an enemy have to do? Be an enemy, that's all." He answered as if he knew quite a lot though in fact he knew very little.

Six soldiers carrying rifles had marched into the courtyard, led by an officer snapping orders, and finally stood at attention along the wall opposite the prisoner. To Madelaina, they resembled toy dummies who wore no expression on their faces. She watched her father standing relaxed, listening to what *El Presidente* had to say. At one point they exchanged words, and her father expressed himself with his hands. He shook his head. His face clouded over darkly like that when he was annoyed with her. But this was worse.

An officer marched toward the prisoner and spoke to him. *El Tigre*, poor wretch, shook his head emphatically, still unable to focus his sensitive eyes on anyone or anything. A black scarf was draped over his eyes. President Diaz nodded and the officer in charge of the crack riflemen shouted an order. Instantly the men braced and raised their weapons to their shoulders. It all happened so fast, she didn't hear the orders. She heard the smart *crack—crack—crack* of the rifles, saw the prisoner fall back against the wall and fall to a heap on the ground like a sack of potatoes, hands tied behind him.

Felipe had looked away. His face paled and he felt sick again. Madelaina watched the sight in a burning silence. Unable to understand why her father permitted such a terrible thing to happen; she resented President Diaz more. How could he command such a violent act? None of it made any sense to her young mind. She had been sheltered all her life up to now, hardly knew anything of the world outside her own world of the military encampments, where she had thought

136

the soldiers played the way the children played. War to her had never been real, only part of a make-believe world in which she played. She had never seen action nor felt the reality of the horrors of war.

"I hate him," she said. "Felipe, promise me you'll hate him, too!"

"Who?" he had asked.

"*El Presidente*, that's who?"

"Are you crazy? He is a hero. He is Mexico! He fought Maximilian. He is *El Presidente*!" He asserted himself with masculine superiority.

Madelaina wasn't listening. She was shaking with rage and fear. She climbed down from the high wall, and when Felipe jumped the last few steps and fell to the ground under the magnolia tree, he saw tears in her eyes.

"I hate him. Promise me you'll hate him, too. Promise!" she implored him. "When I grow up I will not permit a firing squad to kill the people. It is a sin against God to kill! The *padre* teaches us that all the time. The sisters, too."

Felipe had never seen this *Enfant terrible* cry. It frightened him. It also stirred in him that masculinity all highborn Spanish men are endowed with. "Don't worry, *querida*. If you hate him, then I shall hate him." He expressed himself with youthful fervor, exuding machismo.

"I hate my father, also, for not stopping *El Presidente*. Promise you'll hate my father, too."

"But—but, you don't understand," he stammered. "That is too much for me to agree to. Don Alvaro Obregon, major general in *El Presidente*'s army is also my *padrino*—my godfather—whom I love with enormous affection. I can't agree to this without suffering serious consequences!"

"Promise! Promise me. We'll make a pact, and when I return from Spain, we shall hate *El Presidente* together and wish that he is shot before a firing squad!" she cried passionately.

"No! I shall do no such thing!" He got to his feet to

137

assert his macho stubbornness. "You are being infantile. Now get up. You've got a lot of growing up to do. I shan't hate your father, my *padrino*. And you can't make me!"

"Then I hate you, too!" she screamed hysterically. "I hate you. I hate you!" She ran from him into her house and slammed the door so hard the slumbering *dueña* awakened, and seeing the lad close by with a look of perplexity on his face, she figured they had been up to no good. "Go home, little *señor*, before I report you to your father, the *coronel*," she told him. "Since the *señorita* has become a woman, it is difficult to understand her tantrums."

It had all seemed so childish and so foolish then. She left for Spain without saying good-bye. Felipe sulked for days wondering about the words the *dueña* spoke and the erratic change in Madelaina Obregon.

Now they stood looking at each other with deep interest in their eyes.

"Felipe," she said in a husky, almost breathless voice.

"Madelaina."

General Obregon exited instantly knowing he wouldn't be missed. Besides he had ulterior motives.

"I don't know whether to kiss you or put you over my knee," chided Felipe.

Her dark eyes lit up with amusement. "I prefer the first." She ran into his outflung arms.

For an instant, she felt him hesitate and glance about the room. Then he quickly swept her in his arms and kissed her warmly. He thrust her back away from him with a measure of surprise in his eyes. "You *have* grown up, *querida*." He searched her eyes. This was the well-practiced kiss of a courtesan. He kept his thoughts to himself, then held her tightly. "I shouldn't speak with you after you left me so suddenly, never once writing me to let me know whether you were dead or alive. You can't know how deeply I felt your absence."

"If I was so important to you, why didn't you write

138

me? Papa knew where I resided. You could have written, Felipe. Really you could have."

"After you left, I entered the university at Harvard in the United States. Then I went into military training and now am a *caballero* on President Diaz' staff." If he noticed her cringe, he said nothing. He removed a cigarette from his case and lit it.

"Are your manners still lacking, Felipe? Won't you offer me a cigarette?" she laughed softly. "I've picked up many bad habits in recent months."

"So you've learned the brazen custom of smoking," he said politely, offering her a smoke. He lit it for her and accepted the drink she offered.

"Have you dined, Felipe? Have you come a long way? I can have cook fix something—anything you desire." She remained cordial, despite the fact that she would have liked nothing better than to ask him how he could have sworn allegiance to that foul, ambitious dictator who lined his pockets with the blood money he extorted from the people.

"Your father is the perennial cupid. He left us alone. Isn't that frowned on in Spain? Where is your *dueña*?" His eyes sparkled uncomfortably.

"Oh, don't be stuffy, Felipe. Don't be so concerned with protocol. This is the twentieth century. Things are changing. Even here in Mexico."

He sipped the sweet, burning liqueur and felt it coursing through his chest. "Well," he said. "You're home at last. It's been a long time. Many things have changed."

"Yes, many. I was away five years, home nearly two, that makes seven years altogether. We've all changed." She actually felt awkward in his presence.

"Some things never change," he said suggestively.

They both looked into the embers of the fire. Then came the sound of music as the gypsy *campesinas* came to life, dancing and singing their native songs.

"I've been hearing strange stories, Madelaina," he said quietly. "Rumors fly around the presidential palace. I've laughed at them all. I've squelched most of them, but a few persist. You see, I work in the confidence of the Intelligence Office. I'm not telling you this to intimidate you, understand."

Madelaina drew on her cigarette and fought the impulse to lean over, elbows on her knees, as she had done so often seated around the many campfires in the past year. "What sort of rumors?"

"Rumors that the daughter of a fine, stalwart, and loyal general in the service of President Diaz has become a traitor—a revolutionary, a *Villista*. Have you heard such rumors?"

"Diaz is a traitor to Mexico. He has sold the people into peonage. He has provided no schools for the poor and uneducated. He has brought in too many foreigners to share in the spoils." She paused when she saw disapproval in his eyes. "You're disappointed. You expected me to be changed, more of a refined lady? Sorry to disappoint you. My opinions of Diaz haven't changed."

"Yes. I won't lie. I had hoped that you had changed, that none of these rumors were true—that they were unfounded and simply a figment of someone's distorted imagination. How could you have gotten into this impossible situation?"

"It wasn't that easy to set aside my memories."

"You never really understood, *querida*. The people are lazy. They don't want to change. They want things to be given to them, not to work for them. Even sending their children to school becomes an effort with which they refuse to cope. In some areas the *soldados* must act as truant officers, searching the children out and forcing them to go to school. The parents are the worst offenders. They prefer to have a brood of children working for them so they can rest and take a full day's siesta. Face it. Diaz built a few schools. The people refused to send their children."

Madelaina said nothing. She wished that he wouldn't hold her in contempt. He was an old friend from the past. She knew he held her in little regard. It was only because of her father that he was being polite to her.

140

"Why does he imprison the opposition? Isn't thirty-one years of his dictatorship enough for us to swallow?"

"You think it will be different under Madero?"

"Pancho Villa thinks so. He had pledged his life for Madero."

"Pancho Villa is a fool. He thinks with his emotions. He is illiterate and cannot understand the ways of the military. He doesn't know that all politicians succumb to power. Madero will be no better, and perhaps even worse, than Diaz."

Madelaina flipped her cigarette expertly into the fire. Felipe smiled at the mannish pose she assumed. Strange how you don't stop loving someone, he thought.

"You interest me, Felipe. At least when you speak, things are not cut and dry. I belive you when you say power can corrupt even the most idealistic. You think Madero will perpetuate the Diaz regime?" Madelaina asked thoughtfully.

"Madero is too willing to please everyone. He is too willing to forgive his enemies. He is a man who can be persuaded by the most convincing talker. Like all politicians, he bends in the whirlwind and makes deals with men he shouldn't."

"Then who else would you support in a revolution?"

"What makes you think I'd support anyone?"

"How else will the country be primed to change? To make things more equitable for the poor?"

"What did you study in school, Madelaina?" he asked indulgently.

"The usual—history, languages, and the social sciences, needlepoint and the art of being a woman. Why?"

"You didn't immerse yourself in political science— or military tactics? Economics—or any of the things necessary to be able to determine the right or wrong way for nations and their leaders to comport themselves?"

Her red face was answer enough. She bit her lips angrily in a sullen silence.

141

"How do you dare, then, attempt to comprehend the politics of both sides? Emotionally? Is that the way you react? With your emotions?" he asked with love.

"Emotions fire the engine of power!" she retorted defensively.

"Power with no direction is useless."

"Felipe, let's not spoil our first encounter by arguing politics," she said finally, recalling her determination in this new role. "My father has already attempted to show me the error of my ways. And I must admit, since I arrived early this morning, I've begun to lean toward his thinking."

"Truly? Are you truly reconsidering your foolishness?" He seemed relieved. He heaved a sigh of relief as if he'd been constricted in knots for the past ten minutes and just came untied. "What will you do? Return to Cuernavaca and keep house for your father?" Felipe believed her because he desperately wanted to.

"I haven't quite decided to resign myself to that life yet."

"Are you aware, Madelaina, your father is a great man? His greatest desire is to see our country united under one government representing the people equally. One day it is possible he might be *presidente*. I can't think of anyone better suited for the job. He has many friends among the gringos. And for a long time he has been learning their ways. We have had many long talks since I returned from Harvard, and he picks my brain continuously about the constitutional government the Americans thrive under."

"How can you be so sure that my father will not succumb to power as you believe Francesco Madero will do once in office?" This interested her.

"There is a great deal of difference between your father and Francesco Madero. Your father is a man of principle. He will not bargain with outlaws and undesirables to elevate him to power. He will do it the right way."

"Pray tell me, dear Felipe, what is the *right* way?"

Felipe paused a moment. "One day you may be

142

privileged to see it. Now, do you wish to go for a stroll?" He was anxious to rekindle the old fires.

"Only if you do not mind an escort," she purred teasingly.

"I don't understand—why an escort?"

"I am under restraints here, about to be sent to Madrigal de Los Altos at Manzanillo." Her wide-eyed innocence tore at his heart, but the acid of her words cut him deeply.

"I do not believe it!" He was aghast.

"Oh, it's true. My father advised me this afternoon."

"But—but he can't send you there. Not there!" Felipe was agitated. "I will talk with him. You must promise to give up all this talk of revolution. If you don't, it may be taken out of your father's hands. That's why he even thinks to send you to Madrigal. Don't you see? It's for your protection. If the Secret Service feels you are a threat to Diaz, General Obregon and I will no longer be able to protect you. Oh, Madelaina, *querida,* how is it you've come to such an end? You really don't know the peril of your acts!"

She was shaken. Now that the implications were made clearer, she could see that she might be sucked up into a vortex of political intrigue. They were afraid of her. How could she remain here now? They would be watching her, waiting for her to make a slight mistake, then—then—*Dios mios. What have I gotten myself into*? She fought for control. "*Que va*? You act as if I am a spy. So I was a revolutionary. I heard things and my emotions were distorted into feverish, foolish reactions. Am I the first young woman to be led astray? Truly, Felipe, I'm glad to be home."

"But—you are Villa's woman—the communiques speak of nothing else." He stopped short. Already he had said too much. "Oh, Madelaina—"

"*Que va*? Villa's woman? See how rumors spread? I've never slept with Villa. He's never met me. True, I've been in the camps, where I've observed and watched and listened. It became so terribly boring. I was never privy to the discussions he had with his men.

I have never met Francesco Madero. No one even knows I am the daughter of General Obregon. To them I am the Little Fox." She stopped short. Now, *she*'d said too much. Damn! Why had she told him that? His facial expression convinced her he hadn't heard her.

"I believe you, Madelaina, because I want to believe you. I will do my best to kill these ugly rumors. You'll see. You have an ally in me. Now that I've met you again, I intend to be more than an ally. You understand?"

"*Si, querido*, I understand. Now, shall we go for a walk?"

"It's true about the escorts?" he asked, still unconvinced.

"It's true." She patted his hands consolingly, accepting her lot with resignation.

"Then I shall have to ask you to give me your word that you will not attempt to escape. And I shall dismiss your jailers while you're in my company."

"Felipe, you are wonderful! I can't tell you how happy I am that we've met again."

They walked among the peasants, staying close to the outer edges of camp so as not to impose on the *campesinas*. The music and dancing became infectious. Madelaina had always loved the music of Mexico—a combination of the fiery Spaniards and the ritualistic Indians. For a time as they stood watching, she began to tap her foot. Soon she was clapping her hands, keeping time to the savage rhythm. Watching her with amusement, Felipe leaned back against a tree and clapped his hands with her. Instantly she struck a pose and began to move her feet, clicking her heels and moving her arms sensuously over her head as her body swayed back and forth mesmerizing the tall young soldier in his French uniform. She became erect, in the stance of a matador with an arched back. Holding herself with perfect control, she made a few imaginary

144

passes with an invisible *corrida* cape. She was breath-taking.

One head turned in her direction, then other, and another. She shook out her hip-length black hair, and it swirled about her like black silken fans as she twirled and moved passionately. She had no idea of the picture she presented to Felipe de Cordoba. She wasn't aware of the crowd that had gathered, keeping time to the music, watching and applauding her, including several sentries doing guard duty. Felipe noticed a tinge of pride and a flare of jealousy. Had she danced like this in the camps of Pancho Villa, in the presence of those dirty, animalistic outlaws, those uncouth, degenerate coyotes who treated their women like the scum of the earth? He tried not to think of her in that light. Unfortunately, Felipe knew all about her. Well, almost.

Many *campesinas* recognized her. They whispered her name as she approached their fires, and seeing her face, they knew this was the general's daughter. Their voices rose in appreciation, attracting others. General Obregon himself came out on the grounds to see what the commotion was about. When he saw his daughter at the center of attention, his first reaction was to stop her instantly. He noticed Felipe, hypnotized by her sensuous dance. He moved quietly toward him, smoking his *cigarro*, with one eye cut sharply on the figure of his highly sensuous and rebellious daughter.

"Well, Felipe, do you approve of Madelaina's wild streak? She dances with the abandon of the Spanish gypsies—no?"

"She is magnificent," he said breathlessly, unaware of the general's presence.

"Do you think you can tame her?"

"It would be a shame to tame such a stunning creature—with your permission," he said, realizing his position. A blush spread over his face and neck.

"I'm happy you arrived, Felipe. You realize what she knows about our enemies? The value of her knowledge, how it could aid us?"

Felipe turned to face the general, forgetting Madelaina for a moment. "You can't mean what I think you mean?"

"If we can use her without her knowing she's being used—"

Felipe was dismayed. "But she's your daughter—" He paused, recalling what Madelaina had told him about Madrigal de Los Altos. "Is there more I should know about, General Obregon, that perhaps she hasn't told me?"

"Tomorrow at breakfast, we'll talk. I'll explain what must be done. She is no longer one of us, Felipe," he said sadly.

"Yes, sir." He braced himself. His heart sank and he despaired.

"At ease, Felipe. We are not soldiers for the moment. I am only a very concerned father, and you, I hope, besides being my godson, are a true friend."

"I should like to think of myself more than a trusted friend and godson," replied Felipe. "Now that I've seen Madelaina again, I realize I've never stopped loving her. Despite all those affairs with the gringos—my heart has never left your daughter, sir."

General Obregon sighed heavily. "I can only hope we both do the right thing for all concerned." He studied his daughter as the dancing neared a climax. "She is beautiful and most desirable—is she not?"

"Most assuredly. She is superb. It's remarkable the resemblance she bears you, *mi Generale*. Does she take after her mother in any way?"

"If only she did." He sighed. "*Buenas noches, caballero.*"

"Good night, *mi Generale*." Felipe saluted him.

The general touched his forehead and walked back to his quarters, unsure of himself and far less certain of his daughter. What was this demon inside her, sitting detached from her logical, reasoning mind? What had caused these insidious thoughts to germinate into a hot bed of revolution? Where had he gone wrong? Just who was this man Peter Duprez who influenced his daughter so much?

Chapter 7

Peter Duprez was furious after the incident at Vera Cruz. He should have known he couldn't trust them high-class, stuck-up Spaniards. He been warned about them, about their high falutin' airs. After all, wasn't there a dang-blasted revolution going on because of their class disparities? She hadn't wasted a minute while he was gone to notify the *Federales*. Damn the cotton-pickin' cupid who had taken a bite outa' him. Of all the women he had consorted with, he had to go and fall for the Obregon baggage. Anyone else, he coulda' dismissed from mind as he had all the others.

Goddamn her lying lips! He had actually fallen for her—against his better judgment. Well, like all things there'd be a day of reckoning, he'd told himself as he paced the jail cell that night in Vera Cruz. In the darkness, as pale moonlight filtered through the bars, he was glad he'd been given a cell without some loud-mouthed jerk talkin' to him. He was in no mood to exchange pleasantries with anyone. In this mood, blacker than the midnight sky, pacing in pantherlike strides to and fro, he'd paused momentarily, certain he heard his name spoken. He couldn't think clearly. He listened. Nothing.

Madelaina. Madelaina Obregon. Soft, sensuous lying lips. What had she told him. *"I feel like your wife. Even if it's a game of pretend we're playing, I couldn't feel closer to any man than I do to you. I feel like your wife."*

"Pete!"

Duprez tensed. There it was again. Clearer this time. He had jerked his head around and walked toward the window where he peered about in the darkness.

"Duprez! Pete Duprez! Is it you?" asked a voice in the night.

"Who the hell is it?" he whispered quietly, for even a whisper carried in the still of a night as clear as those in Vera Cruz.

"It's me, Alejo. Alex, *señor*."

Peter Duprez took heart. "How did you know I was here?"

"We talk later, *patrón*. First, to get you out of there. *Cuidado*! Take care, *patrón*. Get under the bed," came the voice from outside.

"Oh, oh!" Duprez made haste and slid under the wooden cot. He knew what was coming. And it did— with a loud blast, taking one wall apart. He felt the building had crumbled. As soon as the debris fell all around him in a shower of wood and crumbled adobe brick, he scrambled out from under the cot and made his way through the dust, out the collapsed wall, coughing and shielding his eyes. He ran quickly and jumped on the ready and waiting Don Quixote. With Alejo following, they made their way into the night before the soldiers at the Federal jail knew what struck them.

A squad of cavalry mounted up and rode hard into the night. A mile out of Vera Cruz, in the darkness of the forests, the soldiers lost sight and track of the escapee. Dejected, they returned to Vera Cruz to report a jail break.

Nearly a year had passed since then. Duprez had moved on to El Paso to meet with Tracy Richards, and stopping in Juarez, he met with Madero's generals and other officers of the Antireelectionist movement. He delivered the weapons to the revolutionists and planned with Tracy Richards to join Villa's army a few kilometers out of Juarez, where he learned a big powwow was in progress among the heads of the revolutionary armies.

Captain Tracy Richards, a strapping bear of a man who knew the *latinos* well and spoke the language fluently, wore beige breeches, putees, and double bandoliers over each shoulder. He packed double six-shooters over each hip and wore the sombrero of his Mexican neighbors with more dash than the natives. Richards was responsible for teaching many of Villa's troops the use of artillery.

He laughed a great deal, drank beer and wine like water, cursed worse than Satan's keeper, and fought like a tough-fisted, sharpshooting, dead eye that he was. He did more to boost the morale of Villa's army than any fifty men could have done. He also made love to more *chiquitas* than was humanly possible.

Now, as he watched his friend Peter Duprez pace the floor of their hotel room, he admitted he hadn't ever seen Pete this worked up.

"Dang-blasted little Mexican tart!" Duprez cussed. "How was I to figure she'd give me a stiff dose?"

"That's one thing ya gotta concern yourself with, ya hear? Ya gotta watch 'em—those *campesinas*. It's best if ya bring yore own little piece of baggage. Ya got one?"

"No!" snapped Duprez, puffing angrily on a cigar.

Tracy ignored his anger. He glanced through the Juarez newspaper, thumbing the pages as he scanned them. He paused a moment. "Hell's bells, from the looks o' this, ya ain't gonna need no one. Take a look here, pardner. Plenty o' them little *señoritas* for ten armies. Don't know what makes 'em do it! They follow Villa as if he were some god! He ain't half near as lusty as ole Tracy, here, but danged if them fillies don't moon over him. Ain't a bad-looking one in sight." He tossed the paper toward the foot of the bed on which he lay. "Hey, Pete. How come you ain't told me you've been here before? Ya never mentioned ya knew Mexico."

"Ah haven't. Ah don't." Peter picked up the paper, and seated in the rocking chair, he glanced idly through it, focusing his attention on the photograph of nearly fifty women milling about a campsite. The caption read: "Pancho Villa's *campesinas* grow in number each day, by Miguel Guerra."

"No, huh? Then how come one o' 'em li'l *señoritas* has been asking aboutcha? Ya know anyone called Little Fox—Zorrita?"

"Like ah said, Trace, ah've never been here. They must be looking for someone else."

"Nope. It was Tracy Richard's friend they asked for—and there's only one Peter Duprez ah know—*you.*"

Duprez's eyes focused on a face in a photograph and gave a start. *Li'l Fox! It couldn't be. It just couldn't be. The picture is fuzzy and I'm just wishing too hard,* he told himself. *Christ! Stop it,* he swore under his breath. He should have known better than to let her get to him with all that talk of innocence. If he had only continued to treat her in a standoffish manner and not spoken too freely with her about his own involvement, he wouldn't have fallen for her.

He was so busy with his own biting thoughts that he hadn't really heard Trace. He slammed down the paper in a way that brought a grin to his companion's face.

"If ah didn't know those symptoms so well, ah might let it pass. What's wrong, Pete, old boy? Some little wisp o' baggage get to ya? Ya sure ya don't know anyone called Little Fox?"

"Ah already told ya—no!" he countered, a bit too edgy. "What? What's that you say—Little Fox?" Peter Duprez stared at his friend in open-mouthed astonishment. That's what he had called Madelaina on board the *Mozambique.* It couldn't be coincidence—could it? He eyed Tracy Richards warily. "Where did ya hear about Little Fox?"

"Ah've been tellin' ya. Ah been trying to tell ya some little *señorita* has been asking aboutcha in Villa's camps." Richards told him once again about the word that had reached him.

Peter jumped to his feet and stood over the bed staring at his friend. "Where? Where'd they say she'd been? Who told ya?'

"Hold on, dang-blast it! One o' Villa's men—Ur-

150

bina, ah think—came ta me yesterday at the canteena and asked if ah knew some gringo named Peter—"

"Did he tell ya where she was? How can ah get ta her?"

Tracy sat up on the bed, stretched and yawned. "Ah got no idea. All ah told this here Urbina was that you was a *compadre*, one of us. And if she was some bitchin' li'l fox, ta turn her on ta me right quick."

Pete Duprez glowered. "Cut it out, Trace. It's General Obregon's daughter!" He glanced cautiously about the room making sure there were no eavesdroppers.

"The hell ya say!" He came alive. "Ya been messin' around with *Obregon's* daughter? Shooooooeeeeee!'

"It's the one ah told ya about, dang-blast yer head. If ya didn't get yourself so bloody damn drunk, ya might hear what a pal is tellin' ya."

"The filly ya brought back from Spain?"

"The very same."

"Ya better not let Villa know about it." He frowned. "What the hell are ya telling me? Ya expect me ta believe Obregon's daughter is running from camp to camp like some dang-blasted little whore looking for ya? Ya got any idea whad'd'd happen ta her if anyone was ta learn whose daughter she is?"

"Tell me," he replied flatly, worry lines creasing his forehead. Then he shrugged it off. "It's too far-fetched. It can't be her. It's gotta be someone else. Or maybe she sent someone looking for me, using that name. Yeah, that's more like it," he said, trying to convince himself. "That's what she done." He squashed his cigar to shreds on an ashtray.

"Good. Ah'm glad ya got it worked out in yore mind. Ah sure in hell ain't figured it. Listen, how much time ya gonna devote ta this Mexican chili fry? Ya gonna stay and see it to the end with me?" asked Tracy.

"What else?"

"Good. It ain't gonna take much time, ah can tell ya," began Richards as if he possessed amazing insight. "That there Diaz is gonna be in for some big surprise."

151

"How's that?"

"For thirty years, old Papa Diaz has been taking good care of his army. Uniforms, weapons, all that glitter, pomp, and ceremony. But ah'll tell ya like it is, Pete. They ain't nothing but a bunch of busted-down old winos and deadbeats and old jailbirds. Rumored to be 50,000 strong. All Papa Diaz has is a few well-trained officers and *políticos* who have drained the treasury, and they don't have the arsenal Pancho Villa will have when we get right down to the nitty gritty. All *El Presidente* has is one big jack-o-lantern, empty inside."

Captain Richards stood at the window looking down into the crowded streets of Juarez, studying the increased activity. The door opened and Duprez' trusted sidekick, Alejo, entered. "Señor Duprez, they are moving. We must all go. You also, Captain Richards. We will ride less than a day's journey to where Pancho Villa meets with Presidente Madero. *Vamenos*!" This is what they'd been waiting for! Hallelujah!

Nearly 5,000 men filled the area surrounding the sprawling hacienda of Don Amadeo Cephalona, a day's journey from Juarez. They moved about at their usual duties: currying their horses, cleaning their weapons, eating breakfasts of tortillas stuffed with either meat or beans. They came from all over; farmers, miners, mountaineers, and few citified intellectuals, newspaper reporters, who had all joined in the common cause of ridding themselves of that tyrannical dictator Porfirio Diaz.

Captain Richards waved to many of his friends as he and Duprez milled through the crowded courtyard of the gorgeous hacienda that morning in April of 1911. Dressed in his Texas Ranger uniform, adding only the incongruous touch of the sombrero, to which he'd become addicted, Tracy pointed out some of the notables seated on the tiled portico in wicker chairs.

Peter Duprez wore a beige shirt and trousers with a black leather vest, leather boots, and thickly roweled spurs. A Stetson was pushed back on his forehead. His eyes were covered with dark glasses to keep out the glare. The sun had already begun to warm the desert like the inside of Hades.

"That there li'l man over yonder is Francesco Madero, the man hankering ta be Mexico's president," said Tracy, pointing out the chieftains.

"He's not very old," surmised Peter, studying the small bearded man seated hunched over in his seat talking with a few of the notable dignitaries.

"And that's his brother Raoul what's sittin' across from him—the one dressed in a dark suit—in civvies. He and Villa are some tight buddies."

"And who's that dandy?" asked Peter, indicating the tall, handsome blond, who was highly polished and quite European in manner.

"That's the grandson of Guiseppe Garibaldi—the great unifier and liberator of Italy. Ah think he's Garibaldi III. The man ta whom he's talking is Pasquel Orozco—sonovabitch was just beaten ta a pulp by Diaz' men south of Juarez. As a matter of fact, that there Eytalian, Garibaldi, just had the tar beaten out of him in Casa Grande by one o' General Navarro's best officers. Madero retreated here ta the hacienda, and I'm telling ya, it's gotta be the biggest damn powwow since Geronimo called all the Chiricahuas into a council of war in 1886 and caused the biggest damned uprising in Apache history."

Tracy Richards' words were interrupted by the sound of hard, swift riding. Through clouds of thick sand kicked up by hundreds of horses, a heavily armed stranger, with twin bandoliers of bullets crisscrossed over each shoulder, sprang from his sweating black stallion and quickly tossed the reins to one of the men riding alongside of him. He pulled off his floppy sombrero and smacked it hard against his leather pants, which were caked with dust, his spike-roweled spurs clanked loudly as he walked. Electricity filled the air.

Everyone's eyes were on the stranger. Tracy Richards grinned broadly. "That's him. They ain't no

153

one like him," he said with fierce pride. "Hot damn! Ain't he somethin'?" His eyes never left the spectacular man.

Peter Duprez didn't have to be told who he was. It was Pancho Villa in the flesh. He watched him closely, noting the grand manner of his appearance, picking just the right time to make his entrance. Damned near theatrical, he thought. He and his *vaqueros* in knee leggings, with crossed ammobelts and conical-brimmed hats flopping as they rode, were a fearsome bunch, sober-faced, savage in appearance and manners, and distrustful of their surroundings and the people in their midst. But what a spectacle to see them all together.

All the men on the portico rose to greet him with the exception of Francesco Madero. Villa ignored all the others. It was as if he, with some mysterious homing device, zeroed right in on the man whose cause he had elected to champion. He paused only a few feet away from Madero.

"Tell me, *Señor Presidente*, if it's true you've sent for me?" Villa said gently, with tremendous respect in his voice and manner.

Madero smiled and stood up. "You can only be the great *guerrillo* of our cause, *el señor*, Don Francesco Villa."

The two men embraced, slapping each other's shoulders, and disappeared inside, with the other chieftains following. It was a great moment in history.

"Damned what I'd give ta be a little *cucaracha* and hide myself in Villa's pocket. There's plenty of history being made inside that there hacienda," Tracy Richards told his friend.

Just then a small, dark, weasel-eyed *guerrillo* came up to him and slapped him on the back. "Gringo! Ayeiii, *amigo*, it's you!" He laughed heartily, and heads turned toward all the commotion.

Richards turned, glanced idly at the dirt-streaked face and dust-caked clothing on the man Tomàs Urbina, one of Villa's officers. "*Hombre,* how the hell

154

are you?" grinned Tracy Richards with some reservation.

"*Bueno, amigo.*" He grinned a bucktoothed smile, showing spaces between tobacco-stained teeth. He bit into a chaw of tobacco. "Ah, the *generale* will be happy you came, gringo." With a diabolical leer on his face, he turned and studied the other American. "Is another gringo like you, this one?"

"Meet up with Peter Duprez, *amigo.* He's fighting right alongside with us against the *Federales.*"

"Dat's so, *amigo?*" He laughed again in a deep raucous voice, incongruous to his small frame. "Good. Is *muy bueno.* Is good we keep the gringos our *amigos,* no?" His laughter slowly dissolved. In Urbina's eyes appeared the first signs of deep thought. "Piayter Dur—Dupreayez is thees gringo?" His dark, ferretlike eyes blinked several times and he scratched his *mustacho* thoughtfully. "Ees gringo who knows of Little Fox? Ayyyyiii. Ees some hard name to speak—no, *amigo?*"

"If ya can't speak mah name, Urbina—an' ah gotta admit it's a tongue-twister the way ya say it—then, man, ya'all call me Tom Mix, heah?"

"Tom Mix? Tom Mix?" Urbina's insane laughter rolled from his throat like a steam roller. "Tom Mix is more better. *Hombre,* which are you—cannon or dynamite, eh?" he prodded Peter.

"Neither. Artillery. Crack rifleman Tom Mix. That's me, *hombre,*" he replied, taking an instant dislike to Urbina. "A deadeye shot!"

That desert weasel and number one man to Pancho Villa, a total illiterate like his *jefe,* knew men and sensed instantly that Peter—alias Tom Mix—expressed certain hostility toward him. "Ahhhh." He roared with laughter once more. "Artillery, eh? Is more better yet." His smile dissolved instantly. "Listen, Tom Mix—you are the gringo who knows Little Fox?"

Captain Tracy Richards turned to his friend. "What about it, Tom Mix? You know anyone called Little

Fox?" He gave him the business with his twinkling hazel eyes—and a silent warning.

Peter, who would assume the alias of Tom Mix for some time to come, shook his head dubiously. "Damned if ah knows a filly by that name. Can't say as the name rings a bell."

Before Tracy could warn him of his error, Urbina picked up on the faux pas. "Ahhhh, *si.*" Urbina laughed as if this was the funniest thing he'd heard. Then the smile dissolved as quickly. "Tom Mix knows of no *woman* by name of Little Fox. Is funny, Urbina mentioned no woman. But, now that Tom Mix says the Little Fox does not ring a bell, I tell him. This Little Fox is some *guapa*! *Ayeiii chihuahua!* She goes from camp to camp, this one—no *vieja*—no old woman, these wan. Che is some *chiquita* who looks for her *marido*, husband. Ayeii! Ees sometheeng I have much desire to be—the *hombre* who warms her bed."

Tom Mix was grateful when Eleuterio Soto called to Urbina, and he watched the filthy, foul-mouthed hillsman, dreading what might have happened if Urbina had defamed the girl called Little Fox.

Watching the expression tighten around Peter's lips, Captain Richards said, "Now, hold on, Tom Mix. Don't getcher dander up. That man happens ta be Villa's right arm. They've been through hell together. So don'cha get no ideas o' tanglin' with the likes o' him. He's a devil, that one. Wouldn't hesitate a doggone minute ta sink a knife into ya." Richards proceeded to enlighten Peter on the ways of the Mexicans with whom they'd be fighting side by side. "Soto, too, is a tough *hombre*. They're tight, those *amigos*. Yup, from now on yer name's Tom Mix. Ah like it better fer lots o' reasons. An' ah'll tell ya sumpin else. Ah don't cotton ta the fact that General Obregon's daughter is sendin' out feelers for ya. It's scary, friend." He pondered a moment. "Still, Duprez ain't a name people will remember. If they do, ah guess we can handle it. Ah jus' got me a low-down feelin' that this here *chiquita* spells a heap o' trouble fer us—all bad. Well, that's about it, buddy. Y'all come along, heah? Ah'm gonna meetcha up with the rest o' us gringos who've joined up with Pancho Villa. Hey—there's Dreben!" The captain waved to a scraggly man who appeared older than the others in the Gringo Brigade.

"Hiya Captain Dreben, ya old sow's ear!" Tracy laughed again, then glanced at Peter reflectively. "Tom Mix . . . hmmm. That's as good a name as any." He slapped Peter's shoulder and led him toward the grizzled man in a ranger's uniform.

"Tom, c'mon. This here's Captain Dreben. Captain Sammy Dreben. Known ta his friends an' enemies as the fightingest, scrappiest, goddamn Jew bastard that's ever hit the front lines. Hot damn, Dreben, it's shore good ta lay these here eyes on ya."

The two men shook hands and slapped each other's shoulders with jocular familiarity. "Captain," said Tracy Richards, "this here is mah friend, Tom Mix. A helluva sharpie with artillery. Tom, this here goddamn soldier of fortune has fought in the Philippines, Nicaraugua and the Boxer Rebellion. Sammy, ya just finished in Peking, didn'tcha?"

"Oiy, such a memory you have," moaned the soft-spoken Russian Jew, a dark, square-set man in his forties who spoke in a thickly accented voice. "Nine long years it's been since the Boxers." He shook his head tolerantly. "So it's Satan who dug you up again for Panchito, eh?" He smiled and focused on Peter Duprez. "Some name you have, Tom Mix. From El Paso, too, you come? Not another captain?" He shook his head woefully and turned quickly in afterthought to Richards. "Listen, my friend from Louisiana, you know who's here? Oscar Creighton—that crazy dynamiter—that's who came. For us it's like a union of crazy men, *muy loco*—*mahshuganuhs*—*ni?*" He shook hands with Peter and led both men toward the far end of the courtyard where nearly a hundred gringos, fellow Americans, set up camp. They passed countless *campesinas* who had already set up personal belongings and prepared campfires for cooking.

"Ah thought we wouldn't be here too long. What are the women doing setting up camp already?" asked Peter, his eyes widening at the vast number of women squatting where they automatically staked out their respective domains. He found himself eyeing each of the shawled women, looking for a familiar face, as he stumbled forward following his companions.

Captain Richards turned to glance back at him. "Go along, Sammy, Tom Mix, here, an' ah'll be there in a few moments." Captain Dreben waved them off and continued toward the others. Tracy lit into his friend. "Now, see here, Tom Mix. Ah know what's on yore mind. And ya gotta stop it. Look, you can get yerself killed. Worse here—where ya got no business—than on the battlefield. If that Little Fox o' yourns got sense, she'll leave ya alone—that is, if she's here, which ah doubt, and ah'm gonna find out for ya jus' as quick as ah can skidaddle back to Juarez later tonight."

Peter's eyes lit up.

"If ya think ah'm doing it for ya, forget it. Ah'm thinking o' my own neck, *hombre*. If Villa gets wind mah friend's been consorting with the daughter of his enemy, yer life—an' mine—ain't worth a dang-blasted nickel."

"How'll ya find out, Trace?"

"Leave it ta me. But ya gotta promise me ya won't look at another one o' them fillies in the camp—those Indian knives sink in deeper than any of ours and a helluva lot faster, too."

"Thanks, Trace, but ah ain't no cherry in these matters. Ah'll watch mahself, heah? And—thanks again, friend."

"Yeah," said Tracy Richards flatly. He lit up a smoke he'd just finished rolling in one hand, wet one end, and puffed on it thoughtfully as he watched Peter Duprez move on among the others.

As in all the cases of mercenaries and freedom fighters, thought Captain Richards, if they didn't wanta talk, ain't no one gonna make 'em talk. And old Peter here just warn't no talker. Rumors have a way of circulating about, and word was he was the son of some wealthy Texas cattle rancher from up in the Panhandle. Cattleman. Tough sonofabitch of a man harder than saddle leather. Bastard musta done something bad to his son to cause him to skiddaddle off the ranch at a tender age. Some humdinger of a bastard, Tracy had heard from reliable sources. Peter Duprez was a right kind o' man in his books, and he learned Duprez was no dummy, like most soldiers of fortune. Why, he could tell the lad had been educated in some fancy college, but by his own admission to Captain Richards, he claimed he'd learned more from the world of hard knocks. Well, ain't that the truth, thought Tracy when he first heard the remark.

He learned that Peter had taken the name of his mother and disowned his father completely—or was it the other way around? Once, in El Paso, he and Duprez had been dining in one of them swanky gambling palaces. Tracy swore that some fancy dude had come up to Duprez and called him Denton, Benton, Benson, or some such name. The incident stayed with Tracy Richards a long time. Matter of fact, he never forgot it. With his sharp ears he'd have heard the right name, but the music had been loud and the booze played tricks on him. He never mentioned it to Peter and wasn't about to meddle. The man was entitled to his privacy.

H also learned that Duprez was sure all-fired fussy about the fillies he cavorted with. He'd never seen Peter with anyone short of special. That hadda mean something 'cause Tracy learned long ago that water seeks its own level. Still, there was an air of mystery about Peter Duprez. Like, why in hell he chose to be a freedom fighter when he could be living off the fat of the land.

Tracy scratched his thick shock of hair and told himself none of it was his business. Then he laughed aloud at the name Peter had given Urbina. Tom Mix! Hot dang! If that warn't some imaginative name! He chuckled and glanced over at Peter just as Pancho Villa's *vieja* approached his friend.

"Hey, gringo. You gotta light for Antonetta?" asked a redheaded woman in her late twenties, with a clean, well-scrubbed look on her freckled face. She pulled on Peter's arm, restraining him as Tracy Richards shrugged and moved on ahead of them. Her blue-green eyes, sparkling with warmth, searched his face in a manner that made Peter uncomfortable.

"Sure, *chiquita*. Why not?" Peter struck a red devil on the sole of his boot and held the flame at the tip of her hand-rolled cigarette.

"Call me Antonetta, gringo. Ees more better. What's jur name, eh?"

"Look, *chiquita*," said Peter, gazing casually about for the irate and anxious face of a man who might be lurking nearby to do him in. "Ah don't wantcher man ta get ants up his britches by making more o' this than it's worth, ya heah? Ya got yer light, so be a good little woman and skiddaddle back ta yer *viejo*, yer old man," he drawled with a thick twang. "Name's Tom Mix," he added.

"Villa is no old man, gringo," she replied tossing her hip-length red hair over each shoulder and puffing on her smoke like a man. Her eyes continued to examine his face critically. "Tom Mix, eh? For sure ees Tom Mix?"

"You Villa's woman? The *jefe*'s?" He eyed the hand-rolled, brown-leafed cigarette in her hand and studied the way she inhaled. "What the hell's that yer smoking, *chiquita*?" he asked suspiciously, ignoring her last remark.

"What's wrong with ju, gringo? Ju never see marijuana before?"

"Not in brown leaves—"

She shrugged indifferently. "Here we use what we find. Ju want one?"

"Nope." He shook his head. "Gotta keep mah head screwed on tight. Down heah, south of the border, *chiquita*, a man's gotta keep a step ahead of all the hot

160

politicking. But thank ya, woman. Ah'm very much obliged by the gesture."

Peter tipped his hat politely and moved toward the other gringos. Captain Richards was engrossed in conversation with some of his old *compadres*. Aware that Antonetta's eyes still followed him, he shrugged in annoyance. All he needed was to get himself involved with the likes of Pancho Villa's woman in the middle of this revolution. He'd never have to worry about a *Federale* bullet. The *Villista*'s would make short order of him. Yet, he'd give anything to know why she looked at him in such a manner, as if she were committing him to her memory.

"Gringo!" Antonetta called, catching up to him. "Tell me again—what do they call ju?" Antonetta for so long had been talked to by Zorrita, the one called Little Fox, she almost had an imprint upon her mind of the man Peter Duprez as the girl had described him. "Eyes the color of vibrant blue against a coral sunset, hair of brown kissed by the sun. Shoulders like a bull and a body so firm and strong, it takes your breath away. He walks like a king, and he talks with a peculiar gringo drawl. Strong hands with a golden ring that looks like the mark of a branding iron." She had told her so many times. Strange, thought Antonetta as she watched him speaking with Urbina, this man looks much like the man Little Fox described. The fates of work were about to foil many plans. Peter studied the attractive woman, wondering how she came to be the woman of Pancho Villa—out here in desert. If the woman didn't speak with so thick a Mexican accent, he never would've taken her for a *señorita*. Damned if she didn't look like a gringo herself. "Like ah said before, the name's Tom Mix. Ah'm from El Paso, fighting with Captain Richards, Dreben, an' the others."

Antonetta nodded. "*Muy bueno,* gringo. I mistook ju for another." She looked at the ring. "What it means, these sign—eh?"

"This here brand ring? That's what it is—a brand."

"Jur brand, gringo?"

161

Peter Duprez had probably nearly always told the truth—it never hurt, except in some rare instances when he was running away from an enemy in a war or similar skirmish. But today he had told two whoppers. And to some obscure little *campesina*, who wouldn't have meant a damn, he was about to tell another whopper. "No, m'am. Jus' a trinket I picked up off'n some guy who needed ten bucks."

Antonetta, who knew jewelry, reached over and examined the ring closely. "Listen, gringo. Ju got yourself some pretty goddamn good bargain." She eyed him askance. "I myself would give ju twenty dollars for that brand."

"Ya sure tha' old maryjane ya smoke ain't clouding up yer head? This is nothin' but pure junk," he said lightly.

"Junk, eh? *Pues*. Man, I'd like more junk like this. *Pues*, gringo. *Adios*. I get back to my camp." Antonetta left him, but the initials on that brand disturbed her. There was a large B and a P, but another letter was scrolled around those which made no sense. Zoritta's man was P.D. She dismissed the incident—but not the *hombre*—from her mind.

Antonetta returned to her fires. The memory of this man burned into her memory. But now the glowing feeling of her cigarette began to hit her. She sat down cross-legged before the fire and stared dreamily into it, chanting to herself, wondering how the Little Fox was making out. All round her were the clanking sounds of spurs, creaky wagon wheels, the smell of leather and horses, and the aroma of spicy food cooking over fires.

"Listen, Tom Mix," said Tracy, calling to him as Peter entered the draw. "Ya ain't never been a born sucker fer love—that ah know about—what's makin' ya go seedy out here?"

"Ah just lit the *señorita*'s smoke, that's all."

"Well, jus' so ya know that's Villa's woman," he said, handing Pete a mug of hot coffee, as black as licorice and twice as kicky.

"Ah already got the word, Trace—and what the

162

hell's happenin' all of a sudden? Ya tryin' ta pamper me, wet nurse me? Like ah ain't old enough all of a sudden?" Duprez got a little rattled. "Ah been lookin' out for mahself a mighty long time, Trace. Ah can handle things." He sipped the coffee and winced.

"Let's hope so. Still, Urbina makes a pass at ya, now Villa's woman hits on ya. Ah don' like it," he said, munching a friole tortilla oozing with onions.

"Captain, from where I sit," said Captain Sammy Dreben, "it's better you don't look like such a worrier. Come have a look at the kind of weapons your friend Tom Mix has provided our *compadres*."

The Americans stretched their tall frames and ambled over to the supply wagons. Captain Tracy Richards wasn't settled. He kept glancing over his shoulder in the direction of the redheaded Antonetta. Once in a while he stole a glance at Urbina, who was guzzling wine like a dying man at the last oasis on a desert. He didn't like it. He liked none of it. For the first time, his instinct pulled on him. There were just too many people interested in Pete Duprez and he aimed to find out why.

His attention was arrested by the oncoming figure of a woman wrapped in a *rebozo*. "Alloo, *bebe*!" cried the woman. "Hey, Gringo! Gringo *capitán*!"

The voice was familiar. Tracy shielded the sun from his eyes. Suddenly his face lit up and a lusty growl escaped his throat. "Hello, baby!" he grinned. "It jus' ain't possible that you'd show up smack dab in the middle of action again. Y'all been looking for me, baby?" Suddenly the sun seemed to burst around him.

Rosalia Quintera grinned happily. "No one else, *bebe*, but ju!"

She seemed to spring up on her toes and land in Tracy's bearlike arms where they both twirled around and around, laughing together in a genuine warmth of friendship and lust.

"Hot damn, little *chiquita*. Damned if ah ain't kept both eyes peeled for ya! Been looking all over for ya ever since ah left El Paso. The minute ah crossed the

163

border, ah says to my friend Tom Mix here, my little *chiquita mia* has jus' gotta be waiting for me."

"Ju bastard!" she cried in her pigeon English. "If I got some sense upstairs, I'd spit on ju for leaving with no good-bye, no nothing. But *bebe*, I got some s'prise for ju. *Pues*, some s'prise." She gave him a lusty kiss and he kissed her back.

"Listen, baby, y'all be a good girl and leave us men alone for a while. We gotta handle some business, ya hear. Tell me where yer fire is and ah'll come round as soon as we done finish, hear?"

"The fire is inside Rosalia Quintera. Jus' look for the hottest *campesina* and ju will find us." She let loose a lusty laughter that trailed behind her.

"Shore thing, little *chiquita*." He took off his sombrero and smacked it against his knee. "I'll see ya in a little while, baby," he called to her.

"Hokay, *bebe*," grinned the black-eyed charmer with long raven tresses falling in natural curls over her shoulders, past her cotton peasant blouse. She waved as she made her way past the milling crowds.

"Hey, little *chiquita*," he called frowning. "What do ya mean us?"

But Rosalia had already pranced off back to her campsite, out of sight.

Tracy Richards scratched his thick crop of brownish-red hair and flopped the sombrero on his head backwards, brim off his face. He shrugged and joined the other gringos, already anticipating a lusty bawdy night. "Whhooooooooeeeeee!" he yippied aloud, giving no thought to the curious glances he got from the *campesinas* who shrugged and nodded knowingly. "Some crazy gringo gone crazy on peyote or maryjane, mebbe?"

But Tracy Richards didn't give a damn what anyone thought. His bundle of dynamite, more explosive than the real TNT he handled, had just arrived and all was right with the world. "Yahooooooo!" He slapped his sombrero against his thigh again, with exuberant vitality and happiness oozing from every pore.

164

Chapter 8

Thank God for Felipe de Cordoba. No question but he had become Madelaina's closest friend. She could trust him. Not with all she knew and had experienced, but enough to comfort her. She knew that he didn't observe her with cold, calculating eyes filled with hurt and silent questioning as her father did. The general seemed a lost soul since her return, unable to handle the slurs and innuendoes he knew were common among the men under his command. Perhaps a rest in Cuernavaca, a change in routine would revive and rekindle the former fires of conquest and supremacy in him. All in all, Madelaina hoped the trip home would prove a calmative for all those involved in her immediate life.

She had become addicted to smoking and enjoyed the relaxation of peyote. Finding herself unable to cope with the frustrations brought on by the frowns of disapproval from her father and his companions, she indulged in each vice more frequently than she really wanted to. When they arrived in Cuernavaca, she took to remaining in her own quarters with only Concepción as company for the next two months.

Concepción, usually calm and stoic in her relations with the outside world, began showing evidence of strain. The Indian squaw longed to return to Zacatecas only a few days after the newness wore off. Despite the arduous and exhausting 300-mile trip, she was willing to return to her own humble abode where she felt she could be of more use to her brother. Not that it wasn't all breathtakingly beautiful—this hacienda of General Obregon's. Already she had visited the famous gardens built by Maximilian for Carlotta. Her ironic comment

165

was, "For these flowers he stole food from the mouths of the people? Perhaps he wasn't all bad. For such beauty the peasants would have willingly fasted and contributed two day's food each week. But why is such beauty provided only for the wealthy *hacendados*?"

What magnificent creations of nature had been molded by human hands, thought Concepción as she glanced around Zocalo, the plaza where the palace and magnificent cathedrals faced each other across the enormous square. She stared at the office of the president and considered Diaz. No wonder he knew nothing of the peasants' plight. Seated in that splendor of all splendors, how could he feel the pain of his people? She was impressed by the city, all right—even the rolling verdant countryside of Cuernavaca differed greatly from the vast deserts and mountain country she had known. Still, she longed for the desert, the hot, stifling, almost unbearable desert air and the unendurable broiling sun beating down on her, which for so many centuries had given life to her people, direct descendents of Montezuma.

Madelaina felt as if she were dying a slow, purposeless death. She moved about the hacienda, a silent, brooding figure, unable to interest herself in the duties of the hacienda. She recalled Peter Duprez, more now than when she pursued him across the nation. By now, his image, as vivid as it had been once, was gradually fading. It took a strong will to consciously bring him into better focus. Is this the way it would end—nothing but faded memories left for her? How many times had she relived those memories in Sanlucar, Lisbon, and the more precious moments aboard the *Mozambique*? And that last afternoon they spent together in Vera Cruz, before that worthless son of a six-tongued viper, that little bastard's whore, the room clerk, had reported Peter to the *Federales*. When her father confessed the name of the betrayer to her, she had burned with humiliation and anger—but what good did it do?

There were times she longed to return to Las Marismas among her friends in the swamps—those beauti-

166

ful birds. She even missed her little egret, who died en route to the desert. Poor little creature was apparently unable to withstand the heat. She thought about Armando, hoping he had married or found himself.

She took to walking about the hacienda, always careful never to go near that small *casita* where her father kept one of his mistresses. There had been a loud forceful argument one night, for the general had brought Dolores with him and put her up in a guesthouse, a bit more luxurious than the *casita,* in which *La Condesa*, as she was called by the others, was housed. *La Condesa* had been queen in Madelaina's absence. Now that the general had returned with her and that other *puta*, Dolores, the fights had turned into out and out brawls. Madelaina heard the scuttlebutt reported by Concepción and it was verified by the small bruises and abrasions on her father's forehead and temples one morning at breakfast.

When the general saw Madelaina's curious stares, which she quickly tried to hide with an attitude of indifference, he felt obliged to explain. "It's difficult being a man. Women simply do not understand he must have variety if he's to be sustained."

"Perhaps if women were to adopt the same standards which men can speak of so casually, the world might be a different place, Father."

"True," he said caustically. "The world would simply overflow with bastards, my dear." He tossed his napkin down and told the servant he'd take his coffee in the study.

After the scene of the previous evening, he wanted no truck with his daughter. *La Condesa* had been raving mad when he entered the *casita* for his usual sojourn with her. "So! You come to me at last!" she had screamed at him, hurling uncivilized invectives at him as well as a string of curses.

"You've kept me waiting for two weeks while you frolic with that *puta*—that whore from Zacatecas!" She lunged at him, clawed his face, and beat on him with her bare fists. "I hate you! I hate you, you alley

167

cat! You have brought shame to *La Condesa*. You have reduced her to the level of this whore of the *Federales* and made the *casita* a house of degradation," she screamed.

"Listen, *querida*, calm down," he said, grinning at the overexaggeration of her shame. He tried to reach for her wrists, and so doing he stepped aside, throwing her off balance. She fell to the floor in wild disarray, her negligee falling off her shoulders revealing her brown skin. She was an attractive wench, more seductive in the bedroom than she appeared at other times. Now she was outraged. Her glittering black eyes filled with menace.

She cursed aloud, "You demon—you oversexed, heavy-balled demon!" This was followed by more curses which expressed her indignation, her jealousy, and her shattered pride. "You think I will lay with you after you've lain with that whore," she spat. "Never! Never! *La Condesa* is particular about whom she sleeps with."

"It matters not that *La Condesa* was a worse whore than Dolores? Does she forget where I found her—in those foul cribs in the red-light district in Mexico City? How easily she forgets, eh? She is no longer grateful to her lover for providing these luxuries?" he shouted angrily.

"And what of your daughter—is she no longer Villa's *puta*?" she countered angrily. Obregon reached out and struck her across the face, not once, but twice.

"Shut up!" he snarled. "You shut up, bitch! If you don't appreciate all you have, you can pack up and leave!" He turned around and left her to contemplate his displeasure. But *La Condesa*'s displeasure had been mounting inside her. She slammed the door, bolted it after him, pulled the curtains over the windows, and walking to the far end of the room, pulled back the drapes revealing an altar of Indian devil worship. She turned down the oil lamps, lit two candles, and in the shadowy darkness, she knelt before the altar.

La Condesa was a mestiza—half full-blooded Indian

and half Spanish. She had inherited her father's Spanish beauty, but her fire, spirit, and instincts were fully Indian, including the pagan worship, the idolatry of animal idols, and an overt belief in evil spirits and the supernatural. She wore amulets of Aztec origin which over the years had been refined and combined with the idols of Peruvian Indians.

Seated cross-legged before a brazier with several pottery bowls at either side, she poured a few sprinkles of powder into the fire and watched the fire flare brilliantly. Another bowl contained a few golden mushroom buttons, *amanita muscaria*, a hallucinogen used by her people to help stimulate certain powers of perception. She selected one button, placed it on the tip of her tongue, placed another on her head in ritual, and began to chew the mushroom slowly.

On the floor before her were two images, small dolls; one represented the new threat to her life, Dolores; the other was Madelaina, the woman who had brought shame and disgrace upon the man she loved. Both these women threatened *La Condesa*'s existence, thwarting her expectations to marry the general and become mistress of the hacienda.

Since their return from Cuernavaca, they had caused her a loss of prestige, anxiety and frustration with which she was unable to cope. Since the general had not sought the favors of *La Condesa*, her position with him was in jeopardy. For this, all those responsible would pay. By all that was holy, they would pay, vowed the woman known as Golden Dawn among her own people.

Once, her mother had told her, her ancestors came from royal lineage, that her destiny would be one of greatness, because she had been born with the beauty of a true Spaniard: milk white skin, gray eyes, raven hair, and a body that would bring any man to his knees. In addition, she had innate powers of the Indian to change her destiny.

For Golden Dawn there were many drawbacks in her mother's prophecy. All she'd known was poverty, starvation, and disease. Her mother, a whore, coupled with a soldier in Maximilian's army, and as the issue of this lust, she grew up with a half-dozen brothers and sisters with brown Indian skins. From the start she had been different, and at twelve she was sold to the madam of a whorehouse in Mexico City so that her family could eat for the next six months.

Expertly trained in the art of sexual pleasures, Golden Dawn, who carried herself every inch a princess, was nicknamed *La Condesa* by Obregon, then a colonel, during Madelaina's absence in Spain. He brought Golden Dawn to his hacienda and set her up in her own small house, built to her specifications.

Over the years, as the mistress to General Obregon, she catered to his every whim and caprice, even hosted dinner parties. It appeared she would one day become the wife of this *hacendado*, for they got along famously. Those stories implanted in her mind by her mother at an early age didn't seem too far-fetched after all. Her life was ordained to be special and opulent.

Golden Dawn, an ambitious young woman with vision, allowed no grass to grow under her feet. She educated herself, learned to read and write. In the absence of the general, which left her with considerable time on her hands, she hired tutors to teach her of many things so that when Madelaina returned from Spain, they could be friends and enjoy a warm companionship. After all, she was only two years the girl's senior. The relationship would be idyllic, she convinced herself. Daily she'd walked about the hacienda among the peasants, none of whom knew her real background. She enjoyed affluence, the courteous respect paid her, all the luxury at her fingertips. It was heavenly to her.

For whatever reason, Golden Dawn had been stirred inexplicably toward the study of mysticism and the occult. How could she have known that the more formal knowledge she acquired, the more questions would remain unanswered in her mind. In her quiet moments of solitude, pictures formed in her mind which disturbed

170

and frightened her. She had developed an uncanny talent of precognition—of knowing beforehand what was to happen. She spoke with her mother of such things and her mother grew remote, urging her to push such things from her mind, for they were evil spirits which threatened her sanity. She argued if God intended people to know beforehand what was to happen, he wouldn't have gone to such trouble to keep them in ignorance. These warnings, never satisfying, excited her curiosity to the point that she had to seek answers.

She traveled to the mud adobe hut of an Indian seer near Lake Tetesquitengo where she learned enough of the traditions of her people to comfort her and give her the needed security and knowledge to keep the things she had acquired. Golden Dawn would never again fear the unknown mysteries of the future. She had it within her powers to change that which might happen.

Madelaina's arrival from Spain proved disastrous. If the general had seen fit to bring the girl into Golden Dawn's company, she might have had the opportunity to remove from her mind all desire for joining the revolution. The occasion for her to suggest this to General Obregon didn't present itself. She knew her place, how far she could go, and how much to expect from him. To secure her own position with him, she maintained a position of subservience. When finally Madelaina had disappeared, Golden Dawn listened to the girl's *dueña*, to the comments of the other servants, and all proved her visions to have been correct.

She could have told the general what his daughter was planning. Hadn't she seen it all countless times in her visions? But who would have listened to the mistress of General Obregon, who was kept mostly hidden from his society as if she were a leper?

She had often insisted that she be permitted to accompany him to Zacatecas, but he denied her this. "You will supervise the hacienda, watch over the servants to make certain they don't steal me blind," he had told her gently. Golden Dawn felt instinctively that this meant he trusted her and was in fact making her a de facto mistress of his home. Very well, she'd become indispensable to him, make herself so important, efficient, and refined that each time he came home and noticed the remarkable change in her, he would become immune to his own resistance and marry her. Golden Dawn hadn't really understood the devotion of this man to duty, country, and his own long-range ambitions. If she had, she might have approached him quite differently.

The effects of recent developments were devastating to her. Despite the powers she'd acquired and perfected since the general's entourage had returned, the old insecurity came back to haunt her every moment. She could understand Madelaina's return, even Concepción. But Dolores? Never! This was the blow of all blows. Now both Madelaina and Dolores were her foes, as alive in her mind as enemies as if they held knives to her heart.

Whether or not they knew it, they were in for a shocking life of turmoil, devastation, and heartbreak, to say nothing of the agony, suffering, and violence she was capable of bringing to their lives. No one—but no one—would take from Golden Dawn what she had strived so hard to attain.

The mushrooms had begun to take their effect. At first she sensed a tremendous rush of power, she felt as if she could raise the universe if she had to. But soon came the tingling, almost paralyzing, effects. She had been warned by the old Indian seer of the danger in taking more of this mushroom, for herein lay the cause of many deaths of those not skilled in its proper use.

In the faint glow of the candlelight and flames from the brazier, perspiration glistened her forehead and ran down her face and neck as if she were sitting in a steam bath. She lowered her eyes to the dolls before her, chanting an incantation as old as time. Soon her eyes closed. In her mind were images of clouds, of bright colors, imbued with brighter lights in a kaleidoscope of brighter and brighter colors of such intensity Golden Dawn was certain she couldn't stand it. But

172

this was only part of what must be endured to enable her to penetrate the threshold of the all-pervading power, that ruled all, including infinity.

The convulsions began, and she used all her strength to wade through them without incident. At hand was additional atropine ready to use to counteract the muscarine, for each mushroom contained unpredictable quantities of each drug, and the reaction upon the human body wasn't fully controlled, she had been told.

Her skin became blotchy. Hot and cold flashes churned through her body as the drugs took effect. Now. Now. Now! She felt the sudden drop in her pulse rate. A moment before, it had accelerated until she felt her head would blow off her neck. She was almost there. Smells became more pronounced, the ultraviolet lights in her head were increasing to brighter and lighter intensity until white fire burst in her head. Then, it settled.

In the serene mist that began to clear, she saw Madelaina standing atop a pinnacle of shifting clouds dressed in gold, with bright lights fanning all around her. The spectacle was so brilliant she wanted to dismiss the sight from mind, but she wouldn't. Then, as if a motion picture projected itself in her mind, she saw Madelaina walking down the steps slowly, regally, like a queen. She descended, step by step, into a pool of blood which rose like quicksand to suck her under. Even as she gasped for her last breath, there was no hope for her. She was totally submerged in a lake of blood. The picture shifted.

Now Madelaina stood in tattered garments in a cold, damp cell, her wrists bound in chains, fastened to a wall. She was being brutalized by a shadowy figure, a man who raped her and beat her and mistreated her. Once again the picture changed. Madelaina, close to death, lay on a covered wagon driven across deserts. A stranger drove the wagon, whipping the horses in a fury. The pictures faded.

Into focus came the woman Dolores Chavez, a favorite of General Obregon.

Dolores came to life in these pictures. Arrogant, hip-swinging, spiteful, vindictive, and cunning, she moved in toward the bed upon which General Obregon lay waiting for her, arms outstretched to embrace her. They made love, body thrashing against body, like two mountain cats. A new picture superimposed itself on the first. Dolores, horrified, crouched in the corner of a crude room, her black eyes widening in abject terror, shaking her head, begging, pleading for mercy from a dark shadow standing over her.

Another picture dissolved onto this one: Dolores, her face like a death's head, walked about an alien hacienda with a shadowy figure of a one-armed man. From time to time, the face of Concepción appeared, thrusting itself in and out of focus.

The pictures grew fuzzy, straining under the personal will of Golden Dawn to reject the last one. Her eyes fluttered open. She was wringing wet, soaked clear through her negligee. She blinked her eyes several times; they had become terribly sensitive to light. For a time she sat there, a smile on her lips. She sipped water from a nearby bowl to slake the thirst which followed and diminish the bad taste which remained in her mouth.

Golden Dawn reached for a cigarette and smoked it in silence until the effects of the mushrooms had passed. Now she reflected on what she'd seen, the memory of which would never leave her. She had seen such pictures before, on a wide variety of subjects, and learned only recently, by concentrating on a particular person, she could prophesize their futures. She knew that in the future of Madelaina would come untold horrors. She could of course go to the girl and tell her all this. But she wouldn't. She also dtermined that the whore, Dolores, would also come to a bad end. She had but to wait and the laws of Destiny would work in her future, toward victory.

It was clear to her that Concepción figured in all of this, but, since she hadn't concentrated on the Indian, she was unable to determine the extent of her involvement. Merely another complication, thought Golden Dawn, which can be handled properly when the time comes. She retired that night to an empty bed, but in her mind she was satisfied that all would end very well for *La Condesa*.

She directed her thoughts to Madelaina, wondering what had happened to break her spirit. She was not the same as when she first returned from Spain, and so far no one had told her what had happened—not even the general. She shrugged perceptibly. *As if I care. My day will come*, she said before falling off into a drugged sleep.

Prior to her arrival in Cuernavaca, Madelaina considered how strange had been the effect she had on the people, both men and women, soldiers and their *campesinas,* in the compound at Zacatecas. The men eyed her with mixed feelings of amazement, resentment, hostility—and desire. To think this woman dared to defy her father, the general. How dare she oppose his views? How dare she flaunt her respect for Villa in his face? She was a traitor, wasn't she? If any of them had done what the general's daughter had done, they'd have faced a firing squad. *Como no?*

Instead she was tolerated as a spoiled child who had erred in an adolescent fancy, which was hushed instantly by the authorities as if it never happened. A peon defecting to the establishment would have been shot by his peers. Ah, there was no justice. None at all. Least of all for a peon.

Still, she was a desirable wench whom a great many of the soldiers in the Zacatecas compound felt they could tame. "If she was my woman, I'd dissolve those crazy ideas in her fancy boarding school brain," said some. Others declared the general's daughter needed only one thing—a real man to show her the only function of a woman; a good screwing by a real man would tame her.

The women were more definite. An aristocrat posing as a peasant was destined for the looney bins and was to be treated with contempt. They were jealous, vio-

175

lently envious of her stature in life, resentful and confused by her streak of independence. Her flair for adventure brought forth their contempt and in their class-consciousness, they decided anyone stepping down to their level would find it hard going.

Bigotry and prejudice, Madelaina discovered, were even more prevalent among the earthy women of the lowerclass than among the aristocracy. Rumors that she'd been Villa's woman kept them in awe of her. Nevertheless, Madelaina daily gave thanks these women were not the animals those *campesinas* in Villa's camps had been.

The day her father announced they were leaving for Cuernavaca, she heaved a sigh of relief. The tension had built to a point where she was forced to keep to her quarters to ward off the looks she received from her father's soldiers. Anyway, she needed a change. Concepción would go with her, she would insist upon this to her father. Now that she had arrived, all she could think of was how to leave gracefully. She took more and more to visiting the barns where her father had taken to the breeding of bulls.

"Madelaina! Madelaina!" cried Felipe, dashing into the hacienda one day looking everywhere for her. She was nowhere to be found. Finally he encountered the grumbling *dueña*, Concepción. "Where is she? Where is Madelaina?" he pressed excitedly.

"Out looking at the bulls, where else?" she muttered sullenly.

Felipe found Madelaina seated on the split-rail corral watching some youngsters making passes at a few two-year-olds. He approached her slowly.

"Careful you do not ruin this bull, *chiquito*," she called. "Or the general will have you shot at sunrise. If the bull gets used to you, he will think you are playing with him and he will never become a brave bull—simply an ox." She addressed herself to a young lad in the makeshift bullring.

"*Si, señorita*," cried the little ragamuffin, tightening the rope holding up his trousers. Brown as an overripe olive from long hours in the sun, the barefoot boy arched his back and, in the stance of a matador, challenged the heifer. The bull, fully annoyed, disliked the intrusion on his privacy and, wanting nothing more than to be left alone, decided to rid himself once and for all of this petty aggravation, this little *muchacho* determined to become his master and future executioner.

They faced each other; the boy, who in a second became a man, with his makeshift cape which instantly transformed into a glorious matador's cape, and the heifer, who decided to become a bull like his father. The bull snorted and clawed the earth with his foreleg. Young Juanito stood his ground. He could already envision himself a famous matador, dressed in dazzling attire. He drew himself up, proudly, arrogantly. He could almost hear the applause; both the bull and the imaginary Plaza de Toros were his to command.

Watching this young man, even Madelaina saw the spectacle of the *corrida* come to life. Even she was held spellbound and totally fascinated by the bravery of both the small boy and the young bull. She tensed and watched closely, her eyes taking in everything at once, making certain there was no *real* danger to the lad. She wasn't familiar with the strain of the bull. The stud had been a Chihuahua bull, but the mother, she had not had the time or the interest to investigate. Felipe had stopped several feet behind her, aware that this was a special moment for Madelaina. His eyes were on the activity in the ring.

Juanito advanced slowly, getting closer and closer until he paused a foot from the muzzle of the bull, who stood abnormally still, wondering at the audacity of the young man, waiting for the right moment to teach him a lesson for all time.

Juanito stamped his foot into the dirt impatiently, inciting the animal to attack, and it finally came at him, bellowing and snorting. Juanito passed the cape over its horns as the bull passed him. Cheered on by the few onlookers—a scattering of young boys who adored

Juanito and followed him daily from the city to come and watch him practice for the day he'd become the greatest of all Mexico's matadors—the lad grew braver, more confident. The "*olés*" grew louder. "*Olé*, Juanito! *Olé, muchacho!*" He stood firmly fixed in place, his feet planted in the ground; he moved only to throw his body back as the thundering young bull passed. His eyes flashed triumphantly as the *olés* rang louder. He didn't notice that the incited, temperamental bull had quickly turned and charged to attack him. Madelaina, shouting a cry of alarm, jumped off the fence. Removing her jacket en route, she shoved Juanito aside to avoid disaster and, making a few passes at the bull with her jacket, shouted, "Oho, Toro! Oho!" The bull, furious at the deception, charged her time and again.

Two of the handymen, realizing what was happening in the small corral close to where they attended to their chores, let out wild shouts to distract the bull. Jumping into the corral, they worked together until they led the heifer into a shute where he joined his companions.

"Juanito Campos! It's you again!" shouted the Obregon foreman angrily. "How many times must I kick you off the Obregon *rancho*? If the *generale* is informed of this, he will shoot you at sunrise. Now go! Leave immediately."

"Madelaina!" cried Felipe who watched in panic the instant she jumped into the ring to save Juanito. Climbing the fence, he rushed to her side. "Are you crazy to do such a thing?" He examined her shirtsleeve which had been sliced through by one of the heifer's horns. "You could have been killed!" He wrapped her bloodied arm with his handkerchief.

"Nonsense, Felipe. It was a baby. Juanito could have been killed," she said loud enough for the shame-faced lad to hear. "He is a *niño,* not yet dry behind the ears." She walked over to him in her *matador* pants and torn shirt, unmindful of her bloodied arm or the surprised glances she got from the onlookers. Juanito had paled at the close call, and there was a shame-filled, hangdog expression on his youthful face.

Madelaina lit right into him without preamble.

"You want to be a matador, eh? Then it's best you learn from one who knows how to fight a bull. You come each day at one o'clock. I will teach you to make passes, teach you to know the bulls, *comprender*?"

Juanito stood straight and tall, exuding pride and manliness in every inch of his ten-year-old body. "Learn from a woman? Never! You think I want it known that Juan Campos is a mamma's boy?" With that, he pivoted and spread out his arms signaling all his friends to fall in behind him like the entourage of a very special, strutting matador.

Madelaina burst into laughter, joined by Felipe who was both relieved and astonished by her skill in the ring. Together they began to walk toward the hacienda. He looked at her through new adoring eyes.

"Where did you learn to work a bull?" His eyes lit up with considerable respect. "It's crazy—a dangerous sport and certainly not for a woman."

"You, too, Felipe? Is it not enough I was ridiculed by young Juanito, who didn't even thank me for saving his life?" She smiled fetchingly, amused by the whole thing. "That boy has the will. One day he shall be a matador. Believe me, I saw something special in those first moments he faced that heifer. You know who taught me?" she asked wistfully. "Manuelito Perez, Spain's greatest matador."

"Madelaina, I'm neither interested in bulls, Juanito, or this Perez. I came to see you to ask you to marry me. Will you at least tell me you'll think about it? You can see I'm in love with you." The ardor of his proposal shook her.

"All right," she replied. "I'll think about it. Is that why you braved the sweltering heat all the way from Mexico, to repeat what you've asked me countless times before?"

"That—and to invite you to *El Presidente*'s birthday ball. On the anniversary of his birth there will be a grand celebration in spectacular form. Everyone who's anyone will be there."

"Oh, Felipe," she sighed. "What do I have to do to convince you I am not interested in everyone who is someone? Come inside and let us cool off and drink some tea." Taking his hand, she led him inside the spacious and comfortable villa. "Concepción," she called to the Indian who appeared from the shadows. "Tell Theresa to bring refreshments. And Felipe—do take off that heavy tunic. You must be in great discomfort."

They sat on the cool, fragrant patio off the grand salon, under arbors of flowers. Madelaina seated herself next to him on the leather and mahogany sofa. Before them stood a large hatch-door table in hand-rubbed oak, graced with Indian artifacts.

"Even in those ridiculous, scandalous clothes, I find you totally irresistible, *querida*," said Felipe, love oozing from every pore. "You are enough to drive ten men passionately mad." He caressed her hands in his.

"Because you are my best friend, and I love you as such, I permit you to talk this way," she began. "But, please, Felipe, if you do not wish me to close my doors to you, do not mention marriage again. I can't marry you," she said seriously. "I am already married."

Felipe's face fell. "But when? How? To whom?" He was dumbstruck.

She told him about Peter Duprez. She even told him about Armando, the man who deflowered her, in hopes he'd consider himself lucky to have escaped her clutches. It only made him more determined to have her.

"Don't you see, Felipe, my sweet, since I'm already married, I cannot marry you. Besides you deserve an untarnished woman."

"But it doesn't count. You are not married by a priest," he argued.

"I can't believe you'd permit yourself such undiminished hypocrisy." she retorted. "Once consummated, a marriage is a marriage, no matter who conducts the service. I went in search of my husband for nearly a year. I was unable to find him." She washed her hands

180

in a small enamel bowl brought to her by the serving girl, Theresa, a shy little thing who kept her eyes lowered in the presence of the *capitán*. She wiped her hands on an embroidered linen towel and poured tea from the thickly encrusted silver set before her.

"You must have some of these cakes, sweet Felipe. Cook made them for our homecoming. You know it takes nearly a full day to make these confections." She passed the plate to him. Felipe took several and devoured them hungrily, noticing her finesse in handling these domestic rituals.

"You do this as if you were born to it," he said softly. "It's difficult to reconcile myself to the *matadora* I saw only moments ago and the reports of you as a *campesina*. Where did you look for your—uh—this man, Peter Duprez? Is he not a gringo?"

"Yes, a gringo. Also a freedom fighter."

"Ah, a mercenary. For money he fights other men's problems."

"A mercenary?"

"Of course. You don't believe he does it for an ideal? Are you saying he's fighting on the side of the revolutionists?"

She knew she had said too much, even to dear, sweet Felipe. She had learned that much this past year. Never confide to anyone. Truly, he'd been the only one in whose presence she could for an instant drop all pretense. She grew reserved and reflective and filled with tension. She felt trapped.

"I don't really know, Felipe. I was told he'd be in El Paso or some place where the revolution was active. I just supposed he might be in the north."

"You love him, *querida*?" he asked quietly, sipping his tea from a delicate porcelain cup.

"I'm not sure, Felipe. It's been over a year. I've changed. I believe he might have changed. But he is my husband. That much hasn't changed."

"If you don't love him, there is no problem."

"The problem is that I want to find him. I wish to face him myself to see whether or not I still feel as I

181

once felt. Then I'll tell him myself if I wish to annul the marriage. Is it too much to ask?"

Felipe leaned forward, set the cup and saucer on the table, and from a gold case, he removed a cigarette. He saw her eyeing the thin, white rolls of tobacco, and smiling he extended his hand. "Go ahead, *querida*. It does not offend me to watch you smoke. Nothing you do offends me."

Madelaina wished at that moment she could love him as he loved her. He made it so easy. No threats, no reprimands, no contemptuous looks or slanderous words ever escaped his lips. She took the cigarette gratefully, and he extended a lit match.

"That doesn't mean, *querida*, that some of your actions haven't offended others in higher places." There was a solemnity, a hidden warning in his voice.

"Oh?" She relaxed in the enjoyment of the smoke so much, she failed to detect the concerned look on his face.

"It appears that the rebellious daughter of General Alvaro Obregon has come to the attention of Colonel Vitoriano Huerta."

"And who is this Huerta?" she asked, trying to fathom the serious overtones projected into Felipe's voice.

His eyes caught hers and she studied the sudden bright lights that crept into his, animal-like, almost predatory. "What is it, Felipe, sweet? You act as if a monster has just appeared between us."

"*Aye, querida.* That is precisely what he is, a monster. There is no one like Huerta. Loyal to Diaz as if he were an extension of *El Presidente* himself." He shuddered. "I am not proud to say the man is my superior officer. I do my best to avoid him every chance I get. In fact, I am seriously considering leaving the Intelligence office the first opportunity I get."

"Why is Huerta interested in me?"

"He is interested in a spy named Little Fox. Someone who has been involved in a series of escapades in

182

which messages get to Pancho Villa and the other revolutionaries."

Concepción, about to enter the garden, paused at the mention of Little Fox. She retreated and remained hidden in the *pérgola*, under the grape arbor. A frown creased her bronzed skin, and with a quick movement of her head, she tossed her black braids behind her shoulders. She had refused to give up her usual mode of dress for the more accepted city clothes of a Spanish *dueña*, threatening to return to Zacatecas if such clothing was imposed on her. General Obregon relented since they expected few callers and protocol wasn't vital. Besides, Concepción's services were warmly welcomed. "My daughter seems a different person in your company," he had told the Indian. "Perhaps it's true you people hold within their grasp certain mystic powers over others."

Concepción remained out of sight, her ears attuned to the conversation taking place a few feet from her.

"What has all this to do with me, Felipe?" asked Madelaina.

"Huerta has some crazy notion that you are this Little Fox," he replied, watching her reaction from the corner of his eyes.

Madelaina laughed heartily. "Now, if your spy was named Little Torera, perhaps I'd fall into the game, Felipe. I'm sorry to disappoint this man—uh—Huerta. You tell him for me he is some crazy man. A peyote smoker no doubt—or a chocolate drinker."

"A boozer, for sure," said Felipe with a grimace. "There are times he stinks of alcohol. I get drunk inhaling the fumes from his foul breath."

"And you take the word of such a *borrachón*? Diaz believes such a man?"

"Don't mistake what I tell you. He is the most dangerous man in the entire Diaz regime. His alcoholic excesses are the talk of the palace. But he gets his results, *querida*. He reports nothing but success to Diaz. For this and his phenomenal devotion to Diaz, he is kept in power. He is the head of the Secret Police, *querida.* His spies are everywhere. Believe what I tell you, he is the most dreaded man in the capital. Not even Diaz gets the respect this man receives."

"You mean fear, not respect."

"One identifies out of fear, *querida*, not love."

"And so you say this man is after me? Does he not concern himself that he has selected as a target the daughter of the most respected officer in President Diaz' army, the granddaughter of the General Obregon who fought at his side against Maximilian?" she said haughtily, a tinge of defensiveness in her voice.

None of this was lost on Felipe. He put his cigarette down in the bronze ashtray on the coffee table. Turning to her, he took her hands in his. "Madelaina, if you are involved in any such traffic, I beg you cease and desist this instant. If it were anyone but Colonel Huerta I wouldn't take the time to warn you. For your sake and that of your father's do not incur his wrath or bring yourself to the further attention of this tainted tiger. He'll not rest until he tears you to shreds." Felipe's eyes were filled with concern and compassion and love.

Madelaina laughed superficially. "Dear, sweet Felipe. I do believe your imagination has run away with you. It's best you rope it in again and control it."

"*Querida*, everyone talks of this strange relationship you maintain with Concepción. How is it one Indian *peón* has suddenly tamed the wildcat daughter of General Obregon? That is what they ask within the confines of the palace. Oh, word has gotten about, from Zacatecas. Even your father has found the relationship disconcerting. Your comportment with the woman contains too much respect. Who is she, *querida*? Why do you subdue yourself in her presence? I, too, have noticed it. I've said nothing before. But I tell you Huerta, who is part Indian, cannot be fooled. He will learn her identity and have you both beheaded."

"Felipe! I will not have you saying such things to me! If you are trying to frighten me, you have succeeded. But the rest is quite preposterous. You just don't happen to be around when I put Concepción in

184

her place. I have only attempted to mind my manners and show off my good breeding. That's why I do not yell or rave and rant at the woman. She is my father's servant, not mine! She has been with the general far longer than I've known her and her loyalty is to him, not me." She tossed her cigarette into a brass spittoon as if it had suddenly lost its taste. "If this is why you've come to see me on this day, to bear bad tidings and the demented ravings of, by your own admission, an alcoholic madman—well, you can just leave. If I am to subject to such verbal abuse, it is best I return to the camps of the revolutionists. At least there, each man minds his own business."

Felipe de Cordoba was terribly crushed. What he had hoped to do was draw closer to her, so she would lean on him and confide in him. Now, she acted as if he were her mortal enemy. He watched her pace back and forth on the tiles, the clicking sound of her leather boots beating a sharp staccato.

"If I've offended you, I regret it. I only thought a word to the wise would be sufficient. Just remember my warnings about Huerta. He is a man who operates on the premise that drop added to drop makes a lake." He rose to his feet, reached for his tunic, and slipped into it.

Madelaina turned to him, instant apology etched on her pale face. "Oh, Felipe, I don't mean to be so wretched to you. It's just that I don't understand any of this. Why can't everyone leave me alone? I went through terrible trauma as a *campesina*. Now that I'm back, no one will allow me to be Madelaina Obregon, daughter of General Obregon. Why can't they simply ignore all that a silly, empty-headed child so foolishly involved herself in? Why?"

Felipe reached out for her. She fell into his strong, comforting arms. How good it was to lean against him. She smelled the clean, masculine scent of his body and cologne and sighed wistfully. Why couldn't she just accept him into her life. She could love him. She nearly did now. If only the image of Peter Duprez didn't cloud her mind, pushing out all other images.

"What shall I do, Felipe? Help me. Tell me what I should do to keep all these monsters out of my life?" She was so vulnerable in these moments.

"Come with me to the president's ball, *querida*, and stop all these rumors, once and for all. They have but to see the beauty of Madelaina Obregon, dressed in the finest of all finery, to know she is no rebel. Once they set eyes on you, as I know you can be—every inch a princess—all rumors will be dispelled instantly."

"That's all it takes? For me to attend the Diaz ball?" she asked incredulously. "Are you sure, Felipe? Then they will stop hounding me with these vicious rumors and their contemptuous glances?"

"That's all, *querida*. Let them know, once and for all, that your loyalties lie where General Obregon's loyalties lie. That will shut them up."

She reached up and kissed him. It was more like a kiss between brother and sister, with much affection, endearment, and admiration, not that of two lovers. Felipe, sad and resolute, said nothing. He tried to lift his spirits, forcing a smile on his face, and he walked with her arm through his to the front entrance of the hacienda.

"You must be the most exquisite creature at the ball. Understand? And if you'll do me the honor of wearing my mother's diamond and sapphire necklace and tiara, Madelaina, I will be most honored."

Madelaina curtsied. "*Señor*, it will be the finest honor of my life, to be escorted by the most enchanting Capitán de Cordoba. I promise I shan't cause you to be embarrassed by my presence. Do you believe me?"

"I believe you, *querida*," he said, taking his leave. As Felipe mounted his stallion, he sighed heavily. "That's the trouble, I believe what is not the truth," he told himself. He waved his hat twice over his head to her and galloped toward the gates of the hacienda.

Chapter 9

As the time drew closer to the president's ball, it became obvious that Captain Felipe de Cordoba was ecstatic. Madelaina had reconfirmed her promise to attend the social gala with him. In conveying this to General Obregon, Felipe had to admit he hadn't seen the general as lighthearted in many a moon.

"You've been a good influence on Madelaina, Felipe. I only hope she has seen the error of her ways," remarked Obregon, showing signs of fatigue. "Come, sit with me, my boy." He extended his hand toward a comfortable leather chair.

Felipe bowed and sat stiffly in an almost military brace. "You should see her, General. What excitement she generates. I escorted her and Concepción to the best modiste in Mexico City. She selected a gown that will turn the other women green with envy. Perhaps a few more months among her own people—with whom she can perfect her drawing room manners—will produce miraculous changes. I see them already," he said with supportive enthusiasm.

"You, my dear Felipe, are blinded by love and I by a father's dream. Others won't be blinded by such emotions. Take heed. If she's up to something traitorous, she'll be detected. Try to get this across to her. She'll listen to you." The general sighed. "When we speak, sparks fly. She's unmanageable in my presence. Unfortunately, I'm too aware of this. If her attitude changes in my presence, it's because she has some ulterior motive."

General Obregon pulled at the tunic of his uniform and moved tigerlike to the windows overlooking the courtyard where soldiers and their *campesinas* milled about. Women in their shabby but colorful clothing had always been a part of army life. He hadn't been able to change it and didn't suppose he ever would. Countless times he'd approached President Diaz about providing barracks for the women and children, but Diaz made it clear he intended to change none of this. The pity of it was Obregon lost more good soldiers to venereal diseases and peyote binges than he did to the enemy.

He turned from the scene which depressed him and poured himself a stiff tumbler of brandy. Lately he'd been drinking heavily—more than ever before. Even Felipe was alarmed over this. Since his own father had died, he'd grown terribly attached to General Obregon, who treated him as a son. To watch his hero, the brilliant Alvaro Obregon, dissipate himself hurt Felipe. He smiled brightly in an attempt to elevate the general's spirits.

"I, with your permission, *mi Generale*, intend to ask for the hand of your daughter in marriage."

"With my permission?" exclaimed Obregon. "My dear boy, this is the best news I've heard in two years. You have my permission! You have my blessings! My son, you have my undying gratitude. If she doesn't accept you, Felipe, then we'll both know something is drastically wrong with her mind. She'd have to be demented—you hear, Felipe?—demented to refuse you."

Felipe was annoyed. He shook his head, not wishing to contradict the general. "One thing Madelaina is not, sir, is demented. It's possible she may still be in love with the man she married in Lisbon, the gringo Duprez."

"Nonsense! She told me she married him for convenience only, to get back to Mexico. I've already taken measures to annul the marriage, so, you see, she is or will be a free woman. The ceremony wasn't officiated by a priest. That makes it invalid." The general's exuberance couldn't be dimmed. He poured a glass of brandy for Felipe and smiled warmly. "This is an occa-

188

sion for us both. Let's drink a toast. To Felipe de Cordoba and his bride!"

Felipe smiled. "Although it's premature, I'll drink to it, *señor*." They touched glasses. "Do you know who this gringo really is, General?"

"In two weeks, I shall have a report on him."

The palace of *El Presidente* was a magnificent glitter of bright lights and gay laughter. The air, heavily perfumed by an overwhelming display of floral baskets in every corner of the splendid salon, reached her nostrils as Madelaina, on the arms of her father and the handsome Captain Felipe de Cordoba, entered the foyer. She was breathtakingly beautiful in her exquisite gown of gold lamé and satin, fitted over a whalebone corset which pushed her firm bosoms to the edge of a daring décolletage. Panier drapes a few inches below the waistline fell gracefully over her hips, accentuating her hour-glass figure and caught behind her in a double-billowed flounce blending fully into a sweep train.

"General Alvaro Obregon; his daughter, Señorita Madelaina de San Luca de Obregon; and Captain Felipe de Cordoba," came the footman's announcement as they stood at the top of the circular marble staircase prepared to descend.

Every head in the grand salon turned toward the trio: many out of curiosity to see the rebellious daughter of the elite general, others out of respect to General Obregon, and many more because of the spectacular beauty of the young Spanish *gachupín* on the arms of two of the most eligible bachelors in all Mexico.

President Diaz himself, in full dress uniform instead of his usual dinner clothing, turned in their direction. So this was the general's daughter. He studied her closely as they made their way toward him to pay their respects and offer him hearty congratulations on his birthday.

She didn't look like a rebel or a conspiratorial *Villista* as was reported. Seeing her now, so feminine, he couldn't reconcile the reports that she had been a *cam-*

189

pesina. Ugh, the very word offended his dignity. He watched her nod to a few, smile at others, with her head held high, carrying herself with the aplomb of royalty. What a shapely wench. Fit to be queen. Perhaps these were the most dangerous, he told himself, bracing to meet her.

She curtsied before him. His eyes were on her firm, rounded breasts and her magnificent coiffure and diamond tiara. The scent of her perfume reached his nostrils. As she bowed before him, she lowered her eyes, thickly fringed with dark lashes. Then she stood up and searched his eyes and the false smile he wore. Her dark eyes were filled with warmth, her voice remarkably soft and musical.

"My heartfelt congratulations on this, the anniversary of your birth, *mi Presidente.* What an honor to be sharing these moments with you. Would you think it in bad taste if one of your loyal subjects were to kiss you?"

President Diaz was both pleased and annoyed by such brazenness. General Obregon and Felipe were stunned by both her amazing social graces and her bold audacity. And yet, what daring diplomacy, eh?

Before Diaz could either protest or agree, Madelaina reached up and planted a kiss on both cheeks. Diaz flushed and glanced about at the others in the room, who stared in astonishment. The *doñas* twittered their fans nervously.

"My dear *señorita,*" he explained. "I do believe you've just set a precedent. One I shall encourage most enthusiastically," he exclaimed. Suddenly, the stillness in the room ended. The others nodded and smiled. "Yes. Why not? A president is still a man, even though he gets old and grumpy when his *children* are not happy. It is sad not being appreciated for all a parent has done, when the children rebel. Don't you agree, Señorita Obregon?" he asked with affected passion.

"*Señor Presidente,* you are not old, and you should not be grumpy—the people love you," she said gaily. "It would please me no end, if you would dance with

190

me before the ball has ended. May I write you in my card?" she asked pleasantly.

"Indeed, *señorita*, you may. First, I must beg your permission to borrow these two fine men from you for a time. You know Doña Costanza and her family?"

Madelaina bowed. "Of course. But you must promise not to keep them too long. This is a celebration for you." She fanned herself in that ladylike manner with the golden lace fan while the intoxicating scent of her perfume swept into his nostrils. He bowed his head, a look of flushed excitement in his eyes.

Felipe escorted her to the table of Doña Costanza. "I promise I shall be back as swiftly as my feet can carry me," he whispered.

"Please hurry," she said, exposing her vulnerability. "I do not feel comfortable here," she confided. "I feel the animosity of many."

"What you feel, *querida*, is the envy of every woman here, and the burning desire in all the eligible men. Be patient, you're doing fine."

She watched him walk back to the men and saw them disappear into a salon to the rear of the corridor. The Costanza girls, Clothilde and Ambergris, eyed her for a time. Finally they managed polite conversation. Madelaina purposely spilled wine on her dress and wailed, "Oh, look how clumsy I am, Doña Costanza! Where can I go to have this rinsed off before my gown is ruined?" She could endure the old shrewish bullfrog's company no longer.

"My girls have been taught not to be as clumsy," croaked the frog with glowing satisfaction. "Nor as brazen as you were with *El Presidente*! Imagine—kissing him."

"But, Doña Costanza, it is the custom taught me in the royal court of Spain. If the king desires to be kissed by his admiring public, why not *El Presidente*?" Her naïveté was disarming. And she got in the shot she intended. "Will you direct me to the salon for women, please?"

"It is at the end of corridor just before the courtyard

191

to your right," she said, silencing her daughter Clothilde, a sweet young girl, thoroughly dominated by her mother, who was about to offer Madelaina assistance.

"Thank you for your graciousness, *Doña*. I shall find it by myself."

She smiled tightly, winked at Clothilde, and moved gracefully among the other bejeweled, exquisitely dressed matrons and young women, swishing past them, leaving in her wake a sweet smell of perfume created by special apothecaries in the capital. The light of the overhead chandeliers, spectacular masses of glittering crystal, lit up the jewels worn by several notables. She saw La Marquesa Ottavia, the mistress of Diaz, in the midst of six or seven young dons and officers paying court to her. Along one wall, over a hundred feet in length, were tables overflowing with sumptuous foods and wines. The sight of so much food made her recall with dismay the thousands of hungry urchins she had encountered throughout Mexico; they could thrive on the food to be discarded that evening. She glanced about the room, but hardly anyone noticed her now, for they had begun to converse again, no doubt about her.

She slipped along the corridor and instead of turning right, she entered the salon to the left and closed the door behind her. It was difficult to make out the room, until her eyes adjusted to the darkness. It appeared to be a sitting room. Straight ahead, however, under the double doors, a shaft of light struck her eyes. Muffled voices came at her.

She leaned against the doors, held her breath, and listened. Slowly her hand grasped the graceful curve of the handle. Ever so quietly, she turned it and through the open slit she peered into the room. They were all there—Diaz, her father, Felipe, and countless other *políticos*.

It appeared that President Diaz had cornered General Obregon and Felipe into a small private conference. As she listened, she was aware they spoke about her. Diaz was talking.

"It is my sincerest hope, General, that she has recovered from her recent indispositions."

A polite way of making sure she wasn't a threat either to him or her father, thought Madelaina.

"I can assure you, *mi Presidente*," said Obregon, "it was simply a case of youthful idealistic nonsense she picked up from the radicals in Spain."

"Let us hope it has been eradicated," said President Diaz.

"Not only that," added Obregon. "Felipe has just spoken to me of his intentions to marry her." His fierce pride was evident.

President Diaz appeared relieved. "Well, well, my boy. Congratulations are in order. It would please me no end to make that announcement tonight on my birthday. Will you grant an old man such a honor?"

Felipe seemed flustered. "I could think of nothing more delightful, *señor*, however, I haven't made my intentions known to the *señorita*. I do owe her that much." It will stop many idle rumors and Diaz knew this, he thought.

"Then find her when we're finished and settle it. Before the night's ended, I shall make the announcement," he insisted with pomposity generally attributed him, in what seemed more an order than a statement.

Felipe and the general exchanged concerned glances.

"Then it's settled. Let's get on with our discussion." Diaz slapped each man on the back and drew them back into the circle of men. He sat down with effort behind the gleaming mahogany desk and lit up a *cigarro*. The others present followed his pattern.

"General Navarro has arrived with news which I shall relate to you. Word has come that the rebels intend to take Chihuahua City. We have learned there is dissension in the camp of the revolutionists. Carranza and Villa are sparring like two pugilists, with Madero, that spineless jellyfish, acting as referee."

There was laughter among the gathering of brass, who found the inside joke quite humorous.

"But the day hasn't come when they can fool an old

193

soldado like Diaz," exclaimed the president. He pointed to the map spread out on the desk before him and slammed it hard with his fist. "If I know my enemy—and I swear in my past victories, I knew them all better than they knew themselves—they will not attack Juarez. It's too well garrisoned. Besides, the *Norteamericanos* have already warned Madero in El Paso that any act of aggression against the Diaz government would be frowned upon and would be cause for his immediate incarceration." He stroked his snow white moustache thoughtfully, secure in this knowledge.

General Navarro, a portly man with a rigid sense of morals and unbending military discipline, nodded, clasping his hands behind him and turning his craggy face toward the others. The touch of gray at his temples gave him a distinction belied by his manners. "With the gringos at the border and President Taft on our side, Madero has no chance. Besides, under my strict orders, my men have converted Juarez into a virtual stronghold. It cannot be penetrated. One thing I can say for Madero is, although he labors under many false delusions, he has the intelligence to listen to his officers. They will not attack Juarez. I agree with *El Presidente*. They will go after Chihuahua."

General Obregon had moved in closer to the desk and studied the map spread before President Diaz. He shook his head slowly and maintained his silence. They were wrong, totally wrong, but it wasn't his place to interfere.

President Diaz spoke up. "You are too silent, General Obregon. I see opposing thoughts reflected in your eyes." He patted the gold braid on his uniform unconsciously.

"I am in disagreement with your thoughts, *mi Presidente*—with your permission, of course," he added hastily when he saw the appalled glances of his peers. "It is my contention they will aim at Juarez, not Chihuahua. At least I think Villa's thoughts shall take such action. If they take Juarez, they'll seal Mexico off

194

from the gringo border. That way they control what comes in and what goes out."

"My dear Obregon, attacking Juarez would be suicidal to them. General Navarro has just told you how much strength he has in Juarez. They will need a minor victory first. They will strike Chihuahua!" Diaz was adamant.

"Absolutely," echoed General Navarro. "Only fools would attack Juarez," he repeated himself.

"Villa is no fool, *mi Presidente*," said Obregon firmly. "He's a man who functions on instinct and sheer determination. For instance, word has reached me recently that Pancho Villa is no longer the crude outlaw we have pictured him to be, no longer the *bandido* of his youth. His talent as a *guerrillo* has been surpassed by his skill as a regular, an army trainee. To his camps have come foreign mercenaries who have joined him in his cause. These gringos are specialists in cannon and artillery. He is nearly as skilled as a *Científico*!"

Heads craned toward General Obregon. There were looks of indignation on their faces as they silently contested his words, but at the same time they mulled over Obregon's surprising information.

Skilled as a Científico! Madelaina stood perfectly still behind the doors listening to her words replayed by her father's lips. She had been listening intently to the conversation. *So,* she thought, *my father is using me as I had intended using him? Isn't it clever of him to advance his own career through the betrayal of his daughter?* Had all this had been a part of a plot? Was Felipe involved? They talked of her marriage to him. What utter nonsense! She was still the wife of Peter Duprez. What was her father thinking?

Glancing cautiously about the shadowy room to make certain she was not observed, she pressed her ear closer to the door.

It became obvious no one agreed with her father. General Navarro, who currently held the city of Juarez with his battalions of thousands of men, continued to

195

protest that the stupidest of imbeciles would never dare attack his fortifications and expect to survive. They'd be annihilated, crushed without mercy. Why, the gringo soldiers already lay in open trenches beyond the Rio Grande just to make certain no stray bullets fell upon their soil.

It was agreed that President Diaz would secretly fortify Chihuahua. Meanwhile, as a decoy he would institute provisions for a six-day truce and send peace delegates into the camps of Madero to negotiate certain specific terms which he had no intention of keeping. It would simply be a means to distract their enemy while secretly reenforcing Chihuahua. The meeting ended on that note.

Suddenly Madelaina felt herself grabbed from behind. In the dark she was embraced passionately and kissed in such a manner that she was greatly offended. A hot wet tongue probed hers as she fought and strained against powerful arms, which held her only tighter. She felt the rise of hardness in his trousers and grew even more offended by the daring affrontry and foul, repulsive kiss. She managed to free an arm and slap the stranger hard across the face. Her knee was drawn up in a quick jackknife to the groin, but the uniformed soldier backed away in time.

"How dare you, *señor*? How dare you?" she hissed, not daring to raise her voice. She tried to make out the man's features in the dark but couldn't.

"It couldn't be helped, *señorita*. When I saw the spectacular Señorita Obregon here in this dark room all by herself, I simply couldn't help myself. I beg you a thousand pardons for frightening you, but I do not apologize for the kiss. If I were to be hanged at sunrise, I'd do it again!"

"You, *señor*, are both audacious and too reckless for your own good. You realize I could have you severely punished for this rude behavior." She regained her composure and fanned herself rapidly.

"I doubt you'd do anything so base, *señorita*, not to
196

one of your own kind. I am Captain Simon Salomon, at your pleasure." He bowed graciously.

Madelaina fanned herself nervously, feigning the vapors. "I'm trying to walk off a headache, and now, after the manner in which you accosted me, I am quite overcome."

"Again, my humble apologies. Your displeasure grieves me." He glanced about the dim shadows. "Would the *señorita* prefer a breath of fresh air?" He extended his hands toward the open French doors. "As a matter of fact, I was planning to visit the hacienda of your father soon to have an informal chat with you."

Her eyebrows arched slightly. "Me? Why, what on earth would the *capitán* desire from me?" She skirted around him and moved onto the terrace, where the flowers scented the air with their sweetness. And where the dim lights would disguise her nervousness. "I really don't know what got into me. First, I spill my champagne and now I feel a peculiar breathlessness."

"When a gentlemen hears such remarks, he would like to think he is the cause of such palpitations." The captain's thin lips twisted into a half-smile, one that seemed to mock her.

"Really, *Capitán*, you take too many privileges," she snapped.

"I heard so much about the—uh—unusual renegade daughter of General Obregon that, I must say, you piqued my interest. And when I was assigned the task of interrogating you, it was with much excitement that I set up my schedule for the coming week. Since you're here, would you object to an informal talk—that is— since your father and your fiancé are—uh—still confering with *El Presidente*."

"What sort of an—informal talk—do you have in mind?" she said icily.

"A little chat about your life as a *campesina* for starters. More precisely, your experiences with Pancho Villa." His polite mask of affability remained constant.

Madelaina turned to him with fire in her eyes. "You

197

have no right, *señor*. Must I bring my father into this distasteful conversation? On whose authority—"

He cut her short. "Did I forget to tell you? Forgive me. I'm with the Mexican Secret Service. I'm here on the authority of Colonel Huerta—it is he from whom I accept orders." He bowed curtly with an insufferable air.

"I'm sure *El Presidente* wouldn't appreciate your interrogation of me on the night of his anniversary, *señor*. But since they are occupied, as you pointed out, tell me what you wish to know?" She felt herself tremble and grow pale.

"Just who is Peter Duprez?"

Astonished, Madelaina lost her composure for a brief moment. Out of the blue, he asks about Peter. "I beg your pardon, *Capitán*?"

"Don't bother to deny you know him, *señorita*. It would be best you tell us the truth." He sat on the balustrade looking into her dark, solemn eyes.

"The truth is, *Capitán*, the man of whom you speak is my husband."

"Your husband? A gringo?" Salomon's mouth hung open for a moment in astonishment. He gazed at her inscrutably, then burst into laughter. "The *señorita* is humorous. I can see part of your charm is to bring light laughter into your conversation. Everyone knows you are to be betrothed to Captain Felipe de Cordoba." He spoke as if to imply Felipe was out of his mind to tangle with her. "Now then, how did you come to know the gringo Duprez?"

"Quite intimately. We were married in Lisbon and honeymooned aboard ship," she said without humor. "There are records to substantiate my statements."

Captain Salomon flushed the color of a cockscomb.

"Do you wish to examine the wedding certificate?" she asked with a tinge of sarcasm. "When you come to the hacienda of my father on your planned trip—"

Captain Salomon clasped his hands behind the back of his French uniform in an effort to control himself and paced thoughtfully before her. All this was new.

"—I shall be happy to furnish it for you."

"Then how is it you're to be betrothed?" he said, collecting himself.

"Since you seem to know more than I know, pray tell me, *señor*?" She waved her fan slowly, inhaling the bouquet around her.

"I assure you, I am not playing with you, Señorita Obregon. And if you think you can escape questioning by claiming American citizenship, dispel the thought. No papers have been filed to provide you with such immunity."

She stopped fanning herself. "Why *Capitán*, what a provocative thought. Truly I hadn't given that any thought until this very moment. An American citizen, eh?" She smiled enigmatically, in a way that provoked Salomon to anger.

"It appears to be your game to play cat and mouse with me. Since you don't take me seriously, I shall explain to my superior officer, Colonel Huerta, whom I'm certain won't play parlor games with you. We know that you have been looking for Peter Duprez in the camps of Pancho Villa. We know this gringo has been supplying arms to the rebels. You say he's your husband? You must know of his activities. Are you so blindly obedient that you'd risk your life to save his?"

"Captain Salomon, you go too far. My patience is already at the breaking point. Now, will you step aside and permit me to pass—or shall I break into *El Presidente*'s conference to tell him I've been sorely abused by one of his soldiers?" He was handsome in a cruel sort of way, she thought.

"Perhaps you'll explain to him why you were listening at the door to the conference room then," he said smugly.

"I wasn't listening. I felt faint, nearly swooned—"

"The laws against espionage are severe, my lady. President Diaz himself requested the investigation into the activities of Señorita Obregon—"

"I don't believe you!"

"Would you prefer asking him? Look," temporized
199

the S.S. officer, lighting a cigarette, "I'm only doing a job. Cooperate with me and I'll cooperate with you. No one need know the extent of our conversation."

"Just how do you mean—cooperate?"

"Not in the manner you suggest, *señora*, although I wouldn't mind it in the least."

"You insufferable—" She raised her arm, fan in hand, to bring it crashing against his face. He caught it in midair. "Well, a spitfire as well! I don't like anyone raising a hand to me. I prefer it the other way around." He held her hand tightly and leaned his face in close to hers. "I have the authority to question all suspected revolutionaries—especially the daughter of General Obregon. Do you realize the implications of my jurisdiction? I can execute them, imprison them, do as I see fit to exact the truth from them. I tried to be pleasant tonight, out of respect for the noted General Obregon, but if this dialogue should progress beyond this point, understand, Señora Duprez, the situation can be far from pleasant."

Madelaina wrestled her hand from his as if she touched a loathsome serpent. Her head tilted stubbornly with noticeable defiance. Captain Salomon, no longer smiling, looked positively diabolical to her.

"Do you realize the guns your—uh—gringo husband smuggled into Mexico are used to killed *Porfiristas*? Your own people? Where does your loyalty lie? That is precisely what *El Presidente* desires to know. You, the daughter of General Alvaro Obregon, married to a *Villista*? A rebel of the government? *Señora*, you had better think carefully on this matter—or must I threaten you with arrest and execution before you speak out?"

"I don't take to threats easily, pig! You can't get away with intimidating me with threats of arrest and execution! I'm a citizen of Mexico. This is my residence. I claim no American immunity—but if I must, I will."

"Threats? I assure you that is one thing Captain Salomon does only rarely. However, if you persist in this posture, I shall inform Colonel Huerta and the task shall be his. He shook his head regretfully and smoothed his brown hair into place with the affectation of a dandy. "You'll fare better with me, believe me." He puffed languidly on his cigarette.

"Before you burst a vein, *Capitán*—and believe me I could care less if you do—I assure you you're making much of nothing. Since I am traveling in the land of hunters, let me point out that if there were something worthwhile in the owl, a hunter wouldn't pass it by. I, Captain Salomon, am as worthless to you as an owl. I know nothing. I married Peter Duprez for convenience only to get back into my country—because of a lost passport. I know nothing of him or his involvements, and if your spies told you I've been looking for Mr. Duprez in the northern camps, then they stand to be corrected. Besides, I know nothing." Madelaina's dark eyes flashed angrily. "Now, if you wish to pursue this farce any further, then by all means inform your superior—Huerta! He shall have to deal with General Obregon, within the strict confines of the law. I do have certain rights—even under the tailor-made laws of Diaz!" Instantly an inner voice cautioned her not to voice her true thoughts. This man Salomon was a man to be reckoned with. The thought of dealing with Huerta, after what Felipe had told her, sent a chill through her body.

Captain Salomon bowed curtly, stepped aside, and extended his arm to allow her to pass. "Very well, *señora*, if you prefer the tiger to the pussy cat, you may pass."

Gathering all her queenly poise, Madelaina nodded curtly and swept grandly past him, slowly and sensuously, leaving a trail of her perfume behind her. Once out of the small salon, she glanced in either direction and glided across the hall into the salon of women. There, a lady in attendance managed to blot out a portion of the champagne from her gown, while Madelaina collected her thoughts.

The small scene with the S.S. captain was like a dream—far from the reality she was used to of late.

Mental gymnastics with a man of Captain Salomon's calibre were something she didn't relish and they left her disturbed.

More than the words he articulated were those he'd left unspoken. There were the things that disturbed Madelaina. It became more apparent to her that what Felipe had spoken of not long ago was indeed a reality. She was suspect of some terrible thing other than being a revolutionist. Espionage! The same thing Concepción hinted at. The same thing her father intended to use her for. The government suspected her of it already and she was innocent!

"Please hurry," she told the maid.

"But it is still wet, *señorita*. The spot must dry."

"Well, do something with it please. There—that pale yellow rose in the vase. If you pin it on the gown, it will look as if it belongs."

The maid's eyes lit up. She did as she was told. With the rose pinned into place, it was difficult to detect that any damage had been done.

Madelaina's mind wasn't on the gown. She was thinking of Felipe, of her father, of the secret service agent, and of Peter Duprez. They were on to his gun running, were they? Did her father know—or Felipe? Felipe had tried to tell her the other day, and she made light of everything. Hadn't he explained the seriousness of Colonel Huerta's complaints. After all, it is war! Even Papa and Felipe had obligations to fulfill. They believed in their cause as she did in hers. Why hadn't they left her alone? She'd have been better off up north in the *Villista* camps. But now she knew much more than she did before she arrived. The problem was how to delude everyone into thinking she had been converted back into the Porfirio Diaz corner.

Madelaina went back toward the ballroom. She smiled and raised her fan overhead to catch Felipe's attention. The orchestra was playing a waltz, and Felipe made his way through the crowds, caught her tightly in his arms, and swung her onto the floor, where she immediately became the center of attention.

"You look positively magnificent tonight, *querida*," he told her, holding her at arm's length in the usual stance of a waltz. His eyes looked down into hers. "In fact, *querida*, I wish to express my feelings for you, tonight. I was proud of your behavior. So much that I wish deeply for you to be Señora Madelaina de Obregon de Cordoba."

"Felipe—" she began. She wanted to tell him about the Salomon encounter.

"No. Hear me out. We should have been betrothed as children if our parents had had any sense. If our mothers were alive, they would have arranged it, I'm sure. What do men know? They are soldiers with other things on their minds, not the future of their children. Is it not so?"

"Felipe, please listen." She smiled and nodded to others in passing.

"No, listen, Madelaina. Please marry me. I have never stopped loving you. I know, in your way, you are fond of me. What more can a man ask?"

He twirled her around and around the floor, caught up in the passion of his love. Madelaina began to feel a heady dizziness as she moved in circles. She lay her head back and caught sight of the swirling chandeliers overhead, the breathtaking frescoes on the domed ceiling, and the blurred faces of the other dancers as they twirled endlessly.

Soon caught up in his mood, they both laughed breathlessly. They were the center of everyone's attention as they danced in the unbroken rhythm of two lovers in sexual embrace. When the music ended, they continued for several moments until they became aware they were the object of everyone's attention.

Watching them, General Obregon moved toward the president and whispered to him. President Diaz' eyes lit up and he nodded. He movd his hand signaling to the orchestra leader to strike up a fanfare. The drums rolled. The heads of those in attendance turned toward their elegant white-haired host.

"My people," began Diaz. "It is my great pleasure

and joy on this evening on the anniversary of my birth to make a special announcement. With increased joy, I take pleasure in announcing the coming nuptials of Capitán Felipe de Cordoba, son of my trusted friend, Coronel Jesus de Cordoba, to the daughter of General Alvaro Obregon."

Madelaina turned, her fiery black eyes leveled at Felipe. "How dare you?" she hissed accusatorily. "How dare you assume such a thing without consulting me?" She glared murderously at the flustered young captain.

"Madelaina, I assure you, I gave him no such permission." He implored her with his eyes not to cause a scene. They were at the center of all attention.

Madelaina forced a polite smile and bowed as the crowd applauded the announcement. "I'll settle with you later," she whispered through clenched teeth. They walked together, her arm on his bent arm, nodding and thanking the well-wishers. "Take me home, Felipe. This instant," she said, again with a fixed smile on her face.

She glared at her father, when she approached him. Forced to go through the motions of accepting the president's congratulations, she gave him her hand. The music started up and the couples crowded the floor. Madelaina ran from the room and climbed the spiral staircase with Felipe in pursuit. She ran from the palace and ordered the Obregon carriage from the footmen.

"Madelaina, listen to reason. I promise, I had nothing to do with it. I am not so steeped in old traditions that I wouldn't have preferred asking you firsthand. I simply asked your father's permission to court you, and he oddly enough spoke of it to Diaz."

"I'm not interested, Felipe. In the first place, I'm already a married woman. So how can I marry you?"

He took her cloak from the attendants, wrapped her in it, and pulled her out the palace door to the stone steps at the top of the courtyard. Below them, hundreds of carriages and cabriolets stood in neat order with their drivers waiting for the festivities to end. Impeccably groomed horses stood by idly in total bore-

204

dom. The sound of the Obregon carriage pulling out of file could be heard as wheels clanked against the cobblestones.

"Don't bother to come home with me. Stay here, Felipe, and be one of Diaz' puppets. Let him do your thinking for you! One of a thousand girls inside will end up being your wife. They have been drooling for you, so go inside and play your part in this farce of a life." She entered the carriage and slammed the door behind her, forgetting her confrontation with Captain Salomon for the moment.

"Madelaina!" he cried. "Don't go! Don't do this!"

But the Obregon carriage, approaching the gates leading past the exit, was out of view. Watching the scene from an upper balcony with intense interest were Colonel Vitoriano Huerta and his assistant Captain Salomon.

Torn between his love for her and his duty to President Diaz and Mexico, Felipe, who'd been taught to live by the letter of the law, sadly shook his head and returned to the social function inside, trying to formulate an excuse for Madelaina's absence. How can loving someone be so painful, he asked himself. He had always thought it would be a state of idyllic bliss. Certainly not like this. He'd have to make certain that General Obregon had annulled the marriage between Madelaina and that gringo. Was it possible he'd done it without her knowledge or approval? Perhaps it was just as well that she left. It would give her time to reconsider marriage to him. After all, he suspected it had been a shock coming as it did from the president's lips, like some edict which could not be disobeyed. But something else must have disturbed her to bring on such irrational behavior.

The carriage sped through the city streets. Once on the highway en route to the Obregon hacienda near Cuernavaca, she pulled back the sky hatch and gazed at the brilliant stars nestled in a sky of black velvet. How beautiful it was—the nature and exotic beauty of Mexico itself was incomparable. Flowers, the most

205

tropical and unusual in the world, proliferated in certain areas and gave a scent to the air that no manmade perfumes could match. She tried to think of all these things of beauty on the way home just so she wouldn't dwell on the feelings of hatred and disgust she felt for her father and Diaz. It was a plot to humiliate her, to make her bend to their wishes, and lord it over her. If they had exercised any good sense, they might have waited for her to come around. She liked Felipe, even loved him in her own way. One day she might have accepted him if he could continue to argue away her rebellious stirrings. Felipe made sense, and because he didn't treat her as a brainless child, she listened to him.

But they all wanted instantaneous, unconditional surrender from her. And she balked. Perhaps she was acting childishly in venting her emotions and backing away from anything they suggested. Those conspiratorial political jackals with their senseless arguing were nothing but blundering idiots who deserved to be deprived of power.

It pained her to admit her father had been the only bright one among them. Suddenly, she gave a start. It came to her she'd been privy to certain vital information which might net a stupendous victory for the revolutionists and the brother of Concepción. Fired by the far-reaching impact of such a daring plan, she could hardly wait until she reached the hacienda.

The horses had hardly come to a halt before Madelaina alit from the carriage and ran swiftly to the old Indian's quarters. Thoughts of Salomon evaporated.

"Wake up, Concepción!" she shouted, shaking the woman out of a sound sleep. The Indian, out of long habit, slept on blankets on the floor next to the large four-poster bed provided for her in the luxurious surroundings.

"Wake up, you daughter of a sow's sow!" Madelaina continued to hurl invectives at her in an effort to wake her.

The woman sat up gradually, squinting her eyes and

206

rubbing out the sleep as Madelaina lit the oil lamp on the dresser. "Wake up," she pleaded. "We've work to do."

Finally Concepción yawned and with great effort got to her feet. She shuffled barefooted to the stove, struck a match, and lit the kindling inside. She replaced the iron lid and set a pot of coffee on to boil. Grumbling, she reached for a *rebozo* and tried to make sense out of what the girl was telling her. As Madelaina repeated herself for the third time, Concepción was wide awake.

"What's this you're saying? It had better be the straight of it, *chiquita*, or I shall brand you where a woman should never be branded, hear?"

"It's the straight of it, you silly woman. I tell you I heard it with my own ears. Now will you get the message to your brother, or must I run away and do it myself?" Madelaina had become the spy she was accused of being. A half-hour later, Concepción, who never went anyplace without her special *palomas,* attached three cartridges to the three very special doves she had taken with her to Cuernavaca. Madelaina watched as she assisted each into the air, mumbling a prayer of safe journey. *"Vaya con Dios, muchachos,"* she whispered as they melted into the midnight blackness. "Go with God, little friends."

"How can you be sure they will reach your brother?" asked Madelaina.

"Birds such as these have been handling more important things without interference from man since the beginning of time, *chiquita*. In three days we shall know for sure." They returned to Concepción's quarters to have coffee and talk.

Out of the shadows came *La Condesa*, dressed in her long cotton robe, her hair caught at either side of a center part, Indian style. She glanced thoughtfully at the remaining doves raised for eating, her dark eyes smoldering in thought. She hesitated only briefly before retreating to her *casita* to await General Obregon. Earlier, before he left for the ball, he'd stopped at the *cas-*

ita and instructed her to expect him later. *So, he's tired of his little Dolores, eh?*

Two long, nerve-wracking days passed. Then a third, followed by a fourth and a fifth. Concepción grew agitated, short-tempered. Madelaina became more introverted. She stayed in her room. Her father, concerned that she still resented his interference over the wedding announcement, kept his distance thinking she'd soon get over it. At least she hadn't run off. It indicated she was willing to face her problems.

On the morning of the sixth day, Madelaina looked out her window and saw a dove circling arcs overhead. She ran out the door in the direction of Concepcion's quarters. She called for the woman everywhere.

"Concepción! Concepción! It's here." Instantly a hand reached out from the doorway of the stable and clasped her mouth closed, pulling her inside.

"Silence, girl! Be still!" hissed the older woman, the sister of Doroteo Arango. Madelaina nodded and the woman removed her hand. "Stay here."

They both stared at the bird as it circled lower and lower. Suddenly it lost all power of flight and fell with a thud to the enclosed yard, not twenty feet from its cage. They waited in silence. Concepción's sharp eyes were everywhere at once.

"Do not go near the bird, *querida, comprender?* Under no circumstances are you to go near it!" She had already replaced the missing birds on the third day, so that if a count of her pigeons was made, the same number would be found.

She led the girl to the rear of the stables and out the tack room to the side entrance of the villa. "Go back to your quarters. Say nothing to anyone."

"But what will you do, Concepción?"

"Whatever is essential, *querida.* Go quickly and keep yourself occupied."

She obeyed instantly. She entered the hacienda through the side door and moved quietly to the other wing of the sprawling estate where her bedroom and sitting room looked out onto a floral courtyard. She had

208

been dabbling at a few oils and on the easel sat a half-finished painting of a bull. She removed her shawl and decided to disrobe and put on the matador's black suit she had worn in Las Marismas. She placed a mirror outside against a chair in which to study her stance, and began to sketch a portrait of herself alongside the bull. Thoroughly engrossed in what she was doing, she hardly noted the passage of time.

Outside, Concepción avoided the dead bird like the plague. She could feel eyes on her. The instinct of her people was a part of her, like a built-in alarm warning of impending danger. She began to clean a rug. Hanging it on a thick cord stretched between two posts, she proceeded to beat it with a wire coil as if in a state of frenzy. Slowly she inched toward the dead bird. Once or twice she kicked it out of her way as if it were some offensive obscenity. Finally, she forced herself to look down at it. She picked up her skirts and stared at the inert blood-stained bird. Her eyes saw the message intact in its holder. She pushed her braids off her neck, wiped at the sweat pouring off her face, and went through a series of small movements to give anyone that might be spying on her the impression that her curiosity was piqued. With considerable effort, she leaned over and holding the bird's stiff leg gingerly between thumb and forefinger, she kept it at a distance from her while evidencing an expression of horrifying distaste.

She tossed it on a wooden table close by, picked up a stick, and poked at it. She managed to dislodge the capsule. With mounting curiosity, she opened it, read the message, then screamed aloud, *"Mi Generale! Mi Generale!"*

Instantly the door at the far end of the courtyard opened and two soldiers entered with drawn guns. *"Mi Generale!* Where is Señor Obregon?" she shouted.

"Woman! Stop! What's wrong with you?"

"See? See, what I found! There is a note here with writing on it. I found it on the dead bird. He's been here in the yard all this time, but I gave it no importance. But see! There are words. What do they say?"

"Very well, woman! Come with us," said one of the men, eyeing her sternly.

These were *Federales*, not General Obregon's troops, observed Concepión as she scurried along behind the soldiers. So! It was a trap after all! Had Doroteo received the first message? *Madre de Dios*! This message read: *"Kiss the Little Fox for me. Better, I will do it myself when I meet her."* It was signed D.A. as all other messages. It was difficult for the Indian to know if her brother had received her message. Doroteo was illiterate. He could not read or write. The messages in the past always came in different writing. This itself could be a bigger trap, worse than quicksand, and it might suck her under. She must keep her head.

Now she quickened her steps. *"Ondolay, ondolay pronto,"* she called to the soldiers. "I must tell *mi patrón* about such a thing!"

The general sat at his desk in his study, grim-faced and fuming inwardly. The muscles on his face flexed and his jaws were set in a hard line. His dark eyes leveled on the woman.

"Ah, *mi Generale*. With your permission, I found this in my courtyard. Right in the middle of my rug beating, I find a dead *paloma* and this—some writing." She exhibited a ruffled lack of composure which he'd seen on other occasions when she was possessed by something she didn't comprehend.

General Obregon took the note and read it. "Who is Little Fox?"

"You ask Concepión, *mi Generale*? I know of no Little Fox." She turned to the soldiers. "*You* know of Little Fox? Tell the general," she commanded in her usual manner. "Tell him at once, or I shall deal with you!"

"Concepión!" he called sternly, suppressing a smile. "These are not *soldados* of General Obregon. These come from *El Presidente*'s palace."

"*Si, mi generale*? For sure?" She glanced at them with a slight look of respect. "Ah. But why? Why they come here, *mi Generale*?"

"For the dead bird, Concepción, and this message."

"All this for a dead bird, *mi Generale*?" She tilted her head in that stupid peasant's attitude as if she'd never be done wondering about the waste of time in pursing a dead bird.

Unseen by Concepción, Colonel Huerta sat immobile in a nearby chair, listening to the conversation and observing the woman. As he began questioning his men, the startled Indian woman turned. "*Dios mios*!" She jumped noticeably. "What do we have here—*espectro*—ghosts?"

"Explain what you saw, Corporal," said Colonel Huerta, a stiff-backed, slightly bald officer, dressed impeccably. He moved with effortless, premeditated ease. Behind tinted glasses, his dark eyes probed and filled his victims with disquiet. Even if they were innocent of any wrongdoing, by the time Huerta finished with them, they were eagerly admitting to a crime they never committed. He was a sober-faced, suspicious man whose brittle voice and impatient manner bordered on rudeness.

Concepción, who feared no man, paled in his presence. The corporal related what had happened. "After the bullet hit its mark, the bird circled and fell to the ground. No one went to retrieve it. No one came into the courtyard. After a half-hour, the Indian woman stepped outside and proceeded to beat the hell out of a rug. She stumbled on the bird several times, kicked it out of her way, and finally paused to take a better look. She studied it, picked it up, brought it to a table where she poked at it, seemingly offended by it. She removed the capsule and glanced at the writing. I am certain she had no time to read. She made a quick effort to bring the message to General Obregon's attention."

"What are you called, woman?" snapped Huerta.

"Who me? Everyone knows Concepción Montoya," she said proudly.

"I do not know you," said Huerta, incensed by her lack of respect.

"Colonel, Concepción has been with me for many years—" began Obregon.

"If you don't mind, General—" interrupted Huerta. "You are not *my* superior officer. There is much I shall excuse during the course of my investigation. One thing I'll not permit is insolence or insubordination. Do I make myself clear?" The extent of his power was clear enough to enrage the general.

"Colonel Huerta! You are in my house. While I understand that the nature of your visit is not social, I nevertheless expect the courtesy and respect given to an officer of my rank in the service of President Diaz. Your insolence and lack of manners leaves me utterly appalled. Now state your business and leave my hacienda—or I shall put you on report directly to President Diaz. There is no excuse for your insufferable disrespect or your rudeness. Do *I* make *myself* clear?"

Colonel Huerta clicked his heels together and bowed his head imperceptibly. "As you will, General. We can consummate this *your* way—or the easy way."

"Question the woman as you will and get out of my sight!" snarled Obregon, waving his arms wildly about the air. He lit a cigar with ferocity.

Colonel Huerta spoke in soft whispers to one of his men. The soldier left the room on an errand. "If your daughter had cooperated with Capitán Salomon—well, that's past. Now then, Concepción Montoya. How many homing pigeons do you keep?"

"Homing pigeons? I do not understand." Her face went blank.

"Doves—*palomas*—you know, birds."

"Ah, *palomas. Pues*, many birds. More in Zacatecas. Only three I brought with me. My pets. Without me they die." She spoke with provincial candor.

"The dead bird in the courtyard—it didn't disturb

212

you when you found it dead?" He purposely turned his back to her so she wouldn't see his eyes.

"But why? It is not Concepción's bird. Only the birds I have tamed do I concern myself with. You know how many birds are in the world? Pooooh! If I concerned myself with them, I would have no time to live."

"Who is Little Fox?" he asked softly, getting in the zinger.

"Little Fox? Zorrita? But why should I know who is a little fox?"

Colonel Huerta removed a sheet of paper from his pocket and thrust it before the Indian woman. "Read, woman."

Concepción looked at him as if he were insane. She glanced at General Obregon who stood silent, flexing his jaws in anger. Finally, she hung her head in flushed embarrassment. "*Que va*, read? You wish to humiliate Concepción? When does a *peón* get time to learn how to read? There are no schools to learn to write. With so much to do, *señor*, where would I learn such miracles?"

General Obregon felt nothing but instant dislike for this obnoxious, ugly, and unreasonable old man, whose brilliant military career had advanced him to a highly trusted position with the president's Intelligence Corps. Moreover, there was a limit to what Obregon had to take from this man. The only thing holding him back was knowing Huerta possessed information regarding Madelaina's rebellious past. So, when Concepción claimed illiteracy, he didn't give her away.

"Very well, Concepción Montoya. You are free to go. But you will bring your mistress to this study for questioning."

Concepcion bridled in exaggerated fear. "No, *señor*. Not Concepción. If you desire to speak with Señorita Obregon, you must go to *her* quarters and ask permission yourself." She recoiled as if she'd been asked to contact a leper.

Revolted by her attitude and lack of respect, Colonel

213

Huerta glanced at Obregon for some words of encouragement. The general stood firm.

"Very well, then. Take me to her."

En route to Madelaina's quarters, the corporal returned. "They are all there, Colonel. Three of them. All in their cages."

"*Señor!*" exclaimed Concepción. She turned to Obregon. "*Mi Generale!* What will they do with my *palomas*? You must not let them take them. They are my pets, I have trained them. I have no one else, *mi Generale*," she protested with crocodile tears as she shuffled along the tiled steps behind them.

"Hush! They will not touch your pets." General Obregon led the way to his daughter's suite of rooms. At her door, he knocked lightly. There was no answer.

"Madelaina, this is your father. Open the door." Still no answer.

A cunning look appeared in Huerta's face. He smoked his cigarette European style, holding it between this thumb and fingers.

"Perhaps she is in the garden, *mi Generale*," said Concepción. "She's been painting all morning as she has this past week."

"With your permission," said Huerta. He nodded to his soldiers who both knocked harder. "Señorita Obregon," he called. "You will please open the door."

More silence. Colonel Huerta glanced at Obregon. Behind those insufferable glasses, his eyes were challenging, daring Obregon to open the door. The general turned the gilded iron loop handles. The door pushed open. The salon was unoccupied. They entered after Obregon.

They found Madelaina absorbed in her painting, a study in concentration.

"Madelaina, didn't you hear our knocking?" Obregon was fully perturbed.

She didn't reply. Nor did she look up. Her eyes were on her own trim figure reflected in the mirror. She moved toward the canvas and, with a stroke of her brush, filled in the charcoal sketch she'd rubbed in earlier. Finally she glanced up in utter astonishment. Slowly her face contorted to one of fury. "Who—what—how dare you enter my quarters without asking permission?" She threw her pallet at Concepción, who ducked in time to miss being smeared with the paint. However, the board struck Colonel Huerta's chest, smearing his tunic with a rainbow of colors. The astonishment on his face was all the satisfaction General Obregon needed. He turned his face to the wall to hide a smile. The soldiers instantly moved forward in a menacing manner, blocking Madelaina's path.

"Father! What is the meaning of this? Tell these sons of motherless whores to stand aside or I shall make them wish they had abided by the manners that should have been taught them in the primers!" She picked up a large vase of flowers and held it menacingly in her hands.

Huerta raised his hands and, taking the cloth Concepción handed him, tried to wipe the paint from his tunic. "It's all right," he told his men. "Stand aside." Behind his tinted glasses, his eyes raged with fury.

"Colonel Huerta, this is my daughter, Señorita Madelaina Obregon."

"Madelaina, you will apologize to Colonel Huerta for your rudeness, for your lack of manners," commanded her father with authority.

Madelaina was furious. Despite her rage, she trembled inwardly. This was the despicable Colonel Huerta Felipe had told her about. His superior officer. An intimate of Diaz'. A man thoroughly briefed in the clandestine operations necessary to the intelligence units he headed. He was a hard, sharp field soldier, not a supercilious chocolate drinker. Felipe told her Huerta had trained with the Cossacks in Russia. There were hidden facets to this man's character that no one knew about, a fact which in itself was frightening. Felipe had told her with cold sobriety, "It is rumored that this man delights in torture. Torturing women especially, *querida*. Just thank God you have no truck

215

with such a man." Now they stood face to face. If she read the message in his eyes correctly, she would one day pay for the damage done to his pride in these moments.

"Lack of manners?" she screamed like a shrew. "I shall inform *El Presidente* just how many manners this stupid son of a squealing pig has shown. First your Capitán Salomon accosts me at the presidential ball, and now you push your way into a woman's boudoir, trying to pull rank! And you, Father!" She turned to the general who grew more astonished by the moment at these new revelations about Captain Salomon. "Have you no pride, no shame? You allow him to enter the private salon of your daughter as if she was any *puta*! And you!" she screamed at Concepción. "Some *dueña* you are, eh? Where is your protection—your—" She stopped at the silent warning in Concepción's eyes. She had said enough. She tossed aside her brushes angrily.

Huerta instantly grew cunning and filled with duplicity. "*Señorita*, if I offended you, I apologize. It is on President Diaz' orders that I am even imposing my presence upon the hacienda of one so revered as General Obregon. A man of impeccable character, with so fine a record in the military service of his country." He bowed stiffly, and changing his tactics, he glanced upon her canvas. "Ah, the *señorita* has captured the Concha bull with amazing perception."

Madelaina evidenced surprise. She filled with artful guile. Remembering just who he was, she kept her silence as she simmered down and turned on the charm.

"*You* know the Concha bulls, Colonel?" She smiled brightly in an instantaneous change of personality that left her father staggering and the others in open-mouthed astonishment. "If I had known a man of your stature intended to visit me, *señor*, I would have prepared myself." She glanced about at the others. "Really, Colonel, is it necessary for you to travel with this entourage? And look what I did to your tunic! I'm dreadfully sorry. Concepción! Take the colonel's tunic immediately and see if you can clean the mess off it." She moved in and began to unfasten his buttons.

"No, really, *señorita*. I'm perfectly content to keep this on. Let us just pass this off as one of those accidents," said Huerta, playing her game. "With your permission, may we speak in private?" He glanced at the others. "You may leave us—with your permission, General?" he said mockingly.

General Obregon's face turned purple with rage. He stomped out of the room, followed by the soldiers, who stationed themselves at either side of the door. Only Concepción remained rigid. She refused to leave. Madelaina grew livid.

"Very well then, be the *dueña*, you stepchild of a mountain goat. While you remain, I ordered you to clean off Colonel Huerta's tunic. Now do as I say! or you shall taste ten lashes of my whip this night! And bring some brandy!"

Huerta's dark eyes behind those glasses flared brilliantly. He liked her spirit. What a playmate she'd make. How was it possible she was the daughter of that ultra-conservative, military dandy, Obregon, that milquetoast, who did her bidding. At any rate, she didn't fool him for a moment. Not for one moment.

"You must forgive my attire, Colonel Huerta. I brought this with me from Spain. I often tested the bulls at the *tientas*. I learned many *Verónicas* from Manuelito Perez. I understand he will fight in Mexico City soon. Are you also a fan of the bulls? Please sit down. Do not feel uncomfortable in your shirt. I have seen many a man without clothing."

If she intended to shock Huerta, she succeeded only in increasing his desire to entrap her. He knew her entire background, except for her sojourn with the rebels. It was difficult, while in her presence, to think of her as anything but a spoiled chlid of a *hacendado* in need of a spanking. Her attempt to convince him of this very fact caused him to question her more. He sniffed the game she was playing immediately, but for a time they fenced.

"So you are the young woman who has ensnared the most eligible young man in all of Mexico, Captain de Cordoba."

"My dear colonel, like many people, you presume too much!"

"Now, we are back to being enemies," he said playfully as he might to an erring child.

"I find it both regrettable and irritating that everyone thinks they know what's right for me. And they don't, let me tell you. No one knows how I think, what I feel, or why. And what's worse, they don't care."

"I'm here to learn how you think. What you feel— and why?"

"Really? Why are you so interested in me? Do you check on all the prospective wives of all your officers? Is this something new you've devised to check on your officers? I can attest to Captain de Cordoba's loyalty, his ability, and his dedication to President Diaz."

"Who is Little Fox?" he asked suddenly.

"I beg your pardon?" She glanced questioningly at him. "What did you say?" Her face was bland.

"Who is Little Fox?"

"Is this a game you're playing? Some storybook character of whom I've never heard?" She smiled pleasantly as if it was a game.

He studied her. "You've never heard of Little Fox?"

"No. Should I have?"

"Do you maintain carrier pigeons, *señorita*?"

"The Obregon hacienda raises numerous pigeons, Colonel. They are for eating, however. Precisely what are you getting at? Oh dear, don't tell me you intend being as stuffy as that Capitán Salomon? My dear colonel, he is a bore! I mean simply a bore without manners. How you, such a sensitive, understanding man, can put up with the likes of Salomon is baffling to me. He dares emulate you! That cheap imitation!" she said scornfully.

"When did you declare your loyalty to Pancho Villa?"

"Ah, I see," she replied, nodding her head. "All the

218

old things will not die, eh? Once I was inspired by one of those speeches *you* permit aired in Chapultepec Park, to become a rebel and join the revolution. *Pues*, did I learn about the revolution? I grew sick from hunger, I froze in the deserts, I fought off *campesinas*; both treacherous dogs of women and those lust-crazed peons, who can neither read nor write. Ayeiii, Colonel. It was a very dangerous, frightening, and loathsome experience which I do not wish to repeat. Talking of revolution is different than being in it!"

She had paced about the room, still dressed in her slim-fitting trousers. She struck several attitudes all of which were designed to impress him with a certain hardness, a toughness for which she instantly apologized. "You see, I am not fit, yet, to meet in society with my old friends. Not until I lose some of these wretched habits I developed. I smoke too much. Ugh, what a foul habit. I even chewed peyote, *mi Coronel*. But when I began packing a gun better than any *soldadero*, I reflected on my lot. After I killed my first fifteen *Rurales*, I grew even more appalled. It was then that I decided to come off that miserable broiling desert and return to the house of my father. I prayed each night that he would accept me back. You know how many *novenas* I say? How much penance I do each night in my prayers? Ayeiii!"

Well, there it was—all he knew about her and she told him straight out. All except for her meetings with Villa, why she used homing pigeons and, of course, Duprez.

"You've been so honest with me, *señorita*, I'm sure it slipped your mind to mention that you know Villa. What of your confrontations with him?"

"Villa? Pancho Villa? The *guerrillo*? That loathsome *bandido*?"

Huerta nodded. He drank the brandy served to him by Concepción without waiting for her to drink with him. Madelaina glanced at the Indian and nodded slightly. Instantly Concepción refilled his glass. He drank it down again. Once more she refilled the glass.

He set it down beside him on the table. Concepción placed the crystal decanter at his side.

"*Si*, Pancho Villa, the outlaw, the *bandido*, the *guerrillo*."

"What is it you wish to know, Colonel? I'll tell you anything I know of him. Mind you, it's scant. I hardly saw him. When I did, it was from a distance."

"You never spoke with Villa? You never introduced yourself?"

"Of course not. Do you think I'm crazy? The moment I let anyone know that I was the daughter of General Obregon, my life would be over. I wouldn't dare reveal such information among those people." Madelaina expressed a loud sigh of relief. "*Dios mios.* Each day I was in camp, I shuddered at the possibility that someone would recognize me. The chances of this happening were slim because I had lived abroad for so long. Who would know Madelaina Obregon? *Gracios Dios.*"

"You *never* spoke with Villa? A beautiful woman such as you? Then it's not true that he has roving eyes?"

"I didn't learn how roving his eyes were. I can only attest that in the condition in which I found myself, not even a coyote would desire me. Sometimes I took no baths for weeks. My hair, crusted with the dust of the desert, was baked by the broiling sun. You know how long I soaked in a tub of perfumed water when I returned? *Pues.* At least a week! Still, I smell the desert. Still, I feel the winds hardening my skin and I smell those foul animals who stink of wine. No, *señor*, all that is behind me." She shuddered. "Ugh." *Dios mios.* It's difficult to believe I experienced such a life. But I am no fool. I know the difference between there and here. My only shame is that I gave my father such a bad time. He doesn't deserve such a cat for a daughter. Each time I shout at him, I ask God's forgiveness. It will come in time, I'm told, a complete readjustment, a rehabilitation to the old ways of life."

"When did Villa call you his Little Fox?"

"Again that record, *señor*? What must I do to convince you I do not know of a Little Fox? I have never even seen the real animal. To whom do you refer? Explain. Perhaps I may have seen this fox of a man. Describe him."

She was good. She was very good. *She nearly convinces me*, thought Huerta. He smiled. It was a frightening smile, and Madelaina decided she preferred him tight-lipped and angry, for she read things into the smile that sent shivers down her spine. Concepción left a moment before and returned with Huerta's jacket on orders from General Obregon, who didn't want the man under his roof a moment longer.

Colonel Huerta handed her the message found on the dead pigeon. "Do you know anything about this?" he asked, slipping into his tunic.

She read the message. "No. Should I? I told you I don't know Little Fox. Now what's all this about?"

"We intercepted this bird circling over your father's hacienda. One of my men picked it off. This message was attached to it in a capsule."

"What makes you certain the bird intended to alight here? Is it not possible he pauses only for a while? Is it not possible for birds to make mistakes, *señor*? Oh, for pity's sake. Why am I even discussing such a subject? I know nothing of birds and their habits."

"Really, *señorita*? You lived in Las Marismas, collected stray birds, studied the migratory paths of the strange and exotic tropical creatures, and now you say you nothing of birds? My, my, your inconsistency unnerves me."

"I was of course referring to the doves you mentioned earlier. I have never taken time out to examine their instinctual behavior. Rest assured, if I had this knowledge, I wouldn't have hesitated a moment to flaunt it before you. I thought, *señor*, when you first recognized the Concha bull, that at last I had found a soul mate, for whom I've longed. But I can see you're a suspicious old man, cynical and dried up inside, who can't stand seeing the youth of our nation filled with

221

emotions by the things that probably once stimulated you. Now, if you don't mind, I desire to be alone. I get such migraine headaches when I involve myself in one-sided conversations." She stood up and walked to the door.

"Please give my salutations to the president when you see him. Tell him I still haven't forgotten nor have I forgiven him for announcing my engagement before I had been asked." She opened the door and stood waiting for him to leave. "Now, go. You give me a headache."

He gulped the remainder of his brandy and took his time lighting a cigarette with a match from a small box, studying her behind his dark glasses. He walked toward her with that arrogant strut she would come to detest one day, and he stopped before her.

In the back of the room, Concepción fingered her knife too eagerly. She had listened long enough to know Huerta didn't believe Madelaina. This man was no fool. Not like the usual *Federale*. In fact, there was more disturbing the Indian. How could Huerta have known the pigeons had been sent? It was in the black of night, and by dawn the birds would have been many miles away from Mexico City. She was no fool. Someone here at the hacienda had betrayed them. Who? Who?

The afternoon shadows lengthened, the room grew dimmer than Madelaina's heart. Huerta's eyes gave Madelaina insight as to what might happen to her if she kept up the pretense. He couldn't be fooled, won over, or swayed by any women, let alone the daughter of Obregon. Here was an ambitious man, a man who knew exactly where he was going and what it took to get there. She shuddered with premonition. He'd not mentioned Peter Duprez. Why?

At the door, he bowed. "When we meet again, Little Fox, be prepared to tell me more about Villa. Send another message with any of those doves and my men shall be here before you can cry Pancho Villa. You understand?"

"You, Colonel Huerta, are seeing visions. Perhaps you should abstain from those alcoholic excesses and set aside the marijuana for a time until you are no longer *loco*. As to your charges and your mental abuses, be assured that *mi Presidente* shall hear of your callous, unfeeling nature. Now go. Leave me. I wish to fumigate my salon!" She slammed the door after him and leaned against it, trembling visibly. "Concepción!" Her eyes darted about the room for the *duñea*. The woman held her fingers to her lips as she listened for the sound of footsteps on the tiles below. She peered behind the shutters, just as *La Condesa* walked by. The general's mistress dropped a red rose. Colonel Huerta paused, picked it up, and nodded to her, then moved on into his carriage. She grew thoughtful.

Slipping the shutters back into place, she addressed Madelaina. "They've left. *Dios mios*, we'd better depart to Zacatecas. There, I'm familiar with the terrain. I could disappear into the mountains with little difficulty. An Indian has no chance in the city, *señorita*. That man, *muy mal*, is a bad man. In him is violence."

"I'm going with you," said Madelaina. "I'll not stay here. If Father wishes to stay, he can do so. I'm going back to the desert. Perhaps you can write a letter to your brother, introducing me—" Madelaina heard her father calling her.

"Go to him, child," Concepción urged. "Tell him about this animal, Huerta. Make your peace with him, while I attend to more important matters."

Madelaina was astonished. "This from you? Make peace with my enemy? The man who told Diaz about Pancho Villa and all I disclosed? What matters are more important?" she asked, alerted by Concepción's disquieting manner. The Indian woman seemed possessed by something external to her nature.

"As angry as you may be with him and he with you, he will not sacrifice you to Huerta. He is your father. He will not bargain with the devil for your soul. Now, go to him!" she snapped impatiently.

223

"My father is loyal to Diaz. To Mexico. If a choice had to be made, he wouldn't hesitate a moment in turning me over to Huerta."

"See what he wants. Then tell him you wish to return to Zacatecas. I am concerned with the other two birds, *chiquita*. If they got to Doroteo, I have no way of knowing. If they didn't get to Doroteo, it means Huerta has my messages. So far he believes me to be illiterate. I told him I could neither read or write—"

"And that's something which I demand be explained, Concepción," said General Obregon, standing in the doorway. "I didn't contest you in the study. Now I demand to know what this is about." Both women turned sharply to him.

"Mi Generale. You know how it is for an Indian. If that devil should learn that I write and read, I'd be guilty of whatever crimes he could invent. I lied, *mi Generale*. I thank you for not betraying me. I, too, have doves, and it looked so bad for me, I didn't dare speak out with truth. Punish me if you will. But it's best you hear from your daughter's lips that Huerta believes her to be a spy," said Concepción with marked concern in her deep voice.

"This is not so!" cried General Obregon. "You must tell me, Madelaina! This is not true. A rebel, yes! But not a spy! *Dios mios*, what a disgrace! You know who Huerta is? He is a butcher! He is the most inhuman, unprincipled, despicable butcher, the president keeps in the capital. For his job he is without peer. But I shudder to think what happens to people he suspects even the slightest. They disappear! Never to be heard of again."

"Then you wouldn't mind, *mi Generale*, If I take the *señorita* back to Zacatecas? Now, as soon as it's dusk. We can take the carriage and provisions and two extra horses to change en route," said the *dueña* curtly.

Obregon stared first at Concepción and then at his daughter. "Then, it's true?" he asked with alarm in his voice. "You're a spy," he said deathlike.

"Of course I'm no spy," lied Madelaina with a

224

straight face. "You just said Huerta doesn't care if his victims are guilty or innocent. Anyone he dislikes becomes suspect so he can satisfy his sadistic bent. I insulted him enough today to have to face a firing squad. You see, Papa, Captain Salomon attempted to get me to confess that Peter Duprez, my husband, is running guns to the rebels. I told the *capitán* I had no such knowledge. That's why I was so upset at the ball. I was humiliated!"

"You will kindly not refer to that gringo as your husband," growled the highborn, high-strutting *gachupín*, incredulous over the rapidly developing complications. "You should have told me about Salomon before—I could have prepared for Colonel Huerta." He turned to the Indian *dueña*. "Go, Concepción. Take my daughter back to Zacatecas—to the fort. I'll send along orders to keep the garrison fortified from outsiders until I arrive myself. Understand? God willing, Huerta will have no jurisdiction in my domain."

The Indian nodded. She'd always been an excellent *soldadera*.

"And you, my daughter. I'll settle with you when I return to the fort. Talk with no one. Discuss none of this with a soul. And for the love of God, don't either of you mess with the doves!" he said with mixed emotions.

"Yes, Papa. I understand. And Papa?" Her voice was plaintive.

"Yes, what is it?" he snapped with a brittle voice.

Tears brimmed her eyes. "Will you kiss me goodbye?" Something told Madelaina this might be the last time she'd see him in a very long time.

He turned to her, gathered her in his arms, and hugged her dearly. Tears blurred his vision. "Go now, both of you. Prepare yourselves. I'll send an escort of six of my most trusted soldiers with you. No one will dare stop you. If they do, they'll answer to a firing squad!" He dabbed at his eyes and sent them packing.

Concepción returned to her small house, packed her

225

meager belongings in a bedroll. En route back to the villa, she decided to say good-bye to *La Condesa*, whom she'd spoken to only casually. Ulterior motives spurred her in this. She wondered why the mistress of General Obregon should know Colonel Huerta well enough to nod to him in passing, rather than turn from him as was the custom of her people. Then there was the matter of the rose dropped in Huerta's path. He had picked it up. The looks passing between these two seemed inappropriate to Concepción and spelled bad trouble.

She stopped at the *casita*, dropped her bedroll at the door, and knocked. There was no response. She turned the handle, peered inside, and struck by the pungent odors permeating the room, she entered quietly, her curiosity stimulated. Moving soundlessly across the room, she brushed aside the curtains draping the special alcove of worship. Stunned momentarily by what greeted her, her eyes took in the sacrificial altar and the paraphernalia used for the pagan ceremonial rites. She frowned noticeably, drawing her dark brows together as she scanned the bowls, the dolls, the brazier, and the rest of the accumulated requisites, which she as an Indian knew about but had not used since converting to Christianity. Moving rapidly, she shoved the dolls into the folds of her skirt, retrieved a few of the mushrooms, clutched the bottle of atropine and slipped it into her bosom. She closed the curtains, left the house, and picked up her bedroll. Concepción moved silently between the shadowy buildings and entered the rear entrance to the villa proper, her brain roiling with countless disturbing thoughts.

At the door of the general's quarters, she knocked and opened the door. Standing in the doorway, she addressed General Obregon. "Señor General, we leave at midnight tonight. For the sake of your daughter say nothing to anyone. Most especially, *mi Generale*, not to *La Condesa*." She closed the door and left before the general could reply.

General Obregon glanced in the direction of *La*

Condesa, who sat in the high-backed wing chair, her back to Concepción, invisible to her just as Colonel Huerta had been earlier. "What do you suppose got into that foolish Indian squaw, *querida*?" he asked her.

Golden Dawn lifted her graceful body from the chair, moved silently to his side, and encircled her arms around his neck. "What would I know of the silly superstitious ways of the Indian mestiza, *querido*?" She nuzzled her face into his neck. "Is it not much nicer now we've made peace with one another?"

"Infinitely so," he replied, giving no importance to the words of Madelaina's *dueña*. His mind was on a far more rewarding involvement with his mistress.

While the women and their military escorts began the long tedious trip to Zacatecas, it was unknown except to one man what part these two had played in changing the course of history. And that man, Pancho Villa, with the tools of destiny grasped firmly in his hands, had already begun to make history come to life.

Another man, equally determined to make history himself, had already received news by carrier pigeon that Little Fox and her *dueña* had flown the coop. Colonel Huerta collected his best men, studied maps of the Zacatecas area, gauged the time of their departure, and decided to intercept his prey at Querertaro, just before dawn. "Here!" he shouted aloud to his men, slamming his fist on the map. "Querertaro! Halfway to Zacatecas."

Book Three

Madrigal de Los Altos

Chapter 10

A full silver moon and a thick crust of shimmering stars illuminated the winding, twisting road. The Obregon carriage, driven by six powerful horses and accompanied by a full military escort, sped over the landscape as though pursued by a thousand demons. Having departed the hacienda in Cuernavaca a half-hour before schedule, you'd think they could ease up on the horses, thought Madelaina, suffering the unceremonious jostling about as the carriage swayed and creaked and bumped over the rutted dirt roads. She actually felt seasick.

The labored panting of lathered horses reaching the limit of their endurance, the squeaking of leather saddles and bridle paraphernalia, the intense discomfort of the swaying carriage, and even the chill of the March night grated on her nerves. Shivering involuntarily, she pulled the fur robes about her and drew the hood of her cloak closer to her face. It was winter. Soon would come the rains and howling desert winds, bringing dust storms. Consoling her was the fact that nature prepared its creations to bloom in spring.

Madelaina gave no thought to the possibility that doom might engulf them at any point. She was under the full protection of her father, and no one, not even Colonel Huerta, would dare defy General Obregon's military orders. She felt safe. In the dim glow of the carriage lights, small oil lanterns on either side of the coach interior, she caught sight of Concepción's rigid Indian eyes staring off into space and wondered why she suddenly felt such a suffocation of spirit. A deep depression took hold of her. She hadn't even had time to say good-bye to Felipe. Dear, sweet, sensitive Felipe certainly deserved better than she could offer him. In her mind, she blessed him, then turned her thoughts to the present, trying desperately to show no outward fear.

She lit up two cigarettes, gave one to her *dueña*, and smoked one in silence. It was impossible to talk, to conduct any conversation; you had to shout and strain your vocal cords in order to be heard over the sounds of the horses and the nerve-shattering sounds of the coach.

It's just as well, she thought, reflecting on her life. She was nearly 18 years old. Imagine. What a painful process it was to grow up. Always willing to accept punishment or reward for her own actions, she grew dismayed and felt it unfair that either her father or Felipe should be hurt by her deeds or suffer the consequences of the life she chose or the beliefs to which she held fast. She'd known exactly what she was doing when, after the president's ball, she encouraged Concepción to send the message to Pancho Villa. That night of the Diaz ball, when she gazed upon her peers— shallow, superficial puppets who lived in a make-believe world with little or no touch with reality—she recognized in them the very things she fought against. She made a conscious choice. Indirectly, even Captain Salomon had helped her decide.

In retrospect, it seemed incredible to her that in such a short time such havoc had descended upon her life. That she should be the target of Huerta's wrath. She had never said or done anything to be considered a spy. How could keeping your mouth closed to both sides be an act of espionage? She was thoroughly perplexed by it all. All she had really wanted to do was find her husband, Peter Duprez. Her husband? Husband. Even the sound of that word had a strange, alien sound to it after all this time.

Madelaina had changed considerably since she met Peter Duprez. Had she been so impressionable that she permitted this soldier of fortune—this mercenary, as Felipe had put it—to influence her to his thinking?

232

Everything in her world had changed because Madelaina had changed. All this because of his influence on her? Had he bent her to his will so easily? Or had this rebellion been buried deep inside her all her life, waiting to be expressed? After all, she came from a long line of conquerors, dating back to the days of Queen Isabella. Why then wouldn't it follow that she should inherit some of their fighting spirit? Because she was born a woman was she to ignore the adventurous spirit of the valiant Obregon family? Were her feelings so entirely different from a man's? Oh, it was all too confusing. Life was confusing.

She closed her eyes and as usual the image of Peter Duprez was upon her. She remembered only the good things. How naïve she must have appeared to him those first days aboard the *Mozambique*. She rolled her thoughts backward as if those moments were just happening.

What a fool she'd been to have wasted those first two weeks. If she had known all those memories would have to suffice for so long, she'd have insured there'd be many more. After making love the first time, they'd been consumed with each other. Mornings, afternoons, and evenings of every day for the final two weeks of their trip were spent in sexual embrace. They had both been overwhelmed with love—if this magnetism they felt was love—and were unseparable. It was no wonder she longed for him, ached for him, and chased after him trying to find him for all those many months.

How many times had she asked the *Villista campesinas* about the whereabouts of a Gringo Brigade? The women shook their heads, too occupied in their own miseries to even bother to answer. Even though Antonetta, Villa's woman, had listened attentively for a time, she was far too intelligent to ask such a stupid question of Pancho himself, for fear he'd think her interest was personal.

There was word of a coming meeting between the *Villistas* and the leaders of the revolution. Antonetta had mentioned this to Little Fox. She also pointed out

the woman of Captain Tracy Richards. Madelaina recalled the name vividly—Rosalia Quintera. She had
heard Peter refer to the name Tracy Richards many
times. The news that the Gringo Brigade would be
joining Villa at the outskirts of Juarez had filled Madelaina with such joy that she couldn't wait to take off
for the north. She had encountered Miguel Guerra, the
reporter, several times in her travels. The two got on
famously. One day the two met again on the trail
sloping up into the foothills, where desert scrub, cactus, and mesquite yielded to stunted, twisted trees. It
was on the road leading down along the older trail following the Rio Bravo to Juarez that Miguel Guerra
had caught up to Madelaina once again.

"Chiquita," he had called to her, careful never to
use her name. Madelaina had turned toward the voice
and, recognizing him, ran into his arms with an affectionate greeting. It was then that Miguel had informed
her of the many *pesos* being brandished freely for information leading to her whereabouts. "It seems, the
general, your father, is most anxious for your return,"
he had told her, inspecting the many changes in the girl
since he last saw her. "Take my advice and go home.
The revolution is not for one such as you. You have
too much to offer. You could help in other ways—not
on the fighting front."

She had never told Miguel of her real mission, that
she was in search of Peter Duprez, her husband. Concerned with the fact she might bring unwanted attention to Peter, she kept her silence. It wasn't until she
traveled with the *campesinas* and the *soldaderas* and
learned how to wield a gun against the *Federales* and
those *Rurales*, whom she'd seen brutalize and maim
and harass the people, that she really took up the
cause of the rebels. True, Peter had painted a vivid
image in her mind of conditions under Diaz, but it was
one thing to hear about the injustices and another to
witness them.

She had thanked Miguel for his concern and shared
her *cantina* of water with him. Not less than a half

hour later, Madelaina was accosted by two men dressed as *peóns*, gagged and tied down, and covered under rags in a wagon.

She couldn't recall how long they'd driven, but the first time they stopped was in Torreon, some 200 miles south. She ached, wanted food and water, and needed a bath so badly, she felt nauseated from her own stench. Permitted only to eat, she mouthed her food like a starved animal who hadn't seen food for months. Only then did she notice her assailants had changed into their *Federale* uniforms. She knew her father had caught up with her at long last, that her hopes of finding Peter would have to be set aside.

That night one of the soldiers—which one she couldn't tell, it was too dark—slipped under the wagon beside her. It was the first time Madelaina had slept soundly in months. Life as a *campesina* was hard; she usually slept with one eye open, a knife in each hand and a gun in her boot. She never thought she'd have to worry about her safety while under the protection of General Obregon.

But men were men the world over, soldiers, peasants, or grandees. What did it matter when it came to fullfilling their needs? She felt him first. A suffocation, a feeling of being smothered alive. A grimy hand covered her mouth and she heard a breathless snarl.

"Don't scream or make any noise. I could kill you easily and say it was some *bandido* who molested you, you hear?" he hissed, laughing with a self-satisfied sneer on his face at the squirming girl who lay under him, now stripped naked of her filthy clothing. "When I tell my friends that I fucked the illustrious daughter of General Obregon," he laughed raucously, rolling his eyes skyward, "they won't believe it!"

When Madelaina turned her head in the direction of the second man, hoping to attract his attention, she noticed her waist was tied down to the mat.

"Don't concern yourself with Jose, *puta*. I poured enough tequila in him to keep him asleep till dawn. Meanwhile this soldier is going to live it up first class.

235

Imagine a general's daughter and Obregon's at that!" He laughed aloud.

Madelaina continued to struggle. She tore into him, scratching, biting, trying to kick him, but it only heightened the man's pleasure. "You're like an alley cat," he said, wincing at one of the bites. The next one got him good. He slapped her face so hard she saw shooting stars encircling her brain. For a moment she went limp, her head sagged.

"Bastard!" she hissed at him when she regained consciousness. "I'll have you skinned alive when we get to Zacatecas!"

"The hell you will! Our job's finished in Monterrey. We turn you over to the authorities there. They'll take you to Zacatecas." He proceeded to finish with her. After a few moment's rest, he forced tequila down her throat. "Go ahead, drink, whore. It will make you more willing. You might as well enjoy yourself, you have no other choice. You don't know me and we'll not see each other again. You stink so much—don't you ever bathe?"

Madelaina, who had learned to live by her wits, grew canny. "Let me get up and bathe for you," she said suggestively. "Then we can both enjoy ourselves. After all, you are some man. It isn't often that a woman meets a real man, *señor*."

"That's true," he said laughing. "But the reward is too enticing to chance your escape, simply because I wish you to be cleaner. I shall have to sacrifice cleanliness for expediency." He was back on top of her, his foul, stinking breath enough to asphyxiate her. But he was working hard. He raped her once, then a second and a third time. The degradation done to her on this night was worse than what he'd done to her frail, undernourished body. Pain shot through her body, and she knew she was bleeding internally. The man, built like a stallion, was too large for her and she screamed at each penetration until she blacked out.

When she came to, she had a feeling of choking and gagging and wanting to retch. She couldn't believe what was happening to her. This vicious, demented aborigine had tired of her lower extremities and forced her mouth open to service his enormous cock. He grunted and groaned with animalistic pleasures, laughing a mixture of lust and excitement. A loud scream like a wailing banshee pierced the night air and her assailant jumped into the air several feet after Madelaina's teeth sank into his penis drawing blood.

The noise was loud enough to awaken his partner from an alcoholic slumber. He dumbly reached for his gun and scampered to the scene of the action. It took several moments before he realized what had happened. Picking up a *cantina* of water, he doused himself to awaken his senses. He lifted the lantern and held it close to the deathly stillness of the prostrate girl. He lifted the light and inspected his partner, still nursing his badly bitten penis. Never had he seen as much blood flow or heard such painful laments.

"You stupid son of a shit-headed jackass!" He yelled. "You got something wrong in your head? Fucking around with General Obregon's daughter!" The man named Feliz was wrathful and he clouted the other with a powerful fist to the side of his head. The injured man, named Jorge, hadn't minded the clout to his head; it seemed to counteract the pain in his penis.

"Ayeiii, ayeiii," he groaned. "This miserable, foul, stinking whore has decapitated Jorge Molina! He is without a head," he wailed.

"Serves you right, you stupid idiot. What are we going to say when she tells her father about the treatment she received?" Feliz raised another powerful fist and struck the other time and again. "You know how long we worked to find her and you have to fuck up. Well, it's the last time to screw up with Feliz Galina. We're through! You hear? Finished!"

Jorge Molina could care less what his partner raved and ranted about. All he could concern himself with was that he could no longer load his cannon to fire it. *Demonio!* May the saints curse her forever.

Feliz leaned over the girl, attempting to revive her.

He poured water over her face, slapped it gently. "*Señorita*. Wake up. Wake up, for the love of God!"

"You will tell your father, the general, Feliz Galina had nothing to do with this infamous act. That son of ten lust-filled demons deserves what you did to him. My lament is that you didn't bite it off!" Feliz, a nervous and frail man, concealed a deceptive inner strength. Vitriolic and contemptuous of a man unable to control himself in light of the money this represented, he continued to let loose a continuous string of curses to let his partner know exactly how he felt. Meanwhile he spoke to his important captive. "Please, *señorita*, you must tell your father, the general, I had no part in inflicting shame and humiliation upon you." He continued to tend to her until she felt better and was well enough to sit up.

"I will say nothing of this to my father, Señor Galina," she said coldly. "As for your companion, besides the fact that he may never ever fuck another woman again or subject anyone to such vile, lascivious acts, let him know that I am rotten with disease and need medical care desperately."

These words, untrue of course, brought the desired reaction. Jorge Molina sprang to his feet. He had wrapped his damaged weapon in a handkerchief, and held on to it comfortingly to ease the intense pain. "Diseased? Diseased?" he screamed. "You're diseased!" The bitterly impassioned, cold-hearted brute reached for his gun, violent enough to have shot her if Madelaina hadn't anticipated the move and beaten him to the draw with the gun she slyly removed from her boot.

Slowly she got to her feet, supported in part by the dazed Feliz Galina. She walked over to where the jerking, spasm-filled Molino lay on the ground. Coldly, without compassion, and like a statue of granite, she stared down and spat at him. Feliz Galina, rooted to the spot, watched as Madelaina shot off Jorge's penis.

"Now, then, Feliz Galina, take me to Monterrey. I never want to see either of your faces as long as I live." She got up onto the wagon and wrapped in her *rebozo*, stinking worse than before, with blood and semen drying on her legs and between her thighs. When her captor had collected his wits, they speedily headed for Monterrey where he turned her over to the *Federales*, who finally delivered her in Zacatecas in a zombielike state.

Memories, memories—all of them. Some good, most were terrifying. Yet she went on living, yearning for the day she'd meet her husband, whom she felt certain would wipe away all the bad memories. Peter, where are you? Don't you know I'm looking for you? Can't you remember our love? All the glorious nights we spent together? Memories of Peter had sustained her for these past two years. Two years? *Dios mios*, it seemed like fifty had passed. She felt a hundred after what she'd been through.

But it was too late for recriminations. The night of President Diaz's ball when she committed the act of espionage by sending to Pancho Villa, the plans of fortification of Chihuahua as opposed to Juarez, she had taken the road upon which there was no return. She had made the choice. She was on the side of the people.

Madelaina gazed out at the rapidly changing countryside and sighed deeply. She glanced at the watch about her neck and was amazed to find that three hours had passed so swiftly. The driver had made no attempt to decrease his speed. Too bad Concepción couldn't be convinced to take the train. The Indian was dead set against the iron horse, and no amount of persuasion could induce her to set foot aboard that iron monster. Madelaina glanced at the sister of Doroteo Arango. She appeared to be dozing. Still the same immobile face as expressionless as a mask, she had hardly moved in all this time.

Just when she felt she could no longer endure the rocky movement of the coach any longer, the overhead hatch opened and the driver called down to her.

"*Señorita*, there is a tavern ahead. We will stop to change horses. The soldiers have given the signal."

"Thank God!" she shouted back loudly to be heard over the thunderous sound of galloping horses. "Very well. We stop!"

Instantly she felt the pull of the brakes and the reining of the horses.

She leaned forward in her seat and touched the Indian's face. "We're pausing here to rest. We shall take refreshments and be on our way as soon as the horses are changed."

The silence was heaven. The soldiers dismounted, groaning aloud and rubbing their painful buttocks with vigor. The women were helped out of the carriage, and they too groaned, arched their backs, and stretched their aching bodies.

Madelaina saw a number of tethered horses alongside the tavern, as her father's soldiers advanced with rifles at the ready to sequester the place for them. Inside, she gave no thought to the emptiness of the tavern, thinking the guests must be asleep at this late hour.

Seated before the fire, where her *dueña* settled her before leaving to order their food and attend to certain bodily functions, Madelaina rubbed her hands vigorously, warming them. Her cloak slipped back off her face, and she sat back for a time watching the soldiers light up cigarettes, drink wine, and eat their tacos and tamales. They avoided speaking to her except to discuss her father's orders or indicate how soon they'd be in arriving at their destination.

She didn't care. She was in no mood to talk with anyone about anything anyway. Across the room, she saw Concepción engaged in a conversation with the proprietor, a small, moustached man who wore a dirty apron over his pants and Indian shirt. Hardly a flicker crossed the older woman's face as she laboriously moved across the room to seat herself at the feet of her mistress.

"Listen carefully, *chiquita*, as I remove your boots and rub your feet," she instructed, doing so as she talked. "There is treachery ahead if we pursue the

240

plans we have embarked upon. Already Huerta's men have been making inquiries. They plan an ambush for Little Fox just before dawn, by the time we reach Querertaro."

"But—how? Who? How is it possible such information leaked out?"

Concepción's dark eyes shone with menace as if an internal spotlight had been turned on in her brain illuminating the face of the woman Golden Dawn. The dolls, the mushroom, all she had carried from the little *casita* had burdened her mind during these last three hours of silence. Unnoticed by Madelaina, Concepción had chewed the mushroom, and in the state of psychic awareness, she had commanded her mind to bring forth several answers to what disturbed her. The face of Golden Dawn would not evaporate. It had been a long time since Concepción had involved herself in the primitive ways of her people. Since becoming a Christian, which included a warning by the *padres* to give up all the mysticism that prevented them from becoming a part of Christ, she had reluctantly abstained. She had long since given up the mushrooms and the peyote. She clung stubbornly, however, to Montezuma's gold—marijuana.

These past three hours had been prolific after all.

"Never mind how it leaked, *chiquita*. Concepción will take care of *La Condesa*."

"*La Condesa*? My father's mistress?" She sat back totally shattered. "How did she know? Who could have told her?"

Concepción pulled the dolls out of her skirts and placed them on Madelaina's lap. "The powers of my people burn brightly in this witch. I took the dolls. When I reach Zacatecas, the spell will be removed, I promise."

"Nonsense, Concepción. Don't begin with all the black magic and voodoo. I have no belief in it," she snapped. "Now tell me what you learned about Huerta." She saw the imperceptible shrug, the momentary disappointment as the Indian slipped the dolls

241

back into her skirts. "Despite your disbelief, the sister of Doroteo Arango knows enough to break the spell before untold horrors are inflicted upon you," she muttered. "The other doll must be Dolores."

"Stop this nonsense. Tell me how you learned of Huerta?"

"The *patrón* here is a friend of Zapata, a friend to the revolution," she whispered. "He has promised to help us."

"What shall we do? The soldiers are under military orders. They will not permit me to change them, nor will they listen to any ideas that we may be in peril." Madelaina's instinct stirred. "You think he can be trusted, this *hombre*?"

"Listen carefully, *querida*. We part company here. You will do as I say. First, you eat. Then complain of a headache and go to the coach before me. I will follow in no less, no more than ten minutes. Meanwhile, change into more suitable clothing. When I return to the coach, you will leave by the opposite side while I cover the pillows with your cloak, *comprender*? As soon as the coach leaves, José will provide you with a horse. You will take the back roads through Salamanca and we'll meet in Zacatecas. You will be in safe hands. José will care for you as I would care for you."

"But how? Huerta can't touch me or the soldiers will shoot to kill!"

"What if we're outnumbered? Outshot? What good will orders be then?"

Madelaina concurred. "Of no good."

"Then hurry. Eat," she instructed as food was placed before them.

Steaming hot chili beans and wine. She couldn't look at the food. Her stomach turned over and grew queasy. Trembling, she rose to her feet.

"Lieutenant Flores," she called to an officer seated close by. "I'm returning to the coach. Please take your time eating. I have a terrible headache."

The officer rose to his feet, wiping his mouth with the sleeve of his uniform jacket. He snapped his fingers and he and another soldier flanked her instantly and led her to the carriage. Once inside, a soldier was hailed to stand guard, while the others returned to their food.

She lost no time changing into more suitable clothing, selecting her *matadora* pants and jacket. She wrapped her dark cloak around the black leather pillows and lay them across the opposite side of the carriage to appear as if she were reposing. She blew out the oil lamps. She had just finished tucking her long black hair inside the flat-crowned *caballero*'s hat when the Indian *dueña* shoved her immense girth into the coach. The women embraced.

"Here, little one," she began, giving her a knife in its sheath and watching until Madelaina shoved it inside her boot. "And take this also." She gave her a small hand pistol. "Yes, take it," she insisted, speaking with maternal tenderness.

Madelaina slipped it into the top of her other boot.

"If you need them, do not hesitate to use them well, Little Fox."

Their dark eyes met in the shadows. They hugged once again, knowing they might never see each other again. She poked her head out the window slightly. The soldiers were busy with stable hands, smoking cigarettes and completing last-minute chores, as Madelaina eased herself out the window of the carriage, slipping down quietly, crouching behind the shrubbery.

"Are we ready, *señorita*?" called Lieutenant Flores, flashing a lantern inside the coach. He studied the shadowy form on the seat opposite the Indian.

"Move, you obscene son of an obscene toad!" she cried with her usual gusto. "Let us be off. Can't you see the *señorita* is feeling indisposed?"

He laughed at her, spurring the men into action. They remounted their steeds, and the lieutenant shouted, "Move on, *muchachos*! *Avanzar*!"

A whistling crack of the whips spurred the fresh horses into a fast gallop, and the Obregon entourage was soon lost in clouds of black dust.

243

Madelaina rose to her feet and gazed after the carriage until the dust obliterated it and she had to avert her head to avoid the swirls from blinding her. For an instant she felt a sinking sensation, a feeling of impending danger. She braced herself, and moving lightly on the balls of her feet, she stepped cautiously across the dark dirt road toward the tavern. Now, to find José—this friend of Zapata's.

"Señorita Obregon?"

The voice was painfully familiar. Startled, she spun around, trying to pierce the darkness with her eyes. Her heart beating wildly, her throat constricting, she found herself recoiling at the four shadowy figures, soldiers, moving toward her, rifles at the ready. She wanted to sink back against the darkness and let the night swallow her, but she knew it wasn't possible.

In the faint glow of the orange torch light at one side of the tavern door, she saw a figure move forward to ignite another torch, then another. She saw the figure of another man approach her. Something vaguely familiar struck a note in her memory. As if she didn't already know who it was. Inside she screamed in panic. No! No! It can't be him! No sounds left her lips.

Before her stood Captain Salomon, assistant to Colonel Huerta.

Madelaina tried to convince herself she should scream, but who would hear her? Both she and Concepción had fallen into a trap no child would have permitted to happen. She stood in silence, facing the man who swore to capture her, trying to hide the terror she felt. Behind him she saw movement. The traitorous face of José Limas, the innkeeper, bending over a saddle, was one she'd never expunge from mind. How little she knew of the art of pursuit and ambushes. How little she knew of entrapment. How very little she knew of this devil Salomon.

"So, Señorita Obregon, Colonel Huerta was right. We meet again."

There was little she could say or do. Having left her father's military escort, she had pronounced herself guilty and fallen into the trap set by Colonel Huerta. Madelaina stared with sullen anger into the eyes of her captor and shuddering inwardly, she cursed at not following her own hunch. She felt chilled to the soul with a feeling of betrayal she'd never forget for as long as she lived.

The moon disappeared behind angry black clouds. Then came a rumble, a deep, thundering rumble of thunder. The winds howled through the nearby trees, and she felt a few large drops of rain on her face, as she was hastily led to Captain Salomon's coach behind the tavern where it had sat out of sight. Inside, Madelaina sat opposite this assistant of Huerta's, and once again she felt the unconscious loathing she had for the man the first time she encountered him at the ball, an evil loathing worse than her hatred for Huerta. She maintained a stubborn silence as the carriage traversed the same twisting, winding roads they had traveled earlier, now inundated by a raging storm.

The Obregon carriage, having reached Queretaro as scheduled shortly before dawn, pulled up before the Paso Robles Inn. The soldiers, drenched to the skin in the pouring downpour, had unrolled their rain gear and covered themselves, but still they needed the warmth of a fire and wine to warm their chilled bones. When they opened the door to the carriage and discovered the deception, Concepción, feigning outrage and a drowsy countenance, insisted she'd been duped while asleep. Her mistress must have escaped the carriage and jumped to safety, probably into the arms of some highwayman who'd lain in wait. How would she tell the general, she loudly lamented to them, bringing attention to her dilemma.

Occupied by thoughts of the severe consequences of this dastardly affair, only the Indian woman's formidable reputation at the fort of Zacatecas prevented them from punishing her severely for her blundering stupidity and obvious negligence. They engaged work crews to change horses again. The driver of the carriage made certain repairs to the wheels. He wanted none to come off at an inopportune time, he told the officers. Water dripped off his rain cloak, and his *mostacho* dripped like a leaky faucet.

The soldiers ate a hearty breakfast, lamented their stroke of bad fortune, and talked amongst themselves. Concepción took this time to approach a fellow Indian who'd been eyeing her casually through half-lidded eyes. She stopped to purchase a can of tobacco and papers with which to roll her own cigarettes. She knew the sonofagun. She knew him well. He was Carlos Colimas, one of Zapata's men. What was he doing so far north?

"You," she called to him in her authoritative voice. "Come here, *hombre*. Tell an old squaw which of these tobaccos is the best to roll, eh?"

Colimas, a surly-looking man with a thick *mostacho*, a conical hat, and leggings, the trademark of Zapata's men, had the high cheekbones of an Indian, the small stature of a land *peón*. He wore a colorful scarf around his neck, the sign of a hard, fast rider who must shield himself from the sands of the desert. A *serape* hung loosely from his shoulders, and Concepción was certain that beneath them lay the double *bandoleras* of bullets and double-holstered guns. Judging from the clothing he wore, he was a *vaquero*, a cowboy, one of many who joined Zapata in the recent revolt. He moved a toothpick around in his mouth with noticeable arrogance and the panache of a man who has no fear.

Lieutenant Flores glanced up idly at the two Indians, but, too occupied with his own troubles, he turned back to his food and devoured it greedily. What did he care with whom she spoke? It could be the devil himself and he wouldn't lift a hand to save her. The clean-shaven soldier dourly pondered the consequences of this day.

Speaking in the Indian dialect of the desert people, Concepción questioned Colimas. After they had spoken for several moments, the things she had learned from him turned her blood cold. How could she have been so stupid?

246

"*Muchacho!* It's true what you tell me? It's not a trap?" she asked.

"*Si. Como no*? You think I'm crazy to delude the sister of Doroteo Arango?"

"Know this, Colimas, and know it well in that crazy head of yours: If you are not speaking the truth, Doroteo will find you and slit your throat. If he doesn't, I shall. And if I fail, may the thirty devils of *Te'Hechos* prey upon your soul forever."

"No. No. I have no reason to deceive you. I tell you, woman, José Limas is a traitor to the cause. I passed his tavern but an hour before you. I swear on the graves of our enlightened ancestors I saw Huerta's man, Captain Salomon! *Dios mios*, woman! If I do not know that *bastardo* Salomon, I do not know Zapata!"

"Listen, you son of a demented whore's whore. I am employed by General Obregon under Pancho's orders. His daughter has been kidnapped by Huerta's men, if what you say is true. You must help me convince these soldiers of this fact. *Comprender*? You have the word of Arango's sister that nothing will happen to you. If my words are not truthful, I shall personally give you the knife with which you may slit my throat."

"You are some crazy woman! Have you drunk the gringo's firewater? Or are you truly deranged to think I would fall into such a trap?" He backed off. Concepción grabbed his wrist.

"Do as I say, man. Or shall I scream to the *Federales* that you are heavily armed beneath the *serape*, eh?"

She was gargantuan and loomed over him. It wasn't easy convincing him of her sincerity; the only thing she had going for her was the fact that she was Villa's sister. The knowledge of what would happen to traitors didn't affect him as much as knowing how she'd tend to him.

By the time Concepción, with the aid of Colimas, convinced Captain Saltillo and Lieutenant Flores to return to the tavern of José Limas, it was early afternoon. They found the traitor snoozing before an open fire. It was Colimas, not the *Federales*, who frightened Limas into confessing the betrayal of the general's daughter. Limas considered he'd be better off in the *calabozo* of the *Federales* than at the mercy of those men from Moreles.

The military entourage arrived back in Querertaro, with José Limas heavily guarded, riding in the carriage with Concepción and Colimas. Captain Saltillo placed a *telefono* call to Cuernavaca only to learn General Obregon and his contingent had already left for Zacatecas. Captain Saltillo had no recourse open to him but to proceed to Zacatecas as per orders.

When they arrived, the throat of José Limas had been slit from ear to ear. Colimas had disappeared from the coach. As usual, Concepción had seen nothing. She'd been asleep throughout the balance of the journey.

Captain Salomon's carriage, bouncing and creaking, swayed dangerously over the narrow cliff roads overlooking the Bay of California. They had traveled the entire night in a nightmare Madelaina would never forget for as long as she lived. Seated across from her, Captain Salomon had tried to make her admit she was Little Fox. He tried trickery, cunning, and even threats till finally, in disgust, he nodded to the crude soldier seated next to him, whom Madelaina assumed was his bodyguard. Madelaina had decided that Salomon was actually a stinking little coward, afraid of his own shadow. Only a weak, frightened man would use the devious skills and ploys to degrade her which he found amusing.

When she saw this frightening blob of a man, this walrus, who stank of human excrement and stale fish, come at her, fully intending to rape her, she screamed and fought him off, scratching him and beating his face with her fists. She fought with all her strength but was no match for this giant. He socked her with a tight-fisted blow and she passed out. When she came to, he

248

was on top of her, having already removed her trousers and underpinnings.

Madelaina had never really known the meaning of human degradation until this moment when she was assaulted by this insane lunatic whose weight nearly crushed the last breath from her. Worse, she'd never forget the leering, maniacal lights that shone in Salomon's eyes as he watched the sexual violence taking place before him.

The things Felipe had told her about this secret service agent stormed into her consciousness now, for as she watched him, she knew he was a real psychopath, a demented man who'd stop at nothing to gain his ends.

She continued to fight off the brute, knowing she was powerless against such force. She hadn't the strength, but she certainly had her wits about her. Someway, somehow she had to gather all her strength—right now.

Fear had set in long before this, but the struggle for survival, something she'd learned well in that past year, came to the fore to invigorate her courage.

The occasion of intolerable suffering and shame hadn't ended yet. She had nothing to lose. Slowly her left hand groped inside her left boot, feeling for the knife secreted there. As weak as she was, she gripped it firmly and slowly drew it closer to her. She moaned aloud, hoping to distract her assailant.

"See!" Salomon's black eyes glittered triumphantly. "The whore enjoys it. Give her more, Tadeo. More. More! Let her cry out for mercy!"

Tadeo pumped harder and harder with more sexual fervor and ardent vigor until suddenly his body arched sharply into a backward jackknife, his arm reaching over his shoulder, grasping for something he couldn't see, a flaring look of idiotic lunacy in his animal-like eyes.

"Ayyyyiiiieeeeeeee!" he cried aloud in pain as Madelaina's hand came down again and again upon him. The bloodied knife flashed dully in the glow of the oil lamps inside the carriage. The ogre gasped for breath, made gurgling sounds, and finally fell to one side in a heap as Madelaina pushed and kicked his body from her, vile loathing etched into her face.

She arose unsteadily, grasping the leather seats with clawing fingers as the coach swayed precariously over the rough, muddy terrain. She crouched like a frightened animal into a corner of the coach, her eyes wary with apprehension as she glared at the complacent, seemingly unperturbed secret service officer who glanced down at the dead man with nerve-wracking indifference.

Emulating his superior, Colonel Huerta, Salomon smoked his cigarette in the custom of the Russians, wore tinted glasses, and even affected Huerta's disdaining manner of speech.

"You will, of course, pay for this conduct, Little Fox. Tadeo was a good man. It takes time to train another to fill his place." He pushed open the coach door and shoved the man's body out of the moving vehicle as if the very sight of the obscenity offended him. He picked up Madelaina's *matadora* pants and flung them at her as if she were swine to which he'd flung swill.

Madelaina had contemplated many things in those brief moments. She could have leapt upon him, for her hand still clutched the knife. It would have been worth the chance, any chance to strike at him, kill him if she could. Instinct told her she hadn't given Salomon the importance he deserved. Felipe had told her that like his superior officer, Colonel Huerta, Salomon had trained with the Cossacks. Cossacks! *Madre de Dios!* Having been told many vivid tales by the Sephardic Jews in Spain, who once suffered and were persecuted by the Cossacks, she was unable to make a move against him nor stop the small whimpering sounds emanating from deep in her throat. She still had her gun. As if this was enough, she performed the ultimate act of submission. For an instant she was certain she'd seen Salomon flinch imperceptibly as if to brace himself against an attack.

If only he'd remove those bloody tinted glasses he wore, she could see into his rotten soul, she could tell better where she stood in this matter. Her fingers slowly opened and she released her grip. The knife lay limply in her open palm. She turned her hand and let the knife slip off and fall to the floor of the carriage as if it were suddenly contaminated.

Capitán Salomon made no move to retrieve it. He observed the act as if it were merely child's play, as if none of it had touched him.

Madelaina made no move to pull on her trousers. She was numb. Pain like molten fire shot through her body until she wanted to scream aloud in protest. She pulled a blanket about her so he wouldn't have occasion to leer at her nudity. God! How she hated this man. She recoiled from him as if he were some monstrous obscenity to end all obscenities. Sharing the same vehicle with him was enough to make her retch.

"Get dressed, Zorrita," he said coldly. "You will presently be in the company of the Mother Superior, if we arrive early enough. Have you no shame?"

Madelaina didn't respond. Instead she leveled her hate-filled eyes on him and, forcing a bravado, spoke imperiously to him as a superior might to an insignificant serf. "You realize what you've done, Salomon? What you intend doing will bring the wrath of Diaz down on you."

"He already knows what tidbits I intend for you. You see, Little Fox, we know you've been sending messages to Pancho Villa with those little carrier pigeons your *dueña* carries about wherever she goes."

"You know only that your mother's a tainted whore, you bastard."

"That too," he said with insufferable indifference.

She'd not give him the satisfaction of knowing the extent of her discomfort. Internally she was filled with pain, excruciating pain. Sweet merciful God, she prayed silently, let me die before I'm afflicted with more of Salomon's demented sadism. While she pleaded with God, another voice deep inside her promised she'd live through anything this monster's ugly brain devised and one day she'd make them pay for the humiliating atrocity done to her. Both Huerta and Salomon.

If Madelaina had thought that she'd met Lucifer himself when she met Colonel Huerta, she experienced second thoughts now. This man Salomon, the devil's disciple, was to prove to be ten Mephistopheles rolled into one.

Chapter 11

The fresh salt air was invigorating until she saw in the distance, carved as if from the mountain itself, overlooking Manzanillo Bay and the jewelled sapphire waters of the Gulf of California, the object of her own fright. Madrigal de Los Altos, a remote old fortress dating back to the days of the Spanish *Conquistadores*, loomed in the distance like a frightening spectre of antiquity. Converted in the last century to a convent of sorts, this stone structure, washed white by the elements, resembled an ancient citadel of fable and at times had proven a beacon for ships lost at sea. A golden cross high atop a steep spire, catching the sun's rays, had sparkled with such dazzling intensity it often warned sailors they were too close to the shallows in time to avert shipwrecks. Nothing else about this cold, forbidding place could be considered life giving. Resembling a cloister with newly constructed portions to identify it as a mission of sorts, all was not what it appeared to be. How deceptive, she thought. Felipe had told her enough about the place to make her withdraw and cringe inside.

Beneath the old fortress lay the dungeons where prisoners against the Spanish crown had once been held and submitted to the most horrendous torture known to man. It was the ideal place for all traitors to Diaz. It was also the place where titled and wealthy *hacendados* disposed of their enemies. It wasn't enough to kill them. No. Those who were guilty of speaking out against the inequities and unjust practices of the wealthy class had to remain in these foul dungeons so their accusers could exact their pounds of flesh for every defiant act and antagonistic deed done against them.

Madelaina was about to learn even more. Magridal wasn't only a pseudo-convent and cloister. Here, the bastard offspring of many a Spanish lord or high *politico* was raised in secret, away from the eyes of a disapproving society. A deformed or mentally retarded child or one born with inherited diseases from a weak family strain or those with venereal disease could be provided for with society being none the wiser. As misfits in a society which shunned such stigma or unsightliness, Madrigal was suitable for such pitiful creatures.

In days to come she'd witness the presence of unimaginable monstrosities: humpbacks, misshapen, bent and twisted children whose grotesque malformations were so hideous she'd be forced to turn away from them. Here were the accidental mutations, the hideous mistakes of creation whose parents couldn't bring themselves to end the misery for themselves as well as the unfortunate creatures who sprang from their loins. Madelaina found herself wondering why God allowed such things to exist. Was it to punish their parents? As living monuments to some terrible, horrendous crime they had committed? Surely not to punish those poor helpless souls who must wish every waking moment of life to be dead when they saw their own hideousness reflected in the eyes of all who saw them?

Those recipients of diseases passed on by irresponsible parents were perhaps the most pitiful. Their grotesque deformities, the open lesions on their bodies when they approached advanced stages of their disease, the dirt and foul conditions in which they existed, were all enough to make her retch. In addition to these were the issue of incestuous parents and relatives. Left alone as semivegetables with warped egos and shattered emotions—and many of these frightened people retreated into the caverns of unreality where they found it safer to exist—they were tossed into dormitories with no one really to tend to their needs or care for them properly. Once a day they received food fit for garbage; food that hogs wouldn't swill. It was simply dreadful, this Madrigal de Los Altos, a hideous place, an abomination on earth.

It was certainly not the place for a young, vigorous eighteen-year-old woman like Madelaina Obregon.

There were others. Sexual deviants, psychopathic killers, all who had parents wealthy enough to house them at Madrigal. These people were placed in special quarters and given special privileges upon occasion. Knowing they could never leave Madrigal, many grew up into adults and became trustees who only acted on the orders of a superior. Totally institutionalized, they were as much victims as they were criminals.

The lower dungeons reeked of foul stenches and diseased air. It was here they kept prisoners like Madelaina from whom they expected to exact information to aid in crushing enemies of the state. She was thrown into one of these remote, damp, cells. Madelaina felt it must be at sea level, judging from the distant sounds she heard every minute of the day and night. She identified these sounds as waves rolling up on the shore with the waxing and waning of the tides.

Madelaina had plenty of time to contemplate her foolish rebellion. Every day became a living nightmare. Even at night she wasn't safe. The only thing she could do to keep from going mad was to turn her thoughts inward, shutting out the external world at every possible opportunity. She began to record unusual sounds like the fog horns on ships in the bay or the sound of seagulls which couldn't be too far if she tunneled her way to the exterior of the mountain. Unable to distinguish night from day, since there was no window on her side of the dungeon, she could only guess. When slop was fed to her, it was morning.

Many of these things, she could take, but the most frightening distortion in this entire picture of Madrigal was the bull-necked, heavy-jowled, gargoyle-faced turnkey, whom she learned had grown up in prison. Having been laughed at, mistreated, and tortured all his life, he was certainly the right man to be left in charge of the prisoners. What could he be? In his twenties? He looked nearly fifty. A ghoulish man who moved only on orders. Madelaina surmised that at sometime in his life he had discovered that wine dulled his memory and blinded his perception to a point he could accept himself, for he kept a goatskin of wine on his belt next to the iron circle of keys, far too heavy for the average person to tote about. He swilled from the goatskin as he would water.

He was called Lazaro. He spoke with a peculiar purring drawl, an affectation of sorts, the result of a marked effort to conquer a somewhat unpleasant speech impediment. His left foot was lame; his left arm twisted; three left fingers missing. He was short, yet, he loomed as a giant to her. His head, disproportionately larger than his body, was covered with black hair that stood out straight from his head like magnetized nails. A thick, twisting scar, beginning over the right eyelid, creased one eye and zigzagged over to the remaining half of what had once been a whole ear.

The mere sight of this diabolical work of Satan, enough to send some of the inmates into borderline shock, oddly enough didn't frighten Madelaina after her first encounter with him. Instead, she tried to find the key to his nature. Lazaro? Lazarus indeed. Had he been risen from the dead as had his biblical counterpart? He could have come from no living mortal, thought Madelaina in her more depressed moments.

From the sounds emanating from the prison itself, she also came to know all that combined to create an atmosphere of terror each week on the day Captain Salomon would appear. He'd come to Madrigal four times, by her count, meaning she'd been in Madrigal better than a month. In that time she'd been subjected to one interrogation after another, but after employing every strategem short of torture to obtain an admission from her that she was indeed a spy for Pancho Villa and was known as Little Fox, Captain Salomon knew no more than he had the day she was captured.

On this day, however, he possessed distressing information. Juarez had been captured by the rebels through the efforts of Pancho Villa. He had actually defied Madero's orders and embarked on an almost singlehanded crusade to capture Juarez and end the revolution. April, consumed with nothing but talk, talk, talk, had spurred Villa into action. Naturally Salomon didn't have the firsthand report. All he knew was that the fighting had taken two days. Presently the capital was in an uproar. Diaz, concerned with affairs of state and far too busy to be interested in any general's whorish daughter, was preparing a hasty resignation and exile.

In light of the revolution's imminent end, Colonel Huerta could easily have permitted Madelaina's release. He no longer had jurisdiction over her, yet he intended to make what time was left count. He had more in mind than the defection of a general's daughter. He wanted to show President Diaz his loyalty, that he could always count on Colonel Vitoriano Huerta no matter how the chips were falling in these final hours of the Diaz regime. He instructed Capitán Salomon to take over the case of Madelaina Obregon, to pull out all stops. Salomon sat opposite her now in the prison, overly meticulous in his trim uniform, with that insolent, stiff-back attitude of superiority that rankled her. Under heavy brows, his flaring black eyes lit up weirdly at times. In the dim light of the cell, his eyes were vigilant, apprehensive, with a hint of menace in them. She had already seen the savage cruelty reflected in those agate balls of evil, eyes that had seen death many times and held no respect for it. His thin nose and flaring nostrils suggested the quick breathing of a wild animal. A dark drooping moustache extended beyond the corners of his tight thin lips. There was about Salomon an aura of evil, a sinister quality Madelaina was unable to dismiss.

"You know, Little Fox," he told her in too easy and sure a manner, "it would be easy to condemn you as a civilian by the judgment of a secret military tribunal—"

"Which is both unjust and illegal," she retorted.

257

"You'll never get away with it. Neither you or that despicable Colonel Huerta shall be alive when my father learns of the atrocities I have endured." Her body ached from the abuses and the beatings inflicted upon her. Weals and welts crisscrossed her lower back and bruises, discolored to a purplish hue, were splattered on her face, arms and legs.

"You underestimate me, Little Fox. I could have you shot and simply say you tried to escape. What more proof of guilt would I need?"

"Since when does Lucifer justify his needs? And will you stop calling me by that utterly abhorrent name? I am not an animal, although you are trying your damnedest to turn me into one." Aware of her disheveled appearance and downright filth, she felt awkward and ill at ease under his satisfied stares.

She was dressed in rags—a tattered gray muslin prison dress, a shift, given to all the female prisoners. She had slept in it and lived in it for all this time without a change. There had been no bath for her. Her hair, caked with dust, was matted like a rat's nest. She stank and knew it, but there was nothing she could do about it, except be pleased that in a sense it offended this chocolate-drinking dandy's nostrils.

"You've never told me exactly what it is that I've done!" she snarled at him with a contemptuous air. "Every prisoner is entitled to know why they've been detained and treated in so vile a manner."

It was true. Colonel Huerta and Capitán Salomon had only hearsay to go on. Madelaina's trek to the camps of Pancho Villa had been primarily to find her husband. Even if he was a gun-running freedom fighter whom the Diaz government wanted desperately to catch, what had she to do with any of this? She had told them she was ignorant of his profession, that she'd married him only for the convenience it provided to return to her homeland. Even Felipe de Cordoba pointed out this fact in the report he submitted to Colonel Huerta. After the night of President Diaz' ball, however, Huerta took Felipe off the case entirely and put Capitán Salomon in complete charge.

Madelaina knew that Colonel Huerta couldn't have known for a fact that a message had been sent to Pancho Villa or that it had been sent from the Obregon hacienda. By the time he'd been informed by *La Condesa* that birds had been dispatched northward, there would have been no time to intercept the pigeons. Instead he had to content himself to lay in wait for the return flight, on which two birds were shot, each bearing identical messages as that read by Concepción Montoya. Hearsay and Colonel Huerta's own Indian instinct had pronounced her guilty. The fact that she'd left the military escort of her father when warned of an impending ambush compounded his suspicions. Only a guilty person could have been provoked into making so foolish a mistake. There was little time left in which to entrap her. He had to make time count. Of paramount importance to Huerta was receipt of a signed confession from this brazen tart. All this he had conveyed to his able assistant, Capitán Salomon.

"Under no circumstances are you to inform her of Villa's victory in Juarez," he instructed. "She'll not have the pleasure of gloating over the loss facing the Diaz regime. A confession will solve many things for us. You understand?"

"Even before you issued my orders, Colonel," said the capitán knowingly.

Now, acting upon Colonel Huerta's final orders, Salomon set about the task.

"Enemies of the state are not entitled to preferential treatment."

"You forget my father is General Obregon. He'll find me—if only to preserve the family name from shame and disgrace. And you forget my fiancé, Capitán Felipe de Cordoba. Now that my marriage has been annulled, you think he'll stand still for his future wife being treated like this? I caution you, *Capitán*, tread with caution."

"Then you admit you're a spy?" he said eagerly.

"I admit only that I'm being detained by a half-crazed psychopathic killer, a drunk, a boozed-up alcoholic, a *borrachón, muy mal*."

"You try my patience," said Salomon, tiring of her. He removed a paper from his jacket and took a pen from another. "Do us both a great favor, sign this. Then I'll remand you to the courts in Mexico City to be tried for conspiracy to overthrow the government of Diaz."

"Each moment you prove my point," she said with saccharine tones.

Salomon looked at her. She bore little resemblance to the woman he delivered to Madrigal. Her skin was yellow, her dark eyes considerably dulled. Her hair was a tangle of filth, and the smell about her was atrocious. His eyes traveled down her tattered muslin prison shift. Her wrists were swollen. Wide red gashes on the inner sides. "What are these?" he asked angrily.

"As if you didn't know."

"Lazaro!" he called to the turnkey. "What is the meaning of this? I told you to make sure there are no bruises on her body!" he yelled angrily. Taking his crop from his boot, he struck wildly at the poor freakish man.

Lazaro held his hands over his head to ward off the blows.

"Stop!" shouted Madelaina. "You ignoramus! Lazaro had nothing to do with these bruises. They were self-inflicted. He's followed your orders to the letter. Don't take out your own sadistic nature on a creature who can't fight back! Or is that the limit of your black-hearted cruelty? Women and children and unfortunates who can't fight you like a man. You'll never get me to admit to anything—least of all something I know nothing about. Little Fox! Hah! Even that must be a figment of your distorted imagination, Señor Salomon! You vile excuse for a man! You castrated eunuch!" She spat at him.

Salomon had reached his boiling point. He struck out at her, bringing his fist forward in a quick movement to her jaw. She felt a crushing impact, an explosion of shattering pain inside her head. She fell, staggering backward along the wall, and went spinning through a color wheel lit like Roman candles. She fell to the floor, unable to focus clearly.

"You'll pay for these insults, you whore. You'll pay! By God, will you ever pay! Lazaro! Send for those three devils!" Captain Salomon's dark eyes flared angrily, giving some indication of what was to come.

Lazaro's eyes lit up in expectation. Then, just as quickly they dimmed over in thought. For the first time in his life, he hesitated before carrying out an order. It was so new and frightening to him that he grew confused. His demented brain could not sort out these new thoughts and feelings, so reluctantly he nodded and left the cell.

In a few moments, he returned with three of the most horrifying excuses for God's creatures Madelaina had ever seen. At first she wasn't certain she saw correctly; she thought her vision still impaired from the blows to her head.

She struggled through the pain and color spectrum that wouldn't cease. Her jaw and head, where she banged it on the concrete wall as she fell, ached with agonizing pain. She slowly opened her eyes and saw she'd been strapped down, naked, spread-eagled on a cot. Slowly her eyes focused on the three ghouls, and beyond them a small galleria of four soldiers who policed the dungeons periodically. Despite the dazed, almost total lack of perception as to what was happening, Madelaina began to fit the pieces together. "No!" she screamed, "No!" The thing running rampant in her mind wasn't the horrifying degradation that was about to happen to her or the pain. All she could think about was the cruelty of becoming impregnated by the semen of any of these pitiful mutations, mistakes of God. Oh, dear God, she prayed, let me die instead.

Captain Salomon, seated on a chair like an emperor, viewing all the goings on with the countenance of a Marquis de Sade, loomed more frightening than ever.

261

The first one, called Ciro, stood six feet. His arms and legs were of enormous strength; his shoulders, powerful and heavy; his chest, wide and heavy and covered with thick black hair that extended down to his toes. His face was apelike, his legs short and squat like a gorilla, his manners slow and somewhat dull. He came at her enormously swollen, with lust-crazed eyes, like an monstrous animal, drooling spittle like an over-heated beast.

It was amazing how each of these creatures moved only on Salomon's words. It was as if he'd trained them, and like obedient animals, they did his bidding precisely.

"These, Little Fox, are ingenious men, quite like those used during the Inquisition to loosen the tongues of wenches so that the traitors to God would be captured and punished." Salomon lazily smoked his cigarette. Lazaro had set a bottle of wine alongside this imperialistic gorgon. "Not yet, Ciro. Have patience, my friend, and wait until all the pleasures have been prepared. Wouldn't it be better?"

Ciro, she learned, couldn't speak. He grunted to make himself known. Nodding his head in apelike movements, he slowed down, his eyes grew dull. Standing at the side of the cot on which the girl had been tied down, he moved his hairy hands reluctantly over her body, hardly touching her, in the detached manner of a primate. Shuddering, Madelaina closed her eyes.

Besides Ciro, there was Cipriano and Casimiro. Cipriano was a cyclops, with one eye in the center of his forehead and the other pulled low into his cheek. This revolting creature bore no resemblance to Ciro. Short, squat-legged, he was built smaller and stooped over with a hump behind his neck. His tongue stuck out at the corner of his mouth and hung limp, drooling with spittle. He strongly resembled the Victor Hugo character of Quasimodo. The third, named Casimiro, was just as offensive to behold as his two companions. His resemblance to men called geeks in circuses, hired to perform the most menial of jobs, was characterized by the perennial expression of frozen terror etched into his features as if he were pursued by a thousand invisible demons. Without doubt these three were idiots, severely deficient in mental development, perhaps Mongoloids.

Nothing in Madelaina Obregon's life thus far, or anything she could imagine, would ever match the terror struck in her heart in these next few hours. Time stopped for her. She wanted to die. Death, sweet eternal death, could be the only answer to this. If she lived through this, she'd get even. She was sustained only by the feelings of revenge against this diabolical, sadistic psychopath with voyeuristic tendencies, this madman, Salomon. One day she'd devise enough inhumanity with which to humiliate and torture him as he'd tortured her. Only Satan knew where he extracted the fiendish schemes he was about to put into action. She could excuse him no more than his superior officer, Colonel Huerta, who had hatched this plot.

Madelaina vaguely saw another figure, shrouded in black, dimmed from sight by the shadowy lights from the oil lamps, features indiscernible, yet at times quite distinct. Seated a few feet behind Captain Salomon, with the face of a madonna and the black eyes of satan. She had no way of knowing that this almost nonexistent figure was that of the Mother Superior of Madrigal, the diabolical Mother Veronique who had run the place with marked efficiency for President Diaz for nearly twenty years.

Always in the background, always present, and certainly quite aware of the bizarre and abnormal things taking place in Madrigal, she never lifted a hand to help Madelaina. There was no question in Madelaina's mind, when she had time to contemplate the woman in the proper perspective, that she was a sexual psychopath who under normal circumstances would have been confined for life to a mental institution. She had the same sadistic tendencies as Salomon. A true she-devil, possessing the marked angelic beauty of a madonna and the incongruous sexual sadism of a vile angel of death.

This woman with a horribly twisted libido was known to have witnessed the sexual coupling of man and beast, or woman and beast, and later would watch in utter fascination as sex organs were removed or breasts cut off.

Of course Madelaina didn't know all this at this time, but over the period of her confinement she heard references made to this sister of Lucifer, and rumors spread like a disease from the lips of the frightened inmates of Madrigal. More rumors spread from the soldiers who inspected the lockup and threatened many horrors if the female prisoners didn't respond to their sexual urges. It was all so disgusting and horrifying that Madelaina tried desperately to convince herself that it wasn't true. None of it. It was simply a grotesque nightmare. The power to shut out all the reality from her mind was the only thing that kept her sane in the months that followed.

Her thoughts were interrupted by the sound of Salomon's voice. Her eyes reluctantly unfastened themselves from the shrouded figure and fell upon the speaker.

"Lazaro," said Salomon. "It's time to present our guest with a special wine. Perhaps she'll be a more willing bed partner for our three friends here." The wine, laced with the juice of steeped cocoa leaves, was given to promote feelings of peace and contentment and also to have a stimulating effect on the sexual processes. "Did you mix in the *cantharidin*?"

Nodding dutifully, Lazaro brought the bottle to Madelaina's lips and forced them open, pouring the liquid into her mouth in the same uncontrolled manner in which he drank from his goatskin, animal-like, without the intelligence to provide her opportunity to swallow.

Madelaina's eyes filled with terror the moment she heard Salomon mention the cantharidin. *Spanish fly!* The aphrodisiac for farm animals who don't wish to remain virgins was not meant for human consumption!

264

After being swallowed it finds its way into the bladder and is excreted into the urine, burning the bladder lining and urethra. It causes erection of the clitoris, engorgement of the labia, and an immense irritation of the vagina, and often caused death. She fought at her restraints, clenched her teeth, and struggled in vain to avert her head to avoid the liquid, to obstruct Lazaro's attempt to pour down her throat what was used to breed bulls!

"Easy now, Lazaro, we don't wish to impair our guest's desire to perform," said Salomon in the manner of a patient teacher to a willing student.

Lazaro paused a moment, then with a powerful hand clenched under her chin, he forced open her mouth. He poured the wine in without obstruction. She coughed and sputtered and choked in vain.

One thing these three animals had in common, thought Madelaina, was their expressions of insane and idiotic delight when pleased. Displeased, they grew surly, antagonistic, and vicious, even to the point of attacking each other. No, these were not humans, these creatures. And this realization drove her to borderline insanity.

She strained to move. Her wrists tied down to the wooden posts, her ankles secure, there was no point resisting, she had learned this already. "Very well, do with my body what you will, Salomon," she cried aloud. "You'll never control my mind." Silently, miserably aware of her own desperate predictament, she began to feel an inner glow, something she fought, resisted with all her strength. Her body, shivering moments before, generated heat. They were about to do anything they wished with her and in no way could she prevent it.

"Salomon!" she hissed as the drugs began to envelop her. "With God as my witness, I swear you'll pay for this degradation done to me, to the daughter of General Obregon. The general himself shall bring you to your knees one day. If he doesn't—I shall. Both you and Huerta shall pay!"

"Well, well, well," said Salomon, "Isn't this interesting? Perhaps I should take this opportunity to introduce you to your kin. This pleasant young man, Lazaro, is your half-brother."

Madelaina gasped. She shook her head uncontrollably. "You swine! You filthy, stinking swine! To even say such a thing—"

"Lazaro! Take a good look at the wench. She is your half-sister. Both of you were sired by the same man! You know it, don't you? You know the fine, fancy soldier—the general—who sired you is Obregon, don't you?"

Lazaro paused and turned to blink his eyes blankly at the girl. Growls emanated from his throat. It was as if he were attempting to sift through the foggy haze in his mind and reassemble some giant puzzle that eluded him. He glanced at the Mother Superior for some sign. Nothing.

"Isn't it a shame, Lazaro, that she should turn out so perfect, without deformities, and you should become the corrupt seed of his loins. What justice is there in this, for you?" said Captain Salomon suggestively.

Lazaro growled with discontent. He made funny animal noises deep in his throat again. "S—sister?"

"No! No!" she screamed. "I'll never believe that!" Madelaina turned away.

"You see, even your half-sister finds you too revolting to look upon. Inside, you are like any other man. You have feelings, you can think, you can remember, yet, because of this unsightly outer shell of misbegotten deformity, you must live like an animal, shunned by other humans, no matter how heartbroken you feel."

"Stop it! Stop it! You filthy scum, Salomon!" she screamed. "Do what you will with me, but leave that unfortunate soul alone. It's bad enough you've managed to deceive him and lead him around by the nose to do your foul bidding. Now, get on with what you've prepared for me and may God have mercy on your soul!" she cried, closing her eyes to the degradation she was about to undergo.

Behind these three devils—the three Cs as Salomon referred to them—stood those unvirtuous soldiers remanded to Madrigal for punishment rather than to a military stockade. Guilty of ritual insubordination, dereliction of duty, and a host of countless improprieties, these presumptuous regulars were given duty for unspecified periods of time at Madrigal, in hopes they'd mend their ways and return to the roost as grateful men with their tails between their legs, ready to obey and perform their duties as well-trained soldiers.

It was plain to see they were all revelling in this sordid scene. Animals! Vile, filthy, indecent animals! Madelaina was certain not one among them was man enough to stop Captain Salomon.

Madelaina was wrong. One face, one man among those soldiers recognized her, but he was too stunned and shocked by what he'd seen and heard to move. Frozen like a block of ice, paralyzed by what his senses told him was truth, Corporal Paco Jimenez, sent to Madrigal by order of General Obregon, was stunned at the scene. It was not to rescue Madelaina or attempt to learn her whereabouts that Corporal Jimenez was here. Nothing like that. He was here as a punitive measure for ravaging the daughter of his C.O., Obregon. All by the effort of that spying little bitch, that loose-tongued daughter of Satan's obscenity, that spiteful, serpent-tongued Dolores Chavez! Oh, what Paco had in store for her when he left this chamber of horrors!

For a month Madelaina's disappearance had upset her father. Those soldiers responsible for inadequate protection had been demoted and punished severely. The general, drinking heavily and lacking in good humor, had listened to Concepción's story about Huerta's plot to abduct Madelaina. While he didn't doubt her, he found the story too irresponsible to be believed. Yet the possibility loomed in his mind. There was nothing left to do but confront President Diaz with the allegation. Colonel Huerta, summoned immediately by Diaz, had the question put to him. Had he been responsible for the disappearance of General Obregon's daughter?

Colonel Huerta indignantly denied the accusation. His face lined with duplicity, he expressed profound hurt that Obregon should consider him so crass and in-human as to go above so-well respected a patriot to conspire against his family. He had assumed an air of arrogant indifference. Before exiting the president's study, he demanded a formal apology from the general. President Diaz apologized.

"How certain are you, General, that your daughter hasn't reverted to her old ways? Right now she might well be safe and comfortable in the camp of our ene-mies."

General Obregon, no fool, believed neither Diaz or Huerta. For too long he'd been a *político* himself. He had left the palace of the president, dejected and brooding with concern over Madelaina's disappearance, but he was not altogether without wits. Back in Zacate-cas, he continued to question Concepción to the point of exasperation. Finally, Concepción, in the beguiling ways of a woman who gets a man to do something he had no thought of doing, mentioned casually several things to which the general had given little thought.

She produced the dolls, provided him with a golden mushroom, the bottle of atropine, and placed them on his desk. She explained she had procured these items from the *casita* of *La Condesa*. She explained that she also knew *La Condesa*'s name in translated Indian lan-guage meant Golden Dawn, another mystical meaning of the dawn of awareness produced by the ingestion of the mushroom. She also made mention of the fact that she thought it strange the second mistress of the haci-enda should brazenly exchange greetings with Colonel Huerta. Then, in her affected peasant's ignorance, she asked bluntly, *"Mi Generale,* is it true she was the woman of Huerta before becoming the mistress of General Obregon as rumor has it?"

"Silence, you bitch!" He cursed aloud. "You realize I can have you beaten for this!" he yelled loudly, expurgating his pent-up frustrations. Pacing back and forth in his study, he fumed and let loose a string of curses that would have singed the hair off an elephant's back. "Indians! The whole accursed lot of you! Red Devils! Black magic! Potions! Mushrooms—peyote—marijuana! Is there no decent one among you? I thought you were a Christian."

"*Si, mi Generale*, Concepción is Christian." She crossed herself.

His eyes swept the desk darkly. His hands shoved the items to one side. "Just what do these mean?" He pointed to the dolls.

"One is your daughter. The other is Dolores." She had to say nothing else.

"Why should I believe you?" he snarled angrily.

"The proof is the disappearance of your daughter. I cautioned you to say nothing of our departure to *La Condesa*. Did you tell her?"

Obregon tugged at his moustache and recalled vividly that *La Condesa* had heard Concepción's warning. They had made love for approximately an hour after that. Then he fell asleep. It would have been a simple matter for Golden Dawn to call Mexico and warn Huerta. It was not inconceivable in light of what Concepción had told him.

"*La Condesa* and Huerta?" He glanced uneasily at the Indian woman. "Bring Dolores to me. I shall get at the bottom of this intrigue. And if I find you've been lying, you'd better have explanations ready for me—and far better than you gave for lying to Huerta about your illiteracy!"

"*Si, mi Generale*," said the *dueña*, gravely concerned.

She hadn't seen him this angry since the night of the Diaz ball when Madelaina had walked out on Felipe and him. Having bridled angrily for nearly an hour, cursing the incorrigible young woman, her mother, her mother's mother, and all responsible for wishing such a hell cat upon him, he later, after a few drinks, had gone into the arms of *La Condesa*, ignoring Dolores for the remainder of the trip, and for a time found

269

sweet contentment. Later Dolores had returned to Zacatecas with him.

Dolores, upon Concepción's orders, swaggered seductively into the general's study with the look of a pasha's favorite written in her eyes.

"Come with me, wench," he said boldly. Taking her by the arm, he pulled on her and marched her out into the bold sunshine, past the *campesinas* who stared in amazement at the sight of the fort's commanding officer dragging one of his *putas* by the arm as if she was his recognized mistress. Not that they didn't already know of the intimacy between these two. It simply wasn't customary for a man of his prominence to be seen in public in a posture which declared this intimacy to the world.

Inside his suite of rooms, he pulled the girl to the bed and hurled her angrily on the mattress. "Undress!" he ordered gruffly.

"But—*mi Generale*—what has happened?"

"Do as I say, woman, unless you want a beating."

This role, new to Dolores, frightened her. Usually she was the seductress, the actress, the one who promoted the act, if only to secure her position among the other whores. Now she felt insecure. She wracked her brain to understand what had prompted such unusual behavior on the part of the general. She disrobed, slowly, whimpering, glancing at him with fright and insecurity.

He undressed and fell upon the bed. "Now, do your stuff. Entertain me. Make me feel like the king you keep telling me I am!"

"What shall I do first, *mi Generale*?" she asked, confused to the point of distraction.

"So! You can't measure up to *La Condesa*, after all. You don't know how to please in the manner she knows how to please. You think I don't know you provoked her? You bitches in heat are all the same. You know how to fight amongst yourselves, but now you're alone, you falter." He tossed her back onto the bed savagely. "Spread your legs, whore!"

270

"Please, *señor*, you are frightening me. What has Dolores done that you should treat her so badly?"

He grabbed hold of her long black hair, curled his hand around it, and yanked hard, just as he mounted her and penetrated her body without preparation. He raped her, is what he did, savagely, cruelly, and in a manner quite unlike the gentleman he usually was. She cried out in pain. *"Animale!"* she screamed. "Ugly animal! Savage pig of a whore! Arrogant bastard! *Conquistadore!*"

He slapped her with his free hand. But by then she was lubricated and her screams no longer pierced the usual hustle bustle of the fort.

Outside, the women glanced at each other with raised eyebrows and said nothing. Others, who disliked Dolores, smiled contentedly. Whatever the *puta* had done, she had brought it upon herself, seducing all the men in camp, especially that simpleton, Corporal Paco Jimenez, who had mooned like a sick calf all the time she spent at the general's hacienda in Cuernavaca.

The general had satisfied her in all his brutality. "Is that how you like it, little whore? Is that it?"

Whimpering in a self-consciousness, half-fearful, half-triumphant way, she felt for his manhood and began to fondle him. "No, *mi Generale*. You were like ten Miuras today. What has come over you?" she asked testily.

"Unless you want more of the same, you'd better tell me everything! Else I'll not hesitate to whip you and throw you out of the camp! Understand?"

For several bewildered moments, Dolores had no idea what he raved about. She had concealed nothing from him except the seduction of Paco by the general's daughter. He was in a rage all right. Like nothing she'd ever seen. Ever since he arrived at the fort and found his daughter missing, he'd been uncontainable. He made frequent trips to Mexico City. Even his warring against the revolutionary *bandidos* grew more severe, and he treated prisoners with such harsh measures he had earned the nickname *el serpiente*, the serpent

271

who strikes fast. The disappearance of his daughter had made an animal out of him. Now, all she could think of was that he had learned about the sexual interlude.

"It was nothing, *mi Generale*," she began. "It was on the day she first returned. He couldn't help himself." She made faint excuses.

Aware that he was learning something for which he hadn't bargained or asked, he was about to interrupt her but decided not to.

"He was unable to take his eyes off her, *mi Generale*. He is weak, a man who has not seen the loveliness of your daughter. So when she seduced him—and he is one rooster, too easy to seduce, *mi Generale*—what could he do but succumb, eh?"

Slowly, he slipped his arm out from under her. "You are speaking of course about my—uh—daughter?" he said in a deadly voice.

If she'd picked up on the intonation, she would have stopped and quickly changed the subject. She never counted on the fact that he might be alluding to something quite different.

"Of course, *mi Generale*, your daughter. Who else is so lovely, so alluring that she could sweep that impressionable *burro* off his feet? Ah, that Paco is precisely what you say, *mi Generale*. He thinks only for the satisfaction of his projectile."

General Obregon leapt from his bed as if it had turned into a nest of copperheads. "My—uh—daughter and—uh—that snake in the grass Jimenez? Paco Jimenez and my daughter? Oh, *Dios mios*! No!"

"*Si, mi Generale*. Your daughter and Paco Jimenez. But I thought you knew?" She was aghast of the admission of the sexual interlude. "You commanded me to tell you everything. Everything, *mi Generale*!" Dolores was beside herself. "This is the only thing I've withheld from you—"

She'd never seen him so furious, so red with rage. His face, swollen with outrage, his fists balled and

272

flexed as he paced the room like an enraged cheetah ready for the kill. He was fit to be tied.

"Go! Get out of my sight, woman. Tell that hairless prick to be in my office in ten minutes. Understand?"

"*Si. Si, mi Generale.*" Dolores dressed like a flash of lightning, and was gone before thunder pealed from his lips again.

General Obregon dressed, not really knowing or caring what he did. This was the last of all outrageous acts. Madelaina could go straight to hell for all he cared. Disgrace him, would she? And with a miserable corporal, a former field *peón* from his own battalion. Had she no shame, no sense of decency? Madelaina Obregon! If he never heard her name again, he'd be content. For the past two years she had brought him nothing but grief and humiliation, disgrace and mortification, unlike any he'd ever known—except for once before. A former mistress, a favorite of his, who lived in a small house behind the hacienda when he first married Madelaina's mother, had borne him a boy child, an unfortunate, deformed, less than human creature. Heartbroken, ashamed, and humilated, he had for a long time refused to permit his wife to entertain any thoughts of procreation.

All the time she carried the child Madelaina in her womb, which was a mistake in calculation of safe days by the Catholic calendar, he worried and wondered in a silent hell if the child would be born normal. When Madelaina was born and she appeared normal and healthy, he breathed a sigh of relief and prayed in the small chapel for a week, giving thanks to God. Now he thought about all this. He wondered if it was God's way of punishing him for abandoning the boy. But hadn't he paid for his board and keep? Hadn't he done the right thing by the boy? He had provided at least food and shelter and clothing for him as long as he lived? The doctors claimed they didn't live beyond their teens. Already he was twenty.

Obregon wondered what he had done to deserve

273

such treatment from the daughter upon whom he'd showered so much love and attention. *Dios mios*!

Dressed at last, he brushed his hair into place, buttoned his tunic, and left his quarters with murder in his eyes. He'd tend to that young punk bastard! Bringing such ignonimous behavior down on the head of his C.O. It was scandalous, conduct unbecoming an officer. He'd demote him, whip him to within an inch of his life, turn him out into the desert for coyote bait. No! There had to be something else he could do to make him remember his infamous behavior, something he'd never forget for the rest of his days.

General Obregon racked his brains walking back to this office. Just before he opened the door, the idea struck him. Madrigal! Madrigal de Los Altos! He'd heard of its far-reaching effect on a few of the soldiers who'd been stupid enough to have caused themselves to be sent to that hell on earth. They had discovered too late how easy they had had it.

The general had completely forgotten about *La Condesa* and the reason he had raped Dolores. Certain he might have been able to uncover the treachery which had provoked Golden Dawn into making images of his daughter and Dolores for the purposes of voodoo practice, he had used the super-macho approach. All that was swept aside in favor of more important issues. He would not permit the walls to come crumbing down all around him as they seemed to be doing. By God, he'd take things in hand this minute.

Corporal Paco Jimenez, no coward, was neither a bold hero. When Dolores reached him with the information she'd been tricked into revealing about the interlude between him and Madelaina Obregon, his first instinct was to run. He literally shook in his boots when he stood before the general, and no one could have been more astonished than he to be so quickly disposed of as the general had done with a quick scratch of the pen.

Without one word of recrimination, abuse, or chastisement of any sort, General Obregon said as matter of factly as if he was issuing simple orders, "Corporal Jimenez, you are being transferred to Madrigal de Los Altos for the period of a year for the perpetration of a crime against your general. While not of so serious a nature as to jeopardize the safety of this military encampment or of your companies, I believe the nature of this crime jeopardizes the moral tone of this battalion. The impropriety of which you are guilty leaves me no further recourse but to give you time to think on your actions. I'd be remiss in my duties, if you were permitted to think yourself innocent of entertaining such prurient longings. Assuming you got away with it once, you might be foolish enough to think you could repeat yourself with impunity. There's no question in my mind you were highly imprudent. This should give you ample time to consider your rash lack of discretion."

General Obregon handed the orders to the attending officer and dismissed Jimenez without comment.

How ironic it was that Paco Jiminez should now witness the utter humilation of Madelaina Obregon and be privy to the information which no one had ever guessed about the dark secret of General Obregon's tormented life.

It had only taken Paco Jimenez a few seconds to recall his recent disgrace at the general's hands. Sudden movement by the creature known as Ciro toward Madelaina brought him back to the present.

There was nothing he could do for Madelaina. If he recklessly forged ahead and attacked Salomon, he'd be at the mercy of these other depraved humans, and of course, the other three soldiers whose eyes popped wide in frightened speculation as to what would happen to the girl. They hadn't known beforehand that the prisoner was the daughter of General Obregon. All they heard frightened them, because it wasn't certain they'd ever leave Madrigal with that information under their belt.

Since no outside information was permitted inside

the prison, none of the soldiers knew what was happening in their land, and they wouldn't until they had served their sentences. Meanwhile they, like Paco Jimenez, stood like statues, staring straight ahead at the obscenity about to take place.

"You've been a good lad, Ciro," began Salomon. "You waited patiently. Judging from the size of you, you've also sampled the cantharidin." He remarked, fully impressed by the size of the man-beast penis, as Ciro masturbated, tugging at himself with a half-crazed, fiendish look, trying to abate the irritation of his engorged sexual appendage.

Ciro moved toward Madelaina heavily with that animal-like glazed-eyed detachment as he proceeded to perform a biological function, possessing neither the art of nor desire for sexual foreplay. He grunted, groaned deep in his throat. He grew closer and closer until Madelaina, sensing his presence, looked up into those empty simian eyes. Her mouth opened to scream, but no sound came forth. No! No! Not this! A voice inside her became hysterical. How could this be happening to her? How? But it was.

Ciro mounted her and began the usual motions to satisfy himself and contain the increasing irritation which had to be relieved in any way possible. Against her will, she favored the engorged portions of her anatomy which needed as much relief as Ciro needed. Her body responded in rapid rhythmic movements, powerful thrusts and staccato jerks over which she had no control. There was nothing she could do to stop herself. His penis inside her served only to scratch the tremendous itch which came upon her, an itch which had to be assuaged. She copulated wildly, working herself into a frenzy of motion in hopes of ridding herself of the intense discomfort.

Watching her, everyone, including Corporal Paco Jimenez, was certain she was enjoying herself. To think the slut was actually begging that loathsome creature for more! Finished with her, Ciro backed off. Then, came Cipriano, the cyclops. He received no

276

resistance from her, much to Paco's disgust. But, then, what did an unsophisticated, former *peón* like him know of cantharidin?

Casimiro, the geek, took his turn with her and satisfied himself as Madelaina thrashed about the wooden cot straining at her bindings. Her neck moved in such rapid movements, she was bound to hurt herself, thought Paco. Never had he seen a woman excited sexually to the degree of this wench. He glanced at his companions, all of whom had grown hard, ready for their participation at the first signal from Salomon. Only then did Paco begin to suspect double dealing.

The other soldiers had been here at Madrigal for longer than Paco had been. Not too long ago they'd seen the same thing done to two young *putas* from Zapata's camp. Salomon must be a eunuch, they had agreed, or one of those crazy *muy loco piojoso* who coupled only with men. Too bad for him and good for us, they had declared. Now, they wet their lips in anticipation of this wench. Something beautiful to behold with her white skin and obvious womanly possessions, she whet their sexual appetites and stimulated their imaginations beyond endurance.

At intervals, Madelaina saw the clearing through the foggy mist of her brain. This isn't happening to me, she told herself. It is nothing but a bad dream, a nightmare. When I awake it will all disappear. Huerta, Salomon will dissolve to nothing. She drifted in and out of sanity or what she considered sanity and suddenly found herself aware of a creeping sensation, a terrifying kind of acceptance, uncontrollable by either her will or her mind.

She vaguely heard Salomon's words. "Go ahead, soldiers. Since the general's daughter is so willing, take your pleasure." He had finished the bottle of wine and Lazaro supplied him with another. One by one the lecherous soldiers approached the wild-eyed beauty thrashing about the bed. The secret service agent exchanged satisfied glances with the solemn Mother Superior not far from him.

277

"Yes. Yes," said a voice unlike her own. "Take me, soldier! Show me what you can do."

Salomon's maniacal laughter rang out in an echo in the dismal dungeon.

Aroused to sexual passions unlike any they'd ever experienced, the soldiers tried to enjoy every second with her as if they could never be done with her. The only drawback was they'd had no drug administered to them to prolong their endurance and most shot their loads before they touched her.

She was a stunning wench. Her breasts heaved passionately. They all watched her gyrations, the articulation of her hips, greedily demanding satisfaction with each thrust.

Paco Jimenez was last by choice and premeditation. He mounted her and forced himself to lay heavily on her.

"Take me! Take me!" she cried, impassioned beyond control. She was out of her head, raving and ranting, it was easy to see, thought Paco. Her body burned with continuous irritation and increased sexual sensation she was powerless to control. Her voice was hoarse having shouted deep in her throat for nearly three hours now.

"*Listen to me,*" whispered Paco, his face buried in her neck. "*Listen, Madelaina. It's Paco Jimenez. Don't give me away*, Dios mios. *You understand?*"

"That's it, wench! Give it to me!" he cried aloud for the satisfaction of others.

Her eyes snapped open. She saw his features in the hazy mist of her disoriented brain. His voice came at her like a wild rush of water from a swift stream. "Don't give me away, *chiquita*. Have faith. I will return to free you. I promise. I promise on the grave of my mother, you hear?"

"Yes! Yes! More! More!" she screamed like a banshee. Her nerve-wracked body, exhausted, out of control, moved like a dynamo of perpetual motion.

Paco Jimenez was sickened over the fact that this passionate ball of fire under him was so subjected to

278

the sickened and depraved mind of this Captain Salomon that he suddenly became impotent. There was nothing he could say or do to bring back his potency. Was it possible? It was the first time Paco Jimenez was unable to satisfy himself. Was it possible he had other things on his mind that would not permit him to enjoy himself at the expense of others? Was it something moral? At this point he wanted to do nothing to bring himself to the attention of Captain Salomon. If Salomon should suddenly become curious and examine the orders of Corporal Jimenez and learn he'd been sent by General Obregon, would he not believe treachery was underfoot? That it was possible Obregon had sent him to find his daughter? He would never be able to convince Salomon he'd been sent to Madrigal for the real reasons. He quickly hitched up his trousers, feigning satisfaction, and drifted back into the shadows of the dungeon, sickened by all he'd seen on this night.

Captain Salomon, a smile of satisfaction on his face, moved over toward the girl. "Have you had enough, *señorita*? Are you willing to confess now?" He leered close.

Madelaina let loose a mouth of spittle and it landed on his face. The depraved captain jumped back, slowly removed his handkerchief from a hip pocket and, with the same leering expression, wiped his face. "No, eh? I've got to admit you have endurance. Perhaps I should repeat this performance without the cocaine and certainly without the cantharidin. Perhaps then, you might not be as willing a victim, my dear. Very well." He turned to Lazaro. "Schedule the performance again for next week. On my return, we shall dispense with all the other aids. You understand? Perhaps by then, your half-sister shall be more cooperative." He turned from the obsequious Lazaro. "Oh, yes, you did a fine job. You see how much more I appreciate you than did your father?" He handed the Mongoloid a slender box he carried in his tunic pocket.

"I didn't forget, Lazaro. Here are your special chocolates."

Lazaro grabbed greedily for them. *"Gracias,"* he mumbled, tearing the box open. He grabbed a handful and shoved them into his mouth, chomping noisily.

"Vamenos, muchachos," he told the others. He told the soldiers to take the three Cs back to their dormitory and instructed Lazaro to find two of the prisoners to come in and attend to Madelaina. Lazaro nodded. Salomon and the others left him alone in the dungeon with Madelaina.

For a long time, Lazaro sat but a few feet from Madelaina, munching on chocolates and watching her with mounting curiosity. From time to time, between mouthfuls of candy, he rocked to and fro. "Sister?" he said, unable to understand it all.

Although a fire still burned uncontainably inside her, Madelaina lay very still, looking at his slanted almond-shaped eyes. His lips were thin and deeply fissured, his nose flat and his hands stubby. His trunk was relatively long in comparison to his lower extremities. He walked like Ciro, with apelike movements. She didn't understand his deformities, if she had, she'd have known that Mongoloids are usually affectionate and tender, that their greatest assets are keen emotional response and mimicry. Treated most shabbily at Madrigal, Lazaro was not as playful and puppylike as most. He wasn't an idiot as were the three Cs. His mental level was approximately that of a seven-year-old, able to learn routine manual tasks.

Lazaro set aside his candy. He walked to the other wall in the dungeon and returned with a basin of water. Patiently, he soaked a cloth in the water and sponged her off. It felt refreshing and cool, but even Lazaro's crude gestures kept her in a state of fearful apprehension. He peered about the dungeon several times, threw a towel over her, and hesitated.

"S—sister? S—sister?" he mumbled.

"Yes, Lazaro. I'm your sister. Will you please untie me? I promise I won't scream. I won't give you away. Only please take the chains off."

Lazaro nodded. Slowly, methodically, as if it were

280

an immense chore, he unlocked the iron bands that cuffed her wrists and ankles. They were red, swollen, and bleeding. Without a word, Lazaro poured water over them. She reacted as the pain spasms shot through her. She was in agony. She couldn't sit up, sit down, stand, or walk. She was a mass of sores at her ankles and wrists. Lazaro ripped off strips of the towel. He handed her the old prison shift to put on and draped a blanket clumsily over her shoulders.

The sound of footsteps along the corridor startled them both. They looked into each other's eyes. For Madelaina it was a painful experience to see little or nothing expressed in his eyes. He moved clumsily to the iron door and glanced through the Judas Hole. He turned to her and waved her into the shadows. There was no doubt in Madelaina's mind that Lazaro intended to help her. He mumbled a few incoherent words and opened the door slightly, admitting two young mestizos—a girl of sixteen and another of eighteen. He closed the door behind them.

"Lazaro," whispered Alicia, the eldest, "could you do nothing to help her?"

He shook his head and nodded, pointing out he'd already bathed her and released her. "Good boy. Good boy," said Alicia, a dark-skinned, black-eyed, frail little thing under five feet tall.

They both wore gray prison shifts. Their faces were as grimy and dirty as Madelaina's had been before Salomon had her prepared for this brutal torture.

Amelia, the youngest, wore the look of perpetual terror frozen on her face. She was tall and thin as a rail, with hardly a trace of breasts or hips. The skin on her face was drawn tightly over her cheekbones as if she'd been starved for long periods of time. Her eyes expressed the same haunted expression Madelaina had seen on the children of the deserts who were starving and dying of malnutrition.

"We'll take over, Lazaro. If you wish to leave, you may," whispered Alicia.

He shook his head. "S—sister." He pointed to

Madelaina. "L—azaro s—sister," he stuttered slowly and with great effort.

"She is your sister?" Amelia's mouth hung agape. "Is it true?" she asked Madelaina. "Lazaro is your brother?"

"They told me tonight. He is my half-brother," replied Madelaina dully.

"Madre de Dios!" She crossed herself.

Alicia hissed. "Be still, you fool. Lazaro is good. He obeys all instructions. You should be so tame. There is not a bad bone in his body. Can he help being so unfortunate?"

The girls both tended to Madelaina's injuries. They comforted her and dressed her until every nerve in her body came alive with pain. With the wearing away of the narcotics and other drugs, the pain became unendurable.

She grew feverish and perspiration rolled off her. They wrapped a blanket around her. "Lazaro," called Alicia. "You think it's possible to bring hot soup from the kitchen? You think you can sneak in to warm some? Take care and don't be caught. They will punish you."

Lazaro glanced at Madelaina before he departed. "S—sister," he repeated time and again in that dull, stammering manner.

Madelaina felt sicker by the moment. She was inflamed with burning pain. She had tried to stand up, but her legs buckled under her. Her dark agonized eyes flared wildly as the images of what she had endured earlier kept coming at her, filling her consciousness with myriad pictures so terrifying that she felt certain she was losing her sanity. The dungeons, infested with scorpions, rats, and cockroaches, were terrifying of themselves, but not as frightening as the images of the apelike Ciro, the Quasimodo likeness of Cipriano, the geekish expression of Casimiro which tumbled about in her mind. The demoniacal mental Hades to which she was subjected grew beyond her ability to cope with it.

By the time Lazaro returned with the soup, Madelaina had lost consciousness.

"God only knows what else she contracted from those loathsome, diseased creatures," said Alicia wisely. "She's in fever. One of us had better stay the night. You think I can stay, Lazaro?"

Lazaro shrugged noncommittally. "You—you, stay." He pointed to Alicia. He took Amelia's hand. "Y—you go."

The girls nodded. Alicia curled up at the foot of Madelaina's bed and shivered under the *serape* Lazaro brought. "You think we could have a fire? I promise I'll put it out before dawn. A fire, Lazaro. It's cold. Your sister needs warmth. You understand?"

"F—fire. *Si*." He left with Amelia to return her to her cell. By the time he returned to light the fire in a brazier near the bed, both girls had drifted off to sleep: Madelaina in a fever, and Alicia in total exhaustion.

Lazaro paused a moment. He took a chocolate from his pocket and glanced at it as if he couldn't part with it. He placed it under Madelaina's pillow.

"S—sister," he muttered and left the cell, locking it behind him.

Chapter 12

Madelaina could hardly believe her ears when she learned three weeks had passed since that terrible nightmare had taken place.

She awakened in a bare room, not a cell. She lay on a plain wooden cot in a room with bare wooden floors and no adornments save a table and chair. Overhead was a plain black wooden cross, the first thing she saw when she regained consciousness. For a moment she wasn't certain if she had died and found herself in purgatory or some such drab place. It wasn't beautiful enough to be heaven and it was too cold for hell. So where then?

Pain had miraculously evaporated from her body. A ravenous hunger had set in. She couldn't recall having eaten lately. The sound of a door opening caused her to turn her head. It was Alicia. She slipped inside the door cautiously and held her finger to her lips.

"Take care, *querida*. The sister of Lucifer is coming to see you today."

"I don't understand. The sister of Lucifer?"

"You've been transferred, *chiquita*. You are upstairs now. See? Look out the window at the sea below. Here, I'll help you to your feet. Try to make it. It will do you good to breathe the fresh breeze. Oh, Madelaina! How beautiful it is outside. How I wish we could go down on the beach and lay in the hot sands."

Madelaina's legs wobbled and buckled under her. She grabbed the bed post and leaned heavily on the small, frail Alicia until they made it to the barred window. Below them, the sparkling blue waters of the Bay of California were like a sea of glass, the sun's glare so bright, she had to avert her head.

"So! Our delicate guest is well enough to be on her feet, I see."

They both turned in the direction of the voice. Mother Superior Veronique opened the door and stood poised in the door jamb, dressed in her black habit and white starched headdress like a bird in flight.

If ever a woman looked like a saint, it was the administrator of Madrigal, Mother Veronique, who possessed an almost ethereal beauty. But the moment she opened her mouth to speak, a change occurred that was positively frightening.

"Get back to your duties, Alicia!" she snapped sternly.

"But I am helping Madelaina. She can't walk—"

"Alicia!" Her tone of voice cowed the girl instantly.

Tossing a frantic look at Madelaina, she scurried quickly out of the room.

"You won't have to concern yourself with Colonel Huerta or Captain Salomon. Now that Madero is president, they've been promoted in rank."

Madelaina gave a start. Madero president? The revolution had ended? But why would Huerta suddenly work for Madero? What had happened to Diaz? She tried not to show any interest, but Mother Veronique had already caught the gleam in her eyes.

"So it pleases you to hear the rebels have won? I wonder how your illustrious father feels to know you opposed him?"

"Does it matter? Isn't he now on the side of Madero? Besides, I'm sure he cares nothing in the least what I do."

"He's a fine man, the general. He's met his obligations here at Madrigal each month for the past twenty years without fail. All this time he's provided for your half-brother. I understand from Captain Salomon that you've already had the pleasure of meeting your poor unfortunate brother. Lazaro is a good lad. Dull and certainly an unfortunate creature, but those things can't be helped. We've had no opportunity to inform your father of your presence here. I'm certain when he does

285

learn, he'll be happy to reimburse us with enough to care for your needs."

"Surely you don't intend to keep me here now that the revolution has ended? Madero is president. Why would I be considered an enemy of the state? I demand you release me instantly," she insisted.

"Demand?" The Mother Superior arched her brows in a severe arc. Her true nature showed as her face contorted into surprising ugliness. "Demand?" she repeated. "Where do you come off demanding, you slut? You, the foulest, most decadent of God's creatures, fortunate enough to be highborn, only to misuse your trust, your powers? Bah! People like you who do not appreciate the advantages to which you were born and abuse the privileges deserve to suffer untold horrors. That's why we're here—to do God's work, to punish you as you deserve to be punished. I guarantee, *Señorita La Princesa,* a few years under my careful guidance and you'll know your true place in the world."

Wisely Madelaina kept her thoughts to herself. She grasped the wall for support as she turned from the window and slowly moved back to the bed. She had lost nearly twenty pounds. Her face, gaunt and faded, had taken on a prison pallor. She was weary, without even the strength to talk. Her eyes were unmistakably haunted, with dark circles sunken in their hollows. What more could happen to her now?

As if things hadn't been bad enough with Captain Salomon, this ghoul insists on meddling further. She sighed heavily, and seated on the bed, she made small whimpering sounds. She was unaware she had caused a puddle of blood to splatter the spotless floor. She had been hemorrhaging ever since she'd been sexually abused on that night of horrors, and anemia kept her so weak that any exertion made her lightheaded, and her concentration was poor.

"Well! Blueblood runs crimson after all," sniggered the Mother Superior, her arms folded, her hands hidden in the sleeves of her habit. "Clean it up!" she snapped caustically.

Madelaina turned her head slowly, her dark eyes lifted to meet the cold gray eyes of Mother Veronique. She had no strength to contest the despot, no will to refuse. "With what?"

"Remove your shift and mop it up. Next time you'll think twice before being so careless."

Like an automaton, acting on the other's orders, Madelaina stood up shakily, slipped out of her shift, dropped it to the floor, sank to her knees, and wiped up the blood spots with every ounce of strength left in her. She pulled herself up to her feet, holding on to the bed post. Her knees felt like water.

"Put it on again." The Mother Superior sneered at her, half-daring her to contest the orders.

Once again the general's daughter sighed heavily. What was the use? She did as she was told. If only she had more strength, if only she could assuage the hunger pangs—perhaps then she could contest this impossible bitch. Sister of Lucifer? Alicia wasn't far off. For the first time, her eyes really focused on the woman who had haunted her dreams for the past three months. She glanced with marked curiosity at the unusual leather belt around the Mother Superior's waist. In addition to the thick rosary beads and thick black onyx and mother of pearl crucifix dangling from it, there were an assortment of unusual items: something resembling a nut cracker with wide flat ends; a leather riding quirt; a bunch of unusual keys that opened anything from the dungeon doors to her private office where records were kept on all the business at Madrigal.

She felt too weak to even consider what the other diabolical inventions were. One thing was certain, felt Madelaina, they were for nothing normal.

"It's rare we take one such as you into our care at Madrigal. I've watched you carefully since your arrival. My observations conclude you to be impudent as well as imprudent and irresponsible. You leave me no choice but to make certain you conform to my dictates. We'll teach you civility and obedience."

Madelaina gave a short bitter laugh. "What can you do to me that hasn't already been done? All that's left is death. You know, I'd welcome death. Truly, madam, there is nothing you can do to me."

Mother Veronique struck out at the wooden chair with her quirt. The sound startled Madelaina. "You think not?" she challenged with bright lights in those gray eyes.

"Inflict more pain? Madam, I've learned to become immune to pain. Degrade me? What could be more degrading than what Solomon has already inflicted upon me? You call yourself a sister of mercy? Hah! You sat there watching the abomination, the human degradation, without flinching a muscle. You're the Mother Superior of Hades, you black-hearted witch!"

Without taking her eyes from the highborn Spanish girl, Mother Veronique called aloud, "Alicia!" Hard, brittle, stormy-eyed, she folded her arms into her sleeves, and with implacable rigidity of a stone-hearted despot, she stood and waited until the frail, frightened girl entered the room. It was easy to see the child was petrified and horribly intimidated by the Mother Superior.

"Sit down, Alicia," commanded the frocked tyrant.

Gazing from one to the other like a terrified waif, she moved toward the hard wooden chair with armrests at either side and sat on its edge.

"Sit back and place your arms on the rests." Before either could protest, the Mother Superior quickly pulled out two leather tongs, binding Alicia's wrists to the armrests.

"Whh—at are you doing to me? I've done nothing," whimpered the startled girl, glancing at Madelaina with a silent plea in her eyes.

"Your friend has no fear. She can't be intimidated by authority. Very well, Señorita Obregon. Each time you fail to comply with my orders, your little sniveling benefactor here shall be the recipient of my disfavor."

"No!" cried Madelaina. "You can't do that! Do with

288

me what you will but punish none other for only I am responsible for my actions!"

The Mother Superior had already extracted the small, flat, nutcrackerlike implement and slipped it around Alicia's little finger and squeezed firmly.

Alicia screamed a bloodcurdling cry of agonized pain.

Rooted to the spot, Madelaina was so astonished she could hardly believe what was happening. As one in a mesmerized trance, she watched the satanic nun remove the contrivance, pull off the thongs, and replace the items on her belt as if she'd done nothing out of the ordinary. Breaking both joints in Alicia's small finger came as easily to her as cracking a pecan or a walnut.

"You devil! You rotten scum of the earth!" cried Madelaina. "You indecent, immoral, licentious, scurrilous pig of a whore!" Her voice had risen. "Flesh-eating scavenger! If it takes all my life, I'll make sure you're repaid in kind! And don't take these words lightly, you cretin!"

"Ah!" She grabbed Alicia's arm so tightly, the girl winced. "You haven't learned your lesson yet!"

"No! No!" whimpered Alicia, tears streaming down her face from the excruciating pain. *"Señorita—por favor,"* she begged Madelaina.

"Let her go!" Madelaina rose to her feet. "I said, release her," she commanded in deadly tones. Flushed with adrenaline, she approached the Mother Superior. "Go," she told Alicia. "Go, now. I'll attend to this, you psychopathic madwoman." She directed this last to the nun.

Alicia was no fool. She ran for her life, holding her injured hand tightly with the other. She disappeared through the shadowy corridors, whimpering, tears streaming down her face.

Mother Veronique turned to Madelaina, her stoney face whitening, livid with fury. She sucked in her breath and struck at the girl with her leather quirt. Time and again she lashed out at her, her face contorting with a violent hatred and pent-up jealousies over one so beautiful and young. The quirt struck the side of Madelaina's face where welts began to form and split open drawing blood. Another caught her across the neck—shoulders—upper arms. Madelaina, as if in a trance, kept coming at her, oblivious to the stinging, searing pain, almost against her own volition and under the power of a hidden strength she never realized she possessed. Her dark eyes were glazed with near maniacal lights. From wherever came this strength, it was marvelous and a recuperative nature that invigorated her to action.

In a sudden movement, Madelaina reached out and in typical feline fashion went for the nun's headdress. The two women tussled, fell against the wall upsetting table and chair. Mother Veronique grabbing Madelaina's long hair, twisted it around her hands and yanked severely, throwing the girl momentarily on the defensive. In this moment, the nun reached for the whistle on her leather belt and placing it to her lips, blew shrilly on it, several times. By this time, she held Madelaina in a scissor hold with her legs, pinning the child to the earthen ground under them. No slouch this sister of Satan, she possessed a formidable knowledge of the martial arts. In a sudden lurching movement, Madelaina managed to break free of the hold and grabbing the immaculate white starched headdress, she yanked harder—harder—harder, until she dislodged it entirely from the woman's head.

For an instant, Madelaina recoiled, startled by the gleaming bald pate on the malevolent witch. Despite the tussle, Madelaina began to laugh. It was a slow laugh which rocked with mocking scorn at the pitiful sight of what instantly became a defenseless woman whose tools were a violent loathing and abject humiliation at her appearance. Once again the nun blew her whistle. She caught Madelaina savagely about the waist as the girl tried to rise to her feet.

Madelaina's eyes were impulsed across the room. She froze. Standing in the doorway was Lazaro, the

Mongoloid, her half brother, blinking his eyes at the two of them. She had no way of knowing what went on in his mind in those moments when the Mother Superior screamed at him, "Lazaro! Why do you stand there like a stupid dolt? Take her! You hear? Take her and punish her for what's she's done to me. *Ondolay*! Make haste!"

Fascinated by the nun's baldness, Lazaro grinned with a look of insane lunacy twinkling in his eyes as he neared the struggling women. In those empty eyes Madelaina thought she saw a flicker of satisfaction, as if he debated his next move. Suddenly the Mother Superior seemed as a stranger to him—a threatening stranger. He'd never seen her in such wild disarray or in a position of impotence.

He placed a heavy, powerful arm on the nun and lifted her bodily off the floor. "Not me, you stupid son of a diseased whore," she wailed contemptuously. "Get the girl!" She struggled to free herself from his forceful grip, but the more she struggled, the tighter became Lazaro's grip.

"S—sister?" He looked questioningly at Madelaina.

Madelaina rose to the occasion, and scampering to her feet, she looked into his eyes. "Lazaro. Brother. Brother, it's me—your sister. Punish her, Lazaro. She's the evil who seeks to destroy us. Bind her. Tie her to the bed posts. Sister will help you."

He nodded in full accord.

"No!" screamed the Mother Superior, grappling with her belt.

A powerful fist lifted into the air and fell on her head. Instantly it fell limply to one side, felled as if by a hammer. They both placed the frocked demon on the bed and, making use of her own devices, secured her firmly to the bed. Madelaina ripped up the sheet, stuffed a portion of it into the nun's mouth, and bound her lips, gagging her.

"Lazaro, where is the office? Where this devil does her work? Where can I find Corporal Jimenez? You understand what I ask?"

He nodded and beckoned to her. In that strange limping gait, he led her out into the deserted corridor. She patted her hair into place, smoothed her shift, and told him to lock the door after them. In her hands, she had the ring of keys plucked from the Mother Superior's girdle. She had to move swiftly. "Find Alicia and Amelia. Tell them to meet me at the side entrance. Can you find me a wagon?" She gazed about, orienting herself in the meagerly furnished room.

Lazaro's cumbersome arm moved to his forehead. He scratched it as if to stimulate his memory. He nodded dully and moved limping out the door. She could hear his lopsided gait as he shuffled down the corridor.

Madelaina moved about the drab, sterile office until she located the filing cabinet. She searched through it, then moved to the desk, uncertain of what it was she wanted, but certain she'd know when she saw it. She finally found the release forms. Good. They'd help. She glanced at some of the duplicates, then sat down at the desk and began painstakingly forging five release forms.

She was about to leave when she again glanced at the wooden filing cabinet. She moved slowly, looking under the Os for Obregon. There had to be some record of her and Lazaro's confinement. *Ah, here it is.* She took the file to the desk and thumbed through it. Her eyes scanned the contents with intense curiosity. The papers stipulated that Lazaro Obregon, aged five years, had died fifteen years ago from a rare blood disease. Another official form followed this indicating that another child had taken on the identity of Lazaro Obregon to insure the continuation of those substantial monthly checks from General Obregon. She shuffled further until she came to the name Philip Benson. Lazaro was the real son of a gringo *hacendado* from El Paso, a man who had vast lands in Chihuahua. It meant nothing to her. She shuffled grimly through the files until she located the name Madelaina Obregon. Her eyes scanned the original charges: *Committed to Madrigal, charged with murder, resisting arrest, immoral conduct, prostitution without license or medical certificates.* She smirked when she read the charges leveled against Corporal Jiminez. The files indicated that Alicia and Amelia Scandoval had been arrested as spies for Emiliano Zapata. Collecting the files and release forms, she was about to leave the office when she heard a light knock at the door. She stiffened.

"Madelaina? Madelaina?" It was Paco Jimenez. She sighed heavily. Opening the door, she pulled him inside.

"What is it, *señorita?*"

Quickly, losing no time, she explained the daring plan she had hatched to escape. "We can't lose. Most of the sisters are at prayer to their devils in the chapel."

"You're crazy, woman! Crazy, I tell you!" Paco's dark eyes widened incredibly. "We've no chance. No chance at all. The gates are all heavily manned!"

"We do have a chance, Paco, if you'll do exactly what I tell you." She waved the forged pardons and release forms under his nose.

He stared dumbly at her, his eyes dropping to the papers.

"*Demonio!* You are adding forgery to your crimes? *Pues,* what a crazy woman you are. It's true you make bargains with the devil! Where do you come by such courage?"

"One day, Paco, I'll explain. For now, we must make haste!"

It was a daring scheme, a chance in a million. But for them—Madelaina, Paco and the two young girls— it was now or never! With the combined efforts of Lazaro and the others, they waylaid three nuns, changed clothing with them, tied up the victims, and placed them in another room to be found later by those other *sisters of mercy!*

In less than a half-hour, the escapees, their release papers safely intact, drove up to the heavily guarded gate in a wagon used for obtaining supplies in Manzanillo. They presented a special pass, signed with the Mother Superior's forged signature, and a requisition for supplies. Under Paco's uniform was a heavy ammo belt, which had been secured along with guns that had been hidden by the perfidious nuns. The guards glanced at him and at the papers, and with more to do than be concerned as to why the Mother Superior needed more supplies—twice in a week—let them pass. Paco saluted the guards and the wagon rumbled along, creaking and groaning under the strain, as two donkeys pulled it forward.

Madelaina turned back to study the lonely figure of Lazaro, who had resisted her urgings to accompany them. She'd been unable to make him understand. The fright in his eyes, terror of the unknown, outside world promoted a fearful withdrawal in him.

None of the escapees had any way of knowing that within moments of their departure from the gate, Lazaro returned to Madelaina's room, removed the gag from the Mother Superior, and was about to untie her, when suddenly she let loose a string of curses, letting him know in no uncertain terms what punishment was in store for him. He may not have fully understood her words, but her tone, the hatred and violence in her eyes was enough. Lazaro paused. All he'd ever known from this forbidding figure was harshness, reprimand, and rigid discipline. The only tenderness he'd ever received was from Alicia and Madelaina.

"Rotten, ungrateful bastard! After all I've done for you! So this is the thanks I get! Untie me, you simpering idiot! I'll see that you spend the remainder of your demented days in the dungeons! You worthless blob! You sickening scum of rotting putrefaction! *Pronto! Pronto!* Untie me, you hear?"

Lazaro stopped. Both hands flew to his ears, trying to shut out her voice and those words—the same vile words and ugliness that he had heard all his life. She wouldn't stop! She continued her tirade like an acrimonious fishwife.

Catching sight of the knife in its scabbard at her

waist, his eyes flared open. He removed it and stared at it a moment.

Mother Veronique stopped suddenly. She saw something in his eyes. Was it possible he had understood all she had said? She had no other opportunity to consider this. Quick as lightning, in that detached manner in which he did everything, he plunged the knife into her heart, again and again.

Stunned, the Mother Superior shook her head wildly for several moments in wide-eyed disbelief. It wasn't happening. It couldn't. Not to her. She had taught Lazaro everything he knew. She had been patient with him. He had turned on her. He had turned on her! Her eyes flared wildly before she died.

Lazaro undid her ties. Hoisting her over his shoulders, he moved across the bare floor, leaving puddles of blood behind him. Down the corridor he walked, pausing before her office. He opened the door and deposited the body in the chair behind her desk, propped her up, then left the room, closing the door behind him. He cleaned up the blood left trailing behind them and went about his duties as if nothing happened.

The mystery of Mother Veronique's death was never solved. When it was discovered that four inmates were missing, it was assumed they had killed her. But all this didn't come about immediately. Another violent death occurred in the prison, a fight between two psychopathic killers, who were blamed for killing the Mother Superior.

Three months later, Colonel Huerta was elevated to the post of general in the regular army by Presidente Madero, with orders to destroy the rebel in the south, Emiliano Zapata.

With General Huerta's promotion came another promotion. His protégé, Simon Salomon, became a major. In this capacity it would become the major's duty to make certain Madelaina Obregon didn't tell her story to anyone in the Madero administration, least of all her father. But other duties pressed. This rebel, Emiliano Zapata, was giving Madero problems, and Major Salomon was hastily dispatched to the territory of Moreles, never knowing that the fates of he and Madelaina Obregon would once again be strangely interwoven.

The desert heat was stifling on the afternoon of the day following Madelaina's departure from Madrigal. The three fraudulent nuns sweltered under the blistering sun, yet they didn't dare shed their monastic garb. If stopped by either the rebels or the *Federales*, they would say they were traveling to Xochimilco to attend the Festival of Flowers. Even *bandidos* would permit the holy sisters to pass unharmed.

The wagon lumbered along much too slowly. What more could be expected from two donkeys? They refused to hurry, and Paco Jimenez wasn't one of those men who understood these braying asses. There was little he could do except avoid the main roads and continue doggedly on their way toward Cuernavaca.

Recalling the camps of Pancho Villa, Madelaina assumed those of Zapata would be different. Larger perhaps, more closely guarded due to their proximity to Mexico City, those camps in and around Moreles, the territory of Zapata, had no doubt returned to government control since the revolution ended. Madelaina expected no trouble. However, she had failed to inform her companions of what Mother Veronique had told her about the cessation of the revolution. She had more pertinent things on her mind—like escape.

Alicia and Amelia began to spot familiar landmarks as they approached the village of Ayala. Up ahead, approximately a half-mile distant, pink stucco buildings with tiled roofs caught the reflection of an orange-gold sunset and caused the tile roofs to reflect like gold bars, glittering with opalescent hues, giving an almost fairytale appearance to the squalid, decaying old village. The girls nudged each other, restricting their usual animated gestures to a minimum. They pointed out to Madelaina and Paco the various lookouts and sentries their experienced eyes caught sight of on every hill, tree, and rock they passed. This of itself wasn't alarming to them. It was the dark, deserted village, which at this hour should have been teeming with life, that stirred the Sandoval girls to disquiet. Without being obvious, Madelaina caught sight of Paco, whose twitching moustache evidenced his inner tension and alarming concern.

Instinctively, Paco knew what was happening. With no desire to frighten the women, his eyes, under the sombrero, glanced grimly toward the entrance to the village up ahead. He calculated they'd be in there in ten minutes. He squashed the sombrero down squarely over his forehead to prevent the sweat from running into his eyes. Not even a coyote howled. Overhead in the distance a few soaring buzzards turned arcs against a blinding sun. Corporal Jimenez faced a desperate predicament. As a trained regular, he'd been involved in such plots and ambushes against revolutionaries in Zacatecas. He knew a trap when he saw one and felt the inner responses shooting through him like silent warnings. What to do?

"Slow down, Paco," said Alicia with an edge to her voice that allowed Paco to feel keen respect for her. She knew what was happening, too. As soon as they had lost sight of Madrigal, she had insisted to Madelaina that Paco be made to change his clothing. "We are approaching Zapata's territory. Even as a guard for three holy sisters, his uniform would resemble a sieve before he could praise the Lord or reach for his weapons."

Paco needed no further enticement. He managed to stop a peasant working in the corn fields and persuaded him to exchange clothing. Even at gun point, the peasant showed reluctance to don the uniform of a *Federale*.

"You think I'm crazy?" he said, hardly intimidated by Paco's gun. Only when Paco threw in his boots for good measure, would he consider making the change. Even then, after the wagon was underway, he saw the old man running through the fields in his underwear, holding the boots in mid-air as if he'd been given some noteworthy fortune.

Approaching the entrance, and not wishing to give any outward show of the fact they anticipated trouble, Paco slowed the donkeys down to a walk. He felt unconsciously for his rifle alongside him and the knife strapped to his chest. He wanted to reassure the women that he, Paco Jimenez, would protect them, but he couldn't without alarming them. Somehow, Paco felt they all knew of the danger and were well aware of what might happen.

The wagon turned off the dirt road onto the cobbled streets. The sounds of the creaking wagon and donkey's hooves clippety-clopping in a noisy assault against the cobbles were ear-shattering against the unnatural silence. The feeling they were under the watchful surveillance of a thousand eyes possessed each of the escapees from Madrigal.

"Pretend it's nothing unusual," instructed Madelaina. "Take your beads in hand, bow your heads, and meditate. And you, Paco, keep your eyes and ears open, but do your best to act like a stupid, ignorant *peón*," she insisted firmly.

They passed boarded-up houses, where behind every shuttered window and locked door, the lights had been extinguished. Even the animals made no sounds. Wanted posters offering rewards for the capture of Emiliano Zapata were plastered on all the buildings. Shops were boarded up; the *cantina* unusually silent; even the mission generated a feeling of foreboding. Continuing past the broken walls of the stucco church, the wagon rumbled loudly toward the exit leading from Ayala back into the desert and finally came to a stop at the well. Paco had to water the mules and put feedbags on them if they hoped to travel on to their destination.

He sprang from the wooden seat and stretched; rubbing his aching body. From under the frayed edges of the sombrero, his busy eyes took in their surroundings. He took his time fastening the feedbags to the animals and gazed beyond the village as he did, past the large stables into the mountainous areas.

As the women came off the wagon to stretch and

rub their aching bodies, Madelaina exclaimed softly, *"Dios mios!* Of what are we so apprehensive? If, as that sister of the devil, Mother Veronique, mentioned, the revolution has ended, why should we be concerned? Madero sits in the seat of the president."

"Is this true, *chiquita?*" asked Alicia blinking her wide black eyes in utter amazement. Both sisters exchanged concerned glances, then turned slowly to glance back at the soundless, motionless village square.

"I can't attest to the truthfulness of that bald-headed vulture, but what reason would she have to deceive me? Besides, neither Huerta nor that vile butcher of his, Salomon, has been to Madrigal for three weeks. Does that not suggest something unusual has occurred in our land?"

They all agreed, except Paco Jiminez. He couldn't shake the feeling that something was drastically wrong. Before he could open his mouth, he noticed Madelaina, her eyes wandering beyond the half-spectacles she had taken from the nun to aid in her disguise, slowly approaching him.

"If the revolution has ended, Paco, then what is happening? You're a soldier, what do you make of this deserted village?"

"All is not as it should be. I must insist we do nothing to appear we are anything else but what we are pretending to be," he said quietly to the girls.

"Where are the campsites, Alicia?" asked Madelaina.

"Not far. Something is amiss, *señorita.* What? I don't know." Alicia's eyes continued to sweep the area. She turned to Madelaina and caught sight of her pale face. "Are you all right? You look pale, exhausted, *querida.*"

Weakened considerably from the loss of blood, fatigued, yet fully determined to leave Madrigal as swiftly as possible, she had not mentioned to the others that she'd been hemorrhaging. She had half-hoped they'd cut southeast to Cuernavaca to her hacienda where they'd all be safe and could rest until they got their bearings. Besides, thoughts of her unfinished business with *La Condesa* superseded all personal feelings of discomfort and pain. "I'll be fine as soon as we are on our way," she told the others. "Don't worry about me. We have more problems to concern ourselves with in these next few minutes, *amigos,* than we might be able to handle."

"Stay here, all of you," spoke up Alicia with a special brand of courage seen only in *campesinas.* "I'll discover what's happening. If Zapata's people have been dispersed to the hills, we shall find them. If it's true, Madelaina, that the revolution has ended, we may have difficulty finding our people." She patted her sister's hands comfortingly.

"Where are you going?" asked Amelia, trembling noticeably. "Don't leave me, Alicia." Ever since the girl had been subjected to the brutality of Captain Salomon, who'd taken a shine to her, she'd never been the little hellion she once was. Her spirit had snapped like that of a splendid stallion broken to the saddle.

"You're with friends, little sister," consoled Alicia. "Don't be frightened. It's all behind us. Madelaina and Paco are one of us. I'm just going to the mission to speak with Padre Segismundo. He'll tell me what's happening. I shall return shortly."

"Perhaps, Alicia, if you put on your peasant's clothing, you'd be safer." Madelaina wasn't certain, but she felt this was all wrong. "What if the *padre* asks questions of you about your order? Will you know what to speak of? Your vows? Do you know the vows of any order?"

Alicia stopped in her tracks. "Is it all so complicated? I know the *padre.*"

Madelaina nodded. "What if another *padre* should be there in his place? One you don't know? What if this is some trap? We all feel something. Is it not so, Paco?"

Paco stood next to the mules, pretending to wait patiently for them to finish their oats. His eyes continued to roam about the empty buildings and shuttered windows: "Yes, something. What I do not know. It's a trap. Some sort of trap and we are only incidental. It's best we are on our way. If we have been watched, it will appear strange to suddenly see a peasant girl emerge from a nun, no?"

"You see, Alicia? It pays to talk things over," said Madelaina. "I'll go to see this Padre Segismundo. What does he look like?"

"He is short and fat with a bulbous nose and a paunched stomach. He burps all the time. His indigestion is so bad. He has no hair except for a fringe around the crescent moon of his head. He has kind brown eyes, like those of a calf, and the finger of his left hand—the middle finger—looks like mine." She held up her crushed finger. "You think some Mother Superior cracked his fingers, too?" She smiled ironically.

Paco walked to her side. "You think it's wise, *señorita*? You may be trespassing upon more than you can handle."

"If we go farther, there's no telling what we'll encounter. If we stay here without knowing what's underfoot, we can get trampled unwittingly. I prefer to make some attempt to save ourselves. Give me a pistol, Paco. Make sure it's loaded. And if you have a spare knife, I'll take that, too."

"Oh, Madelaina. You will be careful," exclaimed Alicia.

"I'll be careful. Now, quickly, tell me, Alicia, is the *padre* you speak of on good terms with Zapata?"

She nodded.

"Can you add anything to what you've told me that might help me?" she asked the girl. Alicia shook her head. "What about you, Paco? Any suggestions?"

"You wouldn't listen if I suggested you don't go, *señorita,* so I can only beg of you to be careful. *Vaya con Dios,*" said Paco Jimenez.

Madelaina nodded. With the small arms and knife hidden on her person, she told them to sit on the wagon and say their beads. She suggested to Paco that

301

he appear to be dismayed with the donkeys should anyone stop to question him.

"Hide all your papers and pretend you're an illiterate, if it becomes necessary. And for God's sake, no aggression. Understand? Under no circumstances are you to come after me. If I do not appear in a half-hour, you are to take the women to Cuernavaca. I don't care how you get there, but get there. If you have to use your wits, then do so. We'll all meet at my hacienda. Understand?"

"Si, Capitána!" said Paco mockingly, in response to her abrupt and authoritative voice. "For the love of God, return to us and be careful!" He blushed.

"Forgive me. It was not intended to offend. You will give courage to the women in my absence. And, Paco—" began Madelaina, observing him closely.
"Si?"

"I said only courage. Understand?" She smiled tenderly in understanding.

She was gone before he replied. From where she walked on the rutted dirt roads, she could see the small chapel opposite the fountain in the square of the village. It was strange all this silence. Even the *cantina* was soundless. Not a sleeping *peón* or a small *niño* walking about. She kicked up small swirls of dirt and the black shoes and hem of the habit turned gray.

She passed the stable, slowly gazing at the steeds tethered behind it. The neighing of a stallion caused her to turn in his direction. For an instant Madelaina paused. Again the neighing sound, the short familiar grunts came to her. She shielded her eyes. Was it possible? *Madre de Dios,* Don Quixote! You're imagining things, woman, she told herself. It was difficult for her to see the entire stallion, before a hand reached out and guided it inside the stable. It's the sun, playing tricks on you. How many times in the past have you thought you saw Don Quixote? Woman! Pay attention to the job ahead.

Unconsciously she frowned as the feeling of being under scrutiny intensified. Head bowed, rosary in hand, she plodded along, eyes straight ahead. At last she was there. She stepped onto the cobbles of the two steps leading to the high vaulted door of the mission. Grasping the thick cord in her hand, she shook it hard and the bell sounded loudly, crashing through the unnatural silence.

No dogs barked, no little children's cries were heard, not a horse or mule could be heard now, no one stirred in the marketplace. *Demonio!* A shiver raced through her. She kept her head bowed as she again rang the chapel bell—louder—more persistently.

A small peep hole opened up. "Go away, Sister," hissed a hoarse voice.

"Padre Segismundo, *por favor*. I am Sister Maria Madelaina. I need directions."

"In God's name, go away!"

"I'll not go away. I demand to speak to the holy father," she said, raising her voice authoritatively.

The door opened. An arm reached out and yanked her into the dark dismal courtyard. She glanced about. "Padre Segismundo?"

"He's coming now," muttered a surly peasant with a thick handlebar *mostacho* and a conical sombrero. He looked much like those *compadres* of Pancho Villa. His manners were greatly lacking, she thought as she faced the two six-shooters aimed at her.

"In the house of God, you have need for those irons, *muchacho?*"

The peasant grinned a toothless smile. "You talk like a *campesina, monja*." He called to someone in the building beyond the courtyard.

"*Una hermana religiosa!* A nun wishes to speak with Padre Segismundo." he said to the pear-shaped friar who ambled toward her. In every way, he fit the description given her by Alicia.

"Yes, Sister. What can I do for you? You must excuse our village. We've been under siege by the beast Emiliano Zapata for the past week. The *Rurales*—thank God for them—have saved us from massacre.

303

Right now they await that ferocious animal. Where is your party? How many are with you?'

She hadn't mentioned a party. She grew alert. "At the edge of town. We are lost and need to rest for the night. We are headed to the floral festival in Xochimilco. Can you give us shelter? We won't take much space and promise to be no trouble."

"Let me give you wine to drink, Sister. I'll try to explain further. This is no place for you." He extended his hand and pointed to the inner building.

It was at this moment that Madelaina noticed the friar's left hand. His middle finger was not mutilated. She felt for the security of her gun inside her sleeve and nodded, following him.

Inside the rectory, a modest room with a desk, two chairs, and a few religious icons strewn about, he pulled out a chair for her and waited until she sat down. Her eyes were assimilating the ceiling of cracked plaster, the sweaty dripping walls, and lazy scorpions here and there, when suddenly a thought struck her. She smiled internally.

"Have you traveled far, Sister?"

"From Aguascalientes, *Padre*. We are tired."

"You came from Salamanca—through Leone?" He seemed surprised.

"The backroads, *Padre*. We are not *políticos*. You understand." Madelaina hadn't the faintest idea what she said or why she said it, but it apparently suited the occasion and the counterfeit priest.

"What order are you, pray tell?"

"We are from the Order of the Beloved Mary Magdalene, from the Abbey of Saint Ignacio. There are two other sisters and our guide, a *peón* who has worked at the Abbey for the Mother Superior for ten years. Is there something wrong?"

The *padre* poured wine for her and for himself. "If I may be so bold, you look pale. In fact, if I'm any judge, you look ill."

"Your eyes are quite perceptive. Yes. I've been ill

304

this trip. I suffer from consumption." She coughed effectively, holding her hands to her lips.

She saw him pull away slightly. "My companions both have been quite ill, *Padre*. It is for this reason we go to the festival. It is our understanding that that beloved sainted man, Padre Leopoldo, who studied in Europe with the latest of medicines, will be there. We hope our trip is not for naught."

"What is wrong with your companions?" asked the astute imposter.

"You must have noticed, *Padre,* that our wagon is stationed outside the village. And—well, you see, I don't know how to put this delicately, but—"

"You're not—I mean they aren't—" He was almost afraid to say the words.

"Yes, *Padre*. They are lepers. Are you not familiar with the Order of the Beloved Mary Magdalene? I was certain all the *padres* knew of us—"

"Yes, yes, I just forgot. It's out of the question, Sister. You cannot seek refuge here this evening. Besides, all is not what it appears to be. I am not Padre Segismundo." He flung open his robes. "I am Capitán Pablo Patricio of the *Rurales*. This village is under marshal law. If I were you, I'd get my companions out of here as quickly as possible. I'll see you have a few provisions and put you on the road to Xochimilco. Now make haste. Leave before you are caught in a holocaust!"

While he spoke, Madelaina noticed the manner in which he backed away from her. Nervous, edgy, he recoiled as if she indeed were the leper. She smiled internally. Very well, the story had merit after all.

Caught off guard by this woman, he had agreed to more than he intended. Anything to rid himself of her and the others. "We shall put the supplies on the steps of the chapel. Have your man pick them up and be gone." He handed her a crude sketch of the road, showing her where she must turn off.

"Do not tarry, Sister. You are in Zapata territory."

"Zapata? Emiliano Zapata—the terrorist? The *ban-*

305

dido?" She crossed herself quickly. *"Madre de Dios!"* She prepared to exit. "Tell me, Capitán Patricio, is the revolution not over yet? We were told before we left that Presidente Madero had replaced Diaz. That the rebels no longer rebelled. That is the reason we decided to make the trip, you see."

"Madero, eh? Hah! The people got what they wanted, but that pansy—that shrinking violet is not satisfying anyone, least of all Emiliano Zapata! He has not kept his promises, or so I'm told. Meanwhile we are all back at fighting once more. Under different banners, but nonetheless fighting and slaughtering as under Diaz. I assure you, Sister, you are very fortunate not to be a *político*. It is most confusing. Most confusing. Now, go! Leave before catastrophe befalls you and you are caught in the web of intrigue." He gulped down his wine and bowed stiffly from the waist.

"God bless you, *Capitán*. My companions and I shall pray for you."

"We'll need more than blessings, Sister. But thank you anyway."

Leading the way to the chapel door, the captain walked several feet ahead of her. From the corners of her eyes she saw several of the drab-suited, white-shirted *Rurales* with their narrow pants, boots, sombreros, and leather holsters and rifles, standing in the shadows out of sight. In the upper reaches of the building around the perimeter of the courtyard, she saw sandbagged partitions and the tips of bayonets pointing skyward.

Outside, she pointed to the steps. "Have your men place the food and water on the steps. My man Paco will retrieve them. We shall not push our presence upon you, *Capitán*. We know how sensitive the outside world is to our ills. We respect your rights. Once again, my thanks. God bless you."

"Yes, yes, Sister. Go with God." The door was slammed unceremoniously in her face.

Calm down, she told herself as she retraced the steps back to the edge of the village. Don't be excited. Don't make any sudden move. Keep your head down and give no indication you know anything. There was no question, it came together in her mind. They were at the center of an ambush, a trap. Zapata's men must be expected momentarily in this village, which the *Rurales* had garrisoned. She didn't dare look up or around at any of the buildings.

No wonder they had all felt the same feelings of being watched. She propelled herself around the last building on the street, when suddenly a hand reached out and spirited her off the street. She kicked and struggled and squirmed like an eel, but those strong hands held her in a vicelike grip.

"Be quiet, Sister. Ya ain't gonna be hurt, if ya don't squirm and shout and give us away, ya hear?" The obnoxious man spoke in an unusual, most atrocious Spanish with a drawl. Where had she heard this voice? It wasn't easy moving about in the headdress of the habit. She wondered in that moment, had Mother Veronique shaved her head to keep cool—or was she simply bald? The damned things were not only uncomfortable but hotter than Hades. This idiot who held her so close was behind her, holding her in a half-nelson-like grip. "Ya promise not to scream, Sister—an' I'll remove mah hand from yore lips."

She nodded and turned once more to face him. In the shadowy interior of the stable, she saw two more men, standing with guns poised, peering out the wooden shutters. Her abductor pushed her against the wall. "Now, Sister, suppose ya tell us what happened inside that there chapel? Who did you speak to? Ya might jus' as well tell us. Ya see that man over there with the sombrero? Ya know who he is, Sister? He's a friend to all sisters. He wouldn't hurt ya none and neither would we, ya see? That there *hombre* is Emiliano Zapata."

Madelaina backed away and moved into a shaft of light, trying to see his face. Mistaking her movement as an attempt to flee from him, he gripped her tighter. He smelled of leather and horseflesh, but there was something else. Her fingers felt clammy and numb as she withdrew from him. If only she could see his face—but even if she didn't, she knew him. God in all his mercy, am I seeing things? Is it possible? Can it be? She moved, struggled against him. In the tussling about, the concealed pistol fell from her robes to the dirt floor with a dull thud. His eyes caught sight of the metal piece.

"What's this? A gun? From the person of a sainted sister?"

"Peter!" she whispered. "My God, is it you?"

Her eyes were glued to his, watching the shocked expression on his face turn to suspicion. "Who are you?"

Her eyes had grown accustomed to the darkness, and she could see he looked haggard, worn out. His brown hair under the Stetson had grown longer, and the rough clothing he wore made him appear different than she recalled. He had grown a thicker moustache, and his sideburns were longer. His skin, darker from the sun, only emphasized the bright blue of his eyes.

Peter Duprez' eyes narrowed to slits, trying to search her face for familiar signs. "How do you know me?" He glanced at the others across the stable, all of whom were too busy in their own surveillance to be concerned with them for the moment. Recalling his hatred, his contempt for her that last time in Vera Cruz, she was frightened about revealing her identity. She didn't want to witness that same hatred. But she had to tell him. She must and take the consequences.

She raised her hand and pulled off the cumbersome headdress and shook out her long dark hair. He still didn't understand what was happening. How could he recognize her? Twenty pounds lighter, looking like a skeleton, she bore little resemblance to that little vixen on board the *Mozambique*.

"Peter, don't you know me? It's Madelaina Ob—"

Instantly he covered her mouth with his hand and pulled her over to the shuttered windows, pushing the wooden slat open slightly. A shaft of fading sunlight il-

308

luminated her features. Searching her face, he noticed the sunken hollows under her eyes and in her cheeks, her frail appearance.

"Little Fox?" His brows knit together in puzzlement. Then, recalling their last meeting, he recoiled. "What do you have in mind this time? Another dirty trick to betray me? You had a gun. Have you also a knife and other weapons? Are those companions of yours at the edge of town as phony as you—wolves in sheep's clothing?" He hissed at her, recalling her last betrayal.

No, it can't be like this. Not after all she'd done to find him, to find he still bore her malice.

"Why are you here?" she asked him, suddenly concerned that he might be involved in all this entrapment designed to capture Zapata.

"Wouldn't you like to know? So you can run and betray me again to your loving *Federales*? Once, Little Fox, only once does Pete Duprez get burned. He never gives ya another chance. Ya hear?" His features turned cruel.

"Are you on Zapata's side? Still a freedom fighter?" She lost all her desperation in light of the situation. She spoke in whispers, but her voice was firm, not like the naïve Little Fox he once knew. "In God's name, Peter, will you listen to me? I don't know why you should harbor such feelings—"

"Ya don't, eh? Damn you, you lying little bitch. You showed me yer true color when ya had me locked up in Vera Cruz. Ya think I'll give ya another chance?" His blue eyes were everywhere, hoping no one could hear them.

"Then let me speak with Emiliano Zapata." She stood her ground.

"Are ya crazy? He'd shoot you on the spot, if he knew who you are!" He pulled her back into the shadows. "If yore smart, ya'll put on them nun's duds and get outa here!" His grip was hurting her, shooting pains into her arms.

"You're setting me free? You don't trust me. You still harbor a grudge against me, thinking I betrayed you and you're willing to let me go? Hah! You're not consistent, are you, gringo? Take me to Zapata. If you don't, I'll cry out to him," she said firmly with marked indignation.

Glancing about the shadowy interior of the stable, it was difficult to make out the Zapata brothers. Emiliano and his brother Eufimo wore those conical, wide-brimmed sombreros set squarely on their heads, concealing their faces. Realizing time was flitting by quickly, Madelaina had to settle her business with Zapata and get back to the wagon to either bring them in off the streets or leave the area. Amazing, she thought, the *Rurales* expected Zapata to appear at the other end of the village and he was already but a few hundred feet away from them.

"Release my hand, Peter Duprez. Even though you are my husband, this is my country and I'll do as I please," she said imperiously.

"Ya shouldn't oughta, Little Fox," he said with a great deal of hesitation in his voice, testing her, daring her, and still concerned that she'd get herself into a jam. "This Zapata isn't a man to fool around with." Peter paused a moment. "Your husband? Wait jus' a doggone min—" But she had left his side.

"Emiliano Zapata!" she cried softly, but loud enough for the rebel leader and the others to turn to her. She must have looked a mess, for in Zapata's eyes she saw a mixture of surprise, bewilderment, and a native wariness that made him go for his holstered gun. In a flash it appeared leveled at her.

His dark flashing eyes, canny and oblique, glanced from her to Duprez.

"Que pasa, gringo?" What is this sorry sight you bring upon me at so precarious a time? Is she a holy mother—or not? What, eh?"

Madelaina spoke in Spanish. "If you don't mind I shall speak for myself. I am a *compañera* of Pancho Villa, Doroteo Arango. He calls me Little Fox, *señor*. I and my party have just escaped from Madrigal de Los Altos."

310

She was speaking so rapidly that Pete Duprez didn't catch all of her words. He saw, however, a look of astonishment spread over the *guerrillo*'s face. Zapata's hat was swept off his head in a gesture of humility and respect. Only the slightest trace of a smile softened his features before he retreated with her into a corner.

What the hell was that double-dealing, fast-talking, little bitch up to now? The fact that she had the unmitigated gall to boldly walk up to Zapata irritated Peter. He lit up a smoke and glanced beyond them both at the far corner of the stable where Captain Tracy Richards stood at his position with his dynamiters, ready to give hell to the *Rurales*. Once again he stared at Madelaina and grew sullen. She looked awful. As a matter of fact, she looked downright terrible. She had lost a lot of weight; he wouldn't have recognized her, if she hadn't called out his name. Well, if he and old Trace lived through this one, he'd have plenty of time to ask a few questions of the bitch. So she had been looking for him? He wondered why as he recalled Urbina's comments just before the Juarez encounter. He rechecked his gun and ammo belts, glowering inwardly as he returned to his position, waiting for the action to burst.

"You say this Capitán Patricio has reenforced the chapel? Where is the *padre?*" asked Zapata, frowning in thought.

"I don't know, *señor*. I know only what I've told you. The only reason the *capitán* permitted me to leave is the excuse I used that I'm taking lepers to Xochimilco."

"Lepers, Little Fox!" Zapata stood up. He had been sitting on a barrel keg close to her. His dark eyes flared open. "Lepers?" He crossed himself. "Lepers?" He backed away from her with exaggerated fear.

Madelaina smiled wanly. "It was only a ruse, *señor*. The girls are two of your own people. The man was sent to Madrigal for insubordination." She refrained from mentioning she was the daughter of General

311

Obregon. "As a matter of fact, I have one of your men to thank for betraying a traitor, José Limas. Your man Colimas revealed the traitorous snake in the grass."

"Ah, *si*. I recall, now. Something about the sister of Doroteo Arango. But never mind. If you spent all this time at Madrigal, *señorita,* you must have suffered greatly." He stroked his moustache thoughtfully.

"Yes, it's true. I suffered greatly. But it is all in the past. Tell me what all this is about? While I was in Madrigal, I heard nothing. But we were told that Madero has been seated in the presidential palace. The revolution is not over? What is happening?"

Zapata's eyes grew murderous. "I told Panchito I would help to put Madero in the president's chair, if he would restore to my people the lands Diaz stole from us. Pancho promised Madero was for the people. Well, *señorita,* Little Fox, I believed Pancho Villa. I had his word. Madero is in the palace. Now, he hedges. He tells me there are many complications—that it will take time to legally return the lands appropriated by Diaz and the *hacendados*. I've been waiting. Imagine, he tries to give Zapata a hacienda with land. But I saw, *señorita,* Little Fox, with these eyes I saw the men with whom he has surrounded himself. He can fool Panchito, my beloved friend, but he cannot fool Emiliano Zapata! Close to him stands that misbegotten son of treacherous copperhead, Huerta! Now, he's a general! Imagine! He was Chief of the Secret Police under that dictator and robber of the poor, Diaz! Now, he's a general in the Constitutional Army under Madero!" He pulled grandly at his huge dark moustache. "Listen, Little Fox, I swear to you, one day, between Zapata and Pancho Villa, the world will sit up and take notice of the Mexican people!"

"*Huerta is a general in the army of Madero?*" she repeated slowly. "And what of Captain Salomon?" she asked evenly, half afraid of the answer.

"Captain Salomon? You mean Major. He too has been promoted." Zapata bridled furiously. "You've had

312

encounters with this *animale*?" His eyes flared and he shook his head sadly. "At Madrigal they do unspeakable things to the prisoners."

Listening carefully to the conversation, the brother of Zapata eyed Madelaina carefully. Eufimo Zapata, a born hedonist, lived only to satisfy his manly instincts. He was hard. He was tough, a two-fisted, itchy-trigger-fingered hill *bandido,* with a lusty appetite and penchant to kill his obstructors. When under the influence of whiskey, he was a lusty animal, a tiger with the strength of ten men. No one ever told Eufimo which *campesina* he could take. He took any and as many as he desired, with no man to contest him. Those who in the past had objected to the appropriation of their women were now dead. There was only one man who could control Eufimo Zapata—his brother Emiliano. Only because Emiliano was a faster draw and a better shot.

Between these two was a tremendous love and respect. However, Eufimo never transgressed in the sight of his brother, and this alone led to the almost pure thoughts Emiliano held in his mind for his younger brother. Once they took over a village, he turned everything over to Eufimo, never once questioning him in his judgment unless a *compadre* decided to complain. Complainers among Zapata's men were few, when they realized they first had to contend with Eufimo.

Watching Eufimo through narrowed eyes, despite the shadowy interior of the stable, Peter Duprez recognized the lust that stirred in him.

He didn't even bother to disguise the naked desire he felt for the wench. Madelaina hadn't bothered to even glance at the wild-eyed man, and still he lusted openly for her. With an eye out on the streets, Peter pushed the boarded shutter closed and sauntered over to where Zapata sat with Madelaina.

"Ya gotta pardon me, *Jefe,*" he began. "It's been so long since I've seen my wife that I can hardly stand it."

Madelaina turned her head swiftly in marked sur-

313

prise. She saw the silent warning in his eyes but wasn't sure of his sudden solicitous behavior.

Zapata rose to his feet. "This is a day of surprises, gringo. First I am honored by the appearance of Little Fox. Now I learn she is your wife?" *Hombre!* We should have a celebration instead of this nusiance, no?"

"It don' matter none to me, Emiliano, jus' as long as when it's finished, I can be with my little woman."

"Is done," Zapata declared. "But, first, gringo, we have to make some changes. Little Fox tells me the entire village is garrisoned with *Rurales*. They are in the mission with arms and ammunition waiting for us. What do you and Captain Richards propose?"

For an instant Eufimo Zapata locked eyes with Peter. Then, shrugging, twirling the straw between his teeth, he withdrew. The contest was over. Peter had won Madelaina. It was as simple as that. Eufimo wouldn't contest the gringos who came to help their cause as they'd helped Pancho Villa in Juarez. Who would dare contest a gringo with such courage and *corazón?* Not Eufimo. At least not now. These gringos were ruthless and fast with their guns.

"Trace," called Duprez to the man at the far end of the stable, looking out one of the openings. He beckoned to him.

The flamboyant, swaggering mercenary with his double *bandoleras* criss-crossed over his chest moved toward them. His eyes took in the picture and he frowned. He could smell trouble a mile away and he didn't like what he saw.

"Madelaina, this is Captain Tracy Richards. Trace, this is my wife, Little Fox. You've heard enough about her. Now it's time you meet."

The subtle awareness that crossed the face of this hard-bitten gunman from across the border was expertly concealed. He whipped off his sombrero and nodded respectfully. "So! We meet at last, Mrs. Mix. Gotta hand it to ya, Tom Mix, ya sure know how to pick 'em. A sister of mercy?" He shook his head teasingly.

314

"Ah didn't know it was permitted down here, south of the border."

Madelaina was more confused and growing more so by the minute. Tom Mix? He called Peter, Tom Mix. Was this a joke? Was Peter in hiding? She grew alert and tried not to show her concern. For several moments they ignored her as they spoke of the news she brought. Something about bombs, dynamite, crossfire and *guerrillo* tactics. Apparently something had been decided.

Peter approached her, took her arm, and pulled her to the far end of the stable where they'd been earlier. "You've gotta get out of here. There's gonna be some damn big fireworks, and you shouldn't oughta be here. One of the men is gonna sneak out the back an' escort ya back to Zapata's camp."

"What time is it, Peter or Tom Mix—which is it? Why are you incognito?"

"Haven't time to explain." He glanced at the pocket watch he pulled from his vest pocket. "Why ya so interested in the time?" he asked suspiciously.

"Oh for the love of God! Stop it! I'm too tired to contest you. I've got two women and a man with me. I ordered them to leave for Cuernavaca if I hadn't returned in a half-hour. Now, will you tell me the time?"

"Gladly. 6:15."

"No," she said fully dismayed. "By now, then, they would have left. I should have returned at 5:30. I didn't realize how long I've been here."

"Well, you can't stay here. You'll have to go with Zapata's man."

"Why did you tell Zapata we are man and wife?"

"Why not? It's the truth, isn't it?"

"I didn't think you remembered—or even cared. You never once tried to communicate with me."

"The woman who betrayed me to the *Federales*? Hah! What I said earlier goes," he said quietly, with one eye on Eufimo. "It's jus' that I don't trust the *jefe*'s brother. He was watching ya with desire written all over him. And knowing him like I do, if he lays

315

claim to ya, there ain't no body who'd try to stop him, 'cept me an' I don't aim to be shot up by Zapata himself!"

"For nearly two years I searched for you," she began.

"You think I believe such rot gut? Hah! Look, I got no time for chitchattin', Little Fox. Ya gotta git from here as fast as you can."

"No. I'll stay. I can shoot a gun as well as any *soldadera*. I did so in the camps of Pancho Villa. I can do the same standing next to my husband," she retorted, pulling off the black habit of the nun. She had on trousers and a shirt, something Lazaro had rounded up for her before they left Madrigal. She stood before him stubborn, proud, and determined. Before he could protest further, a shot rang out. It sounded as if it came from the entrance to the village. There was little time for anything. He handed her a rifle. "You asked for it, kid. Now, do your stuff! Damn, don'cha shoot until I give the sign, ya hear? An' when I do, shoot every one of 'em fuckin' *Rurales* in sight!"

From the rear of the stable came a half-dozen or more *guerrillos* carrying handmade bombs, much like the ones Captain Richards and his companions made for the attack on Juarez. They scampered from the stable, each in different directions, with enough dynamite in their hands to blow up the entire village.

The plan, straightforward and neat, had been to ambush the *Rurales*. However, it became apparent from the news Little Fox had imparted that their plan had been betrayed. There was no way they could approach the village from either entrance and not be decimated. This took strategy. With the aid of the gringos, Zapata came up with a plan bound to bring them victory. Zapata's men were to ring the village from the rear. At the signal, they'd hurl the bombs down toward the main arena—the village square. Meanwhile a diversion would be created in the village square drawing the *Rurales'* rifle fire, while the main thrust of Zapata's men would move in with artillery and capture the *Rurales*.

The sunset was growing into twilight. The stable was stuffy; animal smells made Madelaina feel sick to her stomach. If she hadn't been so weak, she might have fared better. But nothing under God's sun would make her complain to Peter Duprez. She thought about him in those next ten minutes of utter silence and mounting tension. He hadn't been happy to see her. He barely remembered her. Well, like all things, this too would pass. Perhaps it was best. At least she'd seen him. Their meeting had fallen short of the expectations of her romantic mind. Very well, she'd finish here with Zapata and request an escort to Cuernavaca, where she could recuperate. At this moment, she hadn't the strength to think beyond this. She was so weak she cared for nothing. In fact, she'd even welcome death.

Then came a rumbling sound of fast riding as a few dozen *Zapatista* horsemen, dragging brush at the end of their *riatas*, raised enough dust for three cavalry squadrons and came charging toward the entrance of the village. Simultaneously, the bombers with their surprise packages rode down the hills to the rear of the village and hurled their leather-wrapped dynamite overhead. The explosions were deafening. Over 200 men poured down the slopes on horseback, trapping the *Rurales* in the village with their cross-fire. The sounds of whooping, shooting men thundered all around them. Artillery cracked loudly. Shouts of *"Viva Zapata! Viva Zapata!"* filled the air.

Peter Duprez, Captain Tracy Richards, and Emiliano Zapata, pistols in hand, moved out along the street, ducking in and out of shadows and doorways on their way to the mission to capture it and Capitán Pablo Patricio.

Snipers overhead, unable to see through the dust, shot wild. One *Rurale* jumped through an open window, landing a few feet behind Zapata. Before he could pull the trigger on his rifle to kill the *guerrillo*, Peter Duprez peeled off two shots from his six-guns. The

317

man fell over, dropping his rifle. Rolling into the gutter, he reached into his shirt and pulled out a grenade. A shot rang out behind Peter. Madelaina had sprinted from the stable, rifle in hand, and caught the soldier. She hurriedly retrieved the grenade and tossed it across the narrow street into a *tienda*, the small shop where earlier she'd seen sandbags and bayonets.

The building crumbled. Peter Duprez ran after her and pulled her up from the ground. He pulled her to safety between two doorways and held her close to him. "You fool! Are you trying to get yourself killed?" he hissed with a mixture of grave concern and anger. He held her tightly. She glanced up at him, and in that moment, with death knocking at both the front and rear doors, they kissed. God, how they kissed.

It wasn't the usual kiss. It was frustration, anger, violence, fierce emotion, the need to make up for lost time; sorrow, hatred, and forgiveness, all rolled into one. His breath came faster, hers was overwhelming as she gasped for air. Suddenly their hearts beat so furiously they had to stop for a second to catch their breath. Two years had suddenly been spanned in the space of a few moments. A montage of pictures flashed into their memories as unlocked drawers sprang open, showering them with hundreds of vivid impressions and bottled-up emotions to correspond with the feelings they experienced. They stared into each other's eyes, unable to believe the joy they felt. In the middle of a goddamned war, with bombs bursting all around them, they took the time to kiss. In those few seconds they had made a lifetime of love with their eyes.

"It's crazy!" shouted Peter Duprez, his face a broken rhythm of smiles. "We're both crazy!" He pulled her to him, holding her tighter than before. "Listen, you get yourself back into that stable and stay there until I get back, ya hear me, Little Fox?" He commanded her with love in his voice. "God! It's been a long time coming, sweet thing. What a sweet night this will be!"

He watched her creep back into the stable, and only

318

when she was safely inside, did he fall in quickly to join the others, shouting, yahooing and cheering.

Machine guns opened fire on the riders dragging brush behind them as they charged down the main street time and again. White flashes of fire burst in the night as gun fire continued in a barrage between rebels and soldiers.

A soldier jumped Peter Duprez, knocking him off balance, but the soldier was instantly hit from overhead. Duprez rolled over and, back on his feet, charged into the chapel.

It was a madhouse. Screams pierced the air. *"Viva Zapata!" "Viva La Revolucion!"* There came more cries and more followed those. *"Viva La Revolucion!"*

The walls of the mission caved in along the southern sector. It was man to man, rebel to enemy, hand to hand, gun against gun, saber to saber. Dead bodies littered the floor, rivers of crimson blood flowed. Peter, unable to find Tracy Richards or Zapata, raced up the side stone steps to the upper attic chambers. He shot the lock off the door and kicked it in. There, huddled in enormous groups, were the women of the village, who had been hidden from sight and locked in with no chance of escape. Seeing the gringo with blue eyes, they rose to their feet, screaming their thanks to God and to him. He herded them out and down the stairs.

A few of the hysterical, wailing women went berserk and scambled in all directions—anyplace for safety. A few more clung to Peter as if he were their saviour. He ordered them to take cover, wherever they could.

"Vaya! Vaya!" he shouted, hoping to disperse them.

A few picked weapons off dead bodies and began to shoot the soldiers in the street. With murder in their eyes and vengeance in their hearts, most of these impromptu *soldaderas* were as good a shot as Zapata's crack snipers. A few took refuge inside the stable alongside Madelaina, where she stood firing away at the *Rurales* who rode by on horseback.

It was over as suddenly as it had begun. It was dark outside. A few women lit torches and ran outside. The

319

dead were everywhere. The women silently walked among the dead men, trying to identify their lovers, husbands, sons, and family. Sobs rang out as some found their loved ones. Screams, shouting, heart-rending sounds. Added to these sounds came those of victory. Yells and wahoos, and *"Viva Zapata!"* *Zapatistas,* wearing four, five, even six ammo belts and double-holstered guns, carrying additional rifles, picked up the dead *Rurales,* moved among the dead bodies littering the street, calling to the older men to clean up the streets.

Unable to stand the suspense and lacking the strength to fight off some of Zapata's men who had broken into the *cantina* to begin their drinking and to seek their women for the night, Madelaina took her chances out on the street, hiding in the shadows, looking for Peter. She avoided the horsemen who had been drinking heavily. On either side of her she saw women scooped off the ground and dragged protestingly to some remote corner where the men could satisfy the urges buried deep in their loins.

Suddenly, out of nowhere came two strong arms, one around her mouth, the other pinning her back against him. She struggled, trying to fight off her abductor. "Be quiet, Señorita Obregon, or I shall turn you over to the *Zapatitas.* When your true name is revealed, they will know how to deal with the daughter of General Obregon."

Madelaina couldn't turn to see her captor, but she ceased struggling. That voice. She shivered inwardly. *Dios mios.* No. Not that *animale!* She didn't have to look to know who it was. The liquor on his breath was enough to make her relive the nightmare at Madrigal.

"Major Salomon!" she hissed when he released her. He held a gun at her temple. She glanced askance at him, trying to face him.

"So, even the stone walls of Madrigal couldn't hold the Little Fox? You'll accompany me back to Mexico, my dear, and stand trial for treason, or any other charge I can trump up against you. General Huerta

320

will consider this disastrous affair at Ayala a victory when I present him with this prize." He pulled her along with him, heading toward the rear of the stables where a few horses were tethered. He walked cautiously, ready for any surprise.

She felt faint. Earlier, through sheer will, she had convinced herself to be strong and endure whatever came. She and Peter would soon be reunited. Now that faint glimmer of hope was dying, and she found herself sinking slowly into an abyss.

She couldn't recall exactly what happened. Only that she saw a blur of motion. Major Salomon, that despotic, devilish monster, had released her and she fell crashing against the stable wall. Another shadow emerged, and now two men fought each other, hand to hand. Shadows moved before her, but her eyes grew so heavy, she could no longer hold them open. She fell into a black pit of uncertainty where everything stopped for her.

When Madelaina awakened, she felt intense discomfort. Her eyes flittered open to the black of night. Wrapped in blankets, she was unable to free herself. No matter how she struggled, it was of no use; she was bound tight. When her eyes grew accustomed to the darkness and her awareness returned, she realized she was in the back of a wagon. She tried desperately to see who was driving.

Her head was backed against the buckboard divider and, even tilting her head back as far as she could, she could barely see the head or shoulders of the person driving. Her last recollection was of Major Salomon. He had told her he would take her to Mexico City. Now he had her. She closed her eyes again. Her head grew befuddled and murky. Thoughts refused to clear and what's more, she had lost all resistance. She let herself sink lower and lower until she fell unconscious again. Not even thoughts of her brief reunion with her husband could stimulate her enough to fight the heavy blanket which pressed upon her.

There were times when she seemed to awaken from

321

a dream, a hazy dream mixed with unrealities, in which she'd tear the clothes off her body, feeling herself on fire and desperately wanting Peter Duprez. Her body, an instant traitor to her mind, ached for his embraces, and she'd shudder through the nights that were sheer torture for her because the need for his flesh against hers, the touch of his lips against hers, and the desperation of unfulfilled moments with him possessed every part of her body and mind. But these dreams, these nightmares, were always accompanied by the faces of General Huerta and Major Salomon, lurking in the background, zooming closer and closer into her consciousness until all traces of Peter Duprez faded from mind.

Book Four

The Gringo Brigade In Juarez

Chapter 13

Many of the *Zapatistas* returned to the hacienda of Emiliano Zapata, a sprawling estate recently appropriated by his brother Eufimo in retaliation for the Madero ultimatum. The men had all been drinking heavily after the last of the fighting. The *cantina* was relieved of most of its stock by the revolutionists, all bent on having a merry time. Most remained in Ayala.

It was their usual way of dulling the reality of the fighting and killing and what must be done following such a battle. The dead littered the streets in numbers Peter had never seen before. Not even the Battle of Juarez had resulted in as much carnage as did this relatively small skirmish in Ayala. All those *Rurales* caught alive in the mission and those rounded up by the *Zapatistas* had been herded together. The officers and noncoms, thirty in all, had been hanged by their their necks on the fig trees at the edge of town. Seventy-five soldiers had been lined up and machine-gunned to death. The rest, dead in the streets, were piled up and buried beneath the desert sands. Zapata, like Pancho Villa, believed in taking no *Rurale* as prisoner.

All in all, ten *Zapatistas* were dead, fifteen sustained minor injuries, and the remaining 275 were drinking, brawling, and coupling with anyone in sight. From someplace came the sound of singing and music, with guitarists strumming lively tunes of victory. There was laughter and sounds of victory. There was laughter and sound of rejoicing from one end of the village to the other—incongruous in the wake of so many dead.

As soon as he had dealt with his responsibilities, Peter Duprez hurried back to the stable to find his wife.

Madelaina was nowhere to be found. He searched among the dead, interrupted couples in their love-making to see if she had been abducted and become an unwilling victim of one of Zapata's men. He even searched for Eufimo, recalling the lusty desire he displayed for Madelaina earlier. Sometime during his search, he began to experience a sinking sensation.

He began to guzzle from a bottle of tequila shoved into his hands by one of the revelers. He stopped to make inquiries of many of the women he had released from the loft in the mission chapel. Had any of them seen a young *chiquita* dressed in the pants of a man? "She was about so high—hair as black as a raven's wing. Eyes the color of midnight sapphires, skin like ivory." The women's answers, laced with raucous laughter and mischievous glances, were the same. "No, *señor*. We've seen no such angel in this village. Whores, yes. But no angels."

Gazing about the stable filled with couples bent on romantic interludes, Peter couldn't have felt worse. When the gypsy *campesina* Lucia sidled up to him, hoping to intrude on his self-imposed privacy, he ignored her for a time, even tried to push her from him.

"Hey, gringo, why you not like Lucia? I am friend to Rosalia Quintera, the *soldadera* of Captain Richards. For too long I like you, gringo."

She leaned against him, rubbing her body close to his. Peter glanced up at her through slightly bleary eyes. By now the tequila had begun to affect him. He'd never been much of a drinker. Beer and wine, yes. But he couldn't take the hard stuff. In the shadows, she didn't look too bad. "Oh, what the hell," he said aloud. He put an arm around her and suddenly felt her hands all over him, like a child cut loose in a candy store.

Lucia wasn't shy or retiring in the least. She leaned over him and kissed him deeply. His body instantly provided the response the girl wanted. Peter's mind was curiously distracted by the recollection of a kiss he'd experienced earlier. For so long he'd harbored a grudge against Madelaina. Then, in Juarez, when Villa's lieutenant, Urbina, asked him about Little Fox, he had so desperately wanted to believe it was Madelaina. Even Tracy had hinted that some young *señorita* was asking about him, but due to the circumstances, he had changed his name to Tom Mix and the inquiries had stopped.

Recollections of Madelaina and their love-making on the *Mozambique* played themselves over and over in his mind. Oh, there'd been many other women, as there had been before he met the young vixen, ten years his junior. But none had captivated him as had Madelaina Obregon. Her naïveté and her willingness to learn about love had automatically placed him in the position of teaching her, and in so doing, he found he had tailored her to satisfy his needs. Many nights he'd lain out under the Texas stars on his modest spread outside of San Antonio, wild thoughts of Madelaina rushing into his mind, accompanied by the exciting pictures of her in the embrace of love with him. At times Peter had gotten so worked up, he'd have to find a woman to get Madelaina out of his system. No one satisfied him—not in the way his own special Galatea had gratified his needs.

All the while he'd been making love to his bit of baggage, Lucia, he'd been thinking of Madelaina. He could hardly believe it was over so soon, when they both lay back in one of the many horse stalls in the stable, momentarily exhausted from their love making.

It wasn't fair to Lucia or to himself to be thinking of another woman, but he couldn't help it. His thoughts always trailed back to Madelaina. She had changed greatly. She was thinner, more haggard than he remembered her. Etched into her pale face had been traces of some tragic episode—something traumatic. That kiss! What a kiss it had been. It promised everything and forgave all instantly. He'd never felt so wonderfully warm inside. At that minute he'd have ridden off into the sunset with her, if there hadn't been more pertinent things to attend to. Dang-blasted maverick.

Wheah in tarnation was she? She promised she'd stay here in the stable. She wouldn't have promised, if she hadn't intended to keep that promise. There was so much he wanted to learn from her. She mentioned she'd been searching for him for two years. Only real love would drive a woman into this life in search of her man. Could he have so misjudged her? It would be difficult for Peter Duprez to really trust anyone in light of all that had happened in his life, yet he was willing to trust Madelaina. It was a first for him. Just to be willing to place his trust in another human being. What was it about Madelaina that suddenly inspired such trust, he asked himself. What?

Peter sat up, disengaging the woman's arms about his neck.

"Don't go, gringo. I have more pleasure for you," she said lazily, trying to trap him in her arms.

"In a while, *chiquita*. All that tequila—yer love-making—all o' that, ah've gotta perform a service to mah body," he said quietly.

"Ah, *si*. Come back soon." Lucia smiled with inner satisfaction.

"Ah'll return as soon as these here legs o' mine can carry me."

Peter Duprez had spotted a woman he'd released from the loft in the mission earlier, moving in and about the cluttered stable. He'd seen her enter the stable and took a chance she might know something about his Little Fox.

"*Chiquita, esperar usted.* Wait for me," he said in his atrocious Spanish. "Did you see a *señorita* earlier, dressed in men's trousers and a shirt?" He described Madelaina and was hard put to disguise his genuine concern for her.

"Ah, *si*, gringo. She was here before. The one with a rifle, no?"

"That's the one, little *chiquita*."

"A *Federale* took her. I think she is the one I saw." She described the man. "I remember that man, an *hombre muy mal*, very bad man." She shuddered in

328

recollection. "I was hidden in the tack room over at the other side of the stable." She gestured. "I saw him grab the woman from behind. He held a *pistola* to her head. She didn't appear to be so willing. I listened. Well, *señor*, I'm no fool. My fingers tightened on the gun, the one I picked up from a dead *Rurale*." She spat the word hatefully. "I followed, ready to blow his guts out if he didn't release the woman. Suddenly everything was A-O.K." She smiled shyly at the use of gringo slang. "The *señorita* was saved by her lover."

Peter stiffened. "Her lover?"

"*Si*, her lover. Who else would beat this son of seven devils and leave him bleeding to death? Ah, *señor*, you should have seen how tenderly he picked up the *señorita* in his arms. You see, she had fainted. But he held her as one would hold his lover, so concerned." She sighed. "They left, *señor*, in a wagon, perhaps one, two hours ago. But do not worry, that *caballero* will take care of that lucky *señorita*." She rolled her eyes suggestively and moved along.

As one in a daze, he returned to the warm, waiting arms of Lucia. Before he could slip down alongside her, Lucia rose on her knees in a catlike movement, her arms encircling his waist. She pulled him down greedily on top her. She fumbled with his belt buckle, unfastened his trousers, and, before he could say Tom Mix, he reacted quickly to her greedy manipulations.

Peter pulled a screen across his mind, shutting out all thoughts of Madelaina. In his arms was a passionate kitten, something tangible, something he could feel and not have to imagine. He was breathing heavily now, responding in kind to Lucia. She wasn't bad, this little one. Maybe he should saddle himself with a *campesina,* just as ole Trace had been telling him for the past six months since Juarez.

She was some woman, this hot little spitfire. She made no pretense at what she wanted—played no little games. She knows what she wants, and by Jupiter she gets it, he told himself with a tight smile. She could make him forget. That's what Peter Duprez needed. To forget. He felt himself sail into an open sky of fire and then come nosediving into sultry clouds of silk until he was filled with peace.

It was nearly dawn. They had made love a half-dozen times or more, he couldn't remember. At some time, he was struck by something Madelaina had told Zapata. She had been en route to her hacienda in Cuernavaca with two of Zapata's *campesinas* and some man sentenced to Madrigal for insubordination. Peter stopped his mind. She told Zapata she'd been detained in Madrigal. Madrigal? Where had he heard the name before? Where was it? What was it?

Lucia stirred and opened one eye. She observed the gringo as he lit a cigarette and sat up on the ground, his knees drawn up close to his body.

"Aye, gringo," she whispered sleepily. "Come back to me. It's cold without you next to me."

"Lucia." He paused. "Look, little *chiquita,* ah got somethin' ta ask ya. Ya ever hear of something called Madrigal? It's a place or a city or something."

"Come to sleep, gringo. Is too early to make with such heavy words—" Both eyes snapped open. Lucia didn't move. Her voice, husky and alarmed, repeated, "M—Madrigal? Madrigal de Los Altos?" She crossed herself and bolted upright, cowering from him. "Why you ask about Madrigal, gringo?" She fairly recoiled. "How you know of such a place, eh?"

Peter Duprez missed none of this action. "What's troublin' ya, little *chiquita*? Ah jus' asked ya a question."

"*Por favor,* gringo." She looked away, avoiding his eyes as if he'd suddenly done something horrendous. "Do not speak of such a place."

It took Peter nearly ten minutes of coaxing, and cajoling, and promising that nothing would happen to her. Would she please explain what was so terrifying about the place? Would she tell him where it was?

Lucia finally complied. When she finished, Peter almost wished he hadn't asked. He had listened to her frightening story, to the incredible tales of what went

330

on inside the prison. She knew about such a place. Two of her cousins, Alicia and Amelia Sandoval, had been taken there by Colonel Huerta's secret police. She spat the name with disgust.

Impossible! Incredible, he thought, listening to Lucia. Such places didn't exist—not here in the Americas—north or south. Then, he recalled that only recently Mexico had been under foreign rule, under despots who knew too well the ancient forms of torture. From the French, Russians, Germans, and Spanish, Mexico had tasted bitter, violent, excruciating tortures.

It was to help further the very principles of freedom enjoyed in the United States that Peter had become a mercenary. The pay wasn't bad—running guns for the rebels proved profitable. How many times had he been approached by Diaz's men to sell arms to them—and he refused. Nearly 100 Americans had joined Villa in what he affectionately called his Gringo Brigade. None of these gringos were so stupid or blind to fight for freedom on their side of the border and let slavery proliferate across the Rio Grande—it was too close for comfort. Why Washington couldn't see it was a mystery to these freedom fighters. For Peter Duprez it wasn't such a mystery. The Wall Street manipulators who romanced the Diaz regime also controlled Washington with their dollars.

As Lucia spoke, he noticed she shivered involuntarily. She was actually trembling. He wrapped her in a blanket. He began to feel the beginnings of a frustrating rage consuming him. He thought about his conversation with the woman in the stable and wondered where this *Rurale* who attempted to abduct Madelaina could be. *"Bleeding to death"* were her words. If it was true, the body had to be somewhere in the vicinity of the stable. In such a condition, the man couldn't have gotten far.

"Stay here, *chiquita*. I've got to find Captain Richards. I'll return for you. If we should get separated, you stay with Rosalia Quintera and I'll catch up to you someplace."

331

"Gringo?"

"What is it, *chiquita?*"

"She must be some woman, eh? *Cuidado, chico*. Be careful."

"Who? Who are you speaking of?"

"The woman you called me all night long. Zorrita—Little Fox."

So, he thought, I mentioned her in my sleep. It wasn't the first time; others had said the same thing to him. Peter had already buckled on his gun belt. He leaned over and planted a firm kiss on her pale lips. "Don't forget what I said. You stay with Rosalia Quintera."

He deliberately sauntered toward the side entrance of the stable, where the woman had told him she'd seen Madelaina and the *Rurale*. In the condition the woman had described, death couldn't be far from him. Either that or he was already dead. In either case, there must be some sign.

Peter stepped over sleeping bodies sprawled everywhere in the stables, side-stepping those who stirred and cracked open sleepy eyes, ever ready to use their *pistolas*. His eyes, steely blue and alert, looked everywhere as the yawning dawn lights rose over the horizon and filtered through holes in the shabby roof. He moved silently over the same route Major Salomon had earlier transported a protesting Madelaina—along the hard-packed earthen flooring where tufts of straw were carelessly strewn about in the tussle of the previous night. The stench was one of pure raw wilderness— horse dung, human perspiration, and the cheap perfume the women doused themselves with to cover their own lack of cleanliness. The traffic in and about this area had been heavy. If only his young Yaqui Indian guide, Alejo, were here, thought Peter. That mestizo could sniff out an enemy ten miles away.

Peter's eyes caught sight of a dark clump of dried earth. Squatting on his haunches, he leaned over and crumbled the dirt with his fingers, allowing it to sift through them. It was dried blood all right. It could belong to any of a hundred men shot in the battle of Ayala. His eyes scanned the countless bales of hay stacked up two and three deep on either side. There were scuffle marks of a dozen or more footprints which of themselves offered nothing concrete. Too many people had wandered through this opening since the previous evening.

The tall, lean Texan had no way of knowing that less than ten feet from him, nestled between two stacks of baled hay, away from curious and threatening eyes, Major Salomon lay bleeding profusely, stopping up the knife wounds with strips of cloth. During the night he'd managed to remove the clothing from the body of a *Zapatista* he'd sliced through the jugular in an unexpected move. Dressed haphazardly in peasant pantaloons and *camisa* of the *peón*, he looked unlike the ultrasophisticated chocolate drinker he was in his French uniform. With luck and time, Major Salomon had hoped to get away.

Those filthy rag-tag bandits had busied themselves with booze and women right before his very eyes, and twice in the dark of night, when the opportunity presented itself, he could have left. Those two attempts to move left him weaker and unable to spring from his hiding place. He knew that he could very well bleed to death and die before anyone was the wiser, but through sheer will power and a determination to live to avenge this atrocity done to his person, he gathered all his force and might, determined to remain alive until all the dirty *Zapatistas* left Ayala. If he didn't die first, he vowed he'd find the daughter of General Obregon and that motherless son of a ball-less coyote who attacked him and make them rue the day they tangled with him. He was a major now—a *somebody* in the service of Presidente Francesco Madero, under the auspices of General Huerta, the man who would be *presidente*. He was too vital to Huerta, too important to die in this godforsaken hole like an animal.

As Salomon contemplated his fate, not five feet from him, Peter Duprez sank down on a bale of hay, sad

333

and dejected that his search had located nothing of importance. His eyes were hypnotically fixed on the antics of a small mongrel dog, yipping, snorting, and tussling with something wedged between the wall of the crudely constructed stable and more stacked hay bales.

"What's up, little doggie? Ya havin' problems?" He moved across the short space, leaned down, and pushed the bales out of the way, facilitating the dog's progress. The mongrel had a uniform jacket between his teeth, a French uniform of the *Federales*, with the insignia of a major. Peter Duprez looked behind the bales and found the pants. Uniform in one hand, his gun firmly grasped in the other, he climbed onto the bales and looked in every nook and cranny. He grew more excited by the moment until reason took over and he told himself that the discarded uniform could only mean one thing: The major had escaped. Had a Mexican found the uniform, it would have instantly become part and parcel of his wardrobe.

Cautiously watching Peter Duprez through a narrow slit made by two bales of hay, Salomon held his breath and drew deeper into his hiding place. He didn't breathe or move; if he could have stopped his heartbeats in those moments, he'd have done so. At one point Peter came close enough for the major to have reached out and grabbed his ankle. Such a move would have been disastrous for the *Rurale,* since he lacked the strength to take flight. He was wringing wet with perspiration, and his clothing was saturated with blood, but he held his breath and sat frozen until the danger passed.

Peter, unsuccessful in his attempt to locate anything more tangible than the discarded uniform, moved out of the area and went in search of Captain Tracy Richards. He found his friend still bedded down with Rosalia Quintera.

"Trace? Trace?" he called out softly.

Instinct made Tracy Richards sit bolt upright; his hands gripped both guns. Rosalia sat up instantly. Seeing a familiar face, she broke into a wide grin, showing her even, pearly teeth. "Gringo, *buenos días.* Is good to wake up to a friendly face. Lucia, she take good care of you?" She wrapped a *rebozo* around her naturally curly, hip-length hair and winked at him.

"If it isn't Tom Mix! Whatcha doin' up so early, blast ya. This is the best time ta get in a little romancin.'" He sniffed the air gingerly. "*Chiquita,* ya think ya can rustle up some o' that coffee for yer old man and his buddy?" The campfires were already active and people moved about preparing the early morning meals. Tracy gave the girl a smacking slap on the rump.

"*Si, querido.* I go *pronto.*" She smiled an alluring smile. None of her sparkling fires were subdued. "Coffee for you, too, handsome?"

"For me, too, *chiquita, gracias.*"

"I go." She moved out of their vision, swinging her hips as only Rosalia could. Many imitated her sensuous ways, but no one was like this fun-loving, female libertine who acted as if the world were made only for her pleasures.

As she moved out of sight, it was obvious to Peter that she wove some sort of hypnotic spell over Tracy Richards. He couldn't take his eyes from her until she disappeared outside. The captain lit a cigarette and shook his head in disbelief. "Ah've gotta marry up with that 'un one day, Pete. Ah tell ya, there ain't no one like Rosalia. She's a goddamned whore. Ah know it. The whole of Villa's camp knows it. Now Zapata's followers know it. But she's mah whore. Ah've fought it for three years. It's her attitude that's got me bug-eyed and bushy-tailed. They ain't no galdarned thing in the whole world that gets her down."

He dragged on his cigarette and into his steely eyes came a soft look of warmth. "Ya know we got ourselves a small *niño*? Little boy. She left him with her grandmother so he wouldn't be exposed to this life. She's got big plans for *our* son. School. An education she never got. Ah jus' don't know, Pete. Rosalia's got more love in her heart than what's good fer her. An' a lot's rubbing off on me. Didja ever seen the day ole Trace'd be tamed?" He scratched his stubbly beard and ran his fingers through his thick mane with a sap-eyed, cowlike expression on his face. He stopped talking for a moment and glanced sheepishly at his friend. That's when he noticed the uniform in Peter's hands.

"Ya look like ya lost yer best friend, Tom Mix. What the hell's up? What's that ya got in yer hands?"

"A major's uniform. Belongs to a *Federale*. Listen, Trace, ah can't find Little Fox. She's plumb gone and disappeared." He explained what the hardened *soldadera* in the stable had told him. "Ya know what this means? A high-ranking Federal officer has escaped in the clothing of one of Zapata's men. Ya better get this news to *Jefe*. Ah've gotta go after her, *amigo*. Ah learned too much to sit back and do nothing to reclaim mah wife, Trace. Ya gotta understand." He explained what Madelaina had discussed with Emiliano Zapata about Madrigal and what she'd endured there recently.

"Ya crazy loon! Ya gotta be careful. Ya know what they do to men like us down here among the jumpin' beans? Together we stand a chance. They wouldn't dare kill Americans if one survives to tell about it. Alone, good buddy, a gringo can be picked off with no one the wiser. We're gringos, yes. But below the border we are revolutionists, subject ta the same punishment as their own people get. Ah won't letcha do it, Pete. It'd be suicide."

"Don't tell me that. Those aren't the words I'm achin' ta hear," countered Duprez. "Y'all are going back to join with Villa again, aren'tcha, now Madero's got the word out ta him? Well, if ah don't have luck findin' her ah'll meetcha in El Paso. Ah'll leave word with that there Miss Antonetta at the Diamond Slipper."

"That's if'n ya live so long, Tom Mix. Ya've had a few close calls lately an' ah jus' don't think ya should be parading around like a barnyard cock in a den of coyotes, ya heah?"

"Ya can't stop me, Trace," said Peter.

"Yep. Ah can see that plain as day," replied the captain, shaking his head ruefully. He glanced up just as Rosalia, approaching them from the rear of the stable, swinging her hips as usual, carried steaming mugs of hot coffee. "Then, good buddy," said Tracy soberly, "ah'll go with ya."

"And leave this gorgeous hunk o' woman behind? You're nuts!"

"Ah need time ta think. Ah know she's somethin' else, Pete, but ah gotta take time ta think. Ya know how it'd be if ah brings me a greaser home ta be mah wife? In Texas? Oooooohhheeee! It might be different in some of them other states, but not in Texas. An' ole Trace here ain't gonna settle down in no other place but Texas. That's mah place an' there's where ah aim ta settle down for the rest o' mah born days, ya hear?"

"Ayeiii, gringos, take the coffee. Ees too hot," exclaimed Rosalia with a winning smile, flashing even white teeth.

The men obliged her instantly. They sat in a circle, sipping the hot liquid in an awkward silence. For a time, Peter began making circles in the dirt with a twig he picked up nearby. Rosalia glanced from her lover to the face of his friend, the usual smile on her face gradually fading.

She could see that her lover was hesitant to speak about something. With their eyes they spoke words which neither could articulate. She rose to her feet and walked to the opening overlooking an enclosure, a small corral, where a few horses were tethered. Rosalia sighed deeply. He was off again. She could always tell when they were getting ready to move on. Only this time, his plans didn't include her. Tracy came in behind her and nuzzled her neck, planting a kiss on it. She remained still and said nothing.

Peter noticed none of this. He was suddenly struck with a name from out of his past, one that had haunted him and now crept out of a deeply buried past which he had tried so desperately to keep buried.

Madrigal de Los Altos! Madrigal de Los Altos, he

said over and over to himself. Suddenly it came to him. His mother had mentioned the place to him shortly before she died. He was six years old at the time. He hadn't understood much of what happened; he only knew that he hated his father.

Life at Seven Moons, the ranch owned by his father near Amarillo, wasn't very exciting for a growing boy. Still, he could have endured it, if the rest of his life had been fulfilling. However, as time passed and he observed the growing animosity between his father and mother, he became more aware of a burning hatred. He loathed William Benson, his father, for having caused his mother to die of a broken heart. Peter loved his mother deeply. She had been the only love figure in his life, the only person to encourage him to think for himself and be his own man. He recalled few scenes of domesticity in the house of his father, a wealthy rancher from the Texas Panhandle, but one scene remained vivid, one that he'd never forget for as long as he lived.

His mother had given birth to another child. Peter had never seen the baby—or if he did, he couldn't clearly recall it. There had been some argument, loud words that echoed through the enormous hacienda. He recalled the servants scurrying about, driven with fright. Peter had left his room and padded down the hall to his mother's room, a room separate from his father's. As usual, his father was screaming, yelling at her something awful. He was calling her names, vile, unspeakable names, at which even the servants recoiled.

"You filthy, disgusting whore!" he shouted. "Degenerate animal. Alley cat!" The words continued, getting worse and worse.

Peter, a mere child, grew incensed at the tone of his father's voice. He understood none of the names, but he could guess, judging from the expressions of the servants who cowered in the upper hallway listening, that they meant something quite horrendous. One of the

338

servants reached for Peter when he left the room. "Stay here, *niño*," she said, clasping her hands over both his ears. "You mustn't listen to such words," she whispered hoarsely.

"It's your fault, Bill! Not mine!" screamed Peter's mother. "You are the filthy, disgusting animal! Not me! You're the one who infected me, not the other way around!" she yelled at the top of her lungs.

Peter could hear them both. He was humiliated, and frightened, and sickened by the whole scene. He broke away from the fat *dueña* and ran into his mother's room. For a time neither parent noticed him. He stood there, his small fists clenched into balls, glancing from one to the other. His mother was sobbing. His father, fierce and terrible, stood over her murderously. He had slapped her across the face. Young Peter glanced about the room frantically. Catching sight of his father's gun belt laying across the back of a chair, he reached for the heavy gun and held it menacingly in his hand.

At age four, his father had had a special small gun made to fit his hand. Already he was a crack shot. This was a big gun, much too heavy, but there was no doubt in his young mind that he could hit his target if he tried.

He screamed to be heard over the two brawling adults. "Apologize to my mother, before I kill you!"

The sight of the young boy standing with a gun pointed toward him shocked Bill Benson into cold sobriety. He made a move toward the boy.

"No, Peter," screamed his hysterical mother. "No!"

A shot went off. The gun, too heavy to be held steadily in his small hands, had missed its target by inches.

"Give me the gun, boy," said his father. "Now, jus' give me the gun and we'll forget about all this."

"Yes, darling, give him the gun. It's all right. He didn't hurt me," said his mother, with bruises on her face and arms. Obediently, he dropped the gun on the floor and ran into his mother's arms.

"I'll kill him if he hurts you, Mamma. I swear, I'll kill him."

Perhaps nothing else in the world could have sobered Bill Benson more than the sight of his own son, ready to kill him if he so much as laid another hand on his wife. He left the room, brutally aware that his son hated him.

Within the next few days, Peter heard more voices, talks with strange men who spoke of a place called Madrigal de Los Altos, just the right place for special cases. The lad was three years old now. Could he be placed in such surroundings? The costs were nominal considering the services one received in return.

It had been settled. One day the housekeeper, a heavy woman with pendulous breasts and a round, full face, was dispatched with two ranch hands to the mission in Juarez, where she'd be met by two sisters from Madrigal de Los Altos. She was to give the child to them and return to Amarillo, bringing back signed receipts for the money and papers attesting to the fact that she had turned the child over to the proper people. Mamacita Inez, following instructions to the letter, returned a week later with her escorts. All had gone as planned.

Until his mother died a year and a half later, Peter never heard another argument between his parents. From the day young Peter held his ground, gun in hand, until the day his mother died, Bill Benson never uttered a word to his wife. He had made a vow that day, a vow he held until the day she died. He sobbed bitterly over his wife's grave and never spoke of her from that day forward. He ordered the servants never to speak her name. It was as if Jennifer Duprez Benson had never existed.

Peter remained on the ranch until he was sixteen. He was sent to college, but he never mixed well with the sons of other wealthy cattlemen and *hacendados,* given preferential treatment in Mexico under the Diaz government. He hated summers most of all, when he had to be close to the man he had grown to detest. Father and son barely spoke. When they did, it was through a third party, which in retrospect was exceedingly childish and grossly immature. But Bill Benson was an iron man, and his son was just as unyielding. Immediately after college, Peter left the Benson ranch, took his mother's name, and became a soldier of fortune, a freedom fighter, a mercenary fighting the problems of others. He hadn't seen his father or concerned himself with him in the least. He had made his own way, and now he owned a handsome spread of land just outside of San Antonio.

Peter never learned the true extent of his father's wealth or of the power wielded by the Benson name, especially in the political corners of Washington. He didn't care. He had no intention of either laying claim to his father's estate or even getting reacquainted with the stone-hearted bastard. Knowing his father, he was certain there'd be strings attached to anything concerning Peter.

Madrigal! How long ago had all this occurred? Some twenty years. No one ever mentioned the boy child to him again, and he'd clearly forgotten about it until Lucia described the evil taking place under that roof. Peter's concern for Madelaina increased tenfold now. He couldn't help recalling how attentive she'd been on the *Mozambique,* hanging on his every word. In a way he felt responsible for having implanted rebellion in her young, impressionable mind. She was the true daughter of a *gachupín*, a highborn Spaniard who'd been brought up with a certain class consciousness. He'd had no right to interfere. He had had no right to fill her mind with things she didn't understand and couldn't handle.

If Peter Duprez had only known the full extent of the horrendous experiences to which Madelaina had been subjected since they'd first met, he might have grown morbid and thoroughly depressed at having been instrumental in influencing General Obregon's daughter to part with her way of life.

Enough of this, he told himself, bringing himself back to the present.

"Trace," he called to his friend, hating to disturb him and Rosalia in what appeared to be a very private moment. Tracy broke away, giving his *vieja* a sharp slap of affection on her well-curved bottom.

"Yeah, Pete."

Peter Duprez lit up a *cigarro* and offered one to his friend. "Let's walk out to corral and talk."

Tracy fell in alongside him, lighting his cigar with a match he struck on his pants seat. Both these Americans prided themselves on their cold detachment from emotional entanglements. They knew their business well, performed their services better than most, and always broke off relations on the best of terms. They maintained good relations with Villa and Zapata and aimed to continue. One thing Pete Duprez prided himself on more than this detachment was the ability to keep his business to himself. He was never one to boast or confide his innermost desires or feelings.

Now he had to tell Tracy, his best friend, that he wanted to go to Cuernavaca alone. He wanted to be with Madelaina to rekindle the fires that once burst into flames for him, as they did only yesterday afternoon when they kissed. He wanted to take her in his arms again and feel the excitement that caused every nerve in his body to tingle. Right this moment, as he walked, he could feel her presence as he did yesterday, as he had in every memory of her with the exception of one. One day he'd know the truth about Vera Cruz. He could wait to find out. After what she must have endured, he could wait forever.

"Ah know whatcher thinking, Tom Mix," began Tracy. "It ain't gonna do ya no good. Ah'm stickin' to ya like glue, buddy. A man in love's a real danger only ta hisself, ya hear?"

"Trace, this is mah business. Ah want no interference."

They were interrupted by a rider coming at them on a fast stallion. One of Zapata's men. *"Señores!*

Gringos! *Espera! Espera!*" The rider, a man named Fuentes, sprang over the top of his saddle horn and slid from his horse, sweat dripping from both the rider and the lathered horse.

"Gringos, the *jefe* desires to see you both on a matter of urgent business. We will ride *pronto* to the hacienda of Zapata," he said in a mixed dialect of *Yaqui* and Spanish.

"What's up, Fuentes? We got us another rumble someplace?" asked Captain Richards coolly. Then with sudden brightness, "Hot damn! Don't tell me the *Rurales* are coming back ta stage a counteroffensive? Ah thought we about wiped them out, *amigo*."

"Fuentes knows nothing, gringos. Only what the *jefe* tells me. You come now."

"As long as it takes ta saddle up, *amigo*." Tracy turned to his companion. "Ya comin', Tom Mix? Ah think we can learn more about your Little Fox at Zapata's headquarters. We'll take the uniform. Can't be that many majors in the battalion we wiped out. Mebbe we can pin down exactly who he was and learn what happened to yer missus."

It was statements like this and clear thinking that made Tracy Richards valuable to men like Emiliano Zapata and Pancho Villa. He thought with his brains, not his testicles. He had a knack for putting matters in the proper perspective. He hadn't been wrong yet, thought Peter as he reluctantly agreed to his friend's strategy. Inwardly he was annoyed by the change in plans, but when Tracy stressed that they were both guests in the State of Moreles at Zapata's request and owed their temporary allegiance to the rebel leader, he knew he shouldn't be running off on his own to solve a personal problem.

It took Captain Richards only a matter of moments to gather Rosalia and Lucia and toss them on freshly saddled mounts. Together the foursome, led by the dedicated Fuentes, broke into a wild gallop across country into the hills of Moreles.

They saw the hacienda of Zapata from the top of a

343

hill. Fuentes halted his party until he received an all-clear signal from the countless lookouts surrounding the sprawling estate. Peter was both impressed and depressed that Emiliano Zapata would stoop to such luxuries, contrary to his rebellious declarations, until they rode into the draw and he saw that the peasant had converted his estate into a mere camp like always. The buildings served only as shelter; the interiors had been stripped clean of all ostentatious furnishings. Only the barest of necessities remained. The Americans dismounted in the corral.

Early as it was, bonfires had been lit and food was cooking. The air filled with scintillating odors of beans, onions, and chili. Musicians played lively tunes on their guitars. Here and there a voice could be heard raised in song. Dancers, always ready to step onto an impromptu stage, demonstrated their talents in every available spot they could find, including the main salon of the villa. Always on duty were the stone-faced guards, wearing their ammo belts crisscrossed over their breasts, with double hip holsters and the constant clanging of heavily rawled spurs, which they never shed, even when they walked on the hand-tiled floors of the hacienda. The carnival-like atmosphere persisted as it did upon each of Zapata's victories. Hardly anyone noticed the gringos as they entered, their weapons displayed openly. They had long since become a fixture, fighting alongside the rebels in a tight bond of brotherhood.

Intrigued by the incongruity of rebels in a hacienda that once housed a noble, Peter Duprez paused to stare at the fire lit in one corner of the room where a pot of beans and coffee were being warmed. He glanced at the spectators watching the dancers. Some clapped their hands keeping time to the music and others watched the dancers make open love with their eyes and bodies. They displayed the gamut of emotions ranging from love to hate and jealousy. The women became seductresses, teasing and rejecting; the men fell victims, accepting then demanding and taking, unaware that they'd already been baited, slain, and quartered from the outset. It was exciting to watch the gypsy dances, which were designed to increase the pulse rate by degrees as they jockeyed emotions to unendurable levels.

"They ain't a one of 'em that can hold a candle to Rosalia," confided Tracy Richards to his friend.

"Ah heah ya," replied Peter as Fuentes hurriedly motioned them along to the corridor beyond the main salon. The gringos fell in behind the *Zapatista*.

Fuentes paused before a door and removed his sombrero, dusting it against his leather leggings. He slicked his stringy black hair into place, eager to make a good impression, and he knocked politely, as if he were being tested in this endeavor.

"Enter!" came the moderate voice of Emiliano Zapata.

Inside the gringos saw the *jefe* seated primly behind an impressive oakdesk, speaking with a woman he called Josefa, his wife. She was a frail, olive-skinned, beauty, highborn and well educated, who'd fallen madly in love with Zapata and married him. Now, besides being an ardent lover, Josefa became a remarkable tutor to the *bandido*, teaching the illiterate hillsman how to read and write.

Moving about the room doing small duties, somewhat unnoticed by their *jefe*, were two younger, dark-eyed, female *Zapatistas*. Astonishment registered on their faces when the guests entered.

Before Zapata could rise and extend his arm courteously to his gringo friends, the voice of Lucia cried out in utter surprise. "Alicia! Amelia!" She broke away from her friends and flung her arms around the Sandoval sisters, who had shed their habits and were dressed in the colorful shifts of their people. "You are both safe! *Dios mios!*" she cried, embracing her cousins. "Only last night, I spoke of you." She turned to Peter. "These are my cousins." She turned to the girls. "I thought you were still prisoners at Madrigal. How did you get here?"

"In due time, Lucia," said Emiliano Zapata, disengaging the girls. He moved his strong, square frame lithely across the tiles and shook hands with the gringos. "My house ees jur house." He spoke English with a crude accent. He smiled politely. Zapata never really smiled. Nor did he laugh as boisterously as his northern counterpart, Pancho Villa. He was more reserved, modest, and reticent in the company of people better educated than he.

"Welcome, *amigos*." To his wife he said, "Josefa, ju will please see that our guests are treated with the cordiality reserved for the trusted friends of Emiliano Zapata."

She smiled a secret smile which only husband and wife understood. It was really the fierce pride she felt for her husband's attempt to be more civilized and she wanted to show him she approved.

She slipped out of the door to do his bidding. The women retired to one end of the room to talk.

"*Gracias*, Jefe," said Tracy Richards, sitting down with Peter Duprez in the chairs designated by Zapata. "By coincidence, we were coming ta talk with ya when yore man Fuentes appeared. Ya see, Tom Mix here has got hisself one doggone problem. His wife, Little Fox, was abducted last night, and he wants ta take a leave of absence ta track her down—this is, unless he's needed here with ya."

"*Si, amigos*? Is not so unusual that Zapata has summoned ju to speak precisely of such an unfortunate happening. But first, please, ju will accept my hospitality," he said with the graciousness of a *hacendado*, receiving an approving nod from his wife, who had reentered the room with bottles of wine and glasses on a tray. The other women stood up to quickly serve their own men.

"*Amigos*, especially ju, Tom Mix, I make jur acquaintance with two of my *campesinas* who escaped from Madrigal due to the kindness of jur *mujer*, jur wife, Little Fox. This is some woman, Little Fox, no?"

346

He introduced the Sandoval sisters to the gringos. "Alicia, this is the husband of jur friend, Little Fox."

Alicia's dark eyes widened perceptibly and she nodded to them both. She began her story. She explained what had happened to Madelaina and themselves in Madrigal, omitting none of the gory details. Two hours and many bottles of wine later, the Americans were tight-lipped, highly incensed, and filled with unspeakable violence, as was the outraged Emiliano Zapata, who snorted and paced the floor like an enraged bull elephant.

"This Simon Salomon—major or whatever—is mine! I shall find him! He shall taste the sting of Zapata's fury!" His fingers rubbed the inside of his palms with marked agitation and a hatred of many years for these *Rurales*, these stinking soldiers of a government which was never for the people.

Peter Duprez fingered his six-guns with menace. "Not if ah find him first," he said with rising anger. He had flung the uniform of the major on the table before Zapata. "Ah found this this morning, hidden in the stable. The *bastardo* must've shed it in the dark of night and taken off, right under ouah very noses!" Peter addressed himself to Alicia Sandoval. "But this man, if it was Major Salomon, you say was badly injured?"

"*Si, señor*. With our eyes we saw Paco stick him many times. We felt certain the man was dead. How could he live with so many stickings?" The sisters exchanged bewildered looks.

"This man—this lover of hers—who saved her from the hands of Salomon—who was he?"

"Paco Jimenez," said Alicia with peculiar lights of tenderness in her eyes.

Peter Duprez took hope. These were the eyes of a woman in love. "He was her lover?" he asked again.

"Not the way you mean, *señor*," said the sixteen-year-old who had grown into a woman in the past year at Madrigal "We all love Madelaina. She saved our lives from a fate worse than death. We would gladly die for her. She is the true spirit of the revolution, *señores*. We know it. We all feel it. When has a *gachupín* taken sides with a peasant? Not those haughty and arrogant piss-stinking *conquistadores*. Little Fox is not like them. She feels deeply for Mexico, for Mexicans—for mestizos like us. It's true, by blood she is not one of us. But, *señores,* she is all of us in spirit. Why do you think Pancho Villa reveres her?"

The room was filled with silence. Lucia glanced at her lover of last night and realized she could not compete with such a woman. She was lost before she began. Her large sad eyes caught the sober expression of Rosalia Quintera; in that instant they both seemed to know the futility of loving a gringo.

Zapata offered *cigarros* to the gringos. He lit his and drew on it thoughtfully while the others lit up. "Tell me, *amigos*, ees true Pancho Villa owes his victory in Juarez to this Little Fox? Is not a story like those romantic crazy stories dreamed up by the fantasies of those *campesinas* who have nothing better to do than carry tales?"

Captain Tracy Richards leaned back in his high-backed chair and nodded solemnly. "Ah tell ya, *Jefe,* it's all true. We were all there from the Gringo Brigade—as Pancho calls us—every last blarsted one o' us. For the whole month of April, the *jefe* had this information supplied him by the woman known as Little Fox, tellin' him o' the changes in plan ta arm Chihuahua."

He hadn't told Peter Duprez this before, and watching the expression of amazement on Peter's face turn into one of wonderment, Tracy Richards told Zapata the whole story of the capture of Juarez. As Peter listened, he realized that while he and the Gringo Brigade fooled around waiting for action outside of Juarez, Madelaina, incarcerated at Madrigal, was undergoing the tortures of hell, if he could believe the atrocities of which Alicia Sandoval spoke. And he did. They were as much alive in his memory now as those days preceding the Battle of Juarez in which he, him-

348

self, almost lost his life. Would Peter Duprez ever forget those harrowing days when the warring cougars and political jaguars gathered outside of Juarez to powwow and send up smoke signals of conquest?

To Peter Duprez, it was one story he'd be able to tell his grandchildren with pride. His mind zoomed back to that critical period as Captain Richards described the silent thunder preceding the contest.

Pancho Villa and the thousands of *Villistas,* congregated at the hacienda where Francesco Madero had gathered them, had grown restless with the time-consuming protocol these Antireelectionists saw fit to spin around their heads. The spectacular *bandido,* Pancho Villa, had had enough. Four weeks of ball-busting inactivity and indecision as they waited for the political *jefes* to make up their ridiculous minds had driven Panchito and his gringos *muy loco.*

Chihuahua or Juarez? Which city was it to be? Which would they capture? Oh, how they wrangled. The conservative Carranza, that gray-bearded, white-haired man, a dead ringer for the American General Custer, stood firm against taking Juarez. He was aided and abetted by Garibaldi, the son of the Italian liberator, Mayortena, and Don Gonzalez. They all used the same excuse that was offered by General Navarro of the Diaz forces on the night Madelaina overheard his argument as to why Madero wouldn't attack the sister city to El Paso: attacking such a well-garrisoned city would be tantamount to suicide. Pasquel Orozco, a former wagon master, who, with a group of miners, concurred Pancho Villa's declaration that they must attack Juarez.

Madero procrastinated. He was intimidated by the pro-Diaz President Taft that he remained ambivalent, undecisive, and afraid of American intervention.

Exactly as Little Fox reported to Pancho Villa, a peace delegation from Presidente Diaz appeared under a six-day truce, negotiating empty promises, while obviously stalling for time.

"Words! Words! Words!" cried Pancho Villa to the warring factions. "Diaz understands only battles, not words. Porfirio Diaz, a tough, hardened army man, understands bullets, not fancy talk by chocolate drinkers. What is Madero thinking of?" the *guerrillo* had exploded with more frequency each passing day.

Against Pancho Villa's advice, Francesco Madero dispatched a formal request to General Navarro asking for the immediate surrender of Juarez.

Is it possible, Villa asked his close associates, that Madero really thinks the request will be complied with? He scratched his head in total bewilderment. And when Navarro's reply, politely declining Madero's request, arrived, Pancho Villa was still unable to cope with such civilized and polite goings on. Certainly wars weren't fought and won by simple requests?

By then, over 4,000 revolutionaries had been recruited by the *Villistas,* and all stood cooling their heels awaiting orders from their *jefe.* Francesco Madero was painfully aware of several considerations: one, the threat of American intervention, and two, his own desire not to oppose the conservatives. Then, there was Pancho Villa to reckon with. It began to appear that Villa's position that the *Maderistas* attack Juarez grew weaker each moment.

Another general, a hero of the Boer War, had joined Madero's staff. General Jan Viloen, a formidable military man, concurred with the conservatives, thereby shaking Madero's trust in Villa. General Viloen agreed with the others that it would be suicidal to attack Juarez. Now Villa stood alone in favor of the Juarez objective.

Across the Rio Grande, 20,000 American troops in full battle array awaited the one act of aggression that would make Madero responsible for American casualties. Madero, fully threatened by the circumstances in which he found himself, was persuaded to forego thoughts of taking Juarez.

The end of April approached, but no decisive action had been taken. As Diaz's peace delegations

350

continued wasting words and time, the Mountain Cougar, the Puma, and the Centaur of the North warmed up in the bull pen. Pancho Villa, bridling under the strain of empty strategy, realized something had to be done and quickly. He had little respect for these army regulars, these highborn, high-falootin' *gachupíns*, sons of *hacendados*, who scarred his life at an early age and caused him to seek refuge in a life of violent crime.

Time was flitting away. Pancho, possessed of the information which Little Fox had risked her life to send him, came to the conclusion that if he didn't act soon, the moments would be lost to history. He contemplated the situation in silence, in the seclusion of the only course he'd ever employed—God.

Meanwhile, the forces of destiny took over to spur the principal characters into activity. It appeared that Juarez was destined to become the battle in which psychological warfare would be employed. All that followed was triggered off by an open letter to the press written by General Navarro's subordinate, an ineffectual man named Colonel Tamborel. The colonel, it was learned, wrote a scathing letter in which he accused the revolutionaries of incalculable cowardice, incompetence, and the grave fear of fighting against army regulars.

In the camp of Pancho Villa, the *jefe* no longer smiled. The twinkle usually present in his eyes was missing as he stood listening to Tom Mix read the open letter to him. His eyes blackened with fury and outrage, and he found himself tensing against the blatant insults aimed at humiliating the *guerrillo* and his loyal followers. Men who'd fought side by side championing the rights of peasants deserved more than the words written by this flea-bitten son of lowly desert cur. *Cowards, eh? So Pancho Villa is a desperado, a cutthroat, a murderer, eh?* The words Peter Duprez read stuck in his brain like hot branding irons to searing flesh. *They'll scurry like frightened cockroaches the moment they face real fighters, eh? That lying son of a whore's pimp,* thought Villa. *That Colonel Tamborel will live to eat those words!*

That night in the privacy of his own camp at the outskirts of Juarez, Pancho Villa made plans of his own. If the Madero revolution was to succeed, he'd have to convince the small Sephardic Jew of the necessity of the Juarez objective. If it failed, Pancho Villa was willing to risk everything and take full blame.

In a shabby building where the *Villistas* were holed up, Captain Richards taught the men how to make what he called Villa's tacos; they later gained popularity as Molotov cocktails. Old tin cans stuffed with gunpowder and tiny hunks of metal were capped and fused and stored in a safe place. Sticks of dynamite, along with a sprinkling of nails and other metal bits wrapped in strips of cowhide, were sewn together into firm, hard bombs. From time to time Captain Richards would explain the "far-reaching" benefits of the bombs, moving the men to inordinate laughter, their eyes glittering in anticipation of the holocaust.

Elsewhere, Francesco Madero gave explicit, foolhardy, and unrealistic orders. Ignoring his earlier campaign rhetoric, he had instructed his followers to abandon all thoughts of capturing Juarez. Instead, the man who would be Mexico's *presidente* told the revolutionists to march southward toward the capital; as they did, they would gather thousands upon thousands of supporters. He felt sure that Presidente Diaz, intimidated by such throngs marching upon Mexico City, would immediately capitulate.

No one was more dumbfounded by Madero's proposal, than Pancho Villa, who believed this to be a hairbrained and ludicrous plan.

Madero, adamant when he saw the look in Villa's eyes, cut off all protest. His decision would stand, he told his men. In the morning they'd all withdraw from the north. Their target was Mexico City. He had spoken. His word was final.

The political *jefes* had filed out of the hacienda where Madero set up headquarters, leaving only the revolution's leader and Pancho Villa eyeing each other coolly.

"You wish something, Señor Villa?" asked Madero, sighing despondently.

Pancho, sombrero in hand, nodded. "Only to tell you I pledged my life to you because you brought to people like me the first hope in centuries of opposition and persecution. But, I tell you, Don Francesco Madero, unless you take Juarez for all those reasons I've been feeding you these past many days—thirty in all—you will have nothing. I beg you, *señor*, attack Juarez. Give the order, *mi Presidente*, and Diaz will be a thing of the past."

"You have my orders," snapped Madero, turning from this devoted animal who venerated him as he would a saint.

"Si, mi Presidente," replied Villa. "I thank you for your time." It seemed Pancho wanted to speak out, but he didn't. He walked out into the night knowing full well what he must do. It was all up to him now. He had to act on the information sent to him by Little Fox. He'd heard from his sister Concepción that the young woman was still missing. *Muy bueno.* Her sacrifice wouldn't be for nothing. Madero or no Madero, Juarez would be taken. Pancho Villa was as stubborn as Madero. Pray God that his mulishness would prove to be a brilliant tactic.

Psychological warfare was about to begin. Pancho Villa put the spur to his men just about twilight, after the sun had gone down, when shadows proved deceptive and frightening. Villa's most trusted men—Tomàs Urbina, Solis, and Dominguez—and all his captains infiltrated the front line trenches, inciting and infuriating the men in the ranks with blurbs from that open letter to the revolutionaries written by Colonel Tamborel. "Cowards! Cutthroats! Mamma's boys still suckling her breasts. That's what they call us in a paper which everyone reads!" There was a rumble of discontent. Roars of disgust and threats of fiery retaliation swept through the front lines like a cry of war. "They dare call *Villistas* cowards?" Those front line men, drinking heavily, grew sullen. Their pride had been ripped apart by such slurs and insults; they were cut to the quick. "No one calls *Villistas* cowards! We're two-fisted, tough, iron-willed *guerrillos* who chew nails for breakfast." The *Rurales*, they boasted, had tried calling them cowards once. Hadn't they all ended up as dead figs on Villa's fruit trees?

The rumble grew and swelled into giant waves, infecting the camp and the front lines. A few took up the challenge, then more and more, until the entire encampment was prepped for action.

It began softly. An occasional shot here and there from the rebels. A burst of enemy fire in return. Insults hurled over the trenches accompanied by spurts of electrifying gunfire. The *Federales*, the army regulars, called out into the night, "Put your pea shooters away, you scum-sucking scums of the earth! Real men are waiting to teach you what it's all about!"

"Come and get us, you rag-bag excuses for men. You haven't hit any of us with your projectiles. Have your eyes been blinded by the diseases of your whorish mothers?"

The insults didn't stop, each side growing more vicious by the moment. Meanwhile, Villa's specialists spread out, sneaking into position. Every now and again bursts of automatic rifle fire broke from the camp of the *Federales*. The marked agitation in both camps betrayed the possibility of an all-out attack.

News reached Madero and he was properly shocked. His aides scampered about, searching frantically for Pancho Villa and Pasquel Orozco with orders from Madero to stop firing. They looked everywhere for Villa. Unable to locate the *guerrillo*, they returned to a sputtering, bombastic Madero, who paced the floor angrily at his headquarters, threatening to court-martial any and all officers who couldn't control his troops. The strain on Madero became more obvious as the night wore on.

He frantically called for a conference of his *jefes*. He

sent a message to General Navarro asking for a suspension of hostilities and nearly lost his mind when reports of increased hostility reached him. Madero began to feel like a helpless bird imprisoned in his own nest.

Jefe Pancho Villa had planned his strategy well. By dawn, nothing could have halted the confrontation between *Federales* and *guerrillos*. Each side, having taken enough insults to explode on contact, was uncontainable. The ranks, raring to go, needed nothing but a leader. Pancho Villa modestly permitted himself to be drafted for the job.

Early that morning of May 9, a day that would forever be burned into the memory of Peter Duprez, it all began when Villa and Major Urbina appeared on the scene with fifty heavily armed men sporting double ammo belts crisscrossed over their chests, carrying leather pouches stuffed with homemade bombs.

"God, they're beautiful!" Peter Duprez had cried, witnessing the terrible, *charro*-hatted hillsmen, loaded to the gills with weapons of every description, riding through the lines. "Everything ya told me about Pancho Villa is true!" he'd shouted to Captain Tracy Richards. "The man knows no fear at all!"

"Ya ain't seen nothing, yet, Tom Mix!" retorted Tracy Richards as he calmly set up his machine guns. "Ah told ya, theah ain't another critter like him."

Immediately Villa stood at the center of his men, riding tall on Seven Leagues, his black stallion. "Listen, *amigos*," he called to the others. "Me and my men intend to blow those *bastardos* out of their holes. Now, listen good. We can't move too fast under all these weapons. So when you hear the bugle blow, shoot to kill. Shoot low into their trenches—make them squat like ducks. When you hear the second blast of the bugle, move! Move as if your pantaloons are on fire and charge! *Comprender?*"

Villa's men had distributed cigars to the bombing squad and ordered them to light up. "When I give you the signal, *muchachos,* light the fuses from the *cigarros* and toss them like you had a wildcat by the tail." Pancho Villa signaled the bugler to play his instrument. "Play it loud!" he commanded.

The bombing detail stood poised. The artillery stood in readiness. Suddenly the *Villistas* released a continuous barrage of rifle fire that shocked the *Federales* into stunned and disorganized movement, allowing time for Villa to surge forth, crawling under the rifle fire until the *Villistas* fell into position halfway between the two front lines.

Villa raised his black kerchief and twirled it twice in a signal to move.

Rising to the occasion, the bombers hurled their homemade goodies across the trenches. Arcs of spitting fire fell on enemy lines blasting open the trenches, leaving gouged-out holes in their wake. Men, bloodied and splattered, zoomed into the air only to fall to the ground in heaps like rag dolls.

The bugle sounded the charge and on they came, sweeping forward, yelling, *"Viva Villa! Viva Villa!"* They used guns, machetes, knives, even pitchforks, anything they could lay their hands on. The *Federales* found themselves losing ground, retreating in panic. The bugle kept blowing loud and clear.

Having achieved his first objective, command of Navarro's defense perimeter, Pancho Villa was prepared for phase two. He had stayed awake all night preparing his plan to seize the city.

General Orozco, dazed and stunned, was spitting bullets at that savage Villa, who had stolen his thunder. He now raced up the irrigation canal which led from El Paso down through Juarez and the trenches Villa had already taken. What he saw led him to believe that Villa had planned too well for this attack, right down to the last details. Sonofabitch! He stood firmly with Villa and Villa told him *nada!* Not to be outdone by this amazing *guerrillo,* Orozco, without orders from Madero, threw his men into the heat of battle, advancing from south and northwest against stiff machine gun fire from Navarro's troops. By now, Madero, who realized he could hold back no longer,

356

dispatched two contingents to aid Pancho Villa and General Orozco.

Led by Captain Dreben, the Gringo Brigade, numbering more than 100, joined in behind Pancho Villa with their expert artillery and cannon fire. The *Federales* opened fire on the rebels as they advanced, but *Jefe* Pancho Villa had chosen carefully to launch his attack from east to north. To Villa's rear lay the city of El Paso. The *Federales* dared not fire directly on Villa for fear of killing some Texan—then there'd be hell to pay. From that point on, Peter vividly recalled, it was Pancho Villa himself, guns smoking, hurling deadly grenades at anything obstructing him, followed by the Gringo Brigade, who set the devastating pace and sent the *Federales* scurrying in every direction.

Villa's brilliant strategy and keen tactical warfare had forced the *Federales* into a period of inaction. They couldn't risk American intervention. Meanwhile, the rebels progressed steadily, infiltrating their way north, then west around the city. Up ahead was the bridge that that crazy dynamiter Captain Creighton had rigged to explode under enemy noses. The *Villistas* crept forward under enemy fire, then Villa gave the signal. Creighton lit the fuse with the burning tip of his cigar and ran like hell in the opposite direction. The bridge blew—shot into the air into broken pieces. Both the bridge and the soldiers came down in a hailstorm of human flesh, bones, blood, and concrete. Everything was transformed into smoldering ruins. Villa's way into Juarez was unobstructed.

Pete Duprez recalled how the *Federales* had converted all tall buildings and strategic positions into sandbagged machine gun nests, and when Villa and the others charged, they were stopped cold. They were unable to move forward. All day the battle raged, and by nightfall, the *Federales* still held Juarez and many rebels lay dead. The day had been a slaughterhouse for the revolutionists. There was constant street fighting in and of houses and doorways. Explosives hurled in arcs through the air hit their targets and machine gun nests

357

were demolished, but as soon as one disappeared, another would appear. From their well-guarded cover positions, the *Federales* were able to mow down the rebels when they least expected attacks.

Villa spent that night working out strategy. Before dawn the following morning he had called a powwow with Captains Tracy, Creighton, Dreben, and Duprez. He told Tracy, "You, Tom Mix, Creighton, and I will ring all the houses and cut through the *Federales*' positions with grenades. We'll outflank and surprise the enemy gunners before they can retreat. *Comprender, amigos?*" He grinned widely, filled with the energy of six men.

The gringos, following Villa's orders, had devastated everyone and everything in sight. Villa and his cohorts had taken time to stop at the city hall to release the prisoners and recruit the inmates into fighting with them. Having made their way to the bullring at the Plaza de Toros across town, Peter Duprez and Creighton fell into a trap. Before they knew what hit them, they found themselves standing stone-faced before a firing squad. Incredibly, the two Americans found themselves staring into the muzzles of twelve rifles held by expert assassins. It happened so swiftly they didn't have time to react properly.

These hard-bitten mercenaries would be taught a lesson, one that would discourage other gringo mercenaries from causing more grief to the *Federales*. These gringo gunmen, thorns in the side of the Diaz regime, were faster than cats sliding on an oil slick, with their trigger fingers. They were utterly ruthless and fought anyone's cause against the establishment. Among such men who fought the causes of others, there was a certain touch of madness, a killer instinct the *Federales* had come up against and didn't relish. Now, they could justify the gringos' deaths.

While one of General Navarro's aides attempted to determine his legal position in the offensive against two gringos, Captain Tracy Richards, viewing the scene at the Plaza de Toros, rode swiftly back to Pancho Villa at the jail and announced emphatically, "Tom Mix and Creighton, captured in the bullring, face a firing squad at any moment!"

Losing no time, Pancho Villa jumped on Tracy's horse and the two of them arrived at the Plaza de Toros amid cries of excitement. The very presence of the redoubtable *guerrillo* leader had a devastating effect on the *Federales.* And when they heard the cries of *"Viva Villa! Viva Villa!"* from the rebels, they seemed to stop and gawk at the overwhelming presence of the legendary Pancho Villa.

"Pancho Villa outside the gate?" they cried. "Is it possible?" The *Federales,* peering with abounding curiosity and adulation, stood transfixed, unable to oppose such fierce strength.

Before the *Federales* could recover from their surprise, Villa and his men, using so simple a strategy as pure guts, arose en masse and took over the entire bull arena.

And so it was that Peter Duprez, on the verge of execution, was saved. Grateful to Villa, his benefactor, he turned to the *guerrillo* leader and, grinning devilishly, found time for levity. "Listen, Pancho Villa. There must be something bettah foah me ta do than bait *Federales.*"

Villa laughed with gusto and slapped Peter affectionately on the back. "You think Pancho would abandon such a gringo? Never!"

The Gringo Brigade, riding confiscated horses, rode up the Avenida Juarez, where for the past two hours that letter-writing sonofabitch Colonel Tamborel had been holed up in a building, desperately fighting with the last of his men.

The dead, the broken, and the maimed lay in the streets, unreal, as in the scenario of a war story, with flies swarming around them like bees to honey. What made the scene even more unreal, thought Peter Duprez, was the sight of American tourists with their box cameras taking photos of the fighting.

The gringos and the Mexican *jefe* galloped swiftly

359

along the streets, weaving their way in and around and over the inert figures sprawled on the cobbles. At the end of the street, Villa sprang from his horse before a old stone building riddled with rifle fire where the remains of the Tamborel battalion were barricaded, determined to die at their posts.

It was dark inside the building. All windows were barricaded, all openings sandbagged. Villa's squad deployed rapidly, sweeping out the first floor and starting upward. Rifle fire blasted them from the stairwell, but the *Villistas* overran the defenders. More rebels arrived to join their *jefe* in knocking out all resistance. The *Federales* had no chance against these hand-picked *guerrillos*.

"Surrender!" came the cries from the rebels. "Surrender, you pigs!"

Replies came in a barrage of bullets. The shooting, loud enough to rupture eardrums, was topped off by a shower of grenades. Subsequently there came blinding flashes of white fire, loud explosions, crumbled walls. Defending Federal soldiers were obscured in the rain of broken plaster, wood, and stones. Colonel Tamborel, a man who'd faced Villa before and cold-bloodedly massacred the *guerrillo's* people, a man who'd had the audacity to call them cowards, now stood naked before his enemy.

Pancho Villa faced his opponent in his moment of triumph without the slightest pang of remorse for what he was about to do. To prove he was a man of his word, he ordered Tomàs Urbina to cut off Tamborel's balls and toss them out the window so the people would all know he went to hell without them.

The sound of Emiliano Zapata's hearty laughter interrupted Peter Duprez' reverie. Tracy Richard's lazy Texas drawl returned him to the moment. "An' so mah good friend, the Battle of Juarez was fought and ended, thanks ta the clear thinking of yer compatriot, Pancho Villa."

"Ayeiii," muttered Zapata. "True. Panchito ees a

360

man of hees word. But, gringo, what happened after that to make Pancho and his little Jew god to part so bitterly?" asked Zapata, sipping his wine delicately under the watchful eyes of Josefa who sat transfixed, listening to the gringo's story.

Captain Richards sat back against his chair, his boots and spurs propped up on a footstool. "Ah'll tell ya, *Jefe*. It's like this. The day after Juarez fell, Madero gets a call from this here General Navarro the officer who held the fort in Juarez. He offered ta surrender unconditionally. Heah's the kink in the cardboahd. Seems Pancho had the same fate in stoah foah Navarro as Tamborel, see? Both Orozco and Villa vied foah this critter's balls. When they arrived at Madero's office, these hombres got the shock o' theah lives. Madero refused ta turn Navarro ovah ta them. Ah'd like ta tell ya, it caused some mighty bad feelin's. By then, news came that Diaz was prepared ta resign office.

"Ya see, *Jefe,* it was all gravy after Villa took Juarez for Madero. The wind changed swiftly. Madero fergot his promise ta Villa. He was a civilized gentleman no longer at war. He thanked Villa for his effort, see? By God, Pancho Villa was plucked hairless in those next few minutes. Ya heah? Plucked hairless! He told Madero how he felt. He bragged on hisself a bit, reminding Madero that while his chocolate-drinking regulars sat around scratchin' theah asses, he, Villa, had displayed the necessary balls ta march on Juarez and seize it foah the revolution.

"Ya could've heard Villa's heart bust in two when Madero pinned back his ears for disobeying orders by attacking Juarez. Not so much as a thank ya for handin' him the revolution—and Mexico!"

"Madero dared tell Pancho this after *he* gave *him* the *presidency?*" Zapata's dark eyes blackened in fury; he sat forward in his seat. "What did Panchito say?"

"Villa was a little mixed up, ya see," replied Tracy. "He don't really understand the lying ways of those crackerjack politicians. An' he was the first ta admit it ta us later. That big bear of a man was hurt, ya can bet

361

me. He took time to warn Madero to be aware of the lying tongues he surrounded hisself with. If he didn't, it would one day mark his downfall. Madero must have charmed Pancho. He embraced the *jefe* and begged him not to condemn him. He told Villa there were things a president had ta do that wouldn't look right ta others, but that he had ta do what was right for the majority."

"And Pancho," interrupted Peter Duprez, "told Madero that he, too, had things ta do that might not look right ta others. An' right theah on the spot, he turned all his troops ovah ta Madero's brother. He said his good-byes ta all o' us. Our last night together, we all got stinkin' drunk and our *jefe* returned to San Andres, his home. The Gringo Brigade disbursed. The captain and mahself returned ta El Paso until we got word from yer men that you needed us, Emiliano."

Zapata paced the floor the last few moments of their conversation. His black eyes flaring angrily, he pounded the table with his balled fists in a fit of temper. "Idiot! Imbecile! And now, the moment that pansy in Mexico City whistles him up, Panchito runs! He's ready once more to make a burro of himself!"

"Ah don't understand ya, *Jefe*," said Tracy Richards. "Whatcha mean?"

"What I say, *Capitán,* is Pancho Villa has already begun to recruit men for the revolution! It has begun again! Madero is not the man for the job! He's not big enough to fit the seat of the *presidente!*" shouted Zapata. "Such a small taco as Madero cannot control the military! All around him are men who will crush him! I tell Pancho this—and ju know what Pancho tells me? Not as long as Villa is alive will one hand be raised against Madero! He is some nut, Pancho Villa! He doesn't see what I see!" He puffed on his *cigarro* as if it were a small volcano. "Listen, gringos. Pancho wants ju to meet him in Parral! Ju give Pancho a message for me—pretty damn *pronto!* Ju tell Pancho that I will defend Moreles as I defended it before Madero arrived in the capital. That I will kill every *Feder-*

ale who sticks his stinking nose into Zapata's territory. But ju also tell Panchito for me, if I learn of any treachery from Madero, I personally will kill him. And if Pancho wishes to fight me because of this act, I will meet him, man to man, *guerrillo* to *guerrillo,* and we'll see whose balls burst first! Pancho Villa's or Emiliano Zapata's!"

Tracy Richards glanced casually at Peter Duprez. In his eyes the message was anything but casual. "You mean, *Jefe,* everything has begun again? The revolution has started up again?"

"Whatssa matter, gringo?" snarled Zapata as he sat down hard in his chair, boots propped up on the desk. "Ju got too much dirt in your hairy ears? The revolution never ended! It just took time to yawn and rub the deceit from its eyes. Why you think Panchito has sent for ju, eh?"

There was silence in the room. At some point during their conversation—Peter couldn't recall when—the women had left the room upon a nod from Zapata, so the men could speak of vital matters. Zapata rose to his feet. He walked to the door and called Fuentes. The man appeared braced in a salute.

"You will bring the gringos their clothing and escort them to Mexico City." He turned to the Americans. "From the capital you will take the train to Durango. Pancho has arranged to have his men meet ju there for the trip to Parral. Is agreed?" He spoke in Spanish.

The Americans nodded reluctantly. "What about the women?" asked Captain Richards.

"We will send them one week later. Do not worry. We shall insure their appearance in Parral—or wherever you wish them to meet you. Is not better you go first, then send word? One never knows when Pancho Villa's wrath will strike. He says Parral, but it could mean Chihuahua when he gets something up his ass!"

The captain nodded. "You're certain they'll be all right. I don't want anything to happen to Rosalia," he said evenly.

Zapata leveled his cold eyes on the gringo. "She is

363

not jus' some *campesina?*" He seemed surprised. It pleased him, however, to learn this. He'd seen gringos before with the Mexican *putas,* and some were worse than the Mexican themselves. It would have pleased Zapata greatly if the men in his camp were married to the women. Single women in the camp always spelled trouble, even among married men. More *putas* had been eliminated by a jealous wife than he cared to think about.

"Then it's settled, gringos. After we eat, Fuentes will take you to Mexico City. Upstairs, you will find your *viejas* in separate rooms, preparing baths for you and your clothing for the trip. Go—enjoy your last moments together. Tonight we have a fiesta to show my appreciation for your combined efforts—and the arms you transported to us, of course."

The gringos rose and nodded, thanking the *jefe.* They walked out of the small salon and made their way through the crowds inside the villa. Fuentes directed them to their rooms.

Tracy Richards stepped briskly in anticipation of his rendezvous with Rosalia. He disappeared behind the door calling, "Se ya in heaven, Tom Mix!"

Peter smiled faintly. He glanced about the area, hoping to catch sight of the Sandoval sisters. He wanted some lead, some idea of where this fellow Paco had taken Madelaina. But they were nowhere to be seen. Reluctantly he entered the room. Lucia was there, freshly scrubbed, perfumed, and wearing a clean lightweight robe. In the center of the room was a bathtub filled with hot water, scented with perfumed oils. He felt awkward, not accustomed to the ways of a Mexican. He hadn't taken to this life as long as Tracy had and didn't feel as secure.

The room was pleasant, not as bare as those he'd seen on the lower level. The bed was a nice size, with clean sheets and a brightly patterned Indian woven blanket over it. A few pieces of furniture graced the room: a bureau with a lamp on it, two chairs, and a wardrobe containing a dark gray business suit with a shirt and tie. Hand luggage, much like a carpetbag, lay in the corner.

Stripped, with his body immersed to his chest, Peter Duprez lay back against the bathtub, where Lucia had placed a wooden headrest, and soaked to his heart's content. He tried to think about Madelaina, to focus on her whereabouts, and while he did, he tried to will himself to think of Cuernavaca. This is where she would go, he felt certain. But something deep inside him told him that the ties between Pancho Villa and Little Fox, whatever they were, would be strong enough to bring them together since the revolution had been fired up again.

With Lucia around it became increasingly difficult for him to concentrate on his wife. Her soft voice and her large, concerned eyes were difficult to withstand as she purred consolingly to him.

"We shall meet soon again, gringo. Rosalia will follow the captain to the ends of the earth—and wherever she goes, I, too, shall be. Is good, gringo?"

"Look here, Lucia, ah can't promise ya nothing like what Tracy and Rosalia have together. Ya gotta know ah'm a married man. Ya already know that, don'cha?"

"*Si,* I know, gringo. Ees a long time you see your *mujer?*"

"*Si.* Right now, ah don't even know if she's dead or alive." He tried to lay back and contemplate Madelaina, but Lucia's busy fingers prevented such concentration, and Peter found himself enjoying the moment with a flush of guilt.

Her full, ripe breasts escaped her wraparound and leaned over into the water as she attempted to retreive a bar of soap that had slipped out of her hand. She felt something else, hard, firm, and eager. Her dark eyes lifted to meet his. Peter reached for her and planted a kiss on her luscious lips. He pulled her across the tub and she fell into his arms, half-immersed in the water herself, uncaring, wanting only for Peter to consume her again as he had the previous night. Only this night would be something very special. Lucia had promised herself that Peter Duprez, the gringo, would never forget such a night.

He heard her gasp when he lifted her in his strong arms and raised her over him and let her sink slowly on top of him. She leaned over and pressed his face into her breasts, holding them taut in her arms, going from one nipple to the other, in and out of his greedy lips. He moved rhythmically under her and heard her sigh and moan like an animal in heat.

Neither of them remembered getting out of the cold tub, or how they found their way to the bed. By now the quantity of liquor Peter had consumed began to warm him, and he delighted at Lucia's moving to his direction. She clung to Peter as if she never intended to let him out of her sight. He was amazed at her skill as a lover. Last night she had given him enjoyment, but nothing like this night. He told her so. She replied that it was only because the setting was right, the mood, the occasion. He had to agree; the proper ingredients had stimulated them both.

Peter learned that Lucia was also a *mestizo*. She had lived in a border town near Laredo and for a time became a whore to support her family. At fourteen she had been abused by a gringo *ranchero,* a beast of a man, and she ran away. She made her way to Monterrey as a gypsy dancer and somehow found herself, at the age of sixteen, a *campesina* in the camps of Pancho Villa, where Rosalia Quintera took her in, hoping to teach her how to elevate herself above the average *campesina*.

Lucia had seen Peter Duprez, whom she knew as Tom Mix, in Juarez at the campsite where Villa and Madero had met for the first time.

"From the minute these dark eyes see ju, gringo, they melted. Ees so terrible that Lucia, like Rosalia, has eyes only for gringo? For ju?" she asked breathlessly.

"No, little cat, ah can't see nothin' so terrible about that."

She lay back, her eyes half-closed, lips smiling in

366

contentment, the face of a woman possessed by a real man. She was enjoying every moment of his sensual thrusts, his teasing, his exciting touch. She grew frenzied, her body twitched and turned, and her fingers dug into Peter's arms and his shoulders. She pulled him down—down—down on her until his mouth pressed against the hollow between the mounded flesh. She was hot and moist and she pulsed heatedly under his lips. Suddenly she screamed and moaned, "Here, gringo, *por favor.* Ayeiii, gringo, how *fantastico* ju are. *Si,* right there, *querido.*"

She moaned and squirmed and thrashed about the bed, bounding like a rippling wave over the surface of the sea. When it was over for her, she pushed him gently on his back. "Now, gringo, the dance is for ju."

Lucia rose to her nimble feet and began by softly clapping her hands above her head, keeping time to some inner native rhythm only she could hear. In a slow, sensuous manner she moved her body, swinging her dark hip-length hair around her like dancing snakes. She swirled about the room, moving around the four-poster like a harem dancer in a pasha's palace. From a nearby vase she plucked a red velvety rose and slipped it between her teeth, flashing a seductive smile at him and dropping her lids over smoldering eyes that filled with promise.

Peter, having lit himself a thin *cigarrello,* lay back on the pillows, contented and fully amused by her. He had found her to be sweet, caring, and somewhat pathetic in attempting to win his affections. He almost regretted that his affections belonged to someone else. At times he'd considered Madelaina simply a figment of his imagination, a distortion for a man as physical as Peter Duprez.

Lucia knew when she had lost his attention. She had stopped dancing and he hadn't even noticed. She sat down on the bed next to him, allowing the velvety petals of the rose to caress his body. She played the rose over lightly over the hairs of his body. She noticed the hair stood up and he shivered involuntarily. It wouldn't be long now. She trailed the rose over his thighs, his genitals, around the coarse hair between his legs until he began to swell and engorge with life. She had his attention. He ground out the cigarette and held her close, opened his lips as she leaned in to kiss him. Slowly, she moved lower and lower until her mouth covered his manhood in soft movements.

Outside, the sound of music swelled as musicians joined other musicians in the early evening. It was growing darker outside; the voices, gay and lively, grew louder and filled with anticipation for the evening's festivities.

There came a loud banging on the wall. "Hey, Tom Mix! Howya doing?" came the voice of Tracy Richards. A smile broke out on Peter's face. "That sonofabitch! He's gotten his fill, now he's gonna do his best ta interrupt ouah fun," he confided to Lucia.

"Ah got me some wild filly!" he called back, hoping to shut Tracy up.

"Oooooohhwheeeee!" yelled the gringo, loud enough to cause the walls to shudder.

Lucia withdrew, an angry frown on her face. *"Bastardo!"* she screamed loudly. "Leave us alone! Rosalia, tell jur man to hold his tongue or I come to cut it off!" She let loose a hailstorm of curses in her native tongue hot enough to derail a train.

"C'mon, little cat, he don't mean nothing by it. We got the whole night ahead o' us. Why don't we take a breather, eh, *chiquita*?" Peter rose from the bed, wrapped a towel around his midriff, and tried the door between the two rooms.

"Hey Trace—open up! Ya started this—now let's get a little cozier."

The door opened with a loud bang. Rosalia stood behind her lover, shaking her head with a half-tolerant look. "When he gets like this, Tom Meex, he wants to love the world. Ees no use to stop him. Go ahead, gringo, you want Lucia, take her." She called to the girl. "Lucia, the *capitán* desires to take ju to the moon with him."

368

"Tell the *capitán* I already have an *hombre* who will fly with me."

"Ju tell him. He won't believe me. He is one *borrachón* tonight!"

Tracy swept into the room in full tumescence.

"See what ole Trace's got fer ya, little *chiquita mia?*" he said, deliriously drunk. "Three times with Rosalia and still not enough. Is that some bull fer ya? C'mon, sweet thing. Ah've been keeping hard jus' fer youah pleasure. Ah can't stand ta wait anothah moment." He held his engorged manhood, proudly displaying it for the others.

Lucia glanced hesitantly at Rosalia, shame flooding her face. Her dark eyes moved to Peter who'd taken time to relight the dead *cigarrillo*. Defiance written in her eyes, Lucia shrugged seductively. "Ju want to fuck, gringo? Ees done. Come with me. I show you the moon."

Rosalia's surprise, mixed with hurt, humiliation, and disappointment, wasn't lost to Peter. In an instant he was moved to action. "Ya stupid sonofabitch," he cussed Tracy out. "Whatcha trying ta prove?" He felt badly for Rosalia in those moments; Lucia was quickly dismissed from his thoughts.

"Ees A-O.K., Tom Meex," said Rosalia, grimly determined not to show Tracy how much she hurt. "That seed bull has too much cum in his balls for me alone—he theenks he's got to spread it around. One day will come too many gringo *niños* named Tracy—*bastardo*—Richards. Eef he cares nothin', Rosalia cares nothin'."

The couple were tussling on the bed. Rosalia tried hard not to witness the goings on and Peter did his best to try to steer her back into her room, but Rosalia wasn't to be moved. He could see the anger, hurt, and disillusionment turn to live coals in her eyes, as she stared at the activity on the bed.

"*Ayyyyeeeeeiiiiii!*" Ya sonofabitch! Ya fuckin' goddamn little greaser whore!" cried Tracy Richards, screaming at the top of his lungs as he held his bloodied phallus. Eyes wide and frenzied, he stared in disbelief at the blood squirting from the sharp teeth marks, where Lucia had bitten into him. He had sobered instantly. The shock and surprise on his face—so overly dramatic—caused a ripple of laughter to form in Rosalia's throat until it broke out into loud, hearty laughter. She turned to Lucia and rushed to her side, embracing her with warm, affectionate hug. Even Peter had to contain a smile that formed at the corners of his lips.

"Ya ring-tailed baboon! Ya asked fer it!" said Peter, forcibly containing his laughter. His blue eyes danced in merriment. Glancing at Lucia, he noticed she glanced at him through slanted, shy eyes.

"Rosalia," whimpered Trace, limping back into his room. "Ya see what that bloody little whore done ta me?"

"Imagine," said Rosalia, winking broadly at Peter as she steered her man through the door, "it may be two months before you can put it back to work, *querido*. What a shame! Tsk, tsk, tsk." She clucked her tongue, shutting the door behind them.

Peter glanced sternly at the girl, then, unable to contain his mirth, he burst out laughing at the funny picture of Tracy Richards, holding his diddling tool like a limp, drying worm. Lucia began to laugh, slowly at first, thinking for certain Tom Mix would beat her for committing so outrageous an act upon his friend. Soon they were both laughing.

"Ah gotta say that ah wouldn't want to be ole Trace for nothing in the world, hear? And ya better not repeat that kind o' stuff again, 'cause some people might not take kindly ta such a carnivorous act. But between youah an' me, ah'm jus' grateful ya had the good sense ta do what ya did 'cause ya wouldn't've had Rosalia fer a friend no more. Ya understand?"

"Is because Rosalia is my *amiga* that I do such terrible thing, ju understand? Somewan has to make him see how wonderful is Rosalia."

"Ah think ah do, little cat. Yes m'am, that's about the quickest justice ah ever saw legislated in mah life."

It was also the first time Peter Duprez had laughed so heartily in a long time. It relieved the tension even better than the sexual interlude.

"Ya gotta understand one thing, little cat—if'n a man's blind, ain't no one gonna make him see, understand?"

"Eef a man not blind cannot see, eet would hurt him none to wear glasses, eh, gringo?"

Peter smiled. He had no reason to worry over this young girl. He felt better about leaving her. Whatever she'd learned, she'd learned plenty from living, and she'd get along all right. This judgment of her took on new proportions when, as they dressed for the fiesta, she casually mentioned that she had learned much about this man Paco Jimenez, who saved the life of Little Fox.

"He ees a *Federale*, attached to the battalion of General Obregon, gringo. Ju know why he was sent to Madrigal?"

"You'ah doing the talking, little cat."

"Ees because the general found out. Paco makes love to Little Fox."

Peter whipped about and stared at her hotly.

"Don'ju get mad at Lucia. Ju want I ask Alicia, gringo. Che told me everything. Also that che loves Paco very much herself. But Paco has eyes only for Little Fox."

Peter felt his throat go dry. They were lovers after all! But Alicia had said they were lovers but not in the sense Peter meant.

"Ju know how far is Cuernavaca from Moreles, gringo?" she asked with the cunning of a tiger ready for the kill.

"No. An' ah don't wantta know. You'ah lettin' youah imagination work overtime. Ah'm here with work ta do."

"Ees over the next hill, gringo," she said softly. "Four, maybe five kilometers. Ju want Lucia to take ju to Little Fox?"

"Four kilometers? That close?"

371

She nodded. "Maybe if Lucia take ju to Cuernavaca, ju get Little Fox out of jur mind?"

"She's mah wife, little cat. Don'cha understand?" He grabbed her shoulder roughly. "If you'ah lyin' ta me, ah'll beat the living bejesus outa ya, heah?"

Peter had dressed in the trim gray business suit with white shirt and tie. He brushed his streaked brown hair off his face, trying to straighten the mass of curls framing his face, but it was no use. Whenever he washed his hair, it remained unmanageable for several days.

"Ju look beautiful, gringo," she said wistfully, devouring him with her eyes.

"No, little cat, it's youah who look beautiful. In fact you'ah ravishing."

"What means ravishing?"

"Good ehough ta eat."

"Señor?"

"No chance! None of that. Weah've got us some business ta attend ta."

Lucia was right. Cuernavaca was just over the hill. He learned this from Eufimo Zapata. And when the *jefe*'s brother asked him why he wanted to know, he said it was simply curiosity, that he had heard the area was breathtakingly beautiful.

Later in the evening, at the height of the fiesta, without saying a word to Tracy or Rosalia of their intentions, Peter Duprez and Lucia sneaked away from the hacienda on horseback. Stopped by the guards at the outer gate, Peter saluted him and called out that they were going for a short ride. Two armed guards instantly converged on them and, taking the reins of their horses, led the gringo and his *señorita* back to Zapata's villa gainst many protestations.

They faced Zapata in the presence of an angry and pain-filled Tracy Richards who periodically stroked the bulge in his trousers while attempting to suppress an expression of pain on his face. Peter, asked to explain why he was leaving the villa, appeared nonplussed by all the fuss.

"We was jus' aimin' ta go for a little romantic ride. Are ya denying me that, *Jefe?*" asked Peter with obvious indignation.

Zapata, dark-faced and stern, shook his head as he spoke in his native dialect. "Beyond the perimeter of my lands I cannot control what happens to you, gringo. You think the *Federales* don't know the boundaries? That any time in a twenty-four-hour day they could rush in and destroy us to the last man if my people didn't keep a diligent watch for them, eh? Tell me what is so important out there?" he asked with native suspicion and an inborn caution. "Collaborators? Friends? People for you to contact—who? Explain to me so I understand." Before Peter could reply, Zapata took his wrath out on the girl. "And you, *campesina*—how is it you didn't come first to me? Haven't you been taught the ways of your people? For the gringo perhaps there's an excuse. Perhaps he wasn't aware of the dangers. But for you there is no excuse." He called to his man Fuentes. "Twenty lashes for the girl so she doesn't forget she violated Zapata's law."

"Now ya wait jus' a doggone second," began Peter, dumbfounded.

"Tom Mix!" shouted Captain Richards, warning him with his eyes. "Don'cha interfeah in the laws of these people. The girl should've known the rules, heah?"

Peter protested as Lucia was dragged out the door. Tracy held him back.

The gaiety of the crowd halted when they saw Fuentes dragging Lucia into the courtyard. Instantly they knew the picture. A flogging intended as a deterrent to anyone breaking the laws of Zapata was respected. Zapata's rules were explicit. The girl was wrong in their eyes. She should have either stopped the gringo or reported his activities instantly to the *jefe*. In being remiss, she deserved to be punished for not only endangering her own life, but the lives of the *Zapatistas*. In this savage land, life was cheap. Only survival counted, and survival was possible only if the laws were obeyed.

The crowd formed a circle around a nearby hitching

post where the girl was tied hands overhead to the rough wood. Fuentes moved forward and with a strong hand ripped the shirt from her back. Behind the circle, off to one side, Peter argued with Zapata. "Let me take the lashes. The girl had nothing ta do with this. It's mah fault, *Jefe*. Ah encouraged her with idle talk of lovemaking."

Zapata stood cold as marble, unyielding. "Ju, gringo are a friend, a freedom fighter who has helped our cause. If we make meestakes, *our* cause—*our* people will suffer greatly. Ju please leave us alone. Go into the villa." He nodded to his men who moved in swiftly, rifles at the ready, with menace in their eyes. They pushed Peter back away from the crowd toward the hacienda proper.

Peter heard the hushed whispers of Zapata's people. Not fully understanding why the girl was being punished, they assumed the worst and that could only mean one thing—she was a spy. He wanted to set the record straight and couldn't. He saw Rosalia run toward him. "What ees happening, gringo?"

Peter, prodded by the drawn bayonets, walked past her, his head in a hangdog expression. "Ask yer people—they seem ta have all the answers, *chiquita*." He disappeared into the hacienda.

Captain Tracy Richards had a front line view of the cat-o'-nine-tails as it whistled overhead and landed with a sharp crack, splitting Lucia's back in two. Lucia gave a start, she bit her lips to prevent the scream from leaving her throat as the skin split and blood oozed between the crevice. Again and again the leather strips slashed down on her until she could no longer harbor the screams. After the sixth lash, Lucia fainted from the excruciating pain. Zapata, watching solemnly, ordered the whipping stopped.

Rosalia came forth to assist the poor, wretched Lucia. "Tend to her wounds," instructed Zapata with surprising tenderness. He turned to his people. "The woman Lucia broke the law. She attempted to take the gringo riding after curfew without reporting to me,

374

thereby endangering all our lives. It was a just punishment." He raised his arm, signaling the musicians. "Commence with the festivities," he ordered, as if nothing unusual had happened.

Inside, Peter, filled with anger and humiliation for Lucia's fate, packed his gear. He converted his gun belt into a shoulder pouch and holstered his gun.

"Ah can't wait ta get outa this crazy country, Trace," he told his friend when the captain entered the room. "Ah'm packed. Are ya coming with me?"

"Ya know ah am, *amigo*. Zapata already told us we were leavin' tonight. What the hell were ya trying to pull off? Ya nearly got us both killed!"

Peter explained about Cuernavaca, how close it was, that he wanted information about Madelaina. "It was that simple. Lucia simply offered to be my guide."

"Goddamnit! Ya should've told me! Didn't ah tell ya before, ya gotta do things right south of the border? These people play for keeps—they can't take no chances. It ain't like it is in the States, galdarn ye!"

"How's the girl?"

"She'll live. She knows the rules, Pete—"

"If ah heah that once more—" he said threateningly. "Are ya ready ta cut this place loose?"

"I've already packed," he said with obvious discomfort. "Served the little hellion right," muttered Tracy, stroking his pain-filled crotch.

Peter glanced at him knowing he was referring to an entirely different transgression. He snapped the bag closed securely. Tracy glanced at his friend.

"Ah know yer hot under the collar, buddy. But ya know the irony of this whole mess? We could've stopped in Cuernavaca en route to Mexico City. Ah could've arranged fer Fuentes ta stop so we could get word of youah little filly. But ya jus' listen heah ta me, big boy. Any mention that Little Fox is a daughter of General Obregon and ya might jus' incite these heah *Zapatistas* ta go on a raiding party some night to kidnap youah *mujer*. Ya wanta gamble with them apples, *amigo*?"

Peter gave a start. He hadn't considered such action. As usual Tracy was right. Peter remained silent during the back-slapping farewells and affectionate gestures. Even Zapata slapped Peter on the shoulders, embraced him, and said gruffly, "No bad feelings, gringo. We take care of Lucia. In time all will be forgiven and she will join you in Parral. *Vaya con Dios, muchachos.*"

Zapata and his followers waved to them as the horses led the gringos along the road leading away from the hacienda. Their rough and ready escorts, wearing conical-shaped sombreros, were hardly discernible until the full orange moon came into sight. They rode for hours through forests, deserts, and rocky terrain, expertly bypassing the road blocks set up by the *Federales* to ensnare *Zapatistas*.

It wasn't until Peter and Tracy were seated safely on the train to Durango, looking like prosperous American businessmen with forged papers and expansive manners, that Peter realized how tightly controlled was the blanket of protection afforded them by Emiliano Zapata. And regretfully he recalled he hadn't said good-bye to either Rosalia Quintera or Lucia.

These past forty-eight hours, memorable to say the least, had been time in which he'd found and lost his wife, learned deplorable, dehumanizing facts about the cruelty inflicted upon her, and witnessed a savage beating among a savage people. He'd been made love to wildly and had nearly been killed in a comedy of errors in which human emotions ran the gamut of emotions from love to hate, from tenderness to violence. Peter knew he'd never be the same man he was before meeting with the *Zapatistas*.

En route to Durango, his silence was consumed with thoughts of Madelaina Obregon Duprez and what she'd endured at that hellish pit, Madrigal de Los Altos. He was unable to put her from his mind. He wondered how he'd ever find her again. Would he have to wait until the new insurrection ended? How would he find her? How?

Chapter 14

Madelaina awakened to strange surroundings. She blinked her eyes several times as she slowly focused on the bare wooden walls. She felt her stomach grow queasy, and for a few mad moments she thought she was back at Madrigal. Her eyes snapped open in alarm. Then, as she noticed the clean sheets and the colorful Indian blanket, as she inhaled the enticing aroma of food, all thoughts of Madrigal were dispelled. She sniffed the air; she couldn't recall ever being this hungry.

Where was she? She tried desperately to stimulate her memory. All that came to her were recollections of many disturbing dreams. She even dreamed she had seen Peter Duprez, her husband. Imagine, dreams so real she could still feel the touch of his cool lips pressed to hers, the warmth of his lean, strong body next to hers. Strange about dreams—they could feel so real.

She sighed heavily, when suddenly the sound of footsteps outside her door alerted her. Under the covers, her shaking fists were balled tightly together. Would the sound of footsteps always do this to her? She trembled in fright and felt perspiration on her face. The door opened and a kindly-looking older woman with snow white hair entered carrying a tray of food. She spoke in a dialect Spanish.

"At last, *chiquita,* you are awake. Our prayers have been answered." Her dark brown eyes twinkled affectionately.

"*Our* prayers?" She didn't understand.

"Your fiancé's and mine. Your *novio*. He's been a lost soul these past many weeks. I've brought you hot broth. You drink now. What's important is for you to gain back all your strength. You've improved. The doctor tells us in time, with good food, you'll be as good as new." She sat on the bed, prepared to spoon-feed the young woman.

"Where am I? Who brought me here?" Fleeting images rushed at her: the Sandoval girls, Paco Jiminez, the trip to Ayala—so close to Cuernavaca—and Peter! Peter Duprez! She'd seen him after all. It was no dream. She raised her hand to her sweating forehead, pushing the black strands from her face.

"Parral, *señorita*. You are a few miles from Parral." The aged woman, with the harsh skin of a puckered fig, raised the spoon of hot broth to Madelaina's lips. "Now drink."

She opened her mouth dutifully and felt the warmth of the broth sear through her chest, just as the face of Major Salomon flashed into her consciousness. She recoiled in fright. "Who brought me here?"

"I've already told you. Your *novio* brought you. Now open your mouth."

"No!" She shook her head, not really listening. "Not him! He wouldn't dare!" She pushed the woman's hand aside. Her brain roiled with thoughts. Hah! That monster would stop at nothing to destroy her. Yet, hadn't he brought her to Parral—to a doctor? She was confused. That bastard wouldn't concern himself with the health of Madelaina Obregon.

"Open your mouth, *señorita*," said the woman firmly. Madelaina obeyed. She was so hungry she let nothing interfere with the rest of the meal. When she was finished, the door opened. Paco Jimenez entered the room, his eyes filled with concern.

"Paco!" She pushed the last spoonful from her. "Paco—what are you doing here?" she exclaimed in relief. Only then did she understand the woman's words.

The old woman stared at her as if she'd taken leave of her senses. "You don't recognize your *novio*?" She shook her head sadly. "We must inform the doctor, *señor,* she has no memory." She rose to leave, taking the empty tray with her.

"She'll be fine," said Paco, closing the door behind her. He moved across the room to Madelaina's side. "At last, you're fully awake. I've worried myself sick these past weeks. February has evaporated into nothing. We are now in the second week of March."

"How did we get so far north? How did you—why didn't you take me to my hacienda in Cuernavaca, Paco?" She asked so many questions she felt foolish. "Please, Paco," she asked. "Tell me everything. I recall nothing after that black buzzard Salomon jumped me."

"Well," began Paco, after he lit a cigarette and walked to the open window, gazing about the countryside. "We waited for you until 5:45 outside of Ayala. When you didn't return, we were all worried sick. I, of course, insisted we must obey your instructions and go to Cuernavaca. So, against the protestations of those stubborn *Zapatistas*—the Sandoval girls—and believe me I had to pick them up bodily and put them in the wagon, *chiquita. Ayeiii!* So stubborn! Like mules. No. Worse. That Alicia—what a wildcat! *Pues,* we traveled approximately one kilometer, no more. In the distance, like a clap of rolling thunder, came the rumble of horses. I quickly pulled off the road. For a time we hid in the foothills. Wouldn't you know—the men of Zapata came to a stop but a few yards from us. *Pues,* those two *loco guapas* leapt from the wagon and moved in closer to listen to what their kinsmen were saying. Before too long a rider came from Ayala on a horse that flew like the wind. He gathered the *Zapatistas* to him and conversed for several moments. Alicia and Amelia, having heard the entire plan, returned to me and explained that the *Zapatistas* intended to attack Ayala and wipe out the *Rurales.* Zapata himself and the gringos hiding in the stables had been alerted by some holy sister that the *Rurales* had garrisoned the mission. *Pues,* it didn't take long for me to understand what was about to happen. I, Paco Jimenez, could not in good conscience leave you to the mercy of either

379

side. I loaded up the girls once more. As soon as the *Zapatistas* tied brush to their *riatas,* we waited for the dust to clear behind them and then followed them to the village. I instructed the girls to wait in the wagon. When we saw bombs bursting, buildings exploding, and bullets flying, my worst fears were growing into panic.

"*Gracias Dios,* the fight didn't take too long—what was it? An hour, perhaps a little longer? By then I had managed to creep into the stables." Paco turned from the window and crossed himself. "When I saw you struggling in the arms of that miserable son of a tainted whore, Salomon, who now wears the uniform of a major," he spat scornfully, "the devil possessed me in those next minutes. I pulled you from his arms. We fought. I pulled out my knife when I recalled all those despicable acts to which he had subjected you at Madrigal. I thank the heavenly Father I knew how to use it. *Pues,* I'm sure I killed the rotten animal. I stuck him, time and time again," said Paco, the reality of his deed flaring brightly in his eyes. "He no longer moved. Even in the dimly lit stables, I could see his body stiffen and jerk as pain after pain caused him to move like a jumping bean, *señorita.*" Paco walked to the side of the bed and sat down. "We traveled nearly two weeks. You've been in fever, out of your mind with delirium," he said soberly, studying her thin, pale features. "Many times I felt certain you had drawn your last breath. Now that we've been here for nearly a month, the doctor tells me you've passed the crisis."

Paco was talking to a woman heavy with sleep. Madelaina had dozed off in the middle of their talk. Understanding, he pulled the bedding up around her and left the room, walking briskly outside into the March air.

Never far from Madelaina, Paco had slept in the room next to hers with the door open in case she might awaken in the night and become frightened. He wondered if she'd ever be the same. She'd been through hell. Anyone else might have given up long ago and taken their own life. He wondered many times if he

380

might have fared as well. She was made of tough stock, something in her favor.

Well, it was nearly over. It was all in the past, a hideous, black past of never-to-be-forgotten memories for either of them. Paco lit up a *cigarro* and moved out under a large fig tree, wondering about Alicia Sandoval. When he had returned to the wagon with Madelaina that night, he'd been frantic because the girls were nowhere to be found. He'd waited nearly an hour on the outskirts of Ayala, hearing the guns and grenades tearing up the village and its people. Finally, concerned over Madelaina, he began to stir the donkeys into activity, making ready to leave. Just then he heard his name being called. He gave a start, cocking his head to listen.

"Paco. Paco?" It had been Alicia. She flew into his arms and held him tightly.

Surprised by this sudden rush of affection, Paco had held on to her, enjoying it immensely. "Where's Amelia?" he'd asked the petite brunette.

"We are returning to our people, Paco. Perhaps one day our paths shall cross again. Take care of Madelaina and remember us in your prayers as we shall remember both of you. Where will you go?" she asked, glancing nervously at the pale face of the girl bundled in the wagon.

He told her briefly he'd found Madelaina being abducted by Salomon—who was now a major. That he'd left the man bleeding to death.

"There are many things that I, Paco Jimenez, do not understand. First the followers of Madero are my enemies, then they are my compatriots, suddenly we become enemies again. Perhaps Little Fox is right. I must think on many things. I am a *Federale*, a soldier, and Zapata has become my enemy. Therefore, you are my enemy, Alicia. Yet, I do not feel you are my enemy. You see how confusing it can be?"

"I, too, am confused. I find no enemy in you, *chico*," she said, tears welling in her eyes. "Perhaps

381

one day we shall meet again, when all this hating and warring ends."

"Perhaps even sooner," said Paco prophetically. "For now, I must go. She is in bad condition and I must find a doctor."

"To Cuernavaca? Many good doctors are there. But, Paco, is best you do not go to the hacienda of her father. I feel something bad awaits you there."

He glanced into her eyes. There was no time to fathom the complicated brew he read in them. *"Adios, chiquita."* He'd paused long enough to gather her in his arms and kiss her lustily on the lips. In an instant, they were both breathless, but Paco had to be strong in those moments. He shoved her from him, jumped onto the wagon, and cracked the whip over the heads of the mules.

"Adelante," he called.

"Paco! Take the back roads! *Adios, querido,"* called Alicia softly, pulling the black *rebozo* over her hair. Tears fell gently on her cheeks. She ran to her horse, mounted it bareback, and kicked her heels into the animal's flesh. She broke into a wild gallop and horse and rider disappeared into the night.

Paco had transported Madelaina in a series of detours. They had stopped in a small village of Zamora, where he sought the aid of a physician. The doctor advised him that the girl had been severely injured internally, that she needed bed-rest and considerable care and good, nourishing food. "There's no way to assess the internal damage done to her for a while, but she may never be able to have children," said the forlorn doctor after he examined her. "Are you her husband?"

"Yes," lied Paco. "She was raped by *Federales.* I returned too late to protect her."

"Hah! What could you against such monsters," said the incensed man, scratching his bald head. "Sometimes I am inclined to agree with the rebels when I see such brutality. We are not *animales!* We are men. Each and every one of us! Why can't we take lessons from the *Norteamericanos*? Look how civilized they are.

382

Mexico desperately needs to rid herself of foreign domination," raved the physician. "I went to school in the north. I was so certain that my duty was to my people and to my country. Sometimes, I almost wish I had remained there, taken up citizenship, and lived among the civilized." He sighed. "There you are, my good man. Take your wife home. Keep her in bed and, if the *Rurales* come back, skin their balls and soak them in vinegar."

And this man is civilized? thought Paco. He thanked the doctor and offered to give him one of the mules in payment for his services. "If you will wait, I can pay you in pesos, but it will take at least two months."

The doctor waved him off. "Why should it be any different for you, my good man? I only get paid in chickens, eggs, or goats, rarely a mule. *Vaya con Dios.*"

Paco had stayed on the back roads, stealing food en route. Some milk from an overblown goat, a few eggs from a chicken coop, and once or twice he'd killed rattlesnakes and broiled them over a fire. It had taken him weeks to get to the outskirts of Parral. Madelaina could go no farther without rest. He made a deal with a farmer to exchange his services for the accommodation of his ailing wife until she was healthy enough to walk.

Rains coming from over the Sierra Madre mountain range in the near distance prevented much work from being done on the modest hacienda of Francesco Lomas and his aging wife. They told Paco they were a retired couple who had donated their lives in the service of Don Diego Ocampo. For their loyalty, the don granted them a small piece of bottom land.

During those next two months while Madelaina continued to heal, Paco helped Francesco Lomas to build another adobe house, one which the farmer insisted was designed to lure his grandchildren to come live with them. The work was easy, the food excellent, and luckily the estate was far enough off the beaten path that neither *Federales* nor *bandidos* had stopped. Beyond the flatland, a deep forest led the way into the Sierra Madre mountains.

Francesco Lomas was filled with the lore and legends of tribes of interior Indians who'd seldom, if ever, seen a white man and still lived as primitively as their ancestors had centuries before. Daily he'd fill Paco's head with intriguing tales. "The closer you travel to the ocean on the other side of the Sierras, the more impossible the land becomes to traverse. Inside there is jungle, swamp lands such as you've never set eyes upon, *amigo,*" explained the white-haired old man with misty green eyes the color of jade. "In there," he pointed to some remote spot beyond the mountains. "In there, *muchacho,* is a place where few men have ventured—Lago Diablo de Los Muertos, Lake of the Devil's Dead."

Paco Jiminez shook his head. "You're *loco,* old man," he said affectionately. He'd grown to love the old man and wouldn't hurt his feelings. Yet he couldn't believe Lomas' statement. "You tell me that in those mountains are swamp lands, jungles, and a lake?" He shook his head with good humor and disbelief. The man was excellent company and kept him amused.

"*Si,* Paco. I'm not *loco*. What I say is true. I myself have never been there, but I listen to men who have traveled there. They told me that approach to this no man's land is barely possible. Only after endless days of exhausting foot travel through treacherous jungle undergrowth and bloodsucking swamplands full of incredible risks, do you come to a clearing where you'll find the Indians of our ancestors living as their fathers before them. Only with their help, I've been told, for which you must first provide them with sweets and tokens of an outside world, are you permitted to begin the slow ride over the broken floor of a strange desert. But once you come face to face with Ii Lago Diablo de Los Muertos, I've been told, miracles will happen. Ah, *amigo,*" sighed Francesco Lomas, "if only these old bones were not so old and creaky, if once again I was young and filled with the spirit of adventure, there'd be no hesitation. I'd go in a moment. There are legends of gold mines, of rare treasures—" His voice would always trail off at the mention of such treasures, his imagination taking over.

Each night after they finished their meal with the Lomas, Paco would walk Madelaina about the small farm, helping her to regain her strength. He'd often relate the fanciful tales to amuse her. They'd both smile and give the stories no further importance. Madelaina was healing rapidly now and with her strength returning, she spoke of their leaving the Lomas *rancho*.

"It's time to move on, Paco," she told him one evening as they sat on the fencing around the corral, watching the several bulls Lomas kept for breeding purposes. A few mongrel dogs barked and yipped, fighting over the remains of a soup bone tossed them by their kindly mistress, an unassuming old woman who had little to say in the past few days.

Paco was silent. A blanket of purples, golds, and white fire draped across the sky at sunset. The heat rising off the floor of the desert assaulted their nostrils, and they could tell the dry, unbearable heat of summer would soon be upon them. Of late Madelaina had been thinking of Peter Duprez again. Uncertain of their destination and knowing more than ever that she had to find Peter, she would let nothing deter her. She knew there could be no other for her. Since their last brief encounter, it was no longer an old affair sustained only by memories. The moment they kissed in the stables at Ayala, she told herself nothing would ever really part them again. Yet, less than two hours later, she'd been stripped of any power she might have exercised to pilot her own destiny. It just wasn't fair! She lamented to herself that Peter must be at least a thousand miles away. A thousand miles! She laughed aloud at the seeming futility of it all.

"*Que pasa, chiquita?* What is it?" asked Paco, searching her face. "For so long I've not seen you smile—now you laugh, which is more precious. Yet I detect irony in the laughter. Tell me what it is so we

385

can both laugh. I ache inside from all the heaviness I carry in me."

"Nothing. Merely my own foolishness. It's incredible, Paco, that you, unaware of what lies ahead of us, remain loyal and true to me. For no reason I can see, you're willing to remain by my side, regardless of consequences. What have I done to inspire such dedication? I've brought nothing but misery to your life. Why do you risk your life—your future—for me?"

"You ask an unanswerable question. Both questions and answers are a puzzle to me. I've been a soldier all my life. My mother, a *campesina*, approached your father, the general, when I was twelve. She begged that I be allowed to become a soldier. At least I'd have clean bedding, clothing, and good food. Such was her reasoning. Your father, the general, whom I betrayed when I coupled with you, had every reason to punish me. After his kindness I repay him with shame and degradation by ravaging his daughter."

Madelaina turned to him in anger. "Didn't my father couple with your mother? Wasn't she his *campesina* at some time? For heaven's sake, Paco, it's possible you could be his son. You were sent to Madrigal for doing what he does each day of his life. I can see punishment, but, *Dios mios*, not Madrigal!"

"Be grateful he sent me to Madrigal, *querida*. If he hadn't, we might not even be here, alive," he said with sudden clear-sightedness.

Madelaina had to agree with him. She retreated into her previous silence, her thoughts trailing back to the time of her convalescence here at the Lomas *rancho*. She'd browsed through Francesco Lomas' collection of books, amazed at the variety of subjects they covered. She had found Francesco to be a well-educated man for his apparent station in life. His reply was that to be first valet and gentleman to Don Diego Ocampo, one had to be well read. On quiet nights at the hacienda of Don Diego, a Creole, a Spaniard born in the Americas, they had spoken in countless conversations on the subject of the occult and the philosophy of the ancients.

Predestiny, a subject which had fascinated him tremendously, had always kept him a spirited match for Don Diego. Lomas proceeded to explain that now, since he was growing old, he knew that his destiny lay only in death. It was too late for him to be inspired by renewed hope. Such indulgence belonged only to the young like Madelaina and Paco, he'd told her. The young like her and Paco, thought Madelaina. What folly!

Paco's words interrupted her thoughts. "For so long I've been a soldier—ten years in all. I obey. I do this or that. Move forward or backward in retreat on command. What more is expected of any man? I go where I'd led by whomsoever decides to lead me." He had a faraway look in his eyes.

"How simple you make it sound, Paco. Stop. Take a good look. Don't you see all the complications added to your life since you encountered me? Does it not make you desire to flee in the opposite direction?"

Paco turned to her, seated on the corral fence. "Listen, I'm no longer the stupid Corporal Paco Jimenez who once lived only to satisfy his manhood. This, for me, is an achievement. I can think for myself, although it's a chore, but not well enough to move on my own commands without fearing the consequences. Perhaps one day, when I have the confidence to believe in myself, I'll stop, face myself, and learn the truth. Until then, what does it matter if I go where you go? What else can happen to us—to me—or to you?" Paco watched in fascination as the bulls came closer and closer to Madelaina. He saw how she made no move to avoid them, how she stared back at them in some mysterious form of communication. Paco had no such form of courage; he was ready to retreat, yet hesitant to be called a *cobardo*. Still, he eyed the bulls warily, one foot over the fence, ready for flight.

Unaware that he watched her cautiously, Madelaina retorted, "Your optimism is to be applauded. You speak with confidence. But, Paco, I confess to you that I sometimes feel I'm under a spell of black magic—

that someone performed voodoo upon me, some Indian mystique that my intellect cannot fathom. You think Concepción could have known what she was speaking of when she told me about the dolls and Golden Dawn?"

"Golden Dawn? What dolls?" Paco, his Indian blood racing through his veins, forgot about the bulls and their apparent danger and turned to her questioningly.

"*La Condesa*. The mistress of my father, the general. Have you not met her in Cuernavaca? As a member of my father's personal escort squad, surely you've seen her—heard of her at least?"

"What about *La Condesa*?" His dark eyes narrowed in speculation.

"She is called Golden Dawn." She told him in detail what Concepción had stumbled upon in the woman's *casita*. "Are you not aware of such goings on?"

Paco crossed himself. "Since I've become a Christian, such things are forbidden by the holy fathers, Zorrita."

"Why do you call me that?" retorted Madelaina sharply, obviously annoyed.

"Just habit by now. I heard Capitán Salomon call you that so many times at Madrigal that in my mind nothing else seems proper. "It's true, Zorrita, you *are* of the people."

They both filled with silence as they gazed off into the distance watching the shifting colors in the sky grow dimmer beyond the mountains. Then Paco spoke. "It's true what you say. Since you came into my life, it has become turmoil. I wasn't forced to succumb to your sexual charms. I should have been stronger, resolved that as an officer in General Obregon's battalion I had no business seeking pleasure with you. What happened between us was forbidden from the first, yet I trespassed. Aye *Dios mios*. Is it possible *La Condesa* has done what Concepción suggested?" he asked with sudden realization. "Concepción is one smart *vieja*. No one fools her."

388

"Paco, I do not know the ways of your people. Only what Concepción told me."

Paco, suddenly enormously excited as the superstition of his people sprang into his consciousness, exclaimed, "Listen, *chiquita*, *La Condesa* is not called Golden Dawn for nothing. *Dios mios*! Golden Dawn is the name given to mushroom eaters, those people who have certain power over others!" He thought a moment. "Two dolls, eh? Concepción declares the second doll to be Dolores?" His head bobbed up and down as things came together in his mind. "It's possible that hot little *puta*, that whore of Satan, made *La Condesa* so jealous and angry that she cast a spell on her." Paco's eyes widened as full knowledge set in. "And I, Paco Jimenez, am caught at the center of this volcano!" He jumped off the fence, snorting and pacing in the dirt, more enraged than the bulls grazing nearby. He slapped his forehead as if to stimulate his memory. The sudden movement and loud exclamation that escaped his lips caused a bull to snort and charge the fence.

Paco instinctively jumped away. "Ayeiii, Chihuahua! Never trust a bull!" he exclaimed, then he quickly returned to the subject of Golden Dawn as if the bull was of no importance.

"What a mess, *chiquita*! Ayeiii, what trouble. Had I known in advance of this Golden Dawn, Paco would have left Zacatecas with the whirlwind. I could have taken the necessary precautions. Now we must endanger ourselves to ward off this evil. Who has possession of the dolls?"

"Concepción. But, Paco—"

"Concepción will know what to do. It must be done or we'll all be doomed," he said solemnly. "All of us who've been sown with the seeds of her displeasure."

"Oh, really, Paco. I don't believe any of this. I was only making conversation."

"Believe it, *señorita*," interrupted Paco. "*Madre de Dios*, believe it. I personally have seen the work of those mushroom eaters. In their minds are buried the eyes of Destiny."

Infuriated, Madelaina retorted smartly, "The difference between the educated and uneducated is we must have proof before we believe such nonsense."

If Paco took momentary rebuff, he didn't show it. He was on another tack instantly. "How is it that neither General Huerta or his devil's disciple, Salomon, never learned that Concepción is the sister to Pancho Villa?"

The general's daughter stiffened imperceptibly and feigned indifference. "What are you saying? I've never heard such stupidity," she said flatly, trying not to appear nervous. She turned her attention to the bulls, never seeing them as she watched Paco roll a cigarette. He lit it and handed it to her.

"You are some talker when in fever, *querida*."

She raised her dark eyes to meet his. How could she deny it now? "What exactly did I say?"

"Everything. So much. *Pues*. I couldn't remember all—only what interested me. You spoke of Peter Duprez, your husband. Of Concepción, of a man named Colimas who betrayed that tavernkeeper, José Limas, the man brought to Zacatecas and locked in prison by your father." Paco was silent a moment and spoke softly. "How is it you never confided to your father, the general, that Concepción is sister to Villa?"

"It's a good question, Paco. One for which I have no answer."

Paco brooded for several moments. He really needed no answers. Madelaina Obregon was a revolutionist. It was that simple. Other things caused his unsophisticated mind to fill with disquiet. In looking back over the calamities which had befallen them, none were the *usual* things that happened to plain, everyday people. Nothing had been—as usual. Not Madrigal—not the boy Lazaro—not that vile obscenity of a Mother Superior—or that foul pig of a whore, Major Salomon! Not the escape or the involvement at Ayala. Nothing was as usual. This knowledge only heightened his fears.

Madelaina, having grown quiet, harbored thoughts equally strange. It was difficult to realize all that had happened to her since her arrival from Spain—that it was all in the past, shut from her memory, if she could help it, forever. She had learned one thing in Madrigal. She could blot things out of her mind by just willing it. Just as she'd done when the pains became acute, when they grew so intense she had fainted from the excruciating agony. While Paco drove the antiquated wagon, every bump grated on her nerves and every ache in her body throbbed. How many times had she employed the principle of self-hypnosis unwittingly, declaring over and again, *I have no pain. I have no pain. I feel only comfort and ease.* Countless times, mile after mile, she'd actually instructed her mind to feel no pain and it had worked. Well, she'd have to will herself additional strength to meet all these new developments head-on.

"We must get to Parral, Paco," she stated resolutely. It was decided they'd leave the next morning. Preparations were made that night.

In retrospect, Madelaina realized her guard had been down. There'd been many telltale signs which normally would have aroused her suspicion. But she paid them no heed. It was as if her mind had been turned off to any possible dangers during her convalescence.

Francesco Lomas and his wife had packed them a basket of food. Tears sprang from their aged eyes during the affectionate farewells. How could Madelaina possibly have suspected treachery from these two warm people who'd saved her life? She and Paco boarded the wagon drawn by their burro and trundled slowly toward the entrance to the *rancho*. Suddenly, out of nowhere, came the dreaded *Rurales*. It happened so swiftly, they could only stand immobile, wagon and burro, waiting to be overtaken. They hadn't even left the gate.

A rattle of gunfire pealed in the distance. It quickly died off and was followed by another round of rifle fire coming from the opposite direction. Over the hill, Madelaina saw *bandidos*. Her dismay gave rise to hope. It took no stretch of the imagination to realize they were caught in a cross fire between rebel forces and the *Federales*. Francesco Lomas and the woman stood by quietly observing the activity with stoical indifference. Even then, Madelaina's suspicion remained dormant, unable to guess what was about to happen.

Paco, acting out of instinct, swept Madelaina off the wagon. "The house! Get into the house," he shouted, running breathlessly behind the elderly couple. Inside the barricaded doors, Francesco Lomas moved—much to their astonishment—with the agility of a much younger man. Filled with the pride of a Mexican national, he took down the rifles from their niches in the wall. He handed one to Paco and kept one himself, against Madelaina's protests.

"Give me a gun, also, Señor Lomas."

The older man complied without question, immediately struck by the authority in her voice. His jade green eyes studied her with keen intensity as she took charge.

"Paco," called Madelaina. "It's time to take a stand. *Rurale* or rebel. Whom will you defend?" Their eyes met and held for several moments. Never had the gunfire outside sounded so close and threatening.

"Does it matter what a lowly army corporal decides?"

"It matters. We can live or die. Which shall it be?"

"Perhaps we should first consult the owners of this estate," he hedged.

"No! First, your decision. You've seen enough of your side. Which shall it be?"

"I'm with you, Little Fox, to the end," he said softly, paying no heed to the inner warning that shook him for some mysterious reason.

"You're certain, Paco?" Her voice grew softer.

"I'm sure."

She lost little time with the Lomas couple. "We're caught in the middle between *bandidos* and *Rurales*. Whom shall we champion?"

"You need to ask, Señora Jimenez?" asked Lomas. *"Viva La Revolucion!"*

392

Even then Lomas' words didn't ring sincere, but she had no reason to suspect duplicity, not after all he'd done for them. However, there was little time to concern herself with the color of his moods. More vital issues were at stake.

Gun in hand, she ran to the window to peer at the activity ensuing between *guerrillos* and *Rurales*. Suddenly the front door was kicked in by two of the fiercest *Rurales* she'd ever seen. They stood before them, rifles ready to blast them.

"In the name of Francesco Madero, president of Mexico, we confiscate this house. You are now under martial law. We are surrounded by *guerrillos* in Parral and retreat to this refuge to reconnoiter. For the use of the soldiers, we take over all food, livestock, and provisions in your storehouse." Two officers stepped into the house behind the corporals. Madelaina recognized one of the officers instantly.

Lieutenant Guiterrez addressed himself to the older man. "You are Francesco Lomas, under the protection of Don Diego Ocampo, a government sympathizer, no?" Handsome, young, dashing, and moving like a graceful panther, Lieutenant Guiterrez was all business. He recognized neither Madelaina Obregon nor Paco Jimenez. For the moment, Paco left it at that, reluctant to introduce himself.

The older man drew his well-muscled body up with an instant change in comportment. "*Si*, Lieutenant Guiterrez. I am Francesco Lomas." He ignored the eye signal sent him by Madelaina to keep silent. He hardly saw her. "I am General Francesco Lomas in the army of the government. My house is your house, Guiterrez. You have our fullest cooperation. Do you wish to requisition supplies from the fort at Chihuahua? There is a shortwave radio in the next room at your disposal."

Lomas bowled them over. Madelaina felt faint. Paco's face turned the color of lead and he lost all energy of opposition in those moments. His hand dropped the rifle on a nearby table in a gesture of submission. Something in all this didn't ring true for

393

Madelaina. She didn't understand and she grew confused. Still, she kept her silence, fighting the desire to pull the trigger on her rifle and put an end to this Judas, Lomas. Francesco Lomas. General Francesco Lomas! They had been trapped for sure, she and Paco. What fools. *Dios mios*, what fools.

Ignoring them, Lieutenant Guiterrez and General Lomas walked into the next room, absenting themselves for several moments. The two corporals who bombarded the doors earlier, demanded that Madelaina drop her rifle. With such odds against her, she complied. One of the corporals left the house to settle the troops which by now were swarming all over the estate, making themselves comfortable wherever they could. The firing had died down to an occasional shot now and then.

It was obvious the *Federales* had been in retreat. Who were the *guerrillos*? In whose battalion did Lieutenant Guiterrez now serve—still her father's? She'd been cut off from the world of Pancho Villa and her father so completely that she hardly knew what was happening. Madelaina once knew who commanded every Federal garrison. Now, she knew very little. Things had changed too frequently of late. For one wild moment, Madelaina was seized with what seemed a logical move, turning herself in to Lieutenant Guiterrez. She would identify herself as the daughter of General Obregon and explain that Corporal Jimenez was escorting her to her father's encampment at Zacatecas the moment she was well enough. With the shortwave they could radio Zacatecas, contact the general himself. What would he say to them? *Dios mios*, he'd tell them he had no daughter. That he knew of no Paco Jimenez. He'd have every right to deny his daughter. When had she really been a true daughter to him? She panicked inwardly and glanced uneasily at Paco, unsure of herself.

Paco was busy watching the soldiers out the window as they took over. The wife of Francesco Lomas sat quietly in a corner, rocking to and fro in a chair, her dark eyes staring trancelike straight ahead of her. Madelaina moved toward the window and saw the courtyard filled with the Cossack-like *Rurales*, their steeds tethered to hitching posts, fences, trees, anything in sight. If she spoke with Paco, would the old woman hear them? She stole a glance at the brown-skinned woman. Where was the compassion of the previous weeks?

All of a sudden, Paco's words rang loudly in her ears. *You are some talker when you are in fever, chiquita!* Had the old woman overheard her in her sleep? She felt a burning itch creep over and under her skin as she contemplated the consequences of so irresponsible an act. She closed her eyes for a moment and grabbed Paco's arm. Speaking softly, evenly, she told him her fears.

"They know who I am, Paco. You said I talked in my fever. What must I have said in the presence of the woman? They must be spies for the *Federales*."

Paco turned to her. "Then I have only one recourse. I must present myself to the lieutenant. Tell him you were my prisoner, that I was taking you back to Zacatecas," he whispered, one eye on the somber-faced wife of Francesco Lomas. "Don't you recognize him, *chica*? He escorted you from Vera Cruz."

Amused by the similarity in their thinking, Madelaina nodded. "I recognized him. It is he who doesn't know me."

The crunching sound of heavy boots walking on pebbles outside alerted them. Suddenly Madelaina felt the viselike grip of Paco's hand on her arm. Wincing at the pain, she glanced up into his eyes. Paco's were frozen at a point over her head. She knew instantly something was drastically wrong. Almost against her will she turned toward the point of his interest. Madelaina sucked in her breath in a gasp of terror when she recognized the officer outlined in the doorway. The sun at his back left his face in partial shadow, but she'd know that arrogant walk anyplace.

Stooping slightly as he entered the low door jamb,

the officer in question was accompanied by two aides. His thin lips spread into a wolfish grin at her reaction. "Señorita Obregon. We meet again," said Major Salomon with artful cunning. He recognized Paco Jimenez instantly as the man who assaulted him. His eyes narrowed and he scowled blackly. "It appears I have become enormously fortunate this day. You, Corporal Jimenez, and I have a score to settle." He turned to his aide. "Arrest this man. Put him in irons until you receive further instructions. Arrest this woman. Put her in the next room until I finish with Corporal Jimenez!" He snapped his orders economically.

"Why do you arrest the corporal?" Madelaina protested authoritatively. "I'm already his prisoner. He was returning me to the battalion of my father, General Obregon. You'd best think twice before you countermand the orders of your superiors, Major. This is not your jurisdiction!"

As Major Salomon paused a moment to reflect, Lieutenant Guiterrez returned to the living room with Francesco Lomas. Lomas, no longer dressed in the garb of a peasant, now wore the full dress uniform of his rank. Instantly, Madelaina recognized the inimitable General Francesco Lomas! She should have known from his educated talk of philosophies and excursions into the mind of man that he was no ordinary peasant. She had ignored the obvious guideposts that should have warned her.

"I am both disappointed and surprised, *señorita*, that you recognized neither my name nor my face. The last time we met was at the camp of Pancho Villa before your father sent his spies to collect you and return you to Zacatecas. But General Obregon and I fought on opposing forces then. Now we are on the same side. If you find that difficult to understand, let me explain. General Orozco has decided to defect. He has started a rebellion against President Madero. Your friend, the man you've revered for so long, has now joined with the Federal forces. Yes, *señorita,* Pancho Villa works for President Madero once again. Soon he will join with General Huerta to oppose the Orozco forces."

"Huerta and Pancho Villa?" Confusion spread through her like a brush fire. "I don't believe you!" Yet, she recalled the dedicated fervor with which Villa had supported Madero. "Then the Mexican revolution has been split apart!" she exclaimed.

"Madero sits in the chair of the president where Villa put him when he took Juarez. The rest of us were given governorships and forts to command. What more can I tell you?" General Lomas took time to light up a long black *cigarro*. "Forgive me for deceiving you all this time. You were extremely ill when Corporal Jimenez brought you here. Despite your pallor and loss of weight, I recognized you immediately. You are the image of your father," he said. She couldn't tell if he meant it to be a compliment or a slur. Madelaina was outraged.

"You must know General Huerta kept me prisoner at Madrigal! That this animal, this pig of a decadent vulture, subjected me to the most vile form of torture. This Major Salomon now stands next to you draped in the most innocent of deception," she cried indignantly. "I demand his life in retribution for the sufferings of many other innocent victims as well as myself!"

"These are serious charges. Are these allegations true, Major Salomon?" asked General Lomas, tossing the match into a nearby spittoon.

Bracing himself, the major explained he was acting under Colonel Huerta's orders in the administration of Diaz at the time. "The moment President Madero took office, we no longer implicated ourselves in the matter. Due to the constant turmoil in the capital, we no longer considered the matter of Madelaina Obregon. However, when we returned to Madrigal to release her, she'd already escaped. There's a matter pending—the investigation of the death of the Mother Superior. Authorities believe the corporal and Señorita Obregon are implicated."

"You lie!" screamed Madelaina. "You lie!" She

397

turned to General Lomas. "It's true we left Madrigal where for so long we were held incommunicado and where violence was done to my person of such a nature it shames me to recall those times. I was forcibly raped, *mi Generale*. Not once, twice, three times. Nothing like that. Common decency and a terrifying dread of reliving the tortures to which I was subjected in that hell hole prevent me from graphically describing the horrors I endured." She addressed herself to Major Salomon, who stood smugly leering at her. "Lest you think you can get away with what you've done, Salomon, be advised I shall relate all the abominable cruelties you inflicted upon me, and I guarantee you shall be court-martialed and properly disposed of for the sadistic brute you are. I promise. Life imprisonment might satisfy your sadistic leanings, but you deserve worse. You forget I have at least three live witnesses to your abominable acts!"

"With your permission, *Generale*, may we speak in private?" asked Major Salomon, his eyes glittering in triumph. They retired to the next room. When they returned a quarter of an hour later, General Lomas stared at Madelaina Obregon as if she'd sprouted ten horns.

"*Senorita*, what the major has told me is not meant for the ears of the world. I respect his discretion. Please be assured I shall personally take up the matter with General Obregon, your father. The matter shall be investigated."

"General!" Madelaina's eyes burned into his. "I am not a fool. Don't treat me as one. Whatever Major Salomon has related to you is nothing but lies, slanted to protect his rotten, stinking skin."

General Lomas lowered his eyes to the tip of his shiny boots. It was obvious something Salomon told him had turned him against the girl. Paco saw it. Madelaina sensed it and felt all was lost.

"You are far from being considered a fool, *señorita*," replied General Lomas. "I've already radioed Zacatecas. Your father has dispatched escorts for you

398

and Corporal Jimenez. For the time being, consider my home your home. Please don't attempt anything as foolish as running away—or you may not live to speak of it. My soldiers will be instructed to shoot to kill anyone leaving or approaching this stronghold regardless of who they are. Understand, *señorita*, we are at war."

He bowed stiffly and left the room with Lieutenant Guiterrez and Major Salomon.

Madelaina paced back and forth nervously, glancing at the woman who had posed as the wife of General Lomas. How easily they had been fooled, she told herself. It was a lesson to be learned. She addressed the older woman. "Is it against the rules to retire to my bedroom? I feel weak and would like to rest awhile."

It was nearly noon by the clock on the mantle. The older woman, rocking in her chair, nodded. Even she could rest awhile now that army reenforcements had arrived, bringing their own cooks with them. Already they'd taken control of the outside ovens.

"Walk with me, Paco," pleaded Madelaina. "I feel shaky." He held her steadily by the arm as they walked toward the corridor and bedrooms.

"We must escape," she whispered. "I trust neither Lomas or Salomon. I will have to hear it from Pancho Villa's own lips before I believe he's joined forces with General Huerta."

"Listen, don't be crazy, *señorita*. It's best we stay. Your father's escorts will be here in a day or two at the most, providing they don't encounter ambushes. You'll fare better with General Obregon than these pigs!"

"You believe them? You really think they notified my father? Hah!"

Paco stared at her. The possibility that she was right turned his stomach and colored the picture drastically.

"If I should escape, Paco," she suggested, "what will you do?"

"At worst they'll return me to your father. A court-martial perhaps—or a firing squad—whatever their heads tell them at the moment."

"You think laws exist for those who aren't favored

399

by higher-ups? *Pues*, Paco, the jails and mines are full of prisoners who are forgotten people. Worse, you think they'll let you live to tell my father what they did to me? You were a witness, don't forget."

"Why do we wait?" asked Paco, getting the picture all too well. "Here, death is our only fate. We must take our chances, *señorita*."

"*Muy bueno,* Paco. Listen. I noticed earlier that the *guerrillos*, whoever they are, have formed a ring around the perimeter of the *rancho* and are probably watching the *Federales* every move. If I know the *guerrillos*, only those they allow to pass will pass, none other. Imagine," she said in exasperation, "a radio. All the time a shortwave radio under our very noses!"

"What good would it have been to know? I don't know how to operate one," he said honestly.

Madelaina shrugged indifferently, not sure why she brought up the subject. "We must do something to attract the attention of the *guerrillos*. Something, Paco. What?" She pondered a moment. Suddenly struck with an idea, she filled with exuberance. "Listen, don't contest anything I say or do. *Comprender?* Just do as I do. Act like my guard, as if you are concerned only with my safety. Now go, bring my bags to me out of the wagon."

Paco nodded, walked outside, and saluted Lieutenant Guiterrez. "Senorita Obregon wishes her bag from the wagon, Lieutenant. May I fetch it for her?"

"We'll get it, Corporal. Why don't you put on your uniform?" He nodded to his aide.

"I have none, Lieutenant. It was taken from me in a skirmish."

His aide returned with the bag. "Open it," he ordered Paco. Paco obliged, suddenly hoping Madelaina had placed nothing of an embarrassing nature in it like weapons. It turned out there were only odds and ends, clothing she'd worn, shirts and trousers of a man. "Very well, take it to her."

Paco saluted the officer, picked up the bag, and reentered the *casa.*

Fifteen minutes later, Madelaina, dressed in pants and shirt, entered the yard.

"*Buenas tardes*, Lieutenant Guiterrez." She greeted the officer with a dazzling smile.

"Sorry, Señorita Obregon. You are not permitted off these grounds."

"Who said I was going anyplace? I merely wish to see the bulls in the south corral. I'm an *aficionada*. Every day I practice with the *toros*. Surely you won't deny me my exercise? You can ring the arena with all your soldiers. It might be a pleasant diversion for them. I see General Lomas and Major Salomon are out on reconnaissance?" She glanced at the galloping horses with the military escorts kicking up dust in the distance.

"*Si, señorita*. They have gone for a little ride. They will be back in a hour or so."

"Then you won't mind if I visit the bulls?" She smiled pleasantly.

Lieutenant Guiterrez, a handsome, clean-shaven Creole, tipped his hat and summoned three soldiers. "The *señorita* wishes to make a few passes at the bulls in the south corral. You will remain with her every moment. Understand? If anything happens to her, it will be your hide I'll take," he snapped.

The soldiers were confused, yet excited. A woman to make passes at the bull? We've seen everything! They laughed amongst themselves until they recalled Lieutenant Guiterrez' warning. Nothing must happen to her, this crazy woman. Very well, they sat atop the wooden fencing, rifles at the ready, prepared to shoot the bulls if they attacked her.

401

To Paco Jimenez, this was absolutely the stupidest thing this crazy woman could do. Fight bulls indeed! She'll be killed, he told himself. But then, what did Paco really know about this enigmatic Madelaina Obregon? Hadn't he seen with his own eyes how the bulls watched her with wary eyes almost as if she understood them? They had charged him—not Madelaina. He turned to the girl who had brought a bright red *rebozo* with her from the *casa*. She had already given him instructions on what to do.

Madelaina stood at the far end of the corral. She had only the vaguest idea of what she was doing and why she was doing it. Past experience taught her that if perchance these *guerrillos* were *Villistas,* the incongruous acts in the corral with the bulls would set someone to thinking—even if it was only to laugh at such ridiculous behavior. Someone was bound to report it to Villa, and he would begin thinking about such odd behavior at the enemy camps. Yet, if what General Lomas said about Pancho Villa and the *Federales* was true, she was lost. The mere thought that her hero should be working hand-in-hand with that satanic Huerta was enough to make her retch.

She looked up and gave Paco the signal. Paco pulled the lever on the crudely constructed chute, and one of the Chihuahuan bulls snorted and came thundering into the small enclosure and stopped short, blinded temporarily by the glaring overhead sun. In those next few moments, Madelaina Obregon became the essence of everything Spanish. She became the embodiment of a proud heritage of conquerors by the very manner of her walk, her carriage, and the way she tossed her long mane of hair like a wild stallion.

There were only a few men watching her to begin with, but word spread swiftly that the daughter of General Obregon, that wildcat hellion who had supported Pancho Villa in the revolution, was now going to attempt to match wits with a bull. A Chihuahua bull, no less! What a crazy woman! This they had to see!

Madelaina's expert eyes took in the figure of the bull in a glance. True, it was a Chihuahua bull—but not too brave. Yet, he hooked a bit to the left. That was bad. It means that he's unpredictable, Madelaina told herself, assessing the animal closely.

This was the first bull of such a size that Madelaina had ever challenged. She tried to control her shaking knees, disguise her trembling hands as she held the carmine *rebozo*. Her mind clearly recollected all she'd learned about bulls. She had learned something of paramount importance—that she was no true genius in the ring. Competent, artful, and fearless, yes, but no genius. Awkward at first, she had invariably made the wrong kinds of passes for one of her size and build. Madelaina had no desire to kill the bulls; she loved them too much and respected their strength. Manuelito Perez had been a fine teacher all right. From him she'd learned to respect a bull. Now she attempted to employ all her knowledge in this foolhardy attempt to attract someone's attention.

If she'd learned one thing well, it was to keep her feet planted firmly in the earth when a bull charged—the most vital factor in bullfighting. She concentrated on the austere, classic passes—none of those fancy cape-spinning passes. She performed slow *verónicas* and a half-*verónica* while holding herself with such dignity that those insufferable, haughty men, ready to ridicule a woman, watched her in amazement, unable to fault her expertise. She must have silently thanked and praised Manuelito Perez a thousand times in those moments.

She stood her ground, surrounded by more than fifty
403

soldiers who'd flocked to the corral and sat on the fence, unsure whether to cheer her or humiliate her with their jeers. But not a man there could fail to give her credit for the courage to stand inside the corral in the company of that massive ton of dynamite and destruction snorting hotly and pawing the earth. Not a man among them would do such a thing for all the pesos in Mexico. A respectful silence came over them in anticipation of what was to come.

The *rebozo* became a living thing in her hands, and when the bull charged her, the easy flow of the cloth, the casual way it brought the bull's horns within a fraction of her legs was incredibly moving. Creating more excitement and dramatizing the effect on the spectators was the serious concentration on her marblelike face. She gave the feeling of an artist carving a masterpiece from stone. No one laughed now. Each pass she completed brought a wave of astonished "*olés*." Thoughts of war and petty differences faded from the spectators minds. They forgot for a while that she was a woman and appreciated only the artistry of her work. She made the animal charge back and forth before her so closely and with such grace, the men couldn't conceal their admiration. They shouted, screamed, applauded, and demanded the fullfillment of a *corrida*.

Paco Jimenez was petrified with amazement. This little *chiquita,* who a few weeks back had been subjected to the worst abuse known to humans, was now contesting a dangerous and unpredictable ton of dynamite. Was there no end to the wonders of this woman? He had watched the entire performance, which lasted nearly an hour, with an outward show of pride.

From wherever it came, Madelaina's guts and sheer determination to give the most outstanding performance of her life combined to make these spectators leave later, talking about the superb artistry.

"*Toro*, hah, ohoh!" she purred in a low voice, holding the cape out in front of her, shaking it, luring the owner of those enormous, glazed eyes.

The animal wheeled at her voice. Its tail shot up and

he came charging across the small corral. As the bull reached the cape, Madelaina swung it slowly before the bull's nose, guiding his head so that the hooking left horn came within inches of her legs. Without moving her feet, she took the bull back in another charge, and the right horn angled sharply, stabbing at the air even closer than the left horn. Nearly a dozen more *verónicas* followed this, and she finished with a half-*verónica*, so close that the bull nearly knocked her off balance. The soldiers, including Paco Jimenez and an astonished Lieutenant Guiterrez cheered deliriously.

Up on the bluff of the foothills directly behind the Lomas hacienda, with a clear view of the corral and the activity in the makeshift ring, six of Pancho Villa's scouts and three gringos were watching with curiosity the crowd that formed around the corral. Captain Tracy Richards and Peter Duprez, peering through binoculars, were attempting to fathom such an exhibition.

"What the hell do ya make o' that, Trace?" asked Peter. "If we had a mind, just a handful of men and the two of us could skirt down this hill and surprise 'em all."

"Must be some exhibition being put on for the morale of the troops," replied Tracy, jotting notes in his little black book. "Hey, Urbina!" he called to the ratty-looking, ferret-eyed *Villista*, a man who laughed a great deal and cried like a baby while drinking in clockwork precision.

"*Sí, gringo. Que pasa?*" grinned the unpredictable Urbina.

"Whatcha make o' that, *amigo*? Take a look." Tracy handed him his binoculars.

Urbina laughed as if these were the most unique glasses in the world. He made a big production of what he saw through them, marveling at their clear sights, hardly aware of what was going on below them.

"Down below, Urbina. In the corral! Check out the bull and the matador! Tell us stupid gringos why them soldiers would be leavin' their posts and other duties ta

405

be watching a demonstration like this in the middle o' the day?"

Urbina's raucous laughter reached the ears of all the men in the scouting party, who turned in the direction of the activity below them, trying to detect what was happening.

"Ees maybe because ees no *matador*, eh. Ees *matadora*! Ees a woman! Boy, some woman to fight a Chihuahua bull! *Amigos,* that is heroism! Phoooh! Urbina would like to tumble and somersault with that little skirt!"

"Woman?" Peter Duprez concentrated on the lithe figure making those phenomenal passes. "Ya sure could o' fooled me!" He saw the long black hair flying every which way, watched as the bull charge her time and again.

"Hot damn! If it's not!" he exclaimed. "Trace, take another look!"

Curiously moved by both Urbina's reaction and Tom Mix's endorsement of the female matching wits with a living bomb, he grabbed the field glasses from Urbina's hands. He focused on the scene below. For a time he grew silent, reflective. "Hey, Tom Mix, when's the last time y'all saw a woman bullfighter?"

"Nevah! Nevah in mah life!"

"That's right, boy. Ah ain't never heard of a female bullfighter either—an', good buddy, ah've been around plenty. Ah jus' don't figure it. Somethin's going on down below—"

Peter Duprez was a step ahead of his friend for a change. Something familiar about that small, well-coordinated body stoked his memory. His thoughts backed up to the boat trip on the *Mozambique* and Madelaina, his Little Fox. She had told him about her secret passion, her love for the bulls, the training she had undergone, the bullfighting, which had been one reason her aunt had become furious with her.

Peter cursed that the binoculars weren't stronger as he stared fixedly at the activity below him. He lowered the glasses and peered about the area. Approximately a

406

hundred yards below him, closer to the improvised bullring, he spied a rocky ledge. "Ah'm going down there, Trace," he called to his friend. "Ah jus' gotta see this closer up," he muttered, leaving the others in the well-shaded and protected alcove and shinnied down the embankment before Tracy could protest.

Captain Richards wondered why all of a sudden Tom Mix should be interested in a female bullfighter. His eyes turned back toward the bullring. He glanced impatiently at his pocket watch and frowned as he glanced at the others. It was time to be heading back to make their report to Pancho Villa. The *guerrillo* was waiting for them on the other side of Parral, stewing over new complications. Villa, concerned that General Lomas had made a secret deal with General Orozco, the Madero defector, had sent this scouting party to determine the sincerity of Francesco Lomas.

"Pancho Villa trusts very few *hombres*," he told Captain Richards and Tom Mix on their arrival at the *guerrillo*'s encampment a few weeks ago. Their meeting was warm and affectionate and their reunion like old times. Villa listened with intense concentration to the message conveyed to him, through the gringo captain, by his compatriot Emiliano Zapata. Despite the fact that Zapata no longer trusted Madero and despite the shoddy treatment given Villa by the president at Juarez, Pancho Villa gave the Americans every indication that his faith was still embedded in the miniscule Jew who sat in the presidential palace in Mexico City.

Pancho had told his friends that he'd retired to his village of San Andres, content to farm, make love, and raise babies, setting aside the name Pancho Villa for a time to become once again the respected husband and father, Doroteo Arango. For a time he felt certain he'd done the right thing in taking up the plow. Wasn't this what it had all been about? Freedom—democracy— the right to plow his own land? The right of free enterprise without intervention and domination by foreigners? He'd danced a lot, sung a great deal, enjoyed fiestas more than any of his compatriots, because he'd tempted death's sirens more often than anyone else. In all this time Pancho hadn't learned to smoke or drink and never felt he'd missed anything.

One day word came. He'd been summoned by his Presidente Francesco Madero. Pancho returned to his *casita* and announced to his wife he was returning to Chihuahua to open a business. He didn't tell his wife that the source of Madero's problems lay in the perfidy of General Pasquel Orozco, one of the most trustworthy men, who behind *El Presidente's* back had carefully plotted the treachery to end all treachery.

Apparently Francesco Madero had found no solace in his own cabinet. Even his own vice-president proved highly impractical and grossly inept. The others, all blow-hards, able to talk up a storm, fell exceedingly short in practical matters. Of all the men in Madero's recent past, the one who stood out as the most fiercely loyal had been the man he'd treated the shabbiest—that tiger, that powerhouse of action and courage, the Centaur of the North who feared no man, Pancho Villa.

And so, upon Madero's orders, Pancho moved to Chihuahua where he ironically opened a butcher shop. With the aid of Don Abraham Gonzalez, the man who had recruited Villa to the Antireelectionist movement and was now governor of the State of Chihuahua, Villa prospered for a time and sold meat to the peasants at prices they could afford, despite protests from other commercial butchers who lamented his cut-price operation. Villa's place of business was inundated with the curious who came just for a look at the powerful *guerrillo* who'd captured Juarez and devastated the *Federales*. None of the fawning masses affected Villa. He was in Chihuahua for one reason alone; to keep his eyes open and concentrate on that villainous and treasonous snake Pasquel Orozco, the man he promised to kill if he ever betrayed Madero.

Pancho confided to his gringo friends that he had become a changed man once again. His business had

408

literally turned into an espionage unit with employees coming and going, bearing vital messages. Once again he carried *pistolas* and saddle carbines. And then one day it happened.

News of General Orozco's resignation reached the National Palace. The Premier General of the Revolution had openly and boldly declared himself an independent. Within two days the Federal garrisons in Juarez and Chihuahua were under his command. From San Antonio, Texas, the Secretary of Foreign Relations under Madero accepted a provisional presidency offered him by the Juarez and Chihuahua rebels.

Madero stood denuded in the international spotlight of revolt, triggered by the well-designed resignation of General Orozco. No doubt remained in the minds of both Captain Tracy and Peter Duprez, as they listened to Pancho Villa, that America was involved in this catastrophic turn of events. Former President Diaz and his cohorts inspired a certain Don Luis Cardenas, the former owner of half the State of Chihuahua with its enormous cattle and mining regions, to prevail upon President Taft to cooperate with Pasquel Orozco. If Madero could be dislodged from power, Don Luis could reclaim his properties and once again Wall Street would be welcome to the wealth of Mexico.

They found a willing subject in Pasquel Orozco, who by the hand of President Madero, controlled the most important military post in northern Mexico and was now ready to become a turncoat for a higher offer.

"One thing alone held General Orozco back for a time," Pancho told his gringo friends. "Me!" The *guerrillo* laughed heartily when he related the story. "General *Turncoat* Orozco contacted me by letter asking me to set aside any personal differences we might have and join him in the establishment of a new Republic. My reply was to remind him that Pancho Villa, a man of honor, made good his promises. I reminded him of the balls hacked off Colonel Tamborel in Juarez."

The men listening laughed along with the *jefe*. Pancho continued the narration. "By then there was no

409

turning back for that six-tongued snake. Official word came on March 3 that General Orozco really revolted. And following this, word reached me from my president that he had put one General Vitoriano Huerta in charge of the Northern Divisional Army—a former Chief of the Secrt Police under Diaz. Imagine Pancho Villa and his former enemies now fighting shoulder to shoulder? Miracles of all miracles! And so, Capitán Tracy and you, Tom Mix, were the first I sent for from the camps of my dearest *compadre*, Emiliano Zapata. It's a sad, sad thing, gringos, that Mexico is once again caught up in bloodshed. This time it is between rebel and rebel with the former allies split apart. I will do what *mi Presidente* expects of Pancho Villa," he told the gringos soberly. "But I have many reservations about the outcome. One man—this Huerta—has been given too much authority. I fear General Huerta stands at the center of an impregnable power. Only time will tell what happens. I for one intend to keep a sharp eye on this blood-sucking vulture."

It was Pancho Villa's basic honesty, his devotion to country and his people, his innate desire to elevate their standard of living that drew most of the freedom fighters, especially the gringos, to Villa's bosom. Villa could have been a wealthy man, but like his southern counterpart, Zapata, wealth alone held no magnetism for him. Happiness, contentment, the right to be his own man with his own land to work and to provide for his family and above all, peace, were his deepest desires. These seemed impossible feats for the *guerrillo*—they kept eluding him, pulling him forward to his true destiny.

These qualities in Pancho Villa made Captain Tracy Richards, Peter Duprez, and others in the Gringo Brigade his most devoted followers.

Captain Tracy Richards glanced down below the ledge, wondering at Tom Mix's insatiable curiosity over the activity at the Lomas spread. He wished Mix would get his ass back to the cover area before that flaky Urbina got suspicious. He smoked a cigar and paced the ground with increasing impatience. Dammit all! So many complications with women!

Peter Duprez returned to the stakeout just as Villa's scouting party was ready to leave. His face had paled considerably under the coppery tan; his blue eyes were clouded with turbulence. Captain Tracy didn't have to ask to know something was wrong.

"Jus' make it short and sweet," he told Peter. "Ah know it won't rock me ta sleep, but ya better speak up. Ya look like some'un cut out yore heart."

Peter nodded. Under the squared sombrero which kept his face in partial shadow, his eyes glanced about at the others trying to make certain they wouldn't overhear. Urbina in particular, a man who grinned like a maniacal lunatic most of the time, was a man he didn't trust. Behind Urbina's calculating eyes, Peter was certain there lurked a devilish brain, one so canny and diabolical, so filled with unscrupulous, scandalizing immorality, that most of the other *Villistas* looked upon him with cool respect and fear. If he weren't in such great favor with Pancho Villa, the man most assuredly would have been done in long before by any one of a number of his companions. The only things in Urbina's favor were unabashed honesty, a scandalous sense of humor, and the fact that he was the deadliest shot in Villa's army. None of these qualities endeared him beyond the point of toleration.

Peter pulled Tracy aside, out of hearing distance. Both men lit up *cigarros* to make it seem a casual talk. As usual, Tracy wore his sombrero backward, the broad brim fanning about his face like a straw halo.

"Trace," said Peter quietly. "That there *matador* is someone we both know."

"The hell ya say?" Tracy's eyes peered down below them into the corral. He puffed on his cigar thoughtfully.

"It's mah wife!"

The *cigarro* dropped from Tracy's mouth, fell onto his shirt, and rolled onto the ground. He quickly

411

brushed the live ashes from his vest and shirt. His sombrero fell off his head. Leaning down, he retrieved both the *cigarro* and his sombrero. He placed the smoke back into his mouth and slapped the sombrero against his leather leggings before putting it back on his head.

"Take a look see," said Peter, handing him the field glasses.

Tracy took the glasses, returned to the ledge, and glanced toward a bluff high above them to draw the attention of the curious *Villistas* away from his real interest.

"Are they looking where ah'm looking?" he asked his companion.

"Yep."

Tracy must have peered at the upper reaches for at least a full minute before he turned and focused on the activity in the corral on the *rancho* of General Lomas. The activity had ended. All he saw was the figure of the *matadora* being led away from the corral by another man, walking through a throng of soldiers whose loud "*olés*" reached faintly up to the scouting party. Their clapping and shouting faded as the girl moved out of sight.

He handed the glasses back to Peter. "You're sure it's her?"

"Ah dropped down some 250 yards closer. Ah saw her face, Trace. Ah'd know her anywhere. How do ya suppose she got all the way up heah? Ya think she's up to something?"

"Damned if ah know, Pete. It's like Pancho says— he's on the side of his former enemies. Even the girl's father, General Obregon, is now a Constitutionalist like all the former army regulars. The moment Madero took office he gave ordahs theah was ta be no reprisals against the loyal soldiers who fought vigorously foah the previous government. They were all given opportunities to swear theah allegiance ta the Madero government. So, what would Little Fox be doing up heah? Ah can betcha Pancho Villa knows nothing about her being in the vicinity."

"Well, for whatever the reason, ah'm gonna get her outa there," Peter said, grimly determined.

"We'd better tell Villa first, before ya run off half-cocked."

"Y'all go. Ah'll stay heah."

"Ya better come, Pete. Those people down theah ain't going no place, not until Villa powwows with that General Lomas. Besides, you ain't gonna get nowhere neah the house with all those *Federales* milling around. Remember Madero didn't grant us amnesty. Some of those *Federales* hate ouah guts. The minute they see a gringo *guerrillo*, they'll shoot first and ask questions later. We'd be wisah ta return heah with Pancho Villa, under his protection. Then, Pete, ah sweah ah'll help ya kidnap the girl, ya heah?"

"Makes sense, as usual," said Pete, slipping the glasses into a case.

"Let's go." They mounted their horses and fell in behind Urbina.

"What's wrong, gringos?" called Urbina with that diabolical grin on his face. "Is best we return *pronto*, no?"

"Nothing, *amigo*," said Captain Tracy, grinning back. "Thought we saw movement on the ridge above us. Theah's no way they could've circled in behind us unless they was theah all along. That not being the case, it's jus' as well we be mosying back to the *jefe* ta tell 'im what we've seen."

Urbina studied the gringos for a moment, then he raised his arms in signal. *"Vamenos, muchachos!"* The party galloped ahead, then began to wind their way down the slopes to the outer perimeter of the *rancho* and disappeared into woods.

At sunset, Pancho Villa and seventy-five well-chosen men rode their horses to the Lomas hacienda. Accompanied by six of his men, Villa walked into the hacienda to meet with General Lomas. Outside, the men dismounted and remained in their own circle, eyes alert, fingers hovering close to their guns. Tracy

413

Richardson and Peter Duprez sauntered toward the well. They touched their hats to the soldiers. Lieutenant Guiterrez stepped out from the shadows.

"May I assist you, gringos?"

"Just lookin' ta refresh ourselves with watah. Mind if we fill ouah canteens, Lieutenant?"

Through tight lips, Lieutenant Guiterrez gave them permission. "Help yourselves." He stood by, watching them closely. He detested these soldiers of fortune, the gringos especially, with their cocky assuredness, their keen artistry with guns, and their knowledge of the latest in weaponry. Most of all, he hated them because they could come and go as they pleased. Their freedom and the ease with which they moved back and forth between the States and Mexico was an enigma to Guiterrez. Why couldn't the Mexicans travel back and forth with the same ease? More than anything else, Lieutenant Guiterrez, an army regular, trained within certain limits of his profession, detested their guts and the high risks they took beyond any call to duty. They were insane killers with incalculable daring and as a result did more damage to the army regulars and their morale than any cannon or artillery could do. These hard-looking, gun-heavy men, with beards and moustaches giving them a fiercer look, were a real pain in the ass to men like Guiterrez, and he took no pains to disguise his contempt.

"That shore was some exhibition that theah matador put on fer yer troops, Lieutenant," said Tracy, filling his canteen and trying to be friendly. "Hey, ya wanna *cigarro*? Ah mean, seeing as how we'ah on the same side, Lieutenant, there's nothing like getting ta know one another, now is there?" He handed the officer a cigar. "This heah is Major Tom Mix. And me, ah'm Captain Tracy Richards."

For an instant, Lieutenant Guiterrez forgot his inherent dislike for the gringos. The name of Captain Tracy Richards had become a familiar name to the regulars, especially since the Juarez victory. Some newspaper reporter had miraculously snapped photographs of the American freedom fighter servicing a piece of artillery used by *Villistas*, complete with the sombrero picturesquely worn backward. The picture and subsequent story written by Miguel Guerra were in all the major newspapers in Mexico City and other large cities in Mexico. Like any pop-eyed, celebrity-struck *hombre*, Lieutenant Guiterrez fumbled with the *cigarro*, accepted the light, and showed his excitement.

His dark eyes lit up and he signaled to one of his men. "Corporal, this *hombre* is Captain Tracy Richards of the Gringo Brigade. And Major Tom Mix, of course," he added. His attention was on Richards, just as the gringos had anticipated. As most soldiers do when the circumstances were right, they exchanged stories and boasted excessively. Captain Tracy Richards, a silver-tongued story teller, had lured the men, while Peter Duprez sauntered indolently in and about the compound.

Certain he wasn't followed or observed, Peter moved in closer to the villa, following the outer patios and courtyards. Madelaina has to be someplace, he told himself, his heart racing with renewed intensity and hope. Finally he came upon the window looking into Madelaina's room. She was alone, pacing back and forth in the room, smoking a cigarette. He picked up a pebble and tossed it inside between the iron grill work. Instantly Madelaina's head spun around. She glanced at the pebble, then moved toward the window.

She didn't speak. She stood silent and still, her dark eyes peering in the darkness. She heard her name called. It was difficult to see, but her heart gave rise to a fierce hope.

"Madelaina! It's me—Peter."

Her hands flew to her mouth to stifle a cry of happiness. "Peter? Where? How? Oh God," she whispered.

"Can ya get out of theah?" He was up to the window now, his hands holding hers through the bars, her face pressed between them, accepting his kisses—awkward and clumsy due to their position, yet, kisses of joy.

"I'm a prisoner here." She told him how she happened to be there, bridging the gap in time. "I'll tell you more later, but first, you've got to help me—get me out of here."

"Ah will, *querida*. Ah promise. Ah will." His voice belied his outward calm.

A noise behind her caused Madelaina to turn her back on Peter. She moved away from the window as the door to her room was unlocked.

Major Salomon stood there leering at her. "Well, Little Fox, you are technically my prisoner. We radioed General Obregon that I would return you to him—that he need not send his escorts. So you see, once again we'll have a score to settle. By morning you'll be back in my full jurisdiction—you and your Corporal Paco Jimenez. Then we'll see who has the last laugh. The tables always turn around. Have you nothing to say to this bit of good news?"

Major Salomon stood very close to her, leaning in toward her, his leering eyes sending obscene messages to her. She felt instantly naked before this brute. All the hatred in her welled up to a ferocity of a volcano. She spit into his face. "That's what I say to your news, Major Salomon! I spit on you!"

He reached for her and pinned her arms down to her sides. "The trouble with you, Little Fox, is that no man has tamed you yet. I've watched all those tableaux you put on for my pleasure at Madrigal, and I concluded you were made for me. I will be the man who will tame you to my perfection—I will make of you something every man will envy. So! Today, in my absence, you entertained the squadrons of General Lomas. I hear you are quite some *torera*. That's it, eh? You have a castration complex! You hate your father and all men, so you become a bullfighter to show your contempt for all men. Well, Little Fox? What a ridiculous name for you. A tigress would suit you better!"

Outside the window Peter seethed with fury. An alien savagery tore inside him. He wanted to kill the man! It would be so easy. Shoot him right through the window.

But how could he get to Madelaina? She was trapped inside with no way of escape, except through a house filled with generals and Pancho Villa. He couldn't risk causing a skirmish between allied factions—yet what kind of man would he be to let this cad, this vulgar obscenity, treat his wife as he did? He wanted to break every bone in Salomon's body! His anger knew no bounds. He stayed there, watching, turning sicker by the moment, listening to the vile and contemptible things he told her. Somehow he got the impression that they knew each other more than intimately. By the hatred and loathing on Madelaina's face, he felt certain that this man was connected with the misery she experienced at Madrigal.

Peter gave a sudden start when he saw the door to Madelaina's room open. Both Major Salomon and Madelaina's attention was focused on the presence of another man. It wasn't until Madelaina cried out, "Paco—be careful," that Peter realized this was the man who had saved her at Ayala, according to Alicia Sandoval, the cousin of Lucia. Paco slipped the bolt into place behind him.

"So—you dare thrust your presence in this room to oppose me again, Jimenez? You realize all I have to do is fire a shot from my gun and the roof will cave in on you?" snarled Major Salomon.

"That's if Major Salomon gets the opportunity to fire his pistol," said Paco, moving in toward him with catlike movements.

"Stop, Corporal! I command you," said the major, reaching for his pistol.

Paco sprang at him, knocking the pistol from his hand. A struggle ensued. Madelaina stood back for a moment, watching them. Paco, getting the worst of it, was no match for the physically fit major whose bodybuilding exercises were the talk of his command. Madelaina, knife in hand, approached the struggling bodies scuffling on the floor. Her hand faltered in midair, hesitant, yet awaiting the right moment to sink the blade into Salomon.

417

Watching this scenario, Peter Duprez was incensed and terrified for Madelaina. He felt hopelessly enmeshed in a melodrama from which he couldn't escape. Major Salomon flipped over on his back and grabbed the pistol just as Paco flew over him, covering him. The blast of the gunshot, diffused by the proximity of Paco Jimenez' body to the bullet, sounded like the dull popping of a champagne cork.

He saw Paco's startled eyes widen in shock. Then, as excruciating pain jolted him, he fell back away from Salomon like a cowering, whipped puppy. His right upper arm close to the shoulder gaped open with blood gushing from it like nothing Peter had ever seen. Madelaina, taking everything in at once, jumped on Salomon and sunk her blade into him, time and time again, like a raving maniac.

"Stop, Madelaina! Stop!" cried Peter. "*Querida!*" he shouted. "Stop!"

Madelaina glanced up at him with the glaring, bloodshot eyes of an animal. In that brief instant, Major Salomon raised his pistol to fire at her. Peter shot first, three times in succession, and blasted the major in half. Madelaina, dazed and confused, wondered what to do first. She stared at Paco's arm, practically severed in two, then at Peter and the major. She faltered in semishock, unable to get her body to obey her commands. The sound of footsteps outside her room made her cry a warning to Peter. "Go," she shouted at him. "Get back to your men! I'll handle this."

If Peter thought to protest her orders, he didn't. He moved quickly back into the shadows, joining the circle of men who listened attentively as Captain Richards refought the Battle of Juarez. The loud brash orders of a top sergeant, accompanied by a scuffling of feet in the courtyard, brought the soldiers to attention. An officer running toward them on the double saluted Lieutenant Guiterrez.

"Lieutenant Guiterrez! You are wanted inside immediately. There's been an accident!" The two fell into step together and, moving through the inquisitive

418

crowd of soldiers who muttered incoherently, they both disappeared inside the *casa*. Peter pulled Tracy aside and explained what had happened.

"Ah think we better go inside ta see Pancho," said Tracy flatly.

Inside was thorough confusion. It was bedlam. General Lomas had just completed negotiations with Villa, when an aide came to him with news of Major Salomon's "accident." Madelaina was dragged into the big salon screaming. "I've got to help Corporal Jimenez!" she shouted hysterically.

Addressing herself to General Lomas, she yelled, "Now do you believe me? That animal Salomon tried to attack me. Corporal Jimenez caught him in the attempt and ordered the major to stop. The major drew a gun and fired at close range. I grabbed my knife and sprang at him! Suddenly from out of nowhere came several shots. From the window, I suppose. And the major fell over, riddled with bullets. That's all there is to it, General!"

All around them, activity bustled with increasing momentum. One of the medics with the battalion was called to tend Major Salomon's wounds. They ignored Paco Jimenez, much to Madelaina's consternation. From time to time Little Fox stole glances at Pancho Villa, not wishing to acknowledge him until he first acknowledged her. Their eyes met in secret understanding. Madelaina appealed to him in desperation.

"Señor Villa, please, you must insist that this man be helped. He has been of great assistance to me, saving me from the clutches of this madman Salomon. If General Lomas doesn't acknowledge him as an officer in the army who should be given priority over Major Salomon, then I implore you to use your influence to help Corporal Jimenez."

Pancho growled gruffly to General Lomas as he removed a pistol from his holster. "Why is the *señorita*'s wish ignored?"

"Pancho! Why are you pulling a gun?" asked the general astonished.

"Just tell me one thing, General—will I need it?"

"With me, Colonel Villa? Don't you remember me from the early days?"

"I remember you, Francesco, so you can cut the crap with me calling you General and you calling me Colonel. Tell me the answer to the *señorita's* request. We haven't time to play games today."

General Lomas glanced up and searched for Lieutenant Guiterrez. He jerked his head in the direction of Madelaina Obregon. "See to it her young man is tended to."

"He's not *my young man*," cried Madelaina hotly. "He is Corporal Paco Jimenez in the Battalion of General Alvaro Obregon of Zacatecas! Stop inserting innuendos into your speech!" She glanced hesitantly in the direction of Peter Duprez, hoping he wouldn't believe what the general tried to make them all think, that she was some soldier's *puta*. She followed Guiterrez into the other room where Paco lay, deathly pale. The medic had done his best with the major while Paco lay bleeding to death.

"Take Major Salomon to the doctor in Parral," said Lieutenant Guitterez, "and for God's sake, be careful. Don't let any of General Soto's men see you. He's joined with Orozco!" he cautioned his men as they carried Major Salomon's body from the room on an improvised litter.

When his body passed by, Madelaina stared at him with hatred. "When will you die?" she said bitterly. "Are you made of iron?"

Behind the pain and obvious discomfort, she saw a gleam of satisfaction in the major's eyes, promise of future retribution. With all his breath he said evenly, "It pays to keep fit. I've cheated death three times, if only to one day pay you in kind, madam."

She turned from him, hatred burning vehemently in her, and concentrated on Paco. "Lift him gently," she told the soldiers as they pulled him to his feet. "Place him on my bed." One look at the hole in his arm and Madelaina shrank back in disorganized panic. *"Dios*

420

mios, Paco! From one little bullet you get such a perforation?" She tried to make light of it, but she felt terror in her heart.

His severed arm, held together by a few tendons, had become a tap for a massive flow of blood, and since a tourniquet had not been applied immediately, Paco was dangerously weakened by the loss of the life-giving fluid. He knew that the bullets used by Major Salomon had been no usual bullets. In addition, one of the shots fired by Peter Duprez had somehow ricocheted and struck him in the same location—a chance in a million—only a few millimeters away from the original bullet wound.

"Quickly heat water," she ordered the medic. "The bullet has to come out!"

The medic replied, "*Si, señorita*, both of them must be removed. You will excuse me for a few moments. I will see the water is heated."

"You are needed here. I'll make certain water is boiled. You must stop the flow of blood!" Madelaina had extracted many a bullet from the bodies of *Villistas* in her early days as a *campesina*. Following skirmishes, all the women nursed the men and tended to their injuries. She knew the first procedures and set about the preliminaries by herself.

"Don't tell me my business," he snapped haughtily. "I must do what I must do!" The medic left the room. When he didn't return in five minutes, Madelaina knew he wouldn't be back. She knew those supercilious sons of Creoles. That Spanish highborn aristocracy wouldn't dirty their hands on a mestiza. Very well then, she'd handle it herself. She ran into the salon and pulled two bottles of whiskey from the table. The men stood up.

Madelaina glanced at Peter Duprez. "You, gringo! Come with me! I need help in here! And you," she called to the fraudulent wife of General Lomas. "Boil some water, *pronto*!"

Peter Duprez glanced at Pancho Villa, who was hotly involved in settling differences with General Lo-

421

mas. Villa winked knowingly and nodded, giving him permission.

Once inside the bedroom, she sank into his arms. "Peter. Oh, Peter, it's dreadful. Paco is so badly hurt and they will do nothing for him."

She clung to him. Peter glanced at the ashen face of the man lying on the bed who hardly had the strength to keep his eyes open. He comforted his wife.

"First things first, Little Fox. What's say we take care of Paco, here, first, since you seem to owe him so much."

Madelaina's reaction to the slight rebuff was to glance sharply at him, then, keeping her thoughts to herself, she focused on Paco. "I bound his arm and applied the tourniquet to halt the bleeding, but it is *muy mal*, Peter." She poured whiskey into Paco as Peter leaned over the wretched man to inspect the crude bandage and what lay beneath it.

He winced inwardly at what he saw and averted his head. "It's bad. Real bad. Ah nevah saw such a wound. What in tarnation did the majah use—an elephant gun? Damnit ta hell! Ya jus' keep plyin' him with whiskey, little one. Make shuah he drinks a full bottle. At least that much—morah if necessary. The bullets gotta come out, then we'll cauterize the wound." Peter kept up the chatter to cover his own concern. He wondered how in blue blazes he could perform a miracle on this shattered arm. One bullet had totally fractured the shoulder socket, the upper arm was nearly dislodged from the shoulder.

He watched as Madelaina poured whiskey into Paco until the bottle was nearly exhausted. "Ya better not stay heah for the rest o' this, little one. Go find me Captain Richards and a couple morah men ta help us. An' ah'll need some rope ta tie him down. Ask the general foah a brandin' iron an' a brazier ta heat it up, heah?"

As Madelaina set about her duties, she could hear the angry voices of Pancho Villa and General Lomas echo through the *casa*. She was in the hallway just outside the main salon where the two *jefes* confronted the other.

"Do you think for one moment I've betrayed Madero?" asked the general with indignation. "Do you mean to tell me, Pancho, that you think me to be a traitor? You and me fought side by side, Pancho. We've always been friends."

"That's what I'm here to find out," said Villa. "In the past we were friends. But half the army wearing the uniform of President Madero have sided with Orozco."

"And you think me to be a traitor? Oh, Pancho, how can you think such a thing?" General Lomas affected great dismay in the presence of all these men.

"It comes very easy, Francesco. Especially when I see such a reluctance on your part to take Parral. Are you afraid of General Soto? How many men does he command in Parral?"

"Four hundred in total. I have 100 here. Soto has 300. Colonel Anglais is in charge of the regiment."

"All right, old man. Now we'll see if you're friend or foe. You will write a note to Colonel Anglais that will bring him here to your hacienda. If you do it, we will have your men and his. That will mean you are with me in this. If you try to trick me, Francesco Lomas, I'll know it when Anglais tries to take me. And then, my *friend*, there may not be many of us left to fight one way or another. If I go down, most assuredly, plan to go down with me."

"You think I'm a fool to turn against Pancho Villa?" asked General Lomas. "At my age?" He pulled a sheet of paper from his desk drawer and scratched a message on it.

"You see how I trust you, Francesco," said Pancho Villa with a sly smile. "I don't even demand to read the note."

"Listen, Pancho, you think I don't know you are illiterate. You never took time to learn to read or write." The general laughed good-naturedly.

"That's true, Francesco Lomas." He nodded. "But

423

you see those gringos over there? They read. They write. Still, I don't insist on letting them read the message. That's how much trust I have in you."

General Lomas laughed heartily. "The trust you have in me, Pancho, is less than three inches from you all the time. Your *pistola*."

"That's true," nodded Villa, reflecting. "Is good you know me so well."

"Well enough to desire never to be your enemy."

"We'll see, *amigo*. We'll see."

Chapter 16

Paco Jimenez, drunk and delirious, had fallen into an unconscious stupor by the time Madelaina returned without help. She wasn't able to find Tracy.

"It's jus' as well, *chiquita*," said Peter, sweat pouring from his face and underarms. He removed the towel Paco had bitten on when the excruciating pain had driven him into a screaming frenzy. Concerned that those present would hear him scream and label him a coward, he had begged Peter for a towel to muffle his screams.

"He's earned that sleep," muttered Peter, probing for the bullet. Because it was lodged inaccessibly between the ball and socket of the shoulder joint, he was unsuccessful in removing the shell. He had located a second bullet close to the indescribably enormous gaping exit wound, which he presumed to be the only bullet until he actually saw a portion of the metal cylinder through the wound itself.

"Tell me, little one, what's a *bruja*?" he asked Madelaina as he continued to probe for the bullet buried in bone.

"A *bruja*? Where did you learn about *brujas*?"

"Paco's been raving out of his head, blaming all this on a *bruja*. It makes no sense at all. He's been ranting about a golden dawn and a countess and a *bruja*."

Madelaina merely frowned in thought. Worn to a frazzle, perspiration soaking her to the skin, she had piled her hair atop her head and speared it through with a bone hairpin. "He's delirious. It's no telling what he's dreaming."

"Ya bettah go out theah and try ta find Tracy

Richards foah me. Or someone. Ah need me a strong man and a pair of shoeing pliers, ya understand?"

Madelaina sighed wearily. "I understand." She moved across the room as one in a daze. Poor Paco. How in God's name could that arm be saved? How?

Ten minutes passed before she found Captain Richards and conveyed to him what Peter wanted of him. "Ah'm on mah way," he said, touching his sombrero. He nodded and moved away from her and paused for a moment to speak with Pancho Villa, who approached the outer portico of the *casa*. Tracy left the *guerrillo* leader and returned moments later with a pair of long-handled pliers with fine tips.

In the interim, Pancho Villa had excused himself from the officers with whom he chatted and pulled his heavy frame indolently along the dirt toward Madelaina.

"Señorita Obregon." He bowed politely. "Is it possible for us to speak?" He led the way to the outside portico.

"It's possible. But is it wise?" she asked softly, lowering her eyes.

She had to take longer steps to keep up with his bold pantherlike strides. The sound of his thickly rawled spurs clanging loudly against the tiles echoed through the courtyard. A soldier glanced up toward them; a *Villista* or two kept his eyes on his *jefe* for some sign that he might need them. In a shaded spot of the early morning sun, away from prying eyes and alert ears, Villa turned to her.

"You understand how it is, Little Fox?"

"You mean do I understand your unwavering loyalty to Presidente Madero? I'm not certain. Perhaps later, when we've finished caring for Corporal Jimenez, we shall talk," she said, ready to return.

"He is in good hands, *chiquita*. It is necessary that you and I should talk."

Madelaina saw tears spring into the dark walnut brown eyes of the fierce *guerrillo* as he looked into her eyes. She was deeply touched to see such emotion from

426

this powerful, fearsome man, whom she and the entire nation held in awe.

"Señor Villa, what is it? What is it that moves you to such feeling?" she asked, shaken to the core. She felt strangely dehumanized as if she should be in tune with his discomfort or in sympathy with his feelings.

"Only recently have I learned what happened to you because of me. Because of the messages you sent concerning Juarez. They can do anything to me. I am a man, a man who whistles a tune they must all dance to. But, you—a helpless woman—" Villa choked over the next few words. "I swear to you, Little Fox, they shall pay. All those who've wronged you shall feel the sting of Pancho's wrath."

"How can you say that, *señor*? The very men who wronged me are now your allies. Your loyalty is to Madero, not to me. True, I don't comprehend your strong feelings toward this weak, ineffectual man. It's a puzzle to me. Perhaps you see in Madero something to which my eyes are blind. For this reason, I do not question Pancho Villa. But I wonder. I think, and my mind becomes confused with the countless questions which race through my brain. Then I ask myself— what do I know? How would I dare contest or offend the most respected *guerrillo* in all Mexico—the puma—the mountain lion—the Centaur of the North? Surely Pancho Villa knows far more than Little Fox. It's not your fault that I don't understand any of this, *señor*. Enemies one day, friends the next. Men who killed each other yesterday embrace each other today. Truly, why are wars fought? What has changed? I see everything as it was—only worse," said Madelaina, shattered by what she heard and what had happened on this day.

"Ave. What you say is true. You wonder why I revere Madero? I shall try to tell you. I, Pancho Villa, knows no other way to do things except through force. I'm an uneducated *peón*, a Yaqui Indian, a stupid peasant. It's true, I don't understand men like your father and General Lomas here, and many other like him who do battle with their tongues and dangle money-belts before the eyes of their enemies to entice them. But the first day I met Madero, I felt *simpatico* to him. He has a heart, *señorita*. He feels things deeply as I do. Only Madero has an educated brain to direct his heart. I, Pancho Villa, has plenty of heart but no brains. Only a gun. *Pues*, that day Madero came to greet me with open arms. He embraced me, he hugged me to his bosom, and gave me a welcome such as Pancho Villa never had before from any man. His heart reached out to mine in deep understanding. In that instant, I laid down my gun for him. I had nothing else to offer him except my heart and my gun, and this I promised to do to the very end. I would die for that man because we both want the same thing for Mexico—and the people. God-given rights to be free men."

"Then why do you suppose Emiliano Zapata opposes him now?" asked Madelaina. "Why does he take up arms against the *Maderistas*? I'll tell you. Because Madero is stalling him. He gives him the same fancy rhetoric Diaz spouted. Madero offered Zapata a fancy hacienda with the wealth that goes with it. Imagine, he tried to buy off Zapata. He gave governorships to Don Gonzalez and to others in the early movement. What did he do for Pancho Villa—except to give him the rank of a colonel?" she scoffed with sarcastic contempt.

"I wanted nothing. I asked for nothing." Pancho scowled darkly as her words sunk in. "It's not true. Pancho wanted that lying, murderous dog, General Navarro. But *el señor presidente* denied me this request It was hard, but I understood. Madero said they were civilized. It's true what he said. Pancho Villa was not civilized. What would he want of such a barbarian, eh, *chiquita*?"

"Yet the minute those lying, traitorous jackals whom he empowered with the strength of armies turn on him, who does he call upon for help? The uncivilized barbarian, Pancho Villa, the man who gave him Juarez and with it the presidency! That's who!"

"That's true, too," replied Villa. "You see, it's not

easy to explain. Affairs of state can be complicated. Too complicated for even this dull brain to understand." He turned his attention to a horseman in the distance, riding swiftly toward the hacienda. Villa grew alert. "Ayeiii, Little Fox. I think Pancho Villa is needed soon."

Before he left to greet the rider, he confided to her that if what he planned to happen came off, he wanted Madelaina and her husband to be bedded down in the finest house in Parral, so they could renew their acquaintance and have a long-anticipated honeymoon. She had thanked him politely and watched as he joined his men beyond the courtyard, his spurs clanking noisily behind him.

Madelaina, ambivalent and somewhat frustrated by her talk with Villa, suddenly thought of Paco Jimenez. A pang of guilt surged through her as she rushed back inside, past the gathering of soldiers who expressed great interest in the approaching horseman. She swept past them and returned to the bedroom.

It was all over. Paco was asleep with a silly inebriated grin on his face, dulled to insensitivity. Peter, finished with the laborious work, stood over him, smoking a cigarette. Then it dawned on her that the talk with Villa had been planned to get her out of the room while Peter did what he had to do to save Paco's life. In a way, she felt grateful to have escaped the ordeal. On the other hand, she felt annoyed that Peter would think women shouldn't be exposed to such atrocities. If Peter only knew what she had been subjected to, he wouldn't be so squeamish over exposing her to such tribulation.

She moved toward him in silence. He extended his arms to her, drawing her close to him. For several wonderful moments she forgot everything.

"Don'cha worry none, little sweet thing, he's gonna pull through. We'll hafta get him ta a real doctor before long. As soon as we can we'll see ta it, sweet." He held her in his arms. She clung to him as if she couldn't be parted from him ever again.

429

"Ya know how ah ache for ya, sweet thing?" he whispered. "God almighty, since we met in Ayala ah've thought of nothing but you." His voice grew subdued and concerned. "Ah learned in part what happened ta ya from Alicia Sandoval."

"Alicia? Amelia? You saw them?" He nodded, and for the next half-hour he filled her in on what happened since Ayala. She began to tell him about their trip north. "You know, then, that the major you shot was the same man who subjected me to those depravities? He won't die, Peter. He'll never die until he comes back and humiliates me further. You wait—" Her eyes grew frenzied; she went on as if she was losing her wits. "You'll see. He won't leave me alone." Rising hysteria and fright consumed her. She grew erratic.

"Madelaina!"

"He'll stop at nothing. Oh, God, this is the third time he's been left for dead! Nothing can kill him! He's indestructible. He swore to get even with me. No one escapes his clutches. No one!" Hysteria mounted. "Peter, what will I do?"

"Madelaina! Stop!" He reached out and slapped her across the face, then held her until she snapped out of the momentary paralysis and fright. She sank against him, pathetic, broken, and numb from the exhausting emotional display.

"Theah, theah, sweet thing. It's all ovah now. You ah safe with me, sugah."

A knock at the door caught their attention. Captain Richards stuck his head in the door, a devilish grin scrawled on his face. "He's done it, buddy! The old puma has done it. Colonel Anglais arrived here moments ago, and together with us, Lomas' men and his, weah on ouah way ta victory. Get moving, buddy. Weah pullin' out, *pronto*."

Peter withdrew his arms from around Madelaina.

"No," she cried. "You can't go. I won't let you!"

"Ah must, sugah. Ah promise ah'll return." He stroked her face lovingly.

430

"Like you did at Ayala? Peter, don't leave me this time! I beg of you!"

"Ah mus' go, *querida*. Ah sweah, ah'll be back. This heah will be an easy victory. The *jefe* has marked his course well."

"Villa promised the finest house in Parral for us at the end of this day," interrupted Madelaina. "And what do I get—separation. I'm coming with you," she announced boldly.

Behind her back, Tracy Richards shook his head at Duprez and mouthed the word "no." Peter understood He couldn't allow her to ride in with an army. The women would follow later. That's as it should be. He thought quickly.

"And what about ole Paco here? Ya can't jus' leave him to fend foah hisself, now, can ya?"

Madelaina, dismayed, filled with sadness. "No, you're right. I can't just leave him." Her duty to Paco took precedence over her personal feelings.

For an instant Peter felt a tinge of jealousy at the quick change in her. There was no time to argue. "Ah promise—this time theah'll be no accursed Major Salomon ta keep me from ya. Wait foah me, ya heah?"

They kissed deeply. He broke away from her as a blush crept over him. She smiled knowingly and pressed her body close to his hardness with a secret smile in her eyes. "I'm tired of promises, *querido*," she teased softly.

He laughed with embarrassment and shook his head. "*Perder la vergüenza*? Have ya lost all sense of shame, little one?" He patted her bottom and was about to take his leave. Pausing at the door, he added, "An' when ah return, sweet, weah'll talk sensibly about ya fightin' them bulls! Understand? Don'cha ever do such a thing as long as youah mah wife. Ah want to keep ya foahevah, heah?"

The door closed behind him. Madelaina stood for a time in a dream state. *I want to keep you forever*, he had told her. She tried to feel for him what he felt for her when they were so close to each other, wanting,

431

needing each other so badly. Madelaina began to wonder how she'd tolerate a man coming close to her after her recent experiences. For an instant she was terrified. *What if I freeze? What if I experience the same frightening emotions I did at Madrigal?* Madelaina grew concerned. She broke out into a sweat; her hands, clammy and cold, fidgeted nervously. Earlier when she faced the bulls, she didn't experience such fear.

Madelaina recalled the words of Major Salomon. *You hate men! You have a castration complex. That's why you fight the bulls! You refuse to be a woman!*

Madelaina paced agitatedly to and fro. *He couldn't be right! Not that foul obscenity! What does he know? Who is he to talk to me like so? Castration complex indeed! Refuse to be a woman, hah!* Peter made her feel everything a woman should feel. Just because not every man left her feeling as breathless as he, did it mean she refused to be a woman? That's what her father had told her. He had lamented, "Why can't you be like the other women, Madelaina? Why can't you enjoy sewing and needlepoint, and running a household?" Even Felipe hinted at certain aberrations, her disinclination to comport herself as other woman did. Madelaina had protested. Why should she be like other women: empty-headed, flighty, thinking only of men, like a common coquette? Couldn't she be herself, a woman who entertained some of the likes and dislikes a man might have? Why must she be tormented because she didn't conform to the ways of her contemporaries? Despite her many experiences, her wisdom, and her vast knowledge, she came to realize that in certain respects she was naïve and didn't understand. Being a woman in the sense her peers meant, she understood even less.

Paco stirred restlessly, interrupting Madelaina's thoughts. She moved toward the bed and wiped the sweat from his face with a cloth dipped in water from a bowl on the stand next to the bed. Peter had bandaged him professionally. She felt a tinge of pride to think he'd done as well as a doctor might. She sat down in the chair next to the bed and leaned her head back wearily. The day had been long, active, and filled with tragedy. *God! Pray it ends up a happy one.*

Later in the evening, Peter Duprez returned. Wrapped in blankets, Paco was placed gently in the rear of a wagon. Madelaina, up on the seat next to Peter, lay her head on his shoulder as the wagon trundled back to Parral. Earlier she'd had a happy reunion with her old horse Don Quixote, who took a few moments to warm up to her, then he nuzzled her affectionately. Now he trailed behind the wagon, prancing spiritedly, his head bobbing up and down, his black mane flowing like wisps of silk in the wind.

Madelaina asked countless questions of her husband. "What happened? Did the fort collapse? Did the *Federales* surrender? Did he find the treachery he expected?"

"Without firing a single shot," laughed Peter goodnaturedly. "Ya should have seen it, *chiquita*. Anglais was put undah heavy guard. We surrounded the fort and caught that there General Soto by surprise. Why, honey, in less than an hour ole Pancho had hisself a trained army of 400 willin' men in his command. What strategy! He sent ole General Lomas on ta Durango ta recruit more men ta combat the Orozco forces."

An hour later, true to Pancho Villa's word, Madelaina was settled in the finest hacienda in Parral. Paco was put to bed by a bright-eyed little charmer named Lola. A vibrant, exotic gypsy, she had unusual blue eyes, auburn hair, and a figure that burst right through the bright yellow Indian shift she wore, red and blue embroidery decorating its low-cut neckline.

Madelaina laughed. "You almost look envious of Paco," she told her husband, noticing with a tinge of jealousy how his eyes assessed the girl's beauty.

"Yes, m'am! She's shore a cute little thing," he whistled breathlessly. "Now, if only ah weren't a married man, little *chiquita*. Mmmmmmuh!"

Before she could offer a protest, she was swept up in his arms and two at a time, he climbed the steps to the

433

second level. Madelaina lay her head against his chest, her arms entwined around his neck. This was all that mattered to her. After two years she had found Peter. It didn't matter what had happened in between. They were together. Sweet blessed Jesus!

Apparently Peter had seen the house before. He knew where to go. He kicked open a large double door and entered the attractive bedroom. Her eyes widened at the cheery room with its fireplace and large French doors leading to the balcony. Peter tossed her on the bed and gripping her even tighter in his arms, he kissed her over and over and over until they were too breathless to continue without pausing.

"Ah've many surprises in storah foah ya, little darlin'." Peter pulled away a folding screen at one end of the room, revealing a wooden bath tub filled with hot water and perfumed bath salts. He bowed with the flourish of a Spanish gallant and announced like a court page: "Mistah and Missus Peter Duprez regret ta infoahm friends that they've taken a temporary leave of absence from the world. Theah'll return only when theah've ravished each other, when theah've no strength left. Y'all approve, Señora Duprez?"

Madelaina giggled. "Most assuredly," she replied in a voice to match his special cadence. *"Mi marido bonito,* how much I love you."

He locked the door, a wicked gleam in his expressive eyes, and moved toward her with exaggerated leonine strides. He tossed his gun belt to one side, his leather vest to another, peeled open the buttons of his shirt, his eyes never wavering from hers. "Ya know how long ah've ached foah ya? How ah've yearned foah ya? Ya better remove those theah trousahs, love, befoah ah do it foah ya," he said with a bold innuendo that excited her. "Sweet thing, this is gonna be the best night of ouah lives—bettah than the *Mozambique,* heah?"

"Oh, Peter," she muttered, a sudden awkwardness upon her. She felt self-conscious, in the manner of an untutored virgin and didn't know why. Her eyes darted uneasily about the room. She slipped off the bed, put

434

off Peter's reach, and scampered toward the tub. She dipped a hand into the water and allowed it to ripple across the surface, carving a path between the soapy bubbles. Moving across to the dressing table, aware that Peter watched her with a disturbed expression in his eyes, she studied the perfume bottle, a smile playing about her lips as she read the label.

"*Querido*? Where on earth did you find this? Surely you haven't carried it with you all this time?" She sniffed the essence of roses appreciatively, then inhaled deeply. "Ahhh," she sighed wistfully. "I haven't smelled this in two years." He had bought her the same essence in Lisbon.

"Ah bought a few things at the *tienda*, sweetheart. Ah wanted ta make things jus' perfect foah us." Fully unclothed, he moved in behind her, standing very close.

She glanced up and caught his reflection in the mirror. "What a handsome, beautiful man you are, Peter Duprez," she said quietly. "I am most fortunate to have found a man who loves me as much as I love him." She snuggled up to him and felt the security of his strong arms around her. She would have been content to remain in this posture for all eternity. Feeling the urgency in him rising, she smiled a secret smile.

"Y'all aren't fair. Ah was shore ya'd be standing naked as a jaybird by now."

She frowned, visibly annoyed. "Not like animals, Peter! Surely there's more to love than *hurry, take off your clothes so I can ravish you!*" Her voice, suddenly brittle, was reprimanding. No one was more surprised than Madelaina at her words and attitude. Catching the sudden hurt look in his blue eyes, the wondering startled expression of a rejected male, she wanted the earth to swallow her so she wouldn't have to see the chagrined expression on his face.

It was a moment of acute bewilderment for both. Peter deigned to ignore her remark. Affecting an attitude of gaiety as he walked to the tub, he said, "Well, little darlin', theah's much more ta love than any one thing. Love's an accumulation of many things, ya

435

know. Listenin' ta the sound of yore voice, watchin' ya flutter them wide innocent eyes at me, feelin' yore body close ta mine, talkin', listenin', finding out what makes ya tick. Ya know, like what's inside that little ole head of yours." He felt the water and let it trickle through his fingers.

"Ah don't know about ya, little one. But, ah'm gonna get me inside o' this here tub an' soak me up a stoahm, ya heah?" He got into the tub and sat back, groaning and moaning with satisfaction. "Now, ya jus' take yer time. An' when ya get yer mind ta it, ya can come on over and scrub yer *viejo's* back. Ah was kinda hoping ya'd join me. Ya see, it ain't all that easy to get more hot water, baby." He began to soap himself, his face, his neck, and head until Madelaina broke into laughter at his antics. He even hummed in a ridiculous off-key manner to cause her to rock with mirth.

Slowly, almost against her will, she began to disrobe, a curious expression on her face that he'd never seen before. Trying to keep up an atmosphere of continued gaiety, Peter began to sing with his atrocious Texas twang.

"La Cucaracha! La Cucaracha. Ya no puede caminar. Porque no tiene, porque la falta, marihuana que fumar."

She winced at his laughable Spanish and soon doubled over in paroxyms of laughter. The more she laughed, the more he exaggerated his gestures and his accent. Peter watched her carefully under a knot of wrinkled brows and affected facial gestures designed to keep her laughing. She stood before him naked, and he whistled in appreciation of her exquisite body. He had almost forgotten how lovely she was. In two years she had filled out considerably and matured to exquisite proportions. Her breasts, firm and well rounded, were just the right size—not pendulous, but more than ample. Her waist was minute, and her hips, never broad, were slightly fuller than the slim-hipped sixteen-year-old he'd met in Sanlucar de Barramedas. He tried hard not to express his genuine appreciation of her beauty and graceful proportions. The Sandoval girls had told him of the abuse to which she'd been subjected at Madrigal. How foolish of him to think she hadn't been affected mentally by what had happened to her.

Above all, he wanted to be tender and understanding. Earlier she'd bridled when he showed the least amount of sexual urgency. Well, ole Pete Duprez could wait. He'd always had enough women to tide him over. If the one woman he loved needed reassurance, love, and consideration, he'd give it to her. Meanwhile he told himself to cool it. She responded to fun like a child. Very well, they would have fun together. The other would come in time. He just didn't want to see that look on her face he'd seen earlier. He began to whistle the tune.

"Ya don't like mah Spanish? Ya mind if ah whistle a mite?"

His whistling was more outrageous. He purposely went off key several times until Madelaina laughingly held her hands over her ears. She stood close to the tub now.

"May I come in, *señor*?" she asked playfully.

"By all means, *señora*. But only if'n ya got no jealous husband around," he teased. "Yer jus' so appealing, little one, ah might jus' get a little fresh with ya. Then wheah will ah be if'n some 200-pound bull snorts his way into this heah room ta gore me?"

"Oh, you *mentecato idiota*—silly idiot." Madelaina laughed and climbed into the tub with him. For an instant, Peter caught sight of the livid, twisting scars on her lower back. He gasped aloud and grabbed her quickly, forcing her to look into his eyes.

"Madelaina—what are these?" He traced his fingers lightly over the purple scars, sickened because he already knew the answer.

Shivering under his touch, Madelaina laughed lightly. "Oh, those. Haven't they cleared up yet?"

"What rotten, scum-sucking snake did this ta ya?" he asked hoarsely.

437

"You almost shot him, Peter. Too bad your bullets didn't do the job."

"Salomon?" He shuddered. "He did this?" He pulled her close to him and held her tight against his chest. He stroked her head, her face, her shoulders tenderly, and rocked her gently to and fro in his arms.

"If it makes ya feel any better, little darlin', ah swear, if he lives through those gun shots, he won't live much longah. Ah sweah to avenge ya. Ah sweah it!"

"Oh Peter." Tears stung her eyes. "Let's not mar our time together with memories of that wretched, depraved devil of the damned." She turned to him and kissed him. They kissed and kissed and couldn't stop.

Madelaina was amazed at the pent-up passion in her body. She quivered and let sensation overtake her. She wouldn't think. She wouldn't let herself think of anything. *Feel,* she told herself. *Let sensation take over. Feel him, smell him, hear his soft tender voice. Look into his azure blue eyes and think of golden sunsets on a sparkling sea of blue jewels. Feel the warmth of his body against yours. Feel the lean, hard firmness. Smell the clean, manly smells of leather and tobacco, his own musky smell. Listen; hear his tender voice as it strokes you and cares for you and whispers all those things you've wanted to hear for the past two years. Touch him, Madelaina. Touch the man you love. Let him know how you love him, how you've longed for him, how you've ached for the feel of his body inside yours. Do all the things you've done in your memory so many times. Do them now. Right now.*

She didn't know when, but sometime during this self-hypnosis, Peter had picked her up out of the tub and transported her lovingly to the four-poster bed. Her memories of their intimacy on the *Mozambique* faded into a misty cloud of sensation. For so long she had told herself she had to make new memories. They were doing it together. New memories to last them a lifetime.

"Dear Peter, how I love you," she purred. "I can't begin to tell you how much I've longed for you. How

438

I've wanted you. I would see men and women couple together and think of you. In the spring when nature came into full bloom, my thoughts turned to you. Every act of procreation reminded me of you and our love. In my heart, Peter, even though we parted on a sour note, there was little doubt in my mind that you would forgive me once you knew I hadn't betrayed you. Oh, my love, you can't imagine how strong our love became. Your words guided me in the darkest days. There were times—yes, many times—when I thought I hated you, because I had traveled so far to find you. My father tried to understand. My best friend and childhood sweetheart begged me to marry him. Poor Felipe. Sweet Felipe de Cordoba. How could I marry him when I was already the property of another? I belong to you, Peter. From the very first moment we met, I knew our destinies lay together. Now, at long last, we've found each other." She clung to him tightly. Peter kissed her trembling lips, almost afraid to penetrate her. She was moist, warm as an oven. No, she was torrid. He wasn't certain how much longer he could last. He'd never felt so desperately lacking in control.

The time came when his passion could no longer be denied. He admitted it hadn't been the same as he remembered her. There was an urgency in her that hadn't been there before, a desperate need to satisfy him. She was trying too hard and he felt it instinctively. He had two options: Stop what he was doing and take the chance she'd grow hysterical, or go through with the act to the finish, hoping for the best, yet knowing she wasn't entirely his.

He chose the latter, talking to her, encouraging her, telling her how much he missed her, how agonized his life had been without her, how he had convinced himself he'd never see her again. "Ah didn't have your faith, little sweetheart," he cooed, as he mounted her. It was a strain for Peter. He entered her slowly and felt her withdraw. She was exceedingly tight, almost impenetrable. He moved off her and let his hand caress her

439

casually, his fingers stroked her gently and he felt the moisture, the heat, the pulsation. He tried as casually as possible to enter her body again. Each thrust, gentle as it was, caused her to recoil internally, he felt the increased pressure prohibiting entry. He felt certain she was willing, but her body rejected him. He tried once more with unlimited patience. Penetration was almost impossible.

"What's wrong, *querido*?" she asked, aware that Peter was having difficulties.

"Damned if ah know, love puss. S'pose we sit back a bit and have us some of this heah champagne we put on ice earlier." He rose to his feet to get the wine and glasses he'd prepared earlier. With aplomb he twirled the bottle expertly as he'd seen many French waiters do in Europe. He popped the cork and proceeded to pour the tawny, bubbly champagne into hollow-stemmed glasses.

The next few moments proved Peter to be a splendid actor. He disguised his concern over the predicament as well as his disappointment.

"This villa belonged ta some wealthy *hacendado* who shook in his bones when he learned the fierce *guerrillo*, Pancho Villa, intended ta return to Parral," he told her, admiring the furnishings of the room. "Knowing Villa's passionate hatred of *hacendados*, the *patrón* and his entourage took all the possessions they could carry and locked up the rest. Little good it did, eh, sweet thing? Imagine, he even boarded up the windows." Peter laughed at the mental picture conjured up in his mind. "Ah can jus' see the expressions on theah faces as they skeedaddled in the middle of the night at the mere mention of Pancho Villa." Peter lay on the bed, propped up against the headboard of the hand-carved oaken bed, with Madelaina pulled up close to him. They touched glasses.

"Heah's ta us, *matadora*," he teased. They sipped their drinks in silence.

In the far distance, at the very center of Parral, a gala celebration had begun. The *campesinas* had ar-

440

rived and the men were ready to celebrate. Guitars, maracas, castanets, muted trumpets played ethnic music endlessly as gypsy dancers moved sensuously in the crowd. Pancho Villa's stupendous victory would be celebrated throughout Parral. In Chihuahua City, that defector, General Orozco, would be pacing the floor waiting to hear of General Soto's victory. Only destiny knew that Pancho Villa's blistering victory in this remote village would soon mark the beginning of the end for this viper.

Rosalia Quintera and Lucia, riding into town, started looking everywhere for Captain Tracy Richards and Peter Duprez.

Meanwhile Peter and Madelaina relaxed, talking and getting better acquainted.

"Ah nevah told ya much about me, Little Fox," Peter told her. "Y'all amaze me with youah trust in me. Ya knevah really knew me and still don't know much about me, yet ya trust me with youah life. How could ah have inspired such faith, such trust? Ah'm nothing but a shiftless soldier of fortune, a mercenary, a killah—a man who lives by the gun."

Madelaina reached up to touch his lips with her fingertip. "I don't know who you are, it's true. Or what you are. I know you and I don't. One day here, the next—who knows? You don't sit still enough for me to know you well, Peter."

She raised her luminous dark eyes to meet his and expelled a sigh of wistful resignation. Once they had been able to look into each other's souls. An electric magnetism had drawn together this man and woman. And it was this same magnetism that could either destroy them or recreate them into new-found hope. The trouble was they both wanted to possess each other in a way no human can possess another. And it seemed that this, too, was becoming more improbable by the moment. What was wrong between them, wondered Madelaina.

Peter turned from her, his blue eyes seething with anger—not at her but at his destiny. Striding to the windows, he opened the shutters slightly and glanced outside into the courtyard with its decadent dried-up fountain. It was insufferably hot, the kind of heat where temperatures rise to 120 degrees and the humidity makes it feel 200 in this western Sahara, the kind of heat that pulverizes everything in sight and renders a person impotent of strength.

Madelaina set down her glass. She wrapped her body in a light towel and moved next to him. "What is it, Peter? Tell me. Something's wrong with me you're not talking about."

"What happened to you in Madrigal?" he asked quietly.

"Are you certain you want to know?"

"Yes."

"Why is it important?"

"Ah'm gonna ask ya a question or two. Don't misunderstand. It's impoahtant ta me and ta y'all. Have ya had affairs with many men since ya left that demon's lair, Madrigal?"

"Peter!" It was shock, hurt, and amazement all in one. "How could you think such things?"

"Ah asked ya ta please understand mah question, little one," he told her patiently. "Ah love ya, sugah, an' ah know ya love me. Ah'm not sure what satisfaction y'all got outa mah bumbling on the bed awhile ago, but neither of us can claim it was of any consequence. Ah'm jus' trying to learn why."

"The answer is no," she replied icily.

"Ah didn't think so," said Peter, walking her back to the bed. "Get in and rest, love. Ah'll be back in fifteen minutes—not later than a half-hour." His attitude, both happy and concerned, sparked her curiosity.

"Why? What's happening? Tell me what's wrong, Peter."

"Ah promise ah will when ah return." He slipped into his trousers and boots. He was almost out the door when he tracked back in to pick up his gun belt. "Wouldn't get too far without these trusty companions," he said grinning.

442

After he left, Madelaina couldn't help wondering what he was up to. The champagne had relaxed her and left her head feeling fuzzy. She attempted to recap their earlier activity, retrace their movements, their lovemaking, to better understand his thinking. She was unable to recall anything that might have triggered his behavior. She felt a numbness in her loins, nothing like the erotica she had experienced aboard the *Mozambique*. Sometimes memories were better than the real thing, she told herself before dozing off.

Madelaina experienced strange and troubled dreams in which she tossed and perspired and thrashed wildly on the bed. Images came to her, alien and disconnected. Ghoulish figures, shrouded and vaporous, ectoplasm with no form, but of a morbid and malignant variety, made her bolt upright in the bed like a terrified child. It was at this moment Madelaina heard strange and hushed voices. Her eyes flicked open and she saw Peter standing next to her bed, speaking with a small, wiry man with a brush moustache and short, steely gray hair resembling a wire brush. He wore a monocle in one eye and stood silent, his thumbs hooked into his vest pockets over a heavily paunched stomach.

"*Querida*," purred Peter, moving in to comfort her. "Ah want ya ta meet up with this heah Dr. Gregorio," he told her. "The doctah an' ah've been talkin' a spell. This heah is mah missus, Dr. Gregorio. Ah'm gonna leave mah missus in youah hands foah a time." He turned to Madelaina, who stared at him in total bewilderment as she clutched the sheets close to her bosom. "He wants ta examine ya, little one. Don'cha worry none, heah?"

"Why are you doing this to me, Peter?" she shrieked hysterically. "I'm fine, *muy bueno*. It's the truth. I need no doctor." Her features turned cold and she retreated on the bed with hostility and anger in her stormy dark eyes.

"Ah jus' want the doctor heah ta make shuah everything's fine." Peter exited quickly. He closed the door firmly behind him and leaned heavily against it, out in the hall. He'd never forget the hurt embarrassment and anger surfacing in her smoldering and bewildered eyes.

He paced the floor for the next fifteen minutes, chain smoking, filled with perplexing thoughts. It took neither a medical degree nor any amount of medical sophistication to know that something was drastically wrong with Madelaina. He was unable to penetrate Madelaina's body with his penis. He never recalled her being in this condition. He knew enough about women to know there was some abnormality underfoot. Something had happened in Madrigal that changed her. Grim-faced, shaking with infuriated anger, he had to content himself with waiting until the doctor had examined her.

His imagination conjured up untold horrors, perhaps even worse than those Alicia Sandoval had related. It stood to reason the girls couldn't have been with Madelaina every moment. Who could guess if she'd been drugged or anesthetized to the point of having no memory of what might have happened. One thing was certain; the nightmare began at Madrigal. Where it would end, only the Lord knew.

"Señor Duprez?"

Peter turned around as the doctor emerged from Madelaina's room.

"Is best we talk, *señor*," said the physician.

Peter led the way downstairs to the study. "Before ya leave, Dr. Gregorio, theah's another patient ah want ya ta look in on. He had a bad injury. He was patched up as best could be. Please." He gestured to a chair. "Lola." He called the pretty young mestizo who stood at one end of the hall watching him. "Please bring wine for the good doctor, honey," he said expansively, enjoying the role.

He offered the physician a cigar from the humidor he'd stocked earlier that day in preparation for his week's stay, a week that was to have been the happiest time of his life. They lit up the smokes and, with the customary amenities out of the way, began to converse on pertinent matters.

444

"*Señor*, I find nothing physiologically wrong with your wife. Yes, she's been injured. Injured quite badly, I might say. I found considerable scar tissue. But there's more. I'm afraid the damage done to her is more of a psychological nature. Something I am not equipped to diagnose. Perhaps in Texas, in El Paso, you can take her to the specialists there. They'll be able to tell you better." He spoke in perfect Castilian.

"But, Doctor, ya don't understand. There has ta be a physiological obstruction. Damnit ta hell, ah can't make love ta her. Don'cha understand? Ah can't get inside her ta—well, you know what ah mean!" Peter chewed his *cigarro* to a frazzle. "Two yeahs ago when we married ah had no difficulty. Ah tell ya, Doc, there's an obstruction someplace down theah in her honey jar."

Dr. Gregorio shook his head. "There's no obstruction—not a physical one that is. It's all up here." He tapped his head significantly.

"Ya mean she's rejecting me?"

Dr. Gregorio shrugged. "Who knows what goes on in the mind, *señor*? Something is troubling her. Something buried inside her, deep in her subconscious. Not knowing the patient's history, I can't even offer you solace, let alone a prognosis. Perhaps in El Paso she can undergo tests. They have some excellent specialists there. Meanwhile I gave her a sedative to calm her."

Peter grew silent. It just couldn't be happening to him or to Madelaina. Whatever it was had to be remedied. It had to. The thought of being near her and never able to touch her the way a man and woman in love would touch shook him up beyond belief. He couldn't conceive of such a thing.

They drank the wine in silence. Peter despairing openly and the doctor, apathetic, with a more clinical approach. He drained his glass and smacked his lips.

"Now for this other patient," he said lightly.

"Lola, show the doctor ta Paco's room," said Peter, dispirited.

He hardly looked at the doctor as he left the room,

led by the young girl. He was still seated there staring out into space when Dr. Gregorio returned.

"This is a day of calamities, *señor*. The man is very sick. He's burning with fever. I gave him medication, redressed the wound, but, *señor*, I have little faith he will heal properly. For three days and nights he must be watched like a baby. If he survives the three days, there's a possibility he will fare well enough, with only a minor loss of mobility. However, if my fears prove true and the infection doesn't pass, we may have to amputate."

Peter glanced up in a daze. "Am—amputate? Ya mean cut off half his arm?" He shivered inwardly.

"A whole arm, *señor*. Right from the shoulder." He shook his head. "I will come back tomorrow. It's a sad day I inflict upon your house, *señor*. I beg your humble pardon. With your permission?"

"Yes, yes, of course." Peter waved him off with an abstract gesture. He was numb.

"*Señor?*" The doctor paused halfway out the room and retreated a few steps. "I didn't tell you, but it's possible that the *señora* will not be able to have children. Of course, this can only be determined with tests. Here in Parral there is little need for specialists. The women are so prolific they could have *niños* every day if the Good Lord hadn't imposed a nine-month waiting period."

If Peter heard, he gave no indication. He sank deeper and deeper into depression. It wasn't possible so much could have happened to one so young and teeming with life. He couldn't believe all this was happening. It was like having the very life taken out of him. Dying was one thing. Existing without living was inconceivable to him. How would he tell her? Could he? Should he?

Dr. Gregorio is right. I'll take her to El Paso. Perhaps there she can gradually grow more secure in my love and she's bound to get well. She has to return to me as she was. Oh, Little Fox! He leaned forward, his head in his hands, a silent scream of agony deep inside

446

him wanted escape. He needed release. God, it had been so long! Had he waited for her only to have such a trick played on them both?

How long had he been sitting there, feeling sorry for himself and Madelaina? This would never do. He pulled himself up from the chair, poured himself a healthy slug of whiskey, downed it, and shuddered involuntarily.

They had both been through too much to have it end without putting up a fight. They were both fighters, both idealists to a degree, but logical enough to handle such problems with insight and intelligence.

"*Señor?*"

Peter turned to look into the palest blue eyes he'd ever seen on a mestiza.

"What is it, blue eyes?"

"What time you and the *señora* will eat?" asked Lola softly.

Peter wagged his hand at her in a disorganized gesture. "Ah'll let you know later. Why? Ya want the night off? Ya should be enjoying the celebration too."

"No, Señor Gringo. I must stay with Paco. He is very sick."

"Yes, Lola. He's sick. Good girl. We'll appreciate all ya can do."

Peter walked away slowly, ascended the steps heavily depressed. Only a few hours ago his feet took wings over these very same stairs. And now?

He entered the warm room. Oblique shadows from an early twilight filtered through the shuttered windows. He removed his boots, shirt, and trousers, and wrapped a robe around himself. He padded across the bare room covered by scatter rugs here and there and looked down at Madelaina. The doctor had given her a sedative. Her nervousness over the surprise examination left her hostile, high-strung, and bewildered. The doc said he'd given her tincture of opium to relax her and put her into a less tense mood.

Peter snuggled in next to her. He watched the perspiration beads pop on her forehead and tenderly brushed a few wisps of that raven hair, the color of live coals, off her face. Madelaina stirred sleepily. "There's mah girl," he whispered. "It's all gonna be jus' fine, ya little sweet thing."

Her eyes flickered dreamily. "Peter?" she muttered. "I love you, *mi amor*."

"Ah love ya, too, little darlin'."

She reached up and encircled his neck with her arms. Before he could move she planted a moist kiss on his lips. He kissed her back. It would have been difficult not to. She forced her hot tongue in his mouth and stirred him to such emotion, he was left breathless. He was about to remove her arms from his neck.

How much of this could he take?

In a somewhat somnolent state, Madelaina pushed off the covers. She was totally nude; her warm moist body felt like velvet. Slowly, she raised her body over his and lowered her hips on his. Peter tried to hold back, recalling vividly the difficulty he had encountered in his attempts to penetrate her earlier. By this time, Madelaina had control of the situation. No matter how he backed off in his effort to avert pain for her, Madelaina pushed harder. No one was more surprised than he when he achieved full penetration.

Realization of what happened almost spoiled their lovemaking. Being a master at his craft, Peter allowed her to dominate him for as long as she desired, telling himself not to be concerned with what was happening as long as it was happening. Later he could dissect the act—and try to fathom it.

They began to move in rhythm. Her body moving with his, his with hers. He couldn't believe it. Where was the tightness he had experienced earlier, the pain? He gently reversed their positions, and the pleasure became exquisite. Their breathing quickened as they filled with burning desire to consummate their feelings in one complete union.

The only disturbing factor in Peter's mind was the fact that Madelaina appeared dazed, not really conscious of her act. It appeared she was moving in an unconscious state. She whispered little endearments and called his name frequently. Peter forced himself to push any thought except for this moment from his mind. When they had both experienced releases, he held her cradled in his arms for several precious moments. He felt her begin to move against him with those same sensuous thrusts he had taught her on board ship.

It all came back, just as he dreamed it would, just as Madelaina wanted it to be. Exquisite love, joy, contentment. What flowed between them was simply wonderful. For Peter it was setting the calendar back two years, all but what was good between them. For Madelaina it was an assurance that she wasn't damaged property, that Peter wanted her no matter what had happened in the past. An acceptance without qualifications. He loved her. She loved him. What else mattered, if they had this?

Gradually he began to feel the cadence of his breathing paced to hers. His thrusts, slow and sensuous, aroused every nerve fiber in her body to an exquisite rapturous sensation. Her body lifted to meet his and together they burst inside one another. For several moments time stopped—the world came to a halt and paradise was theirs. A supreme happiness and contentment engulfed them, an indescribable euphoria possessed them.

Afterward, Madelaina's limbs appeared lifeless and weak. She fell into a deep sleep. Peter lay beside her, smoking cigarette after cigarette for nearly two hours. It was 9 P.M. when he arose from the bed to stretch his limbs. Madelaina slept soundly. He called softly to her. She muttered lazily, opened and closed one eye, rolled over and fell into a deeper sleep. He pulled the sheets and light coverlet closer to her.

Outside, from the balcony, he could see the lights on in Parral. He could still hear the celebrants making a night of it. A breeze, drifting in off the desert, brought with it musty odors of a decaying village, spicy food scents intermingled with the putrid stench of acacia, a

449

faint smell of mint and oily emanations of magnolia. At the rear of the villa, an overgrown garden had been left to struggle through life by its previous owner. The flowers needed pruning and picking to make them more prolific. Peter laughed lightly. He was acting somewhat domesticated, a new feeling for him.

He puzzled over the change in Madelaina. The doctor had claimed her ailment was psychological. He had given her a sedative. Had it relaxed her into such submission as to cause physiological changes in her body? It was all too incredible even for him to comprehend. He had enjoyed himself, but not as he would have had he not known how she acted in a conscious state. Damn the mind! He had tried to shut it out and fared pretty well. Now the wheels were back in motion, bringing reality back into sharper focus with all its many complications.

Most important of all was his grave concern for Madelaina. Patience, the greatest of all virtues, he told himself, is what's called for. He considered leaving the *Villistas* and traveling back to El Paso, where Madelaina could be checked over by the specialists Dr. Gregorio prescribed. Then they could go to his spread outside of San Antone. Madelaina would fare well on the west Texas ranch. Her remarkable passion for bulls could easily be turned to profit. It would keep her occupied and absorbed in something she enjoyed and understood. Yes, he thought wisely, it's a good idea.

Book Five

Lago Diablo de Los Muertos

Chapter 17

"*Señora! Señora!* You must awaken now. It's important!"

Madelaina awakened with a start at the anxious sound of Lola's voice. She bolted upright to a sitting position. Blinking in the darkness, she looked for her husband. In the distance came the sounds of the mariachas, muted trumpets, and guitars.

"Come downstairs. It's Paco. He's raving, out of his head."

"Yes, yes, I'm coming." She sprang from her bed and reached for the sheer cotton batiste wraparound Peter had bought for her. She quickly brushed her midnight black hair off her face and let it fall behind her shoulders.

Catching sight of her pale reflection in the mirror as she passed, Madelaina paused at the unfamiliar image bouncing back at her. Her eyes, haunted, with dark sunken hollows around them, had an unnatural glow. Yet no more unnatural than the peculiar aura about her head. Her hands moved up quickly as if to brush it aside, but the faint mistlike emanation remained. Something other than her own will propelled her to leave the room. Moving as a sleepwalker might, she glided across the length of the upper hallway and descended the staircase which tunneled below her. Something outside herself pulled her, pushed her ahead in the direction of Paco's room.

Vaguely she heard cries in the night, somewhat muffled, not clear in her mind. She cocked her head hesitantly from side to side, angling it sharply to the right, then to the left. Following the sounds, she walked through the large salon along the lower corridor until she came to the door of Paco's room. Her hand grasped the large metal ring and turned it. She pushed on the door. The room was dim and shadowy. Her eyes came to rest upon the tormented body of the corporal who'd saved her life so many times.

Lola, frightened and distraught, stood close to him, bending over his feverish body, wiping the sweat from his face and neck with a cool, damp cloth.

"No!" he screamed in Spanish, "You can't do this! Leave me, *bruja*! I am stronger than you! You've wreaked enough havoc in my life. I'll outlive you. Out with you! Out! Out! Out! I cast you out" He ranted and raved and thrashed about the bed, the sweat-soaked sheets which Lola had already changed twice.

"*Señora*, we must send for the doctor. He's in terrible fever. I've never seen such fever—such madness. He talks out of head—" She stopped, arrested by the glazed, almost opalescent lights in Madelaina's eyes. What she saw in Madelaina's eyes, on her face, frightened her. Recalling instantly the things Paco said in his delirium, she felt her stomach knot tightly. "*Bruja—witch!*" Did Paco mean the *señora*? "*Madre de Dios!*" she exclaimed, clutching the ornate silver crucifix around her neck. "*God protect me!*"

"What is it, Lola?" she asked in a controlled voice.

The girl in all her uncertainty stood there trembling, afraid to speak. If ever she'd seen a woman possessed with evil spirits, it was this woman, right here and now. Her voice, dried and cracked, could hardly speak. Never once did Lola take her startled blue eyes off her new mistress.

"We must send for the doctor," Lola managed to say at last with affected bravado.

"Where is my husband?"

"He's been gone all day, *señora*. On business with Pancho Villa."

"All day?" Madelaina blinked her eyes and shook herself. "All day? What day is this?"

"Wednesday, *señora*."

"Wednesday?" Had she slept two whole days?

454

"Turn up the oil lamps, girl." Madelaina touched her forehead. Two whole days lost. How? Where?

The young mestizo obliged, but she remained cautious, keeping one eye on this strange woman who sleeps day and night while her husband, *un mucho macho hombre*, a gringo at that, walks around with swollen loins, just aching to assert his manhood. She had little respect for a woman who couldn't satisfy a man. Especially a man such as Señor Tom Mix.

Madelaina placed a cool, slender hand on Paco's forehead. What a fever! He continued to emit low growling sounds as he tossed and turned on the bed. She lifted the thick, cumbersome bandage and inspected the wound.

Madelaina recoiled in horror! The stench from the gangrenous wound was unbearable. "Give me a lamp! Hurry, girl!" Whatever it was that controlled Madelaina earlier had evaporated. She was once again in full command of her faculties.

She held the lamp over him and stared aghast at the condition of the pus-filled, infected wound. "Lola. Go! Find the doctor! It is very bad!" She turned away from the horrifying sight, recoiling noticeably. "And for God's sake, try to find the *señor*. Understand? You must find my husband!"

No sooner had Lola straddled her horse and ridden out of the courtyard toward Parral, when several riders descended upon her.

Peter Duprez, Captain Tracy Richards, Rosalia Quintera, and Lucia reined their horses with force to prevent colliding into Lola. She recognized Peter instantly and called to him loudly.

"*Señor! Por favor, señor*. I must go to fetch the doctor. Paco is delirious. *La bruja! La bruja! Aye, Dios mios!*" She rattled off in her Indian dialect which Peter didn't understand. "I go now for the doctor."

She kicked her heels into the horse's flanks and took off like a whirlwind.

The gringos and the women spurred their horses into the courtyard and tethered them to the hitching posts.

Bruja! Bruja! Peter rolled the words over in his mind. Those were the words Paco muttered. He turned to Lucia who had surprised him by arriving with Rosalia Quintera. He'd gathered his friends and brought them to the hacienda to meet Madelaina.

"Lucia," he said, holding her back. "Tell me, what does *bruja* mean?"

Lucia crossed herself. "You mean what that crazy girl was raving about out there?" She gave a little quick jerk to her head.

"Precisely that."

Rosalia Quintera overhead Peter and holding Tracy's hand she moved in closer. "What she said, gringo, is that the man is possessed by an evil spirit. Paco is his name?"

Peter nodded.

"Then, this Paco is possessed. Also that the *señora* is a *bruja*—a witch!"

"That's plumb crazy," said Peter with irritation.

"Hey, gringo, don't get mad on me," said Rosalia, laughing in her usual gay spirit. "Ees not me who say such theengs."

"Yeah," said Peter. "You're right. We better get inside ta meet the missus."

Lucia couldn't help but feel more than a pang of jealousy at the possessive way he said "meet the missus." She had loved Peter Duprez for so long, the ache in her heart had become a part of her. She wrapped herself in a lace shawl she had bought in the *tienda* just before she met Peter. For an instant, when she saw Lola, with those sky blue eyes and that auburn hair, she filled with remorse. Peter always surrounded himself with beautiful women. She sighed and followed the others inside.

"Madelaina!" he called. "Madelaina!" He turned toward the corridor and headed for Paco's room. "Make yourselves ta home," he told the others. "Trace —there's plenty o' booze, buddy. Jus' help yerself, heah?"

He found Madelaina staring at Paco, unable to do

456

anything to help him. She lifted her eyes at the sound of footsteps entering the room, her features lax and lifeless, her expression masked with a harshness he'd never seen before.

He whispered quietly as he approached her. "How's he doing, little one? He any bettah?" Peter moved in closer, reaching out to her.

For an answer she lifted the bandage from Paco's shoulder and held the oil lamp for him to see it in all its putrefaction. Her eyes met his.

"Mah God, darlin'." He looked away, trying hard not to show his innermost feelings. "How's it possible that in three days it could've turned out like that? Good thing ya sent for the doctor." He watched his wife wipe the perspiration from Paco's face.

"He's out of his mind," she told her husband. "Delirious with fever."

"Ya wanna come out and meet Tracy's *vieja* and her friend, Lucia? Lucia is cousin to the Sandoval girls."

"You must be mad to bring company at a time like this—with Paco close to death. Peter, how could you?" she exclaimed with a stinging edge to her words.

Peter's nature didn't allow him to be talked down to by anyone; not a man or a woman—especially a woman he loved. He turned stern and irritable, a deep frown creasing his brow. "There's no need ta shake youah rattles at me." Then recalling all she'd suffered and been through, his manner grew softer.

"Ah didn't know we'd have company. Ah tell ya it was unexpected. But the least thing mah missus can do is ta greet mah guests," he said. "Then ya can get back ta yore—" He stopped in time.

"My what? My what?" she demanded. "My lover— is that it? Is that the word you've tried not to think? Well, why don't you say it, Peter? You're thinking it, aren't you?" She'd never spoken so harshly to him. She threw her hands up in the air in a gesture of helplessness. "Is that why we couldn't consummate our love earlier?"

He was about to slap her, to shake her out of this

mood—anything to end this stupid, ridiculous confrontation. He thought he had explained about the doctor, about his understanding of what she'd endured. He turned to leave, exercising as much self-discipline as he could muster. *Patience, patience, patience,* he told himself.

"Peter!" she cried in alarm. "Peter!" She ran into his arms. "Darling, I don't know what's come over me. I don't recognize myself. I am so confused, so frightened by the changes in me." She clung to him, wrapped her arms about his waist, and inclined her head against his shoulder, tears slashing down her cheeks.

"Theah, theah, Little Fox. Theah's nothing ta be frightened about. Ya just expect too much too soon. Jus' relax. Paco's in God's hands. The doctor will be heah in no time—youah'll see, little darlin'."

"I've been a real bitch! A screaming *puta*! Why do you put up with me?"

"Ya ever heard of a thing called love?" He raised her face to meet his. "It's gonna be all right, youah'll see," he said soothingly.

All of a sudden Paco let out a screeching wail that echoed through the villa and brought Tracy Richards and the girls on the run. Startled, Madelaina and Peter rushed to the side of the bed. Paco had bolted upright, his eyes like burning black balls. He was on fire. Sweat rolled off him like raindrops in a cloudburst. He was like nothing they'd ever encountered—a gargoyle—a demon.

He recoiled, staring at some unseen object. In another fast movement he was on his knees, pivoting from one knee to the other, trying to follow some object in his mind. The others stared in utter fascination. He screamed again, this time, his voice, hoarse and dry, cracked and the words came out garbled. Madelaina, in a strong effort to control herself, clenched her fists and screamed, "Golden Dawn! Golden Dawn! You godforsaken whore of Satan! Begone! Vile, contemptible bitch! Leave him alone! You've done enough damage!"

Madelaina had a clear sensation of panic; her breathing accelerated, her stomach twisted into knots. The others, unable to comprehend, stared at one another. Rosalia Quintera and Lucia became aware of what was transpiring and withdrew in alarm, both girls huddling and cowering against a far wall.

"We go!" cried Lucia in terror. "We go!" She tugged frantically at Rosalia.

The next few moments were moments of acute indecision and terror in the hearts of those observers.

"*Diableros!*" uttered Rosalia Quintera. "*Diableros!* Jesus, Mary, and Joseph! They are possessed!" she cried. The girls crossed themselves over and again. They spoke between themselves in a language incomprehensible to either Peter or Tracy Richards. Rooted to the spot, they focused on Madelaina, who in only seconds appeared to have changed. Her features hardened, her eyes turned to steel points, the expression on her face was unlike anything any of them had ever seen. She contorted, bent over in the manifestation of an old crone. With a voice unlike her own, she let out a howl.

"Die!" she cackled. "Die, Paco! You cannot escape me! You will die. You and Dolores, the both of you— and Madelaina, too. You will all die, because I possess all of you!" The language was Yaqui.

Paco stared at her with violent hatred in his eyes. Suddenly he lunged at her, grabbing her by the neck and before their very eyes trying to squeeze the life from her. It took a moment before either Peter or Tracy had the presence of mind to spring forward and pry Paco from her. He had the strength of ten men and the gringos had all they could do to break his hold on Madelaina.

"Ah hate ta do this, Paco," said Peter, letting out with a strong jut to the jaw. Paco's head snapped back, he wheeled away with a look of lunacy in his eyes. Peter let out another punch and caught him on the side of his head. Paco fell back onto the bed, unconscious.

Madelaina gasped and choked and cackled hoarsely.

459

The wind had been knocked out of her. Her head fell back and she was Madelaina again. A tired, spent, weary, but normal Madelaina who had no recollection of what had happened. She glanced at Peter, then at Paco sprawled out on the bed.

"Peter, darling, what happened? Why is Paco like that? Please help me put him back in bed, under the covers." Madelaina was once again herself.

The Americans were confounded. Peter Duprez stared at his wife as if she had sprouted ten horns. The *campesinas* withdrew in terror, huddling together.

"Darling, please take our guests into the salon. I'll prepare refreshments until Lola returns with the doctor. As long as he's sleeping, he'll be all right." Madelaina fussed over Paco. "I do believe his fever's broken—look, he no longer perspires."

Rosalia Quintera herded the gringos into the other room against their protests. "Is nothing you can do, gringos. For now is over—until he returns again."

"Who returns?" asked Peter in alarm.

"*Diableros*—the devils," she replied softly. "Your wife and this Paco are under the influence of a sorcerer."

"Now look, Rosalia," began Tracy, "don'cha try to spoonfeed that kind o' garbage on ole Peter and me, heah?"

Once she composed herself, Rosalia acted exasperated. "*Hombre*, you are some crazy man. What does Rosalia have to do with such things, eh? With jur eyes ju saw what we saw. Leesten, for her sake—jur *mujer*—ju better find out who put hex on her or else—" She drew an imaginary line across her throat. "Ju don' have her for too long. *Es veridad*. Ees truth what I say to ju, *comprender*?"

When Madelaina entered the salon, the only hint of what had happened only moments before was an unnatural pale hue to her skin. Dark circles under her eyes gave her a slightly mysterious appearance. She moved gracefully, pouring wines and whiskey for her guests as if nothing had happened.

She wore a pleasant smile and adopted a gracious manner as she served them. She moved toward her husband with love brimming in her eyes and, encircling her arm with his, led him toward the leather sofa. If she noticed the strange and unusual pallor in his face, the bewildered expression in his dull blue eyes, she gave no hint. She was the hostess, the *hacendada* of a manor, who was simply entertaining in the manner of a loving wife. She hardly noticed Lucia's dark eyes critically studying her or the quizzical look of assessment in Rosalia's eyes.

"How does the fighting go? Rather the celebration? There was no fighting, was there? Well, at least Pancho Villa is back in business again." She smiled reassuringly at her husband. "You think it will end soon, dearest?"

Peter Duprez sat in total absorption watching his wife. The obvious change in her comportment made it difficult for him to reconcile the things he saw, much less understand them. Earlier Rosalia had insisted someone had put a hex on Madelaina, a spell which must be removed before drastic and irrevocable damage was done her—even death. The shrill ringing of a telephone interrupted Peter's thoughts.

Tracy Richards, on the other hand, took it quite lightly. He was making light talk when Peter moved across the room to pick up the receiver on the wall phone. "Ah'm listening," he spoke into the mouthpiece, his eyes on his wife.

"Is this you, gringo?" came the voice of Pancho Villa at the other end.

Peter hesitated.

"Look, I can't see you, gringo, so you'd better tell me if it's you. I am Pancho Villa at his end. Who is it there?"

"It's Tom Mix all right. Ya wanna talk ta Captain Richards, *Jefe*?"

"Hey Trace, it's the *jefe* foah ya." He held the receiver in his hands until Richards swaggered across the room to his side.

461

Peter glanced up in the direction of the door as Lola rushed inside. Frantic, drenched to the skin in perspiration, she ran to Peter's side.

"I cannot find the doctor, *señor*! He is no place to be found. What will we do?" She grew hysterical.

Rosalia spoke sternly to her in their Yaqui dialect, words Peter couldn't make out. Lola glowered angrily. Snarling like a cat, she glanced at Madelaina and hissed the word, "*Bruja.*"

Madelaina turned to her, her dark eyes flaring with fierce, volatile lights. It happened so fast that none of the spectators were prepared for what happened. Madelaina lept upon the young Lola, and drawing a knife from some mysterious hiding place, she plunged it into her enemy's shoulder.

Peter dove into the melee along with Rosalia who tried desperately to pin Madelaina down. The daughter of General Obregon had suddenly developed the strength of ten men. Lucia dragged the bleeding Lola away from them and attempted to stop the flow of blood with her lace shawl. She had to struggle desperately to hold back the young tigress. "Move!" she commanded Lola. "Go into the kitchen! Move, I tell you!" Finally subdued and breathless, Lola still refused to budge. In a trancelike state she was compelled to watch the sudden madness possessing Madelaina, giving no thought to the wound she had sustained.

They all watched husband and wife scuffle as Peter tried to release the viselike grip Madelaina had on the knife. His shirt had been slashed, blood trickled from the cuts on his face and hands. Finally, in a desperate move, he shouted aloud, "Sorry, little one. Ya gotta understand what ah'm doing." He swung his arm back and with a powerful fist connected to Madelaina's jaw, knocking her unconscious.

She sagged back and fell limply into Rosalia's arms, totally disheveled, her long, raven tresses matted with blood, portions of her cotton shirt torn and blood stained. She was a mess. Peter picked her up out of

462

Rosalia's arms and dutifully took her upstairs to the bedroom, with Rosalia Quintera following at his heels.

"Gringo! Gringo! Leesten to me. Something must be done for her—ju understand me? If the spell ees not broken, che will die."

"Now, look heah, Rosalia," said Peter patiently as he headed for the bedroom. "Ya gotta get all that crap right outta yore mind. There ain't no such thing as witches and goblins and evil spirits. Madelaina has been through terrors no human being evah should experience. She jus' needs time ta shape up. Rest, good food, medical supervision. Ah aim to do that foah her as soon as we get to El Paso."

"Listen, *amigo*. You *saw* what Rosalia *saw*. This Lola is Yaqui Indian, more than Lucia. We all know the special tricks of our ancestors." She crossed herself and pleaded. "Ju, I love like a brother—don't do these to her or to ju. We must remove the spirits of evil, the *diablero* from her." She paused, knowing he wasn't listening. "Ju *gringos* all alike! Bah!"

"Whaddya 'espect me ta do, fiahcrackah? Ah don't know the first thin' about what yer ranting about." Frustrated, Peter turned to her after he placed Madelaina's still form on the bed.

"Gringo, ju know what it is to lose one's soul?"

"That's just a figure of speech."

"Ees no fig—fig— ees no what you say. Jur *mujer* is suffering from the loss of her soul. Soon they come and take it all and she die. Jus' like dat!" She snapped her fingers and tossed her head to one side. "I tell ju, Madelaina is bewitched like Paco. He, too, is bewitched. Ju know sometimes the noise of a bird can trap people who are bewitched and are losing their souls and lead them to their deaths?" She spoke in a whisper, a faraway look to her eyes.

Peter's hands flew to his forehead. "Ah don't believe all this! Ah jus' can't believe what's happenin'. Ever since me an' Little Fox arrived at this here hacienda, crazy things have been happenin'. It wasn't bad enough

463

back at the Lomas *rancho*, when dangers lurked all around us. No, heah we hafta deal with hobgoblins!"

"While ju talk, her life is slipping away, gringo," said Rosalia with such solemnity Peter was forced to take her seriously. A physical change came over the young woman who'd given birth to Tracy Richards' child. Her face grew haggard, her eyes extended into large orbs as she fixed her attention on Madelaina's inert form on the bed. "Rosalia don't know who has trapped jur *mujer*'s soul. Who it ees, ees going to kill her or make her *muy mal*, very sick, gringo. Are ju willing to take a chance weeth Madelaina—or do ju want to lose her? Eef ju weesh to take a chance, Tom Meex, I beg of ju to be *cuidado*—careful—and ju must listen to me. Is possible Rosalia can help. Is not for sure. I try, no? If I get lucky, I can arrest this evil until a true *bruja* can do the job, *comprender*?"

Peter shrugged helplessly. "Whatevah ya say. Ah guess ah've gotta trust ya, Rosalia." He ran his fingers nervously through his curly hair.

"Good! Ju must bring Paco upstairs. Bring another bed in here or place him on the sofa, tied down firmly. *Ondolay, pronto, amigo*. Hurry, quickly."

"Paco?"

"*Si*, Paco. He too is possessed! We shall learn who. Trust me. *Ondolay, pronto! Ala chingada!* Bring Lucia to me. And the girl Lola—if she is strong enough. They will both help me." She glanced about the room. "Candles, gringo—I need candles. Ah, here." Rosalia moved like a fleet-footed fawn. "Gringo!" she called, running to the door after him. "Bring rope. Plenty of it!"

In the room she moved even faster. She dragged, pulled and pushed, trying to get the four-poster bed to the center of the floor. It was difficult to budge. She whipped the blanket off the bed, folded it, and pushed it to the center of the room.

Lucia came rushing into the room. "Rosalia, what you want?" She watched the girl in action and listened as Rosalia spoke rapidly in their Indian dialect.

464

"I need an ally, maybe two. Will you help? Little Fox is about to lose her soul." She couldn't lie to Lucia. The girl had to know the dangers ahead.

"No! You don't intend—" Lucia shook her head and looked at her friend as if she'd lost all her senses. "You crazy woman! Not me! No! Never!"

"She will die if we don't help."

For an instant Lucia's dark eyes flickered with dangerous lights. Glancing at Madelaina's inert figure on the bed, she asked herself why she should care. If the girl died, why should she give a fig? Her way to Peter would be without obstacles. Her eyes lit up with anticipation, an almost victorious look.

"I know what you are thinking," snapped Rosalia in their mestizo dialect. "But if you are thinking—and I pray you are not—you know the consequences, Lucia. The condition of this woman at this moment should prove to you what can happen if you fool around with things you don't understand. You want a hex put on you?" Rosalia became an authoritative figure in those few seconds, imposing and firm.

Instantly Lucia cowered. She shook nervously. "N—no. I will be your ally. My journey into this life has been painfully unbearable up to now. If it became worse, I wouldn't be able to live. I'll help," she said resolutely.

"*Muy bueno*. Those are the most intelligent words to pass your lips, *chica*. *Ondolay*! Go to the butter room and bring back oil and water. If you can, lift up the rocks in the garden and try, Lucia, in God's name, try to find a lizard or two. If you can't, then bring me a chicken from the hen house. Move! *Pronto*."

Peter entered the room with Paco in his arms.

"Here, on the sofa, gringo. Where is Tracy?"

"He returned to Parral. The *jefe* wanted to confer with him. The Redflaggers of Orozco intend to return to do battle with us sometime tonight," he said tightly.

As Rosalia took in the full import of his words, she ordered him to tie Paco down to the sofa. "And do a good job," she cautioned. "Ees important ees not possible for Paco to break through the restraints. Do the same with Little Fox. And, gringo, again I caution ju. Be sure ju tie them both with such firmness that God himself bestowing upon them the strength of ten tigers cannot break through the bindings. And don't argue!"

Peter did as he was told. Then he and Rosalia pushed the bed into the center of the room.

"Why?" he started to ask.

"Don' ask. Ees no time for to explain. Ju trust me. *Madre de Dios!* Ju pray for us, gringo. Ju pray my allies give me needed powers. Now, go. Bring firewood—dry as possible. Outside in courtyard are copper and clay pots. Bring one thees size." She held her fingers before her in a circular gesture, indicating the size needed. Peter nodded and left instantly to do her bidding.

Rosalia double-checked the ties on both Paco and Madelaina. By the time Lucia reappeared with Lola, who fortunately only suffered a superficial wound which had been dressed, she cornered them and spoke to them in their curious Indian dialect.

"I will need you both as allies. Shortly, I will need great power. I will need your strength to help me, advise me, and give me the strength necessary to perform acts required of me in the next few hours—or however long it takes to finish the job."

Peter came in and stood very still while she talked.

"Gringo, light a fire in the pot and place it facing the north at their feet."

"Rosalia," said Lucia shivering. "I am afraid."

"M—me, too," said the frightened, blue-eyed mestiza, Lola.

"There is nothing to fear. You have known me a long time, Lucia. Have you known me to do anything bad or evil?" she asked in their native tongue.

"No, *es veridad.*"

"Will you trust me, Lola? Even though we never met before this night?"

She somberly fixed her attention on the girl's eyes. She took Lola's hands in her own firm, strong hands.

"Trust me, *chiquita*. You both must give me the added strength I need. The danger is in *my* life—not *yours*. When I speak out, you must follow my instructions to the letter. No matter how you are distracted. No matter how much you want to disobey my orders. You must stand within the circle I draw for you and under no circumstances are you to step from this spot. Do I make myself clear?"

The girls nodded. Rosalia took the oil and poured a thin stream of the viscous oil in a circle to the east of the large center circle containing the bed, sofa, and two victims. She poured another stream of the fluid in a larger circle around Madelaina and Paco.

She set the can down, and from a small leather pouch around her neck, she removed a small bottle and another sack containing a powdery substance. Her eyes darted around the room. She found a bottle of wine and two glasses. She picked up one, poured some red wine into it, and with a dropper allowed eight drops of the liquid to spill into the wine. She picked up the glass, swished the contents around, and poured half in one glass. She gave one to Lucia and the other to Lola.

"Drink," she commanded authoritatively, allowing for no refusal.

Finished, the girls gave her the glasses. Rosalia flung them into the fire Peter had started. Instantly a bright flame spurted into a myriad of colors. Peter watched the ritual in utter fascination.

Rosalia took the girls' arms and led them into the smaller circle. She began to chant some Indian song of their ancestors. "You who must have enormous vigor, who must seek to endure fatigue and hunger, will soon experience a strength of *herculeo*. It is this strength you will transfer to me when it begins to appear that I have none. Understand this clearly. Do not give it to me before I need it—or when it might be too late. You must keep your eyes only on me. Not on Paco or Madelaina or any other disturbance that might interfere with your concentration. Understand? You, Lucia, know me well. Let no other image fool you or attempt

467

to deceive you. If you do, my life will be taken in for-feit."

The girl, frightened and shaking, nodded, recognizing the enormous responsibility placed upon her.

She cautioned again. "Only when it appears that I need it and not until then! Soon you will feel a lightness and a strength that will make you feel you can grow wings and fly. But you must not let your mind soar. Be aware every second of what we're doing. It is dangerous only because the *diableros* will take any form. You *must not* pay any attention to them. You are safe within the circle I have prepared. Do not give in to any temptations—be it fear or promises of ec-stasy—nothing!"

The girls nodded. In moments the fear-ridden faces changed into faces that demonstrated strength and fearlessness. Their shoulders pulled back defiantly. They stood firm, feet spread apart, hands on their hips.

It is simply remarkable, thought Peter, *how unreal it all seems. And I stand here allowing this insanity to continue.*

"*Muy bueno*," said Rosalia, observing the changes in the girls. "You will maintain these positions when things get very bad. If something should happen when I'm away, if at any time you should feel vulnerable and think you can't endure it any longer, you are to hop twice on one foot and twice on the other without rais-ing your foot off the floor." She demonstrated an an-cient tribal Indian dance movement the girls knew well. They understood. They nodded mutely.

Rosalia walked to Peter's side. "Is time ju go, gringo. Listen carefully. I will lock the door, bolt it with the bar, and place before it a heavy chair. Ju must not enter the room, *comprender*? Is *muy* important, *amigo*. If ju hear screams, crying, braying—even the howling of coyotes—*do not enter*. If ju hear Madelaina scream and call to ju, cover jur ears. Do not let any-one enter this room until I, Rosalia Quintera *as ju have known her to be*, open the door and ask ju to enter. "Is most *importante* what I say. Do not enter or jur

468

mujer, me, Lucia, Lola, and you will die. Is no joke, *amigo.*"

"But where will you go? I heard you tell the girls you were leaving."

"Aye, is so. I must go to find who has taken Madelaina's and Paco's souls, and if possible, try to get them back." She placed two pinches of the powdered substance into her mouth, under her tongue. "I go inside now. Oh, jes, *amigo,* may I have one of jur guns— loaded. Make sure it is ready to fire."

"Mah God, girl. Ya'll expecting to shoot someone?"

"Only if I am in danger of losing my life."

Peter leaned over and kissed Rosalia tenderly and gratefully. He held her close to him. "Ah'm not good at thankin' ya, m'am. Ah jus' wanna tell ya how much I respect ya and love ya for what yer doing for Madelaina. Ah don't begin ta understand, *chiquita,* what yer up ta. But God bless ya, honey."

Rosalia raised her hand and touched his face tenderly. Once again she cautioned, "Be aware of everything, gringo. No matter *who* comes to ju—for whatever reason—do not permit jurself to be bedeviled or bewitched."

She disappeared inside the door. He heard the lock click shut, the bar bolt slip into place. He could hear her drag heavy furniture into place. Peter's tongue wet his parched lips and a burning sensation flared in his mouth. He recalled her taking the powder, and he quickly wiped his lips with the back of his hand. Instantly his mouth went numb. He wanted to run downstairs to drink some wine, to wash away any powdery particles, but he chose to remain outside the door. He dragged a chair from one end of the corridor, placed it next to the door, and sat down, worrying about his lips from time to time until the numbness left.

What he wouldn't give to be inside that room. He'd like to witness this battle Rosalia alluded to among the devils, demons, and spirits of whatever it was she was going to contact. For some strange reason, Peter Duprez, who hadn't experienced fear since he was a child,

469

began to sense a disturbing fear. Her words had produced a state of anguish in him, a feeling of premonition coupled with foreboding. Something dreadful was about to happen—of this he was certain. He heard a loud, piercing scream rip through the room, one filled with such torment that the hairs on his neck and arms stood up. He sprang to his feet and lit a cigarette. He glanced at the pocket watch in his vest. It was 7:30 P.M. His hands were trembling visibly as he paced to and fro like a nervous cat. A quiet lull hung over the hacienda. There were no noises, only the whistling of winds on the desert. Tension mounted in him, and the strain of waiting grew nerve-wracking.

An hour later, the wind had risen noticeably. He heard horses pull up into the courtyard. He glanced at his watch. It was 8:30 P.M. He heard Tracy Richards call to him. "Hey there, *amigo*. Where the hell are ya?"

Under normal circumstances Peter would have sprung from his chair and hailed Captain Richards in his usual hearty voice. However, with the sting of Rosalia's words still burning his eardrums, he cocked his head, fully alert, and listened again. It was Tracy's voice all right, he conceded, but not the usual tone of voice he was accustomed to hearing. And the words used were slightly different. Trace had rarely called Peter *amigo*. Good buddy, yes, fella, even Tom Mix. Rosalia's words cautioned him further, and he stood his guard at the door as a chill passed through him and he broke out into a cold sweat.

Damned if she ain't got me thinking about devils and spooks, he told himself angrily. He continued to hear footsteps outside the house. He became aware of every sound. Snuffing out his cigarette, he sat in the chair, listening for noises inside the bedroom.

Inside, Rosalia had lit seven candles and placed them outside the greater circle: one at the north, south, east, and west positions, the remaining three in the position of an inverted pyramid around the burning fire. Seated cross-legged before the fire, she closed her eyes. The hallucinogenic mixture she'd ingested had

470

begun to take effect. A series of dreamlike images came to her, in no sequential order, surrounded by vibrant colors swirling through the images in a serpentine manner. A sensation of vagueness began to clear as Rosalia departed her body. She had the sensation of being outside herself, observing the entire scene from some distant point. Her eyes, focused on both Paco and Madelaina, blinked from side to side and she perceived them as if through the eyes of a bird.

A series of changes manifested themselves upon the countenance of Madelaina, beginning with a glow of dull lights and continuing in a mist until it cleared. Rosalia had the clearest recollection of another face superimposed upon that of Madelaina; a white-skinned Indian with black hair and holes for eyes. The vision grew clearer and clearer until she saw the body thrashing about the bed in the sexual embrace of a dignified, dark-haired man in his forties.

Rosalia observed the scene stoically as voices came to her loud and clear. The voice of a man, a stranger, said, "*Querida*, you make me happy, contented. With you I could wish for none other." The eyeless woman lying next to her lover caressed him with passion until the fires in her sensuous body ignited his. "You will never want anyone but Golden Dawn," said the writhing body that had possessed Madelaina. "Only Golden Dawn shall be the desire of your heart, *mi Generale*."

The scene shifted and changed as vibrant splashes of translucent colors thundered into a motionless sea of sharp, painful lights, where the jagged edges of stalagmites and stalagtites, illuminated by an infinite variety of flickering lights, changed their luminosity. In another instant, small blobs, shadows which took human form, came at Rosalia like a battalion of warriors with pointed spears and blazing shields reflecting a blinding sun in her eyes. Recoiling, protecting herself by crisscrossing her arms before her eyes, she tried to fend them off as they swarmed upon her. She brushed them off, swept them aside, slapped her body in an effort to rid herself of these verminlike tempters and tormenters.

471

Now, Tracy Richards entered the room, calling to Rosalia, sternly at first, then loudly demanding she come to him at that moment. Angry at her apparent indifference, he called her vile names, threatened her with hated anger and scorching contempt. "If ya don' come heah this instant, *puta*, ah'll find me ten moah whores ta sleep with, ya lowly side-windin' greaser!"

Before Rosalia's eyes, the captain began to clap his hands and dance an obscene dance before the two girls, Lucia and Lola, tempting them, luring them. His voice became gutteral, lascivious, and suggestive. "C'mon' ya gorgeous hunk o' women," he said to them. "Let's y'all an' me show Rosalia what lovin's all about, heah?" He singled out Lola. "What say ya, little kitten? Come find out what a real man's like."

Lola, shaking like a leaf in a tempest, began to wind up in ritual dance. She hopped twice on one foot, then on the other. She began to chant an Indian song, avoiding as she did the outstretched arms of Tracy Richards. He removed all his clothing and, holding his sexual organs, continued to make obscene gestures as he danced a short jig around her. He leered at Lucia, grabbed for her breasts. "Let's youah an' me fuck, baby," he called seductively. "Youah, too, Lola, baby. Weah'll all three fuck. Weah'll show the ole sow what it's really like, heah?" Hidden in his eyes and visible only to Rosalia were malicious, mocking lights shaded with lust.

Lucia, trembling with fright, began to dance as Lola danced, sang along with her partner, their voices growing louder and firmer until suddenly the apparition of Tracy Richards dissolved and another form manifested itself.

"Come with me, girls," said the voice of a seductress, a woman dressed in diaphanous flowing robes of gold. "I'm Golden Dawn. Come with me and you'll have the desires of your heart. Don't stay with this old whore's whore. This gringo tart can give you nothing but the hard life of a *puta*! Who is she to command you? Listen—" She began to sing a sweet plaintive song that tore at their heart strings. Nothing they had ever heard could match the exquisite sound of that golden voice of promise.

Golden Dawn moved as if on a cloud. She tried to break through the outer circle of protection to reach Paco. His eyes had fluttered open earlier. Madelaina also became aware of the strange happenings. She grew frightened by the things she saw and heard. She tried to move and couldn't.

"Paco," purred Golden Dawn. "I want you to be my lover, Paco. Don't you want to be with me? Say you do and I'll help you free yourself."

Paco strained against his ties. "*Si*, Golden Dawn. I will come whenever you say. Come and get me." He strained at his bonds. "I'll come. I'm ready."

Lucia and Lola stepped up the momentum, their voices grew louder and louder as they chanted and sang their songs. Their dance became livelier.

Golden Dawn moved toward the body of Rosalia Quintera. She reached in closer to the fires to touch her, but instantly withdrew her hands.

"Whore! I know you aren't inside." She cocked her head and glanced about the room. "Where can you be, you little whore? You peasant scum of a mestiza! I'll find you if it takes all our lives. You meddling *puta!* You'll be next to taste my wrath!" Her head whirled around and her eyes landed on an overhead beam where she caught sight of a gray lizard. "I see you, Rosalia Quintera. I know what disguise you've assumed. Heed my words or you'll live to regret the evil of Golden Dawn. Give up, whore. You can't win. Don't you know who I am? You! You dare contest me? You, Rosalia Quintera, the illegitimate misbegotten daughter of a whore's whore. What right have you? How do you dare? I'll see your flesh burn in hell, the same place I've put the bastard son conceived by you and the gringo, Tracy Richards. You know what he thinks of you? A greaser, a Mexican whore not fit to be his wife. You see how he craves the delights of woman? Any woman! But I have something more important than

Tracy Richards. I have your *niño*, your little son—your gringo son!" she cackled.

Outside the door, Peter Duprez' face had turned the color of sickly vomit. He had heard every voice, every word, the screams, the chants, the sound of feet stomping to the rhythm of the chanting. To him it sounded like horses' hoofs thundering over a wooden bridge. He heard Tracy Richards shout obscenities. At one point he shoved his shoulder against the door and was about to break it open, when he remembered Rosalia's warning. *God! Ah can't be that strong,* he told himself. Sweat rippled off his brow. There were times he wanted to run away, get as far from Parral and Mexico as he could.

The sound of Madelaina's voice calling him tore at his heart.

"Peter, Peter," she whimpered. "Come and get me, darling. I'm afraid. Oh Peter, it's terrible. Awful. Tell Rosalia to stop all this. I want to come into your arms and make love with you. Please, darling, tell them all to go away. Don't you remember how it was aboard the *Mozambique*? We can relive all those memorable nights, if only you stop this stupid game these girls are playing. We're fine. Paco and I are going to be fine—just as soon as you tell them to leave us alone. Darling, come and untie me so we can make love. Don't you want me any more? Don't you want to feel my warm passionate body next to yours?"

Peter Duprez clasped his hands over his ears. *Stop! Stop*! he screamed inwardly. He whirled about like a dervish and reached for his gun. He was about to shoot the lock off when once again he recalled Rosalia's words. Suddenly he feared for Tracy's mistress, for the girls, and especially for Madelaina and Paco, but his hands were tied. He could do nothing. It took the strength of ten devils to keep him from busting through that door. If someone had told him this would happen, he wouldn't have believed it. *God have mercy on all o' us!* He repeated this time and again.

Inside the bedroom, shadows and mist formed into

474

swirls of darkness. Golden Dawn had disappeared. In her place came the sultry, impassioned Dolores. "So, Paco, look at the predicament you've gotten yourself into, all because of this whore of Obregon's and his shameless daughter, this nothing. For this woman, you brought the wrath of Lucifer upon you. Have you had enough? Eh? Tell me you've had enough and I'll save you."

Paco strained at his ties. His wild-eyed expression as he banged his head from side to side and screamed was indescribable. "Dolores! It's you! Yes. Yes, all is forgiven. You were right. The daughter of Obregon is a whore! She has turned my world into crumbling ashes. Come and untie me. And we'll go. I promise never to look upon another woman again. Only take me. Take me now." He thrashed wildly on the sofa, moving the furniture with him. It bounced off the floor, rattling and banging loudly. "Lucia! Lola, come and untie me. Free me so I can take my woman home. See? She loves me. She has come for me. Lola, for the love of God, woman, release me."

Lucia and Lola increased their tempo. They were dancing their little hearts out. Their voices increased in volume. The chants grew frantic.

There came the sound of gunfire, a steady barrage of guns firing at a fast clip.

Captain Tracy Richards came through the door, bleeding, full of bullet wounds. "Rosalia—where's mah woman?" He stumbled, fell, picked himself up, gasping and holding the wounds. He paused before the image of Rosalia. "Help me, woman. Help me. I'm dying, can't you see?" He gasped for breath, choked, and made gurgling sounds inside his throat.

As Rosalia observed all this, she felt herself weakening. The feeling came over her of being sucked into a vortex, swirling black waters against which she couldn't fight. Down, down, down she went, swallowed up by an unfamiliar darkness. Her energies waned. Her body ached, every muscle stiff and painfully contracted. She had returned to her body now, unsure of what was happening. She blinked her eyes open and saw her lover bleeding to death inches away from her. She only had to reach out to hold him and protect him. Here was the father of her child, the one she wanted to raise in America, like his gringo father. What was she doing here? Helping two people she hardly knew, endangering her own life—and for what? Not even a thank you would she receive for her troubles. Hah! A mestiza, no, three mestizas helping a *gachupín* and her gringo friends! Are you some crazy woman, Rosalia, she asked herself.

She was in her own circle of protection, just as Lucia and Lola were. Neither could penetrate the others. "Come, Lucia. Come, Lola!" she sneered with an ugly look on her face. "Enough of this. Let us finish this farce. Let that whorish daughter of our enemy do as she wishes. We have done enough. Why should we mix in any of this? She got into this mess—she and that Corporal Jimenez. Let them get themselves out!"

Lucia and Lola stopped for a second. The look on Rosalia's face was not the Rosalia Lucia had grown to know and love. Lola, her resolve weakening, was about to pierce the outer circle of protection. "No!" screamed Lucia. "It is not Rosalia! Sing! Dance! Hop!" she commanded. "Faster! She needs our strength! Now!" She took Lola's hands in hers and held them firmly. Both girls continued their incantations and movements as prescribed earlier.

"Peter? Hey, gringo. It's me, Rosalia. It's over, gringo. Your *mujer* is going to be A-O.K. You hear what I tell you? Come in now. Come and get her." The voice pierced the door and reached Peter's ears.

Peter was bewildered. It was Rosalia all right. He recognized her voice. How could he break into the room? It was locked, bolted, and reenforced with furniture abutting it. He continued to pace as he chain-smoked. It was nearly 11:30 P.M. Goddamn! Four hours of excruciating drama. He felt a profound despair clutching at his heart.

"Peter?"

He spun around. Not three feet from him was Rosalia Quintera.

"What's wrong, gringo? Did ju not hear my voice?" She purred ever so nicely. "Imagine what a dumbbell is Rosalia Quintera? I 'ave lost the key. So, gringo, shoot off the lock, eh? We go and finish this thing. Madelaina is fine. In time she will be most well again. A-O.K. Is good?"

"Thank God," he exclaimed, suddenly relieved. "Ya know what it was like out here, listening ta all that garbage?" He pulled the gun from his holster, but just before he shot at the lock, he caught sight of her face. "You ain't Rosalia," he said sharply. He turned the gun and pointed it at her. "Jus' who the hell are ya?" He took a step toward her, and Rosalia receded far into a tunnel, whirling and spinning into a black abyss.

"Hey theah, Tom Mix," called Tracy Richards scaling the stairwell two at a time. "Who the blazes are ya talkin' ta?" He stopped short at the sight of Peter's distraught appearance, at his menacing posture, gun in hand.

"Stay wheah ya are, partnah. Don'cha move a muscle if'n ya want ta live," ordered Peter, uncertain of who the interloper was at this point.

"Hey, boy, what in tarnation's happening? Wheah's mah woman? The others?" Tracy had never seen him acting so peculiar.

"Just toss yer gun belt down, ole buddy, and if ya make one move—one suspicious move—ah'll cut ya in two. Heah?" Peter's voice had never been deadlier.

Tracy's hands shot up into the air. "All right. All right. Jus' ya take it easy, ya heah? Ah'm gonna lower mah hands, Pete, to the buckle and unclasp it. Ah promise, man, ah won't do nothing wrong." He did as he said he would. The gun belt off, he kicked it forward along the tiles.

Peter kicked the gun belt behind him. "Now, you an' me's gonna sit right heah and wait. Y'all make one move—whoever the hell ya are—and ah'll keep mah promise." Perhaps he was melodramatic, but after what he'd seen. . . .

"Don'cha even wanna hear what ah gotta say? Parral's gonna be attacked in jus' about two hours. You an' me gotta get cracking. Ole Pancho wants ta fight this one. He's got one o' 'em brilliant plans as usual, buddy. We jus' gotta get back to 'im to get ouah ordahs straight. The Gringo Brigade is gonna mow 'em down." Smart enough to know something was wrong, he tried to keep calm.

"Ya don't think ah'm gonna fall for that crap. Now keep yer trap shut, before I shut it for ya." Peter was straining to listen to what was happening inside.

Lucia and Lola had grown frantic in their demonstration. Madelaina seemingly arose from the bed, shedding her restraints as if they were tufts of cotton. She walked toward Rosalia. "How can I thank you, my dear, for all your help. I would have been dead if it hadn't been for you and these nice girls."

Behind her, Paco grew delirious. He gasped for breath. "Untie me also, Madelaina. We'll thank her and the others together."

Madelaina ignored him, with a look of disdain. She continued to walk toward Rosalia. Behind her, the lizards Lucia had brought into the house scurried close to her feet. Rosalia felt numb with fear, her hands slid down alongside her until they gripped the gun. A sudden surge of strength filled her, and in a matter of seconds she felt a rolling, rocking sensation course through her as a scream, beginning at her toes, crept up through her body and out her mouth, like the wailing raging of a demon. It was loud and shrill, a chilling outcry that seemed to rock the villa's rafters. Rosalia, shuddering inwardly, raised her shaking, gun-filled hands unsteadily and fired point blank into Madelaina's face. The apparition continued to move toward the mestiza unhesitantly. With all her might Rosalia hurled the gun into the face of her pursuer. A scream, prolonged and piercing, directed her aim and suddenly the figure of Madelaina staggered backward, clutching at a face filled with holes like running ink blots. It disappeared with a wailing sound of defeat tunneling after it, into a well racing toward infinity.

Outside the door, Peter Duprez angled his head at the sounds of the screams accompanied by gun shots. Tracy Richards heard it, too: the chilling silence, the sudden cessation of all activity; what the hell was going on? What had happened to Peter? His questions were compounded by the urgency he felt at what was happening in Parral, what would happen if he and Pete didn't get back to Villa's camp? He glanced at his watch and murmured in apology, "Look, Pete—"

Pete's gun was aimed at his heart instantly. "Ah said, don't move! Ah mean it!" he growled sternly. "Do ah have ta tie ya up?"

Tracy raised his hands, shook his head reluctantly, and said nothing, but his eyes acquiesced to Peter's command. Sounds inside the room drew his attention as they had Peter's. They both strained to listen.

It was past midnight when Rosalia, drained of all energy, mentally and physically exhausted, stirred slightly. She rose to her feet, picked up two lit candles, and moving into the circle, she inspected the pale, sweating features of Madelaina Obregon and Paco Jimenez. Madelaina's dark, tortured eyes flickered and blinked several times until they opened wide.

"Rosalia," she said weakly. "Where are we? Where's Peter?

Rosalia placed a cool hand on the girl's forehead. It felt clammy and cold to the touch. She brushed aside a few strands of the girl's hair and spoke softly to her. "Don't be worried, *chiquita*. Is fine. Is going to be fine, everything."

The oppressive, stifling air seemed to lift and thin, and Rosalia breathed in deeply as she moved toward the two allies. She smiled as they continued to critically assess her features and behavior. "It's me," she said softly. "It's over." She extended her arms toward the girls. For several brief seconds, Lucia held Lola's arm as she scanned Rosalia's face. When the woman of

479

Tracy Richards stepped over the circle, she knew it was the real Rosalia Quintera. Instantly the girls fell into her outstretched arms and she hugged them dearly to her bosom. With barely the strength to talk, she thanked them in a subdued voice. "Bless you both. Without you it couldn't have been done."

Both girls were drenched in perspiration; Lola's auburn hair a mass of ringlets, her eyes grateful and relieved at the end of the ordeal. Lucia cried like a baby. All three women were exhausted. "If it hadn't ended when it did," Lucia babbled on incoherently, "I couldn't have endured it much longer."

Together they moved the bureau drawers and chairs barricading the door. Outside, Peter, alert and tense, heard the scuffling of the furniture and tightened his grip on the gun. With one eye on Tracy Richards, the other on the door, he backed away at an angle, poised for any new and bizarre occurrence. On this night he'd seen more than his eyes would see in a lifetime. He didn't dare speculate on what else could happen. Filled with disquiet, he heard the key turned in the lock and the bolt snapped back. As the door began to open, Peter could feel the sweat rolling off his face; his stomach was tied in knots.

Rosalia's face appeared first, followed by the girls behind her. They looked at Peter, then at Captain Richards and his menacing posture with little reaction.

"You can go and untie them, *amigo*," said the spellbreaker with considerable effort. "Ah, you're back, gringo." She smiled wanly at her man.

Peter stood hesitant and uncertain, still unsure of anything on this night. For a moment he looked blank, uncomprehending. Suddenly he knew. He didn't know how he knew, but it was clear to him. He rushed into the room as Rosalia fell into the arms of her lover.

Lola followed Peter into the room to help untie Paco Jimenez. She smoothed his hair back off his face and stroked his cheeks gently, murmuring endearing words to him. His fever had broken.

With Captain Richards' help, they got Paco downstairs into his own bed.

Peter untied the ropes binding Madelaina. He sat down by the bed, rubbing her bruised wrists and ankles where welts had formed from the pressure against the confining ropes, deep concern scrawled over his face.

She sat upright and encircled his neck. "Dearest Peter, I can't tell you what horrible nightmares I had. They were terrible." She snuggled close to him. It was as if nothing had happened at all.

"Tomorrow, Rosalia Quintera will tell ya all about what happened in heah, little one," he said softly. "Ah for one will be most anxious ta learn all about it." He stroked her face gently.

She yawned and stretched and lay back against his chest, curled up like a small, vulnerable child. "You were *apasionado* this evening," she told him suggestively.

"Don't ya think ya better get some sleep, little one? Ah can't say as ah'd be so chipper if ah'd gone through what ya'll went through tonight."

"Peter?"

"Yes, *chiquita*."

Her hand felt the hardness in his crotch, and she lay back against him, rolling her eyes at him, daring him, enticing him. It was like old times. He sighed in relief. "Tracy's waitin' fer me. We've gotta get back to Parral. Looks like those *Orozquistas* are bearing down on the *jefe*." He cocked a deliberating eye at her. Her hair was so dark he could barely see it in the flickering candlelight. Her dark eyes, heavy-lidded from lack of sleep, could have fooled him. Beneath the lids they were eager, bright, and filled with the promise of love.

Within moments they had shed their clothing. "Ah never like ta make love with an army waitin' fer me, darlin'. Ah've never been one for quickies—ah like a full production an' ah know y'all do, too."

Her legs, wide open, were as inviting as her lips. He kissed her while his hands moved over her stomach, fingers pulling lightly at the tangle of black curls. His

481

hot passionate lips transferring to her all the pent-up emotion, the frustration he felt this evening and for the past two days. It was over now, thanks to Rosalia. He kissed her and kissed her with passionate urgency.

"I had almost forgotten what it was like with you, Peter," she whispered in his ears, sending a thrilling sensation shooting through him.

Peter was at the point of no return. He couldn't hold back the flood of love, the contents of his heart. He drove deeper and deeper inside her as her body met his in undulating desire. His hands grasped her hips, raised them up to meet his thrusts. He was unable to hold back. He came inside her with a wild, outlandish, animal-like shriek that seemed as if his soul had been ripped out of his body. Peter hadn't rested but a moment or two when he withdrew from her. He pried her thighs apart and lifted her legs over his shoulders as a low moan escaped his throat. His hands held her breasts, playing with her nipples as his mouth found her. Madelaina's body writhed and undulated, and she jerked convulsively when his tongue touched the key to her excitement. Her hands played with his curly hair until she grasped him firmly, pulling him in and out in a circular motion, directing his every move.

Madelaina's head thrashed from side to side. "Ohhhhh," she moaned. "Ohhhhh! Yes—yes—yesssssss!" She wailed aloud in animal sounds and her body bounced into the air and continued to bounce and twist and writhe until the two of them were nearly off the bed. When she was spent, Peter moved up and entered her and began to go through the motions again until it was over for him.

What the hell made him do such a thing, he wondered. He'd never done that to her before, never gave it a thought. He smoked a cigarette, knowing he should have been dressed and out of there with Tracy Richards. Madelaina lay back against the pillows, a sweet look of contentment on her face.

She let me do it without a sense of shame—not even a complaint, he thought.

He heard his name being called with urgency. "Yeah, yeah, Trace, ah'm coming," he shouted. He got up and dressed. Damn, he felt like he needed a bath. Well, as soon as the fightin' was over, he could take all the baths he wanted.

Dressed, he leaned over his wife to kiss her. Her eyes flared open with a wicked grin on her face. She whispered, "Peter dearest, you are the *Golden Dawn of all my desires*." Seduction spilled from her amorous eyes.

He nodded contentedly and moved to the door. Glancing back over his shoulder, he gave a start. His eyes caught sight of a lizard clinging to the pillow sham next to his wife on the bed. By the time he moved back to the bed to scatter it, it was gone.

Chapter 18

The skirmish at Parral staged by Pancho Villa lasted until noon of the next day. The general in charge of the Redflagger *Orozquistas* had misjudged Pancho Villa, as many had done before him and would continue to do. Aware of the *guerrillo*'s reputation on horseback with his mounted cavalry, General Campa's plan was to pelt the town with light artillery fire, then crush the weak defense by overpowering it with infantry.

Villa's uncanny grasp of organization enabled him to place the right men in the right places at the proper time. It was the first time he actually had federally trained soldiers at his disposal and he used them all well. As the Redflaggers' pyramid-shaped attack progressed, the Gringo Brigade opened fire and contained them. Withdrawing, General Campa shelled again and resumed the attack. Again he was sent into retreat. The last attack took place at dawn, when the eerie lights played tricks on a man's eyes. Pancho Villa counterattacked, smashed through the Redflaggers' center, then, as Urbina destroyed one wing, the gringos destroyed the other, bringing victory to Villa and a stinging defeat to the enemy.

Peter Duprez had been shot. He took a bullet in the left shoulder and one tore a hole through his left wrist. The pain wasn't bad and binding his wrist as best he could, he had continued through the three attacks. Before noon, word arrived that three trains were en route to Parral with over 5,000 *Orozquistas*, supported by cavalry and heavy cannon. Villa, no fool, considered the odds carefully. Outnumbered and outgunned, he had little hope of holding the city against such force.

Still, Pancho Villa wasn't about to cede Parral without a fight.

By then, Peter's arm had begun to swell and throb painfully. He was in fever. At one point, his eyes, like seas of blue glass, fairly popped from his head as he flagged Captain Tracy Richards a few feet from him. He sank to the ground just as Richards caught him and laid him under the shade of a tree along one side of the garrisoned fort. Tracy assembled all the necessary equipment to help him get the bullet out of the infected shoulder. A canteen filled with tequila was forced through Peter's lips. He gagged and sputtered but managed to swallow.

"Damnit, why didn't tell me yer arm had begun to swell?" cussed the captain over and over.

While Tracy probed for the bullet, Pancho Villa, close by to aid the gringo, outlined his plans, his facial features wincing with every shove and twist of the metal prong directed by the friend of Tom Mix. At last, when the bullet casing was expunged, Villa sighed in relief, as if he personally had undergone the painful ordeal.

"If I was a drinking man, gringo, I'd have consumed more than what your friend drank," he told Tracy. "Such a bad wound—and he said nothing all night?"

"Nothing. Stupid bastard! If he'da told me when the swelling began, ah could've saved him most o' this pain! He'll sleep for a while, all right."

"What you think, gringo? We'll be outnumbered, so we can't remain in Parral. I'll send the women ahead to Durango with the necessary escorts. Meanwhile, we will give this General Campa and Salazar something to remember us, eh? Is no question Orozco controls the trains from Juarez to Torreon. But not the hills or the desert sands. We can move through both and join Madero's Division of the North at Torreon."

"As usual, *Jefe*," said Tracy Richards with profound respect for Villa's uncanny strategy, "mah hat's off ta ya. As it is, ah jus' can't see how ya managed to multiply the sixty of us into nearly 500 strong. But ya did."

"Only because men such as you and Tom Mix are loyal to me, Captain," said Villa, watching the gringo roll a few cigarettes and place them neatly into his jacket pocket, lighting one with a match struck against a rock.

"Ya wanna a smoke, *Jefe*?" he asked, watching Villa's eyes fill with curiosity.

Villa shook his head. "Imagine a tough, pistol-packing *bandido* like me has never taken time to learn to smoke—or drink. Hah, if it was known by my enemies, they'd laugh me into submission." He laughed as he imagined such a thing happening.

Two days later, the *Orozquistas*, led by Generals Campa and Salazar, and reenforced battalions bombarded Parral. For hours the attack prevailed unceasingly, and the Redflaggers marched into Parral only to find Pancho Villa had long since vanished into the hills. What they had been attacking so relentlessly was a tiny handful of volunteers. So scandalized and angered by this carefully executed plan of Villa's were the Redflaggers, they rounded up this scrawny bunch of scarecrows and executed them on the spot—without mercy.

When news of this abominable act reached Pancho Villa, this pigeon-livered demonstration of chicken shit behavior, he vowed openly that when caught, the Redflaggers of Orozco would never receive any mercy from him. It would be death on the spot for all of them. And Villa was growing more well known as a man who kept his promises.

Unable to determine how Villa had eluded them, the two generals who had co-commanded the counterattack upon Parral concluded it was either luck or a stroke of genius.

News arrived at the hacienda where Madelaina and the other *campesinas* were housed that they'd been ordered south to Durango. Madelaina demonstrated considerable reluctance to travel with Rosalia Quintera and the other camp followers, because the unstable condition of Paco Jimenez necessitated slower travel,

with more frequent rests. Madelaina therefore ordered
the others to progress without them. Lola flatly refused. She insisted upon remaining by Paco's side and
challenged Madelaina openly.

"You'll not get me to leave him. Understand me
well," she said defiantly, her pale blue icy eyes staring
imperiously at the legendary Little Fox.

Madelaina shrugged indifferently. "Do as you please.
Only know you'll not be traveling under the protection
of Pancho Villa's *guerrillos*. We'll be forced to take
back roads, through mountains and deserts. You'd best
make sure you can handle a gun."

"And a knife also," added Lola. There was no mistaking her meaning—the mestizo knew the consequences.

Rosalia Quintera embraced Lola, and as she turned
to Madelaina to express her farewell, a vast shadow
appeared in her dark eyes. She scrutinized the regal
posture of Peter's *mujer*, her eyes narrowing in
thought. "Take care, *querida*," she said with polite
reserve. "You've been through much hell." The women
had spoken of that nightmarish night with reservation,
only to explain pointedly to Madelaina that she had
endured no nightmares, only reality in its most precarious form.

"Tell my husband I shall join him as swiftly as possible," she told Rosalia upon their departure. She
watched the *campesinas* ride out of the courtyard on
their horses. "*Buenos suerte*," she called. "*Adios,
muchachas!*" She waved to them until they rode out of
sight.

In preparation for their trip, both Madelaina and
Lola, dressed somewhat shabbily as peasant women,
rubbed dirt on their faces and arms and scratched their
fingers in the earth to lodge dirt under their fingernails.
Paco lay back in the rear of the wagon dressed in his
peasant pantaloons and shirt with a serape over him
and a wide sombrero shoved forward on his pale face,
partially covering him. Alongside him, concealed by
blankets, were three rifles and a few hand pistols, all

loaded. His arm bothered him considerably despite the doctor's assurance that in time it would heal. He kept his complaints to a minimum and seemed annoyed that Madelaina watched over him like a mother hen. He insisted he could manage for himself, that he was a man, not a child, but she would hear none of it.

"If it were not for you, Paco, I wouldn't be alive today. I won't rest until I see you returned safely to your home in Zacatecas."

It was Madelaina's idea, and the others concurred, to take the back road out of Parral. Rather than travel at night, they chose to rest and arise at two in the morning, then take the roads back along the desert toward the Sierra Madre mountains in the direction of the Lomas hacienda. If needed they could pause there to rest and pick up supplies.

Madelaina and Lola sat forward on the uncomfortable hard seat of the creaking wagon, their *rebozos* wrapped tightly about them in the early morning air. The trio said very little in those first hours. Their concentration was directed at spotting possible *bandidos* or worse, Pasquel Orozco's Redflaggers, now the enemy of Pancho Villa and the state.

When Paco first saw both girls dressed so shabbily, he shook his head in wonderment at the difference clothing and cleanliness make in a woman. He watched this redheaded girl, Lola, and the fondness he felt for her grew into desire, despite the constant pain caused by his injuries. *A man will never lose his manliness*, he chuckled to himself, *not when there's a wench such as this around to possess*. Besides, the girl liked him—perhaps more than liked him—no?

He thought about the gringo, Peter Duprez. He liked the man. There was something very masculine about him, a fierceness, a hardness, yet there had been something he'd seen in the man's love for Madelaina—quite unlike that which a Mexican displays in a relationship. They made a good pair these two. It would be interesting what would happen when General Obregon met the gringo. Ayeiii!

Paco had learned what Rosalia Quintera had done for both Madelaina and him the night they were possessed. Knowing the ways of his ancestors, Paco felt the worst was over and he hoped it would all end soon. However, Lola, skeptical about his love affair with Dolores Chavez, even hating the sound of her name, wondered about this woman who could possess Paco as she herself had done one night when he was feeling chipper and needed to satisfy his *machismo*. Lola had frolicked with Paco enough to know he was her man. That night she laid claim to him and had no intentions of giving him back to Dolores—especially not Dolores.

At the Lomas *rancho*, they found no one, not even a caretaker. Unsure of what this meant, Madelaina moved rapidly. She shot the lock off the door leading to a hidden cellar stocked with foodstuffs. She and Lola took what provisions they needed, hopefully enough to last two weeks, cast a last look at the place, and took off as quickly as possible, taking the road behind them that led into the mountains. They were high into the hills when they saw the Redflaggers below them, winding their way toward the Lomas *rancho*. The red flag fluttered in the breeze, its bold white lettering reading "Reform—Liberty—Country."

Madelaina had pulled up alongside a few trees and turned back to stare at the activity. Using a pair of field glasses she picked up at the Lomas *rancho*, she focused them on the activity.

"They make themselves at home, no?" she asked Paco, handing him the glasses. Her hidden meaning was sufficient. Lomas was an *Orozquista*!

"As if they knew in advance they must camp there. It doesn't seem possible that Lomas could be a man of such insincerity, but then, *chiquita*, he had fooled us, no?"

Lola's eyes were caught by some activity not far from them, where a scouting party had paused for several moments to inspect the area. "Is best we go," she told her companions. "And go with God's speed. It would do us no good to be caught by either side. Advance, *chica*. We have no other way to go."

Madelaina saw the scouting party in a second. She picked up the reins and moved! They moved as fast as the donkeys would move. She purred to the animals and lashed the whip overhead—making certain it never touched them. How they moved for her. The route was growing thickly wooded and the cool air chilled them despite the hot noon sun they'd just driven through. Paco grabbed a blanket and wrapped himself as best he could. The girls clutched their *rebozos* more firmly about their heads and shoulders. Still the mountain air chilled them. They had ridden for more than four hours, when it dawned on Madelaina that the atmosphere had changed drastically as they followed the winding path leading into the interior. Madelaina's forehead furrowed with deep thought as she glanced about the terrain. Where in Mexico, she wondered, would there be such a climate. The thick undergrowth was the most verdant and luxurious she'd ever seen. It was a primitive jungle, overflowing with exotic tropical flora of all species. Before they were aware of the shadowy, mistlike cloud up ahead of them, they had ridden into its center, into a devastating pocket of bugs, flying insects that attacked them in a violent onslaught.

The women screamed. Lola began swatting at them with her shawl. Madelaina, fighting off the attacking insects that were ravaging them without mercy, was unable to combat the pervasive hordes. There was only one avenue open to her—step up the mules, gather more speed, and ride out the marauding bombardment. The mules, as much victims as the humans, sensed the untenable predicament, broke into a stiff-legged gallop, and managed, after several of the longest moments the girls had ever endured, to outride the holocaust.

Only when they reached a clearing where Madelaina felt it was safe to stop, did she managed to reign back the asses. The girls were in a terrible state. Bitten, eaten alive by the rampaging swarm of flesh-loving bugs, their arms, faces, and necks were bloodied and distended. Paco had escaped most of the assault by covering himself with a blanket.

Lola and Madelaina exchanged pain-filled glances. They knew that something had to be done immediately to relieve the unendurable discomfort, but they felt helpless. It was Lola, the mestizo, who spotted a thick bed of succulents along the wooded path beyond the rocks. She wasted no time in jumping from the wagon. Running toward the boulders, knife in hand, she hacked off the verdant, sizable pods and split them into pieces. Hastily, she rubbed the juices onto her arms, neck, and face, seeking instant relief. The juices turned her skin a dark brown, but in seconds she felt the soothing penetration and refreshing absence of pain.

She called to Madelaina and proceeded to rub the juices on her, sniffing the succulents as she did from time to time with native curiosity. "Perhaps, if we spread this on our bodies," she suggested, "we shall be immune to any further such encounters, *señorita. Dios mios*! What an ambush we ran into!"

Without a moment's hesitation, both girls disrobed and rubbed their bodies with the liquid, staining their skins a dark, berry brown.

"Pray it isn't poisonous," cautioned Paco when they insisted he do the same. As he descended from the wagon, his eyes took in their surroundings with a curious, faraway expression. "*Señorita*?" he addressed himself to Madelaina. "You do not think we may be approaching the land that Francesco Lomas spoke to us about?"

For an instant their eyes met. Then Madelaina, pausing in her work, stood up and gazed around with a similar look of apprehension and expectation in her own dark eyes. "You mean Lago Diablo de Los Muertos?" Half-scoffing, half-believing, she shook her head. "Who could believe anything that seven-tongued viper had to tell us!" She dropped the subject instantly.

Finished with their body staining, the trio commenced their journey into the interior. After two more

491

hours of travel, the terrain began to look suspiciously like the land described by General Lomas to Paco, and Madelaina felt an inner trembling that wouldn't abate. Seeing something which corresponded to Lomas' story, Madelaina would often turn to Paco. Their eyes would meet in silence, neither daring to express their thoughts. Growing more annoyed by these secret looks without knowing their meaning, Lola began to show her disapproval. She was just about to air her indignation when she felt the wagon come to a halt.

Up ahead, several hundred feet beyond a clearing, a scattering of unusual natives, primitive in appearance, caught Madelaina's eyes. She felt for the security of her weapons and alerted the others.

"Perhaps, Paco, the legend might come to life," she said slowly, as her eyes glanced about the scene before them. "Tell me what you make of it."

For some time, Paco had been silently eyeing this wonderland of flora and fauna through the eyes of a skeptic. They had pierced the rugged mountains at dawn of the first morning. By noon they had passed canyons and rested in the shade of a hanging cliff. He noticed the mountains in certain areas were solidified lava, weathered over milleniums into dark brown porous rock. Here and there a few weeds struggled for life. But immediately after the beastly attack of the insects—as if they were some armed guard to protect the entrance to another world—the terrain had changed into one of unbelievable beauty. The farther inland they traveled, the more breathtaking grew the panorama. Perpendicular canyon walls contained fiery colors of every conceivable hue. The bright, dazzling sunlight produced an exquisite jewel-like reflection. The setting was embued with such vibrations, as if it were alive and pulsing with life, that the trio had ridden on in a trancelike state.

Madelaina's question shook Paco from his reverie. He hoisted himself up from the back of the wagon. Stretched out before him he saw a scattering of natives unlike any he'd ever seen in all of Mexico. Their scant attire was unique. The men wore loincloths, and their upper torsos were adorned with silver and jeweled amulets and feathers of rare and exotic birds. The women, in sleeveless, calf-length, buckskin sheaths, and fringed with beading, were reminiscent of northern Indians of Montezuma's day. They wore their hip-length hair straight, banded with beads at their foreheads.

"What can I say, *señorita*?" asked Paco in openmouthed bewilderment. "I have never seen such a place or a people like them." He studied them quietly. "Look upon their faces, such calming countenances," he observed. "And upon the men, I see no weapons. At least they aren't visible," he added as they drew closer to the village.

Unlike any Mexican village they'd seen, it resembled an ancient Indian village with mud huts and straw roofs where teepees and tents might have once been used. A few women made exquisite pottery at a wheel, turning it by foot and shaping the vessels by hand. Some made leather moccasins. A few wove fabrics on handcrafted looms that were unique and cleverly designed. There were a few women seated in a circle, listening to a white-haired elder instruct them in the craft of lapidary, gem cutting.

To Madelaina it was as if the pages of history had been turned back centuries, a scene from the Incan civilization, combining Aztec, Poltec, Mayan, Yucatan, even Yaqui, into one. But there was more, much more, to stoke their curiosity. Hardly any of the natives looked up from their work to give the newcomers a second glance. Moreover, what Paco observed earlier was apparently true. The men carried no weapons; they all appeared quite pacific in nature.

Madelaina, possessed of an insatiable curiosity, pulled the wagon onto the sands. "We must find out where we are," she told her companions. Lola, filled with apprehension at the sight of such beauty and calm, had been struck silent. She gazed about the area as one in a dream, as if she had been suddenly thrust into a utopian wonderland that her mind, having witnessed no previous blueprint, was incapable of conceiving.

Madelaina stepped boldly off the wagon, gathered her skirts about her, and swept across the path of polished stones where some women were grinding meal on an ancient *metate*. She addressed them in Spanish. The women glanced up at her, smiled shyly, and shook their heads. Lola, moving in behind Madelaina, spoke to them in her mestiza dialect. She also employed a unique sign language of her people, an ancient, seldom used manner of communicating.

One young woman, who looked no older than fourteen, smiled and nodded her head. She spoke in an ancient tongue the trio hadn't heard before, bowed her head, and absented herself from them.

"I think she went to find someone," suggested Lola, fully enchanted with the unusual people and the immaculate cleanliness of the place. She was standing alongside Madelaina, not far from where Paco stood, when suddenly she felt pressure on her arm. Paco had grasped both their arms and whispered in warning. "Don't move. Both of you remain motionless," he added as two sleek jaguars padded silently into the compound.

The animals, at least six feet long, were a golden tan spotted with black, the texture of velvet, with massive heads and bodies and short, thick, muscular legs. With complete command of the area, they didn't appear threatened or challenged. In fact, they seemed at home among humans as were the natives with them.

One of the sleek cats sniffed at Madelaina from a distance of four feet. She looked into his opalescent black eyes. The cat only hesitated a moment, then languidly slithered over to her. Lola and Paco held their breath, not daring to move, yet wanting to warn her to be careful.

"Don't concern yourself," Madelaina quietly told her companions. "A jaguar rarely attacks man." She allowed her hand to move behind the animal's ears to stroke him affectionately.

494

The young native girl returned, accompanied by what Madelaina felt was the most magnificent man she'd ever seen. He was a tall, muscular man whose body was formed perfectly. His flowing white mane falling below his sun-bronzed shoulders was an incongruity which struck the trio simultaneously. The body and face were far too young for the snowy white hair. He wore a loincloth of soft chamois leather, girded at each side with jewels in the shape of amulets.

Suddenly, without provocation, the second jaguar hissed at Lola. He bared his wet, glistening fangs and stretched his jaws, revealing ugly yellowed teeth. Lola withdrew, sinking against Paco's outstretched arm; the other, still bound tightly, remained immobile in a sling. "Be still," whispered Paco, eyeing the irritated cat.

"I am Tolomeo," said the strapping man whose indescribably beautiful body resembled that of the mythical gods, with rippling muscles and bulging biceps of incredible dimensions. He uttered a few remarks in a language his guests didn't understand. Instantly both jaguars withdrew and moved soundlessly across a small area at the center of the village.

Madelaina became spokesman for her friends. "Tolomeo, I am Madelaina. These are my friends, Paco and Lola. It appears we are lost. We were hoping to reach Sinaloa and travel southward along the coast to Tepic to the land of our people. Where do we find ourselves?"

"You are in the land of Realidad, close to Lago Diablo de Los Muertos, much off the path to your destination. However, since you are incomplete, it is no wonder you've come to us." He spoke gently, in the most wonderful and soothing voice Madelaina had ever heard, using enigmatic words and phrasing.

"Forgive me, *señor*, you speak in riddles. You say we are in the Land of Reality? That we are incomplete?" She looked deeply into Tolomeo's spectacular eyes and felt a stirring in her loins, a rapid beating in her heart.

"When you've cast your eyes upon Lago Diablo de

495

Los Muertos, the riddles will not confound you." He bowed politely. "You need rest and nourishment. You have traveled far." It was a statement, not a question. He glanced at Paco, at the bound arm, and at the pained expression on the Mexican's face. He moved toward him. "You're in pain. What has happened?" he asked quietly.

"An accident. A gunshot wound. One of those freak accidents that occur from time to time, Señor Tolomeo," interjected Madelaina. *"Es muy mal."*

Tolomeo stood tall, slightly over six feet. The muscles in his forearms and legs looked as if they could crush ten men. His unlined coppery skin was beardless, smooth as a baby's buttocks. On his wrist he wore identical solid silver bands, approximately three inches wide, carved with some ancient hieroglyphics. Around his neck he wore an amulet, shaped much like an Aztec calendar, on a narrow strip of leather. The amulet, slightly larger than a silver dollar, was two-sided and convex. Later they learned the hollowed disc contained ground, dried golden mushrooms at least three years old. His loincloth, woven in the shade of natural beige, was held together by thongs over each hip spaced an inch apart. From these thongs dangled a variety of leather pouches and flacons containing special herbs.

Spectacular as he was in appearance, it was his eyes that held the newcomers spellbound, hypnotizing them, holding them seemingly powerless. His eyes, the color of clear amethysts, a pale lavender with green flecks, alternately changed from a light orchid to a deep purple, the shaded hues of an amethyst twilight.

It appeared that only Lola was in rapport with Tolomeo and this obviously bothered Madelaina. She found him most unusual, someone she wished to explore and pursue. But Tolomeo ignored her, choosing instead to make ovations to Lola and Paco upon whom his interest was focused. Pangs of jealousy shot through the daughter of General Obregon in a way she couldn't understand.

Tolomeo extended one arm, indicating he wished them to follow him into a nearby hut. They entered the cool, neatly kept interior which was totally unadorned. "Please be comfortable. If you need anything from your vehicle, our young men will assist you. While that's attended to, may I please see your arm, Paco? Your injury?"

"The wound is serious," spoke up Madelaina in an imperious tone. "Are you a healer—a *curandero*? He needs the professional, expert opinion of a physican."

Tolomeo said nothing. He helped Paco remove his serape and shirt. Slowly, with painstaking effort, he began to unwrap the bindings, layer by layer, until the wound lay bare. Madelaina had moved in close, took one look, sniffed the pungent stench, and averted her head noticeably. Watching her, Paco paled excessively at her reaction. He knew her to be brave of heart and this indication wasn't comforting. Even the look in Lola's eyes, try as she did to conceal it, was revealing of the wound's severity. And if their expressions weren't enough, Paco himself could attest to the excruciating pain and hell he'd endured since the injuries were inflicted.

"Tula," called Tolomeo quietly, summoning the young woman they'd met earlier. She moved soundlessly to his side. Her dark, smoky eyes glanced at the pus-filled, swollen, angry infection that had spread its poison past Paco's elbow clear to his wrist and into his fingers. The arm was nearly twice its usual size. "Bring me the necessary preparations," he instructed gently.

Tula, prepared to do his bidding, hesitated. "It's Navojolla. The cat is restless. His spirit is thinning, Tolomeo," she spoke quietly, looking into his eyes.

Tolomeo turned to Madelaina. "You will not be safe in the same hut with Paco. Go with Tula. She will keep you safe. You must abide carefully by my directives, *señorita*. Do not, I repeat, do not go near the cats. Understand?"

Madelaina's eyes bore into his for several seconds.

"No," she replied. "Since this is your domain, I shall follow your wishes."

Tolomeo nodded curtly. "I can ask for nothing more until I can explain further. I repeat again, *señorita*. Under no circumstances are you to go near the cats—not even an ocelot, if it should appear."

Lola's blue eyes filled with confusion. Deep down inside her, she seemed to know Tolomeo—even though they had never met or known of each other. From the moment they arrived in this strange village, she had the feeling of some mystical experience, something quite rare. Watching Tolomeo as he stroked Paco's arm and muttered incoherent incantations, she was mesmerized. Madelaina had left with Tula. They were alone.

Two young men brought in a table. Paco was ordered to climb upon it and lie down. Overhead was a mobile of three spirals moving in alternate paths.

"Focus your eyes upon the spirals, Paco. Soon your eye will pick out one over the others. Allow your eyes to remain fixed to that particular one and do not take your attention from it. You understand? I will be transmitting my energy to you and soon you will feel no pain. The pain will be gone and all that you felt will flow into my body. Do you believe me?"

Paco nodded almost against his will. His eyes fixed on the others.

"Very well. Take a deep breath." Tolomeo took a small vial from among the items Tula had brought in. He anointed his fingertips and drew an imaginary circle around the wound on Paco's shoulder. "Now, repeat after me: *There is no pain in my body. There is no pain in my body.*"

Paco did as Tolomeo instructed, repeating the statement as many times as requested of him. His eyes stared overhead in the direction of the mobile. First one spiral, then a second and a third shifted into position. Before his eyes, like an optical illusion, the three spirals fused into one.

"Take another deep breath, then push hard in the area of your solar plexus," instructed Tolomeo, touching the area in the upper abdomen. "At the same time, using your powers of imagery, you are to believe that you are pushing the infection and the pain out from your body. Do you understand?"

Lola watched the goings on in utter fascination as Tolomeo massaged the angry and swollen arm, while the incantations progressed. She was startled to see physical changes actually taking place in Tolomeo. She saw them with her own eyes, there could be no doubt. His skin darkened, his left arm began to gradually swell with an apparent infection. She was stunned. Earlier Tula had returned with several bowls containing various potions and herbs on a tray. Several knives of varying shapes and sizes were spread out on a snow white cloth. She had lit a brazier, and when bright orange-red flames shot up into brilliant lights, Tolomeo held a sharp knife over the flame with one hand, while the other, which was swelling rapidly now, firmly held the wrist of Paco's infected arm.

Faster than the eye could see, Tolomeo ran the razor-sharp knife tip expertly around the area of the outer shoulder where pus had turned the skin a gangrenous greenish-yellow. A geyser of pus exploded and overran the sides of Paco's arm, like rivers of molten lava spilling from a fiery volcano. With precise movements, he allowed the pus to drain, then poured the liquid contents of one bowl over the fresh incision. Paco, tempted to remove his eyes from the moving spiral, was softly and encouragingly told to continue the fine job he was doing.

"In a matter of moments it will be over," said Tolomeo. "Do you feel any pain?"

"No, nothing," replied Paco wondrously.

Tolomeo selected a second knife from the collection, held it over the flame, and muttering his incantations, allowed it to turn molten white. This time he worked so swiftly not even Lola realized what he'd done until it was over. He'd cut out a hole approximately a half-inch larger in diameter than the original bullet wound. A cone-shaped, pus-filled corklike piece of tissue

499

popped out and landed on the table. It resembled the root ball of a plant with countless threadlike appendages forming a ganglia of nerve endings. Tolomeo covered it with a cloth.

Instantly he poured the contents of a second bowl over the open wound. Lola would later swear she saw the wound bubble and boil over for several moments. When the aerating properties subsided, Tolomeo applied a thick, yellowish, gooey substance to the open wound and lower incision. He then packed the area with clean green leaves from a plant Lola could neither recognize nor identify, and finally Tula moved in to swathe the arm in clean white strips of material as sheer as onion skin. She worked swiftly, gazing periodically at the swelling on Tolomeo's arm.

All this was done without whiskey, or anesthesia, or drugs, or potions to dull the pain, thought Lola. No one would believe the miracles she'd seen on this day, she told herself. No one, not even Paco. Not even Madelaina! She wondered why Tolomeo hadn't permitted the *señorita* to witness this miracle.

Tolomeo had moved in toward Paco as Tula finished the dressing.

"Paco," he began. "In a few moments, the pain, however slight, will return. It will not be as it was. You will feel only a dullness. I must transfer the pain to its rightful owner since the infection has departed your body." He raised his powerful arm and turned the spiral mobile in the opposite direction. "Now then, Paco, slowly, you'll return to your previous consciousness and awareness. When I count to three, you'll sit up and feel only a slight discomfort. One . . . Two . . . Three."

Oh, the things Lola had seen this day. Miracles on miracles. At the count of three, Paco sat up, completely rid of fever, his arm reduced almost to its original size, and traces of infection totally absent. Paco, with no recollection of what had transpired, knew only that he felt intensely better. He could almost move his arm.

"Paco!" Lola gushed excitedly. "You won't believe

500

what happened!" She turned to Tolomeo. "Oh, *señor, gracias. Gracias!*" She kissed the mystic's hand. Instantly he withdrew it from her lips.

"There's no need for that," he scolded gently. "The things I've done here could be done by any man if he but had the faith to believe in himself."

Lola was woman enough to detect a certain sadness in his voice, but she possessed neither the sophistication nor the knowledge to comprehend the things of which Tolomeo spoke. She grew more baffled when she gazed at his arm and noted the redness, swelling, and momentary discomfort were gone.

As she turned to explain what she'd seen to Paco, a young native boy rushed into the hut to speak to Tolomeo and Tula in words neither she nor Paco understood. One thing they were certain of—it had to do with Madelaina.

When Tolomeo and Tula left the couple, with apologies, Lola lost little time in trying to describe what Tolomeo had done. But if Paco had entertained any doubts about Tolomeo's ability earlier, he'd become a full and devout believer. The excruciating pain which had consumed him the past week was gone. He felt only a dull sensation, as if an army of healers were at work mending his body properly. He was ecstatic. As they spoke of their concern over Madelaina, however, a loud scream pierced the air, shaking the walls of the hut. It was followed by a loud, roaring, animalistic growl.

Alarmed, they left the hut and went in search of Madelaina Obregon.

Outside the hut where Madelaina had been housed, activity ensued. Two young natives, looking more warriorlike than any others, stood guarding either side of the entrance. They were cautioned not to enter the premises by Tula, who employed sign language to convey the directives to Lola. The young corporal and his Lola stood huddled close together, seeing or hearing nothing except the frightening sounds emanating from the hut.

Inside the small enclosure, Navojolla, hissing, baring fangs, and moving with impatient strides from one end of the hut to the other with marked ferocity, stood locked in silent combat with Tolomeo. His slanted cat's eyes, large, black, and glazed, looked upon Tolomeo as his fiercest, deadliest enemy. His huge jaws would open intermittently, and he'd snap viciously at the powerful man who held him at bay through sheer will. A powerful claw with razor-sharp nails reached out savagely and came within inches of Tolomeo's eyes. The cat spit, snarled, and growled angrily at his obstructor who kept him from a delectable feast—the prone figure of Madelaina, lying unconscious on a cot between them.

Tolomeo's smoky purple eyes leveled on the cat as he artfully moved the amulet around his neck to his lips. He tipped it and sprinkled the dried pulverized mass of mushrooms on his tongue. He did all this without disengaging his eyes from the cat.

In a few moments he began to talk with the cat as if it were human.

"I know it is not you, Navojolla. Neither you or Teleco would consider such diabolical depravity. Listen to me, Navojolla. Allow your personality to subside so I can see who is behind the evil who tries to possess the soul of this young woman. Sleep, Navojolla. Listen to Tolomeo. Sleep."

The cat grew languid and its vigor abated. It yawned and lay down. In moments it fell into complete repose. Out of the jaguar came a filmy apparition of mistlike clouds that separated and shifted and kneaded until the figure of Golden Dawn appeared. She faced Tolomeo. Between them Madelaina moved, stirring restlessly, finally sitting up on the cot. She blinked several times, then glancing from one to the other, oblivious that this was a contest to the bitter end over who would possess her soul, she was arrested by the strange powerful emanation that seemed to extend from Tolomeo's luminous eyes. At one point, when Madelaina felt she could no longer breathe, things began to fall away in shifting confusion. Tolomeo's eyes grew more vivid, as if no light in the world could be brighter than that reflected in his eyes. His face and form, lost in shadow, became almost nonexistent as the face and form of Golden Dawn became more prominent. At this point, Madelaina felt as if she were sinking into a black abyss of blood-sucking fluid, as if the very life was draining from her. She felt helpless and became transfixed. Her soul seemed to soar right out of her body like ethereal wisps of transparent silk and hesitate in a fluttering motion before the presence of the powerful sorceress, Golden Dawn, whose outstretched arms with long pointed fingertips awaited greedily like suction cups to draw unto herself these silky wisps emanating from Madelaina.

Renewed mystically by a saturation of fresh energy, Tolomeo obstructed Golden Dawn's progress. The Indian sorceress grew enraged, frustrated, and apparently failed to draw up more energy with which to combat Tolomeo's power. She began to show signs of weakness, a sapping of energy, a fact which enraged her.

Madelaina, fully aware of the inner turmoil and powerful struggle for supremacy between these two sorcerers, was powerless to intervene. Golden Dawn, having met her match, refused to be cowed. Despite her strong determination to emerge victorious, Madelaina could see changes manifesting themselves in the Indian mushroom eater. Golden Dawn withdrew slightly, hands falling limply to her sides, her head drooping slightly like a wilted flower, until she no longer radiated lights from her eyes or energy from her presence. Her vision grew dimmer and retreated, growing smaller and smaller until she evaporated into infinity. The silky wisps of mist, no longer fluttering beyond Madelaina's body, were sucked up in a whooshing sound, returning inside her. Only she and Tolomeo remained in the hut.

Tolomeo, standing rigid and tall with rippling muscles, pulsing and bulging periodically, permitted his supernatural eyes to dim by degrees as he wheeled and cavorted about the interior hut, pausing now and then to cock his head to listen as he suspiciously sniffed the air in the hut.

Watching him, Madelaina's eyes saw all that happened and heard the sounds and felt the enormous power radiated by the two contestants. Yet, more was happening to her. A sense of normality, such as she hadn't felt in many months, was returning to her, an indescribable feeling of contentment and comfort which permeated her being. Now, as if seeing Tolomeo for the first time, her dark lustrous eyes admired his majesty, his posture and body, and his unaffected composure. Something within stirred as it never had in her young life, and she found herself committing to memory all she saw of him.

He had the nose of a bird of prey to give him the expression of primitive fierceness, yet, in his eyes was buried a love such as she'd never experienced or seen in another man. She'd never been taken by the beauty of such a man, and when he moved soundlessly over the earthen-floored hut and lay a lean, hard hand on the head of the reposing jaguar, Navojolla, she was unable to take her eyes from him.

The caressing touch of his hand upon the jaguar awakened the inert cat. Navojolla yawned, his large jaws opened wide, and a deep throaty sound emanated from his throat. He shook himself, stretched his long body, and assumed his former docile manner. He rubbed up against his master, paused a moment to study Madelaina, then turned and indolently sauntered outside.

Tolomeo seated himself on straw mat close to Madelaina and studied her for a time.

Chapter 19

Outside, the frightful heat of the afternoon sun shimmering over the village of adobe and straw huts reflected the beginning of an early fiery-orange and golden sunset. The odors of food cooking over campfires filled the air and Madelaina sniffed hungrily, her appetite stimulated into a ravenous hunger.

She was unable to articulate the many things she wanted to ask this man, for she suddenly felt as young and naïve as a schoolgirl. Thoughts came to her and left as suddenly, leaving her confused and uncertain of everything, including herself. She felt magnetized by the man and was unable to take her eyes from him.

From a small brazier near the mat upon which he sat cross-legged, Tolomeo lit a taper and drew it toward him to light a small hand-carved pipe he'd removed from his loincloth. He finished packing the curious-looking pipe with a powdery substance removed from a pouch and sat back puffing until it was evenly lit. For a time he smoked in silence, inhaling long even breaths from it. His breathing wasn't the normal kind; he gulped at the air as if the very act of intake invigorated him and replenished a diminishing supply of energy. It wasn't until Tolomeo concluded the ritual that he spoke.

He handed her the pipe, suggesting that she inhale the substance. Hesitant at first, she threw caution to the winds. Hadn't he proven himself no enemy?

The taste of peyote wasn't new to her, yet the smoke contained something more, something like the taste of a heavy cigar. It left a more than usual bitter taste in her mouth and she made an appropriate facial grimace. Tolomeo smiled.

505

"The taste will pass. The first is always the worst. It is necessary, however, that you inhale the essence, since you've been through a terrible ordeal. It was an ordeal which you must guard against as long as you live," he spoke soberly with a deep resonant voice which commanded her to listen.

"Your soul, Madelaina, is impressionable, too trusting and without guile. It is necessary that you protect it at all costs. You must never permit another steeped in the knowledge of soul taking to entice it again. Awareness—constant awareness—shall be your only ally, your only defense against such possible invasion."

She shook her head. "I don't understand a word you're saying, Tolomeo," she told him, watching the amber-colored lights slant through the hut's opening. The flaps usually covering the opening had been folded back and the lights permeating the interior were almost hypnotic—or else she was beginning to feel the essence of the pipe she smoke, she told herself. The spectre of her earlier hunger vanished, replaced by the feeling of contentment flowing through her body.

"Are you aware you've been the victim of spiritual possession? You and this man, Paco, were subjected to the wrath of an evil *bruja*. Fortunately for both of you, her work was greatly hampered by what the mestiza, Rosalia, did for you."

"How do you know about Rosalia?" asked Madelaina in total bewilderment.

"Simple. I saw it."

Madelaina stared at him, incredible amazement in her eyes. Still, she wasn't too taken aback. "Then, it's true. Such things can happen? Raised by the holy fathers and sainted sisters to frown on all this primitive mumbo jumbo, you can see it isn't easy for me to put credence into such mysterious ways of your people."

"You saw what happened here moments ago. You know such a person—Golden Dawn?"

She nodded. "Yes." Madelaina once again accepted the pipe, inhaled twice more, and returned it. "No more, thank you. I am experiencing strange things

506

within my body and mind." She held up a restraining hand.

"Because you are still vulnerable to Golden Dawn's sorcery. Only when you fully experience Lago Diablo de Los Muertos will the spell be broken. By then, you'll have learned not to make yourself vulnerable. You'll sense an inner power that will protect you from ever falling slave to any man. A fearlessness will manifest itself in you to take you through this earthly journey unscathed."

As Madelaina studied this magnificent man, a thousand questions formed on her lips. Who was Tolomeo? From where did he come? Why did he content himself to live in the wilderness? He wasn't the usual tribal Indian. His vocabulary, his command of so many languages, and more important, his command of himself intrigued her. He was an enigma to her. Oh, there was so much she wanted to know. Why had he troubled himself with her? The questions wouldn't articulate themselves into words. She seemed powerless to speak out as a self-consciousness gripped her.

"Madelaina." He addressed her sternly as if he read her mind. "You look upon me as a man. Because you do, you'll not learn what I must teach you."

Madelaina lowered her eyes, a flush moved like a wave to bring color to her cheeks. "But you are a man. And I'm a woman. Can you deny this?"

"There is nothing to deny. You are interested only in externals. I gaze upon the internal spirit, the power that allows you to look upon things as they really are—not as they may appear."

"Tolomeo. You speak in riddles. Truly, I understand none of this."

"The answer to a riddle is always obvious. You are not trained to perceive them as readily as I am. You will, soon enough. And when you do, there will be no deception your eyes can't perceive. When you can truly perceive truth—not the illusion with which man deludes himself—only then will you attain the strength needed to protect you in this lifetime. There'll come

507

upon you an inner awareness that you'll perceive as truth—a truth you'll not be able to deny. Once you've seen the light, falsity, like darkness, will weigh like an anchor. You'll know the difference."

"And this truth will protect me? It will make me strong and not subject to the whims and caprices of another? Surely you aren't speaking of will power?"

He smiled indulgently. "Will power is the opposite of won't power. Both are controlled by the vain imaginings of man—not truth. Can you see the difference?"

"I—I think so. No. I don't know." Madelaina grew ambivalent. "I'm overwhelmed by what's happened to me on this day. It's extraordinary to say the least. Yet, I ask myself, why you, with the powers you have, aren't in a place closer to civilization where you could help humanity?

"Whoever needs me will find me, just as you and Paco have done. You could have traveled no farther in your condition without dire consequences. You came to me out of tremendous need. You found me because you had to find me."

Madelaina concurred, even though she was still confused. "But aren't there others with such needs at opposite ends of the world?"

"Those in dire need will find their Tolomeos, just as you did. And that reminds me, child, I must caution you not to reveal my whereabouts, you understand?"

Madelaina nodded. The serious expression on his face touched her to make a solemn oath never to speak of him in the outside world. But there was more.

She began to feel an enormous physical attraction to this man who sat before her like a rajah, and she filled with embarrassment and a peculiar humility that she gazed upon him with carnal desires. She felt a tinge of jealousy toward Tula and the way the young girl moved in and out of the hut as if she belonged to Tolomeo. She saw none of the usual telltale glances pass between them, yet something about the intimacy of their relationship ruffled her feathers.

Tolomeo smiled at her with tolerant understanding.

"Perhaps when you are fully complete, we shall couple, if it stirs you to such impatience," he said with such overt politeness it fairly offended the wife of Peter Duprez.

About to protest, she realized the futility of any such expostulation, for this sorcerer could read her inner thoughts as if they were scrawled out before him on tablets. She blushed, and although she felt perturbed that he had such powers, she was exquisitely pleased at the promise he made so easily.

They spoke for some time. Tolomeo told her he'd left the outer world because he'd observed the needless pain, suffering, privation, and uncertainty, the hardship and struggle with which men needlessly burdened themselves. Unable to assist his fellowman in the achievement of a more perfect life, he and a small band of followers traveled for months, years, until they happened upon this isolated land where few men have traveled. "Here in this marvelous land of beauty and enchantment we've found the way of life to which we are dedicated."

He explained to Madelaina that he was like a watchful eagle. That people like Golden Dawn could easily turn into birds, night owls, and often employed mountain lions and jaguars in which to materialize to lure their prey, so that at the very moment they weren't guarding their souls, it could easily pass on to them. "Most people would be too frightened to contest a jaguar like Navojolla," said Tolomeo thoughtfully. He rose to his feet, extended his hand to her. "I want you to come with me now."

Outside, the dazzling sunset was settling into vibrant amethysts. Two fine and magnificent horses, the color of smoky pearl, readied by Tula, stood patiently nearby. Tolomeo sprang to his stallion and Madelaina expertly mounted the other, barebacked. Tolomeo nosed the stallion out past the village and motioned her to follow.

They rode like the wind for several moments, swift and silent through the canyon until they reached the

509

desert, where the bloodred lights of a dying sun transformed the desert into a wonderland. Huge boulders, black as ebony, crusted with prophyritic sparks, scattered at either side of them as they climbed the steep ravine, created the most spectacular panorama Madelaina had ever seen. They stopped the horses at the edge of the ledge overlooking what to the young Spanish woman seemed like another world, unlike anything she'd seen in her travels. Her eyes gazed slowly around her.

Angled pillars of stone jutted skyward like the ruined gateways to an ancient temple. They had encountered no living person or creature in this blazing universe of red fire and black boulders, sparkling deep purple and crimson earth, and frightful loneliness. She became appalled at the limitless fiery sky and limitless ruined earth imbued with the supernatural lights of hell and unshaking silence of death. Once past the Inca, Aztec, and Poltemic styled ruins, past the slight rise of a shallow terrace, Tolomeo pointed to an unearthly scene below them.

A great misty lake, shadowy blue and violet, lay in a sunken valley, floating cool and lost, catching no flaming lights from heaven. Its waters were as fixed as shadow-filled glass, its shores outlined nebulously. Madelaina felt something terrible in the aspect of remote, motionless water seemingly untouched by man, like a dream in a fiery twilight. Immobile, yet drifting, it seemed within her grasp, then, many miles away, deepening and paling in its hues of murky purple and dulled jade.

Madelaina gazed in awed silence at this magnificent creation of nature, feeling as she did a terrible compulsion to ride down into the valley and fling herself into its cool, calming waters. Sensing her disquiet, an impatient need to satisfy her insatiable thirst for beauty, Tolomeo laid a hand on her horse's bridle, staying her. "It is useless for you to go down there, Madelaina. The lake is not real. The entire scene is but a mirage, like a dream. It appears shortly after sunset transforms itself into twilight, each day, in this very place, unchanging. Men call it Lago Diablo de Los Muertos, a lake cursed by Lucifer. Many men have lost their lives seeking to approach it. During the day, when the sun basks at its zenith, there is nothing but gray, sun-bleached dust, strewn with gray, lifeless stones amd the sun-bleached skeletons of an era passed."

"No," cried Madelaina, uttering a strangled cry of disbelief. "With my own eyes I see it. Can I no longer trust my eyes? I don't believe you. It's real, I tell you—real!"

Tolomeo, a black silhouette against a luminous sky of purple fire, shook his head. "It is merely an illusion. Legend claims once a lake did exist, nestled in a valley of the ancient civilizations, the many forerunners of Montezuma. This is but a ghost of that lake, a lingering evil illusion painted into the landscape by Mephistophles, luring men who pursue the visions to their death."

Stunned, outraged, and impassioned beyond her normal limitations, Madelaina slid off the pearl white mare, and moving closer to the ledge, she felt an irresistible compulsion to descend upon the lake, regardless of Tolomeo's warnings. The mare, with its pink velvet nostrils and candy-glazed eyes, bobbed its head from side to side and whinnied as it moved in closer to the stallion.

Tolomeo slipped off the stallion's back and moved silently behind the girl, unnoticed. Madelaina was so overwhelmed at the deception of the lake that she wept.

Darkness fell upon the earth like the vast lowering of a midnight curtain. Peering over the next ridge, a colossal moon crept boldly into view, illuminating the earth. Stars blinked awake until one by one the entire ceiling of sky was ablaze with crystals of light. Tolomeo's manly smell wafted to her nostrils, and she sensed his presence until the fine hairs on her neck and arms stood up.

Strange, thought Madelaina. In all the time she'd

511

been here in Tolomeo's land, she hadn't thought of Peter Duprez until this very moment. It was only a fleeting thought, so swift it came like a whisper on the wind and lasted less than a second.

Tolomeo took her small hand in his and led her along the ridge, as their horses sauntered along behind them. They descended a slight embankment along the ravine, making their way to another spectacular sight of nature. Some fifty yards ahead of them was a waterfall. Incredible. A waterfall in a mountainous, desert region in the bowels of a land she never knew existed? Was it to be believed?

"Is this also a mirage?" she asked with abated sadness.

"This is no mirage," he replied. "At times I'm given to such thoughts."

The moonlight filtering through the wooded area reflecting upon the waters resembled liquid silver as it cascaded from the upper regions and fell into a frothy pool of midnight blue water. Tolomeo pulled her gently onto the mossy bank that smelled as sweet as clover.

The excitement and thrills coursing through Madelaina's body were indescribable. She felt high on peyote, with the scintillating relaxation brought on by marijuana, combined with the vigorous feeling of an overwhelming love such as she'd never experienced. For a time they looked into each other's eyes as Tolomeo held her hand, stroking it lightly with a feathery touch.

His eyes made the kind of love to her she'd dreamed of experiencing. What next, she wondered. How much more electrifying would their physical contact be? Just seated next to him, his magnetic orchid eyes looking into hers, she must have experienced a half-dozen orgasms—or something resembling such phenomenon. The urgency of burning physical desire set her on fire.

Was this love at its most sublime stage? Was this the love as provided by the Lord in the rapturous Garden of Eden? She attempted to think, but was unable to accomplish anything. She only knew she was his at this moment, at this place in time. She could belong to none other.

Madelaina was in love as she'd never before experienced it. Tolomeo slowly removed her clothing, which she permitted without protest, without shame. When she was completely naked, he picked up her sun-kissed body in his powerful arms and walked with her into the crystal pool, where he kissed her, gently at first, then with increasing fervor. Somewhere, somehow, at some time, he'd shed himself of his loincloth. Now, in the tepid water which soothed and comforted them, he entered her body and Madelaina moaned in ecstasy.

Her head fell back; her dark hair fanned on the water's surface like wisps of black lace; her neck, a graceful curve of ivory satin, reflected in the moonlight. Her body grew electric, sparking at every pulse point and she clung to him breathlessly, growing more passionate with each thrust of his body.

"I love you," she said almost against her will. "I love you. Sweet, sweet Jesus!" she exclaimed. "Never have I experienced such emotion, such love! Speak the word, Tolomeo, and I shall remain with you until my last dying breath." Madelaina's body quivered and trembled with sensations.

Tolomeo heaved her up out of the water and carried her to the mossy embankment, where he lay her clinging body on a slightly rounded knoll. He kissed her lightly with open, wet, inviting lips. His hands artfully caressed her body until it quivered like a field of heather in a light wind. Her body involuntarily jerked from one erotic sensation to the next in a ripple of perpetual spasms that refused to cease. When he touched her, the stimulation was almost unendurable. If he breathed on her neck or ears or lay his cool wet face on her bosoms, she writhed in exquisite pain and sublime pleasure. To Madelaina, Tolomeo was agony and ecstasy all in one. Time had no meaning. She couldn't begin to estimate how long they'd been together, making love, fulfilling the other's needs until she saw a rosy hue in the eastern sky marking predawn lights.

She had awakened in his arms, feeling neither the cool morning air or the need to cover herself. She was in paradise. She never wanted to leave. No other thoughts wafted into her consciousness except for their togetherness. Nothing existed beyond this moment. She wanted nothing else. Her eyes devoured his strong, godlike body. Slowly, she reached out to touch him, feel his warm exciting skin, and she felt a warmth of honey spill between her legs. Her dark eyes, fluttering in ecstasy, opened wider until she noticed Tolomeo's compellingly majestic eyes, which seemed to contain the wisdom of the universe, were fixed smilingly on hers.

She smiled secretly like a child caught doing something rather scandalous. Then she raised her head and pressed a wet kiss on his full lips. He kissed her back until Madelaina moaned and surrendered herself in total submission. She wanted to savor each moment, make them continue for all eternity. Orgasm after orgasm shook her body. She experienced the completeness of woman as Aphrodite might have felt it—as Venus and all the goddesses of love. No one could be as complete as she.

From nowhere, it seemed, Tolomeo produced a slender knife with a two-sided blade. He held it firmly in his hand, inches from her face, to make certain she wouldn't miss seeing it. An inscrutable shadow fell across his face as he contemplated her. Startled, Madelaina escaped his arms and sat up, her long hair spilling over her shoulders, her exotic eyes filled with alarm and uncertainty.

"What will you say, Madelaina, if I severed my phallus?" he asked quietly.

"Y—you wouldn't!" she stammered. "You can't! Oh, Tolomeo, what on earth for?" Her hands flew to her mouth, a look of utter horror frozen on her face.

"Would you still love me as you professed to love me last night? Would you still remain with me until death as you insisted?"

"I'm not sure I understand. Why are you confounding me? I'm bewildered."

"Answer me, woman. Will you love me if I can no longer couple with you?"

"What you ask is unfair. I don't know." She grew nervous and edgy, never thinking for a moment he wouldn't plunge a knife in his life-giving loins.

"Ah, then you don't love me. You love my sexual organs. Good, then I shall cut them off and give them to you so you can take them with you—to love evermore."

"No!" she screamed. "That's not true. I love you—all of you! Oh my God, I don't know what you expect of me!" she wailed, wringing her hands, glancing about the wooded area for some means of escape.

Tolomeo tossed the blade onto the ground next to him. His gentle eyes filled with infinitesimal lights. "You are living in a world where man is unpredictable. Animals are predictable. Birds, also predictable. Man, unfortunately, hasn't evolved to the plane of predictability, therefore you must be on your guard and learn to evaluate the real from the imaginary, the important from the unimportant. You must perceive everything and look at very little. Last night I made love to you. Before I even entered your body, you experienced countless orgasms; therefore, you don't need my body to achieve this. For many hours we were one, on a mental plane where all is perfection. Now, I ask you again, explicitly: If you were never again to experience physical expression, the coupling of two bodies in sexual embrace, could you exist and not make it your god? Could you live without the feel and touch of a man's penis?" He pressed.

"No, I couldn't live like that."

"There's a man in your life, your husband."

"But how did you know?" Her eyes widened in astonishment.

Ignoring her question, Tolomeo continued. "If this man were to cease loving you sexually, would this fact diminish your love for him?"

515

Thoroughly confused, Madelaina faltered. "I tell you I don't know. I've never given it thought. It's too much a part of life—of everything. I'd want to love him with my entire body and soul. Oh, Tolomeo, why do you torture me so? What has all this to do with the development of my strength against an onslaught of unsuspected *brujas*—witches?"

"Simply this. You must conquer all physical urges before you can conquer the mind. If you do not control your body and your mind and your passions, there is no hope against someone like Golden Dawn—or your father—or your enemies."

Madelaina glanced at him sharply as things in her mind fell into chaos and more confusion. She shivered noticeably as a chill coursed through her naked body.

"Put on your clothing, child," he said softly. "Soon you'll be thrust back into the earthly reality for which you must prepare." His voice, so beautiful and strong, so unbearably sweet, clutched at her heartstrings.

Madelaina did his bidding, but she wanted to fling herself back into his arms to recreate the previous night of bliss. Why couldn't she live suspended in time as she had the previous night? She stepped into her peasant skirt, pulled the *camisa* over her head, and tucked it inside the skirt. She sat down again, close to him, as countless changes occurred in her. Something stirred in her.

She drew her legs up to her chin, hunched over, and glanced into Tolomeo's face. Oddly enough, her eyes focused on nothing external; they focused inward on something she felt instinctively was more important than anything she'd ever encountered. Afflicted by a sharp clarity of perception, she closed her eyes, dropped her forehead on her knees, and concentrated on the inner scenes forming in her mind.

The feeling of belonging to part of the universe prevailed. She wasn't a separate entity; she was a part of the whole scheme of things. She'd never given such matters any thought and wasn't certain why it should be in her mind at this time. Yet she was overcome with an immense feeling of detachment, as if she were on the outside of the world looking in, seeing those things which made up Madelaina Obregon. As she viewed herself from this new perspective, she heard Tolomeo speaking softly, in a hypnotic, suggestive voice, which she heard with every one of her senses.

"Knowledge to most men is frightening. Few like changes in their lives. They feel confident and content in an old rut, in the role they've played their entire life. With this special knowledge, Madelaina, the ordinary world will appear mundane. You might feel more special than anyone else. You must guard against this vanity as you guard against letting anyone possess your soul. Know fully that you'll be contested every inch of the way by well-wishers, those who desire for selfish reasons to detain you, and by those who wish to harm you. You must be keenly aware of all obstacles thrown in your path and never allow fear in any shape, manner, or configuration to enter your consciousness."

Tolomeo paused a moment and studied her posture. His hand reached out to touch her but he forced himself not to. "You must remained detached from the world if you wish to understand its riddles. To be detached doesn't mean you must give up living, or go into retreat, or fear the shadow of your own soul.

"On the contrary, you must acquire a natural lust for life—which you have to a great degree—and an awareness of man's natural powers. You must be master at decisiveness, master of your choices. Choice, your sole responsibility, is the only freedom man can express. Once your choice or decision is made, there's no time left for regret or recrimination. They must be final or death will stalk you in countless ways, leaving you no time for attachment to anything. And so, it is with an awareness of death, a needed detachment, and an inner power of self-determination, you can begin life with strategy—with a certain cleverness needed to guide you.

"Let me repeat, Madelaina, so there's no confusion in your mind. The inevitability of your death guides

517

you into necessary detachment and a silent lust for life. The power of making final decisions allows you to choose without regrets, for what you choose is always best for you at your level of consciousness, therefore you'll live with gusto and a lusty efficiency. Above all, you must be patient. When you've learned to see within yourself, the secret to all life and knowledge will reveal itself to you. And if your life is beset with complications, you must take every precaution to rid yourself of those tentacles which rob your peace of mind. So, you must rearrange your life, knowing your first obligation is to yourself—none other."

Madelaina stirred at these words. The guilt she felt over the estrangement with her father had stifled her, preventing her from drawing a free breath for too long. She hadn't been aware that her relationship to him had actually motivated her entire life—until this moment. Having been coerced into living his way of life, the Spanish life of a young, highborn woman, she had every reason to feel incomplete, she told Tolomeo. "How can I think one way, feel another, and expect to be a whole person when my actions negate all three?"

He explained. "You've cut your father loose physically but not mentally. You can never hope for the ideal of self-expression, for you are tearing yourself apart."

His words brought on a terrible melancholy, and Madelaina began to sob. Tears streamed down her face and loneliness engulfed her. Watching her, Tolomeo said nothing to comfort her. In moments the tears were gone. She sat up, arched her back for a second, then fell once again into the attitude of repose she'd assumed earlier.

"Tell me the colors you see in your mind," commanded Tolomeo.

"Green, dark green. No, it grows lighter and lighter, nearly a lime green. No, it's a pale green. Now there's purple—orchids and pale greens and bright yellows. Yes, a golden yellow—lighter, brighter than the shade of a pale gold."

Madelaina rambled. "It's growing lighter, almost white now." She averted her head, eyes closed, as if she focused on a light of super-bright intensity. "It's too bright—I can't focus on it."

"You must—you will. Stay with it and when it shifts, tell me what you see."

"Clouds—like cotton. Bouncing along the sky." She stopped. "I see—I see—" Madelaina gasped. "I see Peter. He's lying in a pool of blood. He's dying, I think. I can't stand it! I want to open my eyes. I don't want to look upon any of this."

"Now tell me what you see," said Tolomeo calmly.

"Men fighting. War! War!" Her voice cracked and grew harsh and filled with venom. "I see General Huerta and Major Salomon!" She grimaced with hatred and vengeance.

"What else do you see?"

"I see a murky red, a dull crimson, deep brown, and black surrounding the bodies of these men, my enemies," she said with a hate-contorted face.

"Now concentrate on them until they dissolve of themselves, and in so doing, admit to yourself they are no longer your enemies. They have no control over you. You must view them with detachment. Your hatred is the fuel they use to control you and bring havoc into your life. Only enemies have power to destroy you. Do you understand?"

An internal struggle commenced within the girl. She wanted to understand, but didn't. There was no way she could remove the hatred she felt for either of these men, her mortal enemies. The struggle grew to sizable proportions, causing her to break into a cold sweat and shake as if afflicted with epilepsy.

"Remove the hatred from your heart. Say to yourself, 'They have no power over me. I am unaffected by their deeds. They have no power over me.' Set them free, Madelaina, in your mind. Only then will you be free of their influence. Set them free—set them free. Absolve them of all their crimes and sins against you," commanded Tolomeo firmly.

Madelaina's body shook and trembled with visible spasms. The internal battle raged for several moments, fighting Tolomeo's suggestions every inch of the way. From the loincloth's belt, Tolomeo removed a small silver flask, the size of perfume flacon. He tipped it to the tip of his tongue, then leaned in toward the resisting figure of the girl. He forced a drop onto her tongue and lay her sagging head back against his inner arm, keeping it there for a moment. Then he allowed it to sag forward into the original position.

Madelaina fought a valiant battle against his suggestion for as long as she could until her resolve dissolved. Consciously, she told herself, she could never forgive Huerta or Salomon. She could never erase all the hatred she felt for those despicable devils. At some time in this mind-bending experience, she suddenly realized that for as long as she was affected by their deeds, she'd forever be in their power. It was hard for her to understand Tolomeo's instructions to free them from her mind. The key words for her became: "The chains that bind you are the chains that will free you. Understand that and detachment will follow in a natural course."

The chains that bind you are the chains that will free you. Over and over and over again she repeated those words. She almost came to life thinking she understood totally what Tolomeo meant. Then he dropped the next bombshell.

"Forgive them. Forgive both Huerta and Salomon and any enemy who may have wronged you. Forgive them in your heart, and you'll never see in them an enemy."

Once again her face contorted with hatred and violent emotion. "No!" she screamed, trying to reject his words. "No! I can't forgive them. I won't. If you knew what they did to me, you wouldn't ask such a thing of me. No, I say!" She protested loudly with uncoordinated movements and the facial gestures of one possessed by fiends.

"And I say yes. A thousand times yes. You must

520

forgive your enemies—or you'll never know a moment's peace. You must also forgive Golden Dawn. You hear? Believing in their evil gives them power. You must release their power from your mind!" commanded Tolomeo authoritatively.

She fought him with trembling lips and twitching facial muscles, wringing her hands together as if she intended to clutch the skin from them. "F—forgive? For—give?" She resisted his commands formidably. "Never!"

"And your father! You must forgive him above all!"

Madelaina's face paled. She jerked and twisted convulsively. "Nooooo!"

"Picture them in your mind, all four of them: Huerta, Salomon, your father, Golden Dawn," commanded Tolomeo gently, then he repeated himself in a firmer tone, more paternalistic. "Do as I say! If you wish to be rid of them forever, forgive them, Madelaina—or you'll never see Peter Duprez again."

Tolomeo removed another pouch from the chamois bag on his loincloth. He spread some powder over Madelaina's navel and rubbed it in a semicircular motion, extending for two inches beyond its diameter. It left a slight ashy residue.

For several moments longer, Madelaina resisted, then she succumbed as if against her will. She began to nod her head, bobbing it up and down slowly.

"I forgive them. I forgive them for all their savagery, their unendurable torture, and the torments inflicted upon me. You, Vitoriano Huerta. You, Simon Salomon. And you, Golden Dawn. All who have seen fit to torture me and use me as a means to your own evil ends, I forgive you with all my heart. You have no power over me . . . no power over me . . . none whatsoever . . ." She repeated after Tolomeo's voice again and again. Finally, she added, "You, too, Papa, I forgive."

Watching her face and body inscrutably, Tolomeo, for the first time in this full day's work with Madelaina, began to relax. A remarkable change came over her face. The strain and worry lines melted away, and she relaxed. She had been through enough for now, Tolomeo told her.

"At any time you wish to open your eyes to join me, you may do so. You've made remarkable progress."

Her thoughts were clear now. She no longer experienced fatigue, drowsiness, or the uneasy sensation in her stomach which promoted an anxious state. She was ravenous and told him so. "After all, Tolomeo, we haven't eaten in a full day and night, have we?"

"It would be impossible to experience miracles so soon," he said, smiling tolerantly as he watched her rise to her feet and walk to the water's edge.

"May we jump into the pool again?" she asked rapturously. "It was such a magnificent experience, I never wish to forget it."

"Of course."

She skipped into the water and fell in with the gaiety of a child. "Come in, Tolomeo," she called. "It's even better than last night."

Tolomeo carefully removed his loincloth and lay it on the bank next to her clothing. Before he entered the sparkling crystal pool of blue water, he touched his amulet to his lips, allowing the dried mushroom powder to spill on his tongue. He recapped the amulet and joined Madelaina in the pool.

For a time they laughed and played and splashed, filled with the playfulness of children. They swam the length of the lagoon and back several times. At one point, Madelaina paused to ask, "What lies beyond the waterfall, Tolomeo?" She swam away from him before he could reply. Catching sight of her direction, Tolomeo dove beneath the waters and, with sure, swift strokes, caught up to her just before she caught sight of the underwater grotto.

He grasped her feet and for a time they both submerged; she, thinking it was a game, and he, fearful she'd see the intriguing world beneath the water and demand to explore it. At this stage, Tolomeo was afraid to rush the truth, sure she couldn't handle it.

His powerful arms reached out to encircle her body

until she lay against his chest as they surfaced, kissing passionately. They tread water a little longer as he steered her into the shallows, where he kissed her with more fervor until she became vulnerable to his love. Tolomeo returned her kisses with increased passion, when suddenly he stopped, his will somewhat shattered.

"You didn't answer me," she purred softly, snuggling in his arms as they lay on the moss embankment. "What's beyond the waterfall?"

"The waters of absolute truth," he replied cryptically.

"Oh, Tolomeo, don't you ever relax? I don't want to think of anything but absolute love, like this," she teased.

For the next several hours or more—Madelaina couldn't tell how long they were there since time seemed to stop for them—they engaged in lovemaking more exciting and fulfilling than their previous encounter. They lay side by side, the warmth of their bodies generating an excitement that dulled any outside cares. They hardly moved, his face next to hers, his body wrapped around her, his hot breath on her neck, her lips, her breasts until she could no longer endure the exquisite and rapturous pain.

"Look into my eyes, beloved," he whispered. "I will stand long where you leave me, the countless days and nights passing with the tedium of a turtle returning to his burial grounds. You've been total in my eyes, indelible in my soul, and will remain with me in each passing face I see. My world has become more magnified. The stars, moon, and skies have never been as beautiful, more alive, and all of nature has become a blanket of jewels in which we wrapped ourselves so greedily." Tolomeo turned her face toward him and silenced her lips with his fingers. "No, listen. How easy it would be for me to say, stay here with me. Stay with me and be my love and we will love forever—"

"Tolomeo—" She wanted to protest, to assure him she'd stay.

He shushed her tenderly and continued. "Soon you will leave my world. And I, who will never be the same since we've touched, must exercise my will, beloved, and thrust you from me. All the things you will be one day, you will be because my love is like the magic touch of heaven, if you will but let me whisper to you and you hear my voice. You will wear my love and my strength, and all those who gaze upon you will know you've been touched by something special—something quite magic. Allow me to work through you, Madelaina, my beloved, and you shall never be alone." He smoothed her wet hair off her face and pressed his moist lips lightly on her forehead, nose, cheeks, and lips, until her body shivered involuntarily.

Tolomeo continued. "And I, beloved, shall be forever a part of you. Although I must forget you to preserve my sanity, visions of your naked body, bronzed by the sun's kisses, lying next to mine as we both soared into eternity, shall fade as all things fade in time. The excitement I've felt with you has been unique—unlike any earthly experience. It is for this I must help you depart. It would be wrong to entice you to stay here. Your destiny lies out in the world beyond Lago Diablo de Los Muertos, where a life awaits you, one which must be lived as only you can live it. While you are here, you will remember me and my teachings vividly. When you venture forth into the outer world, visions of me will fade, but my teachings will remain, deeply implanted in your sub-conscious mind.

"I will make love to you once again—for the final time. Shortly, the time of separation will form an invisible barrier between us. You will remember me only whenever you need my help—not too often, for then you'll not have learned to depend upon your own reserves. When the first star falls, you will depart."

Madelaina heard him and understood every word he spoke with extraordinary clarity. However, something deep inside her, try as it did to resist his words, was unable to do her bidding. She fell into a golden fog of euphoria, into the rapture of a sexual love of such pleasure and erotica that nothing else mattered except what she felt and experienced in these next few moments. She had been looking with torrid intensity into his jeweled eyes. For a time she felt as if she had entered his body through his eyes and now lay curled inside him, forever and through all eternity a part of him. Every touch of his fingers upon her passionate flesh was like an electric impulse of scintillating pleasure to her brain, like the ripples that move outward from a central point when a stone has been hurled into a pool of water. Her entire body became effervescent with bubbles which moved only upon his touch and from time to time burst into tiny explosions of ecstasy in her brain.

She tried to talk, to tell him how breathless and love-filled he made her, but Tolomeo whispered, "Hush, my love, please don't speak. Words are superfluous. Just feel and let your senses do the rest. The time is short."

She could only nod. Tiny bubbles came into her field of inner vision, bubbles that looked like golden teardrops, and she watched them mushroom and multiply and disintegrate and shift in and out of her mind. She saw a series of pictures now, a hacienda in a strange land, unfamiliar to her, except for a brand, an insignia of sorts, that hung over an entrance leading to the property. Madelaina tried to erase these pictures; she wanted nothing to interfere in her interlude with Tolomeo.

Once or twice she shook her head in an effort to rid herself of the unusual pictures. But the pictures persisted. A face out of her past appeared, the face of Manuelito Perez. He stood in an arena, a plaza de toros, strutting and prancing before the *aficionados*, completely oblivious of the dangers that stalked him. He had just finished performing a superb *verónica*, and he turned to the crowds for their cheers. He failed to see the bull turn and charge. The next thing Madelaina saw was Manuelito's body hurled into the air, gored through the left thigh with the bull's horn. He was impaled against the animal's horn for several moments before he was dislodged and his seconds rushed in to attract the beast. The picture faded. Madelaina broke into a cold sweat. She cried out, "No!"

Tolomeo loomed over her, ready to penetrate her body. Her eyes snapped open and in them he saw the truth. "Shall I stop now, *señorita*?"

"No. Please. Let me experience the joy of our final journey into ecstasy," she begged deliriously. "Please, Tolomeo."

"It will make no difference," he said somewhat sadly. "You will not recall the joy for long. A star is about to fall. Soon your dreams will be different."

"Please, my sweet, sweet love," she silenced him. "Don't remind me that I must soon walk alone again. Already I feel you slipping from my embrace, and I'm frightened." She clutched at him as if she were taking her dying breath. "Oh, Tolomeo, you're the essence of life, beauty, the pleasure of all joys. Before distance widens beyond our reach and sight, hold me close, that the gods in heaven may see us and allow us more time. You are what every woman needs to make them complete. If only I could have been more meaningful to you." She sighed sadly. "I see now it could never be." Their strength was waning.

"The pity of it is, I exist in every man and woman, if they'd only look for me."

She stroked his silver white hair as if it were precious. "Will we see each other again, Tolomeo? Perhaps one day, I can return—?" Madelaina shuddered. She reached to him and clinging passionately to him, rained kisses all over his face, arousal once again seeking release in her loins. "Tolomeo, Tolomeo," she purred.

They kissed and walked naked into the clear crystal lagoon, leaving their bodies like old clothes on the shore.

"Madelaina! Madelaina! Oh, *señorita*, please awaken." It was the mestiza, Lola, shaking her shoulders, hoping to arouse her. "You've been asleep for four days! *Dios mios*! Is that all you know to do—sleep?" she asked, recalling vividly the incident in Parral when Madelaina slept for so long.

She sat up on the straw bedding stretched out on the floor of the hut and yawned lazily. Glancing at Lola, she smiled. "Four days?" She yawned again and stretched her arms and arched her back. "*Muy bueno*, it's time we return to our original destination, no?"

Lola sat down on the floor next to her. "*Señorita*, many things have happened to Paco and me since we've spent some time in this crazy place. To begin with, we are in love. We wish to get married, find us a small house to live in, and raise babies. You think your father, the general, would permit such a thing? Must Paco stay in the army and run the risks of getting killed or shot up again?"

"How is Paco?" asked Madelaina. "His arm—is it any better?"

"Like new, *señorita*." She nodded insistently and crossed herself at the sharp look she received from Madelaina. "I swear on the Blessed Virgin de Guadelupe, he is feeling like new! There is something magic about these people," she exclaimed in an almost frightened manner. "This Tolomeo is *muy magnifico*."

"Then Paco will have to return to Zacatecas, to the camp of General Obregon. I will write to my father and explain the valiant bravery Paco has shown in the face of inestimable danger. He should then receive an honorable discharge from the army, Lola. Perhaps with enough of an endowment for you to realize your desires."

Lola's smile was like a ray of sunshine. She was truly a beautiful young woman, thought Madelaina. The azure blue eyes fringed with dark lashes made her think of Peter and she filled with a deep longing.

"What of you, *señorita*? What will you do?"

"Return to Zacatecas with you. What else?" she said with a newborn firmness. "Now that Madero and my father are allies with Pancho Villa, there is no point to the life I once lived."

Perhaps it was because Lola had only seen Madelaina while under the influence of Golden Dawn's possession and she had no yardstick by which to measure the strong-willed determination in the girl. Whatever it was, she couldn't remove her eyes from Madelaina, as if seeing her for the first time in this new role of determination and courage. "When shall we be ready to leave?" she asked finally.

"At the first falling of a star," she replied.

"At the first falling of a star? *Que va*, at the first falling of a star? It makes no sense, *señorita*. Who knows how long it takes to see a falling star?" Lola faltered.

"You heard my orders. Not until then." She watched as Lola, staring at her as if she was some crazy woman, backed away from her and left the hut.

Etched vividly in the deep recesses of Madelaina's mind were pictures which brought a blush to her cheek. She hurriedly stepped into her clothing, unable to understand why her imagination had taken such fanciful flight into erotic vignettes, and of all people, why with this tribal leader, Tolomeo?

She could feel her heart beating rapidly and a peculiar breathlessness coming over her. *It's good we're leaving*, she told herself. *I musn't stay here so close to him. If I do, I'll love him too much. I'll never be able to turn back. To think I've dreamed of him in this fashion. I mean—a total stranger! Could I miss Peter so much that I fantasize over other men?* She felt a hot blush surge through her body as the pictures in her mind continued to form and dissolve. *God forbid that Tolomeo should read my mind!* Dios mios! *I wouldn't be able to look him in the eyes.*

She brushed out her long hair. There was no mirror in which she could study the facial changes which had occurred the two weeks of their stay in the interior. In fact, when she learned two weeks had passed since their arrival, she found it too incredible to believe. It seemed only yesterday.

Consciously, she remembered very little of her encounters with Tolomeo, subconsciously however, she kept getting flashes of pictures. Anyone who knew her before and saw her now could detect a change in her, but, what it was, they were not able to tell and wouldn't for some time to come.

The morning of their departure, Madelaina ran breathlessly about looking for Tolomeo. He was nowhere to be found. Dismayed, she felt saddened, thinking he refused to be present for some foolish thing she may have said or done. She asked Tula and all the others she encountered where Tolomeo had gone. They could give her no answer. Paco, well on the road to full recovery, was anxious to depart. He had many things to consummate, and the sexy and lovely Lola was ready and willing to consummate them with him.

"We will wait, Paco. I cannot leave without thanking Tolomeo for your life and my own. You have your whole life ahead of you," she reprimanded sternly, still marveling over the rapid healing of his arm and splendid health.

Paco angled his head at her. "Unless it is stopped by a *Rurale* bullet or a *bandido*'s *riata*," he said scornfully.

"If you take that attitude," she said coolly with an air of detachment, "you deserve what you get." She moved away from him as if he didn't exist.

"*Si, querida*, it ees true," wailed Paco to Lola. "She has changed. She grows more like her father each day. I give thanks she is not my *mujer*—wife." He gathered Lola into his arms with love and affection. But, like most Mexican men, he did not display his affection for other men to see. So, in the usual custom, he pretended to be brusque and rough with her. "Take notice, woman. You will never be such a macho woman—or it is finished between us, *comprender*?"

Lola reached up and pinched his cheek affectionately. "*Si*, Corporal Jimenez. I see how tough an *hombre* you can be and I tremble before you, respectfully, of course."

"*Muy bueno*, woman." Blushing, Paco gazed about

529

the shaded area of the compound to see if they'd been observed or overheard. If the natives, moving about in their duties, had noticed them, they gave no outward show. "Now, go and prepare the wagon for our journey home. We must be ready—whenever this star decides to fall, eh?" He laughed mockingly and shook his head with growing irritation.

Earlier, Paco had been gloomy and annoyed by what Lola announced were Madelaina's orders. But gazing upon Lola's beauty and adoration erased all his hostility. Paco Jimenez was truly in love—really in love— and it felt wonderful. The miraculous healing of his arm and feeling of love permeating this unusual village had inspired him to the point that he entertained thoughts of defecting entirely—of not returning to the outside world. Who was there to miss him back in Zacatecas? No one. He had everything right here, with Lola and these wonderful people who had fed him, nurtured him, and inspired him to higher thoughts. Perhaps Señorita Obregon may decide to remain here, too, he thought hopefully.

It was twilight by the time Madelaina found Tolomeo standing by the shimmering waterfall, his back to her, staring into the silent pool of liquid silver several feet from the embankment upon which they'd made such scintillating love.

"Tolomeo!" she called out suddenly. "Look—a falling star!" Her eyes followed the blinding streak in the sky as it whirled in an arc and sputtered lifeless. She felt a sinking feeling in her stomach. "It is time to say good-bye," she said quietly.

"*Adios, querida. Vaya con Dios.* Live fully and in peace." His voice seemed deeper, more constrained. Still it excited her as before. He didn't look her way.

"Is that all you'll say? I wanted to speak to you of many dreams I've had, for which I need explanations. Now it's time for our departure. Won't you see us off?"

His manner, calm and dignified, was so remote as to give the impression he moved mechanically as in a dream. Still he didn't turn to look at her.

The sweet smell of earth and clover permeated the air like a heavenly intoxicant, and she inhaled deeply to stir her senses and remember this setting. She heaved a forlorn sigh of sadness. "Tolomeo," she called softly. "Won't you look at me? Say good-bye? I can't believe that you wouldn't grant me that, at least. Is it something I've said or done? I've been known to be headstrong and foolish and independent and nasty in the past. Somehow, I can't seem to recall it. It all must have happened a very long time ago."

Madelaina's soul retreated in confusion to its inner fortress of new and sudden detachment, much to her amazement.

"I came to say farewell, to thank you for your kindness, generosity, and the miracles performed on Paco and myself. I came also to offer you my allegiance. Should you ever want me, I will come from wherever I am."

These extraordinary words, spoken in a firm voice without arrogance but with limitless strength, aroused Tolomeo. Still he did not turn toward her. He spoke quietly. "It was necessary for you to learn to place things in the proper perspective. To know one thing is no more important than another, that pure love transcends all and reduces all else to its own worthless state—nothing. As death can be nothing, so are the stresses of life. The philosophy is so simple. It is overlooked by mankind because the brain desires such things to be complex. Where pure love is, there can be nothing else, and all dangers fall away of their own accord and dissolve into nothingness." Tolomeo paused a few moments. He seemed to be staring straight ahead at the waterfall. His voice softened, became more endearing.

"You will never have to be concerned that a sorcerer can possess you ever again. You have learned how to be a warrior against such threats. Golden Dawn will never harm you again. Now that you've shown your claws to her, she'll never try tricking you. As powerful and relentless as she can be, she will not again trifle with your life, for we've met in the arena. The rattler has no effect on the eagle. Remember, before you can be trapped, you must be willing. You must never abandon yourself. To do so is the crux of all trouble.

"You have acquired much knowledge in the past two weeks, knowledge for which you shall be held to account. You have no choice but to learn more, if only to defend yourself and put your life into better order."

There was something about the way Tolomeo kept his back to her that was truly maddening. She moved a few inches to the right to see him—if only in profile—but Tolomeo would turn to the left. When she moved to the left, he turned to the right. Why did she feel such a palpitation of the heart, she wondered. Knowing she was leaving, knowing she'd probably never see him again, she had wanted the parting to be memorable. She inclined her head sadly and stared at the verdant, velvety knoll on which she stood, then gazed into the aquamarine pool that glistened iridescently in the bright twilight.

"If you won't look at me, Tolomeo, I can only express my deep sorrow and profound disturbance. I thank you for the enlightening and knowledgeable teachings. Truly, I'll never forget them and shall practice them to the end."

"It is one thing to mouth those words, another to put them into practice," he spoke up again. "It is too easy to forget what you've learned if outer things become more important. Outer things: opposing someone, avoiding things, preparing for certain things and not others; something is always more important to us than the self. The world is full of frightening things, and for the most part, people become helpless creatures, surrounded by inexplicable, unbending forces, which they assume cannot be explained or changed. It's like a belief in destiny, the belief that one is powerless against such forces, a fatalistic approach. Knowledge of these forces will enable you to use them by redirecting yourself and adapting to their direction."

"It will make me more powerful than the rest of mankind," said Madelaina, suddenly on the same wave length as Tolomeo.

"It will make you more vulnerable. Make no mistake about this. Your life may become more precarious and cumbersome—"

"Any more than it's been? *Dios mios*," she exclaimed. "Truly, I do not understand. Only a moment ago I was certain that I had been endowed with infinite wisdom—"

"And that would make you swell with vanity, place yourself in a loftier place than your fellowmen. No, Madelaina, knowledge is not for that purpose. The more you come to know, the more you are responsible for. You will perceive things much more readily than others, and because you know the consequences, you will avoid these forces. Knowledge forces you to live your life as a warrior and do battle each and every day of your life. You spoke of your father as an enemy. He is not your enemy except for making you indulgent, soft, and given to custom. The warrior in you combated him, attempted to assert itself, for the spirit of your being isn't geared to complaining or indulging— nor is it geared to victory or defeat. A warrior is geared to struggle, meeting every encounter head on. The outcome is of little importance. Only the necessity to permit the spirit full freedom and complete expression is imperative. And knowing this, striving for this, he can laugh and laugh and laugh at the fraudulent lives lived by others."

Madelaina strained to see his face. She grew dismayed. Her voice had grown husky and thick with emotion. "I'm confused, Tolomeo, by things I don't understand. Please, can't we remain longer? I've no desire to return to what I left before our arrival." She elevated her spirit. "May we go for another swim? It's endurable, this paradise of yours."

"No," he replied firmly. "You're on the threshold of a new life—a new world—and will no longer feel safe in your old ways. You must choose your ways in this

533

new life with premeditated caution. If ever there is doubt in your mind, go into the silence. Your spirit will reveal to you the necessary path to follow." He removed a small silver flacon from his loincloth girdle, reached behind, and held it out to her in his lean, outstretched palm. "Here, take this. If you should find yourself unable to go into the silence, rub this powder in the area of your umbilical cord, speak to your abdominal brain, demanding courage and strength to overcome your dilemma. Command all internal dialogue to cease so that you may hear the voice of the spirit."

Madelaina's hand reached hesitantly for the flacon, then, with her free hand, she grasped his wrist, pulling him toward her. "Please, Tolomeo," she pleaded sadly with a catch in her throat. "Won't you turn to look at me? I want to remember the sparkle of amethyst in your eyes, the sun-kissed glow of bronze of your body. And when the wind whispers and the woods are motionless, I'll remember how an evening star fell and set aglow for all eternity the knowledge of how two bodies like burning candles melted into each other, and where they fused into one, we saw God lit brightly beneath an eternal torch of heaven." Madelaina paused, waiting for Tolomeo to turn to her and express his love. "My lips move, calling to you, Tolomeo. But it is so quiet, so very quiet. Can you not hear me?"

Then, like a whirlwind in slow motion, he turned to her. There was no sun in the sky, yet its dazzling rays caught prisms on the silver amulet around his neck, causing it to sparkle with such brilliance that Madelaina for an instant was blinded by its glare. She blinked several times, averting her eyes. When she could, her eyes fixed themselves on Tolomeo's eyes. All at once the dawn of light broke, as a flaming star shot overhead like burning wick, and in its wake she saw him fully.

They gazed at each other in pregnant silence. An expression, startled and frightened, yet fascinated, moved across her face as one awakened from a terrifying dream by an appalling stranger. Her heart swelled and pressed against her lungs. She couldn't breathe. She grew pale, frightened, and terribly confused, and she stared at him unable to articulate.

"What did you expect from a sorcerer?" he asked. "I did what was necessary. I had to save your life, and I succeeded. Now, you are complete, your soul is yours for eternity if you abide by the precepts you've learned. And my dear, if you don't, I will be helpless to aide you."

Madelaina, unable to speak her thoughts or put into words her feelings in the next few moments, felt her mind growing hazy and cluttered with a montage of pictures of the world and people she knew intimately before entering Tolomeo's world. What seemed to cause more anguish than she could handle was the swiftness with which Tolomeo's world began to fade from her consciousness.

She clutched her breasts as if this movement might help to abate the pounding heartbeats which took her breath away. Her dark eyes blinked hard and rapidly as she tried to wall up an avalanche of tears threatening to break through.

"Noooo," she whimpered softly. "I don't believe it. I'll remember all of it. All, do you hear? I will for all eternity—no matter what you do or how you try to deceive me! I shall never forget our love, regardless of your sorcery!" She was sobbing now, incredibly shaken.

Tolomeo stood before her in all his majesty, the same godlike warrior with a magnificently firm and muscular body; the same she'd loved and had been loved by. Staring at her, *muy dolor*—much sadness—was on the countenance of a leathery, wrinkled old man, skin the color of smoked walnut. Ageless perhaps, but obviously the face of a man in his eighties. Certainly he wasn't the man with whom she imagined herself helplessly in love—or was he?

She bent her head in abject humiliation and, turning from him, ran from this Edenic garden of her most sublimated dreams with the fleet-footedness of a

535

gazelle. Even as she ran, she began to assimilate a comprehension of things that moments before seemed insoluble.

At the village she searched for Tula. Locating her at the well, Madelaina, in a gesture of love, removed the golden locket from around her neck, a gift from Peter Duprez, and placed it around the young girl's neck. The girl shrank away from her in fright. She shook her head, removed the obscenity from her person. Only then did Madelaina recall the Indian superstition that gold brought ill and misfortune to Indians who had the misfortune to adorn themselves in it. "Forgive me, Tula. I only wanted you to have something of mine to remember me. It was just a gesture of our appreciation for your courtesy, your hospitality, and all you and Tolomeo have done for Paco and me. Take care of your master, Tula, there is none like him in the world."

Tula managed with sign language to assure Madelaina that it wasn't necessary to thank them, that she appreciated the gesture of the locket. She removed a leather tine from her buckskin shift and removed the silver flacon gripped tightly in Madelaina's hand, the gift from Tolomeo. Moving expertly, Tula made a slipknot for the flask and tied it around Madelaina's neck. She tucked the silver container between the girl's breasts.

Madelaina kissed the girl on the cheek and joined Paco and Lola, who'd seen the falling star earlier and awaited anxiously for Madelaina's arrival, so they could be on their way, with the overhead stars to guide them.

Paco spurred on the mules, and Madelaina, seated on one side of him, with Lola on the other, never looked back as they left the interior village.

Book Six

Hacienda de Sietas Lunas

Chapter 20

They traveled by day and they traveled by night, taking turns driving the cumbersome, creaking wagon along the back roads to Zacatecas. Their journey was painfully slow, unbearably hard on them. Two weeks of constant stop and go travel, avoiding the *Federales* and hiding to stay clear of marauding *bandidos,* whom they heard stood in readiness to pounce upon, rape, and rob any unsuspecting travelers, kept them from making as much time as they predicted they'd make traveling to the fort.

Madelaina had avoided thinking about the reunion she expected with her father; she dreaded it because her father wasn't a forgiving man. As they drew closer to the fort, however, she recalled what Tolomeo had taught her, and she began to draw on a reserve of energy and concentration to put her in the proper frame of detachment. She could feel a strength surge through her as she drew herself up in a reserved manner which would preclude apology for her past behavior to her father. For a time she was sustained.

Observing the trundling wagon with its three occupants approaching the fort, the soldiers on duty flung open the gates and they were permitted entrance. Odd, thought Madelaina, the atmosphere was as usual, as if they'd never been missed—as if they'd never been away. *Campesinas* milled in and about the main compound as usual, going about their business with sullen resignation and typical boredom.

Paco Jimenez recognized both the uniformed men at the gates who stood now with rifles at the ready, demanding to see their papers. He saluted them briskly, tossed the reins to Madelaina and jumped off the wagon, against her protestation. She continued forward, glancing back over her shoulders to see the men slapping each other on the shoulders as thick dust particles exploded from Paco's jacket. The astonishment was apparent on their faces. Long ago they had assumed Corporal Jimenez to be dead. It was like seeing his ghost.

Madelaina pointed out the barracks to Lola. "This is where Paco will stay. The last building is where my father is housed. If you wish, you may stay in my *casa* with Concepción."

"Whatever is your wish, *señorita*," replied the wide-eyed mestiza who was still trying to handle what Paco had told her about Madelaina. Imagine, she was the daughter of the illustrious General Alvaro Obregon.

"It would go to know the status of the revolution," she said, gazing about. "*Dios mios*, it is strange for Lola to be walking among the *Federales* without fearing for her life," she admitted, glancing apprehensively here and there at the soldiers moving about in their duties.

"You need have no fear as long as you're with me," said Madelaina, reining the burros a few feet before the general's quarters.

Before the wagon came to a full stop, Paco had caught up with them. He was out of breath and filled with a peculiar ebullience. His dark eyes darted about the compound as if he might be looking for someone special. Catching the expression on his face, and knowing that look well, Madelaina spoke up sternly. "It's best you prepare yourself for the ordeal ahead, Corporal, and not go looking for trouble. You've had enough to last a lifetime, no?"

Lola's blue eyes gazed from one to the other, unable to fathom what they were silently sparring over. Both Paco and Madelaina knew he was looking for Dolores Chavez. The guilt of this knowledge brought a flush to Paco's face. He stood up straight, braced himself, and nodded affirmatively. "It's best I prepare myself, wash, and put on a clean uniform before I meet General Obregon."

"*Si*, Paco. It's best. And let no one or anything deter you."

"*Si, señorita*. No one. Nothing." He saluted her and turned to Lola. "Woman, come with me to my quarters." He paused a moment. "What if there are no quarters for Paco? They think me to be dead?" He frowned noticeably.

"Then, find Concepción. She'll attend to you."

"And if Concepción is no longer in Zacatecas? You know how long we've been absent from the fort?"

"I know. Now, stop this. Find someone who can instruct you. If you are unsuccessful, come to my quarters. *Ondolay, pronto*."

"Habit, *señorita*. I am here not five minutes and already I am a soldier again." He smiled sheepishly and helped Lola down from the wagon.

Madelaina watched them walking hand in hand along the dirt path. Here and there, faces turned toward them with expressions of interest as they beheld the stunning beauty of the blue-eyed Lola. Both men and women appreciated such beauty.

She took in a deep breath and all the old familiar odors of spicy foods and tacos and animal excrement and the raw smells of the wilderness brought back instant recall of this place. No more stalling, she told herself. Get yourself inside and face the general. She turned and walked the few steps to her old cottage. She knocked on the door. There was no sound. She opened the door and entered the shadowy room. The blinds had been drawn, admitting no sunlight.

For an instant, she waited for her eyes to grow accustomed to the dimness. She gave a start and stopped in her tracks when she saw the sprawled figure of a woman lying on the bed in which she'd slept most her life. Sensing the presence of another person, the woman in bed sat up abruptly.

Madelaina's dark eyes narrowed to slits, her hand

541

fingered the knife in a sheath at her waist as fires of vengeance stoked her memory.

"What are you doing here?" demanded Madelaina in a cold, hard voice.

The woman blinked her eyes and gave her an amazed look that turned into one of icy contempt. Even as she stood there, the Indian was stunning, so sure of herself. Her vivid Yaqui coloring in that nude lace negligee gave her the look of sun-kissed goddess, thought Madelaina, fighting for control.

"What are *you* doing here?" asked Golden Dawn arrogantly. Her face grew pale, and she drew up the covers close to her.

A strange thing happened to Madelaina. The voice of Tolomeo came at her as clearly and distinctly as if he had been in the room with her. *Forgive her. Forgive her and radiate divine love to Golden Dawn, and she'll no longer possess power over you!* Madelaina struggled against the voice of Tolomeo as if she did mortal combat in an arena with a gladiator of inestimable strength. In those split seconds the formidable feat of strength was tried as forces combated each other.

"How dare you return to the camp of your father?" screeched Golden Dawn. "You traitor! Whore! You'd better leave before the general himself takes measures to liquidate you. It appears you've escaped my clutches, whore, but I assure you what the general has in store for you will not promote your freedom to further humiliate him." As she spoke, Golden Dawn tried to call upon her sorcery to seduce Madelaina's mind.

It was a peculiar sensation for Madelaina to experience. She heard the soft rustle of leaves and a fragrance, one she wasn't familiar with, engulfed her. The wind created a pressure in her ears. It seemed as though the sun had burst into a million fragments behind Golden Dawn. Then, as it slowly rolled around the room, it gathered up all the fragments and formed a fiery ball which remained in the corner of the room like a round spotlight casting its rays on a spot before her.

Forgive her. Forgive her. Remove the hatred from your heart. Say to yourself, she has no power over me. I am unaffected by their deeds. Set her free. Set her free. Absolve her of all sins and crimes against you. The chains that bind you are the chains that will free you. Cut them loose! Madeliana, Golden Dawn is powerless over you when you are filled with divine love! Forgive your enemies in your heart and you'll never see in them an enemy!

Before her eyes, Navojolla, the jaguar, materialized. As quickly as it appeared, it vanished. The sound of dry twigs snapping repeated itself. The sound of rifles cracking in rapid-fire shots sounded. All the unusual sounds came and left like a distant echo. Madelaina stood her ground as the internal strength of Tolomeo manifested itself in her body and mind. Her hand fell from the sheath. When her normal vision returned, she saw Golden Dawn standing before her, a pitiful figure, drenched to the skin with perspiration, fatigue lines etched into her face. Confusion at her lack of power left her disoriented and frightened.

For Madelaina, the incongruity of that moment was her reaction to the phenomenon: Instead of being terrified or moved to violence, she was laughing as if a ten-ton weight had been removed from her shoulders, and she found the entire thing hilarious. The feeling of elation that struck her was like nothing she'd experienced.

Golden Dawn's reaction was an instantaneous loss of her usual aloofness and objectivity. She had unquestionably lost her confidence. Her dark eyes, filled with fright and indecision, darted about the room, looking for something in which she could trust. She appeared to have been seized with stomach cramps. Doubling over, she rolled onto the bed, her knees drawn up tight to her chest. Her face was contorted with the most indescribable expression of half-animal, half-human grotesqueness, as the sounds of flapping wings sounded dangerously close in the room. They weren't loud or intense, but soft and insidious, producing spasms of alarm in Golden Dawn. They stopped as quickly as they had begun, slowly and gradually diminishing until they could no longer be heard.

Madelaina heard something like the swift flight of an eagle outside on the roof of the building. She ran to the window and glanced up into the fiery blue skies. Overhead a flock of giant birds soared and wheeled arcs, then took off to the south.

She quickly flung open the door and went outside to gaze into the distance. Shading her eyes from the hot sun, she peered into empty skies. Madelaina felt a tightness in the muscles of her stomach. She remembered the silver flacon Tolomeo had given her and the instructions he'd given her as to its use. She removed it from around her neck, pulled up her peasant blouse, tilted the flask, and in a second rubbed the powder onto the area of her navel.

She took several deep breaths, and soon she felt a warmth pervade her body with an energy somewhat strange to her, yet familiar enough to be a part of her. Almost as if in a daze, she returned inside.

Golden Dawn lay sprawled out on the bed, arms outstretched, legs dangling over the side, her pale face covered with moisture, quite dead.

Madelaina was unmoved by what she saw—as if it were an everyday occurrence. She walked slowly to the office of her father, General Obregon, only to be told he was on maneuvers. Concepción, it seemed, hadn't been in Zacatecas for many months. Dolores Chavez was no place to be found. Word among the *campesinas* had it she simply disappeared one day, never to be seen again. No doubt the skullduggery of Golden Dawn, she thought.

She spoke with Lieutenant Guiterrez, who was acting C.O. in her father's absence. She explained about Paco. Left a letter with him to give to the general, suggesting Paco be given a commendation for his bravery. She posted a letter to President Madero, suggesting the same thing, just in case her father remained too bitter to be forgiving. One thing was certain: Alvaro Obregon was a true military man. He would always act upon orders. He wasn't as canny and unpredictable as was General Huerta or Major Salomon. At least he had this much in his favor.

Madelaina said her farewells to Paco and to Lola, explaining what she'd done on their behalf, and took her leave, without mentioning Golden Dawn to them.

When at last she arrived in Cuernavaca, she was almost grateful to be in familiar surroundings. She rested for nearly two weeks, babied and fawned over by her old servants, who fed her well and made certain she put a "few pounds of flesh on those scarecrow bones." Her father, it seemed, hadn't been home in nearly five months. He was on active army duty in Sonora, she was told.

It was while she was in Cuernavaca that she learned the status of the revolution. And it was there that she first heard the stunning news that Pancho Villa had been ordered to face a firing squad by General Huerta. That he was subjected to such an atrocity was simply incredible to her. When she and Raoul Madero interceded on Pancho's behalf, directly to President Madero, he stopped the execution just as the soldiers leveled their rifles at the man who had commanded thousands of guerrilla bands. But then she was further appalled that the *presidente* immediately transferred Pancho Villa to the Federal Penitentiary in Mexico City for disobedience, insubordination, and robbery! Why Francesco Madero didn't dismiss the absurd charges against Pancho and censure that vile General Huerta for attempting to execute Villa on his own was too much for her politically inept mind to grasp.

The confusion of alternating facts and opposing loyalties and a leader who was too blinded by his office to see the true loyalties kept her confounded and withdrawn. She hadn't bothered to call upon any of her old friends.

It was on this day in early May that Madelaina sat hunched over in the floral courtyard at her father's hacienda. She contemplated the deplorable state of affairs, over which she had no control, and her own recent experiences, wondering what it all meant and where it would lead her. The sound of voices coming from inside the villa and the clicking of leather heels on the floor tiles attracted her attention and she turned toward the door.

Instantly her face lit up with radiant smiles. "Felipe!" she cried out in genuine affection. She sprang to her feet, denouncing custom and protocol, and dashed madly across the courtyard, dressed in a bright blue batiste dress drawn in tight at the waist and worn over full floor-length crinolines, which didn't encumber her movements.

They hugged and kissed, and he whirled her about in a circle. Finally he held her at arm's length and searched her face. "Madelaina. Oh, my dear Madelaina, how I've worried about you."

"Oh, my dearest Felipe," she said huskily as tears fell freely on her rosy cheeks. "Truly, I never believed we'd see each other again."

"Where, Madelaina? Where in God's name have you been this time?" he asked with open concern. "Are you still in some kind of trouble? What has happened? If you only knew how out of my mind I've been over your disappearance. I—I thought. Well, when we didn't hear, we thought the worst. That you were dead." He sat down on the sofa with her and watched the servants bring him refreshments. Iced tea and small cakes.

"How did you know I was here?" she asked wondrously.

"I didn't. I stopped only for word of your father. And Doña Louisa with tears in her eyes told me you have been here for a few weeks. Why didn't you let me know?" he asked grimly. "You could have let me know, Madelaina." Now he was stern.

She took his hands in hers. "Don't be angry with me. Perhaps when I tell you where I was, you won't want to hear. I half-hoped my father would be here so that I could tell you both. I missed him in Zacatecas, and here, also. But I'll tell you, Felipe. Pray that one day, if I'm not here to narrate the story, you'll do it for me." With this, after she poured their tea, she took him back over the rocky, perilous, frightening road her life had traversed since they last saw each other.

At first, Felipe listened attentively, politely, and with reserve to the story. Soon he showed marked agitation and incredible disbelief as she recounted her experiences at Madrigal de Los Altos. The knuckles on his tightly clenched fists rose like white mounds on his tanned, veined hands.

"Salomon! That devil!" he hissed with venom. "And Huerta! That vile animal ordered such treatment to the daughter of General Obregon?"

She quieted him and continued the story. She told him of their escape, of the boy Lazaro, of the records she'd stolen, and how her father had been cheated over the years. She mentioned she'd met Zapata and once again described her encounter with Major Salomon. How she owed her life to Paco Jimenez, the man her father sent to Madrigal for having coupled with her.

Felipe winced once or twice at the mention of the sexual atrocities, but to learn she'd been a willing partner for Jimenez ruffled his feathers somewhat.

She ignored his reaction and continued with her story. She mentioned how General Lomas had completely fooled her in his role of a small landowner. And how grateful she was to have been reunited with her husband, Peter Duprez.

When she explained she was still in love with her husband, Felipe's hurt and sorrowful eyes struck her like a stab wound to her heart.

"I must be honest with you, Felipe. I love Peter. I'd be deceitful to deny it." She saw the worry lines across his handsome face deepen as she admitted to this love, and reaching up to his face, she stroked it gently. "I'd give anything, if it could have been you, Felipe. But since I am not at the rudder to steer my life in the way I decree—" She paused, forming the words in her mind. "I am at the mercy of destiny—" Once again she

547

paused, trying to stimulate her memory. "I'm sorry, Felipe, I can't seem to think. I seem confused."

"After what you've been through, is it any wonder? Word reached me that you interceded for Pancho Villa, that you approached President Madero on the *guerrillo*'s behalf. Haven't you learned yet?"

With full composure, Madelaina took time to explain. "Mind you, I'm not defending my actions or attempting to justify them. I went to Madero for several reasons. First, the thought that Pancho Villa was to be executed by that contemptible Huerta galled me. Moreover, that the *presidente* permitted Huerta such license was something I wished to speak of to his face. Mark my words, Felipe, Madero gives Huerta too much power. I couldn't believe that Madero would permit the man who handed him the presidency to be executed by a firing squad! Madero is blind—blind—blind! Can't he see that Huerta is afraid of Villa? That he plans to slay Villa because the *guerrillo* stands between him and the presidency?"

"Huerta aims for the presidency—the throne in the palace?" Felipe seemed amazed. "I've heard no such rumors, *querida*."

"You think such a man announces his plans openly while the man he intends to slay sits on the throne? Hah! He's much more clever than that!" she exploded angrily.

Felipe poured himself a cognac from the sideboard and gulped it down. "Didn't I warn you Madero would be no better than Diaz and probably far worse? Francesco Madero abandoned Villa. Isn't that proof enough of the treacheries in high office? Do you still pursue dreams of being a revolutionist, *querida*? Now Madero is in office and another revolution has begun—not the real revolution, mind you, but one between those political snakes who threaten to topple Madero. Won't you give up your rebellious thoughts?"

"I'm no longer a rebel, Felipe. Haven't you noticed? Do you not detect a change in me? I want only to find my husband, make peace with my father, and be left to

548

a life of my choosing. Many things I desire to do are not possible to accomplish here in Mexico. I plan to reside in America where the morals of the past aren't carried over into the future. When moralities imposed upon a nation prevent their progress then something is wrong. The lack of progress breeds stagnation. It is this stagnation that defeats us and permits our oppressors to enslave us. And, *querido,* the stink of it all rises like a nauseous poison that slays us a little at a time, even as we continue to hold our noses and inquire, 'What is it that smells so fetid?' We, none of us, can breathe with such a stench of rotten politics, but nothing is done to eliminate the corruption or the men who prostitute our lives."

"Marry me," said Felipe passionately and compulsively. "Marry me and we'll both go north to make our home. I'll do what you desire, Madelaina. Anything you want. If you don't let me take care of you, I fear for what will happen to you."

His quiet presence, although welcome and calming, wasn't the consolation her soul yearned for. She couldn't help that she loved Peter. Over the last few days, thoughts of him hung heavy about her. She hadn't heard of him or from him since they left Parral. She vaguely recalled the strange dreams she had of him and all that had happened when she'd been under the influence of Golden Dawn, and once or twice she had the frightening feeling that he was in trouble. Where could she begin to find him? Even in their quiet moments he'd told her very little about himself. Something about owning a parcel of land near San Antonio, that he was often in El Paso—but never anything definite.

"Madelaina?"

She turned to Felipe. "I'm sorry. My mind wandered a bit," she apologized. She wanted to tell Felipe more, but her lips wouldn't articulate the words forming in her mind. "Perhaps another time you'll ride to Cuernavaca and I'll tell you more," she told him. She brushed her forehead with a gesture of forgetfulness. "I

549

guess I'm more fatigued than I permit myself to think. Will you forgive me, sweet Felipe?"

"Don't think for a moment that I'll rest until I've brought General Huerta up on charges, *querida*. And that Salomon! He'll get his just desserts, believe me."

She nodded quietly and stood up to walk him to the door. They embraced as friends, and she watched him mount his stallion and ride off with an escort of six soldiers dressed in the uniforms of the Constitutionalist Army. At last Mexico had uniforms of her own design. But, the diehards, the army regulars still clung to their German- and French-influenced uniforms.

Felipe hadn't been gone two hours, when Madelaina arose from her meditation, went to her room, and packed a few belongings. Without preamble or much forethought, she had decided to go to El Paso. Madelaina hadn't really consciously willed herself to go north. In her meditation, she saw herself in a city in Texas which she presumed to be El Paso. Continuous flashes in her consciousness kept coming at her, similar to the psychic awareness she had experienced in the land of Tolomeo, in which Peter had been depicted in some sort of distress. Moreover, she kept seeing Manuelito Perez as she had in a disastrous encounter with the bulls in the Plaza de Toros. These visions prompted her to pack and prepare to travel north. She didn't recall making a decision to leave. She was following some deep silent voice within her that guided her.

From Mexico City she took the train to Chihuahua. In the capital city of that county, she suddenly decided to travel the rest of the distance to Juarez by coach. The uneventful trip grew wearisome, and she questioned her sanity for changing her mode of travel. It was insanely hot, the desert unbearably stifling. Her clothing, warm enough for Mexico City at this time of year, was all wrong for the desert. Her only consolation was having the coach to herself. Most sane people rode the train. What an idiotic sense of timing, she thought. Too ridiculous, she told herself as she bounced unceremoniously in the creaking, swaying coach that never failed to make her nauseous.

She felt the momentum of the coach pick up speed, heard the crackling sounds of the whips whistling over the six team horses as the driver poured forth his energy to yell out a warning. *"Bandidos! Bandidos!"*

The words were loud and clear and perfectly understandable. *Bandidos!* As her body pitched and tossed and jostled about the carriage, Madelaina attempted to move forward in her seat to see out the window. In the distance she saw clouds of dust. Damn their impatience! More delays now. She wasn't frightened, only annoyed and a bit curious. Why would bandits choose to stop a mere stage carrying only a lone passenger? How did they dare maneuver so close to the gringo border? Madelaina was about to learn why the stagecoach carried no other passengers; it carried a large gold shipment which someone intended to intercept. Of course, she knew nothing of this for the moment.

Her thoughts were interrupted as she was flung bodily to the opposite side of the coach when the driver braked the coach. The sudden stop caused the vehicle to shake and shudder and come to a skidding halt against the snorting protests of the six team horses. Outside, Madelaina could hear the loud "Yahoos" and "Yippies" and the triumphant cries of savage barbarians. The coach door was flung open before she could pull herself up from the floor boards, and she was rudely hustled outside by two of the dirtiest, fiercest ruffians she'd ever seen.

"Ah, such a desirable gringa wench!" these hillsmen told each other in their native tongue. They touched their sombreros with a mocking salute and eyed her with sheer animal lust. They were both covered with soot and desert dust, wearing the remains of what she identified as piecemeal khaki uniforms of the revolutionaries. Each man wore no less than four—even five—ammo belts strapped to his person wherever room could be made for them. Low-slung gun holsters over each hip toted six-shooters.

Madelaina pulled herself up from where she'd fallen in the dirt. In an imperious manner, she dusted off her travel costume and deliberately avoided eye contact with either brute. Her eyes skirted past them to the six men who unloaded a heavy metal chest and to those who stood with rifles at the ready, watching the operation and for the approach of any obstructors. Twelve men in all.

Before she knew what happened, sudden movement near the driver's seat brought forth a blast of rifle shots, and both the driver and his assistant, who made the stupid blunder of trying for their shotguns, fell back with a loud scream to the ground, their bodies bleeding from the volley of rifle fire that tore them up. Their fate evoked a round of laughter from the diabolical and terrifying hillsmen.

"Consider yourself *muy tardes*—very lucky," said the man called Ruiz. "One false move and you join your friends, woman," said the largest and dirtiest of the two as he sipped tequila from a canteen and wiped his drooling lips on the back of his shirt sleeve. "You gonna come quietly with me, woman?"

"Move!" called a man on horseback to the six men struggling under the weight of the metal boxes. "Hurry with that gold. *Vamenos! Ondolay! Ondolay!* You hear me? *Vamenos pronto!*" He called out loudly, shooting his pistol in the air overhead. The sweating men moved a beat faster as they loaded the containers of gold into the flat buckboard waiting a few feet from them.

"Hey, *muchacho*?" called Madelaina's captor. "What we do with thees gringa, eh? Ees little time for me to fuck her, no?"

Madelaina decided to use a ploy she once used to save her from such a fate. "Ees plenty time, *muchacho*, especially if you want wan beeg surprise to grow in your projectile," she said with obvious innuendo, alluding to the dreaded disease gonorrhea. "Now tell me *hombre*, who is your leader?"

Ruiz stared at her with open-mouthed astonishment at first, then, with narrowed eyes, he sluffed off her first remark. "Hey, *muchachos,* the gringa speaks with the accent of a Sonoran!" He laughed raucously and sipped more tequila to clear the dust from his throat. As he did, he moved slowly away from her. He'd let the others find out for themselves as was the usual custom, then later he could laugh about it and unmercifully tease the man who became diseased. Madelaina knew their habits and idiosyncrasies well.

The predatory lights she saw flickering brightly in the eyes of these hill bandits intimidated her for a moment or two. Finally, when no one responded to her inquiry, she spoke with an Indian dialect as she'd learned to do as a *campesina.* With her hands on her hips, she demanded to be taken to their leader. She didn't doubt for one minute that all twelve of the men, some of the fiercest, vilest, and most scurrilous dogs she'd ever seen, were about to rape her and rob her of all her possessions, diseased or not.

She let loose a string of expletives and phrases she'd learned and demanded to be heard as one of them. She mentioned Pancho Villa, but not the fact that she was Little Fox, because she didn't know these men. For all she knew they could have been counterrevolutionaries. If so, she'd certainly be killed in a most undesirable manner, but only after they tortured her bestially.

It was obvious from the expressions on the faces of the men they'd been startled by Madelaina's command of the vernacular. Her attitude of fearlessness stayed them off. They weren't used to being sparred with—not by a woman.

A few of the men conferred in excited tones as the men on detail moved the gold from under the floor boards of the coach onto a buckboard, sturdy enough to transport the precious commodity. When they had finished, the men were ordered to return to their camp.

Standing in the dust, averting her head to keep it from smarting her eyes, Madelaina stood in a field of uncertainty. Suddenly, a rider galloping toward her swept her up in his arms onto the rear of his saddle and followed the other bandits into the hills. The stench of the rider nearly knocked her out, but Madelaina had no recourse but to hold on to his waist for dear life as he spurred the horse into an open gallop. In the distance she recognized the Rio Bravo. They were close to Juarez, all right. But where, she wondered. Just when she felt she could no longer endure the hard ride, she caught sight of a scattering of camp followers through a wooded clearing near the river. She heaved a relieved sigh. Her body ached from the abuse given it these past twenty hours, first from the calamitous coach ride and now on this horse's rump behind the saddle. *Dios mios!*

She was unceremoniously hurled from the saddle and dumped with the other *campesinas* near the fires where the evening meals were being prepared. She shuddered as she gazed upon these women. Filthy, unkempt animals, all of them. The ways of a *campesina* were too well known to her. Still she wondered, had she allowed herself to fall into such disrepute when she was one of them? Had she looked as they looked to her now, when her father had her abducted and returned to Zacatecas? She forced the thoughts from her mind because she found herself suddenly sympathizing with General Obregon.

Despite the garments she wore, which destroyed the illusion she wanted to employ as being one of them, she assumed the swaggering walk and stance of the most outgoing. A hard-lined expression formed on her face as she picked herself up from the dust and stared back at the women as they stared at her.

If any of these savage women entertained thoughts of overtaking her and robbing her of her personal effects, the posture she assumed and the look in her dark eyes were enough to deter them. She found a place to sit down and did so, glancing about with ever-watchful vigilance. Curiously enough, she thought she recognized some of the women. Closer examination of their dirty faces convinced her some of these were followers of Pancho Villa.

An older woman, one with soul lacking in the

younger ones, approached her with a mug of black coffee in her dark brown hands. Madelaina gratefully accepted it, although she would have preferred ice cold water. Something of an alarming nature in the older woman's red-veined eyes was enough to cause a shiver to run down her spine. The woman's eyes seemed to spring from their sockets, but it was too late. Madelaina had been attacked from the rear.

Only pure instinct caused her to move in time to avoid the deep thrust of a narrow blade held menacingly in the hands of a shrewish-looking Indian half-breed. Madelaina immediately pulled up the side of her skirt and grabbed for the knife inside her boot. Since her very first indoctrination to the life of a *campesina*, she had never stopped carrying a knife in this fashion. Now, the contest was one to one.

The dark-skinned half-breed, with jet hair braided at each side of a center part, backed away to pace her moves. The other women backed off away from the action, huddling in a circle and watching with blood-thirsty eyes. It soon became obvious to all concerned that this woman in gringa clothing knew how to handle herself. She heard the warnings shouted to the girl called Isabel—her opponent.

"Ayeiii, *cuidado*—be careful, Isabel—this is no usual gringa!"

"*Ala chingada!*" cursed Madelaina in Indian dialect. "Come and get me, you unspeakable obscenity! Daughter of a whore's whore!"

The women circled each other. Isabel, the *puta* of the man who had ridden her into camp, mistook her for keen competition. She meant to cut out Madelaina's heart. Spurred on by the cries of her companions, Isabel was moved to demonstrate her agility with a knife. She wouldn't be shamed by this tramp masquerading as a fine lady. She lunged forward in an unexpected move and pierced Madelaina's arm, drawing blood. Madelaina glanced from the warm blood oozing down her arm to the girl's hate-filled eyes and she blinked hard. Inside, she heard a faint voice stirring her into what she consciously might label an act of stupidity. Nevertheless, as the girl readied herself for another attack, Madelaina, against her will and letting go her earlier resolve to teach the half-breed some respect as well as manners, pulled herself up out of a crouch position and dropped her hands to her side. The knife relaxed limply in her palm in what appeared a gesture of submission.

"They call me Zorrita," she said loud enough for all to hear.

Unfortunately, her timing was off by a hair. Isabel, filled with the venom of jealousy and hatred, didn't hear what the others heard. As a hush swept over the crowd of women, Isabel moved quickly and plunged the knife into Madelaina's left shoulder.

In that instant the name Zorrita registered in the half-breed's mind. She fell back against the others, a look of alarm on her dark face, coupled with fright over the consequences of her enraged act.

Little Fox staggered backward, and caught by several women, she was laid gently on a stack of blankets as Isabel fled through the crowd like a frightened hare running from the hounds.

The women sat in awe-filled silence as they watched Madelaina grasp the the knife buried in her shoulder with the hand of her right, injured arm. Bracing herself for an instant, she paused to gather her strength and then swiftly extracted the knife from her body. She tore the ruffling from her petticoat, and gathering it in her free hand, she lay the thickness against the blood oozing from the wound. One by one, the woman offered to help her. They insisted she lay back quietly and allow them to dress her wounds. They were experts at such duties after all the wars their men had fought, they told her. She, above all, should know of their expertise.

Madelaina reluctantly gave in. She knew of their expertise, all right, but she also knew more men died from the infections that developed as a result of unsterile conditions than from the bullet and knife wounds themselves.

The women insisted they recognized Little Fox, although she didn't look as robust and fiesty as the gutsy *campesina* they remembered. She was some scarecrow now, twenty pounds lighter. The courage she demonstrated by dropping her knife against one of their kind was whispered about the camp.

Luz Lopez, the old woman who had tried to warn of Isabel's treachery, watched over Madelaina for the next three days as a raging fever engulfed her body. The application of countless green leaves and herbs to the infection was to no avail. On the night of the third day, during a moment of clarity, Madelaina recalled the silver flacon given to her by Tolomeo.

She felt between her breasts and, with all the effort she could muster, she lifted the silver flask and weakly signaled to Luz Lopez. "Please, *por favor, señora*. Be kind enough to rub this powder in the area of my umbilical cord."

Nodding, the woman called Luz reached for the flask and stared suspiciously at the unusual carvings on the outside. Her eyes moved from the girl's face to the horrible infection on her body. She'd seen knife wounds before, but, *Madre de Dios*, that Isabel must have dipped her blade into a pot of poison before sticking Little Fox. This was one terrible infection. Her experienced eyes told her the girl wouldn't last the night.

What would it hurt to grant Little Fox a last dying wish, eh? Later, she'd keep the silver flask and the fine clothing as mementoes for the others to grow jealous over. The silver flask was that beautiful!

Behind Luz, several other women, respectful in the presence of death's avenging angels, crossed themselves and muttered silent prayers. They came to gaze upon the face of the legendary Little Fox, who had aided and befriended Pancho Villa. She was one of them, this pale-faced *gachupín*, and they knew it. *Pues*, that stupid, blundering Isabel would surely reap the fruits of that day's bitter labor. When their *jefe* returned to camp and learned of this monstrous attack upon Little Fox, she was as good as dead.

The black angels of death were hovering over Little

Fox, fighting for her soul, insisted the old woman, Luz Lopez, who was herself a *curandera*—a healer. If anyone could save her, it was Luz Lopez. But the old woman shook her head sadly, signaling the others that Little Fox was lost to them.

Their *jefe,* Tomàs Urbina, who had led the clan of *Villistas* since their beloved puma was hustled from the swift injustice of a firing squad to the Federal prison in Mexico City, had been out raising hell some place since they successfully intercepted the gold shipment. It would be up to Urbina to get word to Pancho, who sat rotting in the Federal prison. Poor Panchito, to hear such news while he is so helpless would be too much to bear, no?

The old crones gathered around the campfire to watch Madelaina's life flow from her body. They saw the old *curandera,* Luz Lopez, loosen the girl's skirt and pull up her blouse. What is that old fool up to now, they wondered. The woman must be soft in the head. Little Fox's wound is in the shoulder—not her stomach. Blind fool! Toothless old hag! Blind as a scarecrow at that. The sun must have fried her brains— or else she's on the last legs of her journey also.

Luz leaned in close to Madelaina's parched, pale lips, listening carefully to the words she whispered. Luz Lopez, with whiskers of age on her yellow-skinned chin, smacked her lips together, nodding in understanding. *Que va*—understand? She understood none of this, but she would comply with the dying woman's request. She proceeded to rub the area of Madelaina's navel with the powder from the flask. As expected, the area turned black from the ashy residue. Earlier, when Luz inspected the feet and ankles of Little Fox, she noticed a purple hue creeping up from the toes; now at midcalf, Luz calculated her death would take place at a little after sundown.

The women watched in total absorption.

"What are you doing, Luz Lopez?" they asked in mocking tones, careful lest the angels of death hear them and take vengeance upon them.

Luz, short for Luzmilla, grew annoyed at their constant harassment.

"Be silent, you hags of the desert. Your cackling voices sound as drums for the soldiers of Lucifer. If you don't remain silent, they'll descend upon you and scatter you into the fiery furnaces of hell!"

"But, pray, tell us what you are doing," they insisted. "We've never seen you perform this ritual. Is it something new? Where did you learn such black magic, eh?"

"Shut up!" she snapped. "Don't make fools of yourselves and I'll not make a fool of myself by talking with people who have no understanding. I am performing the last wishes of a dying woman. Are you blind?" She capped the silver flask and was about to slip it into her skirt, but too many were watching her. There'd be time later to remove it from the girl. She replaced it around the girl's neck, lifting her head as she draped the fine chain around it, then laying it carefully upon the blanket. She rubbed her hairy mole-dotted hands together.

Not five minutes passed before Madelaina began to stir. For three days she'd lapsed from consciousness into unconsciousness, recalling little of what happened. There were moments of lucidity in which the face of Tolomeo came to her as if in reprimand, telling her she hadn't abided by the precepts she'd learned. *The more knowledge you amass, the more you're responsible for*, he kept repeating. *Draw on your strength. Command your inner resources to do your bidding. The outer picture is unreal—like Lago Diablo was unreal. Only the mind is power—real power that can command life or death.*

Madelaina's face broke into pools of perspiration. Her eyes snapped open, and blinking hard for several seconds, she attempted to orient herself. Her pale skin flushed with sudden color as circulation was restored to her body. She moved noticeably, and the old woman, Luz, moved in to help her sit up. She reached for a gourd filled with water and lifted the vessel to the girl's lips for her to sip. When she finished, Luz set the gourd aside and continued to rub her hands as if she could feel the residue left by the substance she had rubbed onto Madelaina's navel. She rubbed them on the folds of her skirt with much annoyance, then casually glanced at them. Holding her hands out before her palms down, she stared at them. She turned them over and over in total absorption.

Noticing her interest in her hands, the other women leaned in and stared in astonishment, which changed rapidly into superstitious awe, as the hairs and moles seemed to disappear from Luz's hands. It was not to be believed!

They were so caught up in Luz's hands that very few, including Luz, herself, noticed that Madelaina sat up unassisted, seemingly awakening from a lengthy sleep. She yawned and stretched and scrambled to her feet, favoring her wounded shoulder. The women gasped and drew back, huddling together like frightened sheep. *Dios mios*! This woman had defied the black angels of death!

"Luzmilla! See this! What has happened? A miracle for sure. Ahhhh—and why not?" They murmured amongst themselves. Wasn't this Little Fox? The woman who assisted their benefactor and leader, Pancho Villa? It's true—the stories they tell, she must be enchanted. But see what has happened to Luz's ugly old hands! What miracle is this? Touching Little Fox, medicating her, has passed on the magic to Luzmilla Lopez.

"*Ridiculous*," said some.

"No," said the others. "*Incredible!*"

Some feet away from this bustling activity, turning slowly as he listened to his men, the wicked, perennially grinning Tomàs Urbina tried to pierce the crowd of woman hovering around Madelaina. He wore his usual *charro* pants with leggings, shirt with kerchief around his neck, double bandoliers, and double-holstered guns with a floppy sombrero flung to the back of his head.

"Little Fox, eh? Who gave you this manure to swallow?" he asked his men, when they reported the events of the previous days.

"She did. Besides, she's been raving in fever. Luz Lopez declares for sure it is Little Fox. The women who saw her before are mixed up. She's skinny—no meat on her bones like before. Now you're here, *Jefe*. You will tell us for sure. Oh boy! That Isabel is so scared, she's hiding from her man."

"*Si*, eh?" Urbina flung down his cigar. "We shall see," he said, certain the stranger must be a fraud. He had seen Little Fox in Parral. She'd been sent south with the others. By now, she must be with her gringo husband, Tom Mix, he reminded himself.

In Villa's absence, Urbina was next in command. He moved where he could, but he didn't live and breathe the revolution as Pancho did. Urbina enjoyed life— took as much as he could, exploited every rebel, and provided for a future day when the pickings would be lean. The sound of his thickly rawled spurs drew instant attention, and the women parted to make room for him as he passed among them. It was evident they thought little of this larcenous man and his petty thievery, but still in Villa's absence he was acting *jefe* and was accorded respect.

One look at Madelaina and Urbina not only recognized her, but he filled with wrath and violent anger, knowing full well what would have happened to him if harm had befallen the girl while in his camp. He raged and ranted like a madman, making profuse apologies to the girl in one breath, demanding the life of Isabel in retribution the next.

"Ayeiii, *señorita*," he moaned, lowering his shame-filled eyes to the ground. "If Panchito hears about this disgraceful act, I shall be banned forever from his sight." He couldn't apologize enough. Despite Madelaina's protestations that since she was fine, she desired no harm to befall the girl Isabel, *Jefe* Urbina shook his head. "No. I cannot grant your request. The girl must be punished. And to make it just, it shall be her man who does the whipping."

"And I say no!" shouted Madelaina defiantly. "No. There is enough animalistic behavior among the people. It must cease before there is any hope for the *peón*—you understand?"

Urbina, given to explosions of laughter, especially when he lacked understanding of a subject, grinned obsequiously, nodding his head in assent.

"At your command, Zorrita," he said helplessly.

"Then give me escort to Juarez at once."

"Si, señorita," he replied in complete accord.

While they waited for horses to be saddled up, she told Urbina that Pancho Villa was presently doing time in the Federal Penitentiary at Mexico City. News of such importance traveled fast and Urbina had already heard.

"With *Maderistas* defecting to the right and left of us, Zorrita, there is only one man who can save Madero—and he lets him cool his *culjiones* in prison! All the work Panchito did is gone—it has turned into manure, *señorita*. Pure manure! What good does it do to tell Pancho Madero was a weak man? He will be squashed like the *cucarachas*—you'll see. And you know who'll be the next *presidente*, Little Fox? Huerta! That's who! Huerta! And you know who stands behind *him, señorita*?" Urbina grinned his diabolical, leering grin. "That sleek, well-fed cat in the fancy uniform, that panther who wears medals and gold braids—that General Alvaro Obregon! Already he's responded with his Fourth Sonora Battalion."

If Tomàs Urbina noticed the sudden paleness of the woman, the slight slump of her shoulders as Madelaina digested this piece of information, he gave no indication. The fact was he didn't know she was the daughter of that "sleek, well-fed cat" of whom he spoke.

A horse had been saddled for her, and Madelaina mounted it and fell in behind Urbina and the other escorts who were committed to seeing her safely to Juarez. On the ride back along the desert bed of the Rio Bravo, Madelaina considered this new and stunning information. News that her father had joined

562

forces with General Huerta had shattered her resolve. She wondered how Felipe would take this news. Now, *Dios mios,* there'll be no returning to Mexico as the daughter of General Alvaro Obregon. This one act, this unification with Vitoriano Huerta, had spoken so clearly what she felt all along in her heart. Her father was more ambitious than she credited him with being. They opposed Presidente Madero. Joining forces meant one thing—Madero would soon lose the strength of the *Federales.* With the army against the president, who would he have?

Apart from the obvious political coup intended by these plotting leopards, Madelaina knew in her heart that her father had disowned her. She no longer existed for him. Could she blame him, she asked herself. She had heaped his life with shame and humiliation, and even placed his own life in jeopardy for a time. The one man she really loved with all her being was now her bitterest enemy. Forever and for all time there could be no reconciliation. General Obregon must have known what General Huerta and Major Salomon had caused to happen to her and to Paco Jimenez at Madrigal. Yet, they'd joined forces.

Very well, Little Fox, she told herself. There was one avenue open to her. She would expel all thoughts of him from her mind, just as she'd have to do with her past. She'd break with the past and go forward, carve a new life for herself, a new future which would bring her security and comfort and provide what she desperately craved—the love and affection of a man who loved her desperately. If need be, she'd even forget Peter Duprez, she told herself with an air of secret detachment.

Her escorts left her a short distance from the city's gates, waving their sombreros into the air over their heads. Before their horses reared on their hind legs to gallop off to their refuge, Urbina told her to get in touch with him should she ever need his service. "Urbina is always close by, Little Fox."

Chapter 21

Two Months Later January, 1913

It was Sunday afternoon in El Paso, Texas. Madelaina Obregon strolled along the streets, admiring the fashions worn by the gringas. To her it seemed the entire city was in festival. She saw tourists with box cameras crowding the streets, pausing at intervals to photograph the colorful Mexicans who sold their wares in the vending stands in the old Chihuahua section of the city. Men on flat wagons cranked the wheels of motion picture cameras as they shot the various sights in and around the city.

El Paso, a curious city to her, was a mixture of contrasting architecture: newly constructed buildings standing side by side with rundown, old buildings humiliated in abject poverty. There were fine hotels, private homes, bawdy houses, and gaudy gambling palaces and saloons sprawled throughout the city, and a central depot for cattlemen eager to sell their herds to more anxious northern packing plant buyers. It was a rich town filled with excitement and danger, a carryover from the gay nineties atmosphere of New York and Chicago, much larger than life, but an unmistakable imitation of the eastern cities. The streets filled with Indians, Mexicans, half-breeds, foreigners, so-called American frontiersmen, plotters and planners, intriguing politicians, swashbuckling soldiers of fortune, and not least of all, cowboys toting six-guns and firing them whenever they chose. It was a melting pot—a typical border town despite the whitewashing and face scrubbing given it by the city fathers.

In some sections, the streets were still unpaved. The closer to Juarez one walked, the shabbier became the area. Still, the sun shined brightly in this thriving cattle town, which had already begun to display its carefully structured social levels. El Pasoans had erected a social barrier, an unwritten taboo against Mexicans which obstructed any integration of the two nationalities. Most of the wealth had been acquired by the early pioneers, who, without education or refinement, suddenly emerged as a loud, boisterous ruling class. They were rowdy, uncouth, ostentatious, and crude, conspicuously consuming all things material. Their manners offended Madelaina as she walked among them. Even a lowly *campesina* demonstrated better manners, she observed.

Madelaina had taken lodgings in a small boarding-house run by a quiet widow who, with excellent business acumen, rented to five boarders in all. Uncertain of what she would do with herself, Madelaina lived frugally. She had had enough money to take her through these last two months, but only that morning she discovered her funds were running low. She would have to find work. Uncertain of what kind of work a woman of her calibre could obtain, she had set out on this day to try and puzzle out this new development.

Madelaina had walked through the city streets before. Thrust suddenly among so many gringos, it was only natural she'd search the faces of every man for the one for whom she longed, Peter Duprez. Each time she'd see a man resembling Peter in stature, her step would quicken and she'd catch up to him, only to be disappointed at an unfamiliar face glancing at her in surprise.

She had to tell herself to stop playing such games or one day she'd find herself in trouble with one of those men who wanted to show more than affection for what they assumed was a mere pickup.

She entered deeper into Old Chihuahua. There weren't as many gringos here as there were closer to the main artery of El Paso. This section of town wasn't considered safe by the upper classes, and they kept their distance, unless they decided to come slumming, in which case they brought plenty of protection. Here, the night clubs, saloons, and gambling palaces were jammed together, with barkers standing before each establishment, hawking their specialties and trying to entice customers inside. Mexicans themselves crowded the narrow streets, making it difficult for Madelaina to pass. Mistaking her for a gringa, they harassed her to buy their wares. Little children begged coins from her. She had sewn her costume herself—a pale blue muslin, nipped at the waist over a corset, was caught with sprigs of matching flowers and fell with a panier drape to ankle length. Her high-buttoned shoes and straw hat piled high on her head were quite fashionable and American.

From time to time Madelaina would pause long enough to explain in Spanish that she was one of them and not to disturb her. Most would back off instantly, but others stared sullenly at her, disbelieving her appearance. She didn't have enough money left to be giving it away. Not now. She needed employment. What could she do? She had no skills, no training. Women could hardly find what was considered decent employment except as modistes, dressmaker's helpers, or flower venders begging on the streets.

With these thoughts, she skirted the crowds, picking up her skirts to avoid the dusty debris collecting on the paved areas, and hoping the unpaved paths wouldn't soil her costume. Shopkeepers selling baskets and countless straw items, artificial flowers, and pottery of all shapes and sizes, bargained with the gringo tourists in loud voices. It struck Madelaina as hilarious. The shopkeepers wished to sell and the buyers wished to buy, but they haggled over prices for so long, it seemed such a waste to her. The sellers could have made ten times more sales in that length of time if they'd kept their prices reasonable at the outset.

She continued on her way, her attention suddenly caught by the loud, commanding sounds of an elegant open carriage drawn by four matched bays and driven by a liveried servant, as it came bowling down the dirt street. A fleeting picture of a well-dressed woman with bright, flame-colored hair, brighter than a summer sunset, sped by her. The driver handled both horses and cabriolet with such well-practiced skill that Madelaina couldn't help but stare as the carriage came to a stop before a gambling palace called the Diamond Slipper.

When Madelaina reached the entrance of the spectacularly well-lit club, where elegantly dressed pages hawked the club's specialties, her eyes were drawn to a large billboard at one side of the doorway. Her eyes scanned the billing: *Un Guapa Apasionate*—An Exciting Woman of Great Beauty. *Danzanta Profesional*—A Professional Dancer of Extraordinary Skill. Madelaina couldn't take her eyes from the familiar face and scantily attired body pictured on the billboard. *La Gatitta!* The Sex Kitten!

Madelaina grinned noticeably, her eyes twinkling in amusement. She could feel the inner excitement of old returning to her. Taking a deep breath, she smoothed her skirt and pulled down her jacket. She patted a few wispy curls into place and tipped her hat jauntily. She glanced at her reflection in the window glass covering an array of glossy photographs of other entertainers, squared her shoulders, and entered the bawdy place where music rang loud and raspy over a tinny P.A. system. She plugged her ears defensively.

"Little Fox, is it really you? Are my eyes deceiving me. I cannot believe it! *Dios mios!* Such a rare pleasure!" Antonetta stared at her as if she were seeing an apparition. Finally she grabbed Madelaina and hugged her affectionately until she couldn't breathe. Then she held the general's daughter at arm's length, scanning the smart suit, the updo hairstyle, and broadbrimmed straw hat with nodding approval. "It's you! Chihuahua! Little Fox in the flesh!"

"Antonetta," cautioned Madelaina, drawing her friend into the shadows away from the crowd. "It's not wise to use that name. I am no longer Zorrita."

"What is wrong, child? You look pale. Have you eaten?" asked the former *campesina* of Pancho Villa, her red hair like pink fire. "Look, come into the office where we can talk like old friends, away from so many noisy people."

"The office? Will anyone mind if we are so bold?" asked Madelaina.

"Who is there to mind if Antonetta is the proprietor, eh, Zorrita?"

"Please," she repeated. "Don't call me Zorrita."

"What then?"

"Madelaina."

"*Muy bueno,* Madelaina," she muttered, ushering the girl to a room beyond the bustling barroom filled with laughing, talking men, shouting to be heard over the loud ethnic music.

They were followed by an enormous, brawny, red-necked bouncer named Ed, to whom Antonetta shouted, "Have a waiter bring in refreshments—food also."

She closed the door behind them and seated herself in the charming room done in early El Paso—whorehouse red with velvet sofas, gold tassles, and brassy appointments designed to look "classy."

The room contained two love seats facing each other over a mahogany table before a real fireplace. Marble-topped tables at the ends of the sofas held vases of bloodred roses. At the far end of the room, a large mahogany desk graced the corner with an overstuffed chair of red velvet behind it. A beautiful silk screen partition concealed a wardrobe of numerous exotic dancing costumes.

"Antonetta not only owns the Diamond Slipper, *querida,* she also stars in the shows and personally manages the business from this office," she told her amazed guest.

"I'm so happy for you to be so affluent, Antonetta," she told her friend with genuine pleasure. "It is some lifestyle, especially after seeing you with Pancho, as a *campesina.*"

"I thought I told you about myself," she began, frowning in thought.

"You did, but in truth, I am ashamed to say, I didn't believe you."

Antonetta laughed. "I can see why you wouldn't— not in those surroundings and those circumstances. But, what of you, *querida*? What happened to you? You disappeared from Pancho's camp so suddenly I was certain you had met with foul play."

"Ah, *sí*," replied Madelaina, recalling what happened after her father's men had abducted her from the desert of Mapimi. "You might say that is exactly what happened," she began, giving Antonetta a play-by-play description of those harrowing weeks. She explained about her subsequent encounter with Concepción Montoya, who turned out to be the sister of Pancho Villa. She elaborated on the story of President Diaz' ball and how with the aid of Concepción a message had been sent to Villa to attack Juarez.

"Aha! So that's how Pancho became such a hero, eh?" Antonetta laughed with good humor and patted her dazzling red hair into place. She lit up a cigarette, and puffing inordinate amounts of smoke, she waved her arms about the room.

"All this is mine, *chiquita*. I thank the sweet, sainted Jesus that I didn't give up all I had for that sweet-talking honey bee, Villa. The revolution was over before it began," she chattered on brightly. "And all because you convinced him to attack Juarez instead of Chihuahua!" She shook her head in amusement. "You see, it pays to put enough away for a rainy day. When Pancho returned to his home and family, Antonetta had no place to go, so she came to El Paso to her own home." She waved her hands about the room. "And family, meaning the customers in the outer rooms." She laughed again and poured the ice cold beer which the waiter had brought in moments before. "Drink, *chiquita*. Now, Panchito, lured from the hills, gives 'em hell once more, eh?" She sipped the beer, draining half of it in one tilt of the glass. "You see, Little Fox, how nothing changes."

"Please, Antonetta," urged Madelaina, "try to

remember Little Fox is no more. Forget about Zorrita. She is a thing of the past. Already that snake Huerta has made my life unbearable. I don't intend to give him a second opportunity. To make matters worse, Francesco Madero made him a general in the Constitutionalist Army!" she scoffed ironically.

"So then what is your concern? You make no sense, *chiquita*. If this snake Huerta is on the side of Madero, you are no longer enemies."

"No longer enemies, eh?" Madelaina hesitated. An inner urging tried to caution her. *Bless your enemies and they have no further power over you.* This new thinking was precisely that—new. Madelaina hadn't been fully converted to the teachings of Tolomeo despite all she'd seen and heard. The old role of hatred and vengeance was difficult to rid herself of, so, by the time Madelaina took Antonetta through the terrors of Madrigal de Los Altos and what she'd suffered at the hands of Huerta and Major Salomon, the former *soldadera* had turned chalk white and the fires of vengeance had again begun to smolder.

Antonetta remained silent during the terrifying tales her friend recounted. Only her lips twitched from time to time as she nervously flicked the tips of her long, red-lacquered nails. What depravity the poor child had endured. No wonder Little Fox's hatred of General Huerta twisted her mind.

"You see, Antonetta," continued Madelaina as she nervously tugged the linen handkerchief in her lap. "I don't trust Huerta, not then, now, or ever. It wasn't for the love of Francesco Madero that he joined the Constitutionalists. He's a *Porfirista* through and through. He's always been loyal to Diaz. That *bastardo* even tried to execute Villa before a firing squad." She told Pancho's mistress of the ordeal she'd endured with Madero. "Imagine, Huerta received orders just when the *Federales* cocked their rifles, ready to end Pancho's life."

Madelaina paused to delicately sip her beer. She no-

570

ticed that Tonetta's fragile face had already changed hues several times. The redhead leaned forward.

"And then?" she asked, almost afraid to pursue the topic.

"And then, what do you suppose that spineless cur did, the one who sits on the throne handed to him by the Centaur of the North, eh? He ordered Pancho jailed. Don't look so surprised, It's true. Imagine? Madero ordered Pancho jailed for insubordination and disobeying orders!" Madelaina had risen to her feet. Pacing back and forth in marked agitation, she exclaimed, "Is this to be believed, Tonetta? The thanks Pancho gets for giving Madero all of Mexico is jail. I tell you, Francesco Madero was not the revolution. He is a fraud, no matter how loudly he protests the fact. Only Villa was the revolution. No one but Pancho Villa. Our old *jefe*, who sits rotting in jail, should be made aware of the plottings against him. He didn't believe me, Tonetta."

"What do you wish from me, *chiquita*?" asked the proprietress of the Diamond Slipper. "How can I help ease your pain? It grieves me to see you pressured by so many complications. Sit quietly, *querida*. Rearrange yourself. It doesn't help to concern yourself over matters you cannot control."

"Yes, I suppose you are right. I keep telling myself not to involve myself in such affairs. That's why I insist that Little Fox is no more. The past is over. I try to keep it from my mind—all this injustice and double-dealing. *Querida*, it isn't easy. It makes my blood boil to think they've cornered the only man who ever helped Mexico. Goddamn them all!" Madelaina made a disorganized gesture when she saw the solemn and fixed expression of worry in Tonetta's eyes. "Not to worry, *chiquita*," she told the buxom, leggy dancer. "I'm all right. I need a job to support myself for a while. I came to El Paso in hopes of locating my husband whom I've not seen since the Parral encounter. I tell myself, with more reasoning, that if I do not locate him, it will not matter. I will find a life for me and do what I must."

571

She glanced at her friend with a feeling of awkwardness for not being totally honest with her. "There is something else, something you do not know." She sat alongside Antonetta, picked up her hand, hoping for understanding. "Tonetta, I am Madelaina Obregon, daughter of General Obregon."

Tonetta's sea blue eyes widened. "The daughter of Villa's enemy?" She withdrew her hand.

"Perhaps once they were enemies. The war has ended. Now Obregon works for Madero against the *Orozquistas*. *Si, chiquita*—with Huerta, too. It's too crazy a world even for me to comprehend. Much too confusing." She studied the exotic dancer, fascinated by the shimmering fire in her hair.

"The daughter of General Obregon? Ayeiii! It's a crazy world, as you say—much too complicated for Antonetta's head." She guzzled the remains of her *cerveza*—beer. "*Pues*, you have a job here with me. Can you still dance as you danced once for me in Villa's camp?" she asked, her eyes lighting up with dollar signs. "If you can, *querida*, the Diamond Slipper has just struck oil! *La Gatitta* is going into a quick, much-needed retirement."

"I'll do my best."

"Listen, you mentioned this man—your husband—"

"Duprez. Peter Duprez."

"*Si*, Duprez. All the time gringos come to Antonetta's Diamond Slipper, *chiquita*. Is possible one night he will come. Every now and then, that handsome, virile gringo Captain Richards comes here. We drink. We sing. We dance. We do things people usually do to pleasure themselves. But I have not seen this gringo Duprez. If I have, he has not made himself known to me."

Antonetta arose and, catching her image in the oval floor mirror, she patted her curls into place. "Now, *chiquita*, we go to my house. I have also a boarding-house, like a small hotel, where I rent rooms to respectable people. You will stay there with me. First, you must get well. I never see you so skinny. You must

572

fill out a little, no? The customers here like women with meat on their bones—not the way you are now." She shook her head. "Imagine what they did to Little Fox—forgive me, Madelaina," she said, realizing her error.

An hour later they both entered the modest boardinghouse Antonetta had bought on her arrival in the Texas city after leaving San Francisco. In her cheerful room, connected to Antonetta's by an adjoining bath, Madelaina sank wearily into a large wing chair covered in a bright calico print. A double window gave her a view of the park across the street. After a moment, she crossed to the window and flung it open, inhaling the floral-scented breeze fluttering in through the opening, causing the lace curtains to billow in and out. There was a large, brass double bed and a bureau topped with a marble slab, upon which stood a white milk glass bowl and pitcher. Next to it stood an oval mirror on a hickory base.

Antonetta had stopped at Madelaina's old quarters to pick up her belongings, and now she lay them across the bed, ready to put away.

"It is not the Obregon hacienda, *querida*, but it will be comfortable, you'll see," said the redhead, mistaking the sad expression in Madelaina's eyes for disappointment. She seemed to relax more in the confines of Antonetta's home, whereas earlier at the Diamond Slipper, she seemed anxious that someone might overhear their conversation.

"This is a palace compared to some places I've lived. Not like Madrigal." As Madelaina spoke, her feelings of bitterness dissolved, adding confusion to her mind.

"*Querida*, you mustn't let memories of that hell on earth embitter you forever. You will forget. You must. Leave it behind where all things of the past must remain."

"Forget? You honestly believe I can forget what that animal Huerta did to me?" she blurted out irrationally.

"Huerta again. The same Huerta who sent Pancho

573

Villa to prison. The same Huerta who stands falsely alongside Madero. The same Huerta who plots for the throne. He was the one, eh? The one who did those things to Little Fox." She let loose a string of curses that would have put Tomàs Urbino and Solis to shame. "What is wrong with Francesco Madero?" Her eyes widened to pools of fire. "Has he lost all senses? Has the crazy disease contaminated his brain? Ayeiii! *Desgraciados!* Sons of the sons of black Satan. Before, at the club, Tonetta couldn't express herself. Now I can explode. I swear if Pancho Villa hears of this, he will cut off their balls!"

"If Pancho Villa hears what?" asked a deep voice from behind them. He pushed open the door and stood in the doorway.

Both women, alarm on their faces, turned, holding their breaths as the door opened to reveal the figure of a man standing, observing them both.

There he was, dressed in conservative Norfolk tweeds and a Stetson hat on his head, without a moustache or the long hair he formerly wore. Francesco Pancho Villa, a bit self-conscious, a bit awkward, perhaps, stood there in the flesh, wondering why they didn't know him.

It took only moments for Tonetta to regain her composure, and when she recognized the former *guerrillo,* she sprang forward, leaping in long strides, all ladylike pretentions totally dissolved. She fell into his arms, laughing and crying. A look of insane bewilderment on her face, she twirled about the room in his arms, in sheer ecstasy. "Pancho! You son of a grizzly bear! It's you? It's really you? I knew it! I knew it! There is no prison in the world to keep the likes of Pancho Villa inside its walls." She had straddled him like a horse, and together they whirled about the room, frolicking as they'd done so many times in the past. Finally, Villa dropped her gently from his back and he grew silent. He placed his finger upon his lips in a gesture of silence. He moved back to the door, closed and bolted it shut. He glanced at Madelaina in recognition. Again he held his finger to his lips. He crossed the room and peered from behind the curtain, out the window to the street below. Satisfied, he returned to the women.

"Little Fox, it's you," he said not trusting his eyes. Her pallor and recent loss of weight had disguised her well. "I am enchanted to meet with you once more. To say I am grateful doesn't truly describe my feelings. I learned what you did. But what brings you here?"

"Later, Panchito," interrupted Antonetta, happy to see her former lover safe and sound. "First, tell us how you managed to escape prison? What you are doing here in El Paso?"

"Listen, my little kitten. First, you must forget I am Pancho Villa. I am Doroteo Arango. If anyone should guess my identity, it could prove most dangerous for all of us."

His little kitten understood. *"Muy bueno.* First, we celebrate. A feast, plenty of wine. Then we shall exchange stories. Ayeiii, Pancho—I mean Señor Arango—some stories will prove most enlightening to you." She winked at Madelaina.

"No, my *gatitta.* No celebration. Merely a reunion of old friends. We remain here. Bring in food and we talk. I intend to bring no attention to myself. I have much important business to do here in El Paso."

Tonetta continued to scrutinize him. "There is something very different about you, my big bear. Not your clothing or your moustache—although I must say I like you better with than without," she laughed. "Very well, Doroteo, forgive me if I mention it, but you are not the Panchito I used to know."

Villa's eyes twinkled in merriment. "Of course not. The man you knew, little cat, was illiterate. He could not read or write. The man who stands before has been transformed into a human thinking machine. I read. I write. Imagine? Pancho Villa writing and reading? He understands things now. No wonder Madero had no use for that dirty ignorant peasant—"

"No! That isn't true!" countered Madelaina. "You were loyal! The only true friend and patriot Madero ever had—and look what he did to you! Look what Huerta had power to do to you without even a reprimand from *El Presidente!*" She spoke those last two words with biting sarcasm, as if the words themselves were heinous. "I myself ran to the palace when word arrived you were about to face Huerta's firing squad. *Demonio!* What it took for Raoul Madero and myself before *El Presidente* would send the wire! And to sentence you to prison was the worst infamy. And you, Doroteo Arango, to be so loyal to an undeserving man is beyond my comprehension!" Madelaina was shaking. Tears sprang from her eyes at the bad memories, all the pain and anguish she had suffered for a lost cause. "And now, you stand before me, the man for whose cause I defied my father, my best friend, and the only life I knew, and tell me in so many words that you condone Madero's shabby treatment of you. Are you so blind you can't recognize that you sacrificed your life for the wrong man? A weakling? A man so afraid of his own shadow he hasn't the guts to fight for what he believes in? *You* put Madero into the presidential palace—*not* Vitoriano Huerta! *You* won Juarez for the revolution—not Orozco or Huerta! And even after Madero placed Huerta in charge of the Northern Division of the Regulars, it was Pancho Villa who won victory after victory against Orozco and his Redflaggers. It was *you* who won victory at Torreon!" She stopped, out of breath.

Struck by Madelaina's emotional outburst, Pancho Villa stood transfixed, his eyes staring at her as if she were some apparition. Was he so thick-headed he couldn't understand such dialogue? In prison he'd learned plenty about the rotten politics and intrigues that ate away at the nation's capital. Was he to learn more from this mere slip of a woman? "You think Huerta is a threat to Madero?"

"You amaze me, Panchito," said Tonetta. "Ask yourself why Huerta lined you up against a wall with a firing squad ready to shoot you."

"You're so smart, *gatitta,* you tell me," he replied in

annoyance. A woman trying to tell Pancho Villa his business! Hah!

Madelaina rose to the occasion, not wishing to cause ill will between the old lovers. "Because you were a threat to him. Like I was a threat to him. You, *Jefe*, were fast becoming a legend. You became the power of the revolution. You are strong like iron. Like Zapata you are a stubborn Indian, incorruptible, unpredictable, with a heart that beats for Mexico. Huerta wouldn't be Madero's right arm if he permitted you to exist. It should be the puma, Pancho Villa the conqueror, seated at Madero's right arm—not Huerta!"

"Even without reading or writing?" It was incredible the things she said.

"Even then," said Madelaina flatly. "I, too, stood in Huerta's way, *Jefe*. Shall I tell you what Huerta did to me, *mi Generale*, in detail?" And so once again she gathered up the memories of those bad days at Madrigal and laid them out before him in all their grotesqueness.

Pancho Villa didn't move. At one point he lit a cigarette, took a puff, and quickly snuffed it out, remembering he didn't smoke. Before she finished, Villa shook with rage. His black eyes smoldered and he clenched his fists until his knuckles threatened to break through the skin. At one time he wouldn't have understood such intrigues, such complications. True, he was an Indian. A stupid, stubborn land-tilling *peón*. Once he held fast to a premise, he wouldn't let go.

"I should have told you all these things, *Jefe*, when we met in Parral. You knew I'd been imprisoned against my will, but you knew nothing of the vile treatment which I was forced to endure. Now, you know. I tell you only to acquaint you with the despotic, satanic personalities of both General Huerta and Major Salomon. I will never trust them—allies or enemies."

He stared at her for several long moments as he recalled the countless rumors he'd heard in prison that General Huerta was bent on crucifying Madero. He himself had been asked to participate in a plot, along with the old army irregulars who had fought against Diaz and now plotted against Madero because they found him unfit for the responsibilities of the presidency. Damn them all! Damn the stinking politicians, the *Porfiristas*, Huerta, Salomon, even Pasquel Orozco and his bastard Redflaggers! All those ambitious, corrupt politicians who wanted power—power—POWER had nearly taken his life, not once, but many times. If he lived to be a hundred, he'd never forget the feeling of being marched into the dusty courtyard and backed up against the adobe wall. Someone had offered him a blindfold. Even then he didn't believe what was happening. He refused a last request, offered by a young *capitán,* whom he was certain would at any instant break into a smile and admit it was all a joke.

He had heard the words. *"Atención! . . . Listo . . . Apuntar . . ."*

Still Villa didn't believe it. It was when he caught sight of the flashing steel sword upraised before the *capitán's* face that Villa convinced himself the scene was indeed real. Before the final order was given, in that last breathless moment, Villa raised his arms and cried aloud, demanding to be told why he was going to be shot. He insisted he'd been given no trial. He saw the six rifles leveled against him, when suddenly he heard the sounds of hard riding and the loud, outraged voice of Raoul Madero ordering that the execution be halted. In his hand was authorization from President Madero.

Never, never, never would Villa forget that incident or forgive the man who brought it about—General Huerta. Even after he was imprisoned in Mexico City, he was unable to shut the scene from his mind. He made a silent vow never to trust another man against his instincts. But instinct told him he should still trust Madero—because Madero had no one he could trust.

Madelaina's words had stoked his own memories of Huerta's attempted treachery. Pancho temporized, aware that his stubborn loyalty to Madero, whom he venerated illogically, frustrated both women. He convinced himself women could never hope to understand the logic that came to a new thinking man. This he told himself with newborn, fierce pride. To Madelaina he was more direct.

"In this world, comes time for everything. We cannot settle here and now what will be settled in time, Little Fox," he told her patiently. "I make a solemn oath to you, that I, Pancho Villa, will straighten out this government of Mexico in the near future. I make also this vow. Huerta will pay for the infamy done to you. And that vulture, Salomon, will feel the spur of fear in his ribs before I finish with him. Villa has never forgotten your friendship and what you suffered for him."

Villa paused. He glanced at Madelaina sitting in the stuffed wing chair by the window like a lost soul. She seemed to be in another world. He glanced at Tonetta and nodded when the redhead suggested in a whisper that they leave her to rest. Antonetta led the way to her suite of rooms, through the adjoining bathroom, with Pancho following at her heels. She had gone on ahead. Pancho Villa paused at the door to glance back at Madelaina. He disliked what he was about to say, but his Indian instinct forced the words.

"It is simply *maravilloso* what a man learns by reading, *señorita*. Only this morning I read that General Alvaro Obregon, a new friend and associate to Huerta, Salomon, and Carranza, has reenforced the battalion at Sonora to help defeat that sidewinder Orozco. Even after Orozco's recent departure, the battalion continues to exist. All this against President Madero, it said in the paper. Imagine that, Little Fox?"

Madelaina gave a start, her face as pale as lifeless cloud. "Huerta and my father united against Madero?" she exclaimed softly. "Truly, *señor*, I am doomed." Then Urbina's rumor was true.

Villa stepped back into the room. He squatted on one knee and looked deeply into her gravely concerned eyes. He patted her hand reassuringly.

"No, Little Fox. You are not doomed. Pancho never forgets a friend. It took much courage to break out of jail. One night my way was made clear through much travail. I found my way here—to begin anew what was started before my time. As long as Villa lives, you are not doomed." He kissed her damp hand, blinked his eyes, and placed a cool hand on her feverish forehead.

"The poor child has fever. Is there no doctor you can summon, *gatitta?*

"You can thank that stupid bastard Urbina for this!" snapped Antonetta, listening from the doorway.

"Urbina? Tomàs Urbina?" Pancho's eyes lit up with enormous excitement. "Where is that little devil?" he grinned openly. Just as quickly his eyes clouded over. "What you mean, woman, I can thank him for this? Speak up."

"Come, *mi Generale.* I'll tell you while I summon a doctor."

The next few weeks sped by rapidly for Madelaina. She had fully recuperated from the periods of profound weakness she experienced at Antonetta's boarding-house. The doctor attributed the condition to acute depression and the wounds she'd suffered at Isabel's hand. But Madelaina knew better. She wasn't adhering to the teachings of Tolomeo. How long would it take for her to remain on the track and stop derailing because of her emotional immaturity?

She began to concentrate on her career as a dancer. She rehearsed daily, and with Tonetta's constant encouragement, her faith was restored in both her dancing ability and her womanly charms. "You're a gorgeous woman, talented and young. Ju can capture the heart of many men," Antonetta would tell her. "Ees better ju choose a reech man than a poor man. And here in El Paso, *chiquita,*" she'd say in her pigeon yankee, "ees many reech men looking for such a beautiful meesus. So be smart. Ju, weeth jur face of a gringa, attract for jurself such a reech man."

On the day Antonetta spoke these words, they had

visited the new shop where Madama Fifi of Paris sold Paris- and New York-inspired apparel for women. Under the firm persuasion of Tonetta's excellent taste, Madelaina had ordered many gowns, "far too many for what I really need," she protested.

She'd complained of a severe headache during the fittings and cut the buying spree short. Truth was, she was getting flashes of those same pictures she'd seen in the land of Tolomeo, and they all had to do with her old and sorely missed friend, Manuelito Perez. Vivid impressions of him in the arena came at her with more frequency. They all ended the same way, with Manuelito being gored and trampled by the bull before the picadors and other cape men could divert the attention of *el toro*. She saw him in death, at a funeral held for him in which he was greatly mourned by his people.

Then, because Madelaina forced the pictures from her mind, they'd cease. Such images were not the kind Madelaina relished, and she grew as puzzled as she was annoyed that she should see them with such frequency.

She and Tonetta left Madama Fifi's and crossed the busy thoroughfare, prepared to step into Tonetta's handsome carriage. Suddenly, Madelaina gave a start. A blast of horns and the loud beating of drums announced the coming *corrida* in the Plaza de Toros, as a small procession of dazzling matadors waved to the crowds from the top of a gaily decorated wagon. On an enormous double-sided placard was the image of a man whose face she'd never forgotten. A few years older perhaps, more mature, but still that handsome, dark-skinned gypsy face she knew so well.

"Matador Manuelito Perez!" came the voice over the loudspeakers. "*Señoras y señores, atención, por favor*. Ladies and Gentlemen. Jur attention, if ju please. Direct from Spain, the world's greatest and bravest matador of all time makes hees American debut. Saturday afternoon at four o'clock in the Plaza de Toros, will be Matador Manuelito Perez! King of all matadors!"

Madelaina heard no more. She had fainted in To-netta's arms.

Two hours later, in the privacy of her home, Made-laina awakened on her bed with Tonetta standing over her, concern on her face for her friend.

"Manuelito," said Madelaina frantically. "Where is he? I must see him!"

"Who? What are ju talking about?" The redhead was concerned by these strange headaches and by the unusual comportment of her friend these past few months. "Manuelito—who?"

"Perez—the matador. Who else?" replied Made-laina, sitting up on the bed. She swung her legs over the side and stood up. "I must see him, *chiquita*. I must."

Antonetta understood. "Ju mean thees matador whose name is on the lips of all El Paso? Ju know heem, *chiquita*?"

"*Si*. I do. He is a dear friend from Las Marismas."

Antonetta's eyes lit up once more with dollar signs. "Ju theenk ju can influence these matador to come to the Diamond Slipper, *chiquita*? Ees much good for business," she insisted, rubbing her fingertips together in a gesture of money.

Madelaina smiled lightly. "Perhaps. For now, with the loan of your driver and bays, I will try to go and see him."

"No, *chiquita,* wait. Ees no good dat way. Leesten to Tonetta. I will send my driver with a note, inviting him to see the *Magnifica La Bomba*. Eef ju go, so many managers weel theenk ju are jus' another *aficionada* and will not let ju see him. Leesten to me, I know how eet ees."

"But Manuelito will see *me, querida*. We were very close."

"Dat close?" asked Tonetta with a suggestive smile.

"Not that close, you wicked woman. Like brother and sister."

Antonetta shrugged. "Whatever ju say. Ees no my

business. My business ees Pancho. And for days I 'ave no seen him. I go to find him. Ju sure jur O.K.?"

Madelaina nodded. "I'm sure. And Tonetta—remember, not Pancho. Doroteo Arango."

"How I forget all de time, eh? For so long ees Pancho to me, not dis Doroteo Arango." She tapped her forehead in mock annoyance. "I go now, *querida*. I see you much later, eh. At de club." She moved with a swish of her taffeta dress, leaving behind the fragrant smell of delicate musk. "Madelaina, eef all change their names, why not call me Toni? No? Ees more better?"

Chapter 22

"What exactly did you expect from me, Señorita Obregon, after the shabby way you and my cousin Armando treated me?" Manuelito Perez said coldly as he gazed down at her.

They sat in the drawing room of the hacienda rented by him during his stay in El Paso. She, demure and prim in a pale gray moire suit with her black hair cascading down her shoulders; he, swaggering back and forth in his trim matador's dress suit with a white ruffled shirt open at the neck. He had turned into an exceedingly handsome man, the pox marks on his face hardly noticeable.

Dismayed by his unexpected aloofness, Madelaina's crestfallen expression and her inability to understand such estrangement was like manna from the gods to the formidable matador. For years he had prayed for the day when he could repay the hurt she'd inflicted upon him during that sensitive and tender time in his life. And now, this was his day. He'd let her know exactly how he'd felt all these years, how he'd learned to hate her.

"How can I begin to tell you how sorry I am? I tried to find you that day, Manuelito, but you had left. No one knew where you'd gone. Why? Why did you disappear, *querido*." She paused. "*Your* cousin Armando? Why do you call him your cousin?" she asked with mild astonishment.

"Does it surprise you that I should be of *gachupín* blood? I am the son of Armando's uncle. That makes me his cousin."

"But that is wonderful, Manuelito. Simply wonderful. At least you know your roots. It wasn't so before."

584

"Stop trying to be so agreeable, Señorita Obregon," he countered rudely. "For so long I have remembered you and Armando's treatment of me with hatred in my heart—"

Madelaina interrupted. "Why is that? The letter I received from a most repentant man, which I have memorized in my heart, led me to believe that I was the victim." She quoted by rote. "*Querida*: I am writing to tell you of my wickedness. My conscience tears at me because I permitted a *bruja* to bewitch you. Forgive me. My heart bled with the pain of loving you because I could do nothing to convey my love. When I saw you leaving the bordello of Madama Tarragona—"

"*Basta!* Enough!" he interrupted. "I changed my mind since then. I was emotional and filled with guilt at the moment. But when I took time to reflect, I realized I had always been the wronged person. And this in itself consumed me with hatred."

"Manuelito," said Madelaina softly, rising to go to him and comfort him. "Please, don't let your heart spill over with hatred."

The nearness of her, this wench whom he'd always loved and couldn't stop thinking about, stirred his senses and created in the matador a burning desire for her. He wheeled around and, grasping her firmly and savagely, kissed her with a pent-up ardor that had fermented since his childhood.

"No, Manuelito," she protested, pounding his strong muscular shoulders. "No! Don't do this to either of us!"

"No, eh? Not to Manuelito will you say such a thing again, woman." He bent over and swooped her up into his arms. "I intend to do what I should have done long ago!" He moved to the circular staircase despite her loud protests and climbed the stairs. Holding her squirming, protesting body in his arms, he kicked open a bedroom door. "Now, *querida,* I will show you what it is to be loved by a real man—not a tea drinker like Armando."

"Oh, Manuelito, not like this." She stopped fighting

585

and ceased to protest when he dumped her unceremoniously on the large four-poster bed. "Much has happened since we last knew each other—"

"Silence, bitch! You think I don't know you were deflowered by Armando long ago—and God knows how many men after that. *Dios mios!* I find you dancing like a common whore in a place like the Diamond Slipper, displaying your body like—like—oh, don't pretend to me with your virginlike ways. Why do you blush? Why did you not blush last evening when hundreds of lust-filled men eyed you with desire in their eyes and hearts. To think I have loved an illusion all these years. That I permitted my life to be wrecked by the innocence of my youth. You, Madelaina Obregon, a cheap *puta*—a whore."

She winced under the cruel blow of his caustic tongue. "Don't judge me, Manuelito. You don't know the half of it—"

"Half? You mean your life has been far more sordid than it appears?"

He was irrationally incensed, thought Madelaina. Why, after all these years, he acts as if he owns me. "Listen, my dear friend," she began temporately.

"*Listen, my dear friend,*" he taunted. "*Que va,* my dear friend? Stop with this unnecessary talk!" He pulled off his shirt and stood before her in the dim bedroom lights, his powerful torso exposed. His trousers went next and in moments he stood naked, his body surprisingly muscular. "Now, *querida,* dear friend," he taunted, "remove your clothing or I shall tear them from your body!"

After all Madelaina had endured in her young life, she could still feel the pang of fear. Oddly enough, fear wasn't what motivated her in these moments. She rationalized that Manuelito, for all his loud ranting and raving and injured pride, was perhaps the last person she should fear. In his state of mind, if she fought him off, he'd no doubt pursue her and inflict some bodily harm, if only to relieve the pain, anguish, and hatred stored up in his searing heart.

His voice broke through her thoughts. "I have cursed your name and your memory a hundred times a day, over and over, until the hatred and anger I felt all those days after I left Las Marismas burned indelibly in my brain. Just when I felt sure I had rid myself of your memory, you have to turn up and display your body shamelessly and in such a place. I have suffered enough trying to do the right thing as befits a man of my class!" he snarled with a sudden brute force.

He brought both his hands down over her shoulders, held her roughly in his arms, and began to kiss her with vengeance until her lips felt crushed and parched. In a brief moment of ruthless despair, he thrust her from him and he turned his back to her. "I said undress, *puta*! Or shall I do it for you?"

"Very well, Manuelito, as long as you've decided that we must couple, I shall oblige you." She rose from the bed and began to remove her clothing. She lay her jacket carefully across the chair near the bed. She removed her blouse and skirt next, then her petticoat and lingerie until she stood as naked as he, quite next to him.

"Without protest?" he demanded airily.

"Without protest," she replied softly. It was the only way she could reach him.

He strolled in closer to her and stared at her fragile body as much as he'd stared at her the night before when he caught her act as *La Bomba*.

"I won't lie, Madelaina. You are as desirable to me now as you were when we were children, as you were to me last night when I saw you parading your nakedness before all those impertinent men. It was then I decided that, since you sold yourself so cheaply, I could afford you. First, I wanted you to come begging."

Madelaina felt the heat of his body as he moved in toward her, like the radiation of fire. She quivered inwardly as his arms reached for her. There was no haste in his movements, no urgency—no awkward fumbling of a man who didn't know women. He leaned over and kissed her. She was afraid he'd awaken the fires that

587

she'd kept smoldering for so long. She struggled slightly, and Manuelito misunderstood her movement to be a rejection of him.

"So, I'm still not good enough for the daughter of the illustrious General Obregon," he snarled. "For one moment—for one small moment, I told myself that maybe—maybe we could find those lost moments of our life and come alive. I see now it was folly. But I tell you, *La Bomba,* I shall have you like all the countless other men who've lusted for you!" He pulled her savagely to the bed and began to ravish her with the ferocity of an animal in heat.

"No—o," she began. She wanted to tell him that rape was unnecessary, but filled with uncontrollable violence and anger, Manuelito gave her no opportunity to talk with him.

Talk was not what he desired. It was revenge and the feel of Madelaina's body under his that he wanted. Only this would appease the torment the years had multiplied. To preserve his sanity, he needed this more than life itself.

His manhood stabbed at her body and finally entered her without preparation. Madelaina tried to hold back the scream that tore from her throat. His organ was like a bull's. She felt as if her body would split apart.

After the first few moments passed and her body had lubricated itself for him, she began to feel the pleasurable sensations that she hadn't experienced since Tolomeo. Slowly her body moved to his rhythm. The initial pain had passed. As she responded to him, she felt him grow more gentle, more considerate. She let herself slip into a euphoria of forgetfulness.

"This is what you've missed all these years," he whispered with a tinge of sarcasm. "This, the love of the most devoted man you will ever find."

"Yes," she whispered back. "I know, Manuelito. I've always known the love you held for me. It was written in every gesture—in everything you taught me even as you tried to avoid teaching me about the bulls."

"Silence, wench," he hissed, his body growing more

eager, more fervent. The heat of his body set her on fire. She stared into his dark eyes and clutched his black gypsy hair with her fingers as her body arched to meet his.

But Manuelito, burning and consumed with pent-up passion, couldn't wait. He was unable to control the boiling furnace threatening to explode in his loins. He couldn't. And when it erupted, it shook them both, even the bed vibrated from the enormous convulsions that tore at him as he experienced the raptures he'd dreamed of for so long. A loud, animalistic cry escaped his throat. "Madelaina! Madelaina," he cried with a noticeable tremor.

Madelaina, against her will, embraced him tighter. Unfulfilled, she gave no thought to her satisfaction, only that she could hear a low whimper escape him. She felt the warmth of his tears on her face, tasted their saltiness.

"What have I done? *Dios mios,* I couldn't even be a man for you—even after all these years that I've dreamed of making passionate love. I wanted you to know what pleasures you had missed. And what am I but a failure with you? I must ask your forgiveness. I find no whore in you. I am much ashamed."

"There is no need for you to feel ashamed, *querido mío.*" She reached up and silenced his lips with a fingertip. Instantly Manuelito caught it and kissed it.

"Do you have any wine, *chico*? I am thirsty." She smoothed the hair off his forehead. "Please?"

He sat up and turned on the bedside lamp. His dark eyes searched hers. "You are not angry? You aren't incensed by my unspeakable actions?"

She shook her head. "No."

Manuelito continued to search her eyes, hoping to find some answer to his dilemma. "You won't even slap my face?"

Again she shook her head, not sure of his mood. She learned soon enough.

"You are a cold, lifeless fish. Too elegant for the likes of Manuelito Perez, is that it? I could have taken your wrath! Your anger and desire for retaliation for so brutish an act. But not this detachment. This forgiving, sanctimonious endurance of yours. Why? Why are you doing this, Madelaina? Am I so revolting to you that you just put up with me?"

"Oh, Manuelito," retorted Madelaina with obvious exasperation. "Why do you persist in this self-pity? You torture yourself with self-doubts. You are your own worst enemy!" she exclaimed, moving away from him. She sat up and swung her legs over the bed. It was then he saw the scars on her back.

He reached for her and pulled her back to him with his strong brown arms.

"Who did this to you?" he asked huskily. His fingers lightly traced the scars on her lower back as he searched her eyes once more.

"Oh, those," she replied blandly. "You don't really want to know."

"I do not ask questions for the pleasure of hearing no answers."

"Very well, matador. Bring the wine and we'll fill the gaps between us."

Reluctantly, he let her go and slipped off the bed. He brought the wine and two crystal goblets, placing them on the table next to the bed. He poured the ruby wine in both glasses and handed one to her. "These gringos live well, no?"

"To the rekindling of an affectionate and loving relationship," she toasted.

"It is not necessary to insult me. I know my place," he said drily.

They both drank, nevertheless. "Do you have a cigarette, Manuelito?" she asked lightly.

"A cigarette?" he asked, raising an eyebrow. "What else does the *señorita* indulge in?" He spoke in a scathing voice and she replied with maddening composure.

"We're even. Insult for insult. Although I can't see that I insulted you."

She watched him pour more wine for them both and replace the bottle on the table. "There are far more devastating things that can happen to a young, impressionable woman than simply being *La Bomba*, Manuelito. I am not the sweet, innocent schoolgirl who once captured your heart," she began. For the next few hours, they sat close to each other like long-lost friends, bridging the gaps of time in their lives.

When Maneulito heard what had happened to Madelaina, he felt a remorse so powerful that it brought tears of shame to his eyes. "Why didn't you stop me? Why didn't you explain? Oh, Madelaina, I'm so ashamed to have put you through such torment. No wonder you couldn't respond to me as a woman should. I am an animal—a poor, demented animal without consideration."

"I didn't respond because you gave me no time," she chided. "How could you have known?" Then, on a gayer note, she prompted him to tell her about his life after he left Las Marismas. He began slowly, then as the wine warmed him and loosened his tongue, he began his story.

"Manuelito has lived and loved hard and swift, *querida*. I have buried my loins in the bodies of thousands of willing women, only to be haunted each time by the dark, dancing eyes and gay spirit of the woman for whose body I've longed and who now lies at my side. I am ashamed to say that I've lived and directed all my energies for a time such as this. No, no, let me continue," he said when she began to protest.

"I spent the years since we last saw each other perfecting my craft. I climbed to the top as king of the *corrida*, fighting any bull in any broken-down plaza in the fringe areas of Spain until I made the big time. Ah, *sí*, I've starved and slept in the streets—in the gutters, dreaming of my success. And for what, *querida?* Shall I tell you? Waiting, biding my time for this moment when I would meet you face to face and with vengeance make you ashamed, repentant, and regretful that you wouldn't return the powerful ache of love I held for you in my heart. This love transformed itself over the years into a violent hatred and anger at you.

591

An all-consuming hatred which has driven me to take reckless and needless chances in the bullring." He inhaled deeply, bracing himself, then relaxed.

"You know why I have such a following of *aficionados, querida*? Shall I tell you the truth? It is because whenever Manuelito stars in a *corrida,* he will oppose the fiercest and bravest bulls. Because they know one day I'll not disappoint them. They know that my death in the bullring promises to be the bloodiest, goriest battle between man and beast they will be privileged to see."

"Manuelito—" protested Madelaina, finding the opening for which she had waited.

"No, *querida,* let me finish. It is the fashion in some circles in Spain to make wagers on this inevitability because it is a just and deserving retribution for a reckless man who courts death with arrogance. When Manuelito swaggers into the bullring to challenge his enemies for the afternoon, the crowds cheer and *olé,* knowing the end can come at any time for such a *muy loco* matador who defies every rule in the *corrida* against these killer bulls."

What Manuelito didn't tell Madelaina was the full extent of his recklessness. Such stupidity posing as talent was most apparent to his manager and his *banderillos,* the men who belonged to his *cuadrilla*—his team. These well-meaning men prayed to the Virgin de Guadelupe ten times each day, hoping the blessed saint would find a way to pour sense into this true champion, who could fight a few more years and retire a millionaire if he only ceased this foolhardy recklessness. They had all pleaded with their matador, begged him to use more caution until they could say no more without being fired.

Only recently, Manuelito had given them all a tongue-lashing with enough vitriol to intimidate a herd of charging bull elephants. He had seen how they wore their fear on their faces each time he entered the bullring. Their expressions, tense, taut, and fearful, had disturbed him more than their verbal reproach. His own endurance had its limitations. At his last appearance in Madrid, he had exploded. He cursed his *cuadrilla* up and down, accused them of acting like *viejas*—old women—and told him that if they didn't erase those apprehensive looks from their faces, he'd replace them immediately, before the scheduled tour to the Americas.

Their reaction was a natural one. Very well, they thought. If Manuelito is stupid and bent on suicide, why should they care? His rude, hostile attitude had transformed their concern for his welfare into apathy and detached indifference. Not permitted to show their concern, they began to secretly hope their fears would come to pass, that he'd meet his match one day. Only this way would his arrogance and ego be brought down a notch or two until he might be persuaded to take more precaution.

When she visited him at the hacienda on this night before the scheduled *corrida,* Madelaina knew about none of this emotional interplay within Manuelito's coterie of men. She only knew that she had to somehow deter him from appearing in the bullfights. Her dreams and visions had become more pronounced since she saw bills of advertisement announcing that Manuelito Perez would star in the *corrida.*

Manuelito had done precisely as Antonetta predicted when he received her invitation to be his guest at *La Bomba*'s performance. He hadn't recognized the scantily dressed woman in the photograph, the woman billed as *La Bomba,* dancer *extraordinario.* A special front table was prepared for Manuelito and his party, which included a bevy of stunning woman who fell all over the matador. It was placed at the edge of the stage and filled with elegant viands and choice foods fit for a king. Antonetta, shrewd business woman that she was, had let it be known that Manuelito Perez would be honored that night.

When the Perez party arrived, the countless hordes of *aficionados* who filled the Diamond Slipper to capacity arose en masse and gave the matador a standing ovation. Tonetta thought the rafters would cave in at the loud *olés* and cries of "Matador! Matador!" Manuelito accepted the fanfare and welcome as part of a normal routine. He strutted inside with the imperious attitude of *a gachupín,* with the pomp and panache of a matador. He bowed, waved his flat-crowned black sombrero to the crowds, and took the attention in his stride. Dressed in elegant black silk trousers, white silk shirt, and thin black tie, with a short bolero jacket trimmed in velvet, Manuelito Perez was perhaps the most handsome Spanish celebrity ever to grace the city of El Paso. Even the gringos turned out en masse to catch a glimpse of this romantic figure. The gringas especially fell all over him and he had difficulty brushing them off.

Antonetta had sashayed through the crowd to introduce herself and was politely requested to take the seat next to him.

"*Gracias,* matador," she replied with a dazzling smile. "The seat next to you is reserved for a very important friend of yours. With your permission, I request that it be given to no one else." She excused herself, eager to return to her overflowing cash registers.

Manuelito had given her remark no further thought. Such things happened frequently in his travels. Those eager to stand in the spotlight with celebrities always claimed they were important friends of his. Meanwhile, as he feasted and drank the choice wines, he paid scrupulous attention to one of the gringas in his party who flirted outrageously with him and made promises of the intimacies awaiting him when the festivities ended.

A fanfare of drums preceded the dimming of lights and persisted to beat out a soul-stirring rhythm as the colored lights outlined the scintillating body of *La Bomba.* So wrapped up in the gringa was Manuelito that he failed to be inspired by *La Bomba* for a few moments.

No performer, and least of all *La Bomba,* could stand not being appreciated by the guest of honor. Noting his attention on the gringa, *La Bomba,* it seemed, commanded the energy necessary for turning a mere performance into a spectacular, once-in-a-lifetime show which spectators would remember as the most magical stage moment they'd ever witnessed.

La Bomba concentrated her attention on Manuelito, commanding him, compelling him to notice her. Once he glanced her way, it was as if no one else existed for him. He was loath to turn his eyes from her. Her swaying hips, suggestive eyes, and the exquisite union of body, mind, and spirit concentrated into one effort reminded him of the discipline necessary in his own art. Even then, he didn't recognize Madelaina. Something about her, he thought, something stirred his excitement. An intangible. Perhaps the joy and pride an artist feels for another artist. It was her eyes, dark and penetrating, that seemed to magnetize him. Then suddenly, at the sound of muted trumpets she took the stance of a bullfighter. With the grace of a ballerina, she made passes—*verónicas* and half-*verónicas*—that caused Manuelito to give a start. How could this dancer—this *La Bomba*—have perfected what he had taught himself? How, he wondered. As quickly as one artist can detect a fraud or cheap imitator, so could Manuelito see that these were his own techniques. She was too good to be simply a dancer. He exchanged glances with his manager and a few members of his *cuadrilla*. They had also seen it. Manuelito wasn't just seeing things. Nor had he drunk too much wine. He stared intently at *La Bomba* as she climaxed her performance to a rousing stand-up ovation by the crowds who clamored for more.

She took six curtain calls and then permitted the next act to follow.

Manuelito became engrossed with thoughts of the dancer. How could *La Bomba* have so successfully demonstrated the very passes for which he'd become famous? Such expert imitation was the highest form of flattery.

Manuelito was still discussing *La Bomba* when Madelaina, in more sedate formal attire, was escorted to his table. Instantly the men sprang to their feet.

"*Señorita*," said Manuelito. "*Usted muy encantador.* You are most enchanting, *señorita*. Please, will you be seated?" His excitement was catching.

Madelaina knew that he didn't recognize her. Why would he? She was a mere child when they last saw each other. She had lived a hundred years in the past five. It was no wonder.

"*Gracias,* matador. With your permission."

He pulled out the empty chair until she sat down, then seated, he became most attentive and gracious. "What a superb dancer! What an artist! Truly you are extraordinary! Your billing does you little justice, if you permit me to be so bold." He poured champagne for her. "Tell me," he asked confidentially. "Where is it that you learned to master those techniques of the *verónica*? Especially that half-*verónica* interests me," he added.

"It was taught to me by a most important personality, years ago in a small village near Las Marismas in Spain," she began, half-taunting, her dark flashing eyes fixed on his. "His name was Manuelito Perez. Do you know him, matador?" She took delight in watching the changes on his face as he gave a start, then searched her face until he knew the truth.

Madelaina hadn't been prepared for his reaction. It was the hard and cold look he gave her, the stony expression that etched itself into his features that left her distraught and feeling she had trespassed on hallowed grounds.

"Don't you know me, Manuelito?" she asked when he had regained his composure. "It is not possible you've forgotten Madelaina Obregon?" She was unable to dismiss the terrible sinking sensation she experienced under his hostile glance.

"I know you. I have never forgotten you, Señorita Obregon. Now, if you'll excuse me." He called to his party. "*Ondolay, vamenos muchachos.*"

He pulled himself up to his full, imposing height.

Nodding curtly to her, he and his party immediately filed out in a body, leaving Madelaina red-faced, confused, and humiliated by his iceberg reaction to her.

Not one to be deterred, Madelaina soon learned that Manuelito was staying in the hacienda—rather the mansion—of a gringo named William Benson, an American who had sponsored Manuelito's tour to the Americas. Benson was also breeder of the bulls Maneulito would fight on Saturday afternoon. Specially bred Chihuahuan bulls.

Aware of the fact that she might be insulted and turned away from the Benson mansion, Madelaina nevertheless chanced it. As she anticipated, when she presented herself at the door and gave the servant her name with instructions to tell Matador Perez, he returned with a polite and firm reply: Matador Perez knew no one named Obregon and didn't wish to be disturbed.

Madelaina, more humiliated than the night before and perplexed by this hostility, had left the premises terribly saddened by such a rude reception. Even if Madelaina Obregon deserved his arrogant dismissal, *La Bomba* didn't. Not even a jaded prostitute would be treated with such hauteur. What she had done to displease him and fall into such disfavor, she didn't know. But she had more avenues to pursue. She wasn't finished with him yet. She wouldn't give up that easily.

She returned to her apartment and called Antonetta. She discussed with her friend what it was she needed. A half-hour later, Doroteo Arango appeared at her door. "*Señorita*. Are you ready?"

"*Si, Jefe.* Is it all arranged? I hope that I don't put you in jeopardy, but it is a matter of life and death to the matador. And for some foolish reason he refuses to see me."

"It is arranged. I will take my chances."

Twenty minutes later, the carriage pulled up before the mansion of William Benson. Pancho was impressed. "This is how they live here across a river from us?"

"Not everyone lives like this. This Señor Benson, I

am told, is a wealthy *hacendado* who has much influence in Washington—and with Diaz," she added, unsure whether she should have mentioned *hacendados* to the very man who had good reason to loathe such political tigers.

Villa crossed himself. "*Dios mios.* If it is ever learned that Pancho Villa has stepped across the threshold belonging to such a man, he will be skinned alive, his *culjiones* fed to the coyotes."

"My lips are sealed, *Jefe.*"

He made an expression that was indescribable and Madelaina laughed the heartiest she'd laughed in years.

The door swung open. The servant, recognizing Madelaina, was hesitant to admit them. "Ah beg yer pahdon, suh. Are y'all expected?"

Madelaina translated in Spanish.

Pancho instantly spoke out in his pigeon yankee. "Please to tell jur boss, *el matador,* his guest has arrived."

"Very well, suh. Ah—step this way."

Pancho grimaced at the intolerable airs and winked broadly at Madelaina.

"Señor Villa," called Manuelito from the salon as he stepped forward to greet them. "I cannot express the thrill I feel that the *premier jefe* of all Mexico should honor Perez by his presence—" He stopped abruptly when he saw Madelaina. It wasn't proper that he should ignore her now. To do so would be an insult to Villa.

"It is my privilege, matador," said Villa in Spanish. "May I present Señorita Madelaina Obregon, a woman responsible for my many victories." He spoke with aplomb and the respect due a person of high social stature.

Manuelito bowed. As Madelaina surmised, he wouldn't dare ignore her in the presence of such a powerful figure as Pancho Villa, who was revered by the *peóns* in both Spain and Mexico.

They were both treated with the utmost courtesy and respect. Manuelito, the congenial host, ordered refreshments and after the amenities were out of the way—Pancho lauding the matador's bravery and skill in the arena, and Manuelito, just as complimentary, lauding Villa's feats—the *jefe* rose to take his leave.

"*Buenos suerte* at the Plaza on Saturday, matador," he said. "The *señorita* has informed me that you are great friends, so I leave you both to your fond memories. Ah, one thing more, matador. It would please me if you speak nothing of our encounter. You see, I am on a—shall we say—sabbatical? I am traveling incognito, you understand?"

Manuelito nodded. "I understand perfectly. God bless you, *jefe*. I understand you are attempting to do the impossible."

Villa glanced up at him with those twinkling eyes that gave him the appearance of a benevolent grandpapa. "It is you who attempt the impossible. You think I'd face such machine of power like a bull? Ayeiii, matador. You think Pancho is crazy?" He tipped his hat and left them.

Instantly the atmosphere changed. It was zero degrees between them.

"Please, Manuelito, tell me why you are so displeased with me that you'd force me to put the life of Pancho Villa in jeopardy just to see you?"

The matador had turned on her with anger, venting his wrath.

That was two hours ago. Now they had filled in the gaps of time, and they sat back quietly in bed in the silence that engulfed them.

"So, tell me, why it was that you were forced to enlist the assistance of Pancho Villa to see me?"

"*Why?* You already know. What it is that I must tell you is what I intend doing. Manuelito, please do not ridicule me for what I am about to tell you. You must not fight in the *corrida* on Saturday. You mustn't, understand?"

His silent questioning reached out at her across the bed and she felt herself falter, but only for a moment.

"There is grave danger if you persist in making an appearance. Manuelito, for some strange reason I've been mysteriously given the powers of a *bruja*. I can see the future. And in my mind I've seen you fighting a Chihuahuan bull, in a place exactly like the Plaza de Toros, and the result is disastrous. *Por favor, chico.* I beg of you, do not fight on Saturday."

"For this nonsense, you called upon Pancho Villa and risked my doing you bodily harm?" Manuelito wanted to laugh in ridicule. Why couldn't he?

"I have seen this catastrophe for the past six months, *chico*. Don't dismiss it so lightly."

"Do you usually see pictures of this nature?" he chided.

"Oh, Manuelito. Don't make fun of me. I am new to all this. I have never been so concerned in my life. There is no way you can escape this destiny if you insist on fighting the bulls on Saturday."

"*Basta!* Enough, Madelaina! I have heard enough!" He sprang to his feet, opened a mahogany chest nearby, and slipped into a rich damask robe. His face had darkened in annoyance. "I cannot permit such thoughts of fear to enter my mind. You hear? I must perform on Saturday. I am bound by a contract. Besides, this debut in America will pave my way to triumph in Brazil and Argentina, where I go next to be granted the highest honor ever bestowed upon a matador." He tied the sash around him with angry punctuating movements.

"If you persist in performing on Saturday, you will never reach South America," she said dully.

"Madelaina! Stop! I command you! You say you saw—in these crazy pictures—the Plaza de Toros? What makes you so positive it is the one in Juarez? Why not the one in Mexico City or in Buenos Aires or even Madrid? They are quite similar, no?"

Madelaina arose from the bed, dejected and spent. "I tried, my dear friend, to make you see. But you will not see. Therefore, I can do no more. I will leave and permit you to dwell upon my words, matador. Try to bear in mind that a wise man is one who acts out of wisdom, not fear."

"So, now you say I am afraid? Is that it? Manuelito is nothing but a *niño* who is frightened of his own shadow?"

"Never that, Manuelito," she said, slipping into her clothing.

"Very well, Madelaina, you know me too well. I will speak the truth. I *am* afraid. I *am* scared. Every time I see the announcement of the *corrida* with my name on the bill, I shake in my boots. It begins at the start of the season and the trembling doesn't end until the season is over. You see? I am a fraud."

"You insist on being hard with yourself. It was you who taught me that to fight a bull when you are not scared is nothing. And not to fight a bull when you are scared is nothing. But, *amigo,* to fight a bull when you are scared is something. That is why Manuelito Perez is premier matador of all Spain."

Perez shrugged. "It isn't every matador who gets a preview of his own funeral, *querida,*" he said with a faraway look in his eyes.

Madelaina was dressed now. She walked toward him. "Will you at least say *adios* in good spirits? I'm not certain I understand any of this. Why, out of this entire world, was I chosen to bring you this message? I, too, am confused by such a mission. Since you will not heed my premonitions, I can only say *vaya con Dios*, Manuelito. I wish it could have been different between us. Different for you. You should have claimed your heritage, returned to Las Marismas as Manuelito Cortez. And I perhaps should never have left Spain." She moved to the door. "*Buenos suerte—good luck,* my dear friend."

"Madelaina?"

"*Si, chico.*"

"I thank you for all your effort. Before you leave, tell me one thing. Are you the woman of Pancho Villa?"

She was arrested by the question and tensed for a

601

moment. She shook her head. "Not I. It is the redhead who belongs to him." As soon as she spoke the words she regretted them. It was a foolish move on her part and she spoke only to ease the pain in Manuelito who already thought her to be quite wicked. All his Spanish morality condemned a woman who displayed herself as *La Bomba*. But she was too fatigued to spar further with him.

"*A los toros!*" came the cries. "To the bullfights!"

For an hour, the Avenida Juarez had been jammed by a steady stream of carriages and throngs of people on foot, all hurrying to the edge of town, to the Plaza de Toros. Cowboys on horses maneuvered their animals through the crowds and tethered them in the stables nearby, paying a fee to guarantee no one would run off with them. Fancy horses, gaily decorated with feathers, drew carriages filled with men and woman dressed in their finest, with dusters over their traveling costumes.

Hawkers with sweets and tortillas and tamales milled through the throngs, selling their tidbits, and the crowds poured into the seats of the plaza. In the shade where the seats sold for the dearest prices, the gringos, the Spanish, and the Mexicans of means sat regally in the boxes. In the sun, the broiling, melting sun, sat the commoners, the *peóns*, the *aficionadas* of the *corrida*, who cared not where they sat as long as they enjoyed themselves.

Madelaina, dressed in a pale yellow and white cotton dress with a whalebone corset pushing up her breasts and nipping in her waist until it seemed she had none at all, moved along with Antonetta in the shade and sat down behind five tall, wide-shouldered men who nearly obstructed their view. Chewing tobacco and constantly spitting out the juices, the men annoyed them, but they refrained from venting their feelings.

Antonetta, dressed in emerald green moire with her red hair piled high, wore a straw bonnet trimmed with bird feathers and ribbons. She was a knockout, thought

Madelaina, the epitome of femininity. She tried to recall how she'd looked as a *campesina,* but the image wouldn't form in her mind.

"What a man, that Arango!" exclaimed Tonetta. "What discipline. He refused to come today, however much he loves the *corrida. Pues,* he has so much business, this general with no army, no?" She laughed at the inside joke until she caught Madelaina's stern look.

"Hush, woman! You never know whose eager ears may be listening."

"Ayeiii," said Tonetta, dismayed. "Who can remember all this intrigue without a war or even a revolution around them?" she whispered in their native tongue.

From time to time the five rough and ready cowhands seated before them turned to gaze at the unescorted women. They gestured suggestively to each other. As men of their calibre were wont to do on occasion, they spoke inaudibly amongest themselves and continued to make exaggerated eye gestures over the presence of such women.

The women ignored their ridiculous antics. Their eyes were everywhere, watching the crowds, listening to the brass band, picking up on a conversation here and there. Madelaina glanced at the golden watch fob pinned to her dress. It was nearly four o'clock. Time for the colorful pageantry to commence, she thought with dismay as the stars were announced over the public address system. Manuelito Perez still intended to contest the bulls. Pray, dear Lord, that her premonitions were false, she said silently.

The blaring blasts of brass trumpets marked the beginning of the *corrida.* Familiar refrains of *"La Virgen de la Macarena,"* the *paso doble,* began. The crowd cheered and cheered; their cries reached a crescendo as the matadors entered the plaza followed by their *banderillos* and the picadors on horseback. Bringing up the rear were the drag mules. Leading this spectacular extravaganza were the constables, dressed in sixteenth-century costumes with gold-embroidered jack-

603

ets and wide beaver sombreros with pompoms on one side. Thick yellow padding protected their legs.

The *cuadrilla* dressed a shade less flamboyantly than the matadors, who wore costumes of thickly encrusted gold embroidery, so dazzling in the sunshine that the crowds often averted their eyes from the glare. It was a magnificent spectacle of ceremony, pomp, and grand tradition. Each phase of the dramatic *corrida* was cheered on by the wild and passionate cries of the people: mantilla-draped *señoritas,* elegant *dons* with broad-brimmed sombreros cocked jauntily over one eye, and of course the gringos.

"You know how long it's been since I've seen the *corrida*?" asked Madelaina, enjoying every second of the pageant. She tried not to show the nervousness and fear she felt over Manuelito's scheduled appearance. He had drawn the third bull. Two Mexican matadors would have an opportunity to show up this Spanish import first. The rivalry between Perez of Spain and the Mexican matador created an added note to the excitement already permeating the arena.

"I hope the bulls are brave, *chiquita,*" said Madelaina to her friend. "Some I've seen here in Mexico leave much to be desired. These Chihuahuan bulls cannot compare to the Concha or Miura bulls. Ayeiii, those are some bulls, Tonetta. Strong forelegs, alert, sharp-witted. But these Chihuahuan *toros* are much like the Salamancas—no strength either in force or character."

"How is it you know so much about bulls?" asked the redhead politely; she understood very little about bullfighting, except for its tradition.

Madelaina had no time to reply. The first matador was ready and the first bull entered the ring. She watched the contest between Mexican and bull and declared it had been a waste to see such an abominable showing. "The bulls are worthless. They respond poorly to all elements of the fight. See, Tonetta, they hardly charged the first capes, wandered away from the horses, and ignored the picadors. *Dios mios!*" she

604

continued. "Look, they even have difficulty following the red *muleta* at the finish. It is cruel to kill such oxen! Bah!"

She began to think all her premonitions were false. Truly, she had no reason to fear for Manuelito if he was going to oppose such docile cows. If anything, it might be his pride which would suffer.

The next matador butchered the beast with three bad thrusts of his sword. Madelaina grew as indignant as the booing crowds. She snorted contemptuously, thoroughly caught up in the slovenly show of burlesque between man and beast.

"This is butchery—not a bullfight!" she exclaimed scathingly.

During the first two bouts, Madelaina noticed that one of the men seated in the box ahead of them turned in her direction whenever she remarked about the bulls. His aloof reaction to her statements turned into curiosity, then into a recalcitrant determination to put her in her place. The more he listened to her criticism, the more he realized that she had some knowledge of bulls. His outward attitude of censure gave way to piqued interest.

William Benson turned three-quarters of the way around in his seat to address her. "Pahdun me, ma'am. Ah jus' couldn't help ovahheahing youah comments." Because he spoke in the same west Texas drawl that had sent shivers up and down her spine for so long, she looked at the man more closely than she would normally have.

"Ah'd like to know mahself wheah such a lovely *señorita* gets ta know so much about bulls." He had removed his Stetson hat, revealing salt and pepper hair clipped close to his head and bushy eyebrows over piercing blue eyes.

Madelaina lowered her eyes and nudged her companion. She turned her nose up in the air at him. How dare he speak to her without benefit of a chaperone? Did he take her for some common whore? Tonetta had explained the ways of the gringo women, whose rules

605

concerning such encounters were as stringent as the Spanish custom. She wasn't about to give this stranger the time of day. Why was the intermission so long, she wondered.

"Sorry, m'am. Ah meant no disrespect. Y'all wait heah for a moment. Ah'll be back in two shakes of a bull's tale." He lifted his huge frame from the seat and moved into the crowd.

"Es un muy loco," said Tonetta. "He ees some crazy man, no?"

"No ma'am. Youah shuah wrong theah," retorted one of the men seated alongside William Benson. He turned in his seat to take a good look at Antonetta.

"Hot damn!" he exclaimed recognizing her. "It's *La Gatitta!* Damn, it's shuah good to see ya again, little *La Gatitta.*"

Her eyes lit up in recognition. "Gringo? Ees ju, Waco? Ees long time no see ju. Where ju keep jurself, eh? Leesten, ju meet *La Bomba*? Ees new star attraction at Diamond Slipper."

Madelaina nodded curtly to him and gazed over his head, wondering at the delay in the ring below them. The three men now turned to gaze at her, then laughing at some inside joke, they nudged each other and howled uproariously.

"Something tickles your funny bone?" Antonetta asked icily.

Waco, obviously the spokesman for the trio, took off his hat and smoothed back this thinning hair. "That theah man is ouah boss, little *gatitta.* Name's William Benson. He's a big noise heah in El Paso. Foah that mattah, he's a big noise in the whole state of Texas. What weah laughing at—and no offense intended, m'am—is that Mistuh Benson usually has no truck with gambling house queens." He laughed again and the others joined in finding the situation quite humorous.

Even Antonetta found their confidence amusing. She laughed along with them. Madelaina, however, found nothing humorous in their roughhousing. She also felt they were in some way ridiculing the man for showing an interest in what they called gambling house queens. Not wishing to embarrass either Tonetta or herself or cause her to lose business, she ignored them and kept her eyes on the bullring. So this was Manuelito's host, William Benson, she thought. She hadn't spoken too kindly of his bulls. Well, what of it? She spoke the truth. If he couldn't accept the truth, it was no affair of hers.

"*Chiquita,* what has theese gringo done?" asked Tonetta, nudging her.

William Benson returned to his box, dragging the mayor of Juarez with him. The official resembled Francesco Madero to such an extent that at first she was startled.

"*Señorita?*" The mayor pulled off his top hat with a forced flourish. He spoke in Spanish. "Permit me, with your permission, to present to you Señor William Benson. He wishes me to impart to your lovely ears that he means no disrespect. So enchanted is he with your knowledge of the *toros,* he wishes you to join him this evening at a dinner given in honor of Matador Manuelito Perez, so you can exchange with him such valuable knowledge of the bulls. You are most welcome to bring a chaperone, is Señor Benson's wish."

The nervous official had in the course of his speech recognized Antonetta. Torn by a burning impulse to advise Benson of exactly who she was, he was silently urged not to make such a mistake by Antonetta's articulate green eyes. He faltered and lowered his small bird eyes to stare at the tips of his patent leather shoes. Madelaina saved the moment.

"You may tell, Mr. Benson," she stated in English, "it is not necessary that I bring a chaperone because I decline his offer." Speaking directly to the mayor, she was able to avoid eye contact with Benson. "You will also inform Mr. Benson that the reason I decline his invitation, even if it is to honor a dear friend, Manuelito Perez, is because I am a working girl." She leveled

607

her dark fiery eyes on the three cowboys who flushed uncomfortably at her disclosure.

"I am a dancer at the Diamond Slipper. If he still desires to speak with me on the subject which interests him, the quality of his bulls, he can bring his party to the Diamond Slipper for dinner. I shall, when my time is free, sit with him to answer his questions." She rose to her feet. From the corner of her eye, she noticed his flushed face and rising anger at the rebuff. "Come, Tonetta," she said with polite reserve. "This bullfight is not worth our time. It is best we leave."

"Ah wouldn't do that, m'am," interrupted William Benson. "If ya do, ya might have to stuff youah words. The bull Perez has been puhsuadud ta fight isn't like the bulls y'all have seen tuhday."

The roar of the crowd at this moment drew her attention to the ring. Manuelito Perez had entered the arena. The third bull was his. When it came charging into the ring, she recognized instantly that it was dangerous and unpredictable. But Perez, out to cut an ear, made the animal charge back and forth in front of him so closely and gracefully that even his detractors were up out of their seats, yelling.

When it came time to kill the bull, he missed with the first thrust. The second dropped the animal cleanly. The crowd applauded, but they didn't wave their handkerchiefs. Perez had lost the ear; the crowd demanded perfection from this Spanish matador.

At least the bout hadn't ended in tragedy, thought Madelaina as she watched Manuelito leave the arena. But there was more. The trumpet blew and the next matador, a Mexican, took his turn with a bull. His art was applauded and cheered until the president of the arena granted the Mexican an ear.

Madelaina had lost sight of Manuelito, but now she saw him enter the arena, as the blare of the trumpet announced the final and most challenging bout. He strutted with the majesty of a king. He stopped before Madelaina's box and paused to bow. He removed his *montera*—hat—and waved it in a circle over his head.

608

With a quick, sudden move, he tossed his hat to Madelaina. She caught it and tossed him a lace handkerchief. In this small ritual, Perez had dedicated the bull to her.

All eyes were on her and she basked in the limelight. But suddenly Madelaina saw him. Terror struck at her. She sat down quickly, trying to slink behind the four Texans. She grabbed Tonetta's hand. "Quick, we must leave. Don't ask questions," she urged, her face drained of color. "When I say move, we both move, *pronto, querida.*"

Antonetta was fit to be tied. "Now, at the most interesting moment—just when everyone sees it's *La Bomba* to whom the bull was dedicated?" Her dismay was apparent, but the frantic silent appeal on Madelaina's face brought agreement to her lips. "*Muy bueno*—we go."

Before the crowd had resumed their seats, Madelaina and Antonetta were nearly outside the bullring, well on their way to Antonetta's carriage.

Safe inside the cabriolet, Tonetta, busting wide open for an explanation, heard only these words. "General Huerta saw me. I'm sure he recognized me."

Antonetta turned from her friend. She leaned forward in her seat. "One dollar extra for ju, *chico,*" she told the driver, "if ju get us to the club in less than five minutes."

"All right, m'am!" called the liveried black man. "Weah already theah, m'am!" He touched his hat, grinned, and sent the whip sailing over the heads of the matched bays.

"Ju know who ees theese Meester Benson, *querida?*" she asked Madelaina. "Hee ees Meester Texas. Ees also one beeg man in Mexico, a man much respected by Diaz. Waco tells me thees."

"Diaz is no longer president," muttered the general's daughter, still clutching Manuelito's black *montera* tightly in her hands.

"*Chiquita,* ju know what Tonetta means. The gringo *hacendados* are beeg men here as well as in Mexico.

609

Thees wan has *mucho dolares*. Eef he theenks enough for ju, maybe he could help ju." In her next breath Tonetta proceeded to negate her words. "Waco teels me he ees some terrible man. Ees best ju ignore heem." She laughed aloud over the rumble of the carriage wheels on the stone street. "Ju got some guts to tell heem the truth, straight out. 'I am dancer at Diamond *Sleepar*!' " She repeated Madelaina's words, just as arrogantly as she'd heard them earlier.

"Ayeiii, *chiquita. Un guapa muy tempestuosa* ees what ju are! A real gutsy woman."

But Madelaina heard none of these words. Still shaken from seeing her mortal enemy in the crowd with a few other uniformed *Federales,* her mind whirled in confusion, wondering what he was doing in El Paso. There were other things annoying the daughter of General Obregon—visions of Manuelito just as she'd seen him earlier, falling to his death in the bullring at the mercy of the bull. She hadn't even stayed to observe the animal he drew.

Damn you, Huerta! She cursed inwardly. Will I never be rid of you?

"We must make certain Doroteo Arango hears of his presence in El Paso," she said *sotto voce.* "It is important the *jefe* learns, understand?"

"*Si,* Little Fox, I understand. It is not necessary to explain whose presence it is that must be brought to the attention of Señor Arango." She lapsed back into Spanish.

"*Muy bueno, chiquita.* We are in accord," replied Madelaina. She reached in toward Tonetta in a gesture of apprehension. "I am so afraid for Manuelito," she confessed. She told Antonetta of her fears and visions. "And after all my cautions I didn't even get to see my own foolishness. Pray God I was wrong."

610

Manuelito Perez glanced up into the box seat section in time to see Madelaina exit with Antonetta following at her heels. She was lost in the crowd for a time. Even then the matador gave no thought to the possibility that Madelaina had actually left the Plaza de Toros. In truth he had no time to be concerned with her at the moment. Manuelito was determined to give the best performance of his life. As the gate swung open, the last bull of his entire life came charging and skidding out of the tunnel.

The instant he saw the beast hooking around the ring, he sucked in his breath. One of his men cursed aloud, "This one is bad, bad, *muy mal*. See how it hooks to the left? Stay away from this one, matador," he warned.

"Why?" asked Manuelito, arching his back stiffly. "Because I must go over the right horn to kill?" he retorted with scorn. "I have fought such bulls before. And for what they are paying, these gringos expect a master, not those Mexican *vaqueros* who make tricks and fancy cape twirls instead of art. They are clowns, not masters! Perez will show this crowd the real thing if it kills him!" Never had Manuelito Perez referred to the words, "death" or "kill" in the ring or at anytime during a *corrida*.

His teammate hesitated, struck dumb by his choice of words. Because the timing was not proper, he made no reference to such bad judgment. Later, he would recall with vivid clarity this telltale sign which should have told him tragedy was about to strike.

Manuelito placed the cape securely in his hands, slid through the fence opening and called to the bull.

"*Toro,* hah, *toroooo,*" he called, shaking the cape before him.

The animal wheeled at the voice, its tail shot up, and he charged across the dusty ring. When the bull reached him, not once did Manuelito spin about or swirl the cape or dance around the way his Mexican competitors had done earlier. He merely planted his feet firmly and executed those skilled passes he'd taught Madelaina. He swung the cape slowly before the bull's nose, guiding the ferocious head with the tantalizing red cloth, so that the left horn sailed past ten inches away from his leg.

Without moving his feet, he took the bull back in another charge and the right horn stabbed at him a few inches from his thigh. Six more perfect classic *verónicas* followed, each closer than the other, finishing with a half-*verónica* so close that the bull's neck hit him, nearly knocking him off balance.

The crowd, delirious with excitement, cheered with abandon. Manuelito, in a classic pose, turned his back on the beast and accepted the roaring accolades from the crowd. "*Viva* Perez! *Olé* Perez!" came the hysterical cries. Here indeed was a master—the fearless king of all matadors.

Now, with the *muleta,* cape, his specialty, he worked closer to the thundering charge of dynamite, wondering as he did why he hadn't seen Madelaina's face in the crowd. He saw the face of the gringo Benson, who had dared him to contest this special bull, one he had bred and crossbred from a strain of killer bulls. What was their wager? Five thousand gringo dollars. *Muy bueno,* thought Manuelito. It is not so much the dollars, it was his pride that was at stake and his determination to prove Madelaina wrong. He wanted to win this extra purse, then beg the love of his childhood to marry him and leave this accursed land in which she had suffered so greatly. He could take care of her. He was a wealthy and highly respected man in Spain. He could give her the things to which she'd been born. These were the thoughts occupying Manuelito's mind as he began the Pass of Death and his own perfected and highly dangerous *Perezinas.*

What followed was the most memorable day bullfighting had ever known in that era. He paid no attention to his *cuadrilla* who were shouting, "No, No!" Nor did he give any importance to the crowds crying, "No, Perez! No!"

He performed over a dozen suicidal natural passes, those in which the sword is taken from the cape and only a small ineffective bit of cloth is used to divert the bull away from the body. And then, feeling secure, overflowing with ebullience and a marked cocksuredness, he did his famous and most death-defying fear—a fantastic pass where he looked disdainfully away from the bull up into the stands as the animal thundered by. He wanted to see the look of adoration in Madelaina's eyes. It seemed to the crowd as though the bull couldn't miss—but he did. By now the crowd was hoarse from cheering. What perfection! How superb! This indeed is a master! What domination he has over this beast!

It was time for the kill. He began final preparations, lining up the bull so its feet would be together, shoulder blades open. In the far distance, beyond the roar of the crowds and the smell of baked earth and animal stench, Manuelito heard his *banderillos* shout warnings to him. "Stay away from him! Off to the side and quick!"

Oh no. This wasn't for Perez! Earlier they had refused to grant him an ear. No further humiliation for the King of Matadors. This one—this final and magnificent ecstasy—was to be a gift to Madelaina, his bride, he told himself.

No running offside and stabbing it in the lungs to spoil so magnificent a performance. He'd head in straight, slip in the blade, give the bull a fair shot, and hope to the Virgin it wouldn't hook to the right.

There stood Perez the Magnificent in front of the deadly killer bull, sighting down the sword, rising on the toes of one foot. As the bull lunged forward, Manuelito hurled himself straight over the lowered right horn. The

613

sword was sinking in, the horn cutting right by him. But suddenly the bull jerked its massive head to the right and sank its horn deep into the matador's groin.

Manuelito, trying to fight the horn from his body, was flung high into the air and slammed hard into the sand. The bull in a passion of fury gored him twice on the ground, then staggered, choked on his own blood, and flopped over dead, the sword, perfectly thrust up to its glittering hilt, between its shoulder blades. Pandemonium struck, the hordes screaming loud cries of horror and dismay. Quickly the crowd was stunned into silence. The crimson lake of blood in the sands was enough to inform his *cuadrilla* that Manuelito Perez was mortally wounded.

En route to the ring infirmary, he kept muttering. "The ears and tail go to Madelaina, *querida,* the love of my life."

William Benson and his men arrived at the infirmary. Only he was permitted admittance. Manuelito, laid out on a makeshift table while examined by a physician, raised his blood-shot eyes and fixed them frantically on the wealthy cattleman.

"I win, *señor gringo?*" He gripped Benson's arm, half-lifting himself from the table against the doctor's protest. "Promise me you will give the purse to Señorita Madelaina Obre—" He stopped in time. On his death bed, as he took his last breath of life, he remembered his promise not to give away her true identity. "To *La Bomba,* the star at the Diamond Slipper. Tell her I will love her for all time. I should have listened to her, *señor*. She predicted my demise on this day—"

Manuelito shuddered desperately as death's icy fingers reached out, extracting his soul from his body.

Two hours later, as Madelaina prepared for the evening's performances, she was still listening to the same tune from Antonetta as she exclaimed of the advantages and financial security open to a woman who married a man like William Benson. Finally in exasperation Madelaina demanded that she refrain from mentioning Benson again. "He means nothing to me. I will not occupy my thoughts with such a man who is openly known for his cruelty!"

"Very well, *chiquita*. I will not speak again of this most important *hacendado*."

"Tonetta!" warned *La Bomba*.

"Oh, jur crazy! I go now!" She retorted. "I 'ave enough of my business not to be busy with jurs," she said, slamming the door to Madelaina's dressing room.

Antonetta shrugged her shoulders back and patted the folds of her exquisite turquoise French original, a beaded, form-fitting sheath that flounced out at the knees. It makes no difference to speak of necessity to Madelaina, she thought. The woman still has a will of her own. So forget her. Attend to business. Her eyes lit up as she walked through the gambling palace to see it growing crowded, even at this early hour. The clatter of silver dollars drowned out the music, a sound welcome to her ears. Faro was the house specialty and the latest was a new game of poker, with several varieties called stud and draw that some of the newly rich oilmen seemed so excited about. These gaming tables were jammed packed with men eager to try their luck.

She continued to saunter through the large and brightly lit salon, nodding to some, waving to others, a fixed smile broadening into a grin at the sight of such business. All the while her attention was trained subtly on two exceedingly tall foreign-looking men dressed in civilian clothing, standing in an unmistakable military brace at the end of the bar. Coming toward her was a trusted employee, Jesus Morales, a young Mexican lad who spoke in Spanish.

"Madame," he addressed her respectfully, "two gentlemen wish to speak with the proprietress on a matter they will not divulge to me."

Antonetta glanced past him at these men, who were not exactly strangers to her. She'd seen them once or twice before here in her establishment and then in the vicinity of her boardinghouse. "Very well, Jesus," she nodded curtly. "I shall be there in a moment."

Since the revolution had commenced, these foreign-looking men had overrun Juarez and El Paso both. She approached them with the utmost courtesy and pleasantness, flashing a dazzling smile.

"*Si, señores,* what can I do for ju?" She spoke her pigeon yankee.

It turned out they desired to rent one of her small salons where businessmen frequently met to converse in the intimacy of a private room. The salon, to be provided with drinks and food and other refreshments, was booked and paid for in advance under the name Eric Von Klause.

The news of the tragedy at the Plaza de Toros hadn't yet begun to trickle in. It would take nearly two hours before her informers would run in with such news. Meanwhile she attended to business and busied herself throughout the establishment, wherever her services were needed. No question, she thought, the *corrida* will encourage thirsty men to drink, then gamble. Was this not why Antonetta was in business? To cater to the desires of free-spending men with un-usual appetites.

How many times she had wistfully confided to Madelaina she wanted to operate a brothel, a whore-house *extraordinario* like many of other establishments were running of late. Doroteo Arango, with his convo-luted sense of Indian morality, wouldn't permit it. Since the majority of women would be Mexicans, he would not bring such shameful degradation upon the Mexican woman who was already regarded at a sub-standard level by the gringos.

"Ju don' see gringos operating such places with the gringas! No! So why permit them to satisfy their lust on our women?"

So negative and indignant had Pancho been over this, Antonetta pushed it from her mind. She didn't dare justify her desire by alluding to the immorality so prevalent among his camp followers. Nor did she dare suggest that it would be better for those *campesinas* to be paid whores than unpaid *putas* who struggled against

616

disease and death each moment of their existence.

Periodically she'd mention this secret desire and ultimate plan of hers to Madelaina. "Ju know how much gringo dollars we could make owning such an establishment, *chiquita?* Ayeiii! Eet makes me seeck jus' to theenk about eet. Bot, what can I say, eh? Pancho ees my man and while he ees my man, I do as he desires."

Antonetta moved behind the bar, swishing to one side as she kept her icy green eyes trained on the bartenders whose itchy fingers rang a melodious tune on her cash boxes. Her eyes would signal messages to Jesus, truly the most honest man she'd encountered, who was hired to watch the sticky-fingered men behind the plank. Whenever she spotted foul play, Jesus was an instant deterrent.

Her emerald eyes gazed about the smoke-filled room, alive with voices. For an instant, she froze. She thought she saw several uniformed Mexican officers enter the place. This in itself wasn't so surprising, the Diamond Slipper often entertained *Federales* who stopped in for a bit of fun while in Juarez on official business. Usually these men were of lesser rank than those men who flashed by her. By the time curiosity moved her through the congested room, they had disappeared. Had she dreamed them up, she wondered.

She craned her neck above the crowd and looked in all directions. She saw nothing of them. She shrugged and moved back through the room. She took a moment to glance at the small gold watch pinned to her breast. Half-hour to show time. The dining room was full, with more people arriving each moment. The first two shows had been sold out. She filled her thoughts with how she could keep the patrons happy and encourage them to remain for the last show as she moved regally about in her business establishment.

Elsewhere in the Diamond Slipper, upstairs in the private room booked by Herr Von Klause, a conversation was underway, which might one day change the course of history. Antonetta had seen no illusions ear-

617

lier when she thought she'd seen *Federales* of high rank in her establishment. They had been slickly diverted to the upstairs salon by two foreign agents who prepared the clandestine meetings in their usual cloak-and-dagger manner.

General Vitoriano Huerta and Major Salomon had met their host Herr Von Klause and a clandestine meeting was underway. They spoke in German and often drifted into Spanish. General Huerta had been trained in Germany so language was no barrier. Most high-ranking *Federale* officers were trilingual; French, German, and Spanish, and sometimes English, came readily to them.

Downstairs, totally unaware of the drama taking place in her establishment, Antonetta received another surprise. Shock is more like the emotion she experienced when she saw Doroteo Arango, dressed in a black dinner suit, arrive and approach her quite matter-of-factly. How many times had she encouraged him to experience the excitement of watching *La Bomba*? Many more times, he had resisted. "I don't drink. I don't gamble. *Pues,* I don't even smoke. Why should I occupy the space of a paying customer?" he'd protest. "Besides, I might be recognized."

"But, *amoroso,*" she had protested. "You must come to see the sensation of El Paso. You would never believe *La Bomba* is the Little Fox who followed you as *campesina, Jefe.*"

But he continuously declined. In all this time, her business had picked up. Each night's receipts exceeded those of the previous night. Crowds stood in long lines to see the Latin bombshell each night. Antonetta had even considered adding more tables, opening another section to handle the overflow. The uptown swells, the stuck-up gringos had started coming to the Diamond Slipper, and she had wanted to make the place a bit fancier to attract more of the monied crowd. Whenever she'd speak of these plans to Villa and voice her exuberance over such marvelous business, he'd stroke her face gently and tell her to be patient, to wait a little

618

longer. Each time her enthusiasm would diminish, and as she gazed upon him, she would see in his eyes the gathering of storm clouds.

And now, as he stood before her, dressed like a wealthy *hacendado,* she felt a deep pang of dismay, a suffocation that shook her composure. In these past several months of their renewed vows of love, Antonetta knew she'd follow Pancho to hell and back. She had listened to his quiet words with love-filled calf eyes and had taken no initiative to enlarge the club. His presence at the Diamond Slipper seemed to blast out loud and clear to her, the time was at hand. He would soon be leaving.

"A secluded table for me, *querida,*" he requested, "away from the sight of other partygoers."

Antonetta filled with dismay. The only available place was in a niche at the foot of the back stairs, close to the dressing rooms, at the edge of the stage, well hidden in shadows. Despite her protestations that it wasn't a suitable location for a man of his stature, Doroteo Arango assured his mistress that it would suit him fine. "All I wish is a glass of strawberry pop," he added, patting her hands affectionately.

Madelaina, dressed scantily in a revealing fandango costume, approached them as she left her dressing room en route to perform her number on stage. Doroteo Arango glanced up casually and fixed intent eyes upon her with an expression of mild astonishment. If he came to any conclusions about her, he said nothing. Not a glimmer of recognition passed his eyes or hers.

The house lights dimmed. The nattily dressed mariachi band, in their white satin ruffled shirts, dark trousers, and scarlet cummerbunds, presented a loud musical fanfare. The room was dark as pitch. Then the spotlight exploded into a circle of intense light. *La Bomba* stood at center stage. There came a loud clap of cymbals and the dance began. Two overhead spotlights, operated by men nestled in the rafters, trained on her and followed her every move.

La Bomba began gyrating to the beat of primitive

619

drums. She clapped her hands high above her head and beat a tattoo on the floor with her slipper. Each twist and turn tossed her hip-length coal hair about in satiny cartwheels like circles of black fire. The fandango began slowly, sensuously, growing livelier each moment. Increasing her momentum, Madelaina pulsated in rhythmic cadence as it rose to a crescendo, until the spectators were left breathless.

Upstairs in the private room, General Huerta, tiring of the negotiations, pulled the curtains apart and glanced at the stunning movement on stage to see what the "*olés*" and wild bursts of applause were about. For a few moments they all watched the performance, their interest absorbed by both the star performer and the uncontainable audience.

When the audience, unable to handle the sensuous stirring of their own emotions, reached the pinnacle of their endurance, the dance and dancer ended abruptly, leaving them stuck in outer limbo. For this reason, there followed several moments of stunned silence before the applause began. And when it commenced, it swelled to deafening proportions followed by the uninhibited cheering, whistling, and yahooing usually associated with a rowdier crowd.

When General Huerta and Major Salomon had finished their business, they took the rear stairs to a back exit, followed by their host, to avoid being noticed. Von Klause and his assistant, however, remained inside, pausing to watch the last moments of the show. Their attention was caught by the presence of Doroteo Arango, who hadn't noticed them. Slowly they moved in closer to him.

On stage the spotlights blinked on and off as *La Bomba* basked in the profuse attention showered on her. She bowed and graciously accepted the accolades as would a victorious matador. Finally she waved the spotlights off and stepped from the stage, as another, less vigorous, act followed. Madelaina passed Doroteo Arango's table and was about to pause when she noted the silent warning in his eyes as he turned from her to gaze upon the faces of the two strangers who approached him. She continued on to her dressing room, her face lined with shadows of concern. In the middle of her dance, Madelaina had felt certain she'd seen the face of General Huerta, with the drooping moustache she'd grown to despise and those black burning eyes of terror. She had felt a pang of fright for an instant, but when she whirled back into position from which she thought she'd seen him, there was emptiness. She convinced herself she was creating these images. She continued along the narrow corridor when she felt the tug of hands pulling her into the shadows. Tonetta had yanked at her and wrapped her in a silk shawl, a finger at her lips cautioning her to be silent.

"What is it?" whispered Madelaina hoarsely. "What's happening? Who are those men with Doroteo Arango?"

Again, she was cautioned to be silent. Tonetta whispered, "I am not certain. Come." She pulled her along the narrow corridor. "We can listen from here."

They had circled behind Villa, and in a small enclosure, Antonetta revealed a peephole through which they could both observe and listen to the goings on.

"General?" queried the man Eric Von Klause in German-accented Spanish. "May we intrude upon your privacy?"

"I am no general," replied Mr. Arango. "I am waiting for a friend who is also no general."

"Ahhh, how clever of you to be so cautious," replied Von Klause.

Arango stretched his politeness a hair longer. "My friend might be upset finding me with men I don't know and have no desire to talk with."

"What makes you so sure I am not that friend, General?"

"It's simple. My friend is a fiery-tempered redhead, prettier than you and equipped with more gadgets than you can invent."

"Ahhh, General. You're a man's man after all. I've heard rumors—by God, I'm glad they are true."

Arango grew sullen as his patience diminished.

"Look, who the hell are you and what do you want? I'm in no mood for games."

"Very good. My people have had you under surveillance since your arrival. We've attempted to speak to you in private before. You always evade us. Earlier I reserved a room here. I thought my business had ended until we descended these stairs and spotted you. If you desire, we can retire to the room where we won't be overheard. I presume this will meet with your approval."

"You presume too much," said Arango, growing very quiet. His instinct stirred him to disquiet. "I sit here comfortably."

Herr Von Klause glanced in every direction, then nodded to his companion who retreated into the shadows. He spoke in hushed tones. "I represent a foreign government who watches your every move. Believe me, General, you have a staunch friend and supporter in us."

"A government which has nothing to do but watch the comings and goings of a nobody like Doroteo Arango? Hah!"

"Heh, heh, heh, my friend. You have a sense of humor. Actually, you are greatly admired in my country. May I sit down?" He moved his enormous frame into a nearby chair without Villa's approval. "We wish to help your cause."

"My cause? What cause is it you speak of?" needled Arango.

Von Klause forced a tight-lipped smile. "Heh, heh, heh." He shook his head amiably, as if he found tremendous humor in the clean-shaven man.

"We wish to finance your revolution, *mein Generale*," he said conspiratorially.

"And?"

Again Von Klause looked about him cautiously. He leaned in closer. "We will help you crush your opposition. decimate them, grind them up for dust."

"And?"

"You see, *mein Generale,* we are not too pleased to

622

do business with General Huerta. His government leaves us somewhat disappointed."

"Forgive me," interrupted Arango, feigning temporary confusion. "Huerta's government? Did—uh—President Madero's government suddenly dissolve? Disappear?"

"Heh, heh, heh," laughed Von Klause, studying the Mexican inscrutably with black smoldering eyes as fierce as Villa's had been on occasion. "You are very amusing, General. I like that. A man with a sense of humor is a man to be trusted. Perhaps, when circumstances prove more favorable and we can boast of mutual success, we can indulge in such patter. At this time, I am suggesting to you that my government, a formidable one, *señor*, is interested in signing a peace treaty with your nation."

"Peace treaty? Ahhh, *si*. That's what all this is about?" replied Arango knowingly as his eyes twinkled in merriment. "Imagine—a peace treaty, eh? So, tell me, *amigo*, what else does your—uh—formidable government desire?"

"Why—uh—I—uh—nothing. Simply a peace treaty marking your nation and you, *Señor Generale*, as a staunch ally."

"Ahhh, I see." Arango kept bobbing his head up and down in agreement. "And what else?" he asked in a disarming manner.

"Well, we are fully prepared to back your struggle for the presidency with troops, solid financial backing, arms, and ammunition—the latest in military strategy and the proper propaganda, you see."

"Ahhh, and in return you'll want oil—land—precious minerals—what?"

"Oh, nothing much. A few submarine bases, a place for our battleships to refuel and tie in for repairs. You know, friendly ports." It was a throwaway statement.

"Ahhh, I see." Arango nodded his head as he observed both men. "You have no Castilian lisp, no *gachupín* manner, so you are so Spaniard. You are not stuck up and I can understand your words, so you are not British. You are all business—so you are not Italian—" he said, pushing a bit.

"We are Germans! Sent by the Kaiser, General!" retorted Von Klause, disdainfully tilting his nose into the air. He inserted a monocle into the crease around his eye and studied the man opposite him with apparent dislike.

"Ahhh," sighed Arango as he leaned in with apparent desire to intrigue with him. "Tell me," he asked confidentially, "what will the Kaiser do with the submarine bases? Attack the gringos?"

"Certainly not!" exploded Von Klause, his nostrils flaring. "Our aim is directed only toward a peaceful coexistence in the field of commerce."

"Hah!" retorted Arango. "What do you take me for? A chocolate-drinking *Federale* regular? Your Kaiser is not unfamiliar to me. I *read* about him every day," he boasted pointedly. "First, a war in Europe. He itches for it this very moment. Then he'll puncture the gringos' lifeline from below the border, eh? Pretty soon, we all speak Spanish with a German accent. And the eagle and the snake turn into black, red, and gold bars, eh? Is that it? All this with the help of that illiterate *peón,* Pancho Villa!"

Madelaina and Antonetta held on to each other tightly. They froze. "They know who he is," lamented Madelaina.

"You wait here, out of sight. Don't even go to your dressing room," ordered Antonetta. She moved out of sight, into the next room. Madelaina listened more intently as she observed the duo speak.

"That's absurd," protested Von Klause, stammering in full outrage.

"What if I permit this alliance and the gringos turn on me?"

Von Klause took hope. "Have no fear, General. We will protect you with full force, of course."

"How?"

"Our navy will be at your disposal, in your harbors—"

"Listen, you lunkhead, the gringos can swat flies across the Rio Grande, reach over and bury them before your navy has time to fart in midocean."

"Have you truly seen German power, General?" Von Klause tensed.

"Have you seen Pancho Villa's power?" countered the Mexican puma. "Peaceful coexistence in the field of commerce! Hah!" he roared thunderously. "Listen, *Señor Alemán,* negotiator at large, I am here as a guest of the gringos here, and good neighbors do not promote treachery." Arango rose to his feet, pulled the German up by his lapels, and with a swift right to the jaw, he flattened Herr General Eric Von Klause of the Kaiser's Imperial Army on his dignified rump.

Before another moment passed, two of Antonetta's burly bouncers moved in swiftly and tossed the foreigners out of the Diamond Slipper on their sorely abused behinds. If Doroteo Arango had anticipated the burning hatred in Von Klause's humiliated eyes and the promise of retaliation registered in them, he might have employed more diplomacy in handling the Chief of German Intelligence. However, Doroteo Arango, knew little of the cunning and skilled diplomacy employed by such treacherous jackals. He knew only the ways of oppressed Mexican hillsmen, straight talk— and if that didn't suffice, the remedy lay in the gun, the swiftest justice in man's unpredictable world.

Madelaina came out of the enclosure and seated herself next to Doroteo Arango, whose cover had surely been blown by now.

"That, Little Fox," remarked Villa knowingly, "was the beginning of an ugly sign. Who will this international negotiator seduce now that Villa won't whore for him, eh?"

"Who else?" hissed the fandango dancer, her eyes staring inwardly as if she'd clearly seen the picture— the sudden coincidences in their lives. "General Huerta. They are alike, those two. Speaking of that snake," she confided, "I saw him and and that devil Salomon at the *corrida* this afternoon."

625

"Huerta is here? In El Paso?" His eyes lost their twinkle. "You saw them?"

"What's more," interrupted Antonetta, swishing into the secluded alcove, "I, too, saw them, here in my own establishment earlier. It's true, I thought my eyes deceptive when they were swallowed up in the crowd, but all the time they must have been upstairs with these German negotiators."

Arango opened a small bag he removed from his pocket and passed it to the women. "Peanut brittle?" They refused. He took out a piece, broke it, and stuffed some into his mouth. He turned his attention to the remains of his strawberry pop, beguiled by the air bubbles fizzing to the surface each time he swished the contents of his glass. "Imagine—how do they create these?"

La Bomba retired to her dressing room, her thoughts wandering. How had they learned of Villa's identity? How had they recognized him? He looked nothing like the terrible Yaqui Indian hillsman, the savior of Mexico. Knowing that Huerta and Salomon were in the same city as she shook her. She began to perspire with alternate chills of heat and cold and relive in her mind the torture of Madrigal.

"I don't care what I promised you, Tolomeo!" she cried aloud. "One day Huerta and Salomon will pay for what they did to me. I had no business promising you I'd forgive them. I can't! I can't! I'm not divine! I'm human!" she sobbed.

The thoughts, comforting and confusing both, pacified her enough to apply the finishing touches to her makeup and slip into her new flamingo-red, beaded costume which covered less of her than the previous ensemble. She sipped the last of the brandy she'd taken to drinking of late to reenforce her courage each time she stepped onto the stage. With all her agility and talent and ability to mesmerize an audience, Madelaina Obregon was still embarrassed and self-conscious about flaunting her physical charms before strange men. She found brandy gave her the courage it took to transform her into an uninhibited bundle of dynamite that excited

626

the senses of her audience and left them with a breathlessness that made her to them, the greatest of all entertainers.

Once again she was on stage. Here, with the brandy churning hot through her upper chest and body, she felt free and alive. What power she felt, whirling, twisting, gyrating, knowing every eye in the house was upon her. For these eight to ten minutes, she had perfect control over them and could bend them to her will.

No one, but no one possessed the magic of *La Bomba*. She was filling out in the right places again and no longer reflected the horror of her past life in those dark, sunken eyes that were so much a part of her. She moved to the side of the stage, dancing from table to table, twirling with such swiftness she only saw blurred faces. Around and around she went, again and again until she felt dizzy. Moreover, for an instant, she thought she saw the face of her husband, Peter Duprez. Again and again she moved, the room beginning to spin. Again she saw Peter's face. *I'll make it stop,* she told herself. *I won't let myself be deluded.* The dance finally ended. She stood quite still; only her breasts heaved and bounced as she tried to catch her breath from the strenuous act.

A fixed smile on her lips, her arms upraised, she accepted the applause. The image of Peter Duprez wouldn't dissolve. She blinked her eyes hard, trying to pierce the blinding spotlights and the smoke-filled room. A waft of blue-white smoke circled ceilingward and in its wake she saw him, plain as day.

He was seated at the number one table with others in a large party. Next to him was a stunning blonde, dressed exquisitely in a white satin beaded gown, cut low in front with a portrait neckline. A white fox fur cape was draped over one shoulder and her blue gringa eyes were fixed on Peter with the look of a spoiled vixen and the impatience of a schoolgirl unable to get her way. Peter's eyes were glued to Madelaina as if by a powerful adhesive, and hers on him. It would be an impossibility for anyone not to notice the vibrations between them.

627

It was this look between the dancer on stage and the man seated next to her that produced a sudden unexpected recklessness in Peter Duprez' impetuous companion, Valerie Townsend, daughter of the Texas governor, Hampton P. Townsend. The young woman picked up her cape with arrogant determination, stood up with a pause that cried for attention, and without glancing back at her companions, stalked haughtily out of the gambling palace. Her entire entourage, ten people in all, muttering protests and mild expletives, nevertheless arose and grabbing Duprez's arm, piloted him out the door in pursuit of the hot-tempered social butterfly.

Madelaina wasn't certain how she got to her dressing room. With trembling hands she quickly reached for the brandy, poured a stiff bracer, and downed it in a gulp. She stood before her mirror, staring at her pale reflection.

"It was Peter. It was," she told the image in the glass.

"What's wrong, *chiquita*?" Antonetta had followed her into the room and closed the door behind her. "What is it? What happened? What was that all about?"

Madelaina, unable to articulate, paced the floor a moment.

"You knew them? They recognized you? What? In God's name, stop this walking and tell me."

"It was my husband. Peter Duprez."

"That man was Duprez?" Tonetta frowned in reflection. "That man with the gringa?" Her eyes narrowed to slits. Earlier Antonetta had greeted the stuck-up El Pasoans, those high-society snobs. The man she knew as Tom Mix winked at her in secret understanding, and noting his uptown tuxedo and swanky accessories, she had discreetly refrained from greeting him as she might have if he had appeared alone. Her mind raced back to the time prior to the Battle of Juarez, after Little Fox had been abducted by her father's spies, when she and Tom Mix had engaged in conversation. He had certainly filled the description burned into her brain by

628

Little Fox, but when Peter had introduced himself to her as Tom Mix, Antonetta had let it pass.

"Oh, Madelaina," she cried out in dismay. "To think if he hadn't fooled me by telling me his name was Tom Mix, I would have told him about you and how you had searched for him."

"You know Peter? But how? When? Where—"

"Even that gringo *bastardo,* Captain Richards, called him Tom Mix. How was I to know, *querida*? How?"

"Who was the woman with him?" asked Madelaina. "Not his wife, I hope."

"*Querida,* if only I had known," she punished herself. "Not yet. But soon. It is in all the papers." She broke into pigeon Yankee. "Che is de daughter of the Texas governor. Che is not so beeg a package, bot de father, ah, he ees beeg noise een Texas. They are how you say—*novios*."

"Betrothed," said Madelaina. She couldn't have felt worse. She poured herself another drink.

"Too much of this stuff will make for ju worse troubles," said Antonetta, recapping the bottle. She was conscious of a twinge of irritation in *La Bomba*.

"Listen, *chiquita,* if the house wasn't so filled with people, I would send ju home, ju hear? In fact, *chiquita,* eef ju desire, *La Gatitta* will perform for ju. After seeing *La Bomba,* they will throw tomatoes at me, for sure. Bot at least there will be some show."

"No!" protested Madelaina. "I wouldn't do that to you on such a night. After the kindness you and Doroteo have showered upon me? I even have my own little *casita,* thanks to you. Now, leave me, *por favor*. I wish to think alone."

Tonetta sadly left the dressing room.

Madelaina lit up a marijuana cigarette and lay back on the red velvet chaise longue smoking, although with none of the usual feelings of relaxation, either from the booze or the grass. She thought she heard a knock at the door. No matter, she was drifting into a euphoric state and didn't care who might be wanting to see her. Her eyes fluttered heavily and closed for a moment or two.

629

Suddenly, she felt something heavy on her lap, something that fell with a heavy thud. Her eyes fluttered open and she sat up with a start. On her lap lay a thick canvas sack, the size of a man's traveling case. Her heavy-lidded eyes were forced open by sheer will, and she saw a pair of boots on the floor alongside of her. Her eyes traveled farther up. Black pants, solid gold belt buckle with an indiscernible brand encrusted upon it, shirt, jacket, string tie, large overpowering shoulders, sun-bronzed skin on a cold, marblelike face, black and gray hair, cut short with a crease from a spiffy Stetson.

William Benson stood there staring down at her. He was alone. She glanced from him to the heavy sack on her lap in bewilderment.

"*Señor*, what is this?"

"The money. Five thousand dollars. He wanted y'all ta have it."

"Who? What money? What are you speaking of? I assure you I have no idea what you are talking about," she said irritably, noting the cold arrogance and borderline disgust in his face.

"That there is Manuelito Perez' blood money. Ya told him he was gonna die and he did. Why he wanted ya ta have the money aftah y'all put a hex on him is beyond all mah comprehension, woman."

Madelaina tried to clear her head, to remove the sudden fuzziness that engulfed her like a thick curtain separating reality from fantasy. "Manuelito—blood money—dead?" His words came to her in disjointed bits and pieces which she had difficulty sewing together in any set pattern.

"Suppose you start at the beginning. You make no sense to me, *señor*."

"Hah! Youah'd like me ta think that, wouldn't ya? What exactly did ya mean to ole Manuelito?"

"Manuelito—dead?" Now it came together. She pulled her legs over the side of the chaise longue, removed the canvas money bag from her lap, and touched her head as if this gesture would magically

630

clear it and bring things into better focus. She could feel his hostility as it permeated the room like a cold draft. She saw him wrinkle his nose and sniff the air suspiciously.

"Youah ain't smokin one o' them dopers, are ya? Those reefers that drive a man plumb loco? No wonder Perez was doomed, with such a harlot as you!"

"As a matter of fact, Mr. Benson, I am doing just that. Will you join me in one?"

"Ya can't shock me, woman. Ah've known women like ya before. Ah came ta keep a death bed promise ta a gentleman. He wanted ya ta have the money he won in a wageuh made with me. He bargained ta fight mah champion bull, a real killah ah imported from them Miura ranches in Spain ta intuhbreed with mah Chihuahuans."

Madelaina wasn't listening to him. All she knew was that Manuelito was dead. "If only he had listened. What more could I have done to convince him? Apparently not enough," she sighed wistfully. She wanted to cry, but no tears would come, something which William Benson picked up on immediately.

"Not even a teah for the dead?" he snorted with inborn cynicism. "That's the leahst y'all could do is ta show some concern foah a man who spoke youah name with his final breath. Y'all are some iron woman. No teahs!"

"Mr. Benson, I don't give a fig for either your thoughts concerning my relationship to Manuelito or what you think of me. As for this money Manuelito chose to leave me, I'm not sure I understand his gesture. But, if you'd be so kind as to learn from his managers the source of his personal charity, I'll be happy to turn the amount over to them."

William Benson leveled his surly blue eyes on the woman and saw the faintest quivering of her sensuous lips, giving her a strangely alluring quality. Her arms and shoulders reflected the subdued lighting of the ostentatious dressing room built to her specifications by Antonetta. Her black hair, falling loose over her shoulders, framed her small but defiant face. And those eyes—those dark, jewellike eyes—reflected a way of life imposed against a strenuous code of morality that didn't add up in his mind. Standing there she looked like a young virgin fresh out of a convent. Yet, he knew all too well what she was. Her profession, as sordid and disgusting as it appeared to him, the kind that his contemporaries took in their stride, spelled it out for him. Still, her astute observations on the bulls weren't the patter that spilled from the mouths of whores or unrefined gambling hall queens.

She was an enigma, especially to William Benson. Her kind of women didn't return the purses left to them by their paramours. "Y'all would do that—return the money?" he asked hesitantly.

"To repeat myself is a waste of time," she snapped with an air of detachment. "Now, if you'll excuse me, I must prepare for the final show."

"William Benson is no fool, *señorita*. Will ya tell me why youah've been trying ta shock me and push me outa youah life, like I was some tainted devil from out the dark ages?" He smiled with a private amusement in his eyes. "Ah wasn't born yestahday, little filly. Ah know women. What is it—do ah frighten ya in some way?"

Madelaina paused a moment, surprised by the new tack he'd taken.

"*You* frighten *me*? The man rumored to be the most powerful man in the state of Texas? A man who, it's been said, chews bullets for breakfast and can outshoot, outfight, and outsmart every man around? I've no reason to fear you, sir. You've nothing I desire. Least of all a sour disposition and foul mouth and a propensity to exercise power over helpless people."

"So that's what they say about William Benson?"

"Worse."

"Worse?"

"Much worse."

"Ah admit ah'm ruthless, m'am. A man hasta be all the things ya said. A weakuh man just hasn't the sense ta stay outa mah way an' when he gets hurt, he cries lika baby. What else have ya heard about me?" he

632

asked as if it gave him a measure of importance to be spoken of in awe.

"What does it matter? I make it a practice never to believe what I hear."

"That so?" He brightened. "A woman after mah own heart."

"You've said what you came to say, Mr. Benson. I thought I'd replied as best I could. What my relationship was to Manuelito Perez is between us. I owe no man any explanation. Since Manuelito has left us, it's useless to resurrect the dead past. Now, if you'll excuse me, I must prepare for the next show," she repeated herself with more finality.

The more Benson listened to her words, her voice, and her subtle airs, the more the aristocratic background he sensed in her came through the tough pose. No whore he'd ever known spoke as she did or held herself with such poise, even if she was clad scantily in such revealing threads. No, thought William Benson, in this woman was something rather special. He sensed it earlier at the Plaza. He could have sent one of his men to deliver the money and message, but instead he chose to attend to the mission personally, to prove to himself this was some special filly.

"As a matter of fact, Mr. Benson, I felt certain that after you learned of my occupation in such a place, you'd make it a point never to cross my path." She flung her head back and eyed him defiantly.

"Look heah, little filly, y'all didn't have me fooled a bit. Ah knew all the time you was jus' puttin' on an act ta scare me off." He laughed good-naturedly, easing up a bit. "Ah didn't mean ta be so hard on ya earlier, ya heah? Men like me have gotta make shuah of any filly who intuhrests 'em. Ya see, ah jus' might be all the things youah've heard tell of me. But, then again, maybe ah'm not. Ah came ta tell ya, ah'm intuhrested in ya, see. It don't make no mattuh ta me what y'all had ta do with the matador. Ah'm fixin' ta get ta know ya better, so youah'd bettah fix it in youah mind what mah intentions will be."

633

Madelaina remained silent. She could say nothing else. Her thoughts were centered on Manuelito and why she hadn't communicated with him. Why hadn't she been able to convince him of the impending doom so that he might have been able to circumvent his fate? Benson's voice cut into her thoughts.

"Look heah, little filly. Ah've gotta leave. Ah can't even stay heah long enough ta see ya dance. Ah've already heard from mah men that you'ah a hot torpedo—dancing, that is," he added hastily when he saw her dark eyes flare angrily. "Ah jus' wanta ask ya ta have lunch with me in three days. Ah've gotta get me into Juarez and do some business south of the boahdah. This is Saturday. Ah'll be back on Tuesday. So ah'll warn ya, ah intend tuh pick youah pretty little brains apaht on them bulls y'all know so much about, heah? Will ya jus' tell me this much—wheah did ya learn so much about them *toros*?"

"In Spain at the hacienda of my uncle, Don Diego—" She stopped in time. "Well, I lived in Las Marismas, where the Concha bulls are raised. I am well acquainted with the *ranchos* where the Miura are bred. And the Salamanca as well. Manuelito taught me all I know about fighting the bulls. I was an apt pupil. Believe me, I learned the difference in the breeding of bulls, and I must say it is vast." She fairly glowed at the conversation and Benson noticed the change in her.

"You—a filly, fight bulls?" His eyes widened in disbelief. "Well ah'll be dang-blasted! The hell ya say, woman!" Benson slapped his thigh with his Stetson. "What's that ya said—Las Marismas? By the holy beard of Satan—Las Marismas! Mah dear child. Didja jus' happen to know of an *hombre* named Don Felipe Cortez? Well, it was this heah Don Cortez, mah good friend, who turned me onta breeding bulls. And it was him who allowed me ta meet up with Matador Perez. That's how weah arranged the American tour foah Manuelito. What a small world, eh? Ah tell ya, *señorita*, it will grieve me evah so much ta inform Don Cortez of the matador's fate."

634

Madelaina listened attentively. Her head was clear and free of any fuzziness she experienced earlier from the marijuana. She tensed incredibly at his words. Indeed, it was a small world. She would have to be very discreet not to mention her uncle or allow any tie in to her past to be aired.

"Then y'all will come ta lunch with me? Ah'll send a carriage foah ya. Wheah do ya live, m'am?"

She gave him the address. "I've a small house on Elm Street."

"Mah man will be by foah ya at 1 P.M. sharp. *Hasta luego,* little filly. Ya jus' done mah heart real good." He stood for a time, staring at her with the exuberance of a schoolboy on his first date. "Don'cha let any harsh words spoken about me allow ya ta change youah mind, heah?"

He placed his Stetson on his head, squaring it properly, shook her hand like a clumsy, self-conscious juvenile, and left. The incongruities in his behavior had disarmed her. She wasn't sure why she'd even agreed to have lunch.

The full extent of William Benson's wealth was not known in its entirety. This Texas millionaire, who owned one of the largest spreads in the Panhandle near Amarillo, Texas, presently owned several haciendas and rich cattle lands and bull-breeding farms in Mexico. Under the old Diaz laws, now perpetuated by Presidente Madero, Benson was a *hacendado* of enormous stature in both countries. As one of the most affluent cattlemen in the state, this man, whose political tentacles reached to Washington and the house of the American president, was often conducting business in El Paso and Juarez.

Benson, a tall, heavy-set man in his fifties, with blunt features and eyes that X-rayed when they stared, had a temper rumored to be the worst of any gringo. This brute of a man, reported as a tough, hard-hitting SOB, short on temper and quick on action, was a wrangler never without his six-guns.

When Benson roared orders to his ranch hands, they jumped through hoops like trained animals. He paid them fair wages, but made no bones about telling them he intended to extract twice as much work as he paid for. This self-made man with the bold swagger and impudence of a man of inestimable wealth and power, hired no man who professed to have brains. All he required from his help was physical endurance and the needed stamina to perform results without bitching like bleating sheep.

His own reserve brain power, enough for ten men, succeeded in making him one of the cleverest politicians in the state of Texas. He needed to be on top of things to outsmart the new breed of politician surfacing in the land where manipulation became the byword. It was rumored about that his only wife died quite young, bitterly disillusioned and heartsick over a loveless marriage and the impossibility of living with so ambitious a man. His greatest disappointment was the fact that he hadn't sired at least a half-dozen sons to take over when he died. His oldest son had left the fold at an early age, unable to bear the degradation to which his father subjected him in his efforts to make a man in his own mold out of him. Because he could no longer take the old man's despotic tryanny, Peter Duprez Benson left and hadn't seen his father in at least two decades.

Six months of the year, William Benson lived on his ranch near Amarillo. The remaining six months were spent between the haciendas in Mexico and his mansion in El Paso where he entertained high government officials, oil tycoons, and prominent government officials on both sides of the Rio Grande.

Recently, however, due to the extent of all his holdings and the nature of the political upheavals south of the border, William Benson had been forced to immerse himself more fully in the politics of both nations. Such a man of influence and wealth, who still enjoyed the profits and marvelous fringe benefits afforded a gringo *hacendado,* was bound to be approached by the

636

warring factions to use his monetary powers of persuasion to keep the status quo.

Stepping out into brightly lit *avenida,* reflecting all the electric signs of the countless night clubs, William Benson lit a fat stogie, proud that he'd achieved a pact of sorts with the girl named *La Bomba.* Why, he hadn't even asked her her true Christian name, he thought, chastising himself. Never mind, he'd know it soon enough, and when he presented this Latin bombshell with a string of perfectly matched pearls, she'd not resist him.

Puffing on the cigar, Benson nodded to his driver and stepped inside the enclosed carriage where his two very important guests had patiently waited while he conducted his personal business. The door closed behind him.

"General Huerta? Major Salomon? Ah thank y'all for youah patience in allowing me to conduct the death bed request of a dear friend. Now then, suhs, shall we proceed ta my little spread wheah we can discuss just what it is you need from mah President Wilson?"

"*Muy bien,* Señor Benson. It will be our pleasure to explain precisely what is needed by the government of Huerta and what Huerta will do in return for the American government."

"Ah see, General. By the sound of youah talk, ah take it that youah've got this heah Madero whupped pretty good."

"Señor Benson. Madero is finished. Believe me," said General Huerta with confidence. "At any moment, upon my bidding, Madero's government will dissolve as if it never existed."

"Well, suh, ya'll talk pretty big. S'pose we mosey on tah mah place and get down ta the nitty gritty?" Benson opened the cabbie overhead door. "Waco, get the drivuh crackin'."

"Yes, sir!" replied the burly cowboy, nodding to the driver alongside him. He felt for the six-guns he carried and patted his holster securely. "Move, Charlie."

Inside, General Huerta gave William Benson a pleasant enough look. "Your generosity to this—uh—professional dancer is to be commended, *señor*."

William Benson glanced sharply at his guest. "Mah, mah, news shuah has a habit of movin' befoah the deed's done. Now, tell me, how in the name of the bloody blue blazes, General, didja fasten youah choppers on ta such a morsel?"

General Huerta shrugged noncommittally. "When the death of so reknown a matador occurs on foreign soil, the people who are at his deathbed have a tendency to swell their superstitions beyond all proportions." He used his hands with a flourish in expressing himself. "It was rumored your wager with the deadman was in excess of fifty thousand dollars."

"It was five."

"That he made you abide by a deathbed oath."

"That's the truth."

"That you," Huerta temporized, "that you might not have fulfilled such an irresponsible wish and entertained thoughts of setting aside the last request."

"Nevah, suh! Nevah would William Benson do such a thing. Death ta me is as sacred as life. The responsibilities of both are too deah to fool with."

"That this *La Bomba* and the matador were lovers."

"Untrue! Why, they were raised in the same country, grew up together as children. They could have been brothuh and sistuh. Why, General, my deah friend Don Felipe Cortez loved Manuelito Perez as if he was his own son."

"This Don Cortez, a *hacendado* also?"

"One of the finest bull-breeding ranches in all of Spain. The Concha bulls. Why, General, that little filly, *La Bomba,* knows so much about the animals, ah've invited her to lunch with me. Ah heard her talkin' about 'em at the *corrida* earlier tuhday—" Benson stopped. Usually a quiet man of utter discretion, he wondered why he was suddenly bent on venting his feelings. He wasn't a man taken to boasting. He flushed beet red.

Huerta picked up on it. "Why, Señor Benson, it appears that you have grown fond of this—uh—dancer. It is a shame that Major Salomon and I, so involved in conducting out business, took no time to watch her perform. From the deafening bursts of applause, however, we have decided to make the Diamond Slipper our last stop before we depart for Mexico."

Benson remained sullenly quiet. Whatever possessed him to discuss the woman? Why, if the time ever came that he might ask her to wear his name, he'd have to bury her past. Now these two greasers know about it. Best to let the matter pass. But General Huerta, always anxious to know the foibles and peccadillos of the men he dealt with, and more anxious to acquaint himself with the skeletons such men kept hidden in closets, pressed the subject.

"What kind of a woman would be born in Spain on a hacienda, you say, and grow up close to a man like Manuelito Perez? Even a man like Don Cortez? How does it happen that a woman of such background ends up in El Paso as an exotic fandango dancer in a gambling palace. It bends the imagination, doesn't it, Señor Benson?" Huerta smoked through his solid gold cigarette holder with maddening manner of a highborn aristocrat with insufferable airs.

Benson frowned. "Ah really don't know a thing, suh. Frankly ah'm not sure ah want ta continue such a worthless beating of gums. All ah know is what the matador told me and what came from her lips. Perez apparently taught the girl how ta fight bulls and their friendship sprang up."

If Benson saw the the quick, sharp looks that passed between the general and the major in the dim light of the carriage, he gave it no importance. His manner indicated they had far more important things to discuss than the relationship between two comparative strangers. And he said so in so many words, just as the carriage rode into circular brick courtyard. The men entered the Benson mansion prepared to negotiate their worlds.

Chapter 24

Madelaina Obregon's only thought as William Benson left her dressing room was to finish the last show and go home where she could relax and think about the numerous events that plagued her life on this day.

Her last performance, as erotic and scintillating as her earlier performances, was finally over. She returned to her dressing room to change into street apparel and go home. Only now, as she shed her costume, would she permit her mind to dwell on Peter Duprez. She sniffed the air about her, puzzled.

All the old longing, the desperate need, the ache and need for him began to surface, and she found herself in a terrible state of disquiet. Thoughts so negative in nature kept her floundering as she removed her makeup with a thick white creamy emulsion mixed for her at the apothecary's shop. She hadn't bothered to turn up the lights in her anxiety to leave the Slipper. She completed her dressing in partial shadow. As she piled her hair up off her shoulders and speared it through with a tortoise shell pin, she heard a familiar voice call to her.

"Is it really y'all, Little Fox? Ah thought foah shuah ah had dreamed ya up earlier tonight."

She spun around and saw him seated in the shadows of the dressing room, nearly hidden from view. Quickly she pulled the chain on the lamp nearby. In the flood of light, she saw him. "Peter!" she began anxiously.

Then, collecting her strength and wits, she managed to remain cool.

"Oh, it's you." She sniffed the air, allowing the fragrant aroma of his aftershave cologne to discend on all her senses at once. No wonder she'd smelled something familiar earlier, she thought. She wanted to run into his arms, to tell him how desperately she needed him, to tell him she was all his, that there'd never be anyone else for her but him. It was the hesitation she sensed in him which prevented her from flinging herself into his arms.

Peter rose to his feet, all six feet of him. In his dinner clothing, he looked more gorgeous than she'd ever seen him. He walked toward her, slowly taking her all in, as if he couldn't believe the transformation he saw.

"They told me y'all were dead, Little Fox," he said halfheartedly.

"Whoever told you this was right. Little Fox is dead. Only I have survived her foolish stupidity and impressionable mind with all that idealistic talk of revolution and hope for a lost people."

"Whatcha doing heah in El Paso? Ah mean aside from ya being *La Bomba*? Don'cha know the city is full o' spies? Why, baby, ah've been told by Tracy Richards that General Huerta is in town negotiating a deal ta dethrone Madero—that the revolution is about ta bust wide open. Is that whatcha heah foah?"

"No. Only to begin a new life, Peter. I'm alone now, and I must consider the future. I, too, assumed you were dead. I asked about you wherever we traveled. I was told you were injured in Villa's last skirmish and died on the battlefield."

"Jus' goes ta show ya, ya can't believe all ya heah, sweetness. Can we go someplace, sweet thing, so we can talk and catch up on ouah pasts? We seem ta be strangers ta each other, honey. What's wrong?"

He crossed the room to her in long strides and put his arms around her. He brought his face in closer to hers, and Madelaina felt herself slipping into submission. Oh God, how she loved him. And he was betrothed to another. Her eyes closed instinctively as they always did at his nearness. She felt his moist cool lips cover hers tenderly, then with increased passion and a rising fevor, his arms tightened their hold. "Aftuh all weah've been through tugethuh, Madelaina, ya

641

can't tell me ya don't still love me," he whispered urgently.

"Oh, Peter, Peter," she began, struggling to summon the strength to push away from him. "Aren't you forgetting something important?"

His eyes opened, hurt buried in them at the rebuff. "Forgetting something? What?"

"Your future wife?"

"Oh, her," he said flatly. "Y'all know about her?"

"I learned only tonight from Antonetta. You needn't worry. I'll do nothing to stand in your way," she said in a manner that didn't reveal her inner torment.

"This isn't mah Little Fox talkin' ta me like a cold westerly gale. Why, ah thought ya'd be happy to see me."

"I told you Little Fox is dead—gone and buried. A lot has happened to both of us, Peter."

Madelaina couldn't reconcile this Peter with her *marido* of the past two years. And Peter found himself concerned that Madelaina didn't view him with the same passion she had when they last parted. They both wondered if their romance and feelings for the other had cooled due to the nature of their hectic lives. No, it wasn't that, thought Peter. Something has drastically changed her. Even when Rosalia Quintera had unhexed her, she never acted as distant and cool. Her ardor had always been there to stir his passion to the heat of a volcano. No, something else was stirring her innards, egging her on. Was there someone else? It was then that Peter caught sight of the canvas bag of money, bearing the WB brand on its leather bindings. He tensed.

"What's this?" he asked, suddenly turning frigid.

"What's what?" she asked.

"Don'cha play so cool and innocent with me, *chiquita*. Ah'm speakin' of this heah canvas bag." He picked it up and jingled the heavy contents. "Silvah bearing the William Benson brand?" He studied the circle within a circle brand with a five-pronged crown over it, and his heart hardened in reflection. How politely and calmly he spoke, when all the while he was raging inside, his anger barely controlled. She'd seen him like this before—not too often, but often enough to know what it meant when his eyes turned to blue dull stones and his lips pulled back tightly.

For an instant he reminded her of someone she knew—who was it? She couldn't think.

"That was left to me by a friend who died in an unfortunate tragedy today. It was delivered by a friend of his. I believe his name was the same you just spoke," she replied casually. "Surely you've heard me speak of him, Peter. Manuelito Perez, the matador who taught me all I know about bulls."

He turned to her, sorely ashamed of his thoughts. Still the canvas bore the William Benson brand. "Yes," he said, waving his hand about the air in an abstract gesture, "Ah heard about his death in the ring taday. It's a sad, sad, thing. Ah recall jus' how much ya thought of him. Ah'm sorry, sugah. It's sad ta lose good friends." His eyes lingered suspiciously on the brand and canvas bag.

"It was a wager he made with the gringo, Benson," she told him and explained what had happened afterward. "It is difficult to believe such a gesture," she added.

"Ya'll don't know just how hard it is ta believe, sugah," he added enigmatically. His mind was more concerned with that skinflint land baron, William Benson, his father. That she even knew him turned his stomach. He refrained from further conversation. Knowing Madelaina as he had in the past, and recalling her naïveté about matters of the flesh, she would have told him if there were any strings attached to her sudden inheritance. "Ya better put that in a safe place, little one," he suggested. "People have killed for a lot less. Listen, ah'll carry it safely ta youah house, heah. Are ya ready?" he asked firmly, not about to take no from her. He stood at the door waiting for her.

"Peter—" Her lips began to form a protest. The longing for him, having ached so long, with such intensity,

643

destroyed all her earlier resolve. "Very well, then. Come along. Let's slip out the back way. Antonetta keeps a horse and carriage waiting for me each night to insure my safety home."

"Ya see? Didn't ah tell ya it was dangerous at night? Especially foah *La Bomba.* Such exquisite charms and talent must certainly attract a variety of stage doah johnnies. Am ah right?" he asked, leaning languidly against the door.

She didn't reply, but pushed him instead out the door and turned off the light behind him.

"Oh, mah little sweet darlin', how much ah've missed ya," he whispered later in bed. "Mah God, sugah, why have ouah lives been subjected ta such turmoil and stress and tragedy? What is it with us? Why can't we live like uthuh people? Can ya tell me, sugah? Why?"

Madelaina didn't want to talk. She wanted only to feel and remember the good things between them. She wanted to love him and be loved in return with wild abandon, the same way they'd made love in the past. He had possessed her as no one had possessed her and she only wanted this to continue.

His arms held hers in a viselike grip and together they soared up the mountain to ecstasy, one plateau after another, pausing to savor and enjoy the intoxication of new delights en route. His body, muscular and firm and hard, delighted her senses beyond belief. No one, no man in the world made love like Peter, she thought. For her, he was the only one. Why was it that for him there could be a thousand like her? For an instant, Madelaina tensed. Flashes of Tolomeo crashed through her consciousness, and his words burned in her mind. *"What if I cut off my sexual organ—would you still love me as you profess?"*

Madelaina shook her head wildly in denial. "No, Tolomeo, not now! Not at this minute. Don't do this to me!" she cried out hoarsely. "I don't want to hear your words. You aren't human—and I am!"

"What is it, *chiquita,*" asked Peter, alarmed by her

wild-eyed frenzy and her animal thrashing on the bed, as if she were being dominated by some mysterious force. He watched her sit up in bed, hands clasped over her ears and eyes shut tightly to shut out the inner pictures. "Y'all ain't hexed up again, are ya, baby?"

She opened her eyes, startled to see him and at the same time grateful. "Oh, Peter, my love, don't let them change us. Don't let him make us into people we aren't!" She clutched at him tightly and ran her slender fingers over his warm skin, secure in the feeling of heat oozing from his body. This in itself always excited her, the feeling that she could generate such heat from his body. It radiated from his to hers, setting them both on fire, sending them both into raptures of love of so exquisite a nature, it fairly made her head spin.

And Peter, deriving from Madelaina what he had never got from another woman, filled with unendurable passion. Only his strong will and concentration allowed him to hold back the driving need he had to satisfy his desires until he had first satisfied her. Time and again, she let him carry her over that familiar and ecstatic road to bliss until she felt as if she could no longer endure the agony and ecstasy again.

Peter, unable to further articulate his feelings with words, did so with his body. As they reached the pinnacle of the mountain and exploded, Peter cried out hoarsely, "Ah'll nevah let ya go, mah sweet Little Fox, ya heah? Nevah!"

The explosion burst again into smaller fragments of cloudlike formations that cradled them and sent their souls into the unknown, until a mystifying force greater than either of them pulled them apart and sent them tumbling down into a misty darkness. . . .

After a few moments, Peter reached for her, and held her tightly. "*Querida*, I have something for you—something that belonged to my mother." He slipped off the bed, pulled a small velvet box from his jacket, and returned to her side.

Madelaina's eyes lit up at the solid-gold earrings shaped like a crescent moon. Dangling at the edge of the curve were seven separate crescents with diamond embedded in the tips of each moon. "Peter, they are exquisite. I can't take them—especially since they were your mothers."

"Because they were hers, I want you to have them," he insisted. "Please put them on."

She removed the full circlets from her pierced ears and slipped the new ones into place. She fluffed out her hair and lifted it away from her face and, turning from side to side, she asked, "You like?"

Peter studied her somberly, then, uttering a small gasp, he drew her in closer to him. "I like—I love—I adore you, *querida*."

They clung to one another, their passion rekindled and once again they made love. Afterward, his face buried in the curve of her shoulders and neck, inhaling the fragrant mass of her silken, raven hair, Peter sensed the change in her even before Madelaina did. Her mind had wandered back to Tolomeo, his face flashing before her mind.

Madelaina recalled now, with vivid clarity, every exquisite moment she'd spent with Tolomeo, and she wondered why, of all times, her mind should choose to bring it all into perfect focus now, together with his teachings and warnings. She gazed at her husband and lover with an air of detachment.

"Peter, do you intend to marry the governor's daughter now, after our reunion?" she asked him quietly in a voice that didn't disguise her feelings.

"Ya hafta ask me now? At this time? While mah body still drips with youah love potion? Can't ya wait until this feelin' between us has abated?" He reached for a cigarette on the night table. "Mah, mah, sweet thing, youah not like the bundle of love ah made love ta on the *Mozambique*. Remembah when ya'll wanted ta jus' exchange love with me?" He grinned rakishly, lit the cigarette, and inhaled deeply.

"I remember everything, Peter. Please answer my question. Do you still intend to marry Valerie Townsend?"

"Please, Madelaina, I don't wish to discuss it." He enjoined her to refrain from discussing the matter. "Can't you just let us enjoy each other while there's time?" He spoke with such urgency that she felt instantly there was something drastically wrong.

The woman in her wanted to lash out at him, fill with anger and hurt him as he hurt her with this—this—governor's daughter. "Is it because she represents much money? Is that it? You no longer run guns or fight with the Gringo Brigade, so you must make your money wherever you can find an opportunity. That's it, isn't it?" she pressed.

"Shut up, woman! Ya don't know whatcher talkin' about!" He puffed furiously on his cigarette. "Ah'm shuah ya didn't let any grass grow under yer feet since we last saw each other in Parral. Y'all had that theah Paco ta take care o' ya. Ya shuah was concerned ovah him, eh? An' jus' who is this Tolomeo, y'all rant ovah? Ya been callin' his name while my love wahms yer heart!" he snapped caustically.

He might just as well have slapped her viciously as to say such contemptible things to her. Peter avoided her eyes in the semidarkness, choosing instead to stare intently at some spot on the ceiling as his thoughts, sparked with live coals, were held in check.

"You dare say such things to me?" Her acrimonious voice climbed higher despite her attempt to subdue it. She swung her bare legs over the side of the bed and felt his hands holding her back. "Get out! Leave me alone! Leave my house!"

"No. We'll talk it out!" He pulled harder, drawing her closer to him.

"There's nothing to say! And don't you—don't you dare tell me you love me when I'm angry!" she charged at him. She caught a deep breath and exhaled it evenly, lowering her temper simultaneously. "You never wanted to be married to me—admit it. It was purely a business arrangement for which we both paid dearly. I convinced myself earlier that once we made love again, your obsession to marry this gringa would

647

pass. You can't couple with me as you did tonight and not feel something for me, Peter. Now you give me no satisfaction. You say nothing except you are bound by some mysterious force to marry her. Did you stop to think we are still married? That if I so desire I could stop this farce between you and this blonde emptiness you paraded before me as a woman?"

"Ya wouldn't do that! Ya mustn't. Ya jus' can't expose youahself or me to any such publicity, ya heah?" Peter stopped abruptly, frowning thoughtfully. He had already said more than he should.

Madelaina picked up on his frantic appeal. His words struck at her like a two-edged blade. "What are you involved in, Peter? Let me understand. Don't do this to me, Peter. Don't keep me in the dark."

Peter wasn't listening. He filled with self-recrimination. He never intended for her to learn his activities. Dangerous as his mission was presently, it could be even more devastating to her if she should in any way be linked to him. Here, in El Paso, where government agents and counterspies were thicker than gutter rats, life was as cheap as ten pesos to a willing assassin.

"Ah don't know wheah ya get such crazy ideahs, woman. Ah guess weah've been apart so long that the magic between us is gone. Well, ah'd bettah be movin' along, Little Fox," he said, gathering all his will power and inner fortitude.

Peter dressed in the dim light. He avoided looking into her hurt, bewildered eyes for fear she'd see the truth. What kind of a beast would put her in jeopardy after the travail she'd endured in her young life?

"Ah had half-hoped ya'd let me continue ta see ya, even after mah wedding. Ah mus' admit, Little Fox, the gringa isn't like youah in bed. Ah find mahself havin' ta pretend with her. Somethin' ah nevah had ta do with y'all."

"*Bastardo!*" she cursed in Spanish as rage boiled over in her. Even as she hurled curses at him, something inside her tried to break through the outer picture to whisper the truth to her. Only moments ago, he'd told her he'd never let her go. Just as he had in the past. Their love had been more sublime, more complete than ever before. No, she told herself, no. He is up to something and he doesn't want to involve me. He's protecting me for some reason. Very well, I'll play his little game.

"It's best you leave my house, gringo. I have no respect for a man who marries a woman and wants to sleep with another."

"Really, sugah?" he quipped airily. "Why, ah was certain youah people thrived on such arrangements. All youah *gachupín* whoremasters have wives and a goddamn string of *putas* on the side."

"It isn't necessary to insult me. If you find this gringa more satisfying than Madelaina, then go to her. Sleep with her and dream of me! I curse you for this, gringo! You hear?" She screamed hoarsely at him, hoping he'd believe her performance.

"So, when it comes right down ta it, youah a bitch, like all the rest, eh?" He shoved his shirt into his trousers, slipped into his boots, and slung his jacket over one shoulder.

"Go, Peter, for God's sake, before we say things to each other we'll regret for all our days," she said. "At least we can part friends. You know I could never wish you ill or misfortune."

Peter stared at her in the dim light as she struggled into a thin wrapper.

She knows, he told himself. She knows what I'm up to. He tossed his jacket on a nearby chair and walked across the carpeted room to her. He gathered her in his arms. "Ah should've known bettah than to try foolin' y'all, sugah," his voice grew husky and filled with emotion. He reigned kisses on her, unable to stop. "Ah know that y'all know and unduhstand what it is ah can't tell ya. Ah don't know how ah know and I don't know how ya know. But it's as clear ta me as the nose on youah pretty little face. Jus' trust me. Ah know its askin' a lot. An' if ya heah of my marriage, don'cha believe it. Don'cha let it shake ya, sugah. Ah'm tellin' ya, the minute ah can, ah'll come back ta ya. Ah'll find ya if it takes all mah born days. Heah?"

They made love until dawn. While Madelaina slept, Peter left to return to his hotel. He had to relax in a hot tub and do some thinking. He grabbed a bottle of whiskey from the top of a chest and began to guzzle it down as he waited for the tub to fill. He undressed and gazed at his reflection in the mirror, feeling a terrible emptiness. It had always been this way after making love to Little Fox. He could still feel her hot body next to his, smell the soft sweet fragrance of roses that unmistakably reminded him of her, and taste the nectar of her body. His senses were possessed with the intoxication of his wife, and he knew he could never be done with loving her.

He had to be strong in the coming days, if he hoped to pull off what he intended to achieve. He'd pow-wowed with Villa and Captain Richards for the past two months. With the governor's help he'd managed to gain audience with President Woodrow Wilson in hopes of securing his aid in the inevitable revolution that fermented and threatened to explode at any time.

Peter dispensed with the glass he'd been using and swung the bottle to his lips, guzzling half of it in a few long swallows.

It was necessary that his closeness with the governor be looked upon as a relationship between a father and prospective son-in-law, no more, no less. To carry out his plans, he would marry Governor Townsend's daughter Valerie if he had to. Love had nothing to do with it. As a matter of fact, he detested the empty-headed, spoiled darling of society. There'd been times when he had all he could do to refrain from putting her over a knee and spanking the tar out of her.

One night, she finally seduced him, an act for which he'd never forgiven himself, because it could have meant blowing the entire cause. Peter, with the control of a superman, had permitted the seduction to appease the headstrong, sex-driven harlot who was determined to give the performance of a high-paid courtesan. Long before, Peter had deduced that Valerie Townsend was possessed by a highly inflated estimation of her need for sex. He guessed she had hypnotized herself into thinking she was insatiable. Hell, Peter knew the difference between real emotion and that which was manufactured and phony.

Valerie was a spoiled adolescent at the age of twenty-eight and should have long since matured into womanhood. He had discovered she was incapable of any real emotional depth, and to boot, she was a lousy actress. His own performance that night, which fell way below par, drew phony raves from the woman who had even faked orgasm. If he had really cared for the wench or needed some reason to inflate his masculine ego, he'd have taken her in hand and taught her how it was to journey into the unknown realms of infinite passion, just as he'd schooled Madelaina so carefully.

He didn't even like Valerie and died a thousand deaths when he had to pretend to be in love with her. How many times had he cursed under his breath and began to truly realize how a prostitute must feel when she had to manufacture false reactions to the countless men who pay for her favors. He shuddered.

Soaking in the tub, he dismissed her from his mind. He concentrated on more pertinent things. Why hadn't Villa told him his wife was in El Paso? Why? Was it possible that Tracy Richards knew also and had withheld the information? He'd just returned from Washington yesterday afternoon, where for several days he had met clandestinely with President Wilson.

It had been a difficult chore convincing that professorial man in the White House just what the situation really was in Mexico. It was apparent to Peter, however, that the Commander-in-Chief regarded with undisguised contempt what his predecessor, President Taft, had caused to ferment south of the border. President Wilson himself disclosed to Peter that incalculable graft was running rampant; that the incredibly callous speculation on Wall Street continued without regard or respect for the honor of America. Why, between President Taft and his Latin America ambassador, every effort at internal reform had been confused and abused until Washington had earned the bloody stigma attached to a bestial landlord—*hacendado*.

Peter recollected the encounter he'd had with President Wilson, Governor Townsend, Don Abraham Gonzalez, governor of Chihuahua, and Don Martino Espinoza, temporary governor of Coahuila. They had all met in the oval office to discuss the Mexican situation and Pancho Villa's aims for his nation.

Armed with dossiers on both Villa and General Huerta, documenting their lives and achievements, up to and including the latest obscenities performed under Huerta rule, he'd presented it to the stiffly dressed Commander-in-Chief.

The meeting had been underway for nearly an hour, and in that time Peter had been attempting, with the aid of the other men, to point out Huerta's double-dealing, and crafty, underhanded politics. "He's a dangerous man attempting ta overthrow the Madero regime," continued Peter. "This man's clearly a psychopath, a drunkard with a penchant foah political assassinations. Why, at this moment, suh, he an' political aides, moah butchers, are in El Paso dealing with the Germans."

"Are you trying to tell me, Mr. Duprez, that at a time when the crisis in Europe is at its worst, this ambitious tyrant is dealing with the Kaiser? Our southern neighbors are attempting to ally themselves with foreigners the calibre of the Kaiser?" President Wilson's apparent disgust concealed his wrath. That son of a bitch Huerta had already attempted through his emissaries to demand outrageous concessions from the U.S.A.! He said nothing of this to his guests, although he did a continuous burn during this conference in more ways than one. "If anything, that maniac should attempt to tighten the bonds between us! Hah! Not even in power and he's making ovations like a big gun."

"Isn't that the way deals are made, Mr. President?" asked Peter subtly.

Wilson shrugged. He glanced at Governor Townsend. "What do you have to contribute to all this, Hampton? Are you in agreement with Mr. Duprez' assessment?"

"I fully concur with him, Mr. President," replied the Texan. "I've read the extensive report and find him to be quite accurate."

"And you, Don Espinoza? What have you to say of this report?"

The Mexican governor of Coahuila shrugged slightly and puffed on his Havana. "I know the timbre of my people," he said officiously. "Their pride—their very deep pride. I am fearful of Pancho Villa's motives. Personally, I could never counsel the people of America to take any action which would cause any break in the friendship with the Mexican people themselves. Thousands of miles separate our thinking, although only the Rio Grande marks our boundaries. *Señor Presidente*, we have not sufficient proof that General Huerta has become everything they say he has. In my opinion, you should proceed with things as they are for the moment. But with care—and caution."

"*Señor Presidente*," objected Don Gonzalez heatedly. "Everyone knows that Don Espinoza is a *Huertista*."

"Just as you are pro-Villa and Madero?" President Wilson smiled tolerantly. "Don Gonzalez, if I am to be fair and impartial, I must listen to both sides of any controversy. All sides, as a matter of fact. It's only fair."

"That's true," replied Don Gonzalez, a true promoter of democratic ideals. "I agree with you. But I think you should pay particular attention to what Mr. Duprez tells you. His information is first hand, from a man who has fought in the thick of things."

President Wilson nodded and turned to Peter expectantly.

"Ah'm not prepared to say anything moah than

what ah've already stated. Mah report should give ya a pretty accurate account of what Huerta is up to."

"I wish I had your confidence, Mr. Duprez," replied President Wilson as he glanced at the younger man over his pince-nez glasses. "By the way, aren't you a Mexican citizen? Have I not been told you are married to a *gachupín*?"

"That's right. Ah married her, but then ah considered calling her an American citizen. Ya see, it works both ways. We held decided interests on both sides of the border. Ya see, we both believed in repelling injustice wherever it arises. We fought alongside of Pancho Villa and the revolutionists because we believe in what the man stands for. Mah wife and ah've been too busy ta concern ourselves with the future when the present is in such dubious straits. But now theah's no longuh a future fer her."

The president's eyes flickered with momentary compassion. "You have my personal sympathies. Then you intend carrying the standard for her, is that it?" Wilson mused a moment. "And what does your illustrious father have to say about all this—about your opposition to the precepts in which he believes?" He leaned in on one elbow to hear Peter's reply.

Governor Townsend also leaned forward, his eyes bright with interest.

"The politics of William Benson, suh, are in no way ta be confused with the politics of Peter Duprez. Just as ah've chosen sides and prefer ta speak foah mahself, so ah reckon will William Benson." Peter steeled himself. He'd protested often enough that politically as in every way he was apart from his father. "Ah thought ah made it clear, suh, by mah intervention in this matter that ah am a Villa sympathizer—as are the many hundreds of other freedom fighters fighting the *jefe*'s cause."

"Yes, yes," snapped President Wilson, pushing his glasses up on the bridge of his nose. "I've been made painfully aware of those freedom fighters. Now then, what does your father-in-law think of your political

654

persuasions and his daughter's rebellious attitude? He is General Alvaro Obregon, isn't he?" ventured the president, peering inscrutably over his glasses at the soldier of fortune.

"I've no idea what he thinks. I've never met the man."

"Yet you also oppose him. Are you such a rebel, my man?"

"I oppose injustice to any human being."

"And this *guerrillo* Pancho Villa, a rebel and a fugitive, has become your savior?"

Peter flinched at his acerbic words. "Pancho Villa fights for *his* people and *his* country, for a belief in freedom and equality and justice for all men. I'm only a warrior who supports his theory. How can I, an American who lives across the river from his land and believes what I do, be blinded to what goes on south of that river?"

The president was silent. He studied all the men in his office. All were respectable men with excellent backgrounds, known for their democratic leanings and pro-American politics. He also had communiqués from several men who weren't present, stating their views on this decision he had to make.

"It seems to me that the men with the most to lose in the event of trouble—with the most to gain from Pancho Villa's friendship—those with the largest holdings in Texas and Mexico are the men who urge caution. Why?" asked Wilson, still stinging from the reputation left by his predecessor, Taft.

"Ah urge caution against American intervention to support Huerta—*not Pancho Villa*," retorted Peter, burning at the implication. "Only because of what he stands for and what's he's initiated in order for him to carry the Mexican sceptre. Ah'm shuah youah espionage agents have informed ya of the countless political assassinations paving Huerta's bloody path to the top. Why, suh, supporting such a man indicates ya support his tactics!"

"Peter!" Governor Townsend's stern disapproving voice deterred him from saying any more.

"That's all right, Hampton," replied the president tolerantly. "He speaks with the zealous fervor of youth." He turned to Peter. "When you've lived a little longer, you'll be more tolerant of those men with graying hair at their temples who learned to temper their feelings with age. Experience comes with age, young man, and with it comes understanding."

"With all due respect, Mr. President, in the interest of both ouah nations, Mexico and America, ah've submitted mah findings. Ah feel ah've been impartial in mah reports. Ah also submit that if theah weren't some merit ta the man Pancho Villa, these distinguished men heah with me today wouldn't be in youah presence ta defend him—excludin', of course, Don Espinoza who after all is only an interim governor."

"Ummmhum," replied the president. "An' you feel deeply, Peter, that my deals should be made with Pancho Villa."

"Indeed ah do, suh. Why don'cha ask yer own generals, Hugh Scott and John Pershing? Ah unduhstand they admire the *jefe* somethin' fierce. Why, suh, ah've fought alongside the *jefe* in the Gringo Brigade an' ah've seen the stuff the man's made of. Ah mean he's revered by the people. They'll lay down their lives foah him, suh."

"You're speaking of—so that we both understand—that illiterate animal from Sonora whose maniacal temper has killed off half the population and caused rivers of blood to irrigate the land of Mexico? Why, Peter, he's nothing but a rag-bag bandit, hardly reformed, whose only pardon came about when he enlisted to fight Diaz. He has displayed no political inclination or talent."

"But, don't ya see, suh, that's what makes him so special. He has no political vices, no ambition to sit on the throne. And, suh, he's the first ta admit he was illiterate—"

"*Was* illiterate. Just what does that mean?"

"Well, suh, Mr. President. Recently he was jailed. While in jail he learned to read an' write."

"Jailed—whatever for?"

"Ah'm not certain, suh," Peter was trying to avoid the question.

"Come, come, Peter. You can't allow me to believe you'd let information as vital as this slip by you."

"Well, Mr. President. It was foah a mere infraction of the rules. As ya know, he's an army irregular, and well, suh, the charges were filed against him by General Huerta. That should ansuh youah inquiry. Insubordination and dereliction of duty."

President Wilson, an incurable busybody in foreign affairs, opened a folder and, adjusting his pince-nez glasses, scanned the report.

"Failure to follow orders from his Commander-in-Chief, Francesco Madero. Pancho Villa attacked Juarez against direct orders to the contrary. . . ."

"But, suh, that's just it. Villa had ta countermand Madero's orduhs because Madero, no military man, had no idea of what was involved. By attacking Juarez, Villa ended the revolution. It was a master stroke of genius, Mr. President."

"But the revolution has begun again. Where does that put Villa?"

Peter Duprez had avoided this question and he'd hoped the president would. But now he had to speak up. "He's still loyal to Madero, suh."

"You've gotta be kidding, Peter!" Wilson's pince-nez glasses fell to his lap.

"No suh, Mr. President. Ah wished ah was kidding. But it does say something about Villa, don'cha think?"

The president picked up his glasses and reset them on his nose. "Yes, it does say something. Only I'm not about to tell you what my mind is whispering. He's a neophyte, a political embryo, who one day might deserve American aid, my boy. But I'm afraid I can't wholeheartedly endorse such a man. Now then," he said, sweeping aside the Pancho Villa issue in a clear, clean-cut sentence, "tell me what you know about a Señor Venustano Carranza,"

Peter had grown hesitant. "One-time governor of Coahuila State. Former member of Francesco Madero's first cabinet. An active political and revolutionary figure. Ah s'pose y'all could say he is stately, well-bred, and politically persuasive."

"I know. I know. Just wanted to see if you were on your toes, Peter. I know about Señor Carranza. And while I haven't made up my mind, I do believe he'd be the best man to place on the throne of the presidential palace in Mexico."

Peter's face darkened, but he kept his thoughts to himself.

"Well, what is it? You looked as if the bottom of the world had just caved in."

"Carranza an' Huerta are one and the same."

"Nonsense, they differ drastically in their political views," replied President Wilson in his all-knowing manner.

"At least Pancho Villa is a man of principle. He won't sell out to the highest bidder."

"You feel strongly in this matter, don't you, my boy?"

"Ah wouldn't be heah, tryin' ta make ya see what's goin' on, suh, if ah didn't know the kind o' man this Pancho Villa is in his heart."

"Very well, then. These things aren't solved in a moment. I'll dispatch a special committee to meet with your Señor Villa. If your man meets with our specifications and can promise us he can keep peace south of our borders, I promise I'll see that he gets an opportunity to prove his worth."

"Thank ya, suh, Mr. President. Ah couldn't ask foah moah."

The president then politely indicated that the meeting had come to an end. He bid good day to Townsend, Gonzalez, and Espinoza, but asked Peter stay behind.

"Peter?"

"Yes, Mr. President."

"Is the date set for your wedding to Valerie Townsend?"

"No, Mr. President. It's been mighty difficult convincing Valerie ta give up her freedom to become mah missus. But one o' these days, ah hope ta break down her resistance."

"Good, my boy. She'd make you a mighty fine wife. Knows all the right things to do. Been to the best of schools. Why, she'd be a great asset to any man on his way to becoming a state senator."

"State senator?"

"Oh, don't play the innocent with me. It's all been arranged. The governor insists on something formidable for his son-in-law. And if we can keep our heads and do the right thing for our Mexican neighbors, well, you are certainly entitled to a worthwhile prize. It's only fitting, wouldn't you say?"

"Well, suh, ah'm flabbergasted. Ah can't think of a thing ta say."

"Then don't. You just leave it to the old-timers who know their way around this political jungle. Good day to you. Peter. God bless you."

Peter had nodded and backed out of the office as one did with royalty.

"Good day ta y'all, Mr. President. And thank ya, suh. Thank ya."

Peter had left the White House wondering what he'd accomplished. Nothing! Absolutely nothing! He felt as if he'd been used. He also felt that his opinion of Pancho Villa held no special importance with President Wilson. It all seemed like such a farce. Even after being back in El Paso a day, he hadn't been able to confront Villa with the disheartening news. If Wilson had intended to help Villa, he'd have given Peter his reply instantly, since time was of the essence.

In spite of the rage and disgust he felt, the self-disgust at his inability to make his own efforts count, Peter found himself grinning over the fight he'd had with Valerie earlier over Madelaina. If he knew Valerie, and

659

by this time he knew her well, she'd probably have him followed by Pinkerton men to make certain he didn't frequent the Diamond Slipper.

She'd had screaming hysterics when he and her entourage caught up with her outside the gambling palace earlier that evening, but Peter wouldn't put up with her unreasonable jealousies and childish tirades. He had dumped her at the governor's mansion and bid her a curt good night. She had screamed at him, threatened to break their engagement, and cussing him out in the foulest and most obscene way, she'd threatened to kill herself if he didn't return that very instant and set a wedding date.

He'd hoped that President Wilson would have expedited matters with Villa, so he could have ended it with Valerie. This delay in Washington not only slowed Villa up, but it put him in an untenable position, especially now that he had to be concerned over Madelaina. He just wouldn't put anything past Valerie. She was a vicious, double-dealing little vixen, who had done a real snow job on her father. Why, she had the old goat wrapped around her little finger. He never guessed what a whore he'd sired. She was one of the most mixed-up little wenches he'd ever met. He found himself growing bored with her demands and her tantrums, and unable to face the prospect of a dinner engagement with her.

Inevitably she'd insist on winding up in bed with him, and Peter, who'd never worn a condom in his life, kept a supply on hand. The little bitch couldn't be trusted. She was the kind ta get herself knocked up, just to drag him down the aisle in a shotgun procession.

One night, he wasn't certain what had made him examine the thin rubber sheath before placing it on his penis, but he did. Damned if he didn't find tiny pin pricks in all of them. He could have confronted her— scolded her and brought her down a peg or two—but he chose not to bring it up. He let her think he was a dummy that could be fooled. He duplicated his supply

660

and kept it well secreted. He used the safe rubbers each time. After months passed, he recognized her old surliness return. One day, he'd returned to find his apartment ransacked. It took a moment before he went to his secreted condoms to examine them. When he found them sliced in half, he burst out into roaring laughter. He never mentioned the incident, nor did she. Now he was bored—bored—bored with her.

Peter slid back in the tub, his head on the headrest. The cigar he had been smoking had died out. The whiskey bottle empty, he dozed in a stupor.

He was vaguely aware that the door opened, that he wasn't alone. Earlier, when he had placed the bottle and ash tray beside the enameled tub, he'd made it a point to place his six-shooters on the stool next to him, a habit that he hadn't parted from. Now, as he stirred from his drunken euphoria, he thought, if he tried, he could make a grab for them. He was limp, without a working muscle or nerve in his body. For one split second, in an instinctive reaction for survival, his eyes flared wide open and, like the lens of a camera, snapped a picture of his assailant. His eyes closed tightly and the impression of a lithe figure, dressed in a riding habit, her hair concealed under a velvet helmet, kept flashing in his mind.

Peter heard a loud explosion first. Then he felt a dull thud hit his chest. The sensation was like the bursting of a ball. The whiskey had so anesthetized him he felt little pain. He heard a loud sob, a scuffle of feet, and the door slamming.

He recalled nothing after that, except the fluttering of heavy eyelids as he tried to open them. In the split second of vision, he remembered thinking how colorful the water around him was, crimson, the color of blood.

For the next two weeks, Peter Duprez lay in a private sanitarium on the outskirts of El Paso, hovering between life and death. None of his friends knew his whereabouts.

Two days after this tragic incident took place, an article appeared in the El Paso *Times* announcing the surprise marriage of Peter Duprez to Valerie Townsend. The happy couple, the article went on to say, had left for an extended three-month honeymoon in Europe. This article is what started Peter's friends worrying.

"You believe this, *chiquita*?" asked Pancho Villa thoughtfully, entering Madelaina's dressing room at the Diamond Slipper.

"Do newspapers lie?" she asked solemnly.

"Who can tell? I know only that your *marido* would not leave without first telling Pancho."

"My *marido*! Hah! That's a laugh! Apparently my *marido* doesn't take his marriage vows seriously."

"Little Fox! Silence your tongue. I was unable to speak up before, but now I must. The gringo was working for me. Now I fear double-dealing. Take heart. I go now to find Captain Richards. He will know what such a thing in the paper means."

Villa left the gambling palace, only to return ten minutes later. The look on his swollen face was enough to alert the women. He sat down heavily in an overstuffed chair, newspaper in hand, his shirt soaked to the skin.

"What is happening, *chiquita*?" he asked the woman in a dead voice. "Has the world gone mad? First, Peter's disappearance, now this!"

Antonetta removed the crumpled paper from his tightly clenched hand. She spread it open and gasped audibly. The headline in the Juarez paper read: PRESIDENT FRANCESCO MADERO RESIGNS POST!

The article went on to say that, due to the events of a ten-day siege on the capital, Francesco Madero and his vice-president respectfully tendered their resignations to the honorable Chamber of Deputies. It was brief, terse, and to the point.

After the initial shock wore off, Pancho and Antonetta returned to the boardinghouse. In the seclusion of his room, while he was kept busy taking calls from aides trying to learn what was happening, plans were forming in Pancho's mind, plans which were immediately scrapped when Madelaina Obregon ran into the room, breathless and pale and obviously upset.

It was three o'clock, Pancho recalled it well. The clock on the mantle chimed just as he opened the latest edition of the Juarez paper, a hastily printed special put out on the streets less than an hour after the news was wired to them.

PRESIDENT FRANCESCO MADERO ASSASSINATED BY RIOTING MOB.

Pancho Villa's world and the world of those he loved had just crumbled to pieces. In a sudden burst of anger, Pancho Villa crumpled the newspaper and hurled it at the floor. His eyes were bloodshot, his face purple with rage.

."Goddamn them! Goddamn them all! They will pay for this disgraceful act! They will pay!" He picked up the phone and gave the operator a number. "Gringo!" he shouted loudly to Captain Richards. "Have you heard?"

"All of it, *Jefe*. All the goddamned black-hearted whole of it."

"Ju hear from Tom Mix?"

"No, *Jefe*." Captain Tracy's voice dropped sadly.

"Ju come with Pancho. We must talk. We must find Tom Mix—is understood? What of the story of the marriage?"

"The governor's mansion sticks with the same ole story, *Jefe*."

As they conversed, Madelaina excused herself. She was explaining to Antonetta that she'd be at her own house until show time. Her heart was heavy enough at not hearing from Peter all this time. Now, learning of his marriage from the newspaper instead of from his own lips, she felt terrible, low in spirits. "If you need me, you know where you can find me."

"Little Fox!" called the *jefe*. "Zorrita!"

Madelaina turned, startled by the tone of his voice. "*Si, Jefe.*"

"Is better ju stay here with us. Ees more safe."

"I'll be all right. No one knows where I live besides you and Tonetta. That is, only Peter knew."

He shook his head stubbornly. "Is more better ju stay here."

She shrugged. "*Muy bien, Jefe.* First, I go home and pack a bag. I need some things."

Pancho glanced at Antonetta. She nodded. "It's all right. Madelaina can take care of herself. Take my driver, *chiquita*," she insisted.

"And what do I do with mine?" queried Madelaina.

"Let him go. I trust mine more. Ju come back before five o'clock?"

Madelaina glanced at her watch. "I'll do my best, *chica*."

Madelaina hardly noticed the day had been cool and crisp, rare for El Paso. A wind had arisen and swept in from the surrounding deserts. She tied her straw sailor hat under her chin and dismissed the driver. "Take the rest of the day off," she told him. Waving her hand overhead, she summoned Antonetta's black man. "Take me home, *chico*," she said, giving him a dazzling smile.

It wasn't until she opened the carriage door that she realized that the black man hadn't returned her greeting. But by then it was too late. Her abductors had seized her, pulled her into the carriage, and placed a blindfold around her eyes. They stuffed a gag into her mouth and bound her struggling arms and legs.

The clatter of horses' hooves slapped against the brick streets; the carriage creaked and swayed as it gathered momentum; the stench of the men, animal odors, and the nauseous smell of dirty clothing gagged her. All the old terrors of previous abductions returned, and Madelaina tensed with vivid visions of what might happen to her. She tried desperately to remain calm and detached, knowing that if she did, she might hear something that would give her a clue to the route they took. It wasn't easy, as she strained at her bindings, hoping not to gag. The constant swaying of the coach brought on waves of nausea. She felt as if she would vomit and might strangle if the gag weren't removed from her mouth.

None of this phases me, she told herself. *It isn't really happening to me. It will all pass and I will remain unaffected,* she continued to repeat to herself, wondering at the same time from where came this strength.

The nausea passed. Her mind was clearer and the heightened fear dissipated. She could even think without the earlier terror. *Where could they be taking me? Who is responsible for this?* When she pondered on these questions, she realized her assailants could be any of a number of persons, beginning with her father, and ending with General Huerta or Major Salomon. She understood that it was useless to struggle, so she sat primly in the corner of the coach where she'd been thrown and waited.

"Ah think weah heah, man," said one of the assailants to the other. His west Texas accent was even more pronounced than Peter's, she thought.

Madelaina had lost all sense of time. She felt the coach gradually slow down as the driver pulled back on the reins and braked the vehicle. Then she was lifted bodily from the carriage and carried by a burly man whose stench offended her. She was toted for a short distance and placed on her own feet.

"Now, ya just walk in a bit, m'am. No—no— straight ahead," said the sweaty-faced bounty hunter, Gus Madigan, as he led her to a chair inside a dimly lit, dank, and shuttered room. "Ah'm gonna hafta leave ya fer a while, heah? Now, don'cha try no funny stuff, or mah partnuhs ain't gonna take ta such liberty, ya heah?"

Madelaina nodded dutifully as they removed the gag from her mouth and took the scarf from her eyes. "Jus' don't try no foolish moves, woman, or these two, your escorts, will know jus' what to do. An' ah tells ya it ain't pleasant."

Madelaina's eyes blinked hard until they grew accustomed to the shadowy interior of the stuffy room. Her eyes fell on the face of the gringo, a foul-mouthed, grizzled cowboy with dirty trousers, boots and spurs, and a six-gun at either hip. He had a surly look on his face, but it wasn't the face of a man who'd do her harm. A bounty hunter, no doubt, who had abducted her for the right price. When she gazed at the other two, however, she gave a start.

Two Mexican *peóns*, dressed more scruffily than the gringo, wearing double *bandoleras* over their chests, with more ammunition and hardware at either hip, were eyeing her with narrow, suspicious eyes. It became apparent that she recognized them. They might have had an inkling that they knew her, but her ladylike appearance had them baffled.

Madelaina had committed these madmen to her memory. Jorge Molina and Feliz Galina were the men who'd abducted her from Villa's camp on her father's instructions. *Dios mios!* Jorge Molina especially! The man whose penis and testicles she'd shot off, the man she'd left for dead after his violent assault on her was alive! If he recognized her, it would be the end. She kept her eyes averted from his. Perhaps in this light he'd not recognize her. What folly do I entertain, she asked herself. They would certainly know her identity by name, wouldn't they? Her one consolation was that Jorge Molina could never again humiliate her with his body.

"So, ees *La Bomba* ju are, eh, *señorita*?" asked Jorge Molina as soon as Gus Madigan left them alone.

"Jorge!" hissed Feliz Galina in their native tongue. "What is the matter with you, man? You never learn, eh? Castrated as you were once for this very same thing, you still continue with such foolishness?"

Jorge turned around to face his companion, who at the moment seemed more like an enemy. "Shut up! Keep your woman's tongue locked tight in your head before I slit it for you! For why you think I live, eh?" His red-flamed eyes burned like torches as he stared at Galina. "You think *Dios mios* let me live in my condi-

666

tion if I were not to be avenged? *Demonio!* I will find that tough-livered daughter of a *gachupín* whoremaster to even the score if it takes all my life."

"*Si, si,*" Galina waved him off. "Is better we stick to business and make our money, *comprender*? And is best you forget what that little female tiger did to you. You had it coming, so stop lamenting."

Jorge turned on Galina, snarling like a vicious animal. He pulled his six-shooter, quick as lightning, and squeezed off a shot at his opponent, slicing a finger from the man's left hand. Galina screamed, fell to the floor, and rolled over, taking cover behind a chair and pealing two shots at the other. They were both cursing loudly and Madelaina, caught in the middle, sat stiffly, unable to move, just as the door burst open and Gus Madigan, followed by two gringo cowhands, stormed into the room.

"Goddamn greasers! Ah leave ya alone for two minutes and ah find ya fightin' over the woman! What the hell's wrong with ya? Too much fuckin' has fried yer brains."

"Fuckin'?" shouted an incensed Feliz Galina scornfully. "That motherless son of a *bastardo*'s *bastardo* hasn't got the equipment to do a manly thing." He wrapped his kerchief around the stump where only moments before a finger had protruded. An evil glint in his pain-filled, menacing eyes promised future retribution to Jorge. His gun had fallen to the floor close to Madelaina's feet, unnoticed.

"Issatso?" Madigan's eyes twinkled in merriment. "Now ain't that a pity? Well, at least ah can say ah feel a mite better, knowing ya can't damage the merchandise for Mr. Benson."

Madelaina's mind stopped at that remark. "Mr. Benson?" she asked. "*He's* responsible for this—for my abduction? But why?"

"Ah only follows orduhs, Miss *La Bomba*. Ah learned me long ago nevah ta ask questions of my boss. It's healthier thata way, ya heah?" He turned back to the two Mexicans. "Ya calmed down yet? Look, heah,

667

Galina, ya better get ovuh ta the kitchen and let cook fix yer finger—or ya might loose the fuckin' arm." He turned to Molina and grinned wickedly. "An' since ah knows ya cain't do the little missy heah no harm, ah guess it'll be all right ta leave ya with her."

"No!" screamed Madelaina hoarsely. "Don't leave me with this madman! He'll kill me! Believe me." Her voice climbed in hysteria. "He'll kill me!"

Jorge Molina turned to her with a look of innocence on his face and searched her features with a kindly, overexaggerated shrug. "Molina does a gringo woman no harm. For why do ju be so scared, eh?" He holstered his gun without menace. "Jorge's anger ees with that chicken Galina, not ju."

Madelaina turned her head, appealing to Madigan. "Please, you mustn't leave me here with this sex-crazed animal. I beg you. Señor Benson will punish you dearly if harm comes to me!"

"Ain't nothing ah don't already know. Now ya jus' sit heah quietly. Ain't nuttin' gonna happen ta ya, ah promise. Or ah'll have Jorge's head." He turned to the Mexican pointedly. "Ya heah, Molina?"

"Si, hombre. My word. No harm shall come to the gringa."

They were alone. For a time Molina studied her, then he began to roll a cigarette from a small bag of tobacco. Finished, he wet one end and curled it against moist lips under a thick handlebar moustache and finally lit it.

"Why ju are afraid of me?" he asked her in afterthought.

Madelaina didn't reply. She didn't have the courage to glance at him, not at this point, knowing he possessed so itchy a trigger finger. She'd heard with her own ears how he planned revenge on the woman who castrated him, hadn't she? God, how in hell he had lived after the gunshot wounds, when she and Feliz and the third man, Jose, left him in the desert to die, was a miracle.

Molina stood up and came toward her, eyeing her as

668

he tilted his head from one side to another. When he grinned as he did at this moment, he reminded her of Villa's sidekick, Urbina. It was an evil, lascivious grin that sent icicles through her blood. "Gringa, eh? Ju are *patrón* Benson's woman?"

Madelaina averted her head.

Molina moved in closer, his eyes narrowing. He reached in and with a grubby hand lifted her face so he could see her better. "Listen, gringa, how ju know Molina ees crazy, sexy man, eh?" Before she could reply, he leaned in and planted a wet, foul-breathed kiss on her lips. She struggled and with a free hand struck him hard across the face.

"Animal!" she screamed with burning hatred as memories of his vile abuse sprang into her mind.

Molina sprang back, startled by her reaction. He touched the side of his face lightly where he still felt the smarting of the blow. He laughed raucously, finding her actions humorous. "Ah, *si*, ju know Molina likes a tigress?" His eyes assessed her physical charms. "Because Molina is castrated doesn't mean he can't satisfy a woman such as you." He leered suggestively. "Molina still appreciates what a woman has and to look upon ju—ees something *muy bien!*"

Madelaina spat at him with all the vengeance she could muster. "An animal who knows only to rape a woman cannot appreciate a thing," she countered, wondering why she bothered. She knew she was playing with dynamite if she continued to goad him. *Let it pass, Madelaina. Do not speak to him and he'll not recognize you. You are defenseless without a weapon. Are you crazy to contest this animal?*

The small voices inside her kept nagging at her to keep her tongue. No matter how she tried to abide by their whisperings, something inside her demanded that she take her chances. She had to confront this animal with his own base and foul behavior and the hatred she bore for him and what he'd done to her when she was so defenseless.

"Ju are some brave woman," he said, staring at her

669

with revulsion for her high-toned manner. "Eef ju were no gringa, ju remind me of stuck-up *gachupíns* in my country." He kept tilting a bottle of tequila to his mouth, guzzling it noisily.

Madelaina breathed easier. She hoped they were still in America. She had gazed about the crudely constructed room and had no inkling as to where she was. But her wary eyes never left the face of this repulsive bear of a man for long. Having tasted his special brand of cruelty, she wasn't about to let it happen again. At one point her eyes came to rest on the gun that Feliz Galina had dropped on the floor not far from her feet. It still lay unnoticed by Molina, who apparently had other things on his evil mind.

Molina walked to the window and opened one of the shutters. His dark thoughtful eyes scanned the empty courtyard behind the large mansion of William Benson. It was deserted, he assured himself, as thoughts raced blindly through his mind. He wasn't making enough money on this job Galina had sucked him into. He turned back and glanced at the woman, thinking how much money he could make by selling her to the Mexicans as he made his way to Sinaloa. That is to say nothing of what he could get if he set her up in a house in Culiacan, eh? With her spirit and such a body, a gringa would bring him enough to retire like a *hacendado* himself. This Gus Madigan had called her *La Bomba*, some dancer, so what could she be—a whore, no?

His mind sped up like a turbine as he thought on the matter. Not even to that mealy-mouthed chicken, Feliz, would he tell his plans. His face broke into a more wicked grin than Madelaina had ever seen. It was enough to alert her—he was up to no good. His instructions had been to safely escort her to the Panhandle near Amarillo in a few days. Señor Benson had promised to pay them well for her safe journey to his hacienda. Who was to say what could happen en route to their destination? The more he pondered this, the better he liked it.

For an instant, he walked to the door, opened it, and peered outside. No one moved about in the dusky shadows of night. They were probably at supper, eating themselves sick. He glanced past the stables to the carriage house. If he worked fast, he could be off the estate at the edge of the city and onto southern roads before anyone missed them. For sure, that chicken, Galina, wouldn't return for a while.

In those few seconds Molina took to scan the exterior of the building, Madelaina reached down and slipped the gun into the folds of her suit. And not a moment too soon. He returned to her side, his eyes leveled on her.

"Gringa, listen to Molina. Ju want to escape? I will help ju to leave thees place. Is A-O.K.? Ju follow me and we go to the stable, find horses, and ride to safety. Ju believe Molina wants to help ju?" Craft and guile dripped from his voice.

Not for a second did she believe his turncoat tactics, although she couldn't help but wonder what he was up to, what his crazed mind was telling him. Knowing him, it could only mean more terror for her.

"Believe a castrated *Federale*, a bounty hunter?" She spat at him as her finger tightened on the gun. She let loose a string of curses in her native tongue that left no doubt in Molina's mind who she was.

He'd heard those same curses before, in the same voice, but where?

Madelaina reached up with her free hand and pulled out a few hairpins, allowing her raven hair to fall about her shoulders. "I thought I killed you once, *bastardo*, you obscene son of a fatherless whore, you putrified mass of decomposed humanity! You don't recognize me, eh? Take a good look at the daughter of General Obregon, swine."

For an instant Madelaina filled with a terror she'd never known before. The madman's eyes burned with volcanic fires of hatred. He came at her with death scrawled in his eyes, with a bitterness and a violence that was new to her. His blood-shot eyes fixed on her, his mouth curled back over his yellowed teeth with animal hatred. "I vowed I'd kill you, *puta!*" he shouted in their native tongue. "Only Satan knows the plans I've in store for you." Before she could fire at him, he whipped out his gun and covered her. "No easy death for you, you castrating daughter of a ball-less *gachupín!* Before Molina is through with you, you'll wish you were dead."

He moved in toward her and pulled open the blouse of her suit, ripping the fabric and popping the buttons. As she moved to avoid his attack, Madelaina jerked back in the chair and the gun was revealed.

"Ahhh, what have we here, *chiquita?* A gun? My, my, what things we learn if we're smart." He viciously yanked the gun from her hand, holstering one and tucking the other in his waistband under his *camisa*. With a free hand he reached for one of her breasts and squeezed it so hard she whimpered painfully. Again and again he squeezed, leaving welts in and around her nipples. "You think I'm finished with you, *puta?* Never!" He dropped his trousers and forced Madelaina to look upon his mutilated testicles and penis.

She averted her head and he grabbed a handful of her hair, twisted it, and forced her head back into position. "Now, *puta*—suck! I said suck it! You were responsible for my condition. Now you make it feel better, before I do things to you that will burn in your memory until I kill you, hear?"

Madelaina's head was twisted in such a position, she couldn't free herself. One of Molina's knees was buried in her lap, pinning her into the chair. The other was straddled over the arm of the chair, his foot planted firmly on the floor as he forced what was left of his mutilated manhood to her lips.

So, she thought, *he has little memory of what I did. He dares put the remains so close to my teeth?* In her eyes was a loathing and violence so deadly that if Molina had noticed, he might have been intimidated enough to back away. But he didn't notice, and he wanted his sweet revenge, so he forced himself on her.

672

Madelaina, repelled by this foul animal, felt the adrenaline shoot through her. She wasn't about to succumb to the beast. She heard the groaning gasp first, looked up, and saw Molina grasp his chest, a look of startled anguish coupled with pain on his face. Low animal noises gurgled in his throat, his black eyes bulged enormously, and his body jackknifed forward and fell heavily on top of her. Only then did she see a knife buried to the hilt into his shoulders. Her dark wary eyes lifted to the figure standing in the doorway not far from them. The man walked forward, followed by William Benson and two of his hands.

It was Feliz Galina who had expertly sunk the knife into Jorge Molina's back. "When I learned who you were from Señor Benson," said Galina. "I knew you were in danger—"

William Benson strode quickly to her chair, and removing his jacket, he wrapped her up in it. "Forgive me, mah deah. Ah'd no idea of the danger youah'd face with this brute. But I'm heah on more vital missions. We must make haste. Come with me inside the main *casa*. All is in readiness."

Confused and dazed by the rapid turn of events, Madelaina's head whirled. She was unable to grasp the import of her abduction or understand William Benson's part in all this.

"What's in readiness?" she muttered. "I don't understand."

"Trust me, mah deah. Ah'll let no harm befall ya. Ya must put yoah faith in me. It's the only way ya can be saved." A note of urgency crept into his deep voice.

Madelaina struggled in his arms as they walked the pathway through the outer portico, lined with fragrant flowers, to the main house. She remembered the hacienda, all right. It was the same one she'd gone to to visit Manuelito Perez, the place where she had allowed him to seduce her. Her face flushed for an instant as she recalled the incident. However, more concerned with pertinent facts of her abduction, she protested. "What are you telling me? What missions?"

Her head turned sharply as she saw several people in the dimly lit salon, among them a man dressed in black, holding a black book in his hands. The sanctimonious expression on his face was so obvious that Madelaina frowned.

"What's the meaning of this, Señor Benson? I thought I had made it perfectly clear that I wasn't interested in such arrangements with you."

"Theah, theah, *señorita*. Ah promise ya—it's the only way." He turned to the preacher. "Now do youah stuff, parson—theah's little time to waste."

He nodded to the other men in the room. Instantly they drew their guns and took positions at the door and windows, standing guard.

About to protest that she couldn't marry him because she was already married, Madelaina looked at Benson long and hard, then kept silent. Something in his eyes signaled her to protest no further.

She hardly heard the words spoken. She found herself answering the questions and mouthing the words—love, honor, and obey, as if she was in a wild, distorted dream. Everything had happened so swiftly that she was unable to cope with the disjointed scenes of which she didn't feel a part.

The makeshift ceremony, a sheer mockery of the nuptial vows, had ended. A golden wedding band had been slipped onto her finger. Madelaina, still numb and bewildered by the whirlwind activity about her, studied the heavy-belted cowboys. Most were chewing tobacco, their eyes peeled outside in the darkness. She saw them tense. Waco, one of Benson's most trusted men, turned to his boss, and with burning eyes, he hissed across the room. "Heah it comes, boss. Be prepared." The others tensed, their postures indicating they were prepared to do battle.

She heard the sounds of horses' hooves first. Then the shouting of orders, the sound of marching feet beating a staccato on the brick courtyard outside.

There came a loud rapping on the door. She saw Benson nod to the butler. The liveried man bowed politely and crossed the main salon to the tiled foyer. She heard loud voices, demanding yet tinged with respect. Madelaina gave a start at the familiar sound of the voices. She glanced sharply at William Benson. His eyes silently reassured her that she had nothing to be concerned about. Then six Mexican *Federales* entered.

"Well, suh, to what do ah owe such an unexpected pleasure?" said the wealthy *hacendado*, catching sight of Major Salomon. "Do come in, Major. Ah'd like ya to meet mah new wife, Mrs. William Benson."

Madelaina tensed rigidly under the burning glare of Salomon's eyes. She felt her stomach cramp and knot as hot and cold chills swept through her. Why couldn't she have given Tolomeo's philosophy a chance, she wondered. Salomon's foul, satanic expression, as fearful as she'd once been of this man, didn't revolt her as it once did. For some unknown reason, she felt possessed of an inner strength she hadn't experienced before in his presence.

"Your wife, Señor Benson," Major Salomon stated flatly, as if he knew the daughter of General Obregon would suddenly elude him again. "And how long has this *fugitive* from my nation been *your* wife?"

"Fugitive? Mah deah major, y'all must be mistaken, aren't ya?" William Benson spoke words packed in ice, leaving no mistake as to his annoyance. "It jus' isn't possible that the wife of William Benson, friend to the American President Wilson, could possibly be married to a fugitive, heah? Ah suggest you bring that important information ta yer President Huerta."

For a moment, Major Salomon hesitated. Oh, he got the picture all right. He glanced at the parson, the witnesses, and the cowhands with drawn guns. If Salomon had misunderstood William Benson's words, there was one language that he as a soldier couldn't misinterpret—drawn and ready guns.

"I see. Yes, I see, Señor Benson. I shall relate this vital information to my *presidente* instantly. I am certain when the situation is fully explained to Presidente Huerta, he'll understand."

675

Madelaina paled excessively. *Huerta? President? So!* *He* was responsible for Madero's assassination! *Dios mios!* She could never return to her country—never! Not as long as Huerta was president. She missed the subtle silent interplay between William Benson and Major Salomon, but not the expression he gave her which promised future retribution as he nodded dutifully and withdrew with his escorts from the premises.

"Quickly, Waco," ordered Benson gruffly, shrugging his six-guns into place over each hip. "Y'all bring the carriage around. Is everything ready ta go?"

"Yes, suh. Shore is." He tipped his western hat back on his head and gave a signal to his men to follow him.

Benson walked over to her. He told her she mustn't worry, that as long as she was in his company as his wife, Mexican law wouldn't dare harm a hair on her head. He patted her hand in an unexpectedly paternal manner. "It'll all work out, mah deah. Weah going to mah spread, Seven Moons, up neah Amarillo, wheah y'all can rest up a bit, git a little beef on ya, and try ta foahget any o' this happened."

If Madelaina's lips formed any protest, she was shushed and wrapped into a long sable cloak he removed from a beribboned box. "A weddin' present fer the missus. Not really good enough fer ya, mah deah, but it'll hafta do until ah get ta know ya better."

They left El Paso, heavily cloaked and guarded by Benson's well-armed bodyguards and expert cowhands. Without the fortification of dinner or a snack, Madelaina's hunger pangs grew to the point where she could no longer endure the empty feeling in her stomach. She wasn't certain which was worse, the continuous creaking and swaying of the carriage, the hunger, or the apprehension of what was to come.

She saw very little of the countryside in the black of midnight with no moon lighting up the way. Less than an hour out she began to feel the effects of this hard journey. She kept quiet for as long as she could, and finally, just at the point where Madelaina could take no more, Benson ordered his driver to stop. From the carriage floor he produced a hamper prepared by his El Paso cook, containing cold chicken and wine. She tore ravenously into the chicken, bread, and cheese until she could eat no more. Accepting a glass of wine eagerly to wash down the dry food, she hardly gave it a second thought when wine spilled on her expensive sable coat.

William Benson leaned forward and with a linen napkin blotted the wet drops that clung to the luxurious fur. "Ya must learn ta take good care of youah apparel, mah deah," he said with patient, paternal tones. "Furs are exquisite and should be treated with moah care," he continued as they took a short walk to stretch their bones. He helped her back into the carriage.

"With my stomach fighting for its life, I can give no thoughts to my outer appearance," she said flatly, arranging her skirts. She uttered a sigh of temporary contentment. "When do we arrive at Seven Moons, Señor Benson?"

"Señor Benson? Mah deah, ya bettuh get used to calling me youah husband."

"Listen, Señor Benson," she began with annoyance. "I keep trying to tell you we can't possibly be married—" She stopped. "Seven Moons? Did you say Seven Moons?" On her face was a quizzical look. She opened her tapestried bag and unsnapped the middle compartment of her reticule. There, in the fold of satin, were the seven moon earrings given her by Peter. Coincidence?

"Now, now, let's not spoil ouah trip, mah deah. Theah'll be plenty o' time fer us ta be talkin' about such things when we get home. Yes, ah said Seven Moons. Youah'll love it, mah deah. You'ah just the kind o' woman that belongs theah." He reached across the swaying carriage to pat her hands. His voice raised to a level that allowed her to hear him over the squeaking wagon sounds.

Madelaina shut the bag quickly.

"Wait till we get ta Seven Moons—ah sweah, youah'll nevuh want ta leave."

677

Madelaina stared at him in the dimly lit setting. Burning candles, encased in glass holders the shape of miniature lanterns at either side of the carriage doors, reflected deeply etched sadness on his stony features, despite his bold attempts to conceal his feelings. He was a strange man, this one with many contradictory sides to his nature. Madelaina was still taken by the coincidence of seven moons on the earrings. She shrugged off the strange feeling she got sitting next to this man and changed the conversation. "You might have at least permitted me to pack a bag. There are certain things a woman needs—"

"Ah've already seen ta ut, mah deah. One o' mah men has gone on ta yer place and will bring some of yer necessities. We'll stop off in Lubbock foah a change of horses. What evuh else ya need can be purchased theah."

Madelaina remained silent. The trip took nearly four days. They'd stopped only to change horses, dine, rest at wayside inns, and stretch their muscles. She still didn't understand why William Benson chose to ride in a carriage, when train travel or automobile was quicker. There was so much of Texas, she thought, observing the unending landscape of desert and the emptiness filled with more cattle than people.

Throughout the journey William Benson had maintained an amiable flow of conversation, detailing the vastness of his own lands and of his cattle- and bull-breeding operation. Admittedly, he told her, the sturdier bulls were bred in Mexico—something about the land and climate. As if she didn't already know what made certain strains of bulls more precious than others. He told her he'd have given anything to have taken her to his hacienda near Chihuahua City first, so that in her own land, among her own people, she'd have had a chance to really acquaint herself with him. However, in light of Major Salomon's urgent desire to detain her, he felt it safer to shelter her in his country where no harm could come to her.

"Then, when that President Huerta has had time ta

cool down a bit, an' when he comes to realize wheah the real power lies, he won't dare ta bite the hand that feeds him, heah?"

Madelaina stared at him with sudden hostility. "You're telling me that you're behind Huerta's sudden rise to power, Señor Benson? You financed his presidency?" This was all incredible to her. "A gringo knowingly supports such a man?"

"Let's jus' say, ah'm protectin' mah interests. Ah've plenty o' contacts in Washington. Ya might say ah'm a mighty powerful man," he said expansively, as he lit a cigar and filled the carriage with smoke. "It's only natural ah'd be protecting my properties, now wouldn'tcha say?"

Madelaina waved the smoke from her face impatiently. "But Huerta?" Her face screwed up with distaste, leaving very little to his imagination. "You must realize the kind of man you turned loose on the Mexican nation?"

"Now don'cha worry yer little head ovah matters that don't concern ya, mah deah. Politics don't belong in the head of a lady." He dismissed the subject from their talk and for the remainder of the trip described Seven Moons. "It's simply the most marvelous land in the whole world, mah deah. Can ya jus' imagine seven lakes all shaped like crescent moons on mah spread? Well, that's wheah the name comes from—Seven Moons. Imagine on a Texas ranch?"

It wasn't until they had arrived at Seven Moons and Madelaina had rested for a time that she was asked by a servant to join *señor el patrón* in the south portico for refreshments. It was more of an order than a request. Nevertheless, Madelaina walked down the steps of the sumptuous ranch, built in the style of a Spanish villa, and stepped briskly along the immaculate tiled floor to the portico beyond the French doors. It was a splendid, well-constructed house with huge polished oak beams, stone fireplaces, and highly waxed wooden floors. Hunting trophies covered the walls, including the heads of some of Benson's prize bull studs with

679

bronzed name tags mounted on wooden plaques denoting the prize strains.

"Well, mah deah, will ya join me in a few refreshments? A glass of sarsaparilla—wine—iced lemonade? What's youah pleasure?"

Ignoring him, Madelaina pressed onto a subject which ate at her. "Why Huerta?" she insisted on knowing. "He's a butcher! A chocolate-drinking butcher, a stuffed shirt who lives by treachery, murder, and revenge. There's no love in his heart for Mexico or its people. He is one of a few corrupt *Científicos* who sprang from the loins of the Diaz dictatorship which can't be trusted. Did you know Huerta was the head of the Secret Service? He wormed his way into Madero's trust only to assassinate him! And you help such a man to the highest office of the land? Hah! Señor Benson, you are as stupid as you are foolhardy."

Benson's square jaw flexed and his temples pulsed as he clenched his teeth, trying to contain his indignation. "Ah'll jus' pretend ah didn't heah those words spring from the lips of mah wife," he said with tight-lipped tolerance.

"How many times must I tell you? I can never be your wife!" she stormed angrily. "I keep telling you time and again and you just won't listen!"

Benson turned his back on her, poured a stiff tumbler of whiskey from a glass decanter on a sideboard, downed it in two gulps, and patted his stomach contentedly. "An' how many times must ah convince ya that politics is a man's subject. Don't evuh let me heah mention of Huerta or mah business again," he said with pointed calm. "Nothing like a good whiskey ta cleah the Texas dust from a man's throat." He sat down and indicated that she sit on a love seat placed in a luscious garden setting of trailing vines, blooming roses, and various cacti and succulents. She'd have enjoyed wandering in the garden anytime, but on this day she was too angry and upset by his dictatorial manner to do anything but fume inwardly as she forced herself to listen to him. He reminded her of her father so much, she forced her lips tight lest she say something she might regret. After all, she was miles and miles away from any land or people familiar to her. To think of running away would be as foolish as committing suicide at this point. Although she'd considered it several times over the past week after hearing about Peter's wedding and honeymoon, she had reconsidered. No. She'd be patient. She'd be detached. Wasn't that what Tolomeo insisted would give her inner strength? Very well, detachment would be her key to the future. Detachment and objectivity.

For the next few moments, William Benson attempted to display his charm. He asked her only what good manners forced her to reply—questions about her father and of the people she knew in El Paso. Many times she wanted to protest that their marriage could never be consummated because she was already married. Yet, when she pursued the thought, the knowledge that Peter had remarried weakened her position. Still, she persisted in bringing it to his attention, and each time she was cut off.

"Youah protests aren't all that important, mah deah, foah whatever reasons ya might conjur up. Ya see, one night while at mah villa neah Chihuahua City, while ah entertained that General Huerta and his man—what was his name?—Major Salomon? Yes, that's the one. Well, mah deah, you can imagine how interestin' ah found it when ah overheard Huerta and Salomon discussing how they'd finally located the famed spy of the revolution, Little Fox—Zorrita."

Madelaina tensed, hoping he wouldn't notice her sudden paleness.

"Theah didn't know ah was eavesdropping. An' ah might tell ya ah wasn't about ta listen fer much longer, especially when ah heard talk about this heah Zorrita, a Mexican spy that had half the *Federales* and *Rurales* lookin' fer her. An' when it turns out that she was none othuh than *La Bomba*, dancer at the Diamond Slipper, well, ah tell ya ah was about ta fall flat on mah face." Benson moved his large frame about the courtyard, pausing here and there to examine some of the exotic blooms.

The hot sun shining directly overhead was diffused by the branches of trees and vines shading off the inner courtyard. A dry wind off the prairie moved the air beyond the ranch house, rustling the sparse vegetation close to the estate and creating wheels of tumbleweed, which danced crazily on the surrounding lands.

Benson removed his jacket with a look of apology on his face. He wiped the perspiration from his face and neck. "Youah'll get used to the heat. Soon ya won't mind it a bit. Now wheah was ah? Ah, yes. Well, ya see, ah wasn't about ta let happen ta a friend what those two political snakes were dreaming up. Ah mean, we are friends, aren't we, mah deah?" He moved away from the flowers, one special sprig in hand and returned to the empty love seat. "What ah mean is, youah a friend of a friend, Manuelito Perez. Ah couldn't allow anything ta happen ta ya, could ah?" He placed the unusual flower into her lap. "Ah call it the Seven Moon plant. It's really a *Calceolaria Darwini* and barely resembles a crescent moon, but ah needed a flower to pay homage to my lands and ah chose this species to take the name."

Madelaina glanced in fascination at the curiously shaped bloom with leopardlike stripes on a crescent-shaped, elongated bubble. "They're quite unusual," she replied politely, unable to take her eyes from them. "I can see why you've called them Seven Moons."

"Well, well," he said somewhat pleased. "Ah knew ah'd picked the right woman. You an' me is gonna be soul mates, mah deah." He took her hand.

Madelaina withdrew her slender hands from between his and stood up.

"For all your efforts in helping me escape the clutches of my enemies, Huerta and Salomon, I thank you, Señor Benson."

"Señor Benson?" He laughed amiably and rose to his feet. "Mah name's Bill ta ya, little *chiquita*. Yer mah missus now! Now don't go getting yer dander up," he said quickly, seeing the anger rise in her. "Ah intend ta give ya a little time ta get used ta wearing mah name before we consummate our marriage. Ah promise, ah won't force mahself on ya. Ah tell ya, ah've waited a long time ta find me a filly like ya, and ah shuah don't intend ta spook her up."

Madelaina held back her tongue. What was the sense of protesting? How many times had she tried to make him understand? *Dios mios!* What a stubborn burro. Her anger flared earlier when he called her "little *chiquita*," much like the way Peter addressed her. She resented those words from the lips of any but her husband. Perhaps after a good night's rest, she could draw more courage and tell him about her marriage to Peter Duprez.

Before he permitted her to leave, he took time to introduce to her all the servants and ranch hands serving the hacienda. Nodding numbly throughout the ritual, she acted very much like the new mistress of the house, a fact which pleased William Benson immensely. She'll do, all right, he told himself. Yessiree, suh, he'd picked a champion. He'd let her rest sufficiently and in time he'd demand to know her background. Class always came to the fore, and this woman had to be a champion—a real prize-winning champion, he admitted.

"Just one moah thing, mah deah." He took her hand and led her to another room off the patio. The stench of the animals struck her first, but the foul odor of excrement, urine, and pure animal odor was dismissed from mind the moment she saw the cage along one wall filled with busy, chattering, and indolent monkeys, swinging from vine to vine in what had been rigged to resemble a miniature jungle habitat.

Her love of any of nature's creatures superseded the offensive odors, and in moments she stood in total enchantment. William Benson removed a packet of food from a wall chest and busied himself feeding the animals at random. They flocked to him.

"Watch'em, mah deah. They are quite instructive. Monkeys, ah feel, are somewhat superior ta man. They

683

can only mimic, so theah stay out of trouble. Man has it much harduh. He has ta be someone special. He has ta outshine his fellamen and work hard to get to the top of the heap. An' when he gets theah, he's a target foah all the unkind remarks and sharp spurs put ta him."

Madelaina sensed he wasn't really talking about monkeys, so she let him ramble.

"Theah smart, really smart, these heah monkeys. They nevuh talk back, they know theah place. Theah mind theah own business and stay outa trouble. Ya see, they just don't go about tryin' ta invent ways ta outsmart theah fellamen. Ya know, a person can learn a lot from just watchin' em."

An instinctive dislike for this man came upon her. Still she was intrigued by his line of patter and wondered where it would lead.

"Ya evuh fed a monkey, mah deah? Heah—take some food. Watch 'em flock ta ya. See what it feels like ta be depended on foah someone's life. Why, if I wasn't heah ta feed these monkeys, give 'em watuh and care foah 'em when they are sick, they'd die."

"If you left them in their own world, among other things in nature, they wouldn't be dependent on you. They could fend for themselves. Survival is instinctual among the lower animals," she said matter-of-factly as she tossed a few morsels to the chittering, highly agitated animals.

"But many monkeys leave their natural habitat and roam onto other territories wheah they can't take care of themselves. What are we ta do? Abandon them? Turn ouah backs on them? That would be inhuman. So we care foah them, feed them, and as long as they mind their own business, they can adjust."

"Just what are you trying to say, Señor Benson?" asked Madelaina, brushing her hands together to rid herself of the remaining crumbs.

"Ah'm trying ta explain a part o' me so y'all will get ta know me bettuh. I guess what ah'm attemptin' ta say is that y'all should try ta be like these heah monkeys."

Madelaina's fiery indignation set off sparks of mercurial emotion in her which Benson misinterpreted as belligerence. It was understandable that she'd be furious—she had a head on her shoulders and knew exactly what he intimated. He always preferred to domesticate his own animals. Tame, they were too set in the ways of their tamer and this offered no challenge to him.

"What ah'm tryin' ta say and farin' badly at it is that it's easy to do as youah told, mind yer own business, that way ya stay outa trouble."

"I know what you're trying to say. I only question why you need monkeys to tell me not to cause trouble among your people. I know my place, and believe me, it isn't here at Seven Moons as your wife!" she snapped contemptuously.

"Well, theah, little *chiquita*, it does mah heart good ta see ya get yerself rattled. Ah suppose ah wasn't being too clevuh with ya. It was just mah way of saying, this heah's mah spread—mah lands—mah Seven Moons. Heah, I am the lord of mah manor. Heah, youah'll do only what ah tell ya ta do. It makes things so much simpler."

"Lord of the manor," she retorted harshly. "Insidious, uncompromising dictator is more like it. Listen, Mr. Benson, no man tells me what I do or don't do. The sooner you understand me, the better we'll get along. I had no hand in this flimsy scheme of yours to kidnap me and marry me against my will. Perhaps I should feel obliged to thank you for saving me from the clutches of Huerta and Salomon. Very well. I thank you. Now, you will please make arrangements to return me to El Paso." Her tone and mood reflected her *gachupín* heritage. She made no attempt to cover this streak of aristocratic impertinence.

Benson smiled tightly. "Ah think youah simply tired," he said in patronizing tones that rankled her and added fuel to the fires blazing inside her. "It's best y'all retire foah a while. Ah've got a lot of work ta catch up with." He turned from her and walked away, leaving her to find her own way back to the house.

Madelaina's tranquility had transcended the storm clouds and she tried pulling herself back to her usual composure. She watched the monkeys for a time, then left to go to her quarters, too tired to give them more thought.

Madelaina stirred restlessly on the bed with the covers flung off her. She felt nauseous and feverish. How long had she lain in bed with thoughts of the past few days' events roiling her brain? She wondered what Antonetta would say and how Pancho Villa would take to her sudden disappearance. How would they even begin to find her so many miles to the north? As much as she needed sleep, she'd been unable to close her eyes the entire night. Affected by strange and alien sounds of servants puttering around the villa, of cattle lowing in the nearby lands, of horses neighing, and of the vast empty silence of the night, she had walked the floors before dawn, unable to sleep.

Standing before a large wall-length wardrobe, Madelaina pulled open the doors. Her astonishment at the contents of the closet, filled with negligees, velvet robes, traveling costumes, and riding clothes, knew no bounds. When, for the love of God, had William Benson thought to stock all these items? Why, he'd thought of everything. She reached in and pulled at random a pair of men's trousers and a shirt and boots. She held up the items before her, reflecting on her image in the oval-shaped looking glass, and decided they'd do.

She tossed them onto a nearby chair, crossed the tiled floor of the large bedroom which had a magnificent view of the gardens, and opened a door to the right of the large four-poster bed. The bathroom was a splendid combination of old war and new Texas charm. The white enamel tub stood on languid mermaid-shaped bases of bright shiny brass—or was it gold? The long marble commode with running water in the wash basin had matching mermaid handles. For several moments, she delighted in this.

It wasn't as if Madelaina had never reveled in such luxury before. She'd lived with it all her life, except for those long months spent as a *campesina* and at Madrigal de Los Altos where she lived in the worst squalor of her lifetime. She was actually born to such living and was grateful she could handle both levels of life. What actually surprised her was to find such luxury in the middle of such desolate wasteland. Only a very wealthy man could afford to house such luxuries under one roof, so far from civilization.

Over the next few hours, she found herself thinking more about this man William Benson. Alternately, as she dwelled upon him, she forced herself to eliminate thoughts of him, as if in so doing, her mind would be free to concentrate on more pertinent things.

She turned the bronze mermaid spigots and filled the tub with warm water. Sniffing several scents from an array of colored jars on the marble-topped commode, she poured the contents of one into the tub and inhaled the rose-scented aroma intermingled with steam emanating from the tub. Just as the sun came up in the east and peered over the horizon, Madelaina disrobed and settled herself in the luxury of the tub. She tried to keep her mind blank, to refrain from thinking, but as she lay back soaking in the aromatic waters, she was unable to keep from wondering what would happen to her here at the hacienda of William Benson. What did he really intend for her? No man as lusty as he could keep away from a woman, of this she was certain.

All she knew of him was what Antonetta had told her. She had described his affluence as a Texas cattleman and his success in whatever else he immersed himself in businesswise.

As the early rays of light slanting through the stained-glass windows lit up the room, Madelaina's attention was focused on the unusual décor of the bathroom. At one end of the marble bath tub stood a glass chest, almost like an island, separating water closet from dressing room. Her eyes traveled to the wooden box high on the wall over the water closet and assessed the hand-painted cupids, cleverly designed to hide the function of such a convenience.

Then again as she marveled at the artistry that had gone into such a contrivance, her eyes traveled back to the contents in the glassed-in wall cabinet. A collection of perfume flacons, conchas, tintypes, turquoise stones, and small silver snuff boxes were painstakingly arranged and appeared as if they'd been untouched for years. Someone had gone to much trouble to set this up, and Madelaina was certain no man had conceived so feminine a bathroom. It was only natural her thoughts would drift back to the type of woman William Benson had once married. She wondered many things about her and why their marriage had broken up. No, Antonetta had told her Benson was a widower. Ah, that was it. The wife had died. Too bad, thought Madelaina. It appeared the woman might have had some softening effect on her man, and his losing her might have caused him considerable grief. Strange he hadn't remarried. With such crazy philosophies, those incredibly unfortunate monkeys, and his feelings about people, it was no wonder. What woman in her right mind would have him?

Madelaina sat up with effort and reached for the towel she'd tossed on a small bench near the tub. She'd soaked long enough. With her heart beating so rapidly, she wasn't sure she could take a nap before the entire household awakened. Wrapped in the thick toweling, she rubbed her body energetically until it tingled. Slowly, she walked to the glass chest to examine its contents. She gazed into the oval-framed tintypes, the oil painting of a stunning brunette with the face of a Mona Lisa, the same enigmatic smile on her face. Or was it sadness she'd detected on the woman's face?

She gazed at the others, photos of children. All at once Madelaina's memory sharpened and she began to roll the name William Benson over and over in her mind. Where had she heard the name before—much before Antonetta had spoken the name? An unexpected vision of the face of Lazaro flashed before her.

Lazaro of Madrigal de Los Altos. His name was Benson! What had she done with those files? She'd carted them from place to place long enough and for what reason she wasn't sure, except to one day confront her father with the fact that he'd been paying for the lodging of a son who'd died long ago. In her wildest moments, she never imagined she'd be in the presence of Lazaro's father.

William Benson, Amarillo, Texas. That was what she knew of Lazaro's father. Was it possible he was the same William Benson? She wrapped the towel tightly around her and tucked it in over her breasts, moving in to peer at the other tintypes. There were photos of the stunning brunette with a young man at her side, some with an infant in her lap, but none reminded her of the hydrocephalic Lazaro. She shrugged, thinking her imagination was working overtime. Madelaina unpinned her hair and let it hang loosely around her shoulders. She glanced about for a hairbrush. There was none on the commode or in the drawers. She opened a cupboard next to the glass chest and searched for either a comb or brush. On the second shelf she found a portrait of a young man.

She lifted it and studied the image in the photo. She got the distinct impression she knew this man. He was in his late teens or early twenties, clean shaven, tall, lanky, thin, and dressed in western garb. Something about his features convinced her she knew him. She had another unexpected vision of a face she knew well, of hard blue eyes that could soften and melt all her resistance, of a face that had grown fuller and more mature over the years, one she'd never forget. It couldn't be! It just couldn't be—Peter?

She thought herself imagining too hard, wanting it to be Peter, so he'd be close to her. No doubt it was William Benson as a younger man. But why of all places would the photo be in a woman's boudoir gathering dust? Why not downstairs in the study among the other memorabilia? She replaced the photo and forced herself to dismiss thoughts of Peter from mind. How could he have married Valerie Townsend after that last night they spent together? How could he have been so deceitful and not told her how soon his plans were to be consummated?

She walked back into the bedroom and slipped into the trousers and shirt and boots. The clothing was snugger than she usually wore and the boots a trifle too tight, but they'd have to do until her own things arrived. Every curve—every outline of her trim figure was readily noticeable, and she felt a sudden flush permeate her body and face as she studied her revealing body in the mirror. Why, the shirt barely buttoned over her full, round breasts!

A soft knock at the door brought her head up sharply from her reflection in the mirror, and she focused her attention on the door.

"Señora, con su permiso. . . ."

The Mexican servant, carrying a tray of steaming black coffee, scrambled eggs with peppers and tomatoes, and fresh bread, walked into the room. With averted eyes, she set down the tray on the table next to the bed. *"Bienvenida,* Señora Benson—" The older woman stopped and stared at Madelaina in shocked surprise. She shook her head vehemently. "No, *señora.* No! No!"

Madelaina spoke to her in her native tongue. "What's wrong, woman? What are you trying to tell me?"

"You must not wear those clothes. They belonged to Señora Duprez Benson. *Señor el patrón* will be violently angry. Never touch those things. Only from this chest can you select the proper clothing." Trying to be helpful, she began to remove the shirt from Madelaina's back.

But Madelaina had stopped at the name Duprez Benson. "Who are you speaking of? Who's Señora Duprez Benson?"

The old serving woman shook her head and with great reluctance avoided the subject. She shuffled across the room to the proper chest, flung it open, and told

690

Madelaina to take her pick. "But never, never must you touch those other articles of apparel. Understand?"

"*Como te llamos*? What are you called?" asked Madelaina.

"Pilar, *señora*. I am called Pilar."

Madelaina, flushed with annoyance, nevertheless complied with Pilar's instructions. She shed the articles and watched as the older woman with pendulous breasts and a wrinkled walnut skin picked up the discarded articles, smoothed them out, and reverently rehung them in place. She picked up the boots and wiped imaginary dust off them with the hem of her white apron before replacing them neatly in the wardrobe. Madelaina selected a pair of trousers at random, a shirt from the chest, and hurriedly donned them.

The aroma of coffee invigorated and stimulated her appetite. She hungrily moved toward the table on which Pilar had placed the tray of food and munched on a hot biscuit as Pilar, pouring coffee for her into a china cup, nodded in approval. Madelaina devoured the coffee and held out her empty cup for more.

"You mentioned Señora Duprez Benson, Pilar. Any relation to a certain Peter Duprez?"

Pilar nearly spilled the coffee. "*Con su permiso, patrón*. Please to repeat jur question," she asked in pigeon yankee.

The marked hesitation in her manner as Pilar glanced curiously at Madelaina caused the new bride of William Benson to dismiss the entire subject. "Never mind, Pilar. It was just an attempt on my part to be frivolous. There could be no possible connection between Peter Duprez and Señor Benson." She began to devour the Spanish-style eggs.

"*Los jovenes*, Pedro Duprez? *Ah, si, señora*. He is the son of the *patrón*."

It was something Madelaina hadn't expected. She glanced up from the fork she held in midair ready to taste the omelette and was held spellbound by the frightened look in Pilar's eyes. "*Por favor, señora*, do not tell the *patrón* it was Pilar who tells you such

691

things. There is *muy mal*—very bad—feelings between these two *hombres*. Such a shame, father and son who do not speak, do not see each other for so long."

Madelaina placed her fork across her plate, her eyes glittering with interest. "Are you telling me that the man called Peter Duprez is the son of William Benson?" she asked in disbelief. "Tell me, Pilar, do you have a likeness of this Peter Duprez—a photograph—something which I can look at?"

Pilar's dark eyes widened. She crossed herself religiously and shook her head furiously. "*Por favor, señora,* do not ask Pilar such a thing. She has said too much already." She pulled off the bed covers and shook the blankets vigorously.

The clock on the mantle across the bedroom chimed 6 A.M. It was early. She took the older woman's hands and led her to the sofa before the fireplace. Her voice was soft, tender, and understanding. "Please, Pilar. I must know. I am one of your people, one of you. I am the daughter of General Alvaro Obregon of Mexico City. I promise you no harm shall befall you. I give you my word I shall not betray you. It is important that I know if the man I know as Peter Duprez is that very one you say is the son of your *patrón.*"

She looked deeply into the eyes of the servant for several moments, and in a silent understanding which comes from a knowledge of one's people, Pilar turned on her small feet and padded out of the room. She returned in moments with something hidden under her apron. Glancing about the room in a cautious manner, she closed the door behind her and removed a faded, somewhat worn photograph in a cardboard frame from beneath the apron.

Madelaina moved forward on leaden feet, wondering why all the hush-hush and fear in the woman's eyes. She took the photo from the older woman's work-worn hands, reluctant to gaze upon it. Her eyes left Pilar's face and lowered to the fading photograph of a young man in western attire. She studied the casual stance, the twinkling eyes, the lean, young face of a man ten years younger than the man she knew. It was unmistakably Peter Duprez.

"*Dios mios,*" she uttered huskily and fell heavily into the chair behind her.

"What is it, *señora*? You know this man? He is the same one you know?"

"He's the same one, Pilar." She took another look at the photo and instructed the woman to replace the photo to its proper place and return to her instantly.

When Pilar returned, Madelaina swore her to secrecy. "If I confide in you, Pilar, you must confide in me. I will say nothing of this to the *patrón*. You must promise the same. Now, tell me," she began. "Did *señor el patrón* and his wife have another son—one who possessed an infirmary?"

Pilar blanched. "You ask too much, *señora*. We have not spoken of such things for many years. I cannot answer you." She was visibly disturbed. On her feet, she avoided Madelaina's eyes. "I go now. I will be missed from the kitchens. *Señor el patrón* was up at an early hour. He asked that I bring the *señora* her breakfast and show you the rest of the *casa*. You eat now. When you finish, I shall be honored to show you the duties of the mistress of this house."

"Very well then, go, Pilar. You have my word, this conversation has ended in this room. Please do not fear anything from me."

Madelaina reached for her reticule from a drawer in a chest. "Pilar," she called to the woman. "Before you go, tell me if have you seen these before?" She held out the golden earrings Peter had given to her. The seven crescents glittering with diamonds dangled rakishly.

"*Dios mios!*" The older woman's eyes widened into circles. She crossed herself. "*Por favor, señora,* why do you plague Pilar?" she pleaded.

"Have you seen these before, Pilar?" asked Madelaina again.

"*Si, señora.* They are the property of the *señor's*

693

dead wife." Then Pilar rolled up her sleeve to show Madelaina a terrible scar above her wrist.

"For those golden earrings, *señor el patrón* almost cut Pilar's hand off." They were missing shortly after *los jovenes*, Pedro, leave Siete Luna. *Señor*, *el patrón* think that Pilar take them. I tell him, no, *señor el patrón*. I never see him so *furioso*. Ayeiiieee. *Por favor, señora*, do not show them to *el patrón*.

Madelaina put them back into her bag. Her mind churned rapidly. "You may go, Pilar. Say nothing to anyone about this, *comprender*?"

"*Si, señora. Si.*" The old woman, thick braids over each shoulder, lowered her eyes and exited softly.

Madelaina fell heavily into the chaise longue, unable to think, unable to clearly assess the situation. The facts were clear enough, but what to do? She needed time. Time. Time and more time to know how to handle the situation. A thousand and one thoughts plagued her. Of all the preposterous situations to fall on her. Her mind wandered back to those monkeys in the cage. No wonder Peter had run off at an early age. All Benson wanted around him were human monkeys with no minds of their own to think things out. He wanted automatons to do his bidding without question.

Madelaina fought a burning desire to run swiftly to the cages, open them, and release the poor creatures, she reasoned that most would probably die, unable to forage for themselves. She conceded they were probably better off here where they were fed and cared for. After all, they were animals—not humans. *Dios mios!* For a time she had categorized people as Benson had done!

Chapter 25

For several days, Madelaina had more leisure than she knew what to do with. No longer ruled by haste or forced to conform to a schedule, she took to riding through the surrounding countryside. She kept silent about her findings and continued to study William Benson with intense curiosity, trying with some determination to find the key to his thinking. He ran the hacienda and his men like a captain on the high seas ran a tight ship. Everything ran efficiently at the pace he'd set long ago.

Her presence in no way interfered with the routine of the servants. The library was stocked with many volumes on nearly every subject she could imagine, primarily the breeding of cattle and his second interest— oil. An unusual chess set, sitting on a special table near the large bay windows, remained untouched, as if interrupted in midgame. Whenever she asked Pilar about it, the older woman simply said, "Don't touch it; *señor el patrón* would be furious."

There had been days when she rode alongside William Benson on the bountiful lands of Seven Moons. Admittedly, it was some of the most unusual land she'd seen, with *arroyos grandes* and *arroyos secos*, rounded green hills shaped like the breasts of a woman, prairies, a belt of rolling countryside called the Black Prairie, areas of eroded regions, and isolated tablelands and canyons. The most marvelous of nature's offspring being, of course, those seven crescent-shaped lakes or ponds for which the ranch was named. Shaped like half-moons, these seven bodies of water could be seen in their entirety from the top of Black Mountain, clustered together like a thick chain winding its way through the rolling hills. Graceful willows bordered the crystal ponds. Farther in toward a more wooded area stood oaks and elms, cedar and mesquite trees in great abundance. Thinking the setting looked more like an artist's painting than real life, Madelaina watched as cattle lowed and quenched their thirst in the waters.

The north pastures were thickly dotted with Black Angus, the south stocked with Shorthorns, Herefords, and Aberdeen Angus steer raised for beef. In the east and west pastures Benson kept a breed of cattle called Charbray—white Charolias crossed with Indian Brahman bulls to produce a fleshier stock for beef.

Benson painstakingly explained each of the breeds and told her of the exhausting efforts he'd undergone to produce these prize-winning cattle.

"Why so many various breeds?" asked Madeliana, caught up in the excitement of his experience. "Why not perfect only one or two strains?"

"Well, ah tell ya. Maybe one day when ah've really perfected a strain, ah'll quit. But lookee ovuh yonder, down on the desert land. See them iron towuhs? We call 'em derricks. Oil derricks. One day, this whole land may be covered with them iron ladies, refusin' ta bend in the wind. An' then, little *chiquita*, and then—" He rolled his eyes skyward with vast expectation registered in them. "Then fer shuah, ah'll be the wealthiest man on both sides of the Rio Grande."

Madelaina had listened politely and patiently, hardly responding unless her own curiosity was piqued. Aware one day that her interest might be waning, he promised that the bulls in Chihuahua would be more to her liking since they'd recently imported more Concha bulls from Las Marismas. He seemed highly inspired by her presence, and there were times when Madelaina felt he might attempt to consummate their marriage vows regardless of their validity.

It happened one night at dinner. It was like any usual night, except that William Benson had been away for several days. He returned shortly after noon and secreted himself with his ranch foreman and other trusted cowhands.

Madelaina should have known by the attitude of Pilar and the servant girls, Lupe and Alicia, that something was underfoot. She'd never seen the women so industrious, attending their duties as if bedeviled by demons, then disappearing from sight. Madelaina was left to putter about the kitchen on her own, preparing something special for dinner. This in itself was frequently frowned on by Pilar and the cook. She'd been actually shooed out of the kitchen at times. On this day, they gave her free reign and when they disappeared at about 4 P.M. and didn't answer her summons, she shrugged, annoyed by their apparent petulance, and prepared the table in the dining salon herself, complete with champagne.

Outside, the *vaqueros* had struck up some music, and she thought the Mexicans had joined in what began to appear a festive time. She glanced outside at the cowhands and recognized the fact that they'd been drinking heavily. They shouted and cheered a few daredevil bronco busters in a nearby corral with their unrestrained yippies and yahoos, as the spooked horses attempted to throw their riders.

When William Benson entered the dining room, it became obvious to her that he'd been drinking heavily. His attitude was surly and withdrawn. In an effort to bring him out of the mood, she asked pleasantly, "What's going on out there? Seems like a fiesta of sorts." She wasn't prepared for gruff response.

"Ya hadda tell 'em. Ya couldn't have kept yer mouth shut like the lady of the house is supposed ta do? Ya hadda tell 'em yer one o' 'em."

Perhaps if Madelaina had persisted in asking Pilar about her unusual silence earlier in the day, she might have learned just what kind of a night this would be.

"What is it? What's wrong? I don't understand. Whom did I tell I was one of them?"

"The greasers, that's who. Now the whole crew

knows. Ah'll hafta take special measures ta protect ya. That means bloodshed. Just what ah don't need."

"From what, Señor Benson?" pleaded Madelaina. "Protect me from what?" She threw her hands up in the air. "I don't understand a thing you say."

"Don'cha know what day this is?" He poured another glass of champagne and guzzled it down like an animal. His manner was surly, his tone sullen.

He didn't remove his six-guns, and before he took his place at the head of the table, he strode through the room to the living room and bolted the front door. He shouted orders to two of his men, both armed and carrying shotguns, to make sure the back door and windows were bolted. His loud voice echoed through the rooms and sounded loud and clear to Madelaina. "Jus' ya tell those red-blooded, gun-totin' sidewinders if they dare come near mah missus, ah'll hang their carcasses out ta dry, heah?" The artillery at his fingertips threatened.

Madelaina shivered inside. Why would they come at her? For what? She moved to the French windows and looked outside at the setting sun. The men were still drinking, occupied with the unbroken broncs. They talked louder than usual, laughed with less restraint, but she saw no other reason to fear them.

William Benson ambled back to the dining room, fingered his six-guns and shrugged the holsters into position over each hip, then sat down. He poured himself another glass of champagne and avoided Madelaina's eyes when she served him from the silver chafing dish and placed his plate before him. She took only a small portion for herself, even though she'd labored long on the stuffed braised veal with mushrooms.

Seated, she glanced at him over the centerpiece of Seven Moon blooms. "Now will you tell me why your people celebrate—and why you are so angry with me?"

"It's a Texas tradition. Theah celebratin' the Texas War of Independence. The Alamo—remember the Alamo?"

"No, I don't. Should I?"

"Surely ya remember what that theah General Santa Anna of youahs did ta the people of San Antonio?" Benson chewed his food loudly and smacked his lips together, sipping more champagne. He glanced at Madelaina's sober expression and continued. "Colonel William Travis and his men had withdrawn ta the Alamo and were massacred in the massive assault leveled against them by yer General Santa Anna. Mah people haven't forgotten or forgiven the sound of the *degüello*."

"And for this terrible infamy, your people *celebrate?*" Madelaina's eyes widened in disbelief. "*Dios mios*, you gringos are strange people."

"Ya might call it a celebration of sorts. The men get themselves drunk an' then, they go crazy." He hesitated to elaborate any further and resumed eating. "Ah was thinking earlier ya might've enjoyed seeing the fireworks in Amarillo. Ah had even thought we might have ridden to Black Mountain. From theah we could have seen what the city folk do ta light up the skies."

"No thank you, William," she said tightly. "I've seen enough fireworks and drunken binges in my lifetime to suffice forever." She pushed her plate from her.

"It's outa the question, now, since ya told the help you were Mexican," he retorted as if she hadn't spoken her mind.

"Mexican?" Madelaina puzzled over this. Suddenly her eyes widened ostensibly. "You don't mean—? Is that why Pilar and Lupe and Alicia absented themselves earlier? You permit this brutal savagery? You, William Benson, a man who should know better?"

The fine hairs on Benson's neck bristled. His eyes narrowed. "Ah'll pretend ah didn't heah those words, mah deah." He forced a lighter mood and patted his stomach contentedly. "The food was delicious. Ah know ah have y'all ta thank foah it. Otherwise, I'd have been gnashing mah teeth on cold mutton and beans."

He had simmered down and he seemed to be attempting to assuage her anger. But Madelaina wasn't about to be humored.

Earlier she had sensed that William Benson intended to make ovations to her on this night. She'd seen the look in his eyes for the past two days, that unmistakable look of a man ready to conquest. So she had in a sense attempted to prepare for this encounter. Fill his stomach with good food, ply him with special viands, and perhaps he'd fall asleep early. Good thinking, she had told herself earlier, never counting on this state holiday to thwart her best efforts.

It was as if William Benson was blind and deaf to her manner and mood. He continued as if she hadn't spoken a derogatory word. "Again, ah thank ya fer preparing an elegant supper, mah deah." He lit up a cigar and puffed on it expansively. At intervals he'd cock his ear and listen as if he were monitoring the volume of the raucous hilarity outside.

"Ya see, mah deah, right aftuh 5 P.M. on this day, the decent Mexican women lock themselves up tight in their *casitas*—away from the Texans. Some of the ranch hands get a mite rambunctious when Old John Barleycorn's been pumped into 'em all day long. The greasers keep theah doors locked tight until tomorrow aftuhnoon when it's safe ta come out. It's bettuh that way. Ah wouldn't like nothin' ta happen ta any o' mah people. Ah need both kinds—ya see?"

Madelaina fumed inwardly. Her slender fingers tapped the linen-covered table top in a steady staccato. His bigotry and prejudices protruded like a sharp knife into her heart, inciting her to anger. "Señor Benson, need I remind you I'm a person of Mexican birth? I find your words in atrocious bad taste and a dishonorable gesture to a person of my class." Her personal fears seem to evaporate as she stared fiercely into his steely blue eyes.

"Well, shucks, now. Ain't no sense gettin' yer dander up. Ah didn't mean ta rankle yer bones. Ah ain't talkin about yer kind o' people. Ah'm referin' ta them low-class *peóns* who don't know from nothin' how ta do fer themselves."

Madelaina's attention was caught up in the noises marking preamble to this nightmare of festivities. Loud shouts, continued wahoos and a long wail of yippies permeated the air. Gunshots peeled off time after time like fireworks.

Madelaina had seen the *Villistas* after victory. She'd seen their animalistic behavior, their lust, their drunkedness, even their bloodthirsty ways. It wasn't that she justified such behavior in her mind by telling herself they were entitled to their playtime after the rigors of revolution and war, of previous oppression and savage treatment by the *Rurales* and other government-inspired butchers. But here she was in what was considered a civilized country, seated opposite a wealthy, powerful, and politically inspired man with connections to the White House, watching him do nothing about such barbarism, as if it didn't exist. His refusal to put a stop to this inhuman custom appalled her.

In a voice dripping with sarcasm, Madelaina demanded, "Why do you permit such savage behavior, *señor el patrón*? Why do you permit your men to act like undisciplined, inhuman animals? You of all people should feel shame for this degradation."

Benson laughed aloud to cover his indignation. "A man's gotta keep his help happy—or he ain't gonna have any help ta keep."

Ignoring him, Madelaina rose to her feet, and swishing the skirts of her pink cotton dress, she moved across the room and flung open the doors to the portico.

"What in hell do you think youah doing?" shouted Benson hoarsely. He jumped to his feet and came in behind her to close and bolt the doors once again. "Get back, woman! Goddamnit!" he cursed. "What the hell's wrong with ya?"

He peered through the blinds. Outside, a large Texas moon, orange as a jack o' lantern and a thousand times

701

larger than any normal moon, lit up the sky and gave the earth a hue of flamingo fire. A few shadows moved about, staggering in drunkenness. The men held jugs of whiskey to their lips in a perpetual pose, hardly pausing for a moment's rest. William Benson felt uneasy for the first time in his life.

Watching him, Madelaina wondered what in the name of God she was doing here. Why hadn't she forced the issue with Peter, fought for him, tooth and nail, instead of letting him return to Valerie Townsend? She was furious at him, at herself, at Pancho Villa for involving Peter in his cloak-and-dagger fiascos. Moreover, she was sick with humiliation for not having the courage to escape Seven Moons. After all she'd been through in her young life, why she was so reluctant to leave this temporary sanctuary didn't make sense.

Women's screams pierced the night air and penetrated the walls of the *casa*. Her eyes darted to William Benson's bloodshot, red-rimmed eyes as he ambled back to the table to guzzle more champagne. In these few moments Benson had changed visibly. He'd grown more sullen, his mood more hostile. *Dios mios*, why didn't he do something about such bestiality?

Never had Madelaina felt so lost and forlorn, so completely isolated from everything and all she knew, so alien in a world more alien and frightening to her than Madrigal de Los Altos had been. At least there she had hope of escaping. Here, what could she do? She didn't even know where she was. She could have been a million miles from civilization for all she knew. Riding horseback with Benson, she'd seen no other life for miles. Other than cattle and a few cowhands, there wasn't another family or sign of human life in more than eight hours of riding. Escape from such a place inevitably meant death—thirst, starvation, or falling prey to the lusty men of the range who detested the Mexicans. *Dios mios*.

There was no way she could hide her frustration. Shrill screams pierced the air outside and she gave a start. "What's that?" she cried. "Women screaming!"

702

"Oh, that," Benson said flatly, sipping champagne directly from the bottle. "Probably one o' mah men catching up with a *señorita*, ah reckon."

"And you do nothing about it?" she asked indignantly.

"Well, well, coming from miss goody two shoes, ah reckon ah should consider the source. Ya don't mean ta tell me y'all ain't heard the likes of a woman screaming befoah, *Little Fox*? Ah mean among those filthy camps y'all tracked about in foah so long? Ah reckon them eyes and ears o' yers have seen and heard a mite moah screamin' than youah'll evuh hear at Seven Moons. What's moah, *chiquita*, ah'm not about ta let ya put me off no moah."

He reached for her, pulled her close to him, and roughly, without restraint, he kissed her savagely. After a moment he held her away from him and stared at her through embarrassed and disbelieving eyes. "Ah don't believe ya don't feel nothing fer me. Yer play actin' with me and ah don't cotton ta such temperament."

He struck out at her in anger, leaving vivid fingermarks across her face. Madelaina's detachment, her utter lack of concern and refusal to cooperate irked him intensely. She glanced at him without emotional reaction, with no attempt to shield herself. And this served only to annoy him further.

"Ah've been patient with ya, wench. More than with any other woman. But mah patience has thinned. Tonight's the night ah demand full payment. Ah saved yer worthless life from them two money-grubbin' murderers and this is the thanks ah get? Don'cha have no appreciation? Ah reckon ah've treated ya like a lady fer too long. Maybe if ah treated ya like the whore ya are, ah'd have gotten moah fer mah money. Now, make it easy on yerself, girl, you an' me is gonna have us a fine time." He grabbed her lustily, swung her over one powerful shoulder, and with a free hand grabbed a bottle of champagne and stalked out the room.

In moments he'd dragged the docile woman up the stairs and tossed her onto the four-poster bed in her quarters. "Now, get yerself undressed, woman. Ah intend ta see what I paid fer." His eyes were bloodshot, his voice harsh and angry. He drank from the bottle he toted and reeled unsteadily on his feet as he began to peel off his jacket and shirt. His narrowing eyes seemed to pierce her like daggers.

"Ah said, undress, bitch! Ah found ya dancing in that whorehouse and ah heard from Huerta and Salomon that you were nothing but a lousy *campesina*, so don't think ya can pull the wool down over William Benson's sharp eyes, *señorita puta*. Ah'm William Benson and no one puts anything over on him, heah?"

"What is it you wish, *señor el patrón*? For me to submit to your greedy sexual excesses? You are a petty man with enormous ambition, *señor el patrón*, but I daresay not as ambitious as I. Perhaps I should introduce myself to you, *señor el patrón*." She spoke the words with dripping sarcasm each time they were uttered, while simultaneously keeping an unemotional posture. "I am Madelaina Obregon, daughter of General Alvaro Obregon of Mexico. I am niece of Don Diego Obregon of Las Marismas, and I do not care what that pig Huerta or that butcher Salomon have told you."

For only a moment Benson faltered under the weight of her words. Too much champagne had fuzzed his brain, and determined to have his way with her, nothing would stop him. He stood before her naked. Madelaina now saw where Peter got his physical stature and strength. Benson had the body of a man twenty years younger, lean, hard, and firm. "Ah don't give a damn whose daughter ya are! Ah told ya ta take yer clothes off, woman," he said sullenly, moving toward her. He reached in and tore off her blouse. "Ah see, ya prefer it with yer clothes on? Is that it? Then spread yer legs and ah'll show ya how a real man takes yer kind o' woman."

But Benson, a man used to having his orders obeyed, instantly grew impatient. He reached in toward her and with both hands picked up the torn shreds of her blouse and began to tear it. This being too slow for his pulsating manhood to take, he reached over on the floor for his discarded belt and from a sheath removed a Bowie knife. With a few expert strokes, he slashed through the rest of her garments and peeled the fabric from her trembling flesh. Finished, he cast aside the knife while his hungry eyes devoured the exquisite contours of her body. Spreading her legs apart, he mounted her and said drunkenly, "Now we'll see just how much of a bargain ah got fer mah money."

Madelaina thought quickly. She could take one of many postures. Remain passive and let it be a severe blow to his ego; fight him and chance that his sexual arousal would increase to the point he'd develop the strength of ten men; or kill him at the right moment. What to do? What to do? *Remain detached to understand life's riddles,* had been Tolomeo's teaching. And this was certainly one of life's riddles.

As it was, she didn't have to make an immediate decision. She heard snoring alongside her, and for an instant she sighed in relief. She was suddenly seized with a mad thought. Slowly, silently prodded by the devil, she slipped off the bed and padded toward the forbidden wardrobe. She selected a very sheer pale blue peignoir, slipped into it, and caught her hair high atop her head, speared through with a few hairpins. She paused long enough to loop the seven moon earrings through the holes in her pierced ears. Returning to the bed, she slipped in alongside him. Her movement caused him to stir and awaken. Through his drunken stupor, his bleary eyes stared at her unblinking for a moment and he began stroking her. Drunk and irrational, only God knew what he saw through his disbelieving eyes. It appeared to Madelaina that he was going through the erotic motions with another woman—not her. Someone he saw in the drunken haze of his mind—someone she didn't know and never would.

"Mah God, honey, how ah've missed ya," he repeated tenderly. "Jenny, mah love, how many times ah've come near ta killin' mahself since ya left me.

Theah's nevuh been anyone foah me, sweet baby, 'ceptin' foah youah. Now, aftuh so many years, y'all came back ta me, jus' like ah knew ya would, Jenny baby."

The sound of his melancholy touched Madelaina and she stirred, ready to announce she wasn't the woman he thought she was. It had been a dreadful thing for her to do—dress and pretend to be another. How could she apologize enough? It was an insane, unthinking, and blundering act on her part.

Her movements, as she strained against him, increased his desire for her, and Madelaina found herself raising her body to meet his in an effort to make amends. His voice grew as urgent as his powerful body thrusts and he cooed lovingly to her, whispering sweet nothings. Madelaina's juices, having been worked up for the first time in weeks, seemed propelled by Satan as she responded to him. She had hypnotized herself in these moments into thinking it was Peter.

For several moments, Benson stared at the glittering golden moons on her ears and said nothing. They served only it increase his ardor and make him moan with more anguish.

William Benson, more aroused with each passing moment, was both pleased and excited by her sultry and provocative responses. God, he thought, what passion she displayed. "Jenny, youah drivin' me ta the brink of madness! It was nevuh like this, ya gotta admit. Lord knows how many times ah wanted it ta be such sweet heaven. Why couldn't we have recaptured ouah love like this—why?"

The desire he felt for this woman, whom in his drunken delirium he mistook for his former wife, overrode his sanity. Even as he tried to be gentle, to caress her and give her time to be aroused, he couldn't hide his excitement. Jennifer had come back—returned to him from the grave—and he wasn't going to lose her again. He persisted against her protests, as one in fever and out of control, until he climaxed with a thunderous roar of animal grunts, moans, and primitive screams.

Wafting in and out of her own self-imposed purgatory, Madelaina awakened to the reality of the moment and panicked. She began to beat her fists against him. "Stop! Stop!" she screamed. "I'm not who you think I am! You don't know what you're doing!" She tugged at the hairpins to loosen her hair. She struggled under his weight to remove the pale blue sheer peignoir but was pinned down too tightly. She clawed at the fabric, tearing at it, trying desperately to remove it.

But William Benson wasn't attuned to her misery. He'd suddenly drifted into another world, another dimension of ugliness and bad memories.

He swore at her, cursed her in both English and Spanish, tossing in a few French words that brought a blush to Madelaina's cheeks. Then he held her by her long hair, pulled back savagely on it, thrusting back her head at an angle that nearly cut off her breath. He kissed her so violently, pressing his hard lips against hers until his teeth cut fiercely into her lips. She could no longer scream. She could no longer fight him off. She could hardly breathe. Unable to catch her breath, she moved in a sudden struggle for survival, and concentrating all her strength into a final effort, jackknifed with her knees in a jerking movement so unexpected it threw him off guard. He rolled uncontrollably, nearly falling off the bed.

The movement jarred his befuddled brain and brought him back to reality. He scratched his head and gazed around through bleary eyes, trying to orient himself as he pulled himself up, staggering to his feet. Meanwhile Madelaina hastily shed the sheer peignoir and pulled the sheets up around her. Benson appeared to have no recollection that he'd already taken his pleasure. Swaying drunkenly, he clung to the bedpost for support as he focused bleary eyes on her.

"Why are ya bent on bedeviling me, woman?" He reached over and grabbed her wrist and twisting it forced her to bend toward him. "Damn ya! You're the coolest animal ah've evuh seen." He pushed her back against the bed and fell on top of her, his hands touching her breasts as if he was wrestling a steer.

The blood rushed to Madelaina's head, causing dizziness to blur her eyes. She felt helplessly enmeshed in a situation too grotesque to contemplate and prayed to heaven in those moments she didn't conceive a child of her husband's father. Oh, God, that would be the most despicable thing that could happen to her.

"Damn ya, woman! Makin' love ta ya is like trying ta fuck a stone statue!" he fairly screamed at her in his rage. "Now show some life or ah'll make ya live ta regret tryin' ta make a fool of William Benson!"

"No," she replied flatly with more courage than she ever realized she had. "I don't want a son like Lazaro!"

For an instant, Madelaina was certain he would kill her. He stiffened like a crouched animal ready to lunge at an enemy. Her words sliced through his alcoholic stupor like a clean swipe of a two-edged knife, and when they replayed in his mind, he pushed away from her, his face hard as granite, his eyes like pulsating branding irons. He viewed her with dark suspicious eyes.

"What's that ya said? Speak up, whore, or ah'll tan yer hide!"

"Like you tanned Peter's hide as a child? You heard me, I said Peter. I can't show you the exciting response you desire because I am Peter's wife. Yes, that's right. Peter's wife. The wife of your first-born son. As for your second son, Lazaro, I'm the woman whose life was saved by the son you rejected long ago."

Benson jumped off the bed as if he'd been struck by a bolt of lightning. He stared at her as if she was some malevolent apparition, intimidated by what he saw and heard. "Who in damnation are ya? Who told ya such a pack of lies? Ya better come straight with me, whore, or y'all live ta wish ya were nevuh born, ta wish youah'd never talked such filth ta me! *Pilar! It was Pilar who told ya!*"

In those next few moments, Madelaina saw what it was that Benson's enemies feared. Never, not if she lived for all eternity, would she forget the violent and burning hatred in those black agate eyes that only moments earlier had appeared a bloodshot, bleary blue haze of staggering uncertainty. His face, filled with loathing, had swollen like a bull frog's. In his blind fury, Benson turned from her, staggered toward a chest, and removed a bull whip. He cracked it overhead several times, menace scrawled on his face.

"Tell me ya lied! Tell me or ah'll skin yer lying body alive!" Benson paused a moment. The golden earrings, catching a prism of light, shone brightly. "Where'd ja get them earrings?" he bellowed. "So now yer a thief as well?" He cracked the whip threateningly close.

"I'm no thief. My husband, Peter Duprez Benson, gave them to me. I am the wife of Peter Benson. It's no lie. Go ahead and skin me alive—kill me—do what you will. Nothing matters to me anymore." Her control disconcerted him.

"Do what you will with my body, but you'll never possess my mind. Not Huerta, Salomon, not even my father could bend me to their will. I belong only to your son, Peter," she said defiantly. "You'll never tame this monkey!"

Benson raised the whip overhead and sent it whistling toward her. It cracked across her breasts, splitting the skin open over both mounds. An angry, searing trail of blood seeped through the aperture. Again he struck her, and again, waiting for her to beg for mercy.

Madelaina bit back the screams strangling her throat.

"Lying bitch!" he screamed incoherently. "Why are ya doin' this ta me? After all ah did fer ya—saving youah lying hide from the *Federales*—this is the thanks ah get?" He raised the bull whip overhead, gathering strength for another singing strike to lash out at her in his blind and furious rage. But William Benson never made it. There came a loud swishing sound as something streaked across the room. A Bolo knife was sunk into Benson's shoulder. He staggered back, dizzy, his equilibrium shattered, and fell against an upholstered chair, knocking it backward. Benson fell into a loose heap and blacked out.

Madelaina saw a blur of faces. Wrapped in a coverlet taken from the bed, she was slung across the brawny shoulders of a man she recognized. Captain Tracy Richards cooed to her. "Don't fret, Little Fox, you're in safe company now." He swiftly transported her out the door and down the steps into the foyer. Madelaina remained as still as possible, wincing at the open rivers of blood flowing from her breasts. Each movement was like a step in hell, but still she wouldn't scream.

Outside, drunken ranch hands, taken by surprise, had been herded against the tack room wall by Pancho Villa's handful of men. How they'd gotten past Benson's sober, well-trained guards stationed at the entrance to Seven Moons was one of those marvelous *guerrillo* tactics which had helped carved Villa's phenomenal reputation. Not a single shot had been fired!

Antonetta, dressed as a *campesina*, sprang from her saddle to receive Madelaina into her arms. "Come, *querida*, you must dress. There's no time to waste. Thanks to God Pancho knew where to find you." She glanced horrified at the rivers of blood oozing from Madelaina's breasts. "*Dios mios!* Put on these things, *pronto!*" She handed the girl a peasant skirt and blouse of coarse cotton.

"*Momentito*," whispered Madelaina as soon as she donned the clothing. "Give me your gun, Tonetta, and make sure it's loaded." Her glazed eyes burned like ebony. She was growing weaker from the loss of blood.

"Don't do nothing foolish, woman," cautioned Antonetta. "Ees best we go and *pronto* like I said." She glanced at Tracy Richards, reluctant to give the gun to her friend. "Ju got some bad injury, *chica*. Let's go. Forget what happened."

The daughter of General Obregon turned from her and grabbed the rifle from Capitán Richard's saddle holster. She addressed the gringo freedom fighter.

"Is it loaded, *Capitán*?" she asked without regard to her blood-soaked blouse.

"It's loaded."

"*Bueno.*" Gun in hand, Madelaina ran toward the small, shabby shacks opposite the tack room which housed the Mexican colony working for William Benson. She ran the length of the shacks and stopped only when she saw a door ajar. Cautiously, she crept forward and kicked the door in loudly, shaking the structure on its flimsy foundation. Sprawled on top of the young girl Lupe, brutally ravaging the protesting child, was one of Benson's burly men. Lupe's obvious struggle against the drunken cowboy had earned for her bloody bruises and abrasions.

"Get up, pig!" shouted the arrogant daughter of a *gachupín*. "Up on your feet, beast!"

The drunken, boisterous, abrasive cowhand, reeling and stumbling in a stupor, managed to raise up on one knee to protest the intrusion. Before he actually saw the figure of a woman with a shotgun aimed at him, before he could plead for mercy, Madelaina squeezed off two shots with the Springfield and watched the rolling eyeballs of the drunken cowhand bulge in pain and shock before he fell back against the wall. Lupe, a dark-eyed waif of a girl, no more than fourteen, sprang to her feet and hugged Madelaina. "Save me, *señora*. Save me from thees pig!"

Captain Richards, who'd followed Madelaina at Tonetta's insistence, released the rifle from her frozen grip. "*Ondolay, chiquita.* Pancho can't tarry much longer, ya heah?" His Texas drawl seemed thicker than ever.

"Reload the rifle, gringo," ordered Madelaina brittlely. "There is one more job to do."

"Youah shuah it's important, Little Fox? We'd best get moving."

"It's important, gringo."

"Then maybe ya bettuh take this heah new gun ah jus' got inta my hands, *chiquita*. It's called the .45 caliber *Obregon* pistol."

711

Madelaina turned her head sharply and pushed Lupe gently from her as her eyes searched Tracy Richard's eyes. Her glance came to rest on the pistol in his hand extended to her butt first. She gazed at the weapon wondrously.

The perspiration rolled off her face and her hair clung to her head in long snakelike ribbons. "*Es veridad?* It's the truth? It's named after my father?"

"The truth. Seven shots in the magazine. Go ta it and move like hell. We've gotta make it the hell outa Texas, heah me, *chiquita?*"

But Madelaina had already left the shack and made her way toward the next one, where she'd seen Alicia retire after her day's chores. Cautiously, she moved on the balls of her sandaled feet, grimacing at the pain across her breasts. Her blouse was soaked with blood and the moisture seeping through was weakening her. One moment more, she prayed, and it will be over. Perhaps then, the gringos won't "Remember The Alamo" with such bloodthirsty vengeance.

She found Alicia in a worse condition than she'd found Lupe. Alicia was unconscious, unaware that she was being ravaged and raped by a man too delirious in alcoholic stupor to realize she couldn't cooperate.

"Waco!" she called to Benson's foreman, astounded that a man of his calibre would stoop to rape a mere child of twelve. "Waco!"

The older man half-turned his grizzled face in the dim lantern glow of the shabby hovel and peered blindly at the figure standing in the doorway.

"It's Mrs. Benson, Waco." She hesitated at the sound of the name, then quickly continued. "I understand you wish to continue in the tradition of your people and do what should be done to the filthy greasers that did your ancestors in. Well, c'mon, Waco. I decided it should be you who takes the *patrón's* wife."

She could almost see the diabolical look of glee and disbelief, intermingled with desire and lust, register in his bleary, bloodshot eyes as he struggled to his feet,

712

not bothering to pull up his trousers. The sight and smell of him nearly knocked her over. But she held her own, seducing him with a come-on look in her eyes.

For an instant, a flicker of hesitation in Waco's eyes alerted her that he might not agree to her proposition, but when his face contorted into an almost sheepish grin, she relaxed.

"Ya mean it, Mrs. Benson?" Again he hesitated, unsure of himself. "Does the boss know whatcher up ta?" He drew nearer to her shadowy form, still unable to focus clearly and never once seeing the Obregon automatic in her hand.

"Come, Waco, get it over with. My husband knows everything."

"Yahooo!" he shouted. *"Yippeeee!"* He fairly lunged at her, only to be stopped by seven consecutive bullets shot into his belly. His body bounced back from the impact of the bullets. "Ahhhhieeeeee," he shouted, clutching at his belly which was ripped apart from the missiles. He fell to the floor, writhing and twisting like a yelping dog until he was dead.

In a corner of the room, tied hand and foot to a standing floor pillar, Pilar watched through horror-struck eyes as Madelaina moved in to cut her bindings. "Listen, *chica*," she told the old woman. "Go inside and tend to *señor el patrón*. When he heals, you tell him the *mujer* of his son Peter Duprez Benson has done this to Waco and to the other man who dishonored Lupe."

Pilar's black eyes bugged from under her thick brows. "The *mujer* of Pedro Duprez, *los jovenes*?" She crossed herself, fell to her knees, and kissed Madelaina's hands. "He's alive? My *niño* ees alive?" she asked wondrously.

"Tell *señor el patrón*, only I am responsible for this. If any of my people are punished, tell him I will return to give him another taste of my vengeance."

She turned to Captain Tracy Richards, who stared spellbound at this supercharged *soldadera* before him. *"Vamenos, amigo.* Pancho Villa awaits us."

713

They exited the shack as the astounded Pilar mouthed the words—*Pancho Villa.* "*Pancho Villa? Dios mios!*" She ran from the shack to spread the news to the other Mexicans, so they might catch a glimpse of the legendary Pancho Villa.

Villa and his handful of men awaited the arrival of Madelaina and Captain Richards. She and Tracy mounted the saddled and waiting horses and joined the circle behind Villa, while he attempted to soothe the ruffled feathers of the slowly sobering Benson cowhands who seemed more baffled than frightened by this unusual-looking Mexican holding them at bay with his words.

He had introduced himself to them in his pigeon yankee, but it was plain to see not one man believed that the kindly, patronizing man with a benevolent smile was indeed the fierce and murderous *guerrillo*, Pancho Villa.

Apologetically, Villa relieved them of their weapons, and marched them into the tack room. Before bolting the doors, he asked them with servility not to make any attempts to follow them for at least an hour. "Unless, my gringo friends," he added, "ju do not care what happens to ju."

Villa mounted his horse and reared it on its heels. He waved his sombrero overhead and called to his miniscule army. "*Vamenos, muchachos!* We go to conquer!"

Book Seven

Viva La Revolucion:

Chapter 26

The entourage of six men, two women, eight horses, and eight guns followed him into the night. They rode with the wind at their heels, through back roads, stopping only to water their horses and freshen themselves at friendly bases established by Villa sympathizers.

Madelaina had time to think of the many ways Villa might have tracked her to the Seven Moons Ranch of William Benson. Most distressing of all was the possibility that Major Salomon himself had leaked the information to Villa's aides. It was the only way, he might have decided, Madelaina would return to Mexico and fall prey to his trap. It was the first thought she had in the matter and the one which persisted above all others. Even as she belabored this idea, she began to develop more insight in her involvement. She viewed the ways and means of resolving her future with more maturity. At the time, however, she had no realization that the words of Tolomeo had begun to work their way into her consciousness and that soon she'd be a changed woman in more ways than she could estimate. Having begun, the metamorphosis wouldn't stop.

By the time Villa and his followers crossed the Rio Grande and made camp along one of its tributaries, the River Conchos, Villa had gathered his trusted lieutenants to reconnoiter. Urbina, Soto, and Captain Richards relaxed after the long hard ride and sat by the fire with their *jefe*, drinking coffee laced with tequila and talking of future plans and strategy.

Nearby, as always, seated before another glowing campfire, Madelaina and Antonetta warmed themselves after taking a bath in the waters of the Conchos. Both women had changed into fresh clothing and dried their long hair with cotton toweling. Both had become true *soldaderas* in the past several days, and it would soon fall upon Madelaina to teach the *campesinas* how to shoot and care for their weapons.

The *jefe* had told them in no uncertain terms that the women would no longer be relegated to doing only cooking and female chores. In this all-out revolution to avenge the murders of President Madero, his key cabinet members, and all those other *Maderistas* who'd been massacred in the seige on the capital by Huerta, Pancho Villa would spare the life of no *Huertista*. That meant the entire army of *Federales*.

Madelaina poured coffee for both herself and Antonetta and handed the redhead a steaming mug. She sat down on a felled tree trunk at the edge of the river and sighed wistfully.

"Ju are thinking of jur husband, Little Fox?" asked Tonetta.

Madelaina traced figures in the sand with a stick. "Can you see so clearly into the center of my heart, redhead?"

"Ayeiii. Ees easy, *chica*. Ees written in jur face what I see."

"Why do I bother? Why can't I forget him? He made his choice. He married the governor's daughter. After all this time, I should understand he never loved me at all. I've been chasing a dream, *chica*. A dream that has no beginning and no ending. A foolishness which must cease for me."

"Listen, *chica*, listen to me," began Antonetta. "Pancho will kill me if he knew what I am about to say." She rolled her eyes skyward. "Don' ju believe what ju read in the papers. Jur husband ees doing business for Pancho. I can tell ju no more. But ees not like eet ees in paper."

If Madelaina heard her friend, she gave no sign, her attention was taken by the setting of the desert sun near the western horizon, at the sight of a fast-moving rider galloping swiftly toward the encampment. *"Jefe!"* she called to Villa, her hands cupped over her mouth.

718

Villa and his men stood up, shaded their eyes, and peered in the direction of the rider.

"*Bueno*," said Villa. "It's our man Ochoa. I've been expecting him with good news."

Before the rider pulled up on his reins, kicking up mounds of sand behind him, he'd already slid off the horse with the expertise of a man born on horseflesh. He whipped off his sombrero and dusted his leggings. With his free hand, he slicked down his sweaty hair, leaving streaks in the dust on his face. Someone handed him a bottle of tequila. He guzzled nearly half the bottle, grunted, and now able to speak through a throat rid of dust, he saluted the *jefe*.

"Well, my friend. What did you learn?" asked Villa, watching him closely.

"Carranza has denounced Huerta and the Anti-Orozco volunteers have sided with him. It's been rumored that General Alvaro Obregon has responded with his Fourth Sonora Battalion."

Madelaina gave a start. Had she heard correctly? Her father was against Huerta? For the first time in weeks, her heart burst with hope and joy. She wasn't prepared for Villa's words as he announced he'd personally go into Chihuahua City to secretly meet with Don Abraham Gonzalez, the man who had initially enlisted his aid for Madero, the man who Madero made governor of Chihuahua.

"But, that, my *jefe*, isn't possible," insisted Ochoa, one of Villa's most loyal followers, the man who had related to Villa just how Huerta had killed Madero. "Governor Gonzalez has been arrested for treason. All of Chihuahua is under the military governorship of an old enemy, a *Huertista* to the teeth, *Jefe*. General Rabago."

Villa's dark eyes burned fiercely at this news.

"Is better you wait, *Jefe*," cautioned Ochoa, growing more uncomfortable.

"What do you mean—wait?" countered Villa. "Wait? For what and how long?"

Ochoa, more subdued now, wiped the corners of his

719

mouth with his shirtsleeve. He glanced cautiously about the small circle. "Maybe is better you wait a long time," he began lowering his eyes, unable to look straight at the *jefe*.

"What are trying to tell me? It's not like you to falter—to stammer like a lovesick calf stammers to his woman." Pancho suddenly picked up on the man's thoughts. "Ah, what you're saying is I'm not wanted in the revolution—not needed? Perhaps they think Pancho Villa is finished, eh?"

"Not that, *jefe*," Ochoa said too quickly. He drew a sharp sustained look from Villa.

"Then what? You know, so tell me."

"I've heard that this Obregon is some military man. He's some strategist. He's a regular, all right, *Jefe*, but I hear he employs all the irregularities possible in his combat plans. Is true, *Jefe*, he is some military officer. Is better you know this. He studied the warring styles of the French and Germans, *Jefe*. He ees no fool. *Pues, amigo*. General Obregon is the only hope for Carranza."

Madelaina heard all this. She felt a tinge of pride, yet what was making Villa so angry? She watched him pace back and forth before his men, flailing his arms in the air. It had to be Carranza that he didn't like or trust. Another split in the revolution? What next?

She concentrated her gaze on Pancho Villa as he paced before his small consortium of loyalists. He was simply marvelous to watch, thought Madelaina. If you looked hard, you could almost see the wheels move in his mind as he gathered his thoughts and without silver-tongued oratory delivered his words with impact.

"So! You think Villa cares for the Germans or the French? This is Mexico! And Mexico is Pancho Villa. What the hell does Obregon or Carranza or any of those quarrelsome sons of whores know what is in my guts? I want to give Mexico a chance. I fought for Madero because he believed in me—me, Pancho Villa. He didn't forget about me," said Villa pointedly, looking directly at Madelaina. "He had to choose between his country and me, and I thank God he chose Mexico

because that showed me the kind of man he was."
Villa continued to rant and rave, more to himself than
to the body of men who'd gathered as he spoke, each
anxious to hear the *jefe*'s words.

"All those fake excuses for men, what do they know
of Madero's feelings for Pancho Villa? They gather
storm clouds of war with an outward show of vengeance, and they mean to exclude Pancho Villa, eh?
There's no room in Mexico for that lowly *peón* hillsman? Hah! Well, I tell you, my friends, those stinking
betrayers in the capital, those Judas goats have never
seen rivers of blood flowing, not like the ones Pancho
Villa will cause to flow to flush them and their kinds
out of our Mexico. Not if these pandering peacocks
should invent a second Trojan horse—not if they
should resurrect Napoleon to lead them, will they see
the battles Pancho Villa will inflict upon them. All the
military geniuses in the whole world—in *todo mundo*—
in a lifetime of battle have never seen the holocaust
that Pancho Villa prepares for them in his war of
revenge."

This small handful of men remained silent. In the
great silence of the desert, every man present felt the
enormous power of the puma who stood before them,
his fists upraised to the heavens and the supernatural
glow of a descending twilight at his back. Here stood a
giant of a man, powerful, determined, and possessed of
remarkable zeal and loyalty to a leader who was dead.
Fired by this fierce loyalty, spurred on by his promise
to the ghost of Madero, this Mexican, this Indian, who
had grown into a man stoked by the injustice and inequities meted his people, had transformed himself into a
tempestuous soldier, a leader of men, General
Francesco Villa.

In the awe-filled silence, Pancho Villa dropped his
arms to his side and said quietly, "Your *jefe* knows
what must be done. He is not *loco*. He is not possessed
with fever. I cry aloud, I sing, and, *amigos*, I dream
passionately of a better Mexico for all of us. I may be
a soldier without an army, but this soldier is not with-

out hope. Trust in me. I will leave you for seventy-two hours. You will meet me in San Andres." He turned to Captain Richards and Urbina. "You will be in charge until I return. Avoid any hostile encounter and let no one know of our plans. Understand?"

The gringo and the Mexican nodded solemnly. "What will you do, *Jefe?*" asked Urbina without the usual grin on his face.

"What will I do?" said Villa, staring at some inner scene in his head to which he alone was privileged to see. "What will I do? I will summon up the ghosts of our ancestors to lead us. From the mountains of Durango, the deserts of Chihuahua, from the villages of Zacatecas, and the farms of San Luis Potosi, I will sound the cry of war once again. The people will not deny me the army that is needed."

And Pancho Villa, true to his word, did just that.

In the hills of Sonora he found his sister, Concepción Montoya, and with her aid, he scattered her precious pigeons to the various sections of Mexico. In the north, east, west, and south, those people who received the white birds studied the messages intently:

Mexico needs us once again. Be ready when I come. Arm yourselves well.—Francesco Villa.

And so it was that the great whirlwind of Mexico gathered unto itself the people of the land. From the north, where poverty was extreme, the people dug up their rifles, guns, and bayonets, and saddled their horses. They collected their belongings and told their compatriots that the voice of Pancho Villa had called to them. In the south, where the drought had ruined crops and the Rurales had wrought more devastation than the fierce elements, the peasants tilling their lands laid down their plows and vowed amongst themselves to complete what had been started long ago. Pancho was coming for them. They must be ready. From the east and the west, from the deserts and mesas and arroyos, they came galloping wildly in a northwesterly direction, looking for the spirit of Pancho Villa.

Galloping wildly from the north country, heading in a southwesterly direction, a lone horseman broke cover and plunged across the shoulder-high Rio Bravo toward the Mexican shore. Once in Mexican territory, he waved across the river, holding a white silk scarf in the twilight to be seen. Four more riders joined him, and together they spurred their horses beyond the trees out into the open fields. Two men broke from the others, galloped ahead across the width of the field, and turned in opposite arcs, half-circles which brought them back to where the other horsemen waited silently, expectantly. The two riders brought their horses to a full stop, cupped their hands to their lips, and hooted softly. They stood up in their stirrups, waved their sombreros overhead, and hooted again.

Only the splashing of water against the horseflesh of hundreds and their riders could be heard as they left the protection of the Yankee shoreline to join their brave companions.

"Viva Villa!" came the cries of men and women once again imbued with the spirit of freedom—the spirit of the revolution—the spirit of Pancho Villa.

Listen, cried the people of the land. Listen to the rumble of the earth. Hear the music written in the wind. Feel and be inspired by the call to freedom. We, those pitiful people who sprang from the bowels of Mexico, we unfortunate people who mean nothing to people in high government, are the land-tilling *peóns* who mean the world to Pancho Villa. We who sit huddled on mountaintops, baking in mud huts, dying in the sweltering desert misery, and falling prostrate in the lost world of the cities, are waiting for the sounds of Pancho Villa. We are waiting for you, Panchito.

In that mysterious way Indians of the desert have of picking up vibrations without use of a wireless, the people waited and knew Pancho was on his way.

Deep in the heart of Mexico, Pancho Villa moved with the speed of a winged meteor, leaving behind him in the state of Durango, where his family were all buried beneath the earth, his childhood, his innocence, and all dreams of an immediate peace. In a ritual to his ancestors, he'd prayed for the strength and wisdom needed to help elevate his people to a better world; for the stamina and intelligence to oppose his enemy on the field of battle, and the ability to become victorious. His supplications to God were to wear the laurel wreath of victory, not the thorns of defeat, so that he could help his people and make them human beings entitled to share in the glory of all men.

And so began General Francesco Villa's personal invasion of Mexico.

The war party grew by ones and twos and fours. By morning, after he'd left Durango, over one hundred had fallen in behind him. They commandeered horses, arms, and ammunition wherever they found them. By noon of the first day, they had whistled up volunteers from every tiny settlement in their path with their cry of revolution. Their war cries penetrated remote mountain pueblos, desert outposts, thickly wooded areas of the hillsmen. Men on horseback with their *viejas* waited, ready to fly, waving their weapons overhead, shouting, *"Viva Villa! Viva La Revolucion!"* As the swelling hordes cantered by, more revolutionaries fell into line alongside them, heading northward singing the Marching Song of the Bandits, "La Cucaracha."

"La Cucaracha, La Cucaracha, ya no puedo caminar. . . ."

From the northern deserts and the southern hills came the hordes of men and women. From all parts came the waves of chanting, singing, supplicating Mexicans.

"Porque no tiene, porque la falta, marijuana che fumar. . . ."

In droves they began to arrive at the appointed rendezvous, on horses, on burros, in wagons, on bare feet, braving the hot winds of the desert, exhausted yet filled with the hope and promise of a bright new tomorrow for themselves and their children.

"Una vieja y un vietito, se cayron en un pozo. . . ."

Their hopes and dreams were bound up with Pancho

724

Villa's hopes and dreams. It had been Pancho who aided them in the past. Only he gave them money, food, and shelter when all was lost. Had the government done as much? Hah! He'd beaten off the terrifying *Rurales* and outwitted the *Federales*. Why, that grand and glorious sonofabitch had won the revolution for Madero, hadn't he? Now, Madero was dead. "*Viva Villa!* Long live Villa!"

By the time the pregnant forces reached San Andres, they had exploded into a prolific 800 able-bodied men, not including the women. Villa had returned with hordes of hillsmen, some former *Federales* who'd escaped Huerta's clutches when they defected and crossed over into Texas to avoid the *Rurales*. Others had deserted the famed crack cavalry unit of *Colorados*. Now they had united to become *Villistas* to the end.

Daily, Madelaina searched the faces of all newcomers in Villa's growing army for the face she wanted to see the most—that of Peter Duprez. She wasn't aware that she wore her feelings on her face for all the world to see or that anyone near her could read her innermost thoughts, until one day Captain Richards pulled her aside and, searching her dark troubled eyes, he said compassionately, "Don'cha worry none, Little Fox, he'll find us when the time's right."

But his words had little effect on her. Madelaina had taken to having troubled dreams again. Dreams of Peter always calling to her. She continued to see him in a pool of blood and this in itself became so alarming to her, she couldn't concentrate on her work. She could only remember the ghastly pictures she had seen before Manuelito Perez fell to his death in the Plaza de Toros. Now, she worried constantly, fearing her own sanity.

It became incumbent upon Madelaina to teach the new women recruits how to use and care for their guns, a job she welcomed gratefully. To preserve her own well-being, she threw herself completely into the job of being a *soldadera*. It was a tough job, but one which brought rewards when those she taught responded by becoming dedicated crack shots.

One night shortly after Villa returned with the beginnings of his army, Madelaina was field-stripping her Obregon pistol, which she'd grown fond of as one might a trusty friend. Seated across from her friend, Antonetta, near a campfire in the dusky twilight, Madelaina studied the former sex kitten and admitted she'd never seen her as nervous and high-strung. Of late she had smoked much marijuana. As a matter of fact, it began shortly after Pancho left them on the shores of the River Concho. Since then, the redhead had become a different person, moody, silent, aloof, and given to periods in which she refused to speak, even with Madelaina. It was so unlike Tonetta that Little Fox began to think she lived with a stranger,

Even after they had settled into a confiscated hacienda, which housed many of the warring renegades, Antonetta had remained uncommunicative. Madelaina considered that all the former sex kitten needed was a few hours with her lover. *Muy bien,* she told herself, reaching in to light a piece of twig from the fires. She lit up a reefer and sat back, deliberately concentrating on Pancho Villa, attempting to conjure up his image in the fires. Once his face was fixed in her mind, Madelaina concentrated strongly on him. She sent out mental thoughts to him, attempting to allow her thoughts to filter in and mix with his.

Listen, you fool, Panchito. Listen to me! Here sits one of the most desirable women in the world, waiting for you, and you haven't time for her. What's the matter? Are you for certain some loco *burro? If you were smart, you'd leave what you're doing and find Antonetta before she forsakes you for another of these* muy macho hombres *who throw themselves at her, just for a mere smile. Fool! One day she will not be here, then you'll regret it. Make hay, Panchito, while the sun still shines for you both!*

Antonetta's eyes wandered to Madelaina for some inexplicable reason, and she watched her in fascination

726

as she stared into the bright flames of the fire. Of late Madelaina had been strange, she told herself. She would never forget the severity of the wounds inflicted on her by the bull whip of William Benson. *Muy mal.* She had guessed that Madelaina would forever bear the scars of that terrible night. Not long ago, before they left the River Conchos, she had watched Little Fox sprinkle a fine mist of dust from that leather pouch she wore around her neck. *Dios mios*, when on the next morning those scars had nearly disappeared, Tonetta had been unable to believe what her eyes told her. She had questioned Madelaina about her miraculous curative powers. "Have you turned into a *curandera*, my pet? Tell me. Tell me quickly how you do such things?"

Madelaina had admonished her to please say nothing to anyone of the miracle she had seen. "I myself don't understand it, therefore, I'd be unable to explain it to another," she had told Antonetta.

Since that time, Antonetta was bitten with curiosity, and she stared at the leather pouch each time she caught sight of it, mesmerized by the thought of its contents. As she watched Madelaina in fascination, wondering at her thoughts, some ten minutes had elapsed. Tonetta felt a gentle squeeze on her shoulder. She glanced up into the twinkling, mischievous eyes of Pancho Villa.

"Come, woman," he told her in a warm, seductive voice. "It's been too long since we've been together. Something told me, as I sat down going over reports and listening to my men, that I was wasting too much time for nothing, that I'd best get to you before some other *hombre* claims you and that would be a pity, because Pancho would have to teach him a lesson, eh, *gattita*?"

Antonetta, trying with difficulty to still her heartbeats, pretended to be coy and indifferent. She shrugged. "Who is this stranger speaking to me?" After first glancing at him, she turned her head with a soft toss of her fiery red hair. "This voice sounds familiar, but the face—that face is the face of a stranger. Go away, man. I have no use for strangers."

Watching the scene from her position at the fire, Madelaina sighed. No one could have been more astonished than she when Pancho Villa showed up in reply to her mental summons. She hadn't even thought such a thing would work. Coincidence, she told herself. Merely coincidence! Why, if I had such powers, I'd summon Peter to my side! Instead of dealing with her own thoughts, she was furious with Antonetta's obvious game playing. That fool! Why doesn't she accept Pancho instantly? It's he she's been mooning over long enough!

Exasperated with the whole thing, Madelaina arose and shuffled down the dirt path toward the coral. What she would give for Don Quixote! Peter had told her he'd left the black stallion at his ranch near San Antonio, to be used as stud for the mares. Madelaina slipped a saddle on one of the horses, strapping it securely and mounted it. Just as she was leaving the corral, she saw Pancho and Antonetta, arm in arm, disappear into the hacienda. *Bueno*, she thought, as she signaled the sentries before she galloped out onto the desert.

"*Cuidado,* Little Fox," called one of the men. "Be careful. Enemy spies have been spotted not far away."

"*Gracias, muchacho.* I am well armed. I am not afraid. But, to keep your feelings easy, I promise not to go far. I need fresh air and time to think."

She waved to him and spurred her stallion into the dark of night. Behind her, she left lit camp fires and erotic, animal sounds that carried into the night as men and women found each other as lovers.

She rode swiftly in the balmy night air, trying to think of nothing in particular. A short distance from camp, she climbed a slight rise in the terrain and dismounted. Seated on a dark boulder, she could see the camp in the distance. Her thoughts concentrated on the military problems that might beset Pancho Villa in this attempt to implement a revolution that would count for

728

Mexico. How would he do it? Without money or weapons, the chances were slim. For several mad moments, she considered what she'd heard about her father's apparent opposition to Vitoriano Huerta. Was it possible, really possible that she might be able to help unite her father, General Obregon, with General Villa for the glory of Mexico?

It was a mad, totally insane thought. Wasn't it? Could her father ever come to terms with himself concerning a revolution? Such a union wouldn't be as farfetched as it might have been when she first moved to El Paso. Daily changes brought about strange bed partners in politics, she'd been told. Madelaina had lived enough to know you could never outguess fate. Just when you're certain of a particular destiny, the old sorceress conjurs up another bend in the road and heads you in a totally unexpected direction.

Well, it was something to think about. Something she'd have to take considerable pains to work out in her mind before daring to broach the subject to General Villa. One never tells the singer to sing. It must be his own inspiration. Perhaps a little prodding? What would it hurt?

Chapter 27

The flamboyantly beautiful Antonetta had coupled with her lover and both had felt the familiar quickening of blood in their veins. He explained to Antonetta that he was growing less indolent than he'd been in El Paso, that in the past week, he'd grown to enjoy the weight of his guns over each hip and the clanking sound of his spurs as he walked. "Tonight, *chiquita,* I will be united again with Seven Leagues, my stallion," he said happily.

"And?" asked Antonetta quietly.

"And, little *gatitta,* you know who else."

"I thought so, *Jefe,*" replied Tonetta, moving away from Pancho on the four-poster bed that had belonged to some wealthy *hacendado* before Villa appropriated it for his cause. Pancho glanced at her with dismay.

"*Gatitta,* you and me, we've known each other a long time. *Pues,* I hate to think how long," said Pancho huskily.

"*Es veridad,* it's true," she said testily.

"In that time, between us has been honesty."

"*Es veridad.* That's also true."

"You have always known about *mi mujer,* Lucita."

"*Si. Es muy veridad.* That is very much the truth."

"Then why do you fret? Why do you look so sad? You know I will see her tonight." He reached for her, put a strong, well-tanned arm about her, and drew her to him. They had known each other a long time, had been most intimate, and Tonetta, never one to be shy, let her hands wander all over Pancho's naked body. His body provided an immediate reaction to her erotic touch, a response that gave Antonetta a secure feeling,

730

one that in the past filled her with the knowledge that she hadn't lost her touch.

But Pancho felt a tinge of annoyance. He was a man. It was up to him who he desired to see, and tonight his strength must be saved for Lucita—his wife, his only real wife whom he loved and missed with a passion. He couldn't just up and quarrel with Antonetta as many men in his predicament often did when they needed an excuse to go whoring. So many men would deliberately pick a fight with their spouse or lovers, so they could justify a night away from the marital bed. But this was not the way of Pancho Villa, a red-blooded man who was also an honorable man. No. He would speak the truth with this woman, this green-eyed wench who'd stood beside him through thick and thin.

Antonetta was doing things to him that prevented his concentrating on the duty which faced him that evening. What a seductress she was, his little sex kitten. Even when he wasn't conscious of what she was doing, Villa had fallen into carnal traps time and again. She was always teasing him, tempting him, and growing sullen if in their little games he pretended to be indifferent to her. She was insatiable, this little tigress, and she made him feel the same. There are two of me to satisfy, he had told her so many times and she seemed to understand. One is Pancho Villa the desperate renegade, the *guerrillo* who lives by his wits and must of necessity take what he can in his travels from any lovely *señorita* willing to please him. And then there is Doroteo Arango, the man, the husband, father, and hillsman, who wants nothing more than to till the land and be a loving father, husband, and provider for his family.

Antonetta always assured him she understood. She was the fortunate one. It was she, Pancho made love to more often than his wife. Why should she deny Lucita a few nights a year when Antonetta had him the other three hundred and sixty nights? They had both discussed this, hadn't they?

His thoughts interrupted, Pancho Villa could

731

concentrate no longer. Antonetta had flown him to the moon with her and after a while they were both physically spent.

The room was silent. Only their breathing was apparent. Outside, the camp fires were cooking up dinners for the followers of Villa. He glanced at his wristwatch. He should have left for his house before this. He sat in bed and gazed at the stirring Antonetta, who opened her eyes.

"*Querido*, where are you going?" she asked.

"I told you where. Weren't you listening?"

"I was listening. I thought I had made you forget."

"So that's what I owe that trip to the moon, eh?"

"That and the expertise of Antonetta."

Villa laughed. He glanced at her. "Don't feel badly. Try not to think of me while I'm gone. It will abuse your soul and Pancho doesn't wish for the soul of Antonetta to be abused. It is too beautiful."

Antonetta, feeling terribly vulnerable, reached over and hugged Pancho's waist. "Oh, *querido*, your words are like the kisses of the stars at the deepest hour of midnight." Her long red hair fanned out like ribbons of fire across his naked thighs, and he looked down on her, gently caressing its silkiness.

"If you don't let Pancho get up, you know what will happen," he said huskily as his reaction to her touch and nearness became apparent.

Antonetta giggled with childish delight, and she stroked his manhood with expert manipulations. She was a real woman, this Antonetta. The kind of a woman a part of him needed desperately. Yet, there was Lucita. She would need satisfaction on this night, and if he permitted this green-eyed vixen to have her way, there'd be nothing left for his wife.

"Never did Pancho Villa ever think he'd have the strength to push you away, *querida*," he said firmly, removing her hands. "Now see what you've done. How will I prevent him from intruding upon my presence until I get home to my house?"

Giggling with pleasure, she forced a pout. "See if I

732

care. When you are making love to Lucita, I shall ser~
my little *diableros* to haunt you. You'll see. Just w
you are ready to climax, Panchito, it will be Antonetta's face you'll see, Antonetta's perfume you'll smell,
Antonetta's body you'll feel!"

"Listen, you insatiable cat. Stop it!" he said
abruptly. "Do not even say such a thing in jest." He
twisted her red, silky hair in his fingers and pulled her
head back. "I do not need such complications to confuse me."

Antonetta playfully shoved her tongue out at him.

"And stop that, too." Pancho let her go, and she
rubbed her head and laughed at him as she watched
him step into his leggings and shirt. Dressed, he
strapped on his double, low-slung gun holsters,
checked the barrels of the guns, and holstered them
easily. Next came the double *bandoleras,* ammunition
crisscrossed over his formidable chest. She felt sudden
pangs of dismay.

"I shall always remember you best as you were in El
Paso, dressed in your dinner tuxedo, *Jefe,*" she sighed
in reflection. "When we were both safe from the uncertain horrors of war. You've changed considerably,
querido," she said softly.

A sharp knock on the door brought a quick response
from Villa. He moved over to the side of the bed and
planted a lusty kiss on Antonetta's lips.

"Vaya con Dios, querido," she whispered. "Return
soon to me."

Villa stood over her for an instant. He placed his
sombrero on his head and shoved it back. He slipped a
bullet from his ammo belt and handed it to her. "If
Panchito is so foolish to ever lose you—for whatever
the reason—you have my permission to use this silver
bullet to kill him."

Antonetta's face paled in the darkness. She was
about to protest, but Villa had already left her to the
memories of their togetherness.

Villa's night with Lucita, the wife he also loved pas-

733

sionately, was forced to an abrupt, unexpected halt. Fortunately, he'd finished coupling with her when the information reached him, vital news necessitating his immediate departure.

Madelaina Obregon, while out riding, had encountered an old friend of Villa's, a compatriot who recognized her from Parral. While riding back to camp, the former member of Urbina's brigade imparted information which caused Madelaina's brain to roil with interest. Another old compatriot of Villa's from his spectacular Juarez victory now *commanded* the garrison at Santa Isabella!

Madelaina immediately saw a chance for Pancho Villa to gain a real army as he'd done in Parral. She escorted the old artillery specialist to camp, then broke out in a wild gallop to find Villa in San Andres, but only after she gathered to her side as escorts Captain Tracy Richards and Tomàs Urbina.

Urbina, reluctant to disturb the loving couple, rejoiced when he learned that Pancho had at least enjoyed the first act with Lucita. He hurriedly requested Villa's presence at Madelaina's side.

Before the sun crept up over the eastern horizon, Pancho Villa found himself in possession of a Federal garrison, seven dozen expertly trained soldiers, machine guns, and desperately needed medical and military supplies. The conquest, thanks to Madelaina's fast thinking, was as important as finding his old friend Fidel Avila.

While Captain Richards and Little Fox inspected the garrison, the two old friends exchanged back-slapping hugs and disappeared into a private room. Madelaina and the gringo walked along the ramparts, watching the sun rise over the broiling garrison. "You think you could train Pancho's men to fight like the regulars, *Capitán*?" asked Madelaina.

Tracy Richards glanced at her in a half-amused manner, tilting his head tolerantly. "You *gachupíns* always ask the impossible, don'cha? And damned if'n

734

y'all don't get yer way. All's ah can say is ya woulda made a handsome general at warfare yerself."

Madelaina returned his smile in that same half-amused manner.

"*Vamenos, muchaco.* Let's find Villa and tell him our idea."

"*Your* idea, Little Fox," he corrected her. "An' ah've gotta admit it's a brilliant one. As a matter of fact, while ah've the opportunity, ah've gotta tell ya how much ah've admired ya since ouah acquaintance."

"*Gracias,* gringo. Tell me, where is your woman, Rosalia Quintera?"

Tracy held up a restraining hand. "All right. All right. Ya done went and emasculated me. Ah meant nothin' fresh. Pete's too good a friend, heah? And foah you information, Rosalia will be joining us pretty soon."

"Good," she said. Suddenly Madelaina felt dizzy. She weaved on her feet and held on to the concrete abutment on the walkway.

"What's wrong? What can ah do fer ya? Ya just turned the color of ash." Tracy was solicitous of her. He held on to her in a more than friendly way.

Madelaina felt waves of nausea engulf her. Her stomach felt queasy and she felt like heaving. She hadn't had breakfast yet. Perhaps that was it, she told herself.

"I'll be all right, *Capitán.* Just dizzy. Perhaps a cup of coffee might help." She sniffed the air. Below them in the courtyard, *Federales* were taking breakfast. In her state, she failed to notice the soft look in Tracy's eyes.

"Y'all wait here, *chiquita.* Ah'll go getcha something. Ah suppose ya ain't eaten since sundown." He moved away swiftly, scaling the wooden steps alongside the garrison to the courtyard, glancing back at her with concern from time to time.

Madelaina, unable to stop the rolling heaves, felt miserable. Had she caught a germ or an infection from

735

the others in camp? She was sure she had long since become immune to all camp ailments.

Tracy returned with the coffee and a few tacos. "Chew this first, *chiquita*, then the coffee," he instructed her tenderly.

"No, coffee first," she insisted.

"Ah'm suggesting it the othuh way around," he said ominously.

But Madelaina stubbornly persisted in taking the coffee first. Instantly she regretted her choice. No sooner had the steaming fluid settled in her stomach, than it came up.

"Chew the taco, *chiquita*," insisted the freedom fighter with a light trace of a smile on his face.

Madelaina hastily did his bidding and found, much to her amazement, that she was able to keep it down. She glanced at him in amazement. "But how do you know such a thing, gringo? And why do you smile at me in so smug a manner?"

"Well, ah reckon a smart little fox like y'all can figger it out." He tipped his sombrero to her. "If ya feel better, we'd best get along to see what Pancho's up to." He paused. "Ya can count on me anytime for anything, heah?"

"No!" she said in dismay as it came together in her mind. "It can't be! Not now. Not here. Not at such a time." She put down the coffee and taco and turned from him, gazing out at the blinding light of the sun, already causing radiations of heat to rise from the desert. *Dios mios!* Was it possible she was with child? It was too soon for the seed of William Benson to be germinating in her belly. It has to be Peter's child. It has to be! And he's married to another. She refused to believe it. Even if she did, she wasn't about to let the gringo know. She tried to find possible excuses. "It's the water I drank near the River Conchos. I've felt terrible for several days."

"Whatever ya say, Little Fox," he replied, quietly, noting her consternation.

They found Villa and Avila in the office, comparing

736

notes. In moments she was to learn that her mind and Villas' ran together like twin rivers.

"So, *muchacho*," continued Villa gleefully, "Huerta made you a colonel?"

"What can I say, Panchito? Madero was very generous to me and Huerta has yet to see the color of my loyalties."

"And you learned all this military stuff—marching, saluting, firing cannon?"

"It was either that or till the soil."

"*Muy bien.* Shall I tell you what your part will be in the revolution?"

"I am listening, *Jefe.*"

"*Bueno.* We exchange men, you and me. You teach my men how to be soldiers. March them. Drill them. Make them use bayonets. You'll start a military school for Pancho Villa's soldiers, understand? My friend, when Pancho finishes whistling up his countrymen, they will flock like bees to the honey pot. And they must learn what our enemies already know."

"*Bueno, Jefe,*" exclaimed Madelaina in full accord with his plan.

"Now yer talking, *Jefe,*" marveled Captain Richards over the obvious change in Pancho Villa's mental outlook. "Ya ain't the same man who took Juarez for Madero, *Jefe;* y'all are something else, all together." His eyes lit up in wonderment.

Even Avila couldn't contain his astonishment: "Is this to be believed, *amigo?* Pancho Villa, the *guerrillo,* turning coat into a regular? *Que va?*"

"You think I didn't learn something in the *calabozo?* You think Pancho doesn't profit from his errors? I learned I had to know more about this military business. I give him little credit, but Huerta taught me plenty. He was a fool. A stubborn, ambitious fool who kneels before the altar of whiskey. But that man wore some magic dark glasses through which he performed some miracles. It's true he runs his army with the power of ten generals. Now, then, *amigo.*" he addressed himself to Avila. "I've taught my men to be the best goddamned *guerrillos* in the world. You take over, finish the job, and we'll have an invincible army, one that will wipe the smile from that sleek, well-fed cat, General Rabago in Chihuahua. We'll reinstate Governor Gonzalez—"

Avila interrupted. "Panchito! Is it possible you don't know—?"

"Know what?" asked the *jefe*. "From the tone of Avila's voice he knew the answer.

"Your old friend, Don Abraham Gonzalez has been murdered."

Every nerve and muscle in Villa's body locked. His eyes narrowed. "Huerta?"

"Who else?"

Villa's black, red-veined eyes burned with vengeance. He glanced briefly at Madelaina and the gringo freedom fighter, then averted his fiery eyes. He rose to his feet, shrugged his holsters into place, then braced himself.

"*Muy bien, chico.* Where is your telegraph? Villa has something to say to an old *compadre*."

Moments later, Villa sent the following wire to the military governor of Chihuahua City:

Señor General Rabago: The government you represent has sought my extradition from America. Bueno. To save us both time and trouble, I am already here in Mexico. With my army, I will combat the oppression of that traitorous jackal Huerta. Whenever you are ready—General Francesco Villa.

While the storm clouds of war gathered might, Madelaina grew more accustomed to the physical changes taking place in her body. Once the morning sickness passed, she tended her duties with her usual vigor. She walked tall and proud, her straight back outlined firmly under her clean blue cotton *rebozo*. Instinctive serenity had softened her dark, well-hardened eyes. Her gait had the natural guarded ease of a primitive woman carrying an unborn child. The shape of her body changed, filling her breasts to more than ample fullness, but the rest wasn't extensively distorted. In the sixth month now, she only looked pleasingly rounded.

She had taken to walking rather than riding horses, for fear she might abort the fetus. She'd had one close call in her fourth month and nearly lost the child. But for the help of Antonetta and some of the other women, she might have miscarried. And Madelaina was determined to have this child of her husband's. She wasn't far from the encampment, and approaching a small village of San Martine—near the Rio Grande, she paused under a clump of pepper trees, along a wall of organ cactus. Glancing around, she saw a bridge of loose stones at the edge of town where a hut, bearing the sign *farmacia* crudely scrawled on it, stood in near shambles.

She had come to buy a few simple herbal teas for the headaches and stomach cramps she had experienced of late. She paused at the bridge to dab her feet into the cool water. Her eyes, resting from the hot sun, fixed on the far-off mountain, a smoky blue under a hanging drift of clouds. This was the first time she'd come this far without an escort. True, she had her gun slung behind her and her Obregon automatic in its holster at her waist. But entering this serene little village of people who might have never seen a *soldadera,* she wanted to do nothing to frighten them. Besides, she was hungry, and although she believed none of the superstitions concerning pregnancy, too many of the women had whispered to her the terrors of marking her baby if she didn't gratify even the smallest in food desires.

She peered beyond the thick hedge of cactus which sheered up nakedly like knife blades set about a protected clearing. She reached for her knife and hacked away at a prickly pear cactus. She managed to cut off four, which she quickly plunged into the cool water and dammed by stones to cool off. By the time she headed back to Villa's camp, they would be cool and tasty enough to eat.

Just as Madelaina began to think it was unusually

quiet, she was alerted to the fact she wasn't alone. She felt certain she heard noises. She stopped short, moved off the main pathway, her hand swiftly unholstering her automatic. Shifting the burden of her weight slightly, she bent forward, shading her eyes to see more clearly through the hedge.

Antonetta, red hair shining like fiery embers in the sun, ran between jasmine bushes, lifting her knees in swift leaps, glancing over her shoulder, laughing in a quivering, excited way. Madelaina, about to call to her, realized she must be with someone. Probably Pancho. She had no desire to interrupt them. About to turn away and proceed on her own mission, she saw Rudolfo Fierro, running after Tonetta, nearly catching her. He also laughed in that strange breathless way. His white teeth set, both rows gleaming under his drooping moustache. She'd never seen Fierro smile, like a man blushing with love, and it startled her for a moment, taking her by surprise. Once she gained her composure, she saw Fierro catch up to Tonetta. He was a new man recently joined with the *Villistas*.

He seized her, clenching her so hard that her chemise gave way and ripped from her shoulder. Tonetta, whose turquoise-green eyes glittered in the sun as she stood next to this enormous man whom she'd labeled a vicious killer, melted in his arms. Fierro kissed her savagely; she didn't protest. She kissed him back with equal desire and ferocity.

Madelaina did not stir. She did not breathe. Hot and cold chills ran through her, and she felt a sudden weakness in her knees as if she were a traitor to spy on them. She was afraid the amorous couple would sense her presence, feel her eyes on them, and find her there in so untenable a position. But they didn't pass beyond that small enclosure made by nature to resemble a true lover's hideaway; tall saplings thrust into the earth, roofed with yellowed maguey leaves, flattened and overlapping like shingles, hunched drowsy and fragrant in the warmth of noonday.

Fierro lifted one of Antonetta's breasts and caressed

it gently. Antonetta smiled consentingly and yielded to his passion. Fierro, walking proudly as a game cock, flourished a grandly manner and spread out his jacket on the mossy ground at their feet. They both fell to the ground eager to sate their passion before it consumed them.

Fierro and Antonetta! Madelaina burned all over as if a layer of tiny fig cactus bristles as cruel as spun glass had crawled under her skin. She forced herself to move forward silently, telling herself this was not her affair. Not to involve herself. Her loyalty was to both Antonetta and Pancho Villa. She wouldn't think about them. Not at all. But an empty feeling had filled her. She moved on to the *farmacia* where an old woman, grumbling over being awakened during siesta, greeted her and sold her the needed items for the required amount of pesos.

She took some of the headache powder and drank it down with a ladle of water from the spring well not far from the *farmacia*. She glanced about the village and realized that siesta was the reason for the abnormal silence. She decided to return to camp. How would she go past that love nest without them hearing her, she wondered. Feeling the hot flush of embarrassment over her recently acquired knowledge, Madelaina scolded herself.

Damnit! It's not your business. Forget it. You must pretend that you know nothing! You can't be annoyed, shocked, or moved to any action by this. After all, Antonetta has needs, just as Pancho does, she told herself. None of this touches you. Forget it. She moved back along the path, careful not to be heard, and moving stealthily past the stone bridge, she found herself out on the desert again, the blue of her *rebozo* becoming a dancing spot in the radiating heat waves that rose from the gray-red soil. She had forgotten the prickly pears completely.

Madelaina never mentioned to Antonetta what she'd seen on this day, and she forgot—or tried to obliterate from her mind—the thought that Antonetta hadn't resisted Fierro at all.

It was simply amazing how these two kept their secret from being discovered. Fierro and Villa continued to be as close as cockleshells. Antonetta kept her distance admirably. If they continued their love affair, it never became apparent to Madelaina again. She caught herself watching them to see if they'd slip or give any hint of their intimacy. Nothing. Absolutely nothing. The only change in Antonetta was that she didn't call Fierro a bloody murderous villain as she had from the moment Fierro appeared in Villa's camps.

Madelaina as Little Fox continued with her duties, never shirking, never complaining. She and the other expertly trained *soldaderas* were always in the thick of the war, fighting alongside the military detachments in the field, and with Little Fox always in the lead, the battalion of experienced women of war swarmed the fields like locusts, gathering provisions for the *Villista* army. She cooked with the *campesinas* and ate with them what was left over after the men had finished. After the battles she went with the women to salvage clothing, ammunition, and guns from the slain before their bodies began to swell in the heat. How many times had they encountered women as tough as they from the opposing sides and entered into a second battle even grimer than the first?

Although it became more difficult for Madelaina to keep up, she didn't complain. Antonetta grew alarmed for her friend and tried desperately to encourage her to return to El Paso to have her baby. But Madelaina refused. She grew gaunt, as if something inside gnawed at her; her eyes were sunken and she spoke less and less with each passing day. She worked harder than ever with no complaint passing her lips.

They had traveled to the north and were camped near the Yaqui River when Madelaina bent over suddenly and, clutching a nearby blanket to her mouth to keep from screaming, glanced up at the faces of the women nearby. She couldn't utter a sound. It was as if she were strangling on her own parched and swollen tongue. Her ankles had swollen these past few days and the knowledge that something was drastically wrong hadn't struck her until this very morning. Still she refused to talk to the midwives about the condition.

Now she was helpless. One of the women saw her fall forward, dangerously near the fires. She screamed. Suddenly there was pandemonium as the women fluttered about her and summoned the men to help lift her.

She was carried inside one of the thatched huts nearby and laid out on a blanket, unconscious. Antonetta was summoned, and she huddled with two midwives who tried reviving Little Fox with tequila, potions, and chicory. They used charred owl bones and other concoctions the Indians used to conjure up spirits of healing, including singed rabbit fur, lizards, and the entrails of cats. These were strewn about the hut at random by the women, who paid more heed to this ritual than to the needs of the mother in premature labor.

Four hours later, when the setting orange sun no longer seared the eyes and a spectacular tropical twilight spread plum-colored comfort upon the earth, the premature son of Madelaina and Peter Duprez was born. The midwife spread a concoction of oils on the infant, wrapped him in swaddling clothes, and placed the child in his mother's weary arms.

The news reached General Villa and he stalked into the hut to celebrate the birth of the boy child as if it were his own flesh and blood. He brought force and turbulence into the hut with him and his dark eyes sparkled brilliantly in the candle glow. He looked at the infant, gathered him in his arms, and with a primitive shout raised the child high in his arms, grinning with the pride of a godfather. He shouted an Indian cry of joy, and lifting the child higher toward the roof of the hut as one might do in making an offering to God, he asked for the Lord's blessing.

"He is some handsome *niño*, Little Fox," he exclaimed with amazed delight. "Now, for the name.

What have you decided?" He displayed the baby to Rudolfo Fierro and Tomás Urbina with much elation, as if it were the most amazing miracle ever performed in his camp. His expression was a blend of masculine triumph, pride, and sentimental melancholy.

"With your permission, *Jefe,* I've decided to call him Alejandro Doroteo Duprez Benson." She smiled faintly at Villa's antics.

"Bueno," he said, handing the infant to Antonetta's outstretched arms. "Tonight we celebrate the birth of Alejandro Doroteo Duprez Benson!" he announced to his men. "Fierro, pass out the cigars. Since the gringo papa is not here, his godfather shall officiate at the baptism." He left the hut, excitedly calling to Captain Tracy Richards. "Hey, gringo! Gringo! We celebrate, eh? We got us another damned good yankee to join the Gringo Brigade!"

Hearing his words, Madelaina shuddered inwardly. *Dios mios, pray you close your ears to the words of Pancho Villa. For my son, I do not wish more revolution.*

And then as most women do after the birth of a child, Madelaina cried and cried, without knowing for what she cried. She missed her husband too much. She needed the comforting touch of his arms around her, the feel of his lips upon hers, reassuring her of his love. But there was no one to comfort her—no one except for a replica of Peter, however small. He would have to occupy first place in her life now. Her own exaltation over the birth of a fine son, so small and helpless, was burned out by the pain she had endured. There wasn't an ember of excitement left in her. She was tired, weak, and terribly depressed. For her, it seemed the perilous adventure had ended when Peter deserted her to marry Valerie Townsend. Peter had vanished as if he no longer existed. Their days of marching, eating, and making love between battles had been so few that the memory of them began to fade of late. Now she had another life to think of and to plan for.

She felt her veins overflow with unendurable melancholy. If only she could stop crying. Perhaps then she could think more clearly about what she'd do now that the responsibility of another life was in her hands. She was so tired, so drowsy she could hardly keep her eyes open. Worse, she had no milk for the baby. What kind of mother was she—no milk!

Outside, Antonetta, holding a clay jar in her hand, approached a gentle mother goat tethered to a sapling which yielded when she pulled at the rope's end at the farthest reaches of grass. The kid, tied up a few feet away, rose, bleating, its feathery fleece shivering in the fresh wind. From behind her came Rudolfo Fierro. Scooping up the baby goat in his hands, he brought it to the mother goat and allowed him to suckle a few moments.

"Now," he said gently to the red-haired beauty. "Now reach in and take the milk you need." Their eyes, met for an instant in silent understanding. Then Tonetta quickly and with very deliberate movements drew enough milk for Madelaina's son, while Fierro's dark eyes lusted for her hungrily.

"Mucho gracias, mi coronel," she whispered. For an instant their hands met, then she reluctantly withdrew and returned to the hut to help feed the newborn infant.

"Por nada," said Fierro, watching her long after she'd vanished. The expression of desire on his face abated. But inside him, the proddings of lust and need burst into bright embers. For now, he had to be satisfied with stolen moments. Although used to taking what he wanted when he wanted it, this man felt an immense loyalty to Pancho Villa. And it was for this reason, that he hadn't already named Antonetta his property. He could wait. Meanwhile he'd do all he could to make sure Villa got to his precious Lucita, whenever the urge arose in him, thus leaving the red-haired vixen more free time for him.

745

Peter Duprez wafted in and out of consciousness for many weeks following the near fatal attempt on his life. He knew without being told that he'd courted death, that he was alive only due to his instinct for survival. Moments before the near-lethal bullets tore into his body, he'd lifted himself slightly from the tub, causing the bullets to miss their intended mark—the heart. Instead, the bullets lodged in his stomach and groin.

When consciousness returned to him it came in sprints of recollections, never in its entirety; hazy and vague at moments, other times painfully clear. His memory of the actual shooting itself was fleeting. What stood out clearly in his mind was the nightmarish, jolting ride in the back seat of a Hayes-Apperson auto, wrapped in blankets, more dead than alive. Moments of lucidity brought with it the perplexity of wondering if he were still alive before blacking out into a delirium of intense pain and feverish darkness.

Thoughts waxed and waned, always accompanied by the feeling of being disembowled, causing him to experience a nightmare of agony, panic, frustration, and a helplessness which manifested itself into a total annihilation of self. Pain dissolved his ego and consumed him without abating. His awareness of the passing of time alternated with periods of blinding sunlight, paralysing darkness, and a radiation of pulsating heat engulfing his body.

Peter wavered precariously between the agony echoing in his eardrums and a silent blackness swallowing him periodically, yet there finally came an awareness—slow as it was—prodding and pushing him into reality.

Voices hovered over him, but he recognized none of them. He was unable to open his eyes, despite the warnings made by these alien voices that he must. If it remained incumbent upon Peter to choose, he'd have gladly remained in that euphoric state of outer limbo which followed the administration of medication to ease the intense pain and discomfort he lived with.

When he finally came to and recognized what was reality for him, he was in small sterile-looking room—a hospital? He was restrained in a bed, covered with snowy linens as white as the glaring enamel-painted walls in which a reflection could be seen. His body, from the chest down to the upper thighs, was wrapped tightly in bandages. In what appeared to him to be a senseless precaution, his legs were also strapped to the bed. He couldn't have moved if he tried.

His eyes blinked hard in an effort to orient himself. Yes, it was a hospital all right. He could smell the antiseptic odors indigenous to hospitals, hear the muffled and hushed sounds. All he could see was white—white—and more white. Over the door opposite him was a large white clock with black numbers, the hands pointing to eleven o'clock. A white cloth folding screen on rollers stood to one side of the door. To the left of this was a window overlooking a scene he couldn't see from the bed. Next to the bed stood a white enamel table covered with a collection of hospital and sick room supplies. A white, metal, straight-backed chair sat at the foot of the bed. His eyes fell on a large bouquet of yellow roses. He wondered who'd sent them.

He felt an uneasy queasiness knotting in the pit of his stomach before sleep overcame him. When he awakened, the hands of the clock pointed to seven o'clock. It had to be evening because very little light came in through the window. His awareness came alive as the sound of hushed voices stirred him. One voice in particular seemed apprehensive and concerned. For a moment he felt as though he were looking into the face of Theodore Roosevelt until he recalled how much

Governor Hampton Townsend resembled the former head of the Rough Riders.

"Can you hear me, Peter?" asked the older man. "They told me you regained consciousness this morning." The portly man, dressed in a dark serge suit with a stiffly starched collar and black tie, was duly concerned over him. "It's a miracle you're alive. Valerie is beside herself. I packed her off to Europe while you convalesced here under an alias. What a perfectly idiotic thing for her to do. I must admit when she announced your marriage and a subsequent honeymoon in Europe to the press, I was outraged. But it's certainly provided you with rest—without those sniffing bloodhounds of the press converging on you." Hampton Townsend spoke in subdued tones, careful not to be overheard by the other men standing near the door.

Peter tried to move. "What happened, suh? Ah'm a bit vague. How long have ah been heah?"

"Haven't they told you? How incompetent of the hospital staff. Nearly two months. For a month and a half we were unsure if you'd live. It's a miracle. A real miracle. It's over now, and thank God you're on the mend."

"What happened?" persisted Peter. "How did ah get heah?"

"Dear me, don't you know what happened? Have you no recollection at all?" The governor glanced over his shoulders at the others, then leaned in closer to Peter. "Have you no idea who your assailant was? You were shot at close range—in the belly and groin. I'm afraid, my boy, the injuries are quite serious." He avoided Peter's eyes. "Well, all that's behind us now. What counts is you're alive."

Peter shrugged. "Yeah, ah suppose ah should be grateful foah that, suh."

"When you feel up to it, my boy," said the governor, seemingly relieved, "I'd best fill you in on what's happening south of the border."

Peter had been looking at the three men who huddled close to the door. He felt below par and his

748

instincts weren't performing efficiently. Still, something about the trio unnerved him. He cautioned the governor with his eyes to be aware of their presence. "Who are theah?" he asked confidentially.

"I was told, Peter, they are guarding your life. My boy, I presumed they were hired by you," he whispered.

"No, suh. Nevuh saw them befoah. It's best we say nothing, suh. Ya understand?"

"Just be thankful you're American—on American soil!" said the Governor Townsend, wiping the sweat dripping from his face. "Word's been out that President Huerta is seeking extradition of all war criminals. He especially wants the freedom fighters—namely you, Peter."

Peter's eyes searched his critically. He glanced at the trio at the door who were absorbed in their own conversation. "Namely me? Why me?"

"Seems you were married to a Mexican spy."

"She's an American through marriage, suh. And don't tell me President Wilson intends ta cooperate with that foul sidewinder, Huerta?"

"Up to now, he's stalled the Mexican president. But it seems they've had the cooperation of another very important American—a Texan at that."

Peter's eyes widened with interest. He could see readily that Governor Townsend felt awkward, ill at ease, and obviously reluctant to speak out.

"Dare ah ask who, suh?"

The governor cleared his throat, blinked his gray eyes hard behind those rimless glasses, and stroked his brush moustache. His brown hair was nearly white now, and he resembled Valerie more at this time than at any other, thought Peter. Here the resemblance ended. This man was a true gentleman and a scholar, who operated within a sphere of ethics that made him admirable. Valerie had to have been a bad seed. She had none of her father's laudable traits. As a matter of fact, Peter, having never seen him at a loss for words, grew concerned.

"It's William Benson, Peter. Your father." He spoke the words solemnly as if he had just imposed a death sentence on the young man.

"Governor," began Peter. "Is theah any way y'all might rid us both of those three men? Ah feel uneasy in theah presence, especially since youah words have just hit me with the impact of hurricane." Peter was shaking. He had no reason to doubt the words of the Texas governor.

The portly man moved with the grace of a bull moose. His manner, however, contained the efficacy of a diplomat. "Gentlemen, I wonder if you'd mind moving outside in the hall. The patient has grown weary and would like to rest. You may continue your conversation out there. I'll only be a few moments longer."

One man, an apparent secret service agent in the employ of the Mexican government shook his head. "I regret, Excellency, I must remain in the same room with Señor Duprez. This gentlemen is with your State Department." He pointed to the slim, dark-haired American wearing a plaid suit, stiffly starched collar, spats, and a derby, who instantly prepared to produce papers giving him authority by the state's attorney general to cooperate with the Mexican agent.

"Apparently you aren't aware I'm the governor of this state," said Townsend, drawing himself up to his full stature of six feet. His head arched imperiously, and the manner in which he glanced at the others through his bifocals gave him a more formidable appearance than usual. "Do I take this reluctance on your part to comply with my request as downright insubordination? What's your name, sir?"

"Fenwick, sir," retorted the man in plaid, instantly flushed with embarrassment. "I had no idea the involvement was at the executive level, Governor," he apologized. "My orders from the state attorney general are explicit." He turned over his portfolio for the governor's perusal.

Townsend glanced at them superficially, folded them, and handed them back. "They appear in order,

Fenwick. I have no desire to interfere with the commitment made by the attorney general with our friends south of the border. All I ask is that you permit me a few quiet minutes with an old and dear friend of the family. As a matter of fact, my son-in-law."

Before Fenwick or the Mexican agent could protest further or become aware they'd been politely put in their place, they were escorted out the door by the expansive governor who made light of the situation. Once closed, the door was quietly bolted and the Townsend tilted a chair beneath the handle.

"What is it, suh?" asked Peter, attempting to rise to a sitting position. He watched the distinguished man's antics with mounting curiosity.

Governor Townsend didn't speak for a few moments as he paced the floor thoughtfully. Soon Peter began to recognize those qualities of which President Wilson mentioned in the man who governed one of the most prosperous states in the union. His face grew taut, his eyes more secret. The planes of his face, sharp and angular, contrasted the deep hollows under his cheekbones. He began to speak as if to himself. Yet, added to the delivery of his words was a peculiar quality of strength and power formerly absent from his manner.

"So, Peter. It's worse than I imagined. They went over my head—didn't give a hint of their intrigue and shenanigans. Not even my spies reported what was underfoot." He stroked the outline of his moustache with the tip of his finger. "He's gone too far this time."

Peter's brows drew together in a puzzled frown. "Who, suh?"

The governor's gray eyes lifted to meet Peter's. His color was gone. For an instant Peter detected a marked hesitation before the words spilled from the official's mouth. "William Benson. Your father—that's who!" Then he gathered momentum. "Lucifer only knows how many acres of Mexican land were exchanged for his betrayal! Blasted fool! Doesn't he even guess that one day his lands—even his life—will be worthless if a revolutionary becomes president? And it jolly well seems a likely prospect from where I stand!" His heavy shoulders shook visibly.

Peter couldn't reply quickly. It wasn't that he was surprised at anything his father did. He hadn't put the pieces together with what Townsend had told him.

"He's always been a maverick, suh," said Peter, then added hastily, "Ah'm not saying this in his defense. Ah'm just not clear on what he's done."

"A maverick's one thing, my boy," replied the governor, still moving about the room abstractly. He paused to glance out the window for a moment, then turned to the man in bed. "You're not clear on what he's done, eh? Well, I'll tell you, Peter. I'll tell you exactly what he's done. That son of a bitch just sold his son for thirty pieces of silver! That's what he's done. That legal document I glanced at so carelessly moments ago gave the Mexican *Federales* the legal right to transport you to Mexico City to be tried for treason against the Mexican Constitutional government, during the period of time you were evidently married to some Mexican baggage who, it turns out, is and has been a spy for the revolutionaries—namely Pancho Villa."

Peter grew alert. "But, how did he—how did my father know? I took every precaution to keep my life and my activities hidden from the public eye." As soon as he'd spoken, he realized the futility of the words. William Benson had access to and could uncover any man's secret life if he had a mind. That's what made him so feared among the circles of his peers.

At a loss to explain his father's participation, Peter wanted to set the record straight about Madelaina. "Foah youah edification, suh," he began. "She's not baggage, suh. She's the daughtuh of a highborn *gachupín*, a blueblood. As a matter of fact, suh," he said almost reluctantly, "she's the daughtuh of General Alvaro Obregon who presently commands the formidable Fourth Sonora Battalion, one of Mexico's most important redoubts."

752

Hampton Townsend's chin dropped in astonishment. He sat at the foot of the bed, one foot dangling free over the edge. Suddenly he slammed a fist into the palm of his other hand. "The hell you say, boy! The hell you say!" He compressed his lips tightly, then bit his underlip in thought. For several moments the room was silent. The only sounds came from an open window—a sudden fluttering of pigeons roosting on the hospital eaves when frightened by the loud sounds of horns coming from the new horseless carriages slowly replacing the equestrian mode of travel. Stanley Steamers and Haynes-Appersons were two of the most prestigious automobiles in Texas and could be found any place in El Paso with rambunctuous drivers blowing their horns, frightening people half to death. *Why am I thinking about such mechanical conveyances,* wondered Peter, *when history is about to be made in one form or another by the steamroller of power standing a few feet away.*

Peter turned his attention to Hampton Townsend who continued to pummel his palm with a balled fist. Here, thought Peter, is a man used to all the political ploys at every level of government. Here was an inscrutable wheeler-dealer, who as a young man had fought the Indians for land, a man who'd worked his way through Harvard and fought side by side with Teddy Roosevelt as they charged up San Juan Hill in Santiago de Cuba. Here was a man who knew how to live by his wits and could exercise the diplomacy and cunning of a king. The strength of his personality was such that he projected his mental climate without a word or glance. And Peter knew he was presently preparing to do battle with another formidable Texan, his father, William Benson.

Hampton Townsend rose to his feet, rearranging the starched cuffs under his coat sleeves. One hand slickly caressed his tie into place. He was a tall man and in the next few moments, Peter thought, as deadly as William Benson.

"I've never revealed this to a soul, Peter, but it's

something I must tell you, before I set my plans into motion. I've avoided—literally avoided—confrontation with Bill Benson ever since he lured Jennifer Duprez from my nuptial bed. Oh, don't look so surprised. Your mother and I were lovers long before Bill Benson entered the picture. You didn't know this? But, then, how could you? Jenny died when you were still a young man." Townsend reached into his back pocket and produced a silver flask. He poured himself a jigger of whiskey, offered some to Peter, and when he refused, he replaced it into his pocket. He smacked his lips heartily after he downed it, then continued.

"There's been bad blood between us long before you were born, my boy. We never took time to resolve our differences, mainly at the urging of your beloved mother—rest her soul. I made it a point to keep out of Bill's way, although I'm sure he didn't exercise the same prudence. Later, when I began to hear of the shabby treatment he gave the woman I loved, I had to keep my peace. After all, Jenny did pick Bill over me to marry. He was her husband under God and law. There's not much a disappointed suitor can do when spurned.

"Then one day I received a letter from your mother, telling me all about you, what a fine lad you were, and the aspirations she had for you. Medicine, she said. You intended to study medicine and be a doctor. Was that it?"

Peter nodded. His curiosity piqued by this revelation, he lit a cigarette and sat with rapt attention as he listened to the distinguished man.

"We were close, your mother and I. Went to school together—childhood sweethearts. We should have married," he reflected sadly. "We were meant for each other, but I guess I somehow didn't spark the fires that burned deeply in her at the time. The depth of her emotions was lost to me because I was pursuing a political career at the time which took most of my attention. It wasn't until she wrote to me that I recognized her despondency over the unrequited love that drove

754

her after you were born. You see, my boy, Bill Benson always believed you were my son—not his. But it wasn't true. I wished it was the truth—that you were the seed of my loins, but he was wrong. You're his son all right, but it's easy to see you inherited your mother's compassion." Townsend lit up a cigar and puffed on it as he sat in the white metal chair opposite Peter. He leaned back, tilting the chair against the wall.

"I was proud of you when I heard you left home rather than cowing to Bill Benson. If you were my flesh and blood, I couldn't have been prouder and more pleased that you refused to buckle under his dictatorship. I followed your career from the moment you left Seven Moons to become a soldier of fortune. I hoped many times that we'd be drawn together. I hoped you might even pursue a political career. And then one day—one day while speaking with my friend Doroteo Arango, whom you know as Francesco Pancho Villa—I learned you'd become a trusted friend of his. Oh, I was aware you'd joined his Gringo Brigade in the early days before Madero took the reins of government, but I had assumed you'd gone away, guided by other interests.

"Through your knowledge—firsthand, I might add —I assumed that between us we could help settle this terrible infamy—this butchery taking place in the land of our southern neighbors. You realize, Peter, only the Rio Grande separates America from Mexico, and the differences in our standards of living keep those poor people in virtual slavery? They haven't ever been able to shake the shackles of foreign oppressors. How could they when their own kind sells out to the highest bidder?"

"Why is it that men forget their own roots when tempted with power and wealth?" asked Peter quietly. "Diaz—that freedom fighter who expelled Maximilian—was no better once in office. Graft and corruption ran rampant. Madero fell into the trap—not as much because he was less corrupt—and was killed for his efforts. Now, Huerta—oh, this man, Huerta—" Peter stopped, recalling all the things Madelaina had told him about the man who sat on the presidential throne in Mexico City. "Well, sir, he just can't be permitted to remain in power. Villa is right in fighting for Mexico's life."

Governor Townsend nodded silently. "We were speaking of William Benson. It's something I must get off my chest, boy. I was only a state senator at the time—before I became governor—when I began to smell the brand of William Benson's burning opposition to every bit of legislation I promoted. Hell, I was beginning to become the joke of the capital. 'If Townsend backs a bill, you could bet sure money and win that Benson will oppose it.' Those were the words that permeated the senate. An' if Townsend blocks a bill, five would get you ten that Benson would support it regardless of the issues. If I hadn't been so obstinate and bull-headed in my effort to save face, I'd have used reverse psychology on your father and publically supported those issues I didn't believe in just to make certain they'd get Benson's backing and victory. I didn't have those kind of guts then. A senator's political future depends on the calibre of issues he backs, regardless of their success." He smiled tightly at the irony.

Hampton Townsend paused abruptly. "What in blue blazes am I doing diggin' up the buried past and beating my gums about such things when we've got to resolve the business of your life?" Once again he reached for the silver flask, uncorked it, and tilted it to his lips, gulping freely. "Ahhh." He smacked his lips again. "Now then, we've gotta concentrate on you. Can you walk yet? Have they tried moving you about? What's your prognosis, my boy?" Suddenly the governor stopped. He leaned in and grabbed Peter's wrist, his face blanched whiter than the sheets on the bed. "The daughter of General Alvaro Obregon, you said?" His mind turned inward, struggling for total recall. "Madelaina Obregon?"

Peter nodded, regarding the governor with gravity.

"By the roaring blue balls of thunder," he exclaimed. "She's the very woman William Benson recently married in El Paso!" Townsend sank back into the chair, dumbfounded and aghast at the revolting situation looming before him.

Peter's troubled eyes swept over the governor's swollen features. It was pointless to ask him to repeat his words. He'd heard him loud and clear. There was no point in contesting his words, in insisting that Madelaina would have never succumbed to a William Benson if he, Peter Duprez, hadn't treated her so shabbily at their last encounter. The next few moments were filled with wild despair as the words struck at him deeper and deeper. No, he told himself, Madelaina wouldn't do such a thing. Never! Never in a million years! *She loves me! She loves me! She had to*. But his memories dug up moments that struck terror in his heart. The money bag bearing the William Benson brand in Madelaina's dressing room swam past his eyes. She said it had been a gift from Manuelito Perez. He believed her. He had seen no reason to reveal to her that he was Benson's son. Now, in hindsight, he realized he should have, so she wouldn't have been deluded by his father.

Why had she done this? Had she believed the story planted by Valerie Townsend? Had she intended to teach him a lesson? How could he have told her straight out he was acting as liaison among Pancho Villa, Governor Townsend, and President Wilson? Espionage for the revolutionary forces! To have told her would only make her situation more perilous. Peter forced himself to sit up in bed. His eyes were glazed in disbelief. He tremblingly lit another cigarette, took two puffs, and nervously snuffed them out. He felt like a wild animal in those moments. He wanted to spring from the bed, run outside and find his father, and finish this thing between them once and for all. Instead, he gave in to a feeling of absolute weakness that engulfed him, a feeling of hopelessness and helplessness and fell back weakly on the pillows.

Watching him, Hampton Townsend felt a flush of anger, both at William Benson and at himself for having been so outspoken. He could have waited a few days until Peter gained his strength. The crimson flush on his face deepened. He rose to his feet, and pointing a finger at Peter, he said in a voice as thorny as barbed wire, "I'll fight him, this time. This time I'll fight him with the same weapons, Peter! Bill's gone too far. Did he know of your marriage to this *gachupín*?" he asked, trying to make sense of Benson's last obscenity. "He must have! No one can tell me he didn't. Bill Benson knows everything he involves himself with, and no one can tell me different." He shuddered with rage. "Bastard! He's made his own rules for so long, he has no respect for the rights of others. I'll be damned if I'll let him win this time, my boy." The governor had chewed his cigar to shreds. He moved in closer to the bed and studied the pale, drawn face of the younger, more muscular man. His voice grew stronger, more compelling, his manner more decisive. "His own son! Imagine! His own son! Listen, Peter. You'll have to stay out of it for a while. Complain to the doctors, contrive a few more ailments. Let 'em think you aren't responding to treatment. I'll need time to reconnoiter. Some way I've gotta get you outa here and I'll need the governor's office to do it. I'm not about to let them extradite you. Damnit to hell, you're an American citizen! If I have to induce President Wilson to intervene with his army, I won't let 'em take you!"

"Do that, Governor, and all youah plans with Pancho Villa will go down a sewer," said Peter quietly, watching the smoke from his cigarette spiral to the ceiling. "If ah know mah politickin', suh, Huerta might just make a quick pact with the Kaiser's men, and German-made barbed wire will be strung up across ouah borduhs, and we'll be sucked into a worse war than the one already brewing in Europe."

"I can't and won't let them take you. Not if I have to enlist the militia to protect you!" The inexorable
758

note in Governor Townsend's voice reached Peter's ears.

"Hasn't the governor and his family already demanded too much of you," he asked wryly. "First, I ask your cooperation in this clandestine affair, then you're felled by the bullets shot by my hot-headed, spoiled brat of a daughter—nearly killed, and now this!"

Peter's eyes snapped open. "Then it wasn't some dream? Some figment of my imagination that I saw Valerie before the shots were fired?"

"You saw her and never mentioned a word to me?" asked Townsend, fully overwhelmed by the lad's loyalty.

Before Peter could reply, a sharp rap at the door, a loud pounding, and an attempt to force the door open brought the governor hastily toward the exit. He removed the obstruction under the handle and the door burst open with four men flying into the room in a rage. The Mexican agent, Leopoldo, and Fenwick from the State Department, accompanied by a nurse and a doctor, composed themselves when they saw everything in order.

"What exactly is the meaning of this?" demanded Governor Townsend, affecting to grow more indignant by the moment. "How dare you break into this chamber? Aren't I entitled to a few moments of privacy with my son-in-law?"

Apologies were in order, and while the men spoke their humblest regrets at the intrusion, the nurse moved in to take Peter's temperature. The doctor took his blood pressure and shook his head regretfully.

"I'll have to ask that you all leave. The patient is in stress and must be sedated."

Two of governor's aides appeared at the door, wondering what the ruckus was about.

"It's all right," the governor reassured them, reaching for his hat. "I was just leaving." He walked to Peter's side. "Now you rest comfortably. Don't you be in any hurry to leave. You've had a serious operation and the important thing is that you recuperate. How long do you suppose it will be, Doctor, before the patient is ready to leave?"

"I have no idea," replied the physician, readying a needle to sedate Peter. "His pressure's up—too high, Excellency."

"Then, you think he shouldn't be moved?" The words were loud and clear enough for both Fenwick and Señor Leopoldo to hear.

"Decidedly not, Mr. Governor. This patient shouldn't be moved for at least two more weeks—perhaps four. Any movement might cause the wounds to open up and bleed again."

"Thank you, Doctor." Townsend winked at Peter, who remained unmoving on the bed as the shot was administered. He nodded to the others and left the premises with his aides, stopping briefly at the door to wave to Peter.

Peter Duprez lay on the bed, fatigued and weakened from the conversation. The emotional shock done to him had sapped his energy as well as his hope. Too many things swam about in his befuddled brain. Madelaina—Valerie—his father, William Benson—and his mother's faded picture superimposed above them all.

The narcotic began taking effect and the pain in his lower extremities, as acute as it was earlier when the governor had been there, began to abate. He felt lightheaded. A myriad of scenes formed in his mind, none as heavy as the earlier ones. He felt a sense of movement, saw a flash of strange faces crowd around him. Still more movement. He alternated between lucidity and a murky consciousness in which time had no meaning and thoughts were nonexistent. If there was confusion in his mind, if there was total disorientation to his senses, Peter had no real way of knowing it.

He awakened weeks later in strange surroundings. That he'd been drugged was a foregone conclusion. The identity of the drugs were not known to him.

Their effects—the cold, clammy feelings of withdrawal, stuffed nasal passages, chills and weakness as each ache in his body was magnified intensely each time he moved—remained with him for the next few days. He had no idea where he was, only that the tropical atmosphere and the balmy breezes indicated he was somewhere near a body of water. The room had a tiled floor, heavy oak beams across the ceiling, and a fireplace of polished stones. He wore a robe, and when he first awakened, he managed to get to his feet and tremblingly hang on to bedpost, chair, and wall as he made his way to the open-air balcony. He was in a villa at the top of a mountain overlooking a magnificent spread of blue sea. He inhaled the sea air and held tightly to the balcony as a wave of dizziness engulfed him, causing his head to spin and nearly making him lose his balance. His blue eyes, still dull from the heavy sedation, blurred for several moments until they grew accustomed to the intensity of the glaring overhead sun.

Immediately below him was a beautiful tiled terrace with furniture and a great abundance of greenery. Below that was a sheer drop to the sea. Slightly north of him on the ground floor was an enormous gate with four armed guards. Beyond the locked gate, halfway down the steep incline was a small structure resembling a gazebo. He couldn't make it out, but men, the size of ants viewed from this distance, wore uniforms and were armed equally as well as those closer to him. A few rare and exotic birds flew about in an aviary next to the terraced patio. Never had he seen the likes of such colorful flamingoes and cockatoos and parrots. Some tropical paradise, surmised Peter—*or else I'm dreaming.*

Walking slowly back into the room, he caught his reflection in a mirror. He was thickly bearded, his hair longer than usual. He'd lost several pounds, judging from the hollows on his face and the flatness of his stomach. If only he didn't feel so weak, so fatigued and depressed. He attempted to reconstruct parts of his life, and was frightened when his memory wouldn't respond. It seemed he had no recollection of anything except for this moment.

He knew nothing for certain—not even that he was alive—until he pinched himself. It wasn't until later, when a young man entered his room and introduced himself as Dr. Gonsalvez, that it was confirmed he was a guest of a high-ranking Federal officer in the Mexican government. He was told he was in the hacienda of this mysterious host, near the seacoast village of Santa Rosalia in the state of Sonora. Dr. Gonsalvez reluctantly refused to name the Federal officer's name. "In due time, you'll meet your host, Señor Duprez. Meanwhile, it is my responsibility to make certain your health vastly improves. Perhaps you'll be kind enough to explain what exactly happened to you? Since I have no medical or hospital records on which to base my prescription of medication and therapy, it would greatly assist me in my efforts. I'm overwhelmed by the major surgical techniques performed on your body."

"Ah was stung by a pea-shooter," said Peter snidely.

The high-toned doctor smiled with the unmistakable aroma of aristocracy. "That's some pea-shooter. More like cannon, eh?" He moved away from the bed. "We've taken into account everything to make your stay comfortable. I had hoped for better cooperation from you, but perhaps in a day or two when you grow less comfortable, you'll confide what was done to help heal you. If you need or desire anything—anything at all—don't hesitate to ring." He gestured to a pull cord close to the bed.

"A bottle of tequila, newspapers, cigars, and a roomful of cooperatin' little *chiquitas* might not be bad for a start," said Peter beginning to feel the necessity and urge to couple.

"I'll provide the newspaper and cigarettes, but I can't promise the tequila or obliging women," the doctor said discreetly.

Peter forced a light laugh. The atmosphere was relaxing, and the sun on the balcony would be a splendid way for him to regain the sun-bronzed look that faded into a near-death pallor when Valerie pumped him with lead. Hell's bells! Damned little vixen, he thought. She could've killed me!

The newspapers didn't arrive until the next day, but the accumulation of them for the past six months provided plenty of reading—the kind he relished. News of Pancho Villa's countless victories!

He read and reread them so many times, he could recite the headlines by rote: *VILLA CAPTURES SANTA ROSALIA! VILLA FORCES CAPTURE FORT IN ZACATECAS! DURANGO FALLS TO VILLISTAS! SAN ANDREAS—CHIHUAHUA CITY —JUAREZ—ALL SURRENDERED TO PANCHO VILLA.* Victory followed in Tierra Blanca, Santa Isabella, Conejos, Mapimi, Bermejillo, San Pedro de Las Colimas, Saltillo. There were a few defeats: Zacatecas fell back into Federal hands, but shortly thereafter Villa masterminded a grand military coup, swept out the *Federales*, and recaptured the stronghold.

The solidarity and growing might of General Villa's army had fairly shattered the resolve of Huerta's *Federales* who found themselves retreating more than advancing these days. The futility of resistance to the hordes of well-armed, militarily trained men was well taken by each garrison commander whenever the awesome army of conical sombreros and Winchesters sprang as if from nowhere to launch savage flanking movements to wild, hectic cries of *"Viva Villa! Viva La Revolucion!"*

Peter Duprez smiled when he read the rave reviews of the zephyr Villa, who moved with incredible swiftness and seemed to be in all places at one time. Even in El Dorado, a place remote to the machinations of Pancho Villa, the whispers of the people came in the form of a song, "La Cucaracha." It was on the lips of the lowly land *peóns,* the fishermen, and the hillsmen. Peter heard it morning, noon, and night until he felt he could no longer stand to hear it without taking up arms and following wherever Pancho's trail led.

On one of his visits with Peter, Dr. Gonsalvez had made it perfectly clear that any attempt to escape would inevitably result in death to him. He explained further that the estate was guarded by armed guards—all crack shots. That in kennels at the rear of the villa, a pack of ferocious Dobermans, trained to kill, were housed. He suggested tactfully that as long as Peter remained cooperative and made no attempt to reject the hospitality of so generous a host, he would be afforded the best luxuries at hand.

And until Peter regained his strength and his former vigor, he entertained no ideas of departing from such hospitality.

Shortly after his arrival at the Villa El Dorado, Peter sat on the balcony soaking up the sun as the servants entered to clean his suite. It was the usual routine that had taken place in the past except there was a new girl, dressed in the typical Indian skirt and blouse. She shyly kept her head averted from him as she skirted by the French doors about her business.

Something about her, thought Peter, seemed familiar. No, it's just the sun's heat making me tipsy, he answered himself. She passed him again, and this time her dark eyes stared at him seductively. Just as quickly she darted out of sight. Peter smiled. She's asking for it, he thought. He felt a little excitement stirring in him—not as in the past, but it was there and Peter sighed in relief. The bullet wound had done much damage, and for a time, with little feeling in his manhood, he worried that he might not be the man he'd been in the past. The doctors in El Paso advised that it would take time and he mustn't panic if he was unable to satisfy himself sexually.

Matter of fact, he hadn't the strength nor the desire to participate in any sexual caper for a while, and he felt certain the drugs administered to him to reduce the pain were responsible. He simply hadn't given it much thought until this moment, when the sight of the bronze-skinned mestizo with her fiery dark eyes that oozed seduction stimulated his appetite.

He could hear the women talk as they changed the bed linens and dusted. A guard, armed and ready for anything, always stood guard inside the door as they dutifully went about their chores. When they were finished, Peter remained in the sun, thinking he'd tell Dr. Gonsalvez to return the dark-skinned charmer to him later. He picked up the paper and read of Pancho Villa's recent assault on a Federal garrison, a story by a crack journalist, Miguel Guerra. Monterrey had been taken by Villa in an astounding manner. "But in and around the desert plains and foothills between Bermejillo and Torreon," wrote the reporter, "one of the most dramatic and critical events of the Mexican Revolution took place." The reporter went on to say, "By the sheer magic of one man's name—Francesco Villa—came the hordes of soldiers that composed the entire army of irregulars of all Mexico in one enormous force for a conference of the *jefes*.

"Pancho Villa arrived with a thousand strong. Tiburco with 200. Urbina with 800. Herrera with 400 first-class cavalry fighters, Contreras with 300. Then came the heads of lesser *guerrillo* bands and one man in particular, who instantly made his strength known to Villa. Coronel Rudolfo Fierro succeeded in obtaining a promotion for his unique and indispensable talents in their first confrontation."

Guerra went on to say, "Pancho Villa addressed the conference of chiefs with the suggestion that, 'We the most powerful single army in all Mexico should without a moment's hesitation advance on the vital city of Torreon and crush it!' And that's exactly what they did. Weapons fired overhead, cracking smartly, *vaqueros* shouting their *yiiipees,* and cheers of '*olé*' and '*Viva Villa*' filled the desert air. And as the remarkable force of military strength faced southward toward the Federal redoubt, the air filled with Villa's marching song—'La Cucaracha!' It was the most exciting sight of my life," commented Miguel Guerra. "The thrill of seeing such colorful pageantry within a well-disciplined army, to hear the clatter of horses and rattle of cannon wheels combined with the song of the people. Sombreroed, gun-belted soldiers and their *soldaderas* sung from the tops of trains, from their horses, and on foot. The Gringo Brigade, possibly the most colorful division in Villa's entourage, those Yankees who've been loyal to his cause, sang the loudest. They even drowned out the Indian drums and the guitars played by tequila-drinking soldiers. The song seemed to lift them right out of the depths of despair to which they were born and elevate them to a plateau where hopes, dreams, and aspirations for better life would come true.

"And then," continued Guerra, "It began. With the deadly intuition which has made Pancho Villa, General-in-Chief of the Northern Division, the most powerful military force in all Mexico, the *premier jefe* hurled General Urbina's brigade along the course of the river of Torreon to wipe out the defenses of the *Federales*. Herrera's magnificent Juarez Brigade moved against defenses of the western flank. *Federale* General Campa, entrenched with artillery and men repairing fortifications, put up an aggressive battle against Villa, but it was all to no avail. Even when Villa's artillery hit them, tearing apart massive defenses with shrapnel and explosives; even as Villa's cavalry smashed their flanks and his infantry ripped through the gaps in perfect order, the *Federale*s wouldn't—couldn't—believe that it was General Francesco Villa defeating them by peerless strategy and top-notch soldiering. Two days later General Francesco Villa entered Torreon behind fleeing *Rurales* and Federal soldiers. Arms, supplies, trains, and prisoners all went to Pancho Villa. Correction, please. All *Orozquista* loyalists among the prisoners were instantly executed according to a promise made once by General Villa, a man true to his word."

Miguel Guerra ended his column by adding something of note. "General Villa has embarked on his first attempt to govern a city by establishing a garrison. He borrowed money from the money lenders to pay his war debts and finance future campaigns. The destitute families of the city were provided with food and clothing. Most important, General Villa built hospitals. Using railroad cars, he ordered them scrubbed and repainted and equipped with requisitioned army cots, tables, stoves, and ice containers. And everything covered in clean white sheets. He hired the best doctors and established a medical corps. He enlisted the aid of every sub-chief to locate and return with all the medical supplies they could lay their hands on, including morphine."

Miguel further embellished his column by lauding the efforts of General Francesco Villa and openly declaring that this remarkable and dedicated man had become civilized. "His consuming passion for the welfare of the wounded, dying, and maimed supersedes that of the government's highest office. Presidente Huerta has never seen fit to establish the much-needed hospitals for those poor unfortunates who were willing to sacrifice their lives for their country. Neither Diaz before him nor Madero concerned themselves thusly."

Peter felt pangs of nostalgia as he read the vivid, clear-sighted report. What he wouldn't give to be with and share the glory with his old friends. His mind churned, wondering how this paper could be dispatched to Washington to President Wilson. He had to learn how Villa had truly reformed and become a leader of his people.

"Señor," came the whisper.

Peter's head turned to the armed guard who walked in toward him. He removed his cap and bowed. "Dr. Gonsalvez wishes to inform you, the women are finished. He has left one of them for your pleasure." He bowed and left the balcony and disappeared into the room. Peter followed him inside, abounding with curiosity. Inside, the guard stood at the door, pointing to the voluptuous creature stretched out on the bed, lying naked in a seductive and languid pose.

Peter's eyes shot up in delight. He gazed upon her face and was about to exclaim aloud. He was stopped

767

short by the warning look in her eyes. Turning to the guard, he pointed to the door. "You don't intend to watch us, *muchacho*?"

The red-faced guard instantly left the room, locking the door behind him.

Peter turned to the girl on the bed. "Lucia! Lucia San Miguel! What in the name of Satan are you doing here?"

She held a finger to her lips and spoke aloud for the benefit of the guard in case he eavesdropped. "*Si, señor*. I am sent by the *patrón* to make your visit enjoyable. Your wish is my command." She led Peter in closer to the bed.

There was tequila and glasses and wine and a tray of cheese and fresh fruits on the table nearby. "First, gringo, we make love, then we talk," she suggested in complete compliance with his own feelings.

A shiver ran through Lucia as his lips pressed hers and the old expertise of Peter Duprez came into play. His lips caressed her temples and ears, and her own excitement grew insatiably. Her fingers, strong and sensuous, began to massage his shoulders, the back of his neck, smoothing away the tension as she'd done in the past. Her body rose to meet his, filling out the curves of his lean hard and sun-bronzed physique. Peter kept his eyes closed just to feel the warmth of a woman's body and the urgent need rising in her which used to excite him.

Lucia reached for him and with a teasing laugh kissed his eyelids. Her hands slid down slowly along his arms under his waist and over his hips and thighs. In a slow circular movement, and with the touch of a *mariposa*—a butterfly—her fingertips touched the surface hair. She felt him shudder uncontrollably and laughed with glee. "Lucia hasn't lost her touch, eh, *gringo*?"

"Not that ah can tell, *chiquita*." In a quick movement, Peter turned his body and picked her up, hoisting her over him. She straddled him now, bent over him, her firm young breasts dangling dangerously close

768

to his mouth, teasing him. They played for a time; he reaching for her nipples, she eluding him.

Lucia glanced at his chest, at the twisted railroad track of scars reaching into his groin. *"Gringo!"* she expressed alarm. "What happened to ju? *Demonio!* Ees like a cannon exploded on ju, no?"

"It's nothing," he murmured.

Lucia slipped off his body, reached for the glasses of tequila she poured earlier, and handed him one. *"Dios mios,"* she muttered. "Ees one lucky theeng ju are alive, *chico."* They touched glasses and downed the firewater.

Her hands busily traced the scar and found their way to his most vital part. For an instant Peter felt terrible that it was limp and unresponsive. Usually he was a step ahead in the physical part of any sexual act. All he had to do was think about it and his body would grow hard with overt desire. He'd been in bed with Lucia for the better part of a half-hour and none of the old responses came to life.

"Gringo, what's the matter? Ju don't like Lucia no more?" She pouted, filled with dismay.

He drew her close to him. "Ah don't know, *chiquita.* Ah just don't know. The doctors told me not to force anything. Ah guess ah was pretty badly shot up. It'll take time."

"Dios mios, gringo. Ju don't think they cut something from ju?"

Her fright, overexaggerated, caused him to laugh. "No, *chiquita.* Ah've just been pretty sick. It'll just take time."

"How much time eet takes, eh?" she asked again in that overly serious manner. This time Peter didn't laugh. He grew annoyed.

Caressing her breasts had formerly given him such an erotic response, but now, nothing. Absolutely nothing. He closed his eyes, hoping to concentrate on her and the erotic past they shared together. Again nothing. He forced himself to think of Madelaina—the true love of his life. He sighed deeply and pictured her as they first met, how they loved on the *Mozambique,* and the lingering memories of their countless lovemaking moments. Again nothing.

Impotence was something frightening to Peter Duprez. He never dreamed he might be forced to deal with its frightening ramifications. He tried to tell himself to stop this ridiculous speculation. That it merely took time like anything else in need of repair. After all, a broken arm took time to heal. A leg—anything broken had to be repaired, didn't it?

Covering his temporary embarrassment and his own frustration caused by a willing mind, duelling with an uncooperative body, he turned Lucia over and held her in his arms. "Nevuh mind foah now, *chiquita.* Let's put the time ta good use. Tell me what youah doing heah. How did ya find me?"

Lucia snuggled in closer to him, her lips close to his ear.

"Ju know where ju are, *gringo?*"

Peter shook his head. "Santa Rosalia?"

"Ju are in the hacienda of General Alvaro Obregon, the father of your *mujer,* Little Fox."

Peter held her at arm's length and studied her intently.

"Ees true. Word reached us ten days ago. *Jefe* Villa say to me, 'Lucia, ju go find Tom Meex and bring heem to me,' *Pues, amigo.* Eees a beeg job for Lucia."

"You've seen Little Fox, my *mujer?* Where is she, Lucia? Tell me."

"*Que va,* tell me, be patient and Lucia will explain." She sipped more tequila. "Ju want more?"

"Ah want ya ta talk a bit faster, *chiquita.* Any time we may be interrupted."

"*Bueno. Bueno, gringo.* Ju must give Lucia time to prepare her words." She set the glass on the nearby table. "Ju got a smoke for Lucia—marijuana?"

"No. Cigarettes are on the table." He waited patiently while she lit up two cigarettes. She handed him one and smoked the other greedily, inhaling deeply. "Ees not like marijuana, but ees not bad. Leesten, *amigo,*" she continued in her pigeon yankee. "Ees better I talk so—they weel not understand my words. Is A-O.K.?"

Peter felt like strangling her for the obvious way she was stalling. Meanwhile, one of her hands was busy on his limp sex organ, trying to instill life into its lifeless shape. She was working her little heart out—to no avail.

"Huerta's men kidnapped ju in El Paso. Word came to the *jefe,* and Little Fox has been worried to death over you. Not far from us is Cuidad Obregon, a village taken by General Obregon. Soon Pancho and the father of Little Fox will contest each other in a battle to end all battles. Before all theese happens, Obregon will come here for a holiday to prepare for the beeg explosions."

"Y'all mean ah'm heah under the auspices of President Huerta?" asked Peter, trying to tie in her words to something plausible.

"No, Capitán Duprez," said a voice standing in the doorway. "You are here under the auspices of General Alvaro Obregon."

Lucia jumped from the bed and, gathering her clothing instantly, began dressing with lowered, shame-filled eyes. She glanced at Major General Felipe de Cordoba, waiting to be severely chastised for her feeble attempts at performing an act of liaison between Villa and Peter Duprez.

"Ah'm not certain what all ya heard," said Peter, pulling on his trousers, "but ah'd appreciate it if no harm comes ta the girl."

"Sorry. She'll receive the same treatment all spies receive," he snapped curtly. "Corporal," he called to the guard outside the door. "Take the girl away and lock her in the servants' quarters under guard. I'll attend to her later." He spoke in clipped, precise tones. He remained silent until Lucia left the room with her escort.

"Look," began Peter. "She said nothing. Nothing at all. Ah don't want any harm to come ta her, heah?"

"I admire your chivalry, Capitán Duprez of the Gringo Brigade, but the matter is out of my hands. I don't handle matters for the Secret Service anymore. I am attached to the Fourth Sonora Battalion under the leadership of General Alvaro Obregon. I report directly to him."

"Then you'll promise nothing will happen to the girl?"

"I promise you nothing. Now let's get down to business. We learned through our sources of Huerta's proposed treachery to entrap you in an effort to obstruct Madelaina Obregon, whom I'm sure you understand is the daughter of my commanding general. Despite their political differences, she is, after all, his one and only kin. He wants no harm to befall her at Huerta's hands," said Felipe, unbuttoning his tunic. He removed his snap-brimmed hat and flung it on a table. "Mind if I smoke?"

Peter extended his arm nonchalantly. "Ah'm youah guest, suh. Y'all do just what ya wish, heah?" Peter grew more aware with each passing moment that he was being scrutinized closely by his host. He began to feel a little ill at ease, being stared at by this handsome Mexican officer.

"You understand, *señor*, that if we hadn't intervened, your destiny might have been far more gruesome than this country club atmosphere so generously provided for you."

"Why is it, suh, that the moah you keep talking, the moah ah keep thinking the more gruesome fate might have been less involved?"

"Hardly," replied Felipe, pouring himself a tumbler of tequila. He downed it in two gulps. "Uuuuggghhh," he shuddered. "Why I ever drink this uncivilized fire is beyond me. Mind if I ring for wine?" He pulled the cord at the side of the bed.

Peter remained silent, as he lit a cigarette and puffed on it thoughtfully.

"You are well aware that Pancho Villa's victories

772

have been numerous of late. Have you also been aware that General Obregon has, for a specific purpose, refused to contest Villa? He has to date not sided with Huerta—although he's obligated dutifully to his country with a zealous fervor. He is also *not* committed to Carranza who appears to be the favorite for presidential material. At present, U.S. Generals Hugh Scott and John Pershing are making a report to your American President Wilson on the merits of General Villa. Before General Obregon commits his loyalty to any future president, he wants to make certain his efforts will put the right man in the presidential palace. I'm certain you can understand his concern for both his country and his people."

Peter laughed lightly. He uncrossed his legs and glanced at Felipe through amused eyes. "Ah understand, all right. Ah see that General Obregon has political aspirations that go beyond being general of the Mexican Army."

"Very clever of you to be so discerning. You're right. One day General Obregon will be president of Mexico. No one deserves it more. He has many fine friends across the Yankee border. He's a temperate man with a deep compassion for his fellow man. He's not an incompetent weakling as was Madero whose enemies found him out and made short order of him. His veins don't run rampant with graft and corruption as did his former countryman, Profirio Diaz. Nor does he maintain or support the alcoholic excesses of Huerta or entertain the delusions of grandeur running rampant in his drug-crazed mind. Damnit, Duprez, Huerta's propensity for political assassinations grows more obscene each day and his policies toward your country are nothing short of antagonistic."

"Felipe de Cordoba!" exclaimed Peter in sudden recollection. "Youah Madelaina's friend. Her deah, trusted, and devoted friend. She's spoken about ya often." His face lit up brightly, as he studied the handsome, clean-cut features.

"And you are the gringo husband of Madelaina Obregon," replied Felipe. "The man she sacrificed a royal life to be with. I have long wondered about you, *señor*. I must add, my feelings are not as generous as yours. I have loved Madelaina all my life and probably always will. I find it horrifying that you influenced her to abandon her way of life for one so foul and oppressive. My blood turns cold when I recall how I first saw her after a year as a *campesina* in the camps of Pancho Villa. For this alone, I loathe you."

Peter shrank internally and maintained his outer calm. "If it hadn't been me who opened her mind to the world around her, it might have been someone less concerned foah her welfare, someone who might have loved her less," he said soberly.

A servant brought a tray with wine and crystal glasses. Felipe nodded to her, dismissing her. He poured the wine himself. One for him and one for Peter. He handed the goblet to his guest. They toasted silently and sipped the ruby liquid.

"Ah, much better. A civilized drink, fit for a god," said Felipe, smacking his lips. He sat down in a comfortable chair. "Suppose we get down to business."

"Ah'd like that," replied Peter. Despite Felipe's cold assessment of Peter, the Texan found himself liking the officer in some odd indefinable way.

"My general wishes you to arrange a rendezvous with General Pancho Villa. He wishes to speak with the former *guerrillo* to see where his intentions lie."

Peter's ears perked up instantly. "Y'all realize what youah asking?"

"Believe me, it surprises me as much as it does you."

"Phew." Peter whistled low. He could just picture this confrontation, and the scene he saw wasn't one that might settle any case of indigestion easily.

"There must, of course, be no treachery, no traps, no subversive machinations to do the other in."

"On both sides," added Peter.

774

"Naturally."

"And that's all?"

"Not quite."

"What then?"

"Your promise to return Madelaina to her father, in exchange for your life and freedom."

Peter's blue eyes grew murky, the color of a stormy sea. "She's mah wife. Y'all ask too much."

"You work it out. Those are the terms and conditions."

"If ah refuse ta comply?"

"We turn you over to Huerta's man, Major General Simon Salomon. You'll spend your days at Madrigal in their den of hell."

"Mah life and freedom are worthless without Madelaina," he told Felipe.

Felipe studied Duprez. "I'm glad you made that apparent. At least I can see why she picked you."

"Besides, ah don't reckon Madelaina would go fer that at all. We've been through too much ta have it all end like the devastation done by one of Villa's tacos."

"Are you aware, *señor,* that during the past year that you've been absent from your *mujer,* she's become Pancho's *numero uno soldadera*? You might say she's become an astute adviser to the *premier jefe.* Is that the kind of life you wish for her?"

"None of us wish foah a life of strife, suh. We are born ta do what we must do ta help ease the pain of others less fortunate. We can't turn from the suffering and weah blinkuhs foah the rest o' ouah born days."

"I haven't the time to exchange philosophies, Señor Duprez. My duty has been completed. Now ah await your reply."

"How can ya be shuah ah'll comply with youah request, General? Once ah get outside these heah walls and join up with Villa, ah just might take my woman and cut for the borduh."

"Ah have no doubt you'll be a man of your word, *señor,*" he said calmly. "You see, we have in our possession the insurance needed to make certain you'll return."

"And that is—"

"*Your son.*"

Chapter 29

Madelaina had hardly slept since the abduction of her son. What meager sleep she did get had been a series of nightmares and obsessions which drove her to near hysteria and caused her to awaken, screaming in the night. Who could have been so cruel as to pluck a helpless three-month-old child from the comfort and security of his mother's breasts? In her son's case, born prematurely and in need of tender loving care, his sudden departure compounded her feelings of insecurity and fright.

Antonetta had offered her solace as best she could and in a way helped to subdue the rising hysterics to which Madelaina was prone to give vent in those few weeks following the infant's disappearance. Even General Villa took time from his countless warring strategies to comfort Little Fox. But there were no words, no expressions of sympathy or consolation to assuage the apprehensive fears for her sanity.

Madelaina had endured too many hardships during those early months of pregnancy: hard, fast riding on horseback, long, tedious journeys, battles and skirmishes where she suffered wounds and bruises. She shot her rifles at the enemy as her growing fetus kicked in her womb protestingly. The morning sickness, the near abortion when she hemorrhaged for a time, it had all been enough tribulation for the dedicated militant. Prior to the height of her pregnancy, she mixed in battle with the other *soldaderas*, expecting no favors, demanding no quarters or special privileges, and finally she delivered the child prematurely, a love child whom she doted on each moment up until she found him missing at her side.

For days following her son's disappearance she searched everywhere, asked everyone she met about the child. She wouldn't eat, wouldn't rest, barely handled her duties. Even after General Villa ordered her to rest, to remove herself from the front lines of battle, she resisted, insisting she had to keep busy to preserve her sanity. When it appeared her child was lost to her forever, it was a different Madelaina who plunged into her duties with a dedicated fervor. She grew silent, more introverted, performed her duties with the movements of an automaton without complaint or comment.

She walked barefoot when necessary, rode when horses became available, stole boots of dead *Federales* encountered in battle, gathered the much-needed weapons and clothing from the corpses of the dead, and continued to train the new *soldaderas* who multiplied in droves after each battle. On orders from General Villa himself, and out of respect for Madelaina's position of trust as an advisor—although Villa hardly let it be known that any woman advised him—the men from various brigades kept their distance.

It was General Villa's orders that Madelaina and Antonetta be heavily chaperoned at all times. However, so as not to incite the girls or add to their frustrations, the fact was known to neither of them. Colonel Rudolfo Fierro, who'd arrived a few military skirmishes back and made himself invaluable to Pancho Villa, had long since attached himself to the *jefe* with a fierce, dedicated loyalty not often seen among the stoic hillsmen. It was only natural that Fierro, always close at hand, would be appointed the honor of keeping his eyes on the women when he wasn't occupied in warring duties.

Even before Madelaina had discovered the affair blooming between Fierro and her alluring red-haired friend, the colonel had demonstrated an unusual fascination for both women. Madelaina had felt his probing, animal eyes on her from the day of his arrival at camp, and after that day she saw him with Antonetta in San Martine, she wondered if he knew she was aware of the affair.

On this day, Madelaina scuffled through the raw lights of an early pink sunset toward the adobe *casa* housing Antonetta. Weighted down by crisscrossed *bandoleros* of ammunition, hip holsters, and guns, she carried a rifle in her hand. Her orange and yellow cotton skirt and blouse were soiled. She was covered from head to toe with the eternal red dust of the desert. Sweat rolled off her face and streaks of dirt diffused any beauty that might be lurking under the mask of dust. The dust she raised scuttling among the *campesinas* turned the color of red clay and followed her like a cloud.

She felt dirty, tired, and exhausted when she entered the adobe dwelling.

Antonetta looked up, pausing as she spread out the remains of her tattered clothing. "Ju know how many times I ask Pancho to buy me some suitable clothing, *chica*? Time and time again. But there ees never time for Antonetta!" She sniffed the air distastefully. "*Dios mios!* What happened to ju? Ju know ju stink, *chica*?" She held her nose repugnantly.

"I know. I know. Ride with me to the River Yaqui, *chica*, to bathe and wash out some clothes. It's early. The sun will dry our clothing before we finish bathing." She shook her head at the redhead playfully. "Why don't you wear pants and a shirt, *chica*? I'm finished wearing skirts! It's too much trouble!"

"And be made laughingstock by the men?" Tonetta wasn't up to hearing cat calls each moment of the day, nor was she able to endure the wrath of Pancho himself who detested pants on a woman. "I will wear what I always wear. But in truth, I grow more disenchanted with everything rapidly," she confided to Little Fox.

"*Vamenos,*" replied Madelaina. "We can talk as we bathe in the water. You know for how long I've been dreaming of a bath?"

"From the stink of you, plenty long," retorted the redhead, grabbing her clean clothing and the soiled

779

garments she planned to wash in the river. She rolled them up and strapped the pack to her back. She buckled on a hip holster and gun and followed her friend back along the dusty path toward the corral.

Colonel Rudolfo Fierro, leaning languidly against a wooden support beam in the portico listening to a few of his comrades make jokes, tipped his sombrero forward. Under the shade of the large brim, his dark, beady eyes followed the two women until they mounted their horses and rode off in a northwesterly direction. Desire, craftily concealed behind his cold eyes, was instantly checked so as not to give away his feelings to the other men.

The women found the water delightful. After scrubbing out their soiled garments with bars of soap, they rinsed them out and spread them to dry on a sun-baked boulder at the bend in the Yaqui River, which was hidden by thickets and shrubbery from the passing eye. For a time they swam nude, and then they each took turns soaping their long hair and washing it squeaky clean. They frolicked for a time, like uncaring children, then, when they were spent, they relaxed naked and lazed in the hot sun, close to the jacaranda trees.

Antonette picked up on the conversation they'd begun earlier as if there'd been no break in the continuity. She reflected on her disenchantment at the substantial change in Pancho Villa's comportment and attitude. More than the noticeable change in the *jefe*, she protested the burning presence of Rudolfo Fierro.

"*Dios mios, chiquita*, how in the name of God did Pancho take up with such a barbarian?" she asked in a voice that seemed testy and guileful to Little Fox.

"Ask Pancho," retorted Madelaina, glancing sharply at the other woman.

"*Que va*, ask Pancho? Ju think I'm crazy? Since Fierro arrives in Pancho's domain, he tells me nothing." The redhead lifted herself up on one elbow off the grassy knoll on the riverbank and shook out her damp hair. She glanced at Madelaina's frail body and

780

shook her head negatively. "Ju better put some meat on those flanks, *chica*, or no man will look at ju when this hell of revolution ends."

Madelaina laughed gently, shaded her eyes with her hand, and turned to glance at the stunning redhead with turquoise eyes reflecting a thousand suns.

"Tell me, Tonetta, why do you stay? Why subject yourself to these gross inconveniences when you could be back in El Paso living like a grand lady? You have no stomach for revolution—for fighting, shooting, none of this."

"Listen, why ju think I grow disenchanted? Of late, Tonetta thinks more and more of the life she left behind. Why do I stay? Ah, *chica*. Why for sure? I stay because I love Panchito. But I begin to question such dedication. Each day I ask myself more and more why I stay. Shall I tell you something? Each day I cannot answer myself, so you see?" She shook out her hair to dry. "It's crazy, no? I do not see Pancho. He is too busy to make love with me as in the past. Oh, *querida*," she sighed despondently. "I admit I am not born to such a life. Even ju—why ju stay? From where comes such dedication? Ju don't love Pancho like Tonetta loves Pancho?"

"You think the love of a man could keep me here?" she asked.

"The love of a man drew you to such a life."

"That was long ago."

"Then why ju stay?"

"Because—because—" Madelaina faltered. "Because I have no place to go."

"*Que va*, no place to go? Ju married William Benson, no? Ju can go to the hacienda of Benson and remain his wife. Listen, you recall that hacienda a few kilometers outside of Juarez, where Pancho camped before the battle?"

Madelaina reached over and took a few rolled marijuana cigarettes from the saddle bag, where she placed her leather pouch, given her by Tolomeo. She struck a red devil against the rock and lit one. She took a few hits from it and handed it to Tonetta. The redhead puffed and inhaled deeply, then falling against the rock, she said cryptically. "Like jur earrings, it's called Seven Moons, just like the *rancho* from where Pancho and me and the others took you, near Amarillo."

Madelaina glanced sharply again at her friend. Did she know in some way that Peter and Benson were father and son? She hadn't mentioned it—ever. Had she?

"You know I can never return to him. It's useless to even discuss the subject." Breathing deeply, she allowed a relaxation to overtake her. She needed this rest off by herself. For so long she'd been wound up like a spring, tense enough to snap. She'd been cold, hard, and unemotional for so long, she was afraid she'd lost all her feelings. Since her baby had been kidnapped, she had closed everyone from her.

"Only the other day, I tell Panchito this man Fierro frightens me. Pancho laughed. He told me Fierro is valuable to him, that he was a first-class brakeman who works on trains—that he can even send messages through the air—"

"You mean telegrams?" She puzzled at Antonetta's line of talk.

"*Si*, whatever." Antonetta spoke in Spanish, so she could ramble without stumbling over her pigeon yankee. "That desert weasel Tomás Urbino found Fierro when Pancho was in the *calabozo*. It seems that Fierro is an A-number one combat leader in whom Pancho finds no fault. I protested that he was too bloodthirsty and shall I tell you what Pancho replied?"

Before Madelaina could answer, Antonetta's outrage accelerated. "Pancho said, 'True, my little kitten, the man is a bastard. But when it comes to war, he's the kind I want—not saints.'"

Madelaina managed a slight smile. "Pancho makes sense, no?"

"Oh, ju are terrible!" she exploded in pigeon yankee. "What can I expect to hear from a woman who has become a man—hard like a rock, eh? You and Pancho are alike! Ju know what else Pancho tells

782

me? He swore Fierro killed more than 100 artillerymen by himself—at one time!"

Madelaina's eyes widened. "Without exaggeration—100 at one time?" Her eyes tilted playfully in mild tolerance.

"Urbina saw it with his own eyes. Fierro told the Redflaggers to get off the train. He lined them up along the tracks and told them he was going to kill them. With a .45 in each hand and two aides walking alongside him to hand him loaded pistols when the bullets in each gun ran out, he shot them all."

"Every last one?" She subdued her mirth as she listened to Tonetta's exaggeration.

"Ayeiii, Little Fox. Every last one. That story is what made Pancho take notice of such a man—no, such an animal! And now, I tell you, Madelaina, they are two of a kind—Villa and Fierro. Fierce, bloodthirsty, irresistible, and of late, *muy* frightening to me. Pancho is not like *my* Pancho of the early revolution. He means business this time and it is this business which frightens me."

Madelaina, still naked, sat up on the rock and drew her knees up to her and rested her chin on them. She took a last puff from the rolled grass and flipped it into the water and watched it disappear in the ripple.

"We are none of us the way we were in the early days of the revolution." She turned to face the redhead. "Tonetta, if you feel so strongly against Fierro, why do you let him make love to you?" she asked impatiently.

Antonetta's face grew redder than her hair. She stammered, stuttered, and her lips quivered as she searched for the proper response. She knew that somehow Madelaina had guessed her secret. It was of no use to pretend or to continue to play the silly game.

"How long have you known?"

"Almost from the beginning, I suppose."

"From the beginning?"

"One day at San Martine . . . before the birth of my son."

783

"Ahhh," she said knowingly, recalling that wonderful summer day. "That was the first time." Her eyes filled with mysterious lights she alone was privy to.

"Why do you humiliate yourself by calling him a beast, an animal?"

"So no one guesses what I feel for him."

"And what of Pancho?"

Antonetta shrugged. "He has his Lucita."

"You know what it would mean if he discovers your treachery?"

"I know. I know. I cannot help myself. If he didn't leave me alone so much—"

"What if someone like Urbina had seen you—or any of those other *campesinas* who would gladly pull out your hair, just for a chance to taste Pancho's passions?"

Antonetta shrugged as if she had no control over destiny.

"Think it over, *chiquita*. Think it over very carefully what you and Fierro do at this critical time. Earlier you said they are two of a kind, both Villa and Fierro. That Pancho is not like *your* Pancho of the early revolution. That his business frightens you. *Bueno.* You are far too smart, *gatitta*, to not know how all of us—you, me, Pancho, Fierro, Urbina, Richards—all of us have changed. What is it that makes you disloyal to both men, now? Are you afraid you'll lose Fierro to the same cause as that which Villa has committed himself?"

"I don't know what I think," Antonetta pouted. "I know only that it's Pancho I truly love, but I need a man, too. Sometimes I get so mad—so mad I see fire. Then I go find Fierro. I know I am playing a dangerous game of passions, but sometimes I don't care what happens." Antonetta was breathless.

"It's not enough the *jefe* has to think of all Mexico, but you make for him so many more complications? The small games you play can only end in a passionate manner—bloody and deadly with the sacrifice of one or all three. And for what? Pray tell me for what?" persisted Madelaina. "Listen, *querida*, you above all should know that it's time for survival and victory, not for death and defeat. Thank God we're on the side of the victors. *Dios mios,* Antonetta, you've seen what's happened to those who've been defeated—the wastelands of death left behind us."

"Exactly. For what do you think I've been talking?"

"You expect perfection. It can't be that way. All we've seen—all we've done must affect us. Only one side can win. God, let it be us!"

"Can it not be done another way? Can it not be discussed and negotiated, this hard business of war?"

"If we were dealing with men of honor—men who kept their words—men who believe in humanity instead of its destruction—perhaps. But there are no such men in Mexico, *chica*. The *Federales* are trained to kill, not to barter or negotiate. The *Rurales* are murderers who have no use for the spoken word. Only those who provide them with food, clothing, and shelter are they loyal to. And the *Colorados*—well, they do what they must, just as the others do. They remain loyal to the men they believe in."

"Then we are hopeless as well as helpless to the butchery that pervades our land?" Antonetta paused a moment. "If that is true, how can I believe in what Pancho is doing? How can you be loyal to such a butcher?"

"Antonetta!" Madelaina glanced up sharply at her friend. She glanced about the thicket, frantically worried. "Be careful of your words. You never know who is listening."

"Why? I speak only the truth. Pancho knows how I feel—that I grow more disenchanted each day Fierro is in our company. Villa and Fierro are destined for each other. I know it. Pancho is certain of it. Listen, *chica*, you don't think I know that Pancho Villa—Don Francesco Villa—has become bigger than the revolution itself? You know the adulation Pancho had for Madero? Well, it is now the same. It is Fierro who adores Villa. He is ready to die for the *jefe*! And each day Pancho grows more determined to crush Huerta, as if fuel has been put into his hands by Fierro. Even if it means joining Carranza to oust Huerta! Such complications!"

"If Fierro adores Villa, why does he seduce his woman? You are frightened of losing both, is that it? You intend to play one against the other?" Madelaina was aghast. "Is that the game you play? It isn't worthy of you, *chica*."

"Then it's time for Tonetta to leave Pancho—and Fierro."

Madelaina's eyes widened in fearful speculation. "Pancho will be crushed, *chica*. Listen, I'd hate to venture a guess on Fierro's response after seeing you two together."

"It's not true. Pancho won't notice I am gone. He has not come to me in many weeks. If he doesn't make haste, Tonetta will throw discretion to the winds. She will make her affair with Fierro no longer a secret. Then see the sparks fly," she said with devilish lights in her eyes.

"Tonetta! You wouldn't dare! You realize what will happen? Chihuahua! A minor revolution! Oh, *chiquita*, you expect too much from Pancho. *Dios mios*, look at the advances made by the Revolutionary Army, at the gains we've made. Without Pancho we are lost!"

"And what of me? Does it no longer matter that without him Tonetta would be lost?"

"The revolution is bigger than any of us. Look how many have died that Pancho Villa might lead Mexico to freedom. You can't even think of breaking up Villa and Fierro."

"Why wouldn't I dare break up the Villa-Fierro alliance? Fierro broke up the Villa-Antonetta alliance, didn't he? Besides, what do I care for advances if no advances are made to Tonetta. Maybe I do this before I go, eh? Stir up the kettle good."

"Go? Where will you go? Why are you acting so crazy, *chica*?" insisted Madelaina with overwhelming emotion. "You can't do this to Pancho and you can't

786

leave him either, not now. We can't both leave at the same time."

"Ju, too?" asked the flabbergasted redhead.

"I must find my baby," she said with sudden desperation.

Tonetta's compassion was superseded by an instant intelligence in such matters. "In this land, ju think you can find one little *niño*?" She reverted to her pigeon yankee. Tonetta's instinct made her pause and glance curiously about the immediate area.

"I must. Don't you see, I must."

"Jur crazy. Ees best ju stay under protection of the *jefe*. I will go to El Paso. Ees easy to find me when this mess is finished."

"If you go, I go." Madelaina studied her friend's uneasy comportment. "What's the matter, *chica*—"

Before either of them could move or speak, a loud voice assaulted them from behind.

"Ees more better if you both remain here."

Madelaina and Antonetta made a quick scramble for their guns and were instantly subdued and restrained by two uniformed *Rurales*, military police who stepped on their weapons, preventing their use. With powerful blows struck at them, the women were sent reeling off their feet. Felled by the unexpected clouting done in whirlwind fashion, the women were too stunned and stricken to make a break.

Crouching on all fours, Madelaina tried springing to her feet. She was coldly struck across the face by one of the *Rurales*, a heavily moustached man with a thin-lipped, vicious smile, and sent reeling back off her feet again. Tonetta fought like a cat, clawing, scratching, kicking, and struggling fiercely to free herself of the other man's clutches.

Madelaina called to her in English, hoping these cruel, Cossack-trained beasts didn't understand. "Play coy," she pleaded in silky, sugary tones. "Pretend to cooperate. Don't fight or it will go worse for both of us. Let them have their fill, then, at the right moment,

787

we'll surprise them, *chica*." She could feel the welts and weals rise on her face and swell.

Instantly both girls became docile, seductively batting their eyelids like the lowliest of whores in Villa's camp.

"It's not necessary to rape us, *Capitán*," said Madelaina in her most seductive, whorish manner. "Not when we are both willing."

The *capitán*, called Gerardo, smiled wickedly. "Very well then, woman, let's see you cooperate." He unbuttoned his trousers and removed his swollen penis, brandishing it about like a valor badge, his black eyes glittering evilly.

"Like that—like an animal in heat? Take off your jacket, remove all your clothing so I can feel the strength of your body flowing through mine," cooed Madelaina.

Gerardo grabbed Madelaina's hair, twisted it hard, and pulled her into him. "You will fuck me the way I am, you hear, woman! If I desire to perform the act with my clothing on, it is my business. But you try one funny thing and I'll slit your lying throat. Now, lay down and spread your legs."

Madelaina complied.

Antonetta was dealt with more severely when she snuggled against a corporal named Hugo. Her hands trailed behind him toward the holster at his hips. In a quick, sudden blow, he smacked her hard against the ground. Hugo dropped his trousers and fell upon the redhead, panting. The smell of uncleanliness made Antonetta want to retch, yet she tried to encourage Hugo. With both arms pinned back, it was difficult for her to function. Her eyes darted to the grassy mound where Madelaina's saddle bag lay open. If she could maneuver him two feet over, she could grasp Madelaina's knife laying partially hidden from view. She began to coo, protesting that she couldn't make him feel the real enjoyment he would if he only permitted her to cooperate. "Just let me put my arms around your neck—let me move my hips the way a woman is taught to do by the very nature of her body," she whispered to him, "and I'll make this a time you'll remember for the rest of your days."

Madelaina wasn't faring as well. The *capitán*, a suspicious, hard-line military policeman, wasn't the kind to want more than to relieve the need in his groin. He didn't care for the artful ways of love. He wanted instant relief for the load he carried. When she asked him to smoke a marijuana cigarette, to make him feel more mellow, he laughed at her.

"You think I am a wet-nosed *niño*, still suckling my mother's breast, whore."

"But even tequila would serve us better. You are so tense, so tight, and so hard, *amigo*," she said in her sultriest drawl. "I am used to being used by men, but I tell you, *hombre*, you need more pleasuring than you take." She forced a light laugh and threw her head back teasingly so he had a chance to appraise her more fully. "I am a little too thin perhaps for your tastes, *mi capitán*, but others have found my treasures more enjoyable."

"You have tequila, whore?"

"On my horse is a bottle in a leather pouch. I'll get it."

"No. You come with me. Any funny business and I promise to slit your throat. No one will miss you, *comprender?*"

"*Si, mi Capitán*," she whispered meekly. *Haughty, proud-faced bastards, All you Cossack-trained sons of whoring pigs,* she told herself as she permitted herself to be dragged to the horse. *I'll fix your unworthy souls.* The taste of rage was bitter as bile in her throat. She glanced cautiously at Antonetta to see how she fared and noticed the girl was edging toward the open saddle bag. *Muy bien, the sex kitten has a head on her shoulders.*

The *capitán* found the bottle, and holding it in one hand, he dragged Madelaina back to the grassy knoll. He shoved her to the ground, kneeled over her, and removed the cork from the bottle with his teeth. "Now, drink, girl. You want the tequila."

Madelaina took the bottle from his hand and, raising the bottle to her lips, locked eyes with his in a teasing, taunting, seductive roll of her eyes. So fascinated was he with the promise buried in those dark, wicked eyes, he failed to see her movements. Faster than he could see, she threw the contents of the bottle into his eyes, blinding him with the gasoline. Gerardo bounced back, screaming in alarm and pain. In the space of those split seconds, Madelaina rolled over and picked up the rifle from the ground and opened fire. Thunder exploded all around her.

Hugo, faster than lightning, rolled over on top of Antonetta, grabbed the knife she'd reached for, and plunged it into her neck. By the time Madelaina aimed the weapon at him and pulled the trigger, the rifle was empty. She panicked as she scanned the area looking for a weapon—anything to use against him. Hugo lifted his gun and pulled the trigger, aiming it at Madelaina. Simultaneously two more shots were fired, then two more. It all happened so quickly, she didn't know what happened. The scene was a madhouse of powerful explosions, sights, and sounds.

She saw the *capitán* rise from where he'd fallen in the momentary confusion and pain of blindness. He reached for his holstered gun and fired blindly at anyone and everything in his immediate range. No question that his eyesight, impaired by the fiery liquid, incurred a vengeful anger and he'd gone berserk in an attempt to retaliate in some equal measure to the whore responsible.

Madelaina saw him spin around from the impact of bullets fired at him from some distant point. He whirled like a drunken man unsure of his footing and moved out along the riverbank where he was felled by a round of shots. Madelaina fell to the ground, glancing about, trying to locate the source of the shots. She crept, half-crawled to her clothing, shimmied into her skirt and blouse, her heart beating so fast she felt it would burst.

It was at that moment she looked for Antonetta. When she saw the ribbon of blood banding her friend's neck, her own knife buried to the hilt in it, she screamed and ran to her side without care or concern for the sniper shooting at them.

She kneeled over the girl, her troubled eyes sweeping the redhead's frightening wounds. She reached in and pulled the abominable and obscene weapon from Tonetta's body and dropped it as if it had suddenly turned to live coals in her hands. Swiftly she tore at her petticoat and wrapped the wounds about the girl's neck. Then, as no life emerged from the girl, she cradled her in her arms, rocking her gently to and fro.

"Tonetta," she whimpered. "No, *querida*, not you, my dearest, sweetest friend." Tears streamed down her face. "*Querida*, what will I do without your friendship? What will Pancho do without you? Fierro?"

Faint gurgling sounds came from Antonetta as her eyes fluttered open. Those sparkling, emerald eyes of jewels and blue seas grew duller and duller.

"Go, *querida*," she could barely whisper. "Go while you can. Tell Pancho I will wait for him in the land of our ancestors." Her eyes lit up once more before fading to a murky blue. Sobbing, Madelaina pressed her fingertips over the girl's eyes, closing them for the last time. She crossed herself. "*Dios mios*, take care of this woman. She was the best woman who walked the earth," she said in supplication.

The sound of a twig snapping startled her. Now, only survival counted. She tensed, slipped her arms from around the dead girl's body, and crept back into the bushes, alerted like an animal. She reached for her Obregon automatic, gripped it tightly in her hands, and pulled her saddle bag close to her. Instantly she slipped the leather chamois pouch around her neck. Her hand instinctively felt for her lower abdomen, for the area of the solar plexus, and she silently prayed for strength. Whoever it was stalking about was as clever as she, she told herself, when after several moments with her ear to the ground, she heard only the wild beating of her own heart.

Like the silent whisper of the wind after a storm, she felt the presence of another being. She felt the slight pressure of a hand on her shoulder before she reacted and with a gasp sprang to her feet, ready to do combat.

"Consider yourself fortunate, Senóra Little Fox," said the unsmiling, sober-eyed, and cautious Rudolfo Fierro. "If I hadn't been so fascinated by the charms of Antonetta and followed you two women, you'd have fallen heir to a worse fate." He paused, his eyes sweeping the ground where Antonetta lay dead.

The terrible Fierro—the man whom Antonetta found most threatening in her recent world—moved to her side and knelt on one knee to stare at the sight of the broken woman. He shook his head in disbelief, picked up strands of her red hair, the fascinating red hair with which he'd been mesmerized since he first joined with Pancho Villa, and let it lay like a satin ribbon of fire across his rough, callused hands. He pulled it in close to his face and lay his cheek on it, feeling its softness, delighting hedonistically in the color of fire and the smell of cleanliness. It was a baffling ritual, totally unexpected from a Rudolfo Fierro. Watching him in rapt absorption, Madelaina found the scene incredible. Here, the man Antonetta labeled a barbarian was as gentle with her as she'd seen him the first time with the redhead. No question, Fierro on the battlefield was every bit as hard-hitting, brutal, and bloodthirsty as Tonetta had described. Now, watching him, so vulnerable as tears spilled from those ferocious black eyes, the evil of the man was erased.

He leaned over and tenderly picked up the dead girl's nude body in his arms as if she were the most precious thing on earth to him. He accepted the blanket Madelaina handed him from her bedroll and wrapped it around Tonetta. Slowly, he walked to his horse and draped his saddle with the inert body. He turned to

Little Fox as he removed a Bowie knife from his thigh sheath.

"It's important we go quickly to inform the *jefe* of this atrocity. You wait, only a moment," he told her. He walked over to where Hugo the *Rurale* lay dead, his blood spilled in the dirt. "This is the pig who killed her?"

Madelaina nodded, wondering what he was up to. Fierro leaned over and hacked off the man's bloodied hand. He wrapped it in the *Rurale*'s kerchief and tied it to his belt without a flicker or trace of emotion on his features.

Madelaina felt sick. She wanted to vomit. Controlling herself, she followed him back to the horses and both mounted their steeds. She noticed that Fierro gently picked up the body of Antonetta and cradled her in his arms, as he urged the black stallion into position. They galloped off swiftly, the fading sun at their backs, and returned to Villa's encampment. *Dios mios,* he was in love with Antonetta. Only love could exact such a performance, she thought.

It was a strange sight to see Rudolfo Fierro, credited with being the fiercest of Villa's men, sitting tall in his saddle, like a king returning from a conquest, holding in his arms a queen for sacrifice. Information reached Pancho Villa's ears even before the unusual riders rode into the draw. It was a funereal procession fit for royalty. And Madelaina promised herself to remember it for all eternity. There was a lesson to be learned here—but what it was she had yet to know. They continued in a slow canter as if to some funeral dirge heard only in Fierro's mind. He stopped his horse before Pancho Villa, who had stepped out of the rundown, confiscated hacienda, and stood at attention.

Fierro raised his left leg, turned his body, and slid off the sadde of his stallion, still holding Antonetta. His eyes, without expression, looked glazed as he stared at Pancho Villa. So intent was the message in his eyes that Pancho himself was unable to remove his own eyes from those so compelling as Fierro's. Only when Fierro stood before him and extended the blanketed body to Villa, did the *premier jefe* remove his eyes from the other's and look down at the body in his arms. Fierro snapped off the blanket as a magician might do in a famous table trick when he miraculously separates a cloth from the table keeping the china intact. Then he draped her nudity with it, baring only the incredible red hair.

Villa stared down at the body of his beloved Antonetta in a state of disbelief and shock. He glanced up at the circle of faces moved by curiosity to witness this strange happening. The Indians removed their sombreros, reverently stunned by what they saw. Their brown-skinned fingers formed the sign of the cross.

A hush fell over the courtyard as hundreds began to gather. Word traveled swiftly. When something touched the heart of Pancho Villa, it touched his people. General Villa turned, the body in his arms, and he entered the adobe hacienda as a silent storm of unanswered questions assaulted his senses.

The women hurried inside, preparing for the angels of death to descend upon the house of Pancho Villa. Upstairs, taking the steps one at a time, Villa moved like a phantom toward the bedroom, where he hadn't spent enough time with Antonetta. Inside the bedroom, he moved toward the bed and gently placed his beloved sex kitten on it. In the pulsating silence, he turned to the others, and they knew without words that he wished to be alone with the corpse of his beloved Antonetta. They shuffled out, compassion overflowing their hearts, and closed the door behind them.

Inside Pancho knelt by the side of the bed. He lifted her slender white hands and placed them over her breasts. He pulled a coverlet from the end of the bed as if she were sleeping and he wanted to ward off any possible chill. Suddenly a huge sob wracked his body. He leaned over, his face on her breasts and sobbed like a child.

"*Dios mios*, why did you have to take her? She was a good woman. As good as they came. Forgive me for being so busy with the business of this goddamned war. Oh, my little *gatitta*. Pancho loved you as he loved life itself." He stroked her hair off her fragile white face, which grew more waxen as the lines of fatigue faded.

Sometime in the next few hours, while Pancho Villa grieved his beloved in the custom and manners of his ancestors, the women entered the room unnoticed by their *jefe*. They had brought candles and lit them at either side of the bed. They brought flowers and commenced to silently arrange them as best they could.

Outside the door, Rudolfo Fierro stood guard, his face a stoic mask. He seemed unmoving, like a giant force of power protecting his *jefe* from any outside interference during his private grief. No one, not even Tomàs Urbina dared to violate that inner sanctum. He talked with the others outside, and they all wondered how it happened and who was responsible. Not even Madelaina could be approached in this blackest hour of Villa's life. She was as silent and uncommunicative as Fierro. Until Pancho Villa learned what happened, none other would know.

Madelaina sat in the downstairs salon of the delapidated hacienda. She was hunched over at the end of the leather sofa, smoking endless cigarettes, her eyes swollen with tears.

She saw Rosalia Quintera and Lucia San Miguel from a distance as they walked with Captain Tracy Richards toward the open front doors of the *casa*. She blinked hard. The sun was setting and the shadows playing funny tricks on her caused her to avert her eyes, then glance back at the foursome. Three, she had recognized. But the fourth, a man, she hadn't been able to see as well, since the hot sun glittered on something bright and metallic, possibly a belt buckle?

The Gringo Brigade in their dusty beige trousers and shirts moved in and surrounded the foursome obstructing them from view. Then came members of the other various brigades as they hailed the newcomers with subdued voices. The sun, it seemed, disappeared behind a mountain in the distance. There was no mistaking the free-swinging hips of Rosalia Quintera nor the carefree attitude in which she swung her naturally curly hip-length auburn hair. Even Lucia was the same, thought Madelaina. Then she saw him. There was no mistaking him. She'd know that tall, swaggering walk any place. His face was shielded by a dusty sombrero, shrugged forward on his head, but not enough to disguise his handsome features from her. He seemed taller than ever. Because he'd lost weight, she wondered.

She saw him pause, shake hands, and embrace several men, backslapping the others affectionately. Madelaina trembled, hardly able to form his name on her quivering lips. His brown hair was longer than she remembered, and the shadow over his upper lip turned out to be a drooping Mexican-styled moustache. It emphasized his lean, reckless face with those azure blue eyes so startling against his coppery skin. As he moved forward, climbing the steps to the main *casa*, her heart pounded as if it would never cease.

Peter Duprez stood in the doorway of the open entrance several moments before his eyes grew accustomed to the dimly lit interior. Then he saw her. Their eyes locked fiercely. Madelaina faltered, stalling for time, unsure if she should be thrilled beyond all belief to see him or angry over the last year of agony he'd inflicted upon her. She watched the expression in his eyes turn to one she didn't recognize. Was it possible they could be like strangers to each other?

Remain detached and aloof, she told herself. Don't let him see how much you really care, how much you ache for him and need him. Hadn't his marriage worked out? Had his wanderlust caused an itch in him to get back into the thick of battle. Hadn't his *wife* objected? These and a thousand other questions filled her with confusion. When the silence between them grew too unnerving, she finally spoke his name, "Peter. How good to see you."

Peter strode toward her, the others respectfully remained outside, permitting them to share their reunion without onlookers. Captain Tracy Richards closed the two front-entry doors and took the women toward his encampment.

The air filled with instant hostility and a venom Madelaina hadn't expected. His voice when he spoke was harsh, sarcastic, and contemptuous.

"I finally found you," he said, adding with scorn, "*Mother.*"

If he'd slapped her, she couldn't have been more astonished. "You have no right," she countered, "no right at all to speak to me in that manner. You married another woman first! Even when you had no legal right to do so!"

"And you did, I suppose? You, a married woman, committed bigamy with your husband's father, adding incest to your already depraved life!"

"Stop it! Stop it at once. I don't care what you think of me. All your words and evil thoughts will have to wait. The angels of death hover over this house tonight, and you can at least hold your vile, vicious thoughts until the mourning is over." She averted her face so he wouldn't study her facial bruises so intently.

Peter's features softened. "Death? Who?"

"Antonetta—the woman of Pancho Villa."

"The sex kitten from the Diamond Slipper?"

Tears brimmed her eyes. She nodded. She was feeling worse now that Peter arrived. It was all wrong, terribly wrong, and she was unable to do anything to set it straight between them.

"Ah'm sorry. Truly sorry," he said, moving toward her. "Y'all must ache inside like a thousand bullet wounds." He reached out to her and embraced her. They melted into each other's arms as if there'd never been any distance between them. When he asked about the welts on her face, she couldn't reply.

It was Peter who pulled back first, a strange and peculiar sensation shooting through him. He felt nothing in his body, just as he'd felt nothing in the arms of Lucia. This, added to the pressing reasons for his arrival here, confused and frustrated him. If he could feel nothing with Madelaina after all this time, then the injury done him by Valerie Townsend had to be permanent.

He shoved her from him almost roughly, his troubled thoughts turned inward. At first he experienced a sensation of hostility and anger toward Valerie, toward the whole goddamn revolution that had gotten him into this mess, toward his own inadequacies and stubborn drives and toward his father who shared prominently in the blame for his fate. He flung open the doors, searched for Tracy Richards, and asked where he could find an adequate supply of whiskey.

Before anyone could reply, Madelaina, with the fleetness of a gazelle, was at his side. "If it's whiskey you want, Peter, there's plenty inside." She closed the door behind them again and led him into the smaller salon, Villa's private office. She opened a locked cabinet and removed a bottle of wine and two glasses. "We might as well celebrate our reunion, eh, gringo?"

"Gringo? Not my husband, lover, long-departed sweetheart? So, it's back to gringo, eh?" His narrowing eyes sent shivers through her.

"What brings you here, Peter?" she asked, trying to remain cool and detached.

"I've been sent on a mission to locate the daughter of General Alvaro Obregon, the wife of William Benson," he said snidely, before drinking the wine.

"Don't you have anything stronger than this?" He glanced behind her in the wall cabinet. "Ah, holding out on me, eh? I'll take the Napoleon brandy," he muttered, taking the decanter from the shelf. He poured an ample amount into a glass.

Madelaina watched him with a concerned expression on her face. She'd never seen him deliberately imbibe alcohol like this. When he gulped down the brandy with hardly a pause, she knew something of a black-hearted nature ate at him. He wiped his lips and his moustache with the back of his hand, and Madelaina, watching him even more inscrutably, felt she had to know what lurked inside his heart and mind, eating at him like a sickness.

She pulled his hands and led him to a leather sofa near the window and sat down next to him. Because her holster annoyed her, she removed it, rolled up the gun belt, and set it on the table before them.

Here they were, two people who loved each other desperately and needed each other more than at any other time in life, unable to speak or communicate in any meaningful way. Perhaps, thought Madelaina, it's because the angels of death hover over the house that they couldn't express their true feelings.

Peter wondered if all hope was lost for them. Drinking to excess, keeping busy, and indulging in therapeutic sex no longer could sustain what they once shared. And now, the loss of his manhood, devastating enough, loosened a sulking madness in his brain. How could he tell her? Perhaps it was all meant to be. This way, if he sustained his anger and intimidation, he could convince her to return to her father and son.

He'd begged Felipe de Cordoba to allow him to see the child, but the major general had been adamant. Only at the very last, after Peter had agreed to his conditions, did Felipe relent and against orders permitted him a moment with the infant.

Peter had only to look upon the infant to know he was the boy's father. His eyes, the color of blue sapphires, the physical traits—even at that age—Peter recognized as his own. He'd held the infant in his arms, felt the soft, tender smoothness of the child's skin, the tight, firm grip of tiny fingers around his own and his heart surrendered to him. Peter knew then, as he knew now, that his own life would be utter devastation if he couldn't be allowed to see the son of his loins again. He also knew, by Madelaina's physical appearance, that she'd suffered greatly at the separation between mother and child.

Madelaina thought, has he forgotten how it was when we parted—following the conception of our son? He had married another woman. Madelaina be damned! He's forgotten we slept naked together, that we generated much heat and our kisses were the sweetest of all honeys, the most intoxicating of all elixirs. In his eyes I see nothing of the love we once shared. Her sadness overwhelmed her and she remained silent. No words would form on her lips or in her heart.

"Well, what is it? What did ya wanta ta say ta me?"

"Perhaps it's better if you tell me why you've come."

Peter frowned. The brandy warmed his insides and on an empty stomach he felt queasy after the exhausting ride in the hot desert sun. The combination of all three factors, plus his close proximity to Madelaina, made him feel awkward at first. Then he coughed to clear his throat and removed his buckskin jacket. "Like ah said, ah've been sent on a mission. Youah father, General Obregon, wishes ya ta return ta his side, Madelaina. They made me a proposition, one ah felt to be a fair one. Youah life foah mine."

"*My* life for *yours?*" she exclaimed. "*My life for yours?* What exactly does that mean?"

"I've been the general's prisoner for the past few months. Major General de Cordoba came to me and put it to me, rightfully so, that y'all belong in the house of youah father."

"And I suppose you concur?" she asked icily.

"Ah do."

"And what right do you have to think I'd entertain such a proposal? You think I care what happens to the life of a man who deserted me for another woman?" she snorted contemptuously. "You left me at the mercy of the fates without care, without concern for my life, Peter Duprez *Benson*! And you have the nerve to address me as *mother*! Why didn't you tell me William Benson was your father? You had plenty of time to tell me!" she snapped.

"Why did ya marry him?"

"You think I had any power over the circumstances which made me wear his name for a time?" And then, Madelaina told him the full story and she capped it off with, "I don't give a damn, Peter Duprez Benson, if you believe it or not! It wasn't until I was at Seven Moons and saw pictures faintly resembling you, and I coerced Pilar to tell me the truth, that I knew you were related. Don't you think I died a thousand deaths after he molested me and I learned I was pregnant? I prayed to God it was your child—not his. And when it was born—*when it was born*, I knew it was yours, yet you both look so much alike, who can prove it? Time was the only reward I felt. I counted each day, each night to the moment we made love. Only then, could I be certain." She was shaking, tears brimmed her eyes, yet she continued, her voice barely above a whisper. "He's gone, that son of ours, that love child. Stolen from my bosom. He was all I had left of you. Now, here you are, bold as you please, looking rested after your long honeymoon with a woman you aren't legally married to, and you tell me I should return to the house of my father with whom I have nothing in common, because you've made some agreement with him!" Madelaina was out of breath, her temper was close to the breaking point, and she bit her lip to try to keep from spilling more tears. "How dare you tell me what to do with my life? How dare you!" she retorted. "Haven't you done enough to me already?"

"Ah didn't marry Valerie," he said quietly, his blue eyes boring into hers.

"How can I believe this ridiculous story you tell me about my father? If your story was true, he wouldn't have permitted you to leave. He'd have sent a messenger," she continued not hearing him. She built her anger in waves.

"Ah nevuh went away on any honeymoon," he added in softer tones.

"My father's pride is at stake. Any day now he will encounter Pancho Villa, general to general, and he only wants me at his side, so that history will document it as such. What a blow to his ego! His *gachupín* pride would be shattered if history recorded that the daughter of General Obregon sided with the revolution-

801

aries—that when he fought Villa in the contest to determine total victory or total annihilation, his daughter remained at Villa's side." Her anger precluded hearing a word he spoke.

"Valerie knew we spent time togethuh and in a fit of rage came at me with a gun. Her marksmanship put me in a hospital foah several months until mah father sold me out ta the *Huertistas*, so they could get ta ya through me, heah? Youah father's people intervened and kept me secreted at El Dorado."

"Why—why—I—uh, what are you talking about?" She stopped abruptly as Peter's words replayed in her mind. *"You never married her*? But the papers—the papers all wrote about it." Amazement seeped into her face. "You were at El Dorado?"

"Ya know better than ta believe the printed word, Little Fox. Didn't ah teach ya nothin'?"

"William Benson turned you over to Huerta?" Madelaina was aghast. "Oh, *querido*, whatever for? Your own father? *Dios mios*!"

"The way ah heard it, it was so he'd secure himself and his monetary interests in Mexico with the present administration."

"You never married her? Oh, *querido*! I've died a thousand deaths!" She fell into his arms and for several precious moments, they kissed and hugged dearly.

Then, Madelaina wiped the tears from her eyes and spoke with candor.

"So, it's all power and wealth? That's all that ever really counts, isn't it?"

"Reckon so," Peter replied dully.

Their mood was interrupted by a loud wailing, moaning sound echoing through the main *casa*. It was more than a piercing scream that reverberated and bounced off the walls. Madelaina's face blanched; she cocked her head to listen. Peter, instantly alert, turned to her questioningly. Never had they heard such lament, such soulful cries of agonized longing and wailing over the departure of a loved one. "It's Pancho Villa!" she exclaimed, turning and heading out of the room, across the main salon, and climbing the stairs swiftly with Peter behind her.

They were obstructed by Rudolfo Fierro, who stood motionless as a stone statue, guarding the door to the bedroom. Immovable, unflinching, his head bowed over his rifle, he looked like some fierce god guarding his beloved's temple.

"Fierro, let us pass. This is my *marido*, Peter Duprez," she said softly.

It seemed intolerably long before Fierro raised his head and, revealing red-rimmed eyes swollen from crying, nodded mutely to them. He allowed them to pass.

Inside, Pancho Villa sat in a high-backed throne chair, his hands hanging limply over the cushioned arms. His face, turbulent and drained of color, didn't acknowledge the presence of either Madelaina or her husband. On the four-poster bed lay Antonetta, smiling palely and serenely in her final sleep. A silken scarf of silver threads and pale blue silk wound around her neck concealed the horrid pattern of her death. Her hands were folded over her breasts, and her red, silken hair streamed over her shoulders and milk white limbs. A sheer silk cloth covered her nude body. She seemed strangely alive, as if an unearthly glow hovered over her, illuminating her in this shuttered room of shadows and candlelight that smelled of paraffin and dying flowers.

Outside, the Yaqui drums beat a soft tattoo of steady and arousing sounds as the strange ritual of death began. And outside, the people, all of them, the soldiers and *soldaderas* and *campesinas* whispered and wondered. Their *jefe* hadn't come to them to tell them anything. Fierro had said nothing. Little Fox even less. Soon their *jefe* would come to them to tell them. And then would come the retribution. How had his woman died? In the eyes of those women who hated Antonetta because she was first in the *jefe*'s eyes, there was talk of whom he'd pick next to grace his bed. Their eyes gleamed excitedly with no feelings of remorse for the red-haired beauty whose gringo appearance always made them feel unworthy.

Madelaina felt a terrible urge to comfort Pancho Villa, and she flung herself at his feet and lay her head on his lap, as Peter watched her.

"If there is a God, Pancho, rest assured she is cradled at his bosom."

Pancho's coarse hand reached out and stroked Madelaina's black hair, his face an expressionless mask of gray concrete. His eyes reflected dead black stones. He didn't respond to Madelaina's words. Pancho Villa had mourned in his own way. He was a realistic man now, a man changed by the many adversities in life. He was a man who would keep his emotions to a minimum. He had enjoyed Antonetta every moment of their life together and now she was gone, forever plucked from his bosom. He would never, from this day, speak the name Antonetta again. But until his dying day, he would hunt down those responsible for taking her life and show them no mercy. After her burial at sundown, in the manner of his ancestors, by a fire strong enough to transport her to the heavens of eternal rest, she would vanish forever, escorted by the black angels of death to her next abode. There was one thing more left for him to do. He rose to his feet, pulling Little Fox to her feet with him. He turned to Peter and signaled for him to take her from him.

Slowly he moved in toward the bed, and with his knife, he whacked off a thick strand of that strange and alluring red hair, the color of pink fire. Folding it in two, he quickly slipped a leather tine from his holster and bound the bent end. He laced it through his belt and tied it securely. Once again his black eyes swept over the still, pale face, then he turned and left the room.

At the door he spoke to Fierro and the man fell into step behind him, following him down the stairs and into an anteroom where they closed the door after them. Madelaina and Peter paid their last respects to the dead woman and left the room as others began the pilgrimage.

Downstairs, seated quietly in one corner of the room, Madelaina stared at all the passing faces. The drums outside had stopped beating, and a small group of musicians began to play mournful musical dirges. Madelaina watched in fascination the combination of pagan and Christian funeral rites. She'd never forget the manner in which Pancho whacked off Antonetta's hair. Later Rosalia Quintera explained the ancient rite of the Yaqui Indian in which fetishes were made of the hair of their beloved. With the red hair of Antonetta strapped to his victory belt, Villa would have no trouble recognizing the face of his beloved when he passed on to the next life, where after their earthly separation they'd be united again for all eternity. If he didn't wear the fetish he'd have no way of recognizing her, for often the souls changed appearance. Later, Fierro would also wear such a fetish and amaze Madelaina by his profound devotion to her memory.

In his office, Villa's black mood permeated the room as he listened to Fierro's story. Then he summoned Madelaina to listen to her account of the tragedy.

Madelaina and Peter hadn't had time to resolve their own differences, but in light of the *jefe*'s needs, they postponed their business and hoped to comfort Pancho Villa in his darkest hours of personal grief.

Villa's face lit up when he saw Peter Duprez. Then he glanced swiftly to the face of Little Fox, who stood quietly beside Peter, weighted with sadness.

"We shall be avenged, Zorrita," said Pancho walking toward her. "You and I have suffered the most, felt the deepest, and have little to show for our efforts. Tell me your story. What happened out there?" He inspected the bruises on her face grimly.

Madelaina substantiated most of Fierro's story and more. Two *Rurales*, acting seemingly on their own. No, she didn't know if there were more in the vicinity. Had either Fierro or Madelaina stopped to search the dead policemen for orders? *Dios mios*, no! The shock had been too great. Pancho immediately dispatched Fierro and Urbina to ride back and find the bodies and relieve them of all clothing, weapons, and identification.

"Now, Little Fox, ju please leave me with your *marido*? Ees much we must talk on." Pancho Villa was returning to his former self.

Madelaina nodded and left them together. She hadn't had much time to reflect on Peter's words. He *hadn't* married the gringa daughter of the governor after all. She went outside to be by herself, to think and mull things over in her mind.

Her father wanted her to return to his house. Did he mean all was forgiven? Or did he mean he wanted her to turn on Pancho Villa? Why would Peter's life be sacrificed for her—why? Why would Peter even make such a proposal, knowing how deeply she felt about her father's politics? None of it made sense. Not even Peter's position in the matter. He was out of General Obregon's clutches, why would he concern himself with keeping his word? They were together. Why not just run away? Head for the border and once across the Rio Grande, they were American citizens. They couldn't be touched—could they?

No matter how she thought things out, nothing could convince her to return to the house of her father. Nothing would ever make her do this short of death! How could Peter have made such a pact? How did he ever hope to persuade her to comply with the wishes of her father?

These and many more questions arose in her mind. By the time she walked around the perimeter of the hacienda and returned to the *casa*, she saw a considerable scurrying of activity. She glanced around in the moon-filled night, wondering what the *Villistas* were up to. *Dios mios!* They were packing, preparing to move out!

Her steps quickened. What had happened? In less than an hour—that's all she'd been gone—new orders had been issued. She had to fight her way through the thronging people making haste, rolling up their possessions.

She searched everywhere for someone who could make sense. Captain Tracy Richards called to her. "*Chiquita*, youah husband is looking foah ya. Weah leaving foah Chihuahua City!" He wheeled his horse in close to her.

"Why? What for? Why so sudden? Why are we to suddenly pick up and pull out?" She held the horse's bridle, calming him.

"The *jefe*'s orders. Peter was with him a long time. The decision's been made. So get a move on, *muy pronto*, ya heah?" He cantered back over the path.

Madelaina made her way toward the *casa*, elbowing her way, trying desperately to find Peter. All around her, horses, wagons, and trundling cannon kicked up blinding dust so thick she couldn't see through the congestion. She raced to her quarters, gathered her belongings, and took her place with the *soldaderas*, prepared for battle. There was no time for emotions, no time for regrets. Only the call to duty was important, the cry of the revolution: "*La Cucaracha, La Cucaracha, yo no puede caminar,*" came the song of war. "*Viva Villa! Viva La Revolucion!*"

There was no time for tears. The best of Villa's fighting forces, loaded onto trains, headed for Chihuahua City in a sudden move calculated to capture and control the capital of that state. Villa was determined to control the state, eastern Durango, and southwestern Coahuila, all of vital strategic importance, for it meant controlling all the railroads from Juarez to Zacatecas, the commercial lifeline of all Mexico.

Chapter 30

General Pancho Villa, dressed in his uniformed khakis, with the bright glaring sun overhead catching the fiery red-haired fetish of Antonetta attached to his uniform jacket, sat on Seven Leagues and gave the signal for his men to surge forward into battle.

Three separate attempts were made to rush the garrison. Each time the *Villistas* were bloodily repulsed. Two more attempts resulted in failure, for the fort was heavily armed and manned. Then Villa did something to baffle his enemies. He ordered a total withdrawal of his fighting forces.

Federales, hot in pursuit of Villa's rear guard, returned to the garrison to report their victory. "Villa was in full flight," they rejoiced, convincing the defending General Orozco of the Redflaggers and General Mercado of Villa's bitter and devastating defeat. "I tell you they are gone—all the rebels have disappeared. The deserts around Chihuahua are clear! Not even the ghost of Villa remains," persisted the young officers who drank toasts to their monumental victory over the crafty puma, that Centaur of the North.

While the *Federales* reveled in their smashing triumph over Villa, only General Pasquel Orozco remained uneasy. His Indian instincts told him that it wasn't over. He knew his old compatriot too well.

What Orozco didn't know and had no way of discerning was that General Villa had Fierro and the telegraphers of the Northern Division busy tapping wires, listening and intercepting the Juarez-Chihuahua communications. Orozco also had no way of knowing that Pancho Villa, alerted to the arrival of an ammunition train from Juarez, had sent two of his brigadier gener-

808

als to intercept the train and had already helped themselves to the ammunition and succeeded in loading the empty freight cars with their men and horses.

At a particular substation a few kilometers from Chihuahua, ironically named Madero, Colonel Fierro, looking like a satisfied Cheshire cat, had relieved the startled telegrapher of his post and called to his *jefe* for further orders.

"Take this message to the commandant of the Juarez garrison. Please say: *Villa in full retreat to the south. Am sending you reenforcements of 1,000 men with ammunition and supplies by returning train.* Sign it Orozco."

In a matter of moments Fierro deciphered the return message. "They've acknowledged."

"Tell me," asked Villa. "Any confusion?"

"None. We also learned the code to identify the returning train through all stops and highball us in without problems." Fierro's lips curved into a smile.

"Bueno," said Villa. "Now my friend." He winked at Fierro. "Cut the wires, both ways." He touched the brim of his Stetson and left to command the other brigades, leaving a well-pleased and diabolical gleam in the other's eyes.

At one o'clock, the city of Juarez, except for the casinos and night clubs, was sleeping. In the section known as Old Chihuahua, where the night life was coming alive, the sounds of music and loud, raucous shouting and wild behavior echoed through the streets. Countless people swarmed the *avenidas* and crowds from saloons, restaurants, cantinas, whorehouses, and gambling palaces spilled onto the sidewalks clear to the American border. The gaudy lights of the entertainment center never seemed brighter, as the unending clamor of music and singing and laughter filled the air.

Close by, not far from all this activity, a freight train from Chihuahua City lumbered into the railroad yards at Juarez and was sided while "Federal reenforcements," unloaded in full combat gear, were formed and marched toward the barracks in the heart of town unnoticed.

Troop movements in this frontier city were no novelty. Under cover of this activity, Colonel Fierro, pistols in hand, quietly entered the office of the stationmaster and announced politely that the communication center was now in the hands of General Francesco Villa. He nudged the four men over against the wall while his aides tied them securely and shoved them into an adjoining stockroom with gags stuffed firmly in their mouths.

There wasn't the slightest hint of suspicion that the revolution was about to burst wide open at any moment. Not until the outbreak of revolutionary cries pierced the night air, arresting people on the spot.

"Viva Villa! Viva La Revolución!" came the cries.

Mexicans, *Federales*, tourists, and everyone in that section of town were jolted and terrified by the sudden outbreak of artillery fire. Turning around at every conceivable spot, they saw, as if in a dream, *Villistas* in broad-brimmed sombreros and heavily rawled spurs, chests crisscrossed decoratively with ammo belts, rush into the night clubs, rounding up all Federal officers, while outside machine guns swept away all resistance by their troops.

Madelaina, Rosalia Quintera, and Lucia San Miguel, followed by other *soldaderas*, rushed into Antonetta's Diamond Slipper and did to the people what their male counterparts had done in the other establishments. They herded nearly two-dozen Mexican *Federales* into a corner of the room, amid stinging and snide remarks that Pancho Villa was hiding behind the skirts of women. One officer, showing his contempt for the women, reached for his gun. He never made it. Madelaina cut him in two with her Winchester rifle, oblivious to the screams and terrified wailing of the women and other civilians lined up against another wall.

The *soldaderas* moved in and began to remove jewelry and watches and other valuables. From the tables they took the money strewn about. Madelaina, about to protest that Villa's women were not *bandidas* and force the girls to abandon their thieving tactics, was arrested at the sight of one face in particular.

Through the smoky haze filling the large gambling casino, she saw him. He wore the uniform and markings of a major general, but there was no mistaking Simon Salomon, the enemy of her lifetime. Raising her rifle slowly, her forefinger curling tightly around the trigger of the weapon, she hesitated a split second just as a bullet caught her in the shoulder. Two more blasts were fired, whizzing right past her ear, and she saw a sniper fall from the overhead beams. Rosalia had killed her assailant. The place was sudden pandemonium as Urbina's men swept into the casino like ants and took over before she could protest.

It would have been so easy—just a matter of moments—to have pulled the trigger and ended all dreams for the man who'd so savagely scarred her life. Goddamnit! He lived a charmed life for sure! She looked for him, but in the crowd, he was lost to her. Everything happened so quickly, she thought she'd dreamed him. Only when she felt a hot sticky substance trail down her arm and over her breasts, did she realize she was bleeding profusely.

Madelaina gazed about the room as a misty, somewhat hazy apparition whirled about her head in confusion. For several moments she saw herself dancing on the stage as *La Bomba*. She even heard the sensuous, rhythmic music in the caverns of her mind, saw Antonetta moving about the old haunt. She closed her eyes and felt herself being hustled out the door by Rosalia and Lucia. She tried to shut out the painful pictures. Recollections of Tolomeo came at her and she faltered, swaying in the street, falling against the building walls. She was sweating fiercely, her dark hair clung to her like wiry coils. Her eyes fluttered open and shut as the lights around her began to whirl overhead.

Rosalia Quintera called to her. *"Chica! Vamenos!* Quick, we go to the customs house. *Ondolay, pronto!"*

Seeing the condition of her friend, she rushed back to Madelaina's side. *Que pasa?* What's wrong, *chica?*" She studied Madelaina's pale face under the lamplight, recalling all too vividly the staggering Indian rites she'd undergone to unhex the *mujer* of Tom Mix and Paco Jimenez and exorcise all those *diableros* and *brujas*. Now again she appears obsessed? *"Dios mios!"* It can't be, not again.

"Tolomeo!" cried Madelaina over and again. "What do you want of me? What am I doing that disturbs you so?" Flashes of their precious moments together whirled about her head in a brilliant fog of memories. Pictures of Peter's accident at Valerie Townsend's jealous hands mixed in with hers. She actually saw the gunshot wounds as they exploded while Peter was in the tub. She lost consciousness after that.

For three days after the infectious bullet was removed from her upper arm, Madelaina lay in bed in the house Pancho Villa had commandeered, totally unaware that the victory of the *Villistas* had been total, with General Villa in absolute command of Juarez.

News of his amazing and stupifying victory, reported by American newspapers, flashed the name of General Francesco Villa to the four corners of the globe. The landless Indian peasant from Durango, this man whose soul cried for the injustices of the poor to be righted, became the man of the hour! He'd tricked a garrison of 3,000 well-trained soldiers and captured the most vital and important city in northern Mexico without suffering a single casualty. But this of itself wasn't enough for General Villa. His mind dwelled on that irresistible seat of power, Chihuahua City!

News from his spies reached the *jefe*'s office that Generals Orozco and Mercado were mobilizing 5,000 soldiers to attack Juarez and decimate all Villa's forces. Eleven trains had been assigned by his enemies for their counterattacks on Juarez.

"My, my," said Villa, smiling at the information. "Imagine that. Eleven trains."

Four days later, scouts reported to Villa that the

Federales had departed from Chihuahua City and were en route to Juarez for an all-out war.

Madelaina, recuperating from her wound and still bedridden from fatigue and lack of nourishment, had to satisfy herself learning secondhand of the *jefe*'s spectacular accomplishments. She'd never been so annoyed at herself for stopping that bullet. Now, through the eyes of Miguel Guerra, she was forced to read of the heated and marvelous accomplishments of General Villa instead of being right in the thick of the action.

"When news reached General Villa that the *Federale*'s reenforced columns of soldiers were taking the offensive in attacking Juarez, he gathered his 800 men and marched right out to meet them. Unknown to his enemies, General Villa rendezvoused with the other brigades of his Northern Division precisely at a destination his enemies least expected him to be: Colonel Fierro's mission was to handpick a detachment of railroad men and dynamiters to circle in behind the Federal troop trains and cut the track, preventing retreat. Within twenty-four hours the entire Northern Division stood at attention, resupplied with Villa's vast Juarez stones, prepared for battle.

"Even I," wrote Miguel Guerra, "received a shock when I saw the entire rebel army sprawled across the tracks. You can imagine what went through the minds of the *Federales* when their trains came around the bend to reveal the spectacular and magnificent strength of the entire *División del Norte* already there and waiting for them. Forced to attack prematurely, only half-prepared, the *Villistas* promptly counterattacked, and for the next three days the battle raged. The *Federales* finally attempted to withdraw to Chihuahua City.

"It was then that Colonel Fierro, struck with inspiration, ignored General Villa's orders to destroy the railroad tracks. Instead, he concentrated on the last of the Federal troop trains. Blocking the rails, he and his men charged the train, and surprising the troop escort, he disarmed them and shot the officers. Then, in another mad but workable scheme, he uncoupled the engine

813

and packed the train's cowcatcher with enormous loads of dynamite, woven through the grating with explosive caps. The colonel opened the throttle and leaped off the engine, leaving it to charge ahead, racing northward around a bend in the road, where the ten Federal trains lay stalled, end to end, by Villa's attack.

"As the dynamited cowcatcher collided with the last caboose, an earth-shattering explosion ended all hopes the *Federales* might have entertained for retreat. The explosions burst into flames and triggered off further explosions. Only after a thick cloud of black smoke lifted and the fire died down did this reporter see the remains of troop trains as they lay scattered over a half-mile. A broad stretch of track had been twisted into blackened junk and the *Federales* ran into a hasty retreat.

"Ten valuable engines loaded with war materials sat waiting for General Pancho Villa to take them over. Meanwhile General Urbina of the Juarez Brigade fell into savage pursuit of the panic-stricken *Federales*, cutting them to pieces.

"It was learned that Generals Orozco and Mercado and the entire Chihuahua garrison subsequently gathered the remnants of a once-powerful army and retreated from the capital, leaving it to the *Villistas*. For General Villa, this wasn't enough. He split his Northern Division once more and personally led the attack on Chihuahua on all the remaining *Federale* troops. The last government troops north of Chihuahua have ceased to exist. Those *Huertistas* who could escaped across the American border and have been interned. Those who didn't escape were executed by General Villa's firing squads."

Madelaina laid down the paper, recalling the friendship of Miguel Guerra in the early days of the revolution and how he protected her for a time from her father's spies. She moved to the window overlooking a portion of Juarez beyond the planted terrace of her roof garden. Each morning for the past three days since she regained consciousness, she searched the streets, desperately hoping to see Peter. She knew he'd joined with Tracy Richards and the Gringo Brigade, but Tracy had returned two days ago and made no mention of Peter. She slipped into a bath, prepared for her by Rosalia Quintera, who'd looked in on her and taken care of her with the tenderness of a loving relative. When Rosalia learned Madelaina's baby had been abducted from her side, she expressed her compassion, one mother to another. Still no words could console her friend.

Madelaina lay back and closed her eyes after she'd soaped and scrubbed herself, but finding herself unable to fully relax, she lifted her body from the wooden tub, dried herself and, wrapped in heavy toweling, moved toward the bed. She slipped the leather chamois around her neck. She recalled Tolomeo's words: if she felt poorly, without energy, she should sprinkle some mushroom powder in the area of her solar plexus and meditate on strength. Nothing else had sufficed and she continued to feel sapped of energy.

Why not do as he'd suggested? She felt a pang of guilt for not having tried harder to live by his philosophy. Her life had been just as difficult after she left the land of Tolomeo, hadn't it? Perhaps not as tumultuous and earth-shaking as before she'd encountered him, but none the less quite hard and rocky. She sprinkled a minute amount of the powder on her flat, hard stomach and rubbed in a circular direction, commanding as she did that the second brain of her body give her the needed energy.

No sooner had she closed her eyes to rest a bit than pictures instantly formed in her mind. She blinked hard and opened her eyes with a feeling of dismay. Was she forever to be cursed with these confounding pictures? She tried to keep her eyes open wide, but they grew too heavy and the desire to close them overpowered her. There they were again, a series of pictures like photographs in motion of a place, a location she'd never seen, high above the sea, surrounded by tall graceful trees and a thick vegetation. She was walking

815

through rooms of an unfamiliar hacienda, passing through them as one might on a guided tour, glancing at the wall hangings and art objects with interest until she stopped in her tracks at the sight of a familiar face. She drew closer and closer and there he was. Felipe de Cordoba! She was certain. And there behind him in a brass cradle was an infant. Moving in closer to the cradle, Madelaina was able to look down at the moving child. Her heart filled with joy at the sight of her child. It was her son, Alejandro! Of this she was certain.

Her eyes snapped open and the pictures faded. Madelaina sat up in bed with a start. She glanced around the room as her heart accelerated rapidly. What did it mean? *Dios mios.* These pictures were like the pictures she'd seen of Manuelito Perez and those of Peter when he was injured. For so long she hadn't seen these pictures, she almost forgot they happened. She reached for another cigarette, lit it, and frowned at the pile of butts in a mound in the ash tray. She smoked for a time, inhaling deep breaths, hoping against hope that her heartbeats would subside. She detested this breathless feeling that left her edgy, nervous, and shaken.

She closed her eyes again. In moments the pictures returned. They were different. These pictures were of Peter Duprez in a hospital. Of the comings and goings of doctors and other specialists. She watched them examine Peter and she saw the enormous scar tracks from his stomach to his groin.

"Who are you?" she asked. "And why do you persist in forming pictures in my mind?" She heard herself ask the people in the pictures. She heard a doctor's voice telling Peter that for a while he might be impotent, that he shouldn't concern himself, that in time the situation would resolve itself.

Madelaina's eyes snapped open again. This time she pulled herself up off the bed, just as Rosalia Quintera walked in with a pot of hot coffee. Lucia came in behind her and remained in the background, avoiding Madelaina's eyes.

"*Chica*, where is my husband?" she asked Rosalia.

"He has crossed the border on business with Pancho Villa. He will return with Pancho and we are to progress to Chihuahua City, *muy pronto*."

"Travel again?"

"*Si*. We travel once more. This time in style, not as *campesinas*. Urbina and Fierro will escort us to the capital city." She handed Madelaina a packet. "This is for ju, *chiquita*. Lucia and I will be back with our belongings." The two mestizos left Madelaina to her privacy.

Madelaina hastily opened the envelope when she recognized the handwriting as Peter's. She began to read: "Madelaina, my love, my sweet: Knowing that we, neither of us, resolved our differences, I, in all good conscience had to write you before I left on business for Villa. It's necessary that you know the most important person in your life awaits you at the hacienda of your father in El Dorado—*our* son.

"Yes, my beloved, *our* son. He is safe and has been from the moment your father took him from your bosom. I knew none of this—not even that you'd borne us a son. I wanted no part in this, but, due to circumstances over which I had no control, I am forced to become an unwilling pawn.

"I've thought about Felipe de Cordoba's words. I also sense the deep love he's always felt for you. As things grow more hectic and dangerous in this revolution to which we've both committed ourselves, I grow increasingly alarmed over your safety. It is for this that I insist that you return to the sanctuary of your father where both you and our son will be safe from harm. You've dedicated yourself long enough to the cause of Pancho Villa. Now, with the responsibility of another life, our son, I plead with you—return to him and stay safe.

"It's my hope that you will try to carve a future for yourself and our son. Madelaina, you must know, my darling, that I've loved you from the moment I was approached by that slim-hipped, boyish woman I met in

Sanlucar four years ago. In the past I've learned to memorize all of you until you remain indelibly etched in my mind. Somewhere a clock keeps ticking away for us, taking more precious time from us. My sweet, sweet *querida*, the whole of the love I feel for you has never found time to be consummated except for the god-given replica of us come alive in our son. Take care of him. Take care of yourself.

"There is something I must confess, so that you understand. I am not the same man you married. I never will be. Therefore, it is God's will that you return to your son and prepare for his and your future. There can be none for us. If you do not understand what I am trying to tell you, I can only say—forget me. Our life can never be. May God bless the both of you. Peter."

Madelaina's heart was so full, she felt it would burst. Tears sprang from her eyes and spilled onto the paper. She understood very little of this letter. Her swimming eyes scanned the third paragraph. What did he mean—*I am not the same man you married? I never will be?*

It wasn't fair! He should have told her before he left. She might have been able to convince him they belonged together. God! What hell she'd been through to keep this marriage of hers together! God wouldn't have paved the road with such perilous twists and turns and tumultuous emotional upheavals only to make her give up when the end was near. No! No! She was sobbing now.

She'd flung herself across the bed; the letter had fallen to the floor near her. Sheer desperation and the fear of not knowing what to do in these next few moments was so overwhelming that she couldn't think straight. Even as she gave vent to this rising hysteria, this mixture of joy at learning of her son's safety, coupled with a feeling of haunting at losing Peter forever, something deep within her attempted to stabilize her distraught emotions.

Rosalia and Lucia returned, their bedrolls strapped

to their backs, to find Madelaina still crying. Rosalia's eyes fell to the letter. She picked it up and slipped out of her backpack. Her eyes darted over the letter. She spoke to Lucia in her mestiza dialect. "Her man has left her. Then it's true what you told me about the gringo?"

Lucia nodded halfheartedly. "*Si*, it's true. But it's like I say to him and like Dr. Gonsalvez say to the young major general, that it will take time for him to be a man again. It isn't all lost. But the gringo, *pues*, you think he listens? That stubborn ass. He tries three, four, mebbe five times with Lucia—and nothing. Now he volunteers for the most dangerous job—the most foolish. He looks to be killed, that Tom Mix!"

Hearing their voices, Madelaina sat up and dried her eyes with the hem of her skirt. She glanced at Rosalia hotly when she saw the letter in her outstretched hand. "How dare you read my letter?" she shouted venemously, reaching for it.

"Read jur letter? Shooo, Little Fox, ju theenk Rosalia knows to read? *Dios mios*! Eef only eet was true, *querida*," she lied. "It was on the floor. Rosalia removed it from the floor, that ees all. Are you ready to move with the company of escorts?"

"*Si*. I'm ready." She hastily gathered what few belongings she had and rolled them up as the other women had done. She slipped out of her blouse and skirt and reached for her dark trousers and shirt. She slipped the bandoleros of ammunition over each arm, crisscrossed across her chest, and hooked on her hip holster in which her Obregon automatic was slung. "*Vamenos, muchachas*," she said abruptly in an authoritative manner. Her previous vulnerability was gone.

In coming to terms with herself, Madelaina thought of many things en route to General Villa's headquarters. First, she decided that her baby son was perhaps in the best place possible, at the home of her father. Neither he or Felipe de Cordoba would wish harm to the small *niño*, so her decision to remain with Villa until her own father's position in this revolution was made clear seemed the right one. She was convinced that her father was riding the fence, since he seemed reluctant to declare his loyalty to Carranza and had definitely split with Huerta at some time in the past.

Whatever the reason, he was reluctant to declare himself for Carranza, it appeared that Don Venustano was the heavy contender for the presidential throne. Obregon had to make his decision because the time was drawing closer and closer for the contest between himself and Pancho Villa.

Only destiny, it seemed, would know the outcome of this confrontation, thought Madelaina, and it was certain the fickle whore wasn't talking—not even to the four winds.

The way Madelaina saw it, and it was confusing at times, President Huerta, as the keeper of Mexican power, controlled the *Federales* and the *Rurales*. Determined to dethrone him was Venustano Carranza, self-declared First Chief of the Revolution, who'd gathered unto himself all the former *Maderistas* with the exception of General Pancho Villa, who was just as determined not to seat Carranza in the presidential palace. General Villa, by the very strength and force of the army he'd built, was considered General-in-Chief of the Northern Division of the revolutionists. He wanted a liberated Mexico, free of all oppressors—and that included Carranza. Her father, General Obregon, was the man whose position perplexed her. In truth, he was a *Federale* who'd split from the *Huertistas* and inclined himself toward Carranza, but not quite.

It was clear to her that Carranza needed both Obregon and Villa, but it wasn't until President Wilson showed favoritism toward Carranza that Obregon even threw his Fourth Sonora Battalion in to support Carranza. True, he'd taken a few minor garrisons in Carranza's name, but not wholeheartedly. His determination to stall was what concerned everyone, including Pancho Villa, who'd once declared Obregon his fiercest enemy.

Who can keep up with these political intrigues, she asked herself on many occasions. It's enough to drive a person crazy, with changing loyalties from day to day. Who knew one's real enemies—or friends—in such turbulent times?

Madelaina had been in Chihuahua City for nearly two weeks, working in the office of General Villa, immersing herself in necessary clerical work before she actually saw the general. He had just returned from El Paso after having met in secret with U.S. General Hugh L. Scott and other political supporters in the United States.

For days he remained uncommunicative. If he appeared astonished to see Madelaina busy at work in the building he'd appropriated for his administrative offices, he said very little, except to tell her that her husband was in Washington on vital business for the revolution.

She had said very little to him. Trying desperately to reorganize the office so that the filing system wasn't too complicated for a child to handle, she had enough work to keep her mind off the urgent longings she felt for Peter.

Several times in the coming weeks, as she busied herself across the hall from General Villa's private office, she'd hear him rage to Rudolfo Fierro, who'd become a general since his spectacular, quick thinking in the Juarez siege, that he couldn't in all honesty and decency comply with the recent suggestions made by General Scott that he amalgamate with Don Carranza, contender for the presidency of Mexico, the moment Huerta was ousted. The breach between Villa and Carranza had become too great to be spanned for the common good, he'd told Fierro.

"But what if President Wilson fully endorses Carranza?" asked Fierro.

There was silence for several moments, then Villa roared. "Damnit, Fierro, don't confuse me. How can an honorable man like Wilson endorse so dishonorable a coyote like Carranza? You think he can't see a skunk's stripes under his coat?"

"You think President Wilson can see through a coat?" asked Fierro.

"Listen, that American has much education, see. He can see through anything, *amigo*. Especially since he wears those fancy glasses. He must see twice as much as this uneducated *peón*."

Madelaina hadn't seen the expression on Fierro's face, but she had smiled at Villa's naïveté. He placed so much importance on education and literacy. Why, with no education at all and a thirst to read countless books, General Villa had done more in the short span of months than cum laude graduates did in years. She concentrated on how she could convince him of his own worth.

In Washington, President Wilson was still debating over the most logical man to support in Mexico, and although still at a loss to decide, he finally outlawed Huerta. The man was a psychotic drunk, too dangerous to be allowed to occupy the highest office in our southern neighbor's government. Still he was undecided between Carranza and Pancho Villa. Word got to him that Carranza was encountering difficulties with his Chief of the Northwest Army, General Obregon, who either wouldn't or couldn't carry out Don Venustano's directives. Having met General Obregon in the past, President Wilson found him to be a reasonable man, well educated, and dedicated to his career. He could understand Obregon's position. After all, Huerta was still president. His cooperation with Carranza could very well be considered treason in certain circles.

Other leaders had risen and fallen these past many months of the revolution, yet there was always Villa. The man President Wilson had first labeled a ruthless butcher, an illiterate *peón*, was suddenly emerging a brilliant, outgoing man displaying an astonishing native intelligence that his well-educated counterparts had difficulty understanding. Why, the former *guerrillo* who once had difficulty expressing himself had begun to

822

show an astounding and spectacular administrative ability.

Peter Duprez had been meeting in chambers for the past three weeks with President Wilson and General John Pershing who, along with General Scott, had nothing but praise for manner in which Pancho Villa, using the democratic guidelines of his northern neighbors, grasped the reins of government. Daily they attempted to convince the president of the vast changes taking place south of the border. And it began to appear, after lengthy conversation, that Peter was winning points for Villa. Right after lunch one day, Peter picked up where the conversation had ended before the break. He'd grown bolder in recent days and took considerable effort to point up the plus side of Villa's activities.

"It's clear ta see, Mr. President, that once the firing squads fade away, General Villa's concern centers around his people. He's freed political prisoners, restoring their full rights. He's established schools, making education mandatory. Ya must admit, it's moah than Diaz or Huerta have attempted. Why, suh, he's lowered railroad rates to benefit the poor who wish ta migrate elsewheah foah work. He's permitted Mexicans returning ta Mexico ta bring in furniture and automobiles duty free. Suh, he's employed qualified help ta supervise schools, hospitals, and other government agencies. He's taxed industries and put ceilings on prices to protect the poor from profiteering. Already he's entered into business relations with American industry. He plans ta import better engines, passenger and freight cars. Mr. President, in mah humble opinion, there's no one better than General Francesco Villa to help cement better and stronger ties between ouah two nations."

Woodrow Wilson, that myopic and sanctimonious president, regarded all Peter had told him with an air of sobriety. Even Generals Scott and Pershing had lauded Villa highly after the few encounters they'd had with the former *guerrillo*.

823

"What you say coincides with the other reports I've had on the man and his reforms. It's been brought to my attention that liquor laws have been enforced rigidly for the first time and that U.S. Customs authorities have been given powerful aid to deter the smuggling of drugs across the border."

"Yes, suh. All of that and moah," replied Peter with rising hope.

"Very well, gentlemen," replied the president. "I'm all but totally convinced. Again I must ask your indulgence to give me until the end of this month to make my decision. While I view with appreciation all you've done to bring me a clear picture of the activities of this barely reformed bandit, from other sources I hear that he represents no cause other than his own."

Seeing the flickerings of discontent in the eyes of his guests, the president hastened to add, "Yet, he does hold all the meaningful territory, including vital border crossings which must be kept open to American commerce."

"Yes, suh," said Peter a bit too quickly. "That he does, Mr. President. That he does."

The meeting was dismissed on a high note. After all, thought Peter, winking at General Pershing, the end of the month was less than two weeks away. He could be patient, all right. They all could if it meant victory for Villa's cause.

Unfortunately, none of the men present could begin to imagine what the fates had in store for Pancho Villa. Least of all, Peter Duprez Benson, who was bound to be most affected by the storm gathering in Chihuahua in the office of General Villa.

Deeply engrossed in the filing that had accumulated over the past several weeks, Madelaina and Rosalia Quintera hardly saw the tall stranger charge boldly through the hall, bellowing aloud, demanding to see Pancho Villa. She'd been attempting to teach Rosalia the simple system of filing she'd devised when she heard General Villa's secretary sparring in a conversation with a gringo *hacendado*, protesting the gringo's presence without an appointment.

Their words grew heated and tempestuous, and as they disappeared behind closed doors, the women could hear very little.

"*Dios mios, chica*," exclaimed Rosalia, pausing in her work to swing her hip-length auburn hair off her shoulders. "Even the rafters shake at the booming of such angry voices." She studied Madelaina for a time. "Perhaps it would be more better if I wear my hair as ju do?"

Madelaina's slick, trim look, with her hair pulled back tightly and wound into coils above her neckline, seemed far cooler than her own appearance. Besides, it was hot and stuffy inside these offices. She liked the shirtwaist dress, boots, and belt worn by the *gachupin*, which appeared demure and well suited for the sedate office work. Even her gun belt looked less intimidating.

Madelaina smiled. "It makes things less complicated when you are dressed to suit the work, *chica*. Soon, now, you'll know my work well enough so I can leave for a rest." She spoke half to herself and bent over the work on her desk. Her mumbled words were hardly heard by the auburn-haired, seductive-looking Rosalia, who complained she had no head for business. "Only for making love, *querida*." She laughed easily. "And why not? For what else ees woman put on earth, eh?"

For a time, there was silence as the girls concentrated on the work at hand. They had no idea that what was happening a few feet away from them would turn the revolution upside down.

Inside General Villa's private office, the *jefe* stared over the gleaming walnut desk at the tall, over-powering gringo who dared shove his way into his office.

"What exactly is it ju want from me, Señor Benson?" he asked evenly.

"That tax ya imposed upon unconfiscated haciendas! S'posin' we begin right theah?" William Benson bellowed loudly.

"*Bueno*, Señor Benson. Ju just pay 1,000 head of

cattle and that's that." Villa summoned his secretary. "My man here will attend to details, gringo."

"Just who in hell do ya think ya are talkin' ta me like that, man? We've got unfinished business ta attend ta, Villa," roared William Benson. "Have ya got any idea who ah am?"

"I know who. What the hell do ju mean bustin' in like this? Tell me what ju want."

"If ya think ah'm about ta pay youah bloody thieving tax man, you'ah plum loco. What's moah ah'm sick an' tired of seeing your goddamn thieving brigade marching up and down along mah lands! Theah makin' mah bulls jitterier than hell. And last but not least, we've got unfinished business. Y'all kidnapped mah bride from my Texas ranch, Seven Moons. Foah that, suh, I can have ya jailed!"

Villa stood up behind the desk. Still he had to look up at the big Texan. His eyes blackened and his temper had shoved into first gear. "Ju listen, gringo. Pancho Villa is short on nerves because he's tired, ju understand? First, since the Mexican *hacendados* pay my tax, why should I make exception of ju? Second, consider jurself fortunate that I didn't confiscate jur hacienda. Third, my blood boils when ju call my soldiers thieves. And last, the woman who escaped Seven Moons was not jur bride. She was the legal wife of one of my officers. Now, where the hell do you get off bustin' into my office, mouthing off like some foolish *borrachón* who stinks of bad whiskey?" Villa fanned the repulsive liquor breath from his nose with obvious disdain.

General Villa, in his shirtsleeves, up to his ears in paper, had given no thought to the fact that he was unarmed. Who would dare threaten his life in his own stronghold? His secretary, Carlos Ramierez, a quiet, studious-looking man with rimless glasses, seated at Villa's side at another desk, glanced nervously at Benson, whose temper, fired with rage, hurled insults and threats at Villa over the desk.

Under Benson's greatcoat, the outline of a large gun

formed a visible impression. Villa had no gun at his immediate disposal, nor did he seem to think he needed one.

To Benson's right, slightly behind him, totally ignored by the room's occupants, stood the dark, thickset figure of a uniformed man with black, narrowed eyes. He wore a white campaign hat. Over his shoulders, a long black cape covered a trim uniform caught at the waist with a heavy gun belt. Rudolfo Fierro, tensed and alert, trained his lethal eyes on the American.

"Don'cha think foah a moment ya can scare me, ya whoring son of Satan," yelled Benson. "Ah've got me plenty o' pull in Washington, ya lousy fuckin' peasant—"

"Jur under arrest!" shouted Villa wrathfully. "Jur in the territory of General Francesco Villa. I'll teach ju to speak with such disrespect, *cabrón*—cuckold!"

"Youah'll teach me nothing, ya stinking swine—" Benson went for his gun. In that same instant, Fierro's gun roared. William Benson fell dead at Villa's feet, a bullet through the head. Everything happened in an instant.

The door swung open and Madelaina dashed inside, her face drained of color. Her eyes darted about the room, and seeing the *jefe* unharmed, she sighed in relief. Her eyes fell on the collapsed heap of the gringo. She walked in closer and looked down just as Fierro turned the body over, allowing her to see his face. Her hands flew to her face in shock. She glanced at Villa and at the smoking gun in Fierro's hands. Her body grew slack, her head shook in disbelief. "You know who this man is, *Jefe*?" The consequences of the act shook her.

"I know," said Villa ruefully. "The father of your *marido*. By his own words, a man with much political pull. His death can do much to jeopardize the work of your *jefe*."

"Oh, what a luckless *peón* I am on this day!" he lamented. "Tell me, Little Fox, what would the Americans have done if some half-drunken Mexican had broken into the El Paso City Hall and attempted to shoot their mayor? Are we in Mexico supposed to be fair game for the abuses and caprices of any whoring mother's son of a foreigner?"

"What will this do to Peter's mission in Washington with the gringo *presidente*? she asked without expression.

"You know about that?"

"I know, *Jefe*."

"I care more what Peter will do to avenge the death of his father," he told her.

Madelaina blinked hard. She had no answers. "It's more important to what your enemies will do, *Jefe*. Carranza, for instance. If the American president removes his support from you, rest assured it will be Carranza he supports. Then what?"

"Then what? Then what? *Pues, querida,* then comes more complications. For instance, that fence-riding father of yours will be forced to declare his position. What do you suppose his position will be?"

"Perhaps we'd better think on such a matter, *Jefe*. And pretty damned quick," she retorted.

They didn't have to wait for long to learn how Washington viewed this atrocity done to an American citizen. The government began an immediate investigation. As for the president, in his cool, complacent, aristocratic manner, he told himself and others that he knew all along that Villa was a savage barbarian not fit to rule his country. He informed Peter Duprez of this when the tight-lipped, somber-faced Texan responded to the presidential summons. "Will you continue to apologize for General Villa now? Honestly, Peter, how can you think to defend a man who shot your own father?" His words, spoken emotionally before a mask of political reserve set in, brought color to his lined cheeks. "I'll wait for the investigation to submit the findings before I can reexamine my earlier willingness to support this—uh—er—man, Villa," added Wilson hastily as he endured Peter's long cold stare.

By then, Peter knew Villa's cause to be lost. Just as he booked train accommodations back to El Paso, without waiting for the reports to be resolved, lawyers for his father's estate contacted him in Washington to suggest he return to Amarillo at once. Peter felt obligated to do their bidding, especially since he was urged to cooperate with them by Governor Hampton Townsend.

On the long ride back to Texas, Peter pondered the situation. He wondered what had happened to bring about the fatal encounter between his father and General Villa. Why exactly had Benson been shot? Knowing his father, he readily assumed the worst. Still Benson was his father. He owed him that much at least. Governor Townsend had put it quite succinctly: it was time for Peter to leave the house of Pancho Villa and concern himself with the affairs at the house of Benson.

They had spoken long distance when Peter was in Washington. He'd insisted to the governor that without hearing the facts, he didn't hold Villa responsible and that he felt sure that Villa was justified in defending himself.

Governor Townsend had coughed with embarrassment and sputtered, "It's commendable of you, my boy, to be so generous in your appraisal of the affair in light of the fact that you don't know the circumstances which led up to it. Just you remember, boy, blood's thicker than water. By the way, it might serve ya well, my boy, to head up the investigation against Villa."

Peter went numb. "Governor, did I hear you correctly?" asked Peter testily. "Your shifting loyalties serve only to confuse me."

There was dead silence at the other end of the phone, followed by a rash of embarrassed coughing and the clearing of Hampton Townsend's throat. "You just have to understand, Peter—"

Peter Duprez Benson hung up on the high state official. He stood for a long time in the long distance phone booth staring into the mouthpiece. His problem was that of late he'd been thinking too deeply, more profoundly than usual. Impotence had done this to him. His thoughts of late had been clearer and in sharper focus than ever before. He'd begun to assess his own life and that of Madelaina. Many questions previously unanswered in his mind began sifting, sorting, and clearing.

Well, first things first. He'd go home at last and see why the lawyers were sending up smoke signals. Yes, that was as good a place as any to begin to come to terms with himself. He almost looked forward to seeing Seven Moons again, especially now that he would not have to tolerate the presence of William Benson.

In Chihuahua City, in the lair of that Centaur of the North, General Pancho Villa, the man who'd succeeded in racking up astonishing victories for the revolution had just adjourned a meeting with his chiefs and subchiefs. For several hours Villa had been attempting to find some direct route through the maze of countless complications that had besieged him ever since the shot that killed the gringo William Benson had echoed around the world. Unable to resolve many things, he dismissed his men, just as Madelaina Obregon entered the study of the confiscated hacienda.

"Come in, come in, Little Fox," he called to her as the officers filed out of the room, somber-faced and without their usual jocularity.

The men, Urbina, Richards, and the others she'd grown to know so well throughout all the campaigns, nodded perfunctorily in passing. Rudolfo Fierro touched the brim of his white Stetson and moved past her without expression.

Madelaina in turn nodded easily, hardly glancing at them, and sat opposite the *jefe*. He poured her a glass of wine, offered her a cigarette, and sat back in his chair, selecting a piece of peanut brittle from a silver dish on the desk for himself.

"It's good of you to come, Little Fox," he said, biting into the candy. "Recently my spies tell me that even my friends, my so-called friends, plot against me. So, you see, it is refreshing to know I can trust you. Shall I tell you how much I miss Antonetta?" Tears sprang to his eyes. "Besides being my lover, my *gatitta*, she was my best friend." He crunched on the candy with relish.

"I'd like to think I fall into that category, *Jefe*," she said.

"You? You, Little Fox? What the hell's wrong with you that you don't already know such a thing? You are more than a friend. You are like my right arm. You don't know that? I called for you today, because we must talk."

He finished with the candy and wiped the corners of his lips with his fingertips, his merry eyes twinkling with self-consciousness. "Me—a grown man—liking candy so much," he scoffed with mild embarrassment. Then he began. "Recently, *querida*, I've given much thought to what might happen if I should fall in battle. Who would there be to carry on the standard first lifted by Francesco Madero, eh? Can you help me to name one man?" He sighed heavily when Madelaina, after a slight hesitation, shook her head. "You see? Precisely my feelings. Among my men, there is no one—not even me—fit to occupy the presidential throne in the palace in Mexico City. So why do I fight?

"Freedom for Mexico is my dream, *chica*, my dream for existence. Without it, I'd be lost, whipped back into an ignorance and slavery which dehumanizes, warps, and eventually destroys man's soul. For this I fight. Yet, as I grow closer to my goal, I look for a man to carry on my work. Shall I tell you who I see? Like you—no one. I say to myself, I could make peace with Carranza, back him, and elevate him to lead our beloved Mexico. But he is no better than Huerta—worse than Diaz. He's a German lover prepared to make deals with the Kaiser. You think the American president believes this? Hah! The gringo who sits in the White House believes only that Pancho Villa is a

831

crazy bandit, killer, a man with no education, a *guerrillo*, who has much empty space under his sombrero."

"How can he believe such foolishness after the victories you've amassed?"

"You think I can answer you? Hah! Sometimes I wish I could drink like my men, Urbina and Fierro. I promise I'd get stinking drunk, then perhaps I wouldn't care as much as I do."

"Why do you punish yourself, *Jefe*? What's been done has been done and nothing can alter the facts. Perhaps if you set your thoughts down on paper in a letter to the American president, speak to him through your heart, as you speak to me, he might reconsider. You must tell him that Benson shot first and Fierro shot in your defense. You can't allow this unfortunate incident to deter you, *Jefe*. You mustn't," insisted Madelaina.

"But for who? For who do I fight. Even if the American president assists me by sending arms and reenforcements to oust Huerta—for whom do I sacrifice the lives of thousands? In good conscience, there is no one I can place on the presidential throne."

Madelaina was aghast. "You can't just give up and turn Mexico over to the political predators who would eat it up and suck it dry." Their eyes met long and hard.

"Listen, Little Fox, I've been preparing to attack Zacatecas, so I control all of the north to that southern point. Is plenty, no? Word comes from Carranza. 'Unite our forces,' he tells me. 'Take Saltillo, first. Forget Zacatecas.' "

Madelaina's forehead screwed up in thought. "If you do that, you'd be sacrificing your campaign for his benefit and glory. Saltillo is the capital of Coahuila—Carranza's home state, no?"

"You see how clever you are, Little Fox. If you were a man, it would be you I would place in the presidential palace—*como*, no?"

"*Jefe*," she said, flushed with embarrassment and

enough sobriety to make Villa think. "Such an honor could never be accorded a woman. That golden throne isn't for the likes of a woman with my past."

Villa agreed with her first statement, shrugged at the second. Then they both laughed at the utter absurdity of his statement. A woman—indeed.

"You know, perhaps it's not so bad an idea." He entertained the thought with a merry twinkle in his eyes. Then he grew serious.

"The question is, *chica*, if I take Saltillo for Don Carranza, am I giving prominence to a worthy man? Or will the sacrifice of sufficient red blood be done to dignify an ignoble lout? I must be certain of what I do, that it is for the good of Mexico, because, you see, the price I will pay is the lives of many good men."

His words struck at her emotions. "What a good man you are, *Jefe*. I saw such nobility in you when first I skulked around your campfires waiting to serve you. For this I sacrificed my former life, to serve you in the revolution for a better Mexico. If those gringos in Washington knew this side of you, if they could see the tenderness in your eyes when you speak of Mexico, they'd whistle up a brilliant madrigal for Pancho Villa and allow their troops to march to its tune."

Watching him, Madelaina saw this wasn't the reply Villa wanted. Compliments, although welcome, bounced off his back when more pertinent issues were to be examined. "What is it, *Jefe*? Are you asking me to tell you the kind of man Carranza is? What do I know of him?"

He nodded slowly, allowing a piece of peanut brittle to melt in his mouth. "Ayeiii, perhaps that is what Pancho is doing. Listen, *chica*, if I throw 20,000 men into a fight, one of every twenty will die—perhaps more. What will I say to their *soldaderas* when their babies suffer and they themselves weep with sorrow and loneliness? You think that a few pesos, a little food and shelter will erase the fact that I, Pancho Villa, ordered them to their deaths, if I support a man who turns out to be a *bastardo*—a second Diaz? You understand I must justify this to myself as well as their women."

Madelaina, visibly moved, rose from her chair. She walked across the room, opened the shutters, and glanced out at the courtyard filled with moving figures: *campesinas, soldaderas*, with their men and children, milling about the fires making preparations for ser. She knew Villa awaited her words as a hungry man might be ready to pounce upon a meal denied him for a week.

"What I know of Carranza, even from childhood, is perhaps an old story to you. My observations of Don Carranza and his stuffy family are colored by my own emotions." She gazed out the window, seeing nothing in particular.

"Naturally. Why else would I ask, if not to know Little Fox's opinion of such a man? The eyes of children always speak in truth and record their thoughts in truth. It is only after they grow up that they shade the bad things to conform to all things around them."

Madelaina turned to him. "Carranza's a four-tongued viper. He is crafty, full of guile, and has the duplicity and cunning of a four-sided man. He pretends patriarchal concern for the nation like Diaz. And like Diaz, he's a stuffed shirt, an opportunist whose real desire is to reestablish the old Diaz regime with himself in the seat of power. He is not a militarist like you or my father, even though he's conferred upon himself title of *el premier jefe*, since President Wilson shows an inclination to favor him as possible presidential material. Yes, First Chief of the Revolutionary Army is what he calls himself. But whose army, *Jefe*? Yours? Obregon's? Mercado's. *Aye*, Carranza is a fox. He's a snake. He's a badger. All three rolled into one. It is for this that my father, General Obregon, refuses to lay down his sword for this chocolate-drinking pansy."

"All this leads me to the question I intend putting to you, Little Fox. The question of General Alvaro Obregon."

She knew what was coming. It's just that she didn't expect it so soon.

"I hear that General Obregon has found the exploits of my colorful *Dorados*—" Villa's hands rolled in a circle in the air before him, groping for a word,—"exciting?" he finally said for lack of a more descriptive word.

"Why wouldn't he? The best-trained crack cavalry troops in all of Mexico. Any military man worth his salt would find them a glorious group—especially since they are the brainchild of Pancho Villa."

"*Bueno*. You think it's time to arrange between us—a meeting—under the white flag of truce?"

The fact that this was precisely the thought she'd entertained for the past few weeks gave her a jolt of satisfaction. But she was wise enough to know it would have to be Villa's decision. Even so, thought Madelaina, there was always the question of her father's reaction. The animosity between these two warring tigers was vast. Could Obregon set aside his personal feelings toward the man who'd won his daughter's loyalty in the revolution? Could he? Would he? Her silence was misunderstood by the *jefe*, who began to drum his fingers on the table in a slow, almost calculating manner.

"I know what you must be thinking. Politics. Stinking politics again. Perhaps you think I'm a traitor to our cause to even consider dealing with an enemy—a formidable one at that. But I've come to learn that anger in a debate causes the argument to be forgotten. And the argument here is the glory of Mexico, not any one man. Truth of the matter is, *chica*, these past many weeks since the death of the gringo *hacendado* I've given much thought to victory and defeat. In my campaigns, I've wounded and wounded deeply, knowing full well that after such a battle, nothing is sweeter than the peace which follows. For these severe tactics, I've been chastized, criticized unjustly by our gringo neighbors."

"What do they know of the suffering here? They remain deaf and dumb and blind to our pleas. They won't listen to the cries of the people whispering in the wind," said Madelaina in his defense. "It remains for a man like you, *Jefe*, a man with heart, soul, and conscience for his people to take up the standard and carry it through to perch atop the highest steeple at Zocalo."

Villa tried hard to blink back the tears that watered his eyes at her touching words. He shook his head slowly. "What will happen if I *cannot*—or *will not*—rule our liberated Mexico? That is the question. Who will rule Mexico once Villa has won the revolution? You see, nothing is easy. Even victory presents more complications than I've bargained for. Since the light was turned on in my mind, all I do is worry, worry, worry. Such is the fruit of a thinking man."

"What good will it do to prepare a parley with my father?"

"It is useless to shoot arrows into an iron statue, *chica*. Obregon grows in strength daily. Make no mistake, Little Fox, General Obregon is better trained in the military than is Pancho Villa."

"He's been in the military all his life. It's only natural that he thinks like a *Científico*. But do you deny that your conquests are greater than his?"

"Obregon's campaigns are far less complicated than the bloodbaths we've left in our wake. Where I hit heavily fortified garrisons, your father is more clever to conserve his forces and he continues to win territory and a reputation."

Madelaina retorted hotly. "Why wouldn't he, *Jefe*? Whenever you attack, you attract all the *Huertistas* from the coast, giving Obregon the opportunity to take over the weakened garrisons, and so doing, he comes out smelling like a rose." To emphasize her point, Madelaina pointed to several areas on the map tacked to the wall along one side of the room. "Not only that, after you've captured a town and moved on, leaving a

836

flimsy crew in charge, he assaults the village and takes it back, weakened and in desperate straights, without booty."

"Precisely," said Villa smiling. "Perhaps working hand in hand, we can march into Mexico City side by side. It is not for naught that my people have a saying—'Two that are of the same opinion can conquer a city.' "

Madelaina got the picture, but she shuddered inwardly at the complications this scene posed in her mind. "*Jefe*, my father is an ambitious man. It would bear well to remember that among my people there is another saying—'The fox favored by fortune conquers the lion favored by strength.' "

"Ayeiii, *chica*, but remember, all those sayings work both ways."

"My father lacks political polish—"

"*Muy bien*. What you are saying is that Obregon needs Carranza to gain this—uh—political polish, eh? Perhaps as much as Carranza needs Obregon's strength—"

"And both of them need you, General Villa, to grind the *Federales* of Huerta into cattle feed!" retorted Madelaina, pouring herself another glass of wine. "With your permission, *Jefe*?" She held the glass up toward him.

"That's true, what you say. Very true."

"Recently, in an interview with Miguel Guerra, you publically labeled my father a chocolate-drinking, pig-headed, mad goat."

"That's true, too," said Villa, suppressing a wicked smile.

"That means my father must be out of his head to beat you at every turn."

"That's also true. You think you can arrange such a meeting between us before I meet with Don Carranza?"

She gave him the shadow of a smile. "Insults stir his *gachupín* blood to boiling. You have a parley planned with Carranza?"

"Of course. The spider is from birth a weaver. It's important to see the sort of web this spider Carranza weaves. Now, what you say, Little Fox?"

"It's been said, *Jefe*, that we *gachupíns* always demand the impossible and somehow get it accomplished."

"Then you'll act as emissary to General Obregon?"

"First, I must tell you what it entails."

Madelaina proceeded to explain that her son was in the hands of her father, and of the purported deal made with Peter Duprez for her return. "I don't know how the general will take to such a proposal. If I go, it may mean I will be detained longer than I intend to be detained."

"Then it's out of the question, Little Fox." Villa paused and looked at her intently. "Unless, of course, you desire to go of your own free will."

"He has my son. I have longed to see his face, *Jefe*."

"I will send an escort with you. Obregon will not dare to detain you as long as you're an emissary of mine. In war, father or not, he's a military man."

Before any decision was made, General Villa and his guest were interrupted by an announcement that Don Venustano Carranza had arrived to speak with General Pancho Villa under a white flag of truce.

"Speaking of Lucifer—" began Villa with amused eyes. "He's ahead of time."

"I will go and think on your proposal, *Jefe*," said Madelaina. "I leave you men to your politics. It's best that Carranza doesn't see me if I'm to confer with Obregon on your behalf. Who knows what treachery lies beneath that white-haired, aristocratic benevolence dressed in a German coat?"

"*Bueno*. Go this way." He indicated to a side door.

Madelaina pulled a black scarf over her head, partially shielding her face, and left the premises. Outside, she trudged along the parched, cracked earth, kicking up little puffs of smoke in her wake. She had much to think about concerning Villa's request. She thrashed a small riding crop alongside her boots as she walked, absorbed in her thoughts.

Approaching her from another direction, his back to the sun, came the imposing figure of the man recently labeled "Villa's Butcher." Rudolfo Fierro's steps were slow and languid, in the rhythm of a great cat. He called to her.

"*Espera, señora*. Wait for me.'

Madelaina stopped, shaded her eyes against the hot, glaring sun, and recognizing him, waited as his steps quickened to catch up to her. Fierro removed his hat with a sweeping gesture of courtesy.

"You have a guest, *señora*, who insists upon seeing you immediately." Fierro's stone face indicated neither pleasure or displeasure over this. He did add apprehensively, "Be careful of this one. She appeared like a bird in flight from nowhere. How she got past our sentries is what I intend to learn as soon as I escort you to her. She is in your quarters at the hacienda."

Madelaina nodded and fell into step alongside him, filled with curiosity. A woman? Clever enough to get past the cadre of officers guarding the military compound? Most interesting. She continued to strike her boots absently with the riding crop as they made their way to the rambling building and entered the villa proper.

Inside, Madelaina discarded the *rebozo* covering her head and shoulders and jerked her head back, swinging her long dark hair off her shoulders. Her eyes, adjusting to the cool, dimly lit interior, scanned the room for the uninvited guest.

The young woman, dressed in a full-skirted, Indian peasant's dress with a low-cut blouse, was seated primly in a highbacked chair, a backpack at her sandaled feet. She was thinner than Madelaina recalled, but it wasn't difficult to recognize the one-time *puta* of General Obregon and Paco Jimenez.

"Dolores Chavez," she said in a moderate tone. "What brings you to the camp of Pancho Villa?"

"*Señora Obregon! Dios mios!* I am happy to have found you after all this time." She rose to her feet and ran to Madelaina's side, expecting a warmer greeting than the frosty reserve shown by the daughter of her one time paramour. She recoiled instantly and immediately fell into a subservient role. She glanced at Rudolfo Fierro, and sensing the cold brutality in the man, she lowered her eyes and stared at her open-toed sandals.

"Please, *señora*, it is in private that I must speak to you."

"You may speak before General Fierro," said Madelaina.

The girl shrugged. "It is your *niño*, your baby. He is *muy mal*. Has much fever. Generale de Cordoba, he say you come, *pronto*."

Madelaina's dark eyes were leveled on the girl. She stepped in toward her, fingering her knife with menace. "Hear me, woman. If you are not speaking the truth, I shall finish the job *La Condesa* apparently forgot to finish." For added emphasis, Madelaina struck the palm of her hand with the leather crop.

Dolores Chavez fairly cringed. "*La Condesa? Dios mios*, no! *Por favor*, not that evil one, Golden Dawn. I have not seen her long since I leave Zacatecas."

Madelaina relaxed somewhat, but not entirely. She didn't trust the girl. "What is the matter with my baby? Where is he?"

"In Zacatecas. He is with a strange fever. *Muy mal*— much fever, *senora*."

"Not at El Dorado? What exactly did General de Cordoba say to you?"

"Only to find you and return with the wind, *muy pronto*. Only a mother knows how to care for her *niño*."

"Why didn't they think of that before they snatched him from my breast? Oh, never mind. Why didn't he think to return the child with you? It would have been better and saved us all time."

"Why so many questions, *señora*? Is it not enough that I risk my life to find you?"

"Perhaps, Dolores," she temporized, leveling her dark, cold eyes on the girl.

"Besides," added Dolores, a bit hastily. "The major general was concerned that the child should fall into the wrong hands—for instance, Major General Salomon." Her eyes secretly challenged Madelaina, then the fire died out.

Madelaina's dark eyes smoldered at the sound of Salomon's name. She forced herself to keep in check. "Now then, be kind enough to explain to General Fierro and myself just how you got past our sentries."

Fierro's appreciation of Madelaina Obregon increased considerably. *What a cool one, this Little Fox. She asks the right questions*, he thought. *Now, let's see where it gets her*. He fingered the red-haired fetish at his belt.

"You forget I am a *campesina* of the *Federales*? For years, I, too, know how to gain access to forbidden places. I am a Mexican *peón, señora*. I know the land. I may be a common whore to you, used by your father whenever he had the need, but I am of the people, a Mexican."

"How did you get past the sentries?" Madelaina repeated patiently.

"You think it was difficult? I hid in one of the wagons filled with supplies coming from Chihuahua. No one stopped to inspect the contents. They just waved the driver, Pepe Rodrigues, on into the compound. I made my escape while he unhitched the burros. It was easy." Glancing at Fierro and the fetish, Dolores shuddered involuntarily.

Madelaina's eyes lifted to Fierro's and carried a silent message, which he'd already picked up. He'd make certain a man named Pepe Rodrigues had actually hauled supplies from Chihuahua, that all supply wagons were to be stopped for inspection, even if Pancho Villa himself should drive one onto the compound.

"You may leave us, General," she told Fierro.

"With your permission, I'll remain until your decision is made."

"Then, it's done. I must see to the safety of my child." She pulled Fierro toward the door and spoke confidentially to him, so Dolores would not hear. "I leave on a mission for the *jefe*. Tell him I'll do his bidding. I shall return when I've obtained the proper reply." Then she spoke aloud. "General, have the men prepare a wagon for me with enough supplies for two to last until we get to Zacatecas."

"You don't intend to make such a journey by wagon, *señora*?" called Dolores aloud with obvious dismay.

"And why not?" countered Little Fox, turning abruptly to the girl.

"Time. Too much time! By train we can be in Zacatecas in a day—not five. Unless you wish to accept the responsibility of your baby's life!"

Madelaina's eyes narrowed. She stared at the girl, studying her brazen, outspoken manner. She turned to Fierro. "The girl makes sense." She rang a bell summoning a servant woman. "Feed the woman, she's traveled far," she instructed the older woman. Madelaina led Fierro out the door and told him Dolores was the *puta* of her father, that she'd known her for some time, and although she didn't understand why she'd be given such a sensitive mission, she could understand that a *campesina* would fare far better than an officer of the *Federale* army in an attempt to pierce enemy lines.

Fierro hardly flickered an eyebrow at this. He touched his hat and left to attend to his work. She watched him head toward the front gates of the compound, then joined the former mistress of her father inside.

"While you fill your belly, I'll pack a small bag of necessities. Tell me, did they summon a doctor for my child?"

"I'm certain everything that can be done has been

842

done. They tell Dolores nothing. Only to summon you."

Madelaina, uneasy about the whole thing, still persisted in her questions.

"Why didn't they send a Federal courier—or a military attaché—even a military escort under a white truce, if they knew my whereabouts? Even a wire?"

"Perhaps because your father's memory serves him well. You might have run away or resisted as you've done in the past."

Dolores' momentary naïveté sprang from an effort to pretend to a lack of worldliness and was weakly enacted. Madelaina saw that the girl was indeed a poor actress. Why, for *dos* pesos, she'd have tossed the girl out. Not for a moment did Madelaina trust her. She excused herself when the older serving woman brought food and Dolores pounced hungrily upon it.

Outside, once again, Madelaina's steps quickened as she headed toward the telegraph station. She hastily scribbled a message and handed it to the clerk with orders to send it immediately. The bespectacled clerk, a thin, young man with a thick crop of black hair, scratched his head wondrously. "But this is incredible, *señora!* To receive an answer before a message is sent is not how this machine works! *Dios mios!* Miracles of miracles!"

"Stop your jibberish," she said sternly. "What are you talking about?"

"Perhaps, he means this, *señora*," came the voice of Rudolfo Fierro behind her. He was holding a message in his hand, outstretched to her.

Madelaina was given to surprises, but never had she been so amazed and at the same time grateful for the astute thinking of General Fierro. No wonder he was so invaluable to Pancho Villa. She read the message:

To Federal Garrison Commander, Chihuahua City. Be advised that the mission of which you inquire, by one Dolores Chavez, is legitimate. The child is critically ill. The mother's presence is needed. Code F ac-

knowledged. *Major General Felipe de Cordoba, Fort Zacatecas.*

"You had your doubts as I did?" Madelaina folded the message and tucked it into her camisole. "Perhaps you'd better send another wire, General Fierro. Announce that Madelaina Obregon is en route as emissary from General Villa and seeks audience with General Alvaro Obregon."

"Are you crazy?" he spoke in faultless English. "The message might be intercepted by *Huertistas*, and thinking you might be an excellent prize, kidnap you for ransom. I'm sure both General Villa and General Obregon might be encouraged to make many concessions to secure your release."

"Damn!" she cursed softly. "Of course, I wasn't thinking! How stupid of me." She paced before him in the small, wooden structure serving as a wireless room: "*Bueno*, General. Let's walk back to the hacienda. I have a plan," she told him.

An hour later, Madelaina was dressed in the smart gray travel suit and matching hat, her hair piled atop her head, looking every bit like a gringo tourist, with the proper papers identifying her as Mrs. Peter D. Benson, giving her resident address as Seven Moons, Amarillo, Texas. She was accompanied by Dolores Chavez, traveling as her maid, with papers to indicate she, too, was from Amarillo, Texas.

If Madelaina saw two well-dressed businessmen enter the car and sit to the rear, never taking their eyes from the women, she paid them no mind. Two additional men, boarding the car ahead of them, and two more in the car behind them brought no suspicions to her mind. They had all taken specific seats, each with their eyes fixed on the panes of glass separating the cars, through which they could see the women.

The train ride, dull and boring, was considerably faster than a wagon. She noted it was far more comfortable than the jostling one was subjected to in a carriage. With the advent of progress, things were vastly

844

improving, she admitted. The train made several stops en route to their destination. At lunch time, Dolores opened a food hamper and handed Madelaina a package containing dainty American-style sandwiches, a small bottle of wine, and figs. Madelaina munched heartily on her food as did the other train passengers, and for a long while the unusual aroma of food was difficult to ignore.

Before midnight the train stopped in Torreon, the midway point. They got off the train, stretched their legs, purchased newspapers and a few sweets, and after making use of the public convenience facilities provided for travelers in the train depot, boarded the train once again.

Marveling at the progress made since the revolution first commenced, she had hope that Mexico might one day become as progressive as their American neighbors.

Once the train pulled out of Torreon, Madelaina began to squirm uncomfortably. She wanted to smoke a cigarette, but for women in the first-class section, this was forbidden. She was growing increasingly uneasy, attributing it to the need to smoke. Finally, she forced her eyes closed, as the overhead lights dimmed, allowing those passengers who wished to sleep to do so without annoyances like lights to disturb them.

Madelaina's thoughts began to shift and change as pictures formed in her mind. For several moments she saw what appeared to be ghouls in purple shrouds with empty black holes for eyes. Then this shifted and the pictures appeared. She saw herself running frantically, pursued through a strange, thickly wooded place. Blood dripped from her hands and she seemed unable to catch her breath. She couldn't breathe; she felt a terrible struggle inside her as if her heart would burst if she didn't get some air. She stirred frantically, struggled, fought with all her strength as the face of Simon Salomon flashed before her. God, how she grappled and exerted herself, thrashing about. She attempted to blink her eyes, but they refused to open as if a powerful adhesive had been applied to glue them shut. A peculiar odor filled her with nausea, and she felt herself falling, catapulting into black abyss. Then it was total darkness and complete immobility.

Chapter 31

As consciousness returned to her, Madelaina became fully aware that she was no longer on a train. An aromatic odor clung to her, and she tried desperately to orient herself. She couldn't move. Her body, she felt certain, was spread-eagled on a bed, judging from the feel of a mattress. Her arms, spread back and tied to the posts, were as rigid as her feet and as firmly secured. Unable to see due to the blindfold tied over her eyes and unable to cry out with the gag stuffed into her mouth, she was helpless.

She was sweating profusely, the drops rolling off her face and neck like raindrops. The room was sultry, and she was aware that her clothing had been removed. The knowledge of this left her feeling more despondent. She had no weapons to defend herself with. What had happened?

The last thing she recalled was lying back in her train seat, the lights dimming overhead—then nothing after that. Absolutely nothing.

Madelaina cocked her head and listened. She tried to familiarize herself with natural noises. Was that water falling? Rain? The ocean? A river? What? She couldn't tell. She heard voices speaking in hushed tones, nothing loud or clear enough to discern. At least she had her senses, and outside of the discomfort she felt, she didn't feel wounded or harmed. How long she lay there, trying to piece together parts of a puzzle, she didn't know.

Someone had entered the room. She tensed and strained against her bindings. The panic she experienced reminded her of the diabolical exposure to the sadism of Heurta and Salomon. If only she could speak or cry out. If only she could see. *Dios mios*, this was worse than anything. Without eyes to see or a mouth to speak, of what good were the other senses except to instill a morbid fear in a person? She attempted to tilt her head back to see under the blindfold, but the room was in total darkness. She wanted to cry out, to ask who it was in her room, to plead with someone for mercy, to remove the gag choking her lips, but, of course, she couldn't.

Whoever it was in the same room with her had seated himself alongside her on the bed. She knew it was a man by the heavy way in which he fell onto the mattress. She heard an unfamiliar rustling sound, labored breathing, the faint flopping sound of boots being removed. Then she felt her flesh shrink and quiver as the touch of human hands lightly caressed her body. She felt her body recoil from the touch, yet simultaneously she found the feeling pleasurable.

A voice whispered huskily. "You and I, Madelaina Obregon, have unfinished business to attend to."

A sudden feeling of terror made her gasp and choke on the gag.

"If you promise to cooperate, I'll remove the gag," whispered the man seated on the bed with her. "No one will hear you if you scream, so you might as well understand that. And if you do scream out, I can easily allow you to inhale more of the floral scents you inhaled last evening. Do you wish that?"

She shook her head furiously.

She felt the gag being untied and the strips of cloth removed from her parched lips. The blindfold was still intact.

"Would you like some water?" he asked, tilting her head up to receive some of the desperately needed liquid.

Madelaina swallowed, fairly gulped the water as it streamed down the corners of her lips onto her face, neck, and shoulders. But she didn't care. Anything to relieve the dire thirst that pervaded her for the past hours of consciousness.

848

"I'd remove the blindfold, too, if I didn't think you'd cause harm to yourself when you see me. For the time being, I'll leave it on. Then, after we've enjoyed ourselves and I've succeeded in taming you, I'll remove it."

"Please," she begged. "Who are you? Why are you doing this? I'll pay you money. You have mistaken me for someone else. I am Mrs. Peter Benson from Texas. I don't know any Madelaina Obregon."

"Lies, dear Little Fox, will get you no place," came the hushed voice of Major General Salomon. "You didn't think I'd let you get away with all the minor victories you've lorded over me, did you?"

Madelaina recognized the voice. As hard as she prayed it wasn't the man she knew it was, she visualized him clearly as the man in her visions pursuing her through the forests. She fought against her restraints, all to no avail.

He pinned her down to the bed with his strong hands. "Tonight we make up for all the injuries meted to me at your hands, you understand me, *chiquita*? From the first time I saw you, I knew what you were, a whore at heart, and I decided to make you mine. I was patient, wasn't I? I watched you at Madrigal and I lusted for you. I've lusted for you from the first time I set eyes on you at President Diaz' birthday party. Do you know the extent of my desire? I've won you. Yes, I've honestly won you. President Huerta wanted you— your neck hanging from a noose on his most cherished tree inside the palace courtyard, but I won you from your fate. And now you are mine to do with what I please."

Salomon continued: "I don't intend removing the blindfold from your eyes, not yet. I want you to feel the body you've tried to kill with such vengeance that you almost succeeded. I want you to feel first what you've been missing."

Madelaina blinked several times under the blindfold. No question about it, she'd know that voice, the scent of his overpowering colognes anyplace. She fought the urge to lash out at him and found herself relaxing her lips from a loathsome sneer into an inviting smile.

"So! Simon Salomon, it's you. We meet again." She spoke with a calm that momentarily unnerved him.

His laughter filled the room. "What a woman! What an incredible woman you are. Just the right sort for me. I always knew it. Pity you've remained blinded to the fact that we are suited to one another, madam." He delighted in her unusual powers of emotional recuperation whether feigned or real. "Even when your life is on the line—and this time there is absolutely no one to come to your rescue—you still have the monumental audacity and courage to speak so imperiously." He chuckled again. "You *are* something special. Not that I haven't always known it," he said, softly caressing her breasts with his fingertips in a circular brushing motion causing her nipples to stand erect.

"Feel how your body responds and is eagerly awaiting my artistry? Now, my pet, when your mind also bends to my will—and touch—I shall truly perform for you in a manner you shall be unable to resist."

How she loathed this man. Words couldn't describe the anguish, pain, and violent disgust this man had inflicted on her and now this! How was she to cope? If she could see him, she could command her senses to obey her—not his touch. Through the blindfold she could discern nothing, for the room itself must have been thrust in semidarkness. She could only feel him, and this in itself was maddening because her body responded to his touch. What to do? What to do?

She tried to writhe and recoil from his fingers, but she was helpless. She decided to change tack. "So the mighty Salomon imagines himself to be a descendant of Eros, is that it? A man who thinks he's been given a godlike power over women, to make me swoon helplessly in your arms? Very well, go ahead. Take your fill. Do what you will with my body, but know in advance that my mind will never bend to your will—never!" she told the man who'd once devised countless sexual tortures and forced on her various drugs which

850

prevented the mind from exercising any power over the pleasure of the flesh.

"My pet, I have the power within me to make you succumb to anything."

And now, Madelaina heard more clearly what she earlier thought was a river or water of sorts. It was raining outside. A crashing peal of thunder split open the skies and rain gushed forth in a tropical storm. Lightning streaks illuminated the room for split seconds and the sound of rain startled her.

Simon Salomon was evoking the proper sexual responses he wanted from his captive, even though she tried with all the will power she could muster to keep herself frigid and unresponsive. God, how much longer could she resist this man she loathed with her body and soul?

Involuntary moans and sighs escaped her lips as his manipulations aroused her erotically. She sensed him leaning in close to her face, holding himself inches from her lips. Repeatedly she jerked her head from side to side to avoid his lips on hers. He patiently held her head between his hands until she no longer squirmed.

"Might as well enjoy it," he said huskily. "It's going to happen whether or not you want me." He moved in closer and closer, barely touching her and with the tip of his tongue traced the outline of her full lips. A quiver shot through her and she tried not to enjoy it, to hate each moment of it, but God wasn't going to let her off easily. She found herself responding to his touch with a pent-up passion new to her. Blindfolded, even the sound of rain excited her as never before.

Salomon took a sip of wine from the bottle on the nearby table and moved toward her and kissed her, letting a little of the wine seep inside her lips. In her prone position she was forced to swallow the drops and found the warmth of the wine invigorating. He permitted some of the wine to spill over each breast, then with loud sucking sounds, he lapped it up with his tongue, watching her breasts grow firmer and harder as if they might explode at any moment.

He was too well practiced, too well schooled in his art to be a bumbler. He knew every erotic zone in her body; and in a matter of moments had her responding far too willingly to his machinations. *Demonio*! He was right. Her will was bending to his and to make matters worse for Madelaina a powerful desire swelled in her loins and throughout her entire body for him. *Dios mios*! What was wrong with her? Why couldn't she force her body to reject him—to remain cold, frigid, and hateful?

Salomon watched his captive respond to his touch with an expression of calculated strategy, the look of a man awaiting a specific reaction from an experiment he conducted. There was a certain degree of lust registered on his face, but there was more, something more than Simon himself could fathom.

She continued to writhe and squirm and quiver under his intimate, exploring touch, and when for a moment he stopped to cross the room to open a case and remove a few articles, Madelaina found herself straining to listen. What's more, she found herself anxious for his return to finish what it was he began.

"You miss me already, my pet?" he asked, watching her head move toward him. "I'll only be a moment. Would you like more wine?" Finished with what he was doing, Salomon returned to her side. He poured a glass of wine and held it to her lips. "That's it, it will relax you." He set the glass down and continued with his artful strokes. "Ahhh, my pet, I see the honey begins to drip between your thighs. You see—you've wanted me all the time. All these years of wasted time and emotion between us. Why, we could have been the toast of all Mexico, you and I. Our bodies together will warm this bed and many other beds where lovers might lie." He raised himself over her body and lowered himself into position. His lips devoured hers hungrily.

At the same moment, Madelaina felt a stabbing shaft of agony between her thighs that tore all the way into her belly, causing her body to arch up against his in a shock of pain. She felt as if she was about to be ripped to pieces. She heard whimpering, moaning sounds like an animal agonizing pain and realized those sounds escaped her own throat. He's killing me, she thought. He's finally killing me and I can't resist him. She tried to drag her legs up, to jackknife and expel his body from hers, but it was no use. She couldn't move. And she'd not give him the satisfaction of knowing how badly he'd hurt her. Whatever her movements they only increased his apparent lust. He drove himself deeper and deeper inside her body, forcing his tongue inside her mouth, probing and stroking until she needed air to breathe.

It was no use. She was as helpless as a child in the grip of a satanic monster bent on violating her, a demon for sure.

All at once, Madelaina tensed. She felt a hot sensation searing her insides, more shocking than the earlier pain, like a flooding warmth of liquid spilling out from her body, between her legs. "What's that?" she asked, half-reluctant to speak out. "Am I bleeding? Have you torn me apart?" she whimpered, unsure of the sensations shooting through her. "I'm burning up. What have you done to me?"

"I knew you'd enjoy it. You do like it, don't you?" he asked suggestively.

"No. I don't know," she stammered. She desperately tried to isolate the countless sensations shooting through her. The mixture of pain and pleasure, agony and ecstasy was driving her wild. Her head reeled and the room, despite the blindfold, was swirling round her head. Colors flashed in her mind and she felt a sudden elevation, a floating sensation, one of suspended animation where feelings blended into a tremendous wave of erotic delights far superior to anything felt on a carnal level. Tiny explosions of light burst in her mind. Sensations of floating, of transcending the terrestrial limits of earthly beings transported her higher and higher until she was lost in infinity.

A soft, self-satisfied chuckle brought her back to reality. "My, my, what a little tigress you are," he told her. "What would happen if I untied your legs?"

Her throat was parched, but she managed to whisper hoarsely. "Untie them and see for yourself."

"And if I untie your arms?"

"See for yourself."

"You'd like that, wouldn't you? You want to claw at me, scratch at me, and bite into my flesh, don't you?"

"Yes! Yes! Yes!" she hissed between clenched teeth. "All that and more."

"Tell me how you've wanted me. Tell me!" he commanded her.

"Yes," she growled low in her throat. "Yes, I've wanted you. I've always wanted you."

Simon Salomon laughed softly, pleased with himself, as he watched her react to his commands with no will or volition of her own. "And now, tell me what you feel when I perform my next speciality."

She felt him unloosen her legs. She moved her ankles in a circular motion, trying to get the circulation back into them. Instantly she drew them up to her chest.

"Don't be so greedy yet," he told her. "In a moment you'll feel a sensation you've never felt. Then I'll know you'll be my slave for all eternity, Little Fox." He spread her legs apart and slipped his body down over hers and positioned himself between her slender limbs. "From the French came the art I'm about to perform on you," he told her.

Madelaina felt the warmth of his heated breath, first, then a velvety softness, as a thousand little shocks burst all around her. Suddenly she knew what he was doing and she didn't care. All she wanted to do is experience the sensations—every one of them. Madelaina had no control—not over her words or her body. And when she spoke the next few words, it was as if someone else uttered them. "Had I know how it would be with you, I'd have succumbed sooner, my dear, sweet, Simon."

Her legs straddled his back and she pressed him in closer to her, harder and harder. If she had any recollections of this man and what he'd caused to happen to her in the past, they were dimmed by the powerful intoxicant of uninhibited sexual desire. Madelaina wasn't certain of how long she remained with Simon Salomon or he with her. She remembered only the pleasurable sensations and immediate gratification of a deeply rooted physical need which hadn't been fulfilled since the night she and Peter conceived their only child.

Madelaina had been kept forcibly drugged for nearly two weeks before she gained insight into her true predicament. Permitted to wear her own clothing now, she dressed simply, even though Salomon had placed several lovely gowns at her disposal. On this day, as she eagerly awaited Simon's arrival, she selected the seven moon earrings to wear as the only jewelry adornment. She stared at her reflection in the mirror for a long time, watching them move fragilely, then forgot them.

She'd been unaware of the passing of time and had forgotten the reason for her mission to Zacatecas. She hardly gave thought to Dolores, gave no mind to Pancho Villa, the revolution, her husband, not even her father or son. She lived only for the moments she could spend with Salomon. She no longer entertained the pain and longing she'd once endured. It was as if no memory existed of her life before these past few days of sexual fulfillment with Salomon. She thought only of him and the satisfaction of her physical needs and desires.

Simon Salomon was by normal standards a handsome man in his thirties. After seeing the sheer bestiality in the man and his many brutalities in Madrigal, his features had brought loathing and disgust to Madelaina. By the manner in which she greeted him on this day, you'd never imagine that she once detested him with uncontrollable emotion.

Madelaina heard his soft whistle and ran to fling open the shuttered doors, her heart all aflutter like a young schoolgirl. He smiled with unusual tenderness, and looking well pleased with himself, he brandished a bouquet of bloodred roses, which he'd concealed behind his back. Dressed in his immaculate khaki uniform, with the brass buttons and braid and decorations of a major general, he cut a dashing figure for any woman who glanced at him.

She thanked him profusely for the flowers and waited for him to take her into his arms as he'd customarily done each day since they had coupled.

She took his hands and pulled him into her room, one of many in an old convent situated close to Ojocaliente near Zacatecas. Madelaina, of course, had no knowledge of her whereabouts, nor did she care. She eyed Simon with the eyes of love and pouted when he sat down alongside her on the long sofa, refraining from making his usual ovations to her. She placed the flowers on the table nearby.

"My dear," he began. "I must leave you for a while. It's unfortunate that we must be parted, but until these savage and despicable rebels can be halted, our time must of necessity be postponed."

"Rebels? What rebels?" she asked in all innocence.

"You aren't aware of the revolution in our country that tries desperately to oppose our love and all the things it stands for?"

Madelaina glanced at him with the petulance of a spurned lover. "You mean, Simon, that you'll be leaving me? But why? Can't you tell the world to get along without us for a time? It's not fair. We've only just met and already you're called back to duty."

"Don't you worry. I'll try to return as soon as I can. If only I knew a way to put that bloody *guerrillo* in his place. We've sent out spies to try to pierce his network of activity, but they can't penetrate the tight cordon of loyalty that surrounds him. His people pretend to stupidity. His soldiers, when caught, prefer torture at its worst, rather than betray him, and he seems inclined to recruit our own soldiers who defect to him by the dozens daily." Salomon sighed. "What a pity. I will miss you." He eyed her testily as if he were baiting her.

"Oh, Simon," she cried with a burst of disappointment. "What will I do without you? I'll be so lonely, I'll die. Is that what you wish for me to do—die?"

"Of course not, my dear. If only we knew what Pancho Villa was up to—what he intended doing—then it would make my job so much easier. I'd be finished and back to your bed before the week is ended." He watched her craftily, as her reactions, confused and irrational, mounted. She perspired a bit and couldn't seem to breathe, but none of this phased her at the moment.

A servant appeared with hot chocolate, a beverage Madelaina in the past had learned to detest. Now she looked forward to drinking it two and three times a day. Usually after drinking the chocolate, Madelaina perspired freely from the hot liquid. On this day, after her first cup, she shivered noticeably as if she'd suddenly come down with a chill.

"What is it, my dear?" he asked, forcing himself to exercise more patience.

"N—nothing. It's nothing. I suppose the news of your leaving has left me somewhat nervous and upset." Again a chill ran through her and she shivered. "Isn't that strange," she told him. "It must be 100 degrees outside and I'm shivering."

"Oh, my dear. What can I do for you?" Instantly he became solicitous of her. He placed an arm around her and held her protectively. "Does your head ache again? You've complained several times this past week. Perhaps I should summon a doctor for you?"

"I've complained before? Oh, dear, I don't even remember. Nothing seems to matter to me except for our time together. I swear, at times I feel intoxicated by you, Simon. I can't recall anyone having such an impact on me. My love for you grows deeper each day."

"I can't believe that," he said, "when you continue to wear those foolish gypsy earrings. I've bought you several beautiful things, including those fine negligees—the latest from Paris, I was told—and you still

857

cling to that absurd wrap and those—those peasant earrings."

Madelaina's hands flew instinctively to her ear lobes and felt for the small bangles of crescent moons. "Oh, these? Does it matter so much to you, Simon? I shall remove them at once. I shall put on the maize negligee if you promise to remain with me and not go off to that silly war. I don't want you to leave me. You must stay with me, you hear? You must stay!"

"I would if only you'd cooperate, my dear. You, as Little Fox, would know exactly what Pancho Villa has in store for us, and if you wanted, you could keep me at your side forever." He slowly removed her arms from around his neck, where she'd clung to him in an almost maudlin manner. His face close to hers was wiped clear of any emotion. His dark, concentrated eyes bore into hers.

"Little Fox? Me? I know of Pancho Villa?" she asked, a puzzled look swimming across her face. She changed expressions. "You must be confused. I know of no one by that name."

"Oh, but you do, my dear. Think. Think carefully, difficult as it might seem. You do know him. You are called Little Fox, his most trusted confidante," he said in a suggestive manner.

"Simon, why are you bent on deviling me like this? If you are trying to frighten me, you've succeeded. Now stop it and don't make me feel so despicable. I have nothing whatever to do with your going off to war." She poured another cup of chocolate, trying to sift through the crazy thoughts suddenly illuminated in her brain. She fairly gulped the hot liquid in a desperate attempt to warm up.

"I'll leave you to think on my words. I'll return in an hour," he said finally, glancing at his watch. In an hour she'd be feeling worse. Withdrawal would be setting in, and her memory, as painful as it might be, would return to her. Then he was sure to secure her cooperation.

An hour later, as Salomon predicted, Madelaina was

in a worse state of mind. Alternating chills and hot flashes, a state of anxiety and marked agitation possessed her. Memory returned in spurts. Thoughts that she'd been a willing participant in love trysts with a man she'd vowed once to kill filled her with insurmountable guilt. Memories of her life before the abduction compounded the increasing waves of guilt. She grew more anxious, more depressed, and decidedly phobic. She paced the floor in a flurry of agitation and at one point tried to open the door to walk on the terrace, only to learn it had been bolted from the outside. She ran to the shuttered windows, tried to open them, and noticed they too had been secured from the outside. She grew claustrophobic.

Her hands flew to her face. Desperately she tried to subdue a rising hysteria gnawing at her stomach. She felt as if she'd been put through a wringer. Pausing before a mirror, she caught sight of her reflection. Earlier she'd admired herself. She hadn't eaten much these past two weeks and the loss of weight had begun to be noticeable. Now, as she stared in the mirror at her skeletal appearance with dark circles under her eyes, she no longer recognized herself.

Her body shuddered with chills, and she grabbed a shawl to cover herself. Sweat rolled off her face even as ice flowed through her veins. She felt a heaviness in her hands, and her arms sagged, pulling her shoulders down. Her nose began to run and she wiped at it with the back of her hand. Madelaina grew alarmed. One moment she felt as if the flesh were melting off her bones, the very next, she felt as if she'd turned into an icicle.

She scurried across the room and quickly set about building a fire in the fireplace. In moments a fire blazed on the hearth and she grew so hot, she felt as if once again she was on fire. She felt suffocated. Her hands flew to her throat as she glanced wild-eyed and frantic about the room. Spying a pitcher of water, she dashed it on the fire. It sputtered, crackled, and popped, then flamed again as the fire caught hold. "No!" she screamed. "Damnit, no!" She ripped at her clothing, tearing it to shreds, trying to cool off. She grabbed a blanket and began to smother the fire with it, as her eyes flared frantically and her breath came in spasms. Finally subduing the fire, Madelaina gave a thankful sigh and picked herself up from the floor where she'd flung herself to obliterate the fire. She was exhausted.

A shudder of chills tore at her, and she grabbed for anything in sight to drape around her to keep warm and to prevent her teeth from chattering. She pulled at the scarf from the top of the dresser and in so doing scattered her few belongings. For an instant she didn't care what had been disrupted, then her eyes came to rest on the chamois bag of dried, powdery mushrooms.

She glanced at it feverishly, then glanced away, giving it no importance. Once again her eyes traveled back to the bag lying on the floor not far from her. She reached for it instinctively, not certain she knew what it was or what to do with it. She held it in her hands for several moments and continued to shiver.

She fell onto the sofa, drew the covers around her, and sat huddled in a heap, staring down at the leather pouch in her hand. Slowly, as if led by some force unknown to her, she pulled the bag open and peered inside. There was very little left, but whatever it was, she grew curious. She wet her fingertip with her tongue, reached in, and when a few particles clung, she raised her fingertip to her lips and tasted it. She repeated the ritual, and as the bitter powder mingled with her saliva and was swallowed, she began to feel an easier, more relaxed glow permeate her being. In her desperate search for a rational explanation to what was happening, Madelaina concluded that she didn't know anything except for the distortion of depth and sensation, which cleared as quickly as it appeared.

As the haze in her mind cleared, a sudden and instant recall of everything up to her abduction from the train came to her. What remained unclear was how she'd gotten here, to wherever it was she was being detained. Moreover, the recollections of her intimacy with

Simon Salomon became so clear, the pangs of guilt she experienced made her want to retch.

How could she? How could she have willingly permitted that beast to make love to her? Worse, the memory that she'd enjoyed it gave her the feeling that she'd been submerged in dirt with the foulest, most revolting creature on God's earth, and her shame was intensified tenfold by the increasing disgust at her weakness. Why hadn't she killed him as she'd threatened to do so many times in the past? Twice before she had him in her gun sights and hadn't pulled the trigger! Why? Had she really wanted him to make love to her all along just as he'd intimated so many times? Her horror-stricken feelings of despair and disgust began to dissolve as the mushroom powder took more effect.

And she began to recall more—and more. Tolomeo! *Rub the powder on you if you need strength and power.* Yes, yes, she told herself frantically as she rubbed the powder on her lower abdomen. You need strength, Madelaina. You need power. You must never reveal the secrets of Pancho Villa to this odious General Salomon.

Love your enemy and you rob him of his power! "Oh, Tolomeo!" she cried dispassionately. "Whatever do you mean—*love your enemy*? Even that didn't work. It only made me more vulnerable! What is the mystery behind those words? What?" she agonized. "What? Show me and release me from this purgatory!"

Madelaina grew quiet and subdued. She began to think methodically over her predicament. It occurred to her that despite the answer she received from Zacatecas to her inquiry about Dolores Chavez, nothing ruled out the girl being a double spy. After all, no one had more good reason to despise the Obregon family than Dolores. They'd robbed her of her paramour, Paco Jimenez, and after the Golden Dawn affair, her relationship with General Obregon had certainly deteriorated. She had lost everything meaningful

861

to her, so she'd be a ripe target for Huerta and Salomon's admonitions to retaliate against the Obregons.

Very well, thought Madelaina, *where does that leave me? So Dolores is a spy. Now what?* She threw off the blankets and coverings as her temperature returned to normal and began pacing the floor, chain smoking in the process. Tolomeo's words preyed on her mind: *Love your enemy and you rob him of his power.* The words spoken over and over burned in her memory, but still they formed a riddle in her mind.

She gave thought to Pancho Villa's encounter with Carranza. What had been resolved? She hadn't even seen her father to discuss Villa's proposition. What could they be thinking? Before she left, she told General Fierro she'd send him a wire, somehow, even it was only to advise him of her safe arrival. Surely they missed her, didn't they? How on earth would they find her?

While Madelaina struggled hard for answers to her dilemma, a loud rumble from the north was beginning to grow into an outrageous roar.

Pancho Villa's encounter with Carranza hadn't resolved a thing. What it had served to do was to define each man's position in the revolution more clearly than before. Villa had tried to cooperate with Carranza. He'd even decided to set aside his planned attack on Zacatecas. Abandoning his plan, he captured Saltillo instead. Just as Little Fox had suggested, the victory merely advanced Carranza's image. And Villa, in a rage when Carranza announced he'd sent another general to attack Zacatecas, greeted the white-whiskered, self-declared First Chief of the Revolution, cowed by the announcement that President Wilson sanctioned the tricky old bastard, despite the growing rumors of his German leanings. Now, to cap it off, Carranza had the audacity to visit Villa again and ask him to cooperate with the general he'd sent to attack Zacatecas.

"No," countered Villa. "I refuse to send my good

862

men to get your man out of difficulties. Goddamnit! You knew I wanted Zacatecas! You send another man to take it and you ask me to keep my tail between my legs and cooperate? Hah!"

"I do what's necessary for the revolution," replied Carranza in that slow, deliberate, nerve-wracking speech designed to enflame Villa's heart.

Villa stormily paced the confines of his study, staring daggers at the man who continuously rocked his boat. He'd been a fool to fall for his sweet talk. Yet, until Little Fox returned with word from Obregon, he had felt it necessary to cooperate with this lout. But Carranza asked too much! Too much, by damn! He saw readily that Carranza was out to get his goat, to shame and humiliate him by goading him into an animal-like reaction. *Very well*, thought Villa, determined not to be used or outwitted, *I'll play his little game.* Suddenly, he saw the way for Carranza's defeat. He bowed graciously, suddenly quite submissive.

"Very well, First Chief of the Revolution," said Villa mockingly. "You tell me General Natera needs help in Zacatecas? *Bueno.* He gets help."

Carranza eased forward, eyes filled with suspicion. "What sort of help?"

"Everything! Isn't that what you desire? Full cooperation from Villa."

"What you mean—everything? Explain."

"Everything is—everything. All of it. Have no fear. Zacatecas will fall."

"What you mean—everything?" Carranza persisted.

"I will send Natera the whole Northern Division."

"Ridiculous," scoffed Carranza, puffing on his Havana cigar.

"With me alongside."

"Preposterous! I won't permit it."

"Permit it? You won't permit it? You forbid me to move my own army?"

"General Villa, I am doing exactly that. You will send 6,000 men as I've directed, not one more or less.

Unless you wish to branded insubordinate to your commanding officer!"

"Ah," said Villa. "*Muy bien*. Then please consider my resignation tendered."

Carranza, unable to fathom this move, assured Villa that his joke was not amusing.

"What joke?" He sat down at his desk and wrote, "I resign" and signed it Pancho Villa. "There is my resignation. I assure you, it's no joke."

"If you think you are being clever, I'll be a step ahead of you. Before Mexico wonders why you've resigned and asks why you lost your army, I'll announce my reward for the hero of Torreon and Saltillo. I'll make you governor of Chihuahua."

It was Villa's turn to be stupified. "*Que va*, me a governor? Me—a governor?" he repeated wondrously as if Carranza was truly one crazy man.

"Why not? Already you've done an excellent job of running things, but I may have to rescind your order giving the lands to the *peóns*."

Villa saw red. Like Zapata, whose intent it was for the peasants to own their own lands, Villa stood adamant. "You touch one inch of those lands, and I swear by the sainted hair of my mother's head, I'll kill you! Yes, I, Villa the barbarian, the bloodthirsty *guerrillo*, will do such a thing, civilized or not."

With that he moved toward the door, his uniform jacket slung over his shoulder.

"You step through that door, General Villa, and I'll immediately summon all the leaders of the Northern Division, instruct them to elect a new *jefe*, then I shall order 6,000 men to Zacatecas. Do I make myself understood?"

"Summon whoever you please, take my army, my rank, the whole fucking state of Coahuila, and stick them up your ass. Do I make myself understood?"

He stalked out of the door, motioning to his two aides in the outer office to follow him. "You hear it?" he asked as the trio moved out of the building.

864

"We heard."

"Well, there you are. He's your new boss."

"Not mine," said Urbina.

"Nor mine," said Fierro.

"Nor mine, either," said Tracy Richards joining them.

"We go where you go," Urbina insisted, grinning incorrigibly.

"*Es veridad.* That's the truth," offered Fierro.

"Me, too," echoed Captain Richards.

Pancho Villa stopped and turned to his friends, a smile radiating his features. "*Amigos,* I don't know about you or the entire Northern Division, but Pancho Villa goes to Zacatecas. And he will take it as planned at one big party."

"Who else is invited to your party?" asked Urbina.

"Whoever wishes to come," Villa retorted.

"Departure time?" queried Urbina, tilting his sombrero rakishly over an eye.

"Departure time? Departure time?" Villa mused. "It depends on how much luggage we carry. What you say to that?"

Fierro smiled. "May I have the first dance at your party?"

Don Carranza heard the staggering news while seated in the office of the governor's mansion. Villa had left during the night, but he didn't depart alone.

Every man, gun, cannon, war wagon, war bonnet, cartridge, and train belonging to the Northern Division had pulled out for Zacatecas. Villa had not ordered them out. He merely loaded his 300 *Dorados* and his new woman on his personal train, and the whole of the remaining division followed him.

Madelaina Obregon thought at first an earthquake had struck. The earth itself rumbled and shook under her. The walls of the old adobe convent shook, plaster ripped off the wall as cracks split the severed structure in more places, leaving a maze of fine lines like cracked porcelain. Running to the windows, she struck at the louvered shutters with her bare hands, breaking slats at random. Outside, she saw nothing in the ebony darkness. Muffled sounds of familiar artillery fire came from the distance. "What is it?" she cried aloud. "What's happening? Let me out someone, please!" She banged on the door until her fists were swollen red.

Outside, she heard the sounds of marching feet shuffling about the courtyard. She ran to the window, picked up a chair, and smashed the shutters into pieces. Barred windows obstructed any chance of escaping, but at least she saw a contingent of *Federales* forming in the yards below, rifles at the ready, preparing to board a few motorized vehicles, while others mounted their horses and headed out the gates. Madelaina strained to see in the distance, and she realized she was approximately ten miles from Zacatecas as the crow flies. Zacatecas! If only she could escape, she could make her way there easily.

What was happening? She tried the door again—no chance to escape. She was stuck, stuck in this stupid place, until someone came to her rescue. What a revolting situation!

She had no idea that history was being made in Zacatecas by Pancho Villa and the entire *División del Norte*. That at the signal given by Villa, wave after wave of horsemen surged forward at a brisk gallop as the roar of cannon echoed through the nearby mountains. Over 20,000 men transported by Villa's trains faced 15,000 *Huertistas*. The entire Federal garrison was surrounded by artillery, cavalry, machine gun snipers, and every last man in Villa's army.

Buglers sounded calls echoed by other buglers from each brigade.

All were in readiness as Villa shouted: "Brigade Juarez . . . Advance!"

"Bri—gade Fierro . . . Ad—vance!"

"Bri—gade—"

The earth exploded in flames. The mighty Northern Division moved forward like a loud, flame-throwing, prehistoric monster determined to pulverize its enemy into mounds of broken bones that would crumble to dust. Within three hours, the Federal garrison was in shreds, their trenches broken, their cannon overrun. By nightfall, General Francesco Villa was master of Zacatecas.

General Fierro, having captured several officers, put the questions to them that brought instant results. Without informing his *jefe* of his mission, he rode off in a southwesterly direction in the company of two other men.

They stopped at an appointed tavern. After the exchange of a few pesos with the innkeeper, Fierro took the steps two at a time and followed the dark hallway along the centuries-old building, falling prey to time, and knocked softly at the door three times in the signal given him. The door opened a wedge, Fierro's huge shoulders shoved it open, and he stood face to face with a terrified Dolores Chavez.

"Now, *puta*, you and I are going to have us a nice talk," he said in the most syrupy voice he could muster, one that sent chills of terror through the traitorous soul of the whore. He slammed the door behind him and bolted it without the faintest trace of menace either in his voice or his face.

867

At the end of this day, June 23, 1914, Madelaina, unsure of what was happening not far from her, walked the floors of her prison at the convent, chainsmoking one cigarette after another. Her supper, brought on a tray hours before, remained untouched. She knew something had happened militarily, but what? She had no idea of the time. She guessed it might be about eight or nine o'clock in the evening. Outside, she heard the cooing of doves, the rustling of a mild wind.

She picked up a few magazines and periodicals brought to her by one of the servants, thumbed through them for the dozenth time, and finally tossed them all aside in annoyance. Perhaps, she thought, it was best that she tried to rest. Lord only knows what was in the offing for her.

Her thoughts traveled to Peter. She wondered why he hadn't contacted the *jefe* from Washington. Why he hadn't sent her a message by courier or wire? Where was he? Had he returned to Seven Moons to attend to the funeral of his father? A thousand and one questions about her infant son plagued her. Was he really in Zacatecas? If so, was he free from harm during the apparent attack on the fort? She had assumed whatever artillery fire she'd heard earlier that day had to have been directed at Zacatecas. *Dios mios*, pray take care of my son.

Dios mios. Villa had told her he wanted to take Zacatecas. He'd also told her he'd wait for the reply from her father. What had happened to accelerate his plans, that is, if it was Villa who attacked the fort? She was unable to stop the constant barrage of questions forming in her mind or halt the fears over her son.

Madelaina paused in her hysteria to make some common sense assessments. Villa wouldn't have attacked the fort knowing Madelaina was there. Apparently General Obregon wasn't there, either—not if Villa really wanted to come to terms with him. Of course not, she told herself. Then it followed, if General Obregon were not at Zacatecas, her son wouldn't be there either! Neither would Felipe de Cordoba. She took heart. Then it all was some plan of treachery. Even the wires must have been intercepted as Fierro hinted they might be.

Madelaina's wretchedness began to dissolve. Her thinking came into better focus. Taking all that had happened to her into account, she realized that by the time Simon Salomon returned to her—if he returned—he'd expect to find a highly irrational, extremely nervous, and high-strung woman, one who might be overly dependent on him and acquiesce to any thing he suggested. *Yes,* she thought, *I'll have to be far more clever than Simon Salomon could ever guess.*

With this in mind, she began to plot and plan and calculate her next move. It wouldn't be easy, but she'd have to be the most consummate actress in the world. Madelaina washed and perfumed herself and did her hair up atop her head. She donned the most fetching of fur-trimmed negligees furnished by her paramour of the past weeks. Disgusted as she was with herself over their intimacy, she had to force herself to drain all the maudlin self-guilt. She hadn't been responsible for her acts while under the influence of whatever potion had been administered to her, so with strength of mind, she used suggestive means to absolve herself of any guilt feelings. *Listen,* she told herself, *while you sit back and wallow in guilt, you'll not have a clear head to think, nor the courage to follow your plan. So forget everything, except the need for survival.*

Madelaina was prepared for many things, but certainly not the news brought to her by Major General Salomon a half-hour later.

"Simon!" She gushed at him and fell into his arms, when he entered her boudoir. "Oh, my dearest, I've missed you so." She was superb.

Simon Salomon himself wasn't prepared for this demonstrative gesture on her part. He held her at arm's length, studied her face, imbued with adoration, and tried to assert himself as best he could, even as disbelief struck at the very heart of his emotions.

"Madam, I've come to transport you to Mexico City. A change in our plans necessitates an immediate departure," he said, clearing his throat self-consciously. He gestured abstractly and eyed her askance, unsure of what to make of her.

"Simon, beloved, must we? My dear, you've been so good to me these past days that in your absence I've designed a most special night for you, full of all the delights that will titillate your senses. Pray, say you'll abandon your other plans at least until this night is over."

Salomon, totally disarmed by her manner, stared at her wondrously.

"May we please have some hot chocolate, my dear?" She fluttered about him like a jittery *mariposa*. "I'm not certain what that hot toddy contains, dear, dear Simon, but I've been so nervous and cantankerous all day without it. How naughty of you not to have left orders with Josefa to serve me some while you were away. But now that you're back, I can have some, my sweet, sweet lover. Can't I?"

The *Huertista* stood stiff, almost in a military brace, as he watched her in utter fascination. Recalling all he knew about Madelaina Obregon, he grew testy at this new personality emerging. Could the drugs have had such an effect on her? Goddamn, she was too downright amorous. She must have had time to come off the drug—certainly she'd be showing signs of withdrawal. What had happened?

In any event, he had a duty to perform. Huerta

870

wanted to talk with her. Since Villa had captured their most important stronghold—Zacatecas—*El Presidente* was a mighty worried official. He wanted to use her as a weapon to keep Obregon in his stable. Already the General-in-Chief of the Fourth Sonora Battalion was gaining too much popularity and strength. Added to that, word had reached *El Presidente* that Villa and Carranza had merged. Now, if Obregon defected to their side, all would be lost.

So it had been decided: Madelaina would be the pawn to keep either Villa or Obregon out of the capital. Whether or not it would work, it was something Huerta had to try. Simon Salomon knew all this and he had to prevent Madelaina from learning she was headed for the presidential palace. Moreover, he intended to say nothing of Pancho Villa's victory for the time being. He'd humor her. It was the only way. Then, when she wasn't expecting it, he'd use chloroform as his men had used it on the train when they abducted her. It was best that she remain docile during their travels. This little tigress was too clever, too wise in the ways of escape, and he could take no chances.

"It's chocolate you desire, my pet?" He spoke softly, falling into her mood. "But, of course. And while we're at it," he added, unbuttoning his tunic, "there's no reason not to take advantage of our solitude. As you say, Mexico can wait."

Salomon pulled the cord, summoning an aide. He ordered chocolate. "The usual for the *señora*," he said, winking his eye to the aide behind Madelaina's back. He turned to her. "Now, then, my pet, you were saying earlier, you'd planned something rather special for me. I can hardly wait."

"And I, neither," she gushed, helping him out of his tunic. "Oh, let me help you with your boots, beloved." Once they were off, he removed his gun and holster, took out the gun, checked the clip, and shoved it into the waist of his trousers.

"Oh, Simon," she pouted like a spoiled courtesan, "I could hardly sleep this afternoon with all your men

871

shooting outside. I thought we'd had an earthquake for certain with all that artillery fire. My dear, what was happening?"

"You heard from that distance?" he asked, watching her pour him a small glass of wine from the liquor cabinet.

"I tried to sleep, to rest up for your return. I was planning such erotica for you, and I daresay the noise interfered with my concentration." She handed him a glass, took one for herself, and linked arms with him, drinking a toast. "What will happen to us in Mexico City? Can we take an apartment and continue to be lovers?" she asked without shame.

Salomon, embraced totally by this sudden new personality, was on his guard, yet quite flattered to think he'd had this much influence on her. "You may not be interested in me when we arrive in Mexico City. You might have a change in heart, then where will that leave me?" he asked artfully in a beguiling manner.

"Bite your tongue, Simon. My dear, don't you know how much I love you? I never dreamed, when you first told me, you were capable of enchanting me, of loving me, and performing magic with your expertise. Well, I'm living proof. Dear, sweet, sweet Simon, can't you make them hurry with the chocolate? I have such a craving for it. I just can't explain it, sweet." She fluttered her hands.

"It will be here shortly. Now come give me a sample of what treasures are in store for me, my pet." He reached for her, embraced her in a passionate near-savage manner, and with clenched teeth, he tilted her head back and commanded, "Now, kiss me as you've dreamed of kissing me. This may well be our last night together for a while, so we might as well do it up right."

Madelaina gave a small gasp as his mouth closed over hers. She wanted to bite him, scratch his eyes out, reach for the gun between them and pull the trigger. Then what? How would she get past the small army camped outside her quarters and those in the courtyard? She shoved such thoughts from her mind, prepared to give the best act of her life. She forced her body to go limp against his, to become as yielding as a paid whore. She shivered noticeably, forcing her teeth to chatter.

"What's wrong?" he asked, pulling back to watch her face.

"I don't know." She hugged her arms about her and rubbed them with her hands, affecting an excellent pose of one going into withdrawal.

"You'll be all right as soon as the chocolate arrives. Now, my dear, you know the rules. Get the blindfold."

"Blindfold? Oh, not again, Simon. We've done it your way all this time, now can't we do it my way for once?" Her voice held a tremor or two, convincingly.

"You know better than to ask, pet. That's the excitement—the unusual thrills that spring from the fact that you can't see what it is that I'm doing. You don't want the thrill to pass?"

"Well, no," she pouted again. "But it would be nice for me to look into your hypnotizing eyes, which make me shudder and tremble under their power."

"It's enough that I untie your legs to give you more pleasure. Now, don't you wish to give me the same pleasure?" Simon was growing annoyed, playing the silly game with her. The things he did for *El Presidente*! He removed the perfumed, lace-edged handkerchief from the cuff of his shirt and held it under his nose, inhaling deeply. "Ahh, that's more like it," he rhapsodized for a few moments. "The only relief I get from inhaling this perennial dust of Mexico. Does everything here stink of cornmeal and stale chili peppers and *ceverza*? Please, my pet, put on the pale yellow chiffon negligee for me."

Madelaina nodded and opened the hand-painted wardrobe. She slipped out of the negligee she'd selected and donned the pale yellow one he'd requested. She moved about the room, circling around like a fashion model. "Does this suit your imperial highness?" she

873

asked making light of the situation and not certain which road she would embark upon shortly.

"Much better, my dear. Much better." He walked into the adjoining bathroom and looked around the room containing a bathtub, commode, toilet basin, and overhead chain pull. He inserted a key into the wall cabinet and removed a small box of tablets. He returned to the bedroom, poured water from the jug on the dresser into a glass.

"Here's a tablet for your headache, my pet. I don't want anything to spoil our last night here. I'm going to take a bath. By the time I return you will be more relaxed and totally free of any headaches." He watched her slip the tablet into her mouth and sip the water.

Madelaina had thrust the tablet under her tongue and sipped the water, pretending to swallow. "Ugh," she said. "Why is it so bitter?"

"Aspirin is always bitter. Is it not?" He returned to the bathroom.

"What do I do if the chocolate comes?" she asked, lighting a few more candles and a few sticks of incense. She spit the headache powder in a spittoon.

"Tell the corporal to use his own key, leave the chocolate, and lock up again as usual," he called back to her.

Madelaina, finished with the candles and incense, lit a cigarette and paced the floor in agitation. Salomon acted as if nothing had happened. And it had. She knew it. The sound of artillery fire for most of the afternoon told her something was underfoot. She hadn't been a *soldadera* for nothing. She could smell the odor of gunpowder in the air. She gazed into the courtyard below. Except for a few sentries, the usual hustle and bustle were missing. Earlier she heard sounds of wagons lumbering out of the courtyard as if the army contingent housed in this facility was on the move.

Yet Salomon himself remained cool and complacent. What did he have in mind? She had to know. Was that really a headache powder—or something else? To keep

874

up the pretense, she assumed it to be a sedative of sorts. So, she had to fake being drowsy for a time.

By the time Salomon emerged from the bath, more relaxed and refreshed than he'd been earlier, Madelaina lay prone on the bed in an affected state of drowsiness. Clothed in a royal blue damask robe with velvet shawl collar and cuffs, he walked to her side, lay a cool perfumed hand on her forehead, and studied her face. He leaned over her, forced open a thickly lashed eyelid, and then let it flutter heavily back into place.

He poured himself a glass of wine from a decanter on the dresser, then from a drawer he removed a few pieces of silken rope. Returning to the bed, he proceeded to tie her feet to the bedposts. "Are you asleep, my pet," he asked softly.

"Uhhh," she replied lazily as her eyes fluttered open. "I'll wake up in a few moments. Whatever made me so drowsy?" she asked.

"Your hands, pet," he ordered, waiting to tie them to the bedposts above her head. Before she extended them to him, a knock at the door interrupted them.

He placed the rope on the nearby table, picked up his automatic, and crossed the room to the door. The room in partial illumination from the glow of candlelight, with flickering shadows playing tricks along the walls and ceiling, made it difficult to see clearly. Salomon opened the door. "Set the tray down on the table," he instructed the aide. "Leave us. I'll knock when I wish you to unlock the door."

He turned from the aide, allowing him to pass without glancing at him.

The heavy-set man moved silently across the room and placed the tray containing the hot chocolate on the table. Madelaina glanced casually at him and felt a sudden jolt of excitement which she instantly attempted to subdue. She quickly averted her eyes at the silent signal telegraphed to her from the glittering eyes of Rudolfo Fierro. Her heart, beating wildly, thundered so loudly in her ears, she was certain Salomon could hear it. She tried with superhuman effort not to give either herself or Fierro away.

Sweet, sweet Jesus! They hadn't abandoned her. They'd found her!

Salomon waved Fierro out of the room with his gun tip and locked the door behind him. He waited to hear the double lock from the outside. Satisfied, he shoved the gun into his robe pocket and walked toward her.

The radiant glow on her face was due to Fierro's presence, but in gazing upon her, Simon Salomon misinterpreted this radiance as a genuine affection bestowed upon him by this woman he'd succeeded in taming. Puffed up with importance, he sat down next to her on the bed and opened her negligee to lift out her firm, full breasts. He took one wrist and tied it to the bedpost.

"Why won't you let me be free so I can reciprocate your love?"

She feigned a few amorous gestures, knowing they stimulated him sexually.

"Let's not discuss it further," he retorted, tugging firmly on the ties. "I've already told you how important this is to me." He secured her other hand, then arose to pour some chocolate for her. He returned to her side and allowed her to sip the contents of one cup. He refilled the cup and brought it back to the bedside, placing it on the nightstand.

"And now, my dear," he said, his face glowing with super macho ego, "we begin out night of a thousand delights." He placed the blindfold around her, tied it securely, and planted a brutally hard kiss on her lips, as Madelaina struggled for air. Apparently this time, Salomon didn't secure the blindfold tightly enough and Madelaina could see under it. She'd been besieged with an overwhelming desire to see what it was that he was so secretive about, but knowing that Rudolfo Fierro wasn't far away lessened her desire and increased her edginess.

She saw Salomon rise to his feet and remove the robe. Madelaina gave a start and gasped aloud.

876

Strapped around his middle, just above the genitals, were the largest penis and testicles she'd ever seen. No wonder she felt as if she'd been ripped wide open. The apparatus was harnessed around his hips with a series of smaller straps. It was difficult to make it out, and she wouldn't have if it hadn't been for the fact that Salomon seemed to be trying the apparatus out. From the sac of the testicles there extended a small bulb that released a fluid from the tip of the penis.

She wanted to speak, tried to find the adequate words to say, but didn't dare because he'd know she'd seen. But the utter farcical quality of this entire scene as everything came together in her mind stimulated her to scornful laughter.

His head jerked around to her. "Why are you laughing?" he demanded scorchingly. "Can you see? Has your spying, sneaky mind compelled you to force this humiliation upon me?"

Madelaina's laughter froze. She was helpless again, unable to move. Why didn't Fierro come for her? Now, before anything terrible happened.

Salomon savagely tore the blindfold from her eyes. "Very well, you tainted whore, take a good look. See what it is that's made you bend like a reed in the wind. Yes, that's right! Not even flesh and blood!" He paraded before her, one hand on the inflated false appendage as if it were the standard of a proud flag. He began to gallop around the room as if he were astride a wild stallion, pumping the dildo as if he were ejaculating. His eyes turned fiery and swollen as he moved in toward her. Holding the hollow rubber penis in one hand, he pressed the bulb and squirted fluid all over her breasts.

"It's better than flesh and blood! Has more endurance. How well you know that, my pet, don't you?" he asked, his voice growing hoarser. "I hadn't meant for you to learn of this yet, not until I had won you over totally."

Madelaina fairly shrank from him. She tried to turn away from him. The whole episode was sickening, and she felt like vomiting from the sight of him. She was right the first time, when she labeled him a sexual pervert, a psychotic who needed institutionalizing. She wasn't prepared for the next move on his part. He jumped on the bed and forced the repulsive thing to her lips.

"Open your mouth and taste the elixir," he commanded.

She shook her head, clenched her teeth, and pressed her lips firmly together. She was in a state of frenzy.

"Open your mouth," he commanded again, his face hardening.

She shook her head fiercely. Salomon pinched her breasts with such force, she screamed out. He took that moment to shove the rubber dildo into her mouth. His hand squeezed the bulb and her mouth filled with a fluid she readily recognized by its offensive odor. She shook her head from side to side, dislodging the apparatus, and spat the fluid into his face. "Filth! Pig! You bastard!" she screamed. "Fucking low life, the worst obscenity of a pig!"

Her words were drowned out by his raucous laughter. "You were better at Madrigal, my pet, when I let all those creatures have a go at you. I should have remembered to use more Spanish fly, as I did last week, then you'd have been more amenable to this."

One of Madelaina's hands had tugged free of its restraints. So surprised was she at this, she didn't allow him to see it for a moment. When the time was right, however, she'd fix his tail. Earlier, she taken her seven moon earrings apart and had slipped a few pointed crescents under the mattress. At the right time she'd planned to pierce his eyes with those sharp points. Once again, he'd chosen to tie her down. She had hoped he'd have left her free when she suggested she wished to reciprocate. Now, realizing why he hadn't, she had to think of a different plan.

It all happened so swiftly that later, when she tried to reconstruct the continuity of events, she wasn't certain which came first. She saw Simon Salomon stiffen, his head shot up and arched backward. At that moment, Madelaina's free hand reached out from behind her and she tugged at the crazy contraption he wore, breaking it free from his body. Her eyes widened in amazement as she stared in the area of his loins. Simon Salomon had the sac and penis of an infant boy! Why, her son Alejandro had more than this man had, she later recalled thinking. She looked up into his eyes, glittering maniacally like an animal's in the night. Simon Salomon was pulled off her bodily, and she shrank back away from him as Rudolfo Fierro's large frame loomed from out of nowhere, enveloping the *Huertista*, his elbow caught around Salomon's throat, pressing, pressing, pressing until Salomon's struggles ceased and his body went limp. Only then did Fierro release the former secret service captain who'd risen from the ranks to enjoy the title of major general in the *Federale* army, and now departed earth to meet his maker. Fierro dropped the dead body to the floor and removed his knife from Salomon's back. He wiped the bloodied knife on his trousers and called imperatively to Little Fox as he slashed at her bindings.

"Quick, we have no time to lose. Get dressed." He glanced at his watch as she hurriedly donned a pair of trousers and a shirt. "Follow me, *señora*. Do only as I do and once you've mounted your horse, ride with the wind. In less than ten minutes, this place will explode. Understand?"

"*Si, mi Generale*. I understand. Fierro?"

"*Si?*"

"Thank you for saving me."

"We've no time to give thanks. *Vamenos!*"

"One moment, please." Madelaina rinsed out her mouth with wine and shuddered as she recollected the earlier events. She reached under the mattress and collected the golden earrings. "*Bueno, muchacho. Vamenos!*"

It was Rudolfo Fierro's turn to stare down at the childlike genitals on the overgrown man, almost reluctant to tear his eyes from the spellbinding malformation. "So this was Huerta's *vieja*, eh? He spat at the man, silently hating the pot-bellied, hairless man with rounded hips proportioned as a woman. It was almost as if his own manhood was threatened by the sight of him.

He shuddered and shoved Madelaina out the door. They made their way down the steps, past the courtyard, stumbling over a few dead bodies Fierro had disposed of en route to free Little Fox. Crouching down in the shadows, hugging the building, they moved swiftly like silent Indians, until they reached the stashed horses. Instantly they mounted and rode off into the night, making their way out onto the desert and nearby hills like riders born to this earth.

From the top of the hill, both Fierro and Little Fox, panting and out of breath, relaxed their lathered horses briefly to watch the old convent at Ojocaliente be reduced to rubble. One explosion, two explosions, three—one after another—shot debris into the air, as the very earth beneath them roared and rumbled in angry protest. Flames shot into the air, as fire spread rapidly in every direction.

The sound of fast riding came at them and Fierro tossed her a rifle. "Those crazy dynamiters," he grinned in a rare moment. "They did it again." He waved to Captain Tracy Richards and two more men from the Gringo Brigade, and the foursome rode swiftly to the fort at Zacatecas.

Central Mexico was in a state of confusion, with *Huertistas* attempting to recuperate their losses, and *Villistas* enjoying the fruits of their labor, and the men of Carranza unsure of who would reach the capital first.

On July 8, General Obregon patiently and methodically threw his 20,000 men against Guadalajara and won his greatest victory to date. The *Federale* garrison lost 2,000 dead and 5,000 prisoners. Obregon's booty was twenty cannon, twenty-nine locomotives, and an enormous warehouse of small arms and ammunition.

On July 15, *El Presidente* Huerta, seated on that throne in the presidential palace, reassessed his position. With western ports cut off, main railroads and cities blocked by Pancho Villa in central Mexico, and an army of Mongol-like hordes led by Emiliano Zapata coming from the south, Vitoriano Huerta took his best shot. He pilfered two million pesos from the national treasury and beat it the hell out of Mexico City and for a time was exiled in Cuba. Huerta's iron rule of terror and conspiracy, deception and disgrace was over at last, and the man responsible for his downfall was the man he'd once set before a firing squad and on whom the fates had shined.

Huerta's flight brought about another defection. Orozco, abandoning his Redflaggers, fled to the American border asking for asylum.

The news reaching Zacatecas was cause for celebration and the entire fort was in fiesta. Only General Villa, happy as he was about the departure of his two worst enemies, couldn't drink or get drunk enough to forget the revolution, not with the same abandon his men employed to relax and celebrate.

Madelaina had wandered about her old haunts at the fort in Zacatecas, reliving old memories when as a child all she had to concern herself with was playing soldiers with Felipe de Cordoba. In the past few years, she'd grown up to know a world entirely different than the one on which she'd been weaned.

Every nook and cranny of her old home stoked up powerful memories; some good, some bad, and many others which no longer had meaning for her now that her life had come around to a complete circle. She had much time to think over her recent circumstances and wonder over her strange involvement with Simon Salomon. Somehow she began to justify his satanic behavior. She recalled all the vile and contemptible insults she'd hurled at him at Madrigal de Los Altos. She'd called him a half-crazed psychopathic killer, a boozed-up *borrachón*. She had also called him a poor excuse of a man—a castrated eunuch! Little did she know the

881

pain and anguish he must have carried all his life to have been born. She understood now why he chose to be a voyeur instead of a participant in those sadistic parlor games he inflicted upon her at Madrigal.

Preposterous! Am I suddenly going soft in the head, she asked herself. *What the hell's wrong with me? Justifying his malevolent behavior!* She shuddered and recalled all that had happened at Madrigal. She found her fists clenching and unclenching as waves of guilt fell upon her once more when she remembered the intimacies shared with Salomon and that giant false phallus! *Dios mios!* Would she ever forget it?

Oh God, Peter! Where are you? Why didn't you take me away from all these bad memories? Why did you ever open my eyes to the suffering and pain in the world? Better that I'd been born blind—with no feeling—without the capacity for compassion! By the time it all ends, I'll be an empty shell, without feelings, without shame or conscience. She moved into the rear courtyard of their old villa, next to the gates where she and Felipe had witnessed their first execution before a firing squad order by Diaz. She could almost hear the crunching of pebbles as boots marched to the point of execution, the clicks of bolts as they were pulled back before the bullets exploded to fell the old man. What was his name? El Lobo? Something like that. Seated under the jacaranda tree, Madelaina couldn't stop the flow of memories or thoughts.

She must have been there at least two hours. *Finally,* she thought, *here I am again, only a different man, not my father, sits in command on the fort.* What had really changed over the past few years? Nothing. The same petty thoughts, restricting ideas, and the greed for political power was ever present. The people were still hungry, living in near-destitute conditions, with disease and death hovering close to them. Only the faces of the people changed around her, replacing the dead and gone.

General Villa was right. Yesterday he had addressed his chiefs of staff after the revelry had died down. He had told them of his plans and ended by admitting, "There is still so much more to do!" Madelaina agreed with the *jefe*. There was so much more to be done. The question was, could it all be done?

Madelaina's hopes and aspirations weren't as optimistic as Pancho Villa's. Especially not on that August 15 when news reached Zacatecas that General Alvaro Obregon had marched on Mexico City to claim the capital for the Constitutionalist government of Don Venustano Carranza. Nor were her hopes raised further when five days later on August 20, Carranza made his triumphant entry into Mexico City. Word reached the fort that Emiliano Zapata and his swollen hordes, some 20,000 strong, waited in Cuernavaca for word from General Villa. Meanwhile, the Centaur of the North had left 30,000 *Villistas* along the northern garrisons outside the capital and returned to Chihuahua City to continue his important work in agrarian reforms.

It was from reading the newspaper columns of Miguel Guerra that Madelaina gained insight into what was happening in that den of political lions, tigers, jaguars, and snakes in Mexico City. The nonconformist reporter, who rode herd with *Villistas*, told it like it was:

"Carranza made his position clear to new Revolutionary Chamber of Deputies," stated Guerra. "But reception to this man was polite and remote. It appears that three distinct political groups have formed. Pro-Carranza, Pro-Villa, and pro-conventionists who feel that the Chamber of Deputies should rule Mexico through a neutral president. Carranza sought to win over these factions by delivering a character assassination speech against General Villa. After a long, drawn-out, and windy speech, he concluded by labeling Villa a power-crazed despot who seeks to become an omnipotent militarist and wishes to dominate all powers of the union by maintaining a formidable army, which could overwhelm the power of the Republic. He

883

also stated that he viewed General Zapata in the same vein.

"Carranza's statements, aimed at frightening members of the convention into naming him president, fell flat when General Villa's immediate reply was read to the deputies. It was terse, to the point, and devastating: *Carranza contends that Pancho Villa constitutes a danger to Mexico. I contend Carranza is the one to fear. Since we are at an impasse, I propose for the good of our nation, we both meet before this delegation, or at some appointed place, where we both commit suicide and thereby remove all threats to our nation.*"

The message, greeted by thunderous applause and cheers, deadlocked the convention and the conventionists chose General Eulalio Guiterrez as interim president. Guiterrez' first act was to confirm Villa as General-in-Chief of the Northern Division and select that division as protector of the convention's rights. Furious at this gross disregard of his virtues, Don Carranza disavowed the convention and left for Veracruz where he established his "government" in exile.

The talk had ended. Hordes of gun-heavy men who fought together to defeat Huerta stood looking at each other with friendship for the last time. They turned and left Mexico City as enemies. Pancho Villa and Venustano Carranza were openly at war.

The morning of December 6, a year since he'd escaped Mexico as a Federal prisoner, General Francesco Villa, magnificently garbed in a field commander's uniform and gold braid, seated regally on Seven Leagues, his stallion, shared the spotlight with General Emiliano Zapata, dressed in a splendid *charro* uniform. They rode together at the head of the combined forces of the northern and southern armies. On either side of them rode Villa's Generals Urbina and Fierro and Zapata's Rafael Buelna. Behind them came the stellar and colorful *Dorados*. These were followed by Villa's crack shot *soldaderas* headed by Madelaina Obregon. Then came the artillery and what the newspapers affectionately came to call the Terrifying Horse-men of the Northern Division. These were followed by countless more brigades and regiments of the two for-midable forces. Zapata's quaint peasants in pantaloons and sandals provided music from the south. Villa's khaki-clad bands played music of the north.

The 50,000 first-class fighting men marched down the Paseo de la Reforma, Avenida Juarez and Plateros Avenues into the Royal Plaza—Zocalo. Villa and Zapata, side by side, flushed with victory and power, marched toward the National Palace, not fighting over the spoils like mad dogs, but doing what two sane men could do with victory, with freedom—give it to the people.

It was a day to remember, thought Madelaina, as swarms of people moved like gigantic ocean swells all around them. How much more wonderful it would have been to have Peter by her side instead of the six bodyguards surrounding her. On orders from General Villa, every precaution was taken to protect Little Fox. Concerned with what had happened to her recently, he was doubly squeamish over the fact that if General Obregon caught sight of his daughter, a kidnap plot might be effected.

The victorious generals, swamped by reporters and cameramen, dismounted before the palace and walked inside, accompanied by their staff members. They stood in the balcony receiving the accolades, then, ac-companied by President Guiterrez, they walked back into the main reception chambers where the enormous, golden presidential chair sat.

General Villa stood staring at the chair for which he'd fought for years, never intending to sit in it, but certainly intending to see someone seated on it.

Not far from him, yet unable to see what transpired, Madelaina stood on the balls of her feet to see what was causing the commotion. The newsmen jokingly wanted to take Villa's picture seated in the ostentatious presidential chair.

"Just one picture, General Villa. Just one. It won't take a moment," they cried.

Villa's half-embarrassed, half-joking smile couldn't deter them. He was led toward the chair. Villa coaxed Zapata. "Let's go, Emiliano. You take the big one. I'll sit next to you and Urbina."

"No," said Zapata. "The gold one's more your style."

"Not mine, damnit."

Madelaina tugged at her escorts to push up front. She wanted to see this comedy. By the time she got in the front line, Villa was seated in the gold chair Zapata, in the chair alongside; and General Urbina to Villa's right.

The photographers got their photo and cried for another. Villa resisted. "That's enough," he told them, waving his hand in a self-conscious manner. He spotted Madelaina in the front lines and called to her.

"You know what, Little Fox?" he confided. "That damned chair's too big for me. I'd get lost, you hear? *Vamenos*. Let's get out of this crazy place of gringos and *políticos* who connive to rob man of his eyeballs. *Dios mios*, when a man is up to his ass in alligators, its pretty damned hard to remember his intention was to clean out the swamp."

Madelaina and all the *Villistas* returned to Xochimilco. The campfires blazed brilliantly and the air filled with the aroma of spicy, tantalizing foods. Listening to the soldiers singing and dancing with their *soldaderas* and *viejas*, Madelaina felt overwhelmed by nostalgia and sorrow. She had to be by herself. By the time she reached the water's edge and sat on a mossy tree bough swinging low over the magnificent array of exquisite floating gardens, she began to sow the seeds of discontent in her mind. The fragrance of the sweet-smelling tropical flowers intoxicated her, creating a hungry yearning for Peter and their son.

She was tired, very tired of this life. She missed Antonetta like life itself. She hadn't taken to Villa's new woman and had no desire to extend herself in any

886

more useless relationships. She hardly saw Rosalia
Quintera or Lucia San Miguel. They were always with
their gringo men. And Madelaina was always alone.
She was lonely enough to give thoughts to sneaking off
to Cuernavaca to gaze up upon the house of her childhood, but sensible enough to take no more unnecessary
chances. She wanted her son desperately—and her
husband. She was obsessed by this desire.

Madelaina remained camped here with the other
Villistas and watched General Villa go back and forth
to Mexico City on business, pleasure, or whatever the
agenda provided. She watched General Villa unwind
and relax to the point that his posture in the capital
grew more scandalous each day.

Newspapers carried red-hot stories of his affairs with
one young whore or another. And Madelaina, in reading all the accounts, felt a burning anger at this civilized society—and at Pancho for not recognizing the
pit he was falling into.

His crude, unpolished behavior, his provincial
manners and quaint peasant eccentricities, however
charming, practical, and formidable they might have
been in the deserts and hills, became the laughingstock
of snobbish Mexican society. The women who teased
him, flirted, played coy and hard to get confused him,
puzzled him, and incited him to anger. Thoroughly
rankled when called to task over his macho attitude
toward these same women who openly made ovations
to him and declined to accept his genuine masculine responses, Villa shouted to the reporters eager to pen his
unguarded remarks. "To hell with protocol. To hell
with propriety. Where I come from a woman's invitation means action! The only action I know in this instance is to tumble the skirt in the hay, what else? Is it
any different here in Mexico City than in our deserts,
plains, and mountains? Fornication is the same here as
the world over, no? Perhaps not in China," he temporized much to the reporters' delight. For some reason
Villa was never partial to Chinamen because they were
the money lenders, the men who charged interest,

something he could never understand. You borrow—you pay back. *Que va*, this business charging for the service? Wasn't it enough to get your money back?

Having tasted the bitterness of ridicule and a growing distrust among the disdaining *políticos* in Mexico City, General Villa, perplexed and homesick, informed Presidente Guiterrez he was leaving. "Let those *políticos* sink or swim. Pancho Villa has work to do."

Shortly after the Christmas holidays, General Villa reassigned his units, shipped his *Dorados* and their horses by train back to Juarez. He gathered his men and Madelaina, and with what appeared as a secretive glimmer in his eyes, he informed her they had much work to do.

For the first time since she'd willingly dedicated her life to him, Madelaina bridled under the strain. "Perhaps it's best, *Jefe*, that I search for my son. I've procrastinated long enough. Besides, you don't need me any longer."

"You've come with me so far toward victory," insisted Villa. "Do you not wish to join me in our total victory at the final outcome?"

"From where I observe the goings on, it will be a long time before those *políticos* in the capital make up their minds—as usual," she added ironically. "No, *Jefe*. I'm tired. I think it's time for Little Fox to retire."

Pancho Villa had never learned how to wrestle with the mental gymnastics of a woman as complicated as Madelaina Obregon. It was perhaps this, plus an inborn set of ethics and behavior toward such women, that never allowed him to make ovations to her of a romantic nature. She had viewed him from the first in a paternalistic light and he was satisfied to remain so. However, now he had to insist on her making this trip, for more reasons than one.

He had planned this surprise for a long time. If it meant abducting her, he'd find a way to keep her close to his side. In the name of good conscience and good sense, he knew he wouldn't force her against her will. Knowing Little Fox well enough, he knew she'd find a way to do as she pleased. No. He'd have to resort to trickery and guile with her. God forgive him.

"Where will you go, if not with us? You can't return to the house of your father, not now, while things remain unsolved between you. Believe me, it's best you come with Pancho. It's not far where we'll be from the northern hacienda of your father in El Dorado. I will send my spies to locate your *niño*. When we locate him and are sure of no trouble, I shall instruct my men to abduct him back for you. Is A-O.K.?"

Madelaina had no other way to go. Villa was right. Then, with her son, she'd return to El Paso and raise him there away from revolution. "Very well, *Jefe*. I understand and believe you. My trust is in you."

Chapter 33

Two days before the *Villistas* finally departed Mexico City, Madelaina felt the need to go shopping. She was in dire need of undergarments, soaps and perfumes, and those small things which make life more endurable for women.

She took Rosalia Quintera with her, and in her appreciation for what the girl had done for her in the past and the nice courtesies extended her by the mestizo, she showed her the glories of Mexico City.

First, they hired a carriage for the day. Accompanied by a lone *Villista* bodyguard, who waited on them patiently, their first stop was at the baths. The steam baths featured in the beauty salons along the Avenida Juarez. They giggled like schoolgirls and luxuriated in the soothing, relaxing waters and even had their hair dressed and toes and fingernails manicured. They put on airs like those displayed by the haughty *modistas*. Nothing was too elegant for them: lingerie, camisoles, the latest in fashions were brought out for their approval. They purchased sailor-type suits, with middy jackets, large white collars and cuffs, belted at the waist with a contrasting ankle-length skirt.

"Bustles are gone?" Madelaina asked the uppity shopgirl.

"*Oui*," she replied in a Spanish-accented French. "But of course, *señorita*."

The shopgirl put on such airs that Rosalia on impulse would have enjoyed pulling the girl's hair. Madelaina cautioned her not to make a scene, and instead she took over. Did the clerk carry other, more elegant creations? Something perhaps by Doucet, Worth, or even Amelie?"

"You know of such fashions, *señorita*?" asked the bug-eyed clerk.

Employing all the aristocratic airs of a *gachupín*, Madelaina stared scorchingly at the girl. "Bring what you have at once. And don't tarry. We haven't all day."

The clerk stared at them, their peasant dresses strewn on the floor, and shrugged her shoulders in a disdaining manner. "Very well, at once," she said with overpoliteness as she exited the dressing room. *One can't ever tell who has the money in these days of hectic political upheavals*, she told herself. Why, only two days ago, one of the rebel soldiers came in, put down several thousand pesos, and gathered all the garments, regardless of size and color, his arms could carry. He left them speechless, but a lot richer.

Ten minutes later, Madelaina was garbed in the most spectacular and elegant gown she'd ever seen. A pale mauve shade, graduating into darker tones from the bustline to the hem, the evening gown was low cut, off the shoulder and caught under the bustline in empire lines. The hobble skirt was asymetrically draped with embroidered beads, colored to match the shading of the filmy English net at the hemline where it formed a train at the rear. The shimmering bugle beads and glittery stones caught the spotlights trained on her from overhead, and Rosalia Quintera gasped and sucked in her breath .

"*Dios mios, chiquita*. You look like a star in the heavens, shining from the sky," she rhapsodized with peasant candor. "You must have thees dress."

Madelaina stared at her image for a long while. She didn't recognize herself. Her hair, piled atop her head, was caught with a brilliant tiara. She shook her head at the reflection. "What would I do with such a gown? Where would I wear it? Can you just see me stumbling through the camps, holding up my train, trying to look like an elegant lady?" Her wistful voice wasn't convincing, even to herself, but she had spoken these words only in the clerk's absence.

"Listen, ju take it, hear me?" Rosalia was enraptured with such a dress. When the clerk returned to the dressing room, carrying other creations, Rosalia turned to her. "How much it costs such a—such a—*como se llamos?* What you call such a dress, woman?"

"A ball gown," replied the snooty clerk. "It is 1200 pesos."

"Ayeiii! So much for so little?" Rosalia's face turned a berry red, more at the clerk's arrogant and unbearable manners.

"I'll take it," snapped Madelaina, watching the interplay between the two women. "And hurry it up. I'll take all the accessories and these other items also." She indicated the other garments stacked on a chair.

"Do you have an account with our house, *señorita*?" asked the offensive clerk.

For a moment Madelaina was tempted to answer in the affirmative and charge the items to the account of General Obregon—just to rankle the shopgirl. She changed her mind. "What's the matter, you don't take cash in this bourgeois establishment?" She slipped out of the shimmering creation of net and beads and let it lay on the floor for the clerk to pick up. From the canvas money belt she'd lain carelessly on the chair in the dressing room, she pulled out a thick stack of pesos and tossed them at the girl "If that isn't enough for everything, charge the balance to General Francesco Villa. Tell him Little Fox made the purchase!"

The name Little Fox had been publicized in all the Mexican newspapers from the very moment Villa's *soldaderas* marched into the Zocalo, the square outside the presidential palace over a month before. Newspaper reporters had interviewed many of the willing publicity seekers, the *soldaderas* who thrilled at having their pictures taken on their horses with rifles at the ready.

Headlines had captured the imagination of every young woman who yearned for the adventures of a *soldadera*, touting them to become one of the foxes trained by the best *soldadera* of them all—Little Fox.

892

They had never mentioned Madelaina's real name, probably because they didn't know her true identity. For this she was grateful. For some reason she wouldn't even admit to herself, she didn't want to hurt her father any more. Was this a sign of maturity—of growing up, she had asked herself on occasion.

It was difficult for both Madelaina and Rosalia to keep straight faces when they saw the expression of electrifying shock on the face of the shaken clerk as she rushed from the dressing rooms, purchases flung over both arms, to complete the transaction.

They were still laughing when they left the *modistas* and stopped to give their parcels to the driver of their carriage and their waiting bodyguard.

"We're going across the street, to the café across the square next," she told the solemn-faced, well-armed young man. "We'll return soon enough."

He tipped his Stetson and kept his steely black eyes on the two smartly attired women, unable to believe they were the same two he'd escorted into the city that morning. "Chihuahua!" he muttered. "What beauties!"

"And now, *chica*, I shall show you how the other half lives," she told Rosalia, admiring the figure cut by the woman of Tracy Richards in her new sailor suit. "My dear, you look like a fashion model. With your gorgeous auburn hair done up so fashionably and your make-up done so impeccably, you fairly take my breath away."

"Ju aren't so bad jurself, Little Fox," laughed Rosalia, pleased at the compliment. "I still see the face of that stuck-up girl when you mention Pancho Villa. You see what she did when she learned she was in the company of Little Fox? *Dios mios.* I'll wager her pantaloonies were not too dry, eh, *chica*?"

They both laughed heartily and with good humor. Looking the epitome of fashion and a bit daring since they were unescorted and without the company of a *dueña*, the two young women sat at a table outside among the other fashionably dressed people in the sparkling sunshine of a beautiful day. All around them it seemed the conversation on the lips of the people was about Pancho Villa and his utterly abhorrent behavior in society. For a time they listened to the snide remarks and obscene jokes made about their *jefe* without flinching.

"Imagine? That fool wants to marry every woman he seduces. Don't ask me why? Some primitive and savage rite among those barbarians, I suppose."

"Why, only the other night, he was bent on taking the daughter of the French ambassador to bed. All she'd said was the whole world knew the name Pancho Villa, and he turned to her and declared they were to be married on the spot."

Madelaina grew angrier by the minute. Rosalia leaned in to ask her friend why everyone was so disrespectful to the man who was liberating Mexico for them. Madelaina proceeded as best she could to outline the differences between the two societies, unaware that she was being inscrutably observed by a group of *Federale* officers seated a few tables away.

"For two pesos I'd give those lying sons and daughters of whores a lesson in respect," hissed Rosalia, her sparkling brown eyes leveled hotly on the people surrounding them.

"You mustn't let it upset you. People will talk no matter what a man does. One thing for sure, it would be an impossible task to defend the *jefe* to such people who have no knowledge of the life we live or what we do to win victories. Let it alone, Rosalia. Things over which we have no power shouldn't affect us, and the thoughts of others and their words shouldn't disturb us."

"*Bueno*," said Rosalia, catching a glimpse of the officers ogling her. Fighting to keep a straight face, she whispered to Madelaina. "Oh, *chica*, if these *hombres* knew we were *Villistas*, the desire on their *gachupín* faces would turn to shocked impotence, no?" She laughed brightly, enjoying the attention. "It would serve my gringo lover right if I were to flirt with them," she flipped with outrageous overtones. She

894

sipped her lemon ice through a straw, making loud, slurping noises, prompting Madelaina to show her the proper way to drink through a straw.

"Why must I *sip* through a straw, for the love of God?" she said in frustration. "Is much easier to pick up the glass and drink."

"But, it's not ladylike, *chica*. Dressed in clothes as fine as yours, you must act the part of a woman of finesse and high refinement. Only *campesinas* and *soldaderas* act rough and tough like men. There is a saying, 'When in Rome do as the Romans do.' It means you should adapt yourself to the mood and manners of the place you're in."

"Why?" asked Rosalia naïvely. "Are you saying this dress makes me someone else—not Rosalia?"

Madelaina smiled at her own asinine attitude. "Why? Why, indeed? To be honest, I'm not sure why I bothered to explain. Don't listen to me. I've been trapped between two worlds for so long that I find it difficult to know to which I truly belong," she replied wistfully.

"Ees too complicated, too confusing to be civilized. No wonder the *jefe* is most unhappy here. We don't belong here, him and me. You, yes. But not the likes of Pancho Villa or Rosalia Quintera. Aye, is best we go, for sure." Rosalia removed her broad-brimmed sailor hat, unpinned her hip-length auburn hair and let it fall into shiny bright, coppery coils on her shoulders and down her back.

"*Chica*," cautioned Little Fox. "You mustn't do that. Not here. Not only isn't it ladylike, but it might be dangerous as well as unaccepted behavior."

"Not ladylike? Is true, Rosalia is no lady. So I do what makes Rosalia comfortable."

Madelaina's face burned with embarrassment when she glanced about and saw they were the center of attention. Their eyes on her made her uncomfortable. "It's just that the others will think we're common whores if we don't restrain ourselves in this section of the city."

"So? Is that not what we are? Whores?"

"Rosalia!" Madelaina was aghast at her crude manners and her outspoken candor. She quickly searched her reticule for a few pesos, placed them on the table, and suggested to her companion they'd best leave. Madelaina felt terrible. Ordinarily Rosalia's brutal candor wouldn't have phased her in the least. Suddenly, back in her old environment of social mores and staid protocol, she'd taken umbrage at the truth. What a hypocrite she'd turned into. How would she ever adjust to the old ways, she wondered. Burdened with the guilt of her conscience and of her double moral standard, she steered Rosalia away from the café.

Waiting for the traffic to pass before they crossed the street where their carriage awaited them, Madelaina failed to see a carriage gathering speed as it headed toward them.

It happened so fast, without forewarning. The carriage came to a stop before them, obstructing their path. A door opened and Madelaina alone was whisked off her feet and hustled into the carriage before a startled Rosalia Quintera, who jumped back out of the way to avoid being trampled by the frisky horses.

No one heard the warning from Villa's man who'd seen the four-horse carriage coming down the *avenida* at a fast clip. Catching her breath, Rosalia ran swiftly across the street, dodging on-coming sedans and hansoms, screaming at the driver and escort to hurry and pursue the carriage in which Madelaina had been abducted.

By the time the horses gathered speed, the first carriage had circled Chapultepec Square and disappeared on one of the several streets branching out from the circle. Dismayed and highly agitated after an hour's search, Rosalia suggested they hurry back to General Villa, who waited for them at the Reforma Hotel to report Madelaina's plight.

Inside the swiftly driven carriage carrying Madelaina and her abductor, Major General Felipe de Cordoba, the two old friends were renewing their acquaintance.

The horses had slowed down and cantered along the winding path in and about the wooded section of Chapultepec Park.

"What a dramatic and clever way to say hello," she told him when her astonishment at his daring feat died down. Glancing through the window of the carriage behind her, she saw no one was in pursuit.

"I had to see you, to speak with you, *quireda*," Felipe told her. "Ever since I saw you riding in the parade at the head of the *soldaderas*, I tried to locate you." He took Madelaina's slender hands in his and stroked them affectionately. "We miss you. Your father is protrate over your absence and misses you more than he'll admit."

"I doubt he has time to miss anyone. He's still too in love with his work," she said caustically.

"Aren't you?" he countered.

His eyes turned the color of jade reflected against azure skies, she thought, gazing into them. "I think not, Felipe. I find myself growing disenchanted with the life of a *soldadera*, even if it does bring a certain prestige being a *Villista* these days."

They talked for over an hour, bridging the gap of time between them.

"Come home," begged Felipe. "You're needed there."

"I don't seem to know where home really is these days, *querido*. So how can I go home? Besides I have many things to do and searching for my son is one of them." She leveled intent eyes on him. "Felipe, do you have him? How could you have been a party to such a cruel ploy. When I heard, I refused to believe it."

"*Querida*, hold off a moment," he said, a look of bafflement on his face. "Surely you are jesting with me?" He looked intently at her, searching her face. "Are you telling me the child isn't with you?"

Madelaina paled. "If this is some kind of a joke, I don't appreciate it."

Felipe's face screwed up in thought. "The child was returned to you three months ago," he said in a voice barely above a whisper.

"You're saying you no longer have my son?"

He nodded reluctantly.

"How is that possible? I don't have him. I haven't seen him since he was stolen from me." She panicked. "Felipe! What have you done with my son?" Tears sprang into her eyes, her throat constricted, and she felt unable to breathe.

"There, there, *querida*. There has to be an explanation for all this. I left El Dorado to march with your father, the general. We were in Cuidad Obregon for two weeks before I returned to the hacienda. When I arrived, I was told you'd come after your son. My instructions to the servants before I left were to protect him from all dangers. I never thought you'd arrive with a court order from the capital of Hermosillo, or I might have warned them not to have turned the child over to anyone. They were positive it was you who claimed them. Matter of fact, the papers are still locked in my desk at El Dorado."

"Oh, Felipe," she wailed. "It wasn't me. Who then? Who has my child?" She grew hysterical, unwilling to be comforted. "How could you, how could you do this to me?"

Felipe felt terrible. "I had no business in this, *querida*. From the beginning, it was your father's plan to lure you away from the *Villistas*. When we heard you'd had a child, he was concerned that you should bear the child in the wilderness. His concern grew into a plan to kidnap the child and bait you to return. Your father misses you dearly."

Madelaina dried her eyes. "It was a horribly brutal thing to do—to take my child from me. If you only knew the anguish it caused, the fears and insecurities, the nightmares and endless frustration, you'd not have been a party to such a dastardly act."

"Yes, I can see it might be inhuman to take the child from you, but the intent was well meant. Try to see it in that light."

"Oh, Felipe, how can you say such a thing, especially now, since my son is missing and I haven't a clue in the world as to where to begin to search for him." She dabbed at her eyes and swallowed the lump in her throat.

"And it's all my fault," he said bitterly. "For once I should have refused to aid the general."

"You've never been able to refuse him, Felipe," she said flatly with a tinge of contempt in her voice.

Felipe pulled back the top hatch cover and instructed the driver to get back to Zocalo. "Your friends are probably looking for you. I'd better get you back as soon as possible. I'd prefer to keep you here with me forever, but now that I know your child isn't with you and hasn't been, I am incensed. Appalled that I should have been a party to influence you so unfairly to return. You'll come back some day, and when you do, it will have to be of your own accord—when you're ready—and not before."

"Thank you, Felipe," she said gratefully.

"Where can I reach you if I must, Madelaina? Surely we can trust each other, now that we've been candid," he said when she instinctively pulled away from him. "Incidentally, as difficult as it was to find a likable and admirable quality in your gringo husband, I confess I could see why you chased the country over to find him. I liked the man. Truly I did. I even told the general that I did."

Madelaina lifted her wet eyes to his and observed him for a moment. "Write me in care of general delivery, El Paso, Texas. Or the same in Chihuahua City. I'm not certain where I'll be. I'd give you our wireless code, but it can be too easily picked up by an enemy."

They had entered the square opposite the presidential palace at a canter. Glancing out the window, Madelaina suggested, "It's best you let me off here. I'll find my own way. I shouldn't want any of my companions to see me in the company of a *Federale*," she said tightly. "It might cause complications for both of us."

The carriage pulled over a slight distance from the front gates leading to the palace. Felipe shoved the carriage door open, alighted the cab, and helped Madelaina out. He gazed about the square, looking for a free carriage. "It would mean nothing, *querida*, for my driver to drop you off at the Reforma," he insisted.

"No. It would be too dangerous. There's a free carriage," she called, pointing to one dismissing his fare.

Felipe told his driver to hail the man and hold the vehicle for them. It was nearly dusk, a time when shadows played tricks on the eyes. He pulled her in close to him and kissed her ardently.

"*Vaya con Dios, querida.* I'll be in touch as soon as I can."

"Bless you, Felipe. Bless you," she told him and ran off toward the waiting carriage.

Three loud shots rang out, blasting her eardrums. Madelaina stopped in her tracks and took cover near the waiting carriage. Horses bolted into the air, spooked by the loud sounds, their forepaws clawing the air as a cursing driver tried to calm them. She turned to glance back at Felipe in time to see him clutch at his chest, wheel around as one hand clung to the carriage door before it slipped off, and fall to the ground, blood gushing from three holes in his body.

"No!" she shouted. "No, Felipe!" She ran toward him, just as a pair of strong arms swept her off her feet and tossed her into another waiting carriage. She pounded her fists against the man holding her tightly, beat on his chest protestingly. When, in the dim light of the carriage interior, she recognized Rudolfo Fierro, she collapsed in a dead faint.

Book Eight

Madelaina of the Seven Moons

Chapter 34

Less than three weeks later, Madelaina was in El Paso in the house she'd bought when she worked at the Diamond Slipper for Antonetta. Standing before a mirror in the exquisite gown she'd purchased in Mexico City, she was preparing for a private party given in honor of General Villa by the political dignitaries of Texas who had promoted the *jefe*'s revolution in the interests of freedom and justice for his people. Madelaina had agreed to attend the ball primarily to act as his interpreter; and she almost had misgivings over her promise.

She'd been a virtual recluse since Felipe's death, and in the security of her own little *casa*, she attempted to pick up the pieces even as turmoil erupted in Mexico City. She kept asking herself why any of it should matter to her any longer. She was a woman—not a man. She wanted only to be a woman, live like one, be loved and exist for the rest of her days in a quiet, serene atmosphere where she could forget those terrifying days of the revolution, those horrifying times when her life meant little or nothing and she'd survived for some mysterious reasons not fully known to her. She wanted nothing more than to erase all those bloody scenes of misery and hardship where death raged around the clock, memories burned so indelibly in her memory, that they prevented her from drawing an even breath.

God, what she'd do to relive her life with different values. What had driven her? Why had she been so stubborn, willful, and foolishly determined to show her father she had a will of her own? Why? If only she'd learned what had stimulated that stubborn streak of

903

obstinance, that need for self-assertion and approval, all her experiences wouldn't have been for naught. Why did she have to be different than most women? Why couldn't she accept—without questioning—the things she read in the papers or what she read in books? Why did she feel she had to ask perpetually, why—why—why?

She'd cried enough over the lost years. In May she'd be twenty-two years old. Twenty-two! She felt 102. Somewhere she had a husband and a son. Had she been some sort of a demon to have lost the people she loved most in the world? Her father, Peter, the baby, Manuelito Perez, and now Felipe de Cordoba.

She stared at her reflection in the mirror, unable to determine or care that she posed a picture of grandeur and such magnificence it would generate excitement from any of the guests planning to attend the evening's gala.

She sprayed a fine mist of her favorite cologne from an atomizer shaped like a graceful swan, patted her up-styled hairdo into place, and allowed the wispy tendrils to fall around her face and neck. Her diamond tiara and earrings were set into place, and before the general arrived to pick her up, Madelaina draped her fox cape on the chair in the living room and poured herself a bracer of brandy. Madelaina gulped it down and stared at her reflection in the mirror over the mantle. The diamonds in her hair and ears glittered with silver and violet and yellow fire. *If only I could sparkle like diamonds*, she told herself, trying to elevate her spirits. She could at least be a suitable companion for General Villa on this night, perhaps one of the most important of his entire career.

"This is Little Fox?" asked Pancho Villa, staring at the apparition before him. "Fierro," he called to his constant companion. "Please to take a look. Is this the *soldadera* of Pancho Villa, or is it some majestic queen who honors us with her presence?" he asked, utterly enthralled by her appearance.

Fierro's face flushed with appreciation. "Incredible.

What a transformation. Such a woman bears no resemblance to a *soldadera* of Villa's camp!" He whistled low. Her appearance intimidated Fierro almost as much as it did Pancho Villa, for they remained silent all the way into the elegant residential district of El Paso.

"I am happy you honored me with your presence, Little Fox. *Que va,* Little Fox. I can't call you Little Fox in the presence of all these social butterflies, *señora.* What shall I call you?"

"Why not Señora Benson?"

"Ayeeiii, another name that is painful to me," lamented Villa. "Obregon is bad enough, but Benson? I shouldn't wish to remind these gringos of that name tonight. Señora Duprez? Does that name offend you, *chica?*"

"Let it be Señora Duprez," she replied, not really caring.

"I am happy ju came," he said, switching to pigeon yankee. "Ees best I talk gringo, out of respect for our northern friends, *si?*"

She nodded.

"Jur heart ees no longer een revolution, eh, *chica?*"

"I've tried to conceal it—" she began.

Fierro smoked a long black cigar opposite them in the carriage. As usual, he never opened his mouth to speak unless spoken to. Tonight even he looked more acceptable. He and the *jefe* wore formal dinner clothes. But not far from their reach were hair-triggered six-shooters. She wondered how they'd fare when asked to check their firearms before entering the party. The thought brought a smile to her lips.

It was a beautiful April night, with a full round moon shining overhead, lighting up the bricked streets. New street lamps had replaced the old with brighter electricity lighting up the shadowy paths formerly lit by gas jets. The graceful street leading to the governor's mansion was lined with tall eucalyptus trees and magnolias, filling the night air with a sweet fragrance pleasing to the senses. Up ahead the sprawling estate built much like a Southern manor was ablaze with lights, and the sounds of laughter and music spilled out into the night.

The circular driveway was lined with both horseless and horse-drawn carriages. Liveried chauffeurs gathered together in a body, comparing notes as their masters and mistresses attended the festivities inside. The carriage carrying Villa and his guests pulled to a stop at the gates, where two uniformed rangers flashed a light inside the carriage inquisitively.

Instantly one of the rangers braced in a military salute. "Pleasure ta meet ya, General Villa. Hey, Jack, it's Pancho Villa himself," he called to his companion, waving the carriage on through. He tipped his hat and returned to inspect the next carriage. At the front entrance to the house, two liveried footmen sprang forward to open the doors. Madelaina, draped in a floorlength white fox cape, emerged first, followed by Villa and Fierro.

"Ju know what, *chica*? I like the way the gringos make a party. Ju watch me so Villa doesn't do something foolish like wanting to marry the first girl who flirts, eh?"

A rush of music greeted them. A small mariachi band hired for General Villa's pleasure wove its way through the large rooms, singing and making music. Everywhere people milled about in small groups, talking, sipping champagne.

From the moment they entered the splendid manor all lit up like a festival, Madelaina's stunning appearance drew the eyes of every awestruck man and envious woman in the main salon. She felt their eyes on her, wondering, staring, whispering, who's the woman with Pancho Villa? She wouldn't deny she enjoyed every moment spent basking in the limelight as much as Villa and Fierro did. How long had it been since she had entertained the feelings of being someone special? Too long ago. How marvelous for the ego, she thought, as the attention paid her rekindled a sense of worth she thought she'd lost somewhere in her journeys.

She heard their names announced by a major domo: "General Francesco Villa . . . General Rudolfo Fierro . . . Senora Peter Duprez."

The assembled guests fell silent. Whispers began slowly and swelled like a wave. "There's Pancho Villa and his butcher, Fierro. So that's the man who killed Bill Benson? Who is this Señora Duprez? Daughter-in-law to William Benson? In the company of the man who killed him? How shocking." No matter what their thoughts were concerning the Benson affair, these people had gathered under the governor's roof to pay homage to the legendary Pancho Villa and this is precisely what they would do. Awestruck by General Villa's imposing presence, they began to applaud him as the trio moved along the receiving line, caught up in the rush of introductions.

So many faces, so many names to remember, thought Madelaina. Governor and Mrs. Townsend, General Hugh L. Scott, General John Pershing, Major Mickie, and so many more, including prominent statesmen from both the military and State Department in Washington. They all clustered around the man of the hour, complimenting him, firing questions, badgering him, even joking with him over his spectacular achievements. Madelaina was relieved when General Fierro, who spoke impeccable English, stepped forward to interpret for Villa. She felt an instinctive resentment on the part of the gringos that a woman should translate their words. She was to learn later that Fierro had already been designated for the job and that her role in the evening's festivities were to be bound up in an altogether different mission.

When she found herself nodding mechanically, and the frozen smile on her face beginning to ache from the strain, she excused herself and walked out on the terrace, unable to endure the forced gaiety any longer. She wanted a cigarette so badly, she was shaking. She opened her beaded bag, uncertain that El Paso society would accept such a gesture and removed a cigarette. She didn't want to do anything to place the *jefe* in a

907

bad light. The publicity in Mexico City had been devastating enough without adding to his discomfort here in El Paso. She lit it with a miniature red devil struck against the concrete balustrade and puffed on it. She took two more puffs, inhaled, and began to calm down.

She walked along the outer portico, inhaling the floral scents of the garden, enjoying the peace and tranquility among the well-kept lawns and shrubbery, listening to the music that drifted out the windows and open doors. Madelaina paused outside the French doors of a room filled with male guests who were engaged in talking with General Villa. She was unaware that from another terrace, some thirty feet from her, she was being observed through the Dresden blue eyes of Peter Benson, her husband. Coming toward her from another direction, she was hailed by a voice from her past. "Madelaina! Madelaina Obregon. Is it really you?"

She turned toward the owner of the voice and gazed upon the tall figure of a handsome, well-dressed man whose steps quickened until he reached her. Her dark, luminous eyes searched his face for some recognition. He looked familiar.

Behind them, Peter moved away from the lights, closer to the building, so he wouldn't be seen, his eyes intent on the scene a few feet from him.

"Do I know you, sir?" asked Madelaina, still uncertain as to the man's identity.

"You don't remember me? My dear, I am crushed. Absolutely crushed, that you'd forget me after only six years." His twinkling blue-green eyes seemed all the merrier for her awkwardness.

"Armando! Armando Cortez!" she exclaimed as his features became clearer. He picked her up in his strong arms and whirled her about, and for a few moments, they were like happy children.

"*Dios mios,* Madelaina, you are something to behold! Could I ever in my life believe that you would have blossomed out into such a ripe beauty? Look at you." He extended her at arm's length and twirled her about

908

as if she were on parade like a model. "My dear, you are positively ravishing. But I am very unhappy with you—running off without so much as a good-bye, after all we meant to each other."

Madelaina blushed in spite of herself, "We were children, Armando. Mere children. So much has happened since then."

"Well, we've got all our lives to reminisce, *querida*." He grinned irascibly. "Let me look at you again and drink you in with these eyes," he began eloquently.

Madelaina smiled. "You've not changed at all, Armando. Still the romantic, no?"

"And why not, *querida*?" He drew her closer to him. "We have many marvelous moments to remember."

"I'm a married woman, Armando," she said. "Tell me, what brings you here to Texas, *chico*?"

"Alas," he sighed. "I, too, am married. To a gringa. Imagine? My father was incensed when he heard the news. His *conquistadore* blood turned cold when I brought my bride to meet him. Not even the fact that she was the Texas governor's daughter would appease him."

Madelaina stiffened. "You married Valerie Townsend? I can see why Don Felipe was displeased," she replied acidly.

Armando's smile dissolved. "She's really a fine person in her own way."

"Armando, I'm sorry. I meant nothing by it. It was unfair of me to make any remark since I've never really met the woman. I can only hope that you both will be very happy." She reached to pat his hands reassuringly.

"She drives me insane, *querida*. I'm not certain what it is she does that drive me mad, but she married me and for a time it was all fine—romance and parties and the gay life—you know. Then suddenly there are more men in her life. It is something my Spanish blood will not tolerate, so when she left me in Madrid, I followed her to Paris, London, New York, and here to El Paso. But I got here only yesterday and already she managed

909

to leave. Out of respect to her family, I promised to spend the week before I go looking for her. *Querida,* I swear, she's a cat!"

"Poor Armando," said Madelaina, drawing him close to her in a gesture of friendship, never knowing that this act would later be misunderstood by the man who was watching this interplay between old friends.

For a time, she led the conversation back over their youth and the passion she had for bulls. They had both grieved for the loss of their childhood friend, Manuelito Perez. "If it's any consolation, *chica,* in Spain, he had risen to the greatest of heights. He became *el grande matador* of all Spain."

They were interrupted by a servant who informed Armando his presence was requested in the library by his father-in-law.

"You will excuse me, *querida.* But you must tell me where you live, where I can reach you. I have so many questions to ask the *soldadero* of Pancho Villa." He bowed and kissed her hand, then clicking his heels together, he said suggestively, "*Mi querida,* until later then. We have so much to catch up on."

Madelaina nodded and remained on the terrace. Behind her, having observed the tête-a-tête, Peter Duprez put out his thin *cigarro* and went inside to confer with the men in the library. His eyes had turned to steely points.

Inside, the conversation turned to accolades for General Villa. Madelaina could hear every word spoken as if she were in the room with them. She sat down on a garden chaise and lit another cigarette.

General Scott had the floor and was explaining to the room's occupants the agenda of the afternoon. "Did you know, gentlemen, that General Villa owns four military airplanes? Yes, it's true. This afternoon, the *jefe* took me to one of his factories, a foundry, to demonstrate the prototype of an armored vehicle far in advance of anything owned by the United States Army."

"I'll vouch for that remark, gentlemen," said the

governor, nodding as Armando entered the room to join the others. He puffed on his Havana cigar in a grand imperious manner. "I told you the man's a genius. Far ahead of his time. He's already conceived the idea of air warfare. He's convinced that when things pop in Europe—war's inevitable—air warfare will decide the victor. My son-in-law, Armando Cortez from Madrid, has already informed me the Germans are working to perfect airplanes." Armando nodded his head in agreement with the governor's words.

Keeping General Villa informed of the remarks made by each of the speakers, Fierro translated into Spanish exactly what the others said. The pleasant smile and twinkling friendly eyes never changed, even at some of the acerbic remarks and candid opinions expressed by a few who related the personal opinion of President Wilson, which Fierro didn't bother to disguise.

"If ya gentlemen think those achievements to be rather unusual foah an unlettered man of dubious origin," began Peter Duprez Benson, moving to the center of the group, "youah are in foah a surprise."

Governor Townsend smiled and extended his arm. "There you are, my boy. Gentlemen, you all know Peter Duprez—uh—Benson, I'm sure." The men nodded to each other. "Peter should know firsthand. He rode with the General Villa in the much-publicized Gringo Brigade."

Outside, Madelaina gave a start. Had she heard correctly? Her heart began to beat rapidly. Peter was here? She sat up on the chaise, swung her legs over the end, and on tip toes, moved in closer to the French doors. Her eyes tried to pierce the smoke-filled room, sweeping past each face. She stopped.

There he was. It was her husband. Only when she saw those remarkably blue eyes, tanned handsome features, and powerful shoulders as he towered over the other men, did she allow herself to believe it. She slipped back away from the window as her pulse quickened and she heard Peter's voice continue.

"This man, General Francesco Villa, known ta his men as Pancho, has risen from virtual obscurity and transformed inta the role of a true leader. He deserves much moah recognition from ouah nation than he's received. Do ya know how many foreign nations have courted him, trying ta woo him inta selling the United States inta the sewer? But the *jefe* heah is loyal ta his northern neighbors. Ah jus' hope y'all can convey this ta Mr. Wilson." Peter lit up a thin *cigarro* and strutted about like a man born to affluence and influence.

"Did ya tell 'em, General Scott, about the *jefe*'s rollin' airdrome?"

"Haven't had a chance, Peter. Since you are more learned on the subject, suppose you go ahead."

"What those two words, 'rollin' airdrome' mean," continued Peter, "is that General Villa can transport his aircraft by train to the rendezvous of battle, service them, and launch them from any spot along the tracks, and drop bombs on his enemies."

"Incredible!" exclaimed General Pershing. "Not even the Europeans have made such progress." He turned to Peter. "You were a member of the much-lauded freedom fighters that went south to assist General Villa?"

"Yes suh, from the early days when Madero mobilized the revolutionary forces," replied Peter, knowing what was coming.

"And you are also the son of William Benson?"

Pancho Villa didn't move a muscle. Fierro's dark eyes scowled.

"Affirmative, suh."

"Yet you laud General Villa for all he's done—despite the unfortunate and tragic results of the altercation? Mighty commendable to have such charity, sir."

The men in the room tensed. Governor Townsend's face colored brightly. Armando Cortez stared at Peter Benson with arched brows. The other statesmen leaned forward in their chairs, not sure of the outcome of the moment's discomfort.

"That ah do, suh." He laughed. "Why, theah ain't a

912

man among ya that hasn't tasted the scorching temper of William Benson—including me. Knowing him like ah do, ah believe the *jefe*'s version of that confrontation. Why, the general heah was unarmed. General Fierro did what any other man might have done in the same circumstances, when a man draws first, ready ta kill."

Well, there it was, thought Governor Townsend. *They heard it first from Benson's son.* Now, by damn, he hoped the air was clear of this stigma. A murmur of mixed feelings and thoughts swept through the room, but Peter took hold again and led them in a body over Villa's talented achievements.

"Ah can't laud General Villa more than he deserves, gentlemen. With hundreds of my fellow Americans, who fought at his side, we all came to respect him in moah ways than one. Let me jus' dwell on his many achievements and accomplishments in what can be called modern warfare. He thought ta mount cannon in armored railcars ta aide us in warfare. Did ya know the *jefe* dreamed up the ideah of hitching explorer cars before the engines ta trigger off enemy mines along the tracks?" Peter paused a moment until he was certain every eye in that room, including Villa's, was on him. Then he continued. "So far all ah've told ya is what he can do and how good he does it in war. And like ah say, it's mighty damned good. But, mah friends, moah important is the fact that General Villa has given every spare centavo, every free moment ta the people of his land. In all my time with him, ah nevuh saw an ounce of graft or corruption flowing through the veins of this red-blooded man. Why, if any of ya have any influence on Mr. Wilson, ya must point out ta him that no man befoah Villa has done this. Not Diaz. Not Madero. Certainly not Huerta. Not even that unprincipled chocolate drinker Carranza has done a thing for his people." Peter paused, out of breath. He caught the appreciative twinkle in Villa's eyes as Fierro translated his words.

There were pros and cons and arguments offered to

substantiate the theory that Villa had promoted graft and done a few shady things during his career. They were too polite to refer to him as a bloody, murdering *guerrillo* in his presence. But Peter offered more arguments on behalf of Villa.

"Will you accept the word of an American citizen who knows firsthand what transpired—or will you believe the propoganda ground out by Huerta's malevolent and diabolical Secret Service, a carryover from the Diaz regime, which Carranza hopes to reinstate?"

"Well," said General John Pershing, rising to his feet. "I for one am highly impressed with everything I've seen and heard. Rest assured I'll do my darndest to convince President Wilson of this man's incredible loyalty and his phenomenal achievements." He turned to Villa. "Tell me, General, how long did it take you to build this magnificent army of yours?"

"All of it?"

"The whole military strength and organizations, including those stupendous and simply amazing *Dorados.*"

"Tree jeers," said Villa, holding up three fingers. "I talk Eengleesh for ju, *mi amigo.* For to make frenship weeth United Estates always and too for Mexico. Ees hokay?"

"*Mucho bueno.* Is okay," said General Scott, moving in to shake hands with Villa. "You are some fine general. As far as I'm concerned, I'll stand behind your qualifications and your character, one hundred percent."

"How far will your president stand?" asked Fierro imperatively.

"Mr. Wilson?" General Scott drew himself up and pulled down on his tunic. "Well, sir, the most of us here are behind General Villa. And General Pershing and myself are advisers to the president. That's why he sent us together this time. It's likely he'll take our advice. Now, if we could only convince Señor Carranza that Americans desire peace in this hemisphere."

"You convince Wilson," said Fierro expansively. "We convince Carranza."

Madelaina had all she could to do sit still and listen. She'd been so thunderstruck by Peter's presence, that she found herself actually disbelieving it was truly him. Waves of dizziness engulfed her and that powerful feeling stirring her loins, sometimes referred to as butterflies, had been uncontrollable until she forced herself to calm down. She had entered a dialogue with herself, an internal dialogue that left her shaken but filled with resolve.

For the past many months, she told herself, since you last saw him, all you've done is mope, wishing for him. Now that he's here in the flesh, are you going to let him slip past your arms without putting up a fight for him? Now's your chance, woman. Plead. Beg. Do anything you can to resurrect your marriage. Only in God's name don't let him evaporate from your life again, for no one. Not for Pancho Villa—not for Mexico—for nothing. You hear?

Confronted with these absorbing, whirlwind thoughts, she scarcely knew the meeting had ended inside. She hadn't heard him approach her. Only when she felt a hand on her shoulder, did she spin around from instinct and see him.

"Madelaina," he said softly.

She sank against him, into his arms, unable to speak. They kissed for a long while, fierce, hot kisses alternating with sweet, tender, and incredibly passionate kisses. When they paused to stare into each other's eyes, the look of love glowed and came alive. Her throat burned and swelled, constricting words.

"Come, beloved. You're coming with me," he said gruffly, leading her by the hand.

"Wait. Where are you taking me?" she asked hoarsely.

"Does it matter?" he asked abruptly.

Her face burned. "No. I'll go wherever you want me to go," she replied submissively. She filled with unendurable excitement and an indescribable thirst and hunger for him as happiness engulfed her.

They skirted around the house, avoiding those rooms where crowds congregated, and made their way toward the front entrance. Not once did Madelaina give any thought to General Villa or Rudolfo Fierro until she heard his lusty laughter coming from one of the salons.

In the foyer to the mansion she paused once again. "Perhaps I'd best tell the *jefe* where I'll be," she began as he wrapped her fox fur around her.

"You'ah a big girl, now, sweet *chíquita*. Or haven't ya noticed? Ya think it's time foah ya to foahget all this revolution business?"

"It's time, Peter. Dear God, it is time!" she said, leading him out the door, past the liveried butlers.

At a quarter to midnight, Peter's open touring car drove into the Benson estate in El Paso. Madelaina felt a chill run through her as countless memories flooded her consciousness. She recalled Maneulito Perez and the night she spent with him. Her marriage to William Benson replayed in her mind. Why did Peter have to bring her here? Why? Why not her own house that filled with pleasant memories of their last night together, when they conceived their son. Her heart fell. She would have to tell Peter about their son. Dear God, if it wasn't one thing, it was a hundred that kept them pried apart.

He helped her out of the touring car and picked her up in his arms unexpectedly. In a few long strides he had her at the front door of the painfully familiar Spanish-styled villa. Inside, in the foyer, he let her slip from his arms, and clinging to her cohesively, he kissed her with increasing passion. For several wild, ecstatic moments, Peter felt a tingling in his groins that had been absent for too long. His feelings gave rise to hope as he removed her fur wrap and flung it on a nearby chair, and he grew ecstatic.

Holding her hand like a child's, he moved across the

916

large living room to the bar. For a moment he released her, long enough to pop the cork on a bottle of chilled champagne that stood in a bucket. She didn't remark on the prepared bottle or the glasses on a tray, although she wondered who he expected to entertain. She didn't care. She didn't want to know. He poured the sparkling amber-colored liquid into both glasses, handed her one and took the other.

"An' now mah sweet Little Fox, mah dearest, sweetest wife, ah toast ta ya and ta us." He clinked glasses with her and drained his entirely.

"What's the mattuh, darlin'? Don'cha like champagne? I prepared it especially foah you."

Madelaina placed the glass on the bar. She lifted her dark eyes to meet his. "Peter, we have to talk. There's something I must tell you—" she began.

He placed his fingers on her lips. "No, not now, sweet. Don' let's spoil it foah us. First, ya gotta trust in me, heah?"

She attempted to speak once again, to interrupt him.

"Ah said, not now." He looked lovingly into her eyes. Once again, he kissed her and held her tightly. Peter was ecstatic when again he felt the tingle in his manhood. He felt himself quiver with passion and his hopes were high, so high.

"Now, enough of this foolishness between two grown-up people. Ah've got a surprise fer ya, mah love."

"All right," she said submissively. He was so alive, so filled with ebullience, she hadn't the heart to bring him down to reality.

"Come with me, sugah," he said, leading her up the stairs, her hand in his. With the other wrapped around another glass of champagne, he led her up the circular stairs and paused before the same door to the room in which she made love to Manuelito. He felt her pull back and was prompted to say above a whisper.

"It's all right, honey. Youah'll see." He opened the door softly, peering into the dimly lit room. Then, turning to her, he nodded. "It's all right. Come in."

The room was in shadow, partially lit by a very small lamp on a chest. Her eyes, adjusting to the darkness, found nothing familiar. The room had been redecorated since Manulito occupied it. Suddenly, she saw it. Right before her eyes. Her heart raced madly and she turned to him with wide-eyed wonder. "Peter—it was you! You who rescued our son!" She sprinted from his side, reached the crib at the end of the room near the bay window, and her eyes widened with delight, happiness, and contentment. Tears of joy misted her eyes as she lifted the mosquito netting and stared down at the peaceful repose of her cherubic baby.

So strong was the inner desire to pick him up, squeeze him, smother him with kisses that she stood shaking nervously, not knowing what to do first.

"Well, is that all ya can do—stand about like a stone statue?"

She turned to Peter, tears streaming down her cheeks, and leaned over the crib to tenderly pick up the infant. She held him close to her, recalling everything sweet and loving about the child and between the joy and tears murmured sweet nonsensical things. "Thank God you're safe, *niñito*," she cooed. "How you've grown. Your mama has missed you more than you'll ever know."

She glanced at her husband who had moved in behind her and held the two of them silently, possessively, and for all eternity.

"Let him sleep, *chiquita*. You'll have the rest of your life for him. Tonight belongs to the both of us." He took the bundle from her arms and placed him back in the bassinette, brushing a tear from his misty eyes.

Madelaina took a small hand into hers and felt the tightening grip around hers with exquisite pleasure. "He's grown so, I hardly recognized him," she whispered, gazing down on the child. What happiness she felt. What joy!

"Let's hope you'll say the same thing about me," he whispered back with a devilish grin to his face.

Madelaina couldn't have asked for anything more when she left the nursery holding Peter's hand. She was consumed with happiness. Her baby son was safe, she was with the man she loved, and nothing else mattered—nothing.

They walked through the upper corridor to his bedroom where he paused to embrace her. "Madelaina," he whispered hoarsely with a new urgency to his voice. "Mah dearest, sweetest evuh lovin' *chiquita*."

Inside, they clung to each other tightly. Her hands felt the familiar muscular play rippling under his shirt. The warmth he generated when excited stimulated her intensely, as it always had in the past. She couldn't think. Time stood still for them both as he did all the exciting things that generally turned her into putty for him. His slightest touch, the lightest caress caused her to thrill and shudder with ecstasy. It was time only for feeling and love; music to which souls dance.

Dreamily she half-closed her eyes as she felt him undo the hooks and eyes of her beaded gown. "Mah sweet, sweet love, ya can't imagine how ah've longed foah ya, how much ah've missed ya," he said softly with a catch in his voice. Her gown slid to the floor unnoticed. She stood naked before him except for the garter belt and silk stockings she wore beneath the gown.

Astonished that she wore nothing under her gown, Peter gasped appreciatively. He leaned over and swept her up in his arms and carried her to the large, oversized bed, and with a free hand as she clung to him, arms around his neck, he pulled back the covers and laid her gently on the silk sheets.

"Hurry, beloved," she whispered dreamily. "The desire in me for you is overwhelming."

Peter paused to pour himself a stiff drink of whiskey from a crystal decanter on a nearby table. He commenced undressing in the shadowy room, his back to her. When he approached the bed, standing nude before her, and she saw the ghastly tracks and scarring from his stomach to his groins, she cried softly in compassion. Her hands tracing the scar brought a shiver of sensation to him.

"Oh, my dearest *querido*," she whimpered. "What pain you must have endured." She reached out for him and hugged him about the waist, lying her feverish face against his bare stomach. "Make the world go away, Peter. Make it go away. We've been too much a part of it. And I'm so tired of responsibility."

"Ah'll try, sweet suguh. Ah'll try. But first youah an' me is gotta have us a talk, heah?" He gulped down the whiskey bracer, avoiding her eyes.

"Can't we talk later?" she implored.

"No. Now."

The tone of his voice alarmed her. She backed away from him and looked up into his blue, blue eyes. He sat down on the bed alongside her and unhooked her garters. "Madelaina, a lot has happened to us, both of us." He slowly peeled off the wispy hose.

"It's the God's truth, *querido*. Too much, to both of us. There is so much you don't know about me." She began thinking this to be a moment of personal confession between them, and she was willing and eager to own up to every moment of all indiscretions, whether voluntary or done under duress. "It's best to talk, my husband, to erase all the bad that's happened so we can make a fresh beginning."

Peter studied her closely. "Ah'm not shuah ah understand ya, sugah. Look what ah've gotta tell ya may make the difference between ouah staying togethuh foah all eternity—or you gettin' a divorce."

"Divorce? *Dios mios*, are you crazy, Peter? Why would I desire a divorce? I have everything I've dreamed of having these past many months, all any woman could want." She reached for his hand, removed the silk stockings from them, and turned fully to him. Only Peter slipped out of her arms and moved toward the whiskey bottle again. He refilled the glass and gulped it down, letting the fiery liquid burn a trail in his chest.

"Mah fathuh thought of everything when he built this heah villa. Ah nevuh gave it much thought until now that ya might a spent youah honeymoon in this heah room."

"Peter!" she cried softly, hurt that he should even bring up the subject. "I told you all about that part of my life—all of it. The ceremony was performed downstairs, but it was at Seven Moons that he—that he—" she faltered, her face burning.

"Seduced you?" he laughed harshly. "Ah, then that explains it."

"Explains what?"

"Why he left Seven Moons to you. All of it."

Madelaina couldn't believe her ears. "To me? You mean to us?"

"To *you,* my dear. *Your* performance must have been superb!" As soon as the words were out, Peter felt terrible. He hadn't meant to say such things, but he couldn't help himself. He gulped the drink and poured another.

Madelaina recoiled and eyed him through curious, hurt, and wondering eyes. "Have you brought me here to humiliate me, to bring up the past over which I had no control, and lay it before me at its worst implications?"

Peter moaned softly, lay across the bed, and pulled her into her into his arms. "No," he whispered hoarsely. "Damnit, honey, ah've no intention of hurtin' ya. Ah'm not shuah what's gotten inta me."

"If you persist, I'll turn back into the iceberg I've been since our son was born," she said coolly, in a voice that hinted at detachment.

"Iceberg? You?" He laughed ironically. "Mah deah, sweet wife, that could nevuh happen ta ya. Maybe if it did, ouah problems would be settled."

"Problems, Peter? What problems?" she scoffed. "We are together. All else is in the past. All the bad dreams with those frightening pictures will evaporate now that we've found ourselves. Why are we using strange words to build walls between us?" She shook her head when he held a whiskey glass up to her. "Neither of us are to blame for what happened. Thank God that we're alive. So many died. So many—" her voice trailed off. "Give thanks that we found each other. Nothing else matters." She sat up and fell into his arms, and her hands began immediately to explore his body.

Catching her hands, Peter removed them gently from his body. Madelaina, hurt, confused, and shaken by this subtle rejection, sat back against the headboard and watched him pour another tumbler of whiskey. Confronted with an absorbing inconsistency of thoughts, she was unable to express her quandary at his behavior.

It never occurred to her until this precise moment that something was drastically wrong. In all the time she'd known him, including those first days aboard the *Mozambique* after the ice between them was broken, he'd never been an inhibited man. Whenever he'd wanted her, he'd taken her. Of course, she had always been willing, for only with him had she felt the overwhelming passion of love and fire of any duration. Only with Peter . . . and Tolomeo. *Damnit! Forget Tolomeo! You're with Peter now. He's the only one who counts. Don't let any other thoughts beguile you or influence you.*

"Heah, sugah, drink this up," insisted her husband, forcing a drink into her hands.

"If you want me to," she said reluctantly. She recalled vividly when Peter drank too much he was unable to make love as he desired. Why, now, does he pick this night to become a *borrachón*, a drunk? Gulping the drink down quickly, she turned the empty glass upside down on her nightstand. "You have a spare cigarette around?" she asked.

Peter lit two, gave her one, and smoked the other. "Want a refill?" he asked, gesturing to the glass.

922

"No, thank you," she replied, puffing on the cigarette, inhaling and expelling the smoke. "Too bad this
isn't marijuana. It would relax you and me both."

Peter cautioned her about the use of reefers in
Texas. "It's against the law, heah, so ya be careful who
ya tell ya smoke it. Texas ain't Mexico, heah?"

Peter watched her as an enemy watches his prey.
How could he tell her? Earlier, when they kissed so
passionately he'd felt a hardness in his loins that
silently gave rise to hope that his impotency had
passed. The moment he faced her nakedness and his
desire mounted, his manhood had deflated into a total
lack of response.

God, how he tried! He had used a few of the Mexican girls from Old Chihuahua every night, sometimes
twice a night and nothing! Absolutely nothing had happened. When General Villa wired him that he was
bringing Little Fox to El Paso, Peter's hopes had
soared and he put them all on the line. If anyone could
stir his manhood into pulsating joy and stimulate him
as a man should be stimulated, it was his wife. Madelaina could jolt him back to life again. He was certain
of it. Love transcended sex anytime. He had every
right to believe his wife was the only one who could
restore his manhood. She wouldn't fail him, not his
Little Fox. She'd lift the curse that had afflicted him for
the past year. He'd confide in her. He felt deeply that
he had no right to hold her to a marriage in his condition, but before he threw in the towel, he would ask
her to help him.

He hated being so vulnerable. Goddamn it! Some of
the whores he'd brought for a night had looked upon
him as less than a man. They'd laughed contemptuously at him when he couldn't perform. Well, all that
was over, now. Madelaina was with him. She'd put an
end to those frightening feelings of desperation and
hopelessness he'd experienced in the past.

With a light curse of despair, Peter rose from the
bed and said, "We've gotta talk, Little Fox. We've
gotta."

"So, talk, my husband," she replied patiently. "I'm listening." Then suddenly Madelaina was afraid to hear what it was he was trying to tell her. Her body tensed and she knew what he was trying to communicate to her. All those visions that came to her, primed to illuminate her mind, had been ignored. She gazed covertly at his limp sex organ, hoping he didn't see her for fear he might misinterpret her interest. And she knew. *Oh, Tolomeo! What wisdom you had stored inside of you. What do I do now? You tried to tell me. You made it quite clear, and I ignored and misunderstood your warnings. You tried to impress me with the right values, and what did I do? I ignored your wisdom.*

Clearly she recollected the time Tolomeo held a knife upthrust in his hands, prepared to cut off his precious manhood.

What will you say, Madelaina, if I severed my phallus? Would you still love me? Would you remain with me until death as you insisted? Will you love me if I can no longer couple with you? Ah, then you don't love me. You love my sexual organs. Good, then I shall cut them off and give them to you to take with you and love evermore.

Dios mios! Madelaina shuddered inwardly. Here it was, just as Tolomeo had tried telling her it might be. What to do? What to do? This was moment of truth. What she did and said in these next few moments would affect three human beings for the rest of their days. *Help me, Tolomeo. Help me, God. Help me, anyone. Have I become a seer? A psychic? Or am I going mad? What is happening to me that I have been gifted with vision? I don't want it! Take it away. It's best that I remain blind to such things,* she agonized desperately.

Tears spilled from her eyes. She turned her head from Peter so he wouldn't see. *This must be a terrible time for Peter, and here I am acting the fool. He expects more from Little Fox and he shall get it,* she told herself.

924

Peter handed her a robe. "Heah, put this on," he told her, slipping into another himself.

It was something he'd never done in the past, cover his nudity. He'd always been proud of his manly, well-proportioned body. Never one to mince words, Peter, as he'd always done in the past, faced her abruptly and spoke straight out. "Madelaina, ah'm impotent."

"Yes, I know," she said quietly, her dark wide eyes fixed on his in love.

"You know?" He was aghast. His eyes narrowed suspiciously. "How do you know? Who told you?"

"No one. I've known almost from the start," she said in truth.

"But how? Who?" He didn't believe her and told her so.

"Don't ask me how. I couldn't explain it so you'd understand." How could she tell him about Tolomeo? He'd think she'd turned into some crazy woman. And it would only add more fuel to the fire smoldering inside him.

"Ya say ya knew all the time? Yet ya were prepared to let me make a fool of mahself tonight?" Now Peter grew angry at her, resented her.

"Things aren't always what they appear to be—" she began.

"That's disgustin'. Youah were waitin' foah me ta make a jackass outa mahself. Why, that's a pretty low thing—"

"No! No," she interrupted. "That wasn't my intention. And calm down, Peter. It's not the end of the world!"

"Hah! That's easy foah youah ta say!"

"Why is it any easier for me than you?" she demanded fiercely. "If I remember correctly, I, too, was unable to function as a woman for a time. Who came to my aid? My husband. So, husband, here I am to help you, to love you and help ease your pain."

"Pity, ah don't need," he said scorchingly.

"Pity?" exclaimed Madelaina hotly. "Who speaks of pity?"

"And don't give me that wifely duty business, either!"

"Are you so hurt, so humiliated, so terribly ashamed of your condition that you won't give me a chance to help you, Peter?" she asked softly.

"The only way youah can help me is ta give me an erection! That's the tall and short o' it!"

"No!"

"No?" He stared at her dumbfounded and resentful.

"No! You heard me. Not when you demand it. You're trying too hard. It's not that important, at least not to me."

Peter laughed uproariously at the ugly joke this presented to his mind. "Not important? Why, Little Fox, without a piece o' tail, you'd be outa youah evuh loving mind! A hot little piece of baggage like youah has gotta have a stud bull in the barn or ya couldn't live. Poon tang is youah life, mah sweet," he said bitterly.

Madelaina stared at him contemptuously. "How little you know me, gringo," she said, standing, her hands on her hips, feet spread apart like a *campesina* from the early days. She undid a few hairpins from her upswept hairdo and let her raven hair fall to below her shoulders. "I tell you it is not important. You don't believe me. I tell you we hardly know each other, that we must first get acquainted. Will you listen to Little Fox?"

Peter, tense and wound up to the point of cracking, had wanted desperately for a miracle to happen this night, like in a story book when the prince walks off into the sunset with a princess to live happy ever after. He reached up for her and pulled her down on the bed, his head against her wildly beating heart.

"Ya think it might help, *querida*? Ya think ya can do it—make a man outa me?" His voice reflected his inner torment.

"What you ask is impossible. You already are a man—some wild, crazy man," she said lightly, hoping to raise his spirits. She stroked his forehead, quietly as-

926

suring him of her love for him. "We can do it, *mi marido,* together we can accomplish miracles." Inwardly she thought, *God, show me how to perform such a miracle.*

They fell asleep in each other's arms. Peter, first. Madelaina, when dawn erupted in the sky, fell exhausted from the countless thoughts burning in her mind.

Chapter 35

"It saddens me, Little Fox, that you and your *marido* will not join Pancho Villa in his most spectacular of battles," said the *jefe* over luncheon a few days before his departure for Mexico. "It will not be the same without you seated at the head of my *soldaderas*. They will feel your absence as much as I will, but I shall learn to get along without your expert counseling," he said, smiling brightly with a twinkle in his eyes. "Ain't that right, Fierro?" He addressed himself to the unsmiling, bearish man who sipped champagne and enjoyed the lavish spread at the buffet table by making short order of it.

Madelaina glanced at Fierro with a smile on her face. She would miss this adoring animal, even though at times his might and cold-blooded nature had frightened her. He still wore the red-haired fetish on his uniform, dangling from the Sam Browne belt he wore over his tunic. She wondered if Villa ever learned of his affair with Antonetta. Somehow she felt deeply that he knew and had accepted it as a human and natural everyday occurrence.

"Please know, *Jefe,* that I, too, will miss you and the others. But I must devote time to my husband and child. They both need me. And if you will pardon my candor, I am tired of revolution. We both are, aren't we, Peter?"

"Shall I tell you that I, too, am tired? *Chica,* this past trip to El Paso has given me hope—new hope. Our gringo friends in Washington have begun to hear my tunes, so perhaps now they'll help us waltz our way to the capital."

"Let's hope so, *Jefe*," she replied, wondering why Peter had remained silent.

"Not yet," said Captain Tracy Richards, entering the patio where the gathering took place. He removed his Stetson, gave it to a servant, and ran his fingers through his stringy brown hair. He wore a strange, taut expression on his face.

Peter walked toward him, hand outstretched to shake hands, a champagne glass in the other to thrust in Tracy's hands. The look in the man's eyes arrested his host. "What's the mattuh, pal? Ya look like ya lost yer last friend."

Tracy nodded and moved in toward General Villa. He saluted the *jefe* and removed a wire from inside his tunic. "Sorry, *Jefe*. I raced as fast as I could. This just came in from Chihuahua City." He handed Villa the paper.

Villa accepted the wire, his dark eyes, unsmiling, were fixed on the captain. He glanced at the message and read: *Obregon back in Mexico City. Carranza back from Veracruz. Presidente Guiterrez fled with 10 million pesos from treasury. Hell has erupted. Advise, Manuelo Isabel.*"

General Villa handed the wire to General Fierro. "Confirm this," he ordered. Fierro's eyes scanned the contents without expression.

"Ah already did, *Jefe*," replied Tracy Richards. "Ah took the liberty of checking with the Juarez wireless office. They just got the word from Mexico City."

General Villa turned to Madelaina. "Let Little Fox see the wire."

Madelaina glanced from her husband to Fierro to Villa, then read the message. Her eyes lifted to meet his.

"Ju know what theese means, *chiquita?*" asked Villa gently.

"I know. Your battle with Obregon—my father."

"I wished for a different result."

"I know. Time was our enemy. Then go. *Vaya con Dios* and may the best man win," she told him tearfully

929

as Peter put a strong arm around his wife. He read the wire and handed it to Villa. The *jefe* directed his words to them.

"Is best ju stay here for theese wan. There will never be a bigger, more forceful thrust than this war against Obregon," he said tersely. "For a long time it's been coming," he told her in Spanish, as he buttoned his tunic. "Come, Fierro, we go. You too, gringo?" he asked Tracy Richards.

"Try and keep me out of this one. Ah got me a feelin' this one will be the beginnin' o' the end of revolution for Mexico, eh, *Jefe?*"

"Perhaps, gringo. Perhaps," he said sadly, taking his leave.

Watching him and the entire entourage leave their home, Peter and Madelaina stood in the courtyard, waving to them with a feeling of great loss.

Peter turned to his wife and smiled tenderly at her. "Foah a while, sugah, ah felt shuah youah were going ta leave me. Ah know y' all wanta be right alongside of the *jefe*. Ah find mahself weakening every moment."

Madelaina turned to him and pressed her fingertip against his lips. "No! I want to be with my husband and child. We shall have to content ourselves with reading about the war from Miguel Guerra's columns, *querido*. Oh, *amado mío,* haven't we had enough? I thought we had made our decision."

"We did, sugah. We did," he said solemnly, embracing her tightly.

It was to be a considerably long while before Madelaina and her family would go to Seven Moons. Peter had immersed himself in pressing business matters. He'd changed so drastically in personality and temperament that Madelaina felt the need to consult with the physician who performed the surgery on her husband. Without Peter's knowledge, she paid a visit to Dr. Clancy Towbridge. The man in his late forties with salt and pepper hair, wearing a stiffly starched round collar with a narrow tie under his white coat, recalled the case intimately.

"Why, shucks, m'am, ah was shuah that Peter had become as frisky as a two-tailed burro by now. Theah's no medical reason why he shouldn't be performin' like a jack rabbit. If theah are problems in that department afuh so long, it's gotta be all in his head. An' youah jus' tell him ah said so, heah?"

"That may well be, Doctor," she said politely. "And if it is as you say, perhaps you can explain better to me what I must do to help him get back his manhood. I don't wish to compound the state of mind he's in by saying or doing anything that might cause him more anguish."

"That's a right sensible gal, ya are, Mrs. Benson. Ah admire such spunk. It isn't every day ah meet such a brave woman." He paused reflectively. "Ah jus' don't know wheah ta begin. It could be from many things— such as a very poor home life. What ah mean is not poverty, ya understand, but a wrongful relationship between parents. What ah'm attemptin' ta say ta ya, Mrs. Benson, is something that medical science tuhday doesn't understand. Sometimes childhood frustrations don't manifest themselves in a person until the late twenties, thirties, and sometimes in mid-life. Ya understand?"

"No, Doctor. I'm afraid I don't. Are you trying to tell me my husband has a sick mind?"

Dr. Towbridge laughed. "Not quite. But ya might say a little bit like that."

"I'm truly confused. He was shot, sustained severe injuries, and he was told impotency might result. It did. Now you tell me, impotency isn't a result of the surgery, that it's in his head. Couldn't you be more specific?"

"If ah could, ah would, m'am. There just isn't enough known about abnormal pyschological behavior."

"Abnormal psychological behavior? You are the most confounding doctor I've ever spoken with," she

931

said, fully irritated. "Dr. Towbridge, my marriage is at stake. What can I do to help it stay together?"

"Be patient and understanding."

"Words, Doctor. Those are just words. How can I be patient when I'm not certain of what I must be patient? How can I be understanding when I don't know what I'm supposed to understand? For a doctor you are incredibly uninformed!" she quipped as her aristocratic *gachupín* blood boiled. "Can't you at least refer me to someone else? Someone who might be more knowledgeable on the subject? Forgive my impatience and somewhat boorish manners, but, Doctor, if I don't conjure up a miracle, my marriage will end."

Dr. Towbridge glanced at her over the top of his rimless glasses and nodded as if to himself. "Yer Mexican, aren't ya?"

Madelaina bridled angrily. "What has that to do with anything?"

His face flared with a pink flush. "Well, I—er—well, sometimes, Mrs. Benson, a man marries a woman in her country and when he brings her ta his land, she jus' don't fit no how. This can make a man regret—" He found words more difficult under Madelaina's hot, melting gaze. "Ya understand it's nothing personal. What ah'm trying ta say is that a man might feel he made a mistake and he feels strangled and he can't be a man."

"Thank you for your honesty. I assure you this isn't so in our case," she told him imperiously with controlled anger.

"Ah gotta say one thing in yer favuh. You'ah a persistent filly." He picked up a pen and scribbled several names on a script pad. "Y'all have ta mosey ovuh ta San Antonio foah the answers, ma'am." He handed her the information she needed and wished her the best of luck.

"Let me just say a word about the man youah gonna meet. Dr. Thaddeus Oemolot, pronounced *Amalot*, isn't what ya might refer ta as the average physician ya see about El Paso. Or anywheah else, foah that matter.

932

He's a little unorthodox. But most of them head shrinkers from Freud on down were a little tetched in the head, according ta theah contemporaries." Towbridge sighed. "Well, mebbe in the next fifty yeahs, theah'll be a few changes in ouah society and people will begin ta wake up the real values. Thaddeus Oemolot is unique among men, the only one of his kind, if ya ask me. He's bright, he's well informed, an it ain't all outa books that he comes by his uncanny perception and his phenomenal diagnostic abilities. But why do ah rant like this? Y'all meet him, decide foah youahself. Ah think the two of ya might hit it off fine. Ya see, he was married to one of youah people. He can tell ya plenty about the difficulties that face ya in Texas."

"I thought the Alamo incident took place over seventy-five years ago," she snapped caustically. "Texans probably have it all over the elephant! *Buenas tardes, senor el doctor. Muchas gracias.*" She spoke Spanish purposely.

She was shaking when she left the physician's office. Damned if she'd admit to this—this—doctor that of late she'd been entertaining similar thoughts. No question she'd encountered the racial prejudices, bigotry, and narrow-minded biases of her neighbors, who hadn't come to call on her since her arrival.

Thank God I have the blood of a high-born Spaniard, she said to herself a thousand times over. *If I'd been a peón with no education, I'd probably walk around like a wounded animal, ready to dig my own grave.* It wasn't fair, she told herself. In Mexico the gringos are treated like gods. Here in America we are treated like dogs. She hadn't brought the subject out in the open to discuss it with her husband, not yet, with all the problems besetting him presently.

But—one day—one day she'd settle this Alamo business so her people wouldn't have to suffer what strangers had done to each other nearly a century ago.

Enough for racial prejudices, she reasoned. Get back to Peter. He'd changed drastically from the reckless, easy-going, freedom-fighting libertine he was when they met. She hardly knew him anymore. He'd grown more introverted, hardly communicating with her. Something rankled him. Something ate away at his insides and the pity of it was she couldn't get close enough to him to find out what it was that was causing such alien behavior.

She'd observed him in silence, hoping to instill in him the old feelings of security and self-assurance she found so attractive in him. A few times she'd chided him about his personality change and he'd stare at her as if seeing her for the first time.

"Ah'm a property ownuh now, a man with responsibilities. Ah jus' can't run off inta the world lookin' ta save humanity. Ah've got mah own little world heah ta set straight first."

What frightened Madelaina more each day was the startling resemblance between his actions and those of his dead father. His impotence had changed him into a hardened, two-fisted, gun-toting *hacendado* who was skillfully manipulating himself into the political sphere of action that kept El Paso at the center of international intrigue. Worse, he refused to confide in her over the nature of his mysterious covert involvements which kept him absent from the villa for longer than she cared to dwell upon.

In a way she was grateful for the time to herself, because it allowed her to spend more time with her son. He'd grown into a fine, strapping two-year-old who kept the entire Benson household gravely concerned because he hadn't taken his first step yet. Peter remained the most anxious, and his concern that it might be something physical rather than the normal way of things kept Madelaina in borderline frustration, trying to reason with him that boys took more time to walk.

"Not to worry, Señora Benson," Pilar would tell her. Peter had brought her from Seven Moons to care for the child in Madelaina's absence, and she was perfect for him, playing with him, giving him the care and attention he needed. "Ees you, Pilar concerns herself weeth. Ju and your *marido*. Are theengs hokay?"

934

Madelaina would smile and nod her head. "As long as we're together, Pilar, nothing can be wrong." But the old woman knew better. Her Indian instinct told her it wasn't right for such newlyweds to be sleeping in separate bedrooms.

Even Madelaina found this unacceptable, but Peter, who had become nocturnal, stayed awake most of the night worrying, and in his desire not to disturb his wife, he insisted on their occupying separate quarters.

Peter had made no sexual overtures to her and Madelaina hadn't pushed. Instead, she attempted to build an emotional closeness with him, tried to share his interests, and did nothing to raise any suspicions in his mind. She exercised all the patience she could muster. She had tried to figure some way she could go to Dallas without raising questions in Peter's mind. His overt possessiveness was beginning to grate on her nerves. She was unable to go to market without his asking her incessant questions about who she'd seen or spoken to.

Then one day it happened. Peter came home in the early afternoon and announced he had to make a short trip to Washington. Unfinished business, he told her. He'd return in less than a week, he reassured her when she expressed her disappointment in not going with him. She'd said nothing when she entered his room and he quickly shut his travel case, so she wouldn't see its contents. But she'd seen his six-shooters and holster. How she wanted to ask him more about his secret comings and goings, his mysterious behavior, midnight callers, and the like. She felt if she pried, she'd disturb the rapport she'd hoped to build to inspire his trust and confidence.

They kissed warmly. "You'ah shuah y'all be fine?" he asked with concern.

"Yes, Peter. We'll be fine. I promise. Remember I managed to survive the revolution in your absence."

"Ya hafta bring that up all the time? Damn! Ah thought all that was in the past. Ah thought we agreed not to talk about it no moah." He stormed out the

935

door, briefcase, travel bag, and coat in hand without saying goodbye.

It would have been easy for Madelaina to resort to tears and feelings of humiliation. Instead, she summoned all her strength and cool temperament and grew more determined to fulfill her mission. It was San Antonio for her. She was going to get her answers—or die in the attempt.

She told Pilar where she could be located in the event of an emergency and left stern instructions not to tell anyone of her whereabouts. She packed an overnight bag and booked passage on the train to San Antonio.

During the long train ride, her thoughts again turned to Peter and his unusual behavior of late. They were more like strangers these past five months. One night, in one of his foulest moods, he addressed her with a hardness she'd never recalled in him before.

"Why don't ya take on a lover, for God's sake? That—what's his name—that Armando fella—the one that took yer virginity!"

She had been astounded. "Why do you think of him now?"

"Listen, don't play the innocent with me. Ya shuah carried on with him at Townsend's villa the night of the gala for the *jefe*."

Madelaina could say nothing. She knew he spoke out of sheer frustration. And her words in defense of her own innocent actions could be easily twisted to suit his own depressive mania. Her silence only incited him to lash out at her, to hurt her by bringing up all she had tried so desperately to forget.

"How many lovers have possessed that body? Ah remember what y'all told me of Madrigal and that theah Simon Salomon—that ya hated him. Well, deah, sweet Little Fox, ah also learned that ya were shacked up with him foah ovuh two weeks. Now tell me that ya hated him?"

Madelaina had glanced sharply at him, totally as-

936

tounded by his words. "How—where ever did you hear that?" she asked.

"Don't deny it. Ah hate liars!"

"I don't intend to deny the truth."

"Then ya admit ya were with him, close as turtle doves?"

"Why are you doing this?" she asked gently. "Why didn't you speak of this long ago? Why are you trying, like an angry child, to hurt the one you love most in the world?"

Peter had no defenses to fall back on. In a voice steeped in agony, he told her to leave him. "Get a divorce. Or we'll end up like my father and mother, hating each other, creating a living hell for us."

"I haven't given up yet, my husband," she told him. She was desperate and it showed. It also served to increase Peter's guilt feelings that he wasn't properly performing his role as husband to her.

This trip to San Antonio was Madelaina's last chance. She had to learn what was wrong with Peter, how to cope or go stark mad.

Chapter 36

Dr. Thaddeus Oemolot, an eccentric, was everything and more the El Paso physician had described him to be. He was a man in his late forties, with well-tanned, unlined features and marvelously warm turquoise eyes which reflected the dancing rays of the sun streaming in through curtained windows in his cluttered office. He had a high, wide forehead framed by a thick shock of snowy white hair. His nose was straight with flaring nostrils, somewhat Grecian in shape, his square jaw with a cleft in it gave him a strong countenance, one which inspired confidence.

He greeted her in a curt, professional manner in thickly accented English, which she later learned was a combination of Swiss, French, and German. Please, she asked, could he speak in either Spanish, French, or Italian to enable her to better understand him? He nodded and then proceeded to speak in impeccable Spanish, complete with a Castilian lisp.

As he began to outline the complexities involved in cases of impotency and the ramifications surrounding the onset of symptoms, Madelaina found herself totally bewildered by the alien and incomprehensible words he used. *Dios mios!* She should have brought with her a dictionary, she told herself. As if she had to be told that impotence was an impairment in the desire for sexual gratification! For this she had traveled hundreds of miles.

Madelaina complained of his semantical snobbery, his use of words she didn't understand. The inveterate chain-smoking, coffee-drinking addict who kept both coffee and cigarettes within reach of his roll-top desk smiled, begged her pardon, and spoke more in layman's language.

"Senõra Benson, I'll try to speak with less complications for you. As I was saying, fatigue, worry, and a long list of seemingly innocent ailments can temporarily impair sexual potency. In my opinion—and I do not make light of the situation—prolonged or permanent impotency before the age of 55 is generally the result of psychological conflicts. It's a study that we of the medical profession specializing in this field know little of at this time."

"Certainly you can give me more encouragement than that?" she asked, gazing at the white cockatoo perched in a corner of the messy office, contentedly eating sunflower seeds.

"Perhaps, if you persuade your husband to explain his own case history, I could make a swifter diagnosis. It isn't customary to work in this manner without first examining the patient or at least speaking with him. You see, whatever the mental block preventing him from performing with you, it must be dissolved—totally removed. Personally, I don't see how I can do anything for him without seeing him."

He glanced concentratedly at the medical report she brought from El Paso, containing the history of the gunshot wounds, subsequent surgery, and the superficial case history compiled of the psychological studies done by Dr. Towbridge.

"This Towbridge was thorough enough. He sewed your husband back together well enough, no?"

"Apparently not good enough or he wouldn't be in such a sad state."

"Señora," he said patiently. "Believe me when I tell you his problems are mental—not physical," he said, tapping his forehead. "How can I convince you?"

"Very well, where are we? We rule out physical impairment. *Bueno*. You can eliminate any feelings of shyness or inferiority with the opposite sex. My husband has been a lusty man from the moment I first met him, and I'm sure he was even before our acquaintance some six years ago," she said candidly.

Dr. Oemolot nodded in approval. "You've been doing some reading, *como no? Muy bien.* Then if you will, tell me more about him, this freedom-fighting soldier-of-fortune business. His thirst for adventure, desire to champion the rights of the downtrodden. Tell me all you can of his background," he instructed.

She did the best she could for some two hours of constant narration.

"Can we rule out any guilt feelings he might harbor over an extramarital affair, *señora?* What I mean is, has he been unfaithful to your married vows?"

"Such a question! A man with his lusty macho qualities? But of course. He is only human, no? Perhaps you weren't listening when I described our roles in the revolution, Dr. Oemolot?" She dug a sharper spur into him than was intended, with more candor than she thought herself capable of. Then she flushed under his melting gaze. "Perhaps not since the accident, if I can believe my husband—and I do." Madelaina squirmed uncomfortably in her chair and lit a cigarette to cover her discomfort. The cockatoo ruffled its feathers and closed its eyes.

From the moment she'd entered his modest, efficient-looking office, surrounded by walls of books, dark leathers, and living plants, she had a strange feeling they weren't strangers. Logically she knew they'd never met before, but there was that intangible energy, that force of attraction stronger than a magnet which compelled their lives to cross. What was it, she asked herself countless times during this initial visit. Had she known him at some time in her life? Madelaina, whose memory was too acute at times, searched every open drawer in her mind for the connection to him. She found none. Still the feeling persisted.

He listened patiently and smiled from time to time at her eagerness, this determined effort on her part to find a solution to her present dilemma. Thaddeus Oemolot admired her spunk and wondered what sort of a man

940

wouldn't have come himself to solve his own quandary and unmanly behavior. Didn't it mean enough to him? It apparently meant a great deal to his wife.

"You are married to a gringo, *señora*? And you are —French—Spanish—what?"

"It makes any difference?" she asked frostily. "I am a Mexican."

"Everything makes a difference and can be vital in such a case," he replied, giving it proper importance. "*Señora,* please tell me of any significant quarrels or arguments that have passed between you and your *marido*? Are there any hostilities between you?"

"Is it necessary to know such personal things, Doctor. Much of what you suggest sounds quite preposterous to me, if you must know my feelings."

His voice had an instant mesmerizing richness and a depth of understanding, but he seemed a bit impatient with her at times. "If you expect me to help restore your husband's potency, yes. It's necessary that I know, however personal or ridiculous my questions sound."

Madelaina glanced at her watch with an attitude of annoyance. "How much time do you have?" she asked in a challenging tone of voice.

"How much do I need?"

"However much time it takes to tell you our full story. It's long, involved, and at times highly incredible even for me, one who's lived it."

Dr. Oemolot impatiently pounded the small bell on his cluttered, oversized roll-top desk. Across the room, the white cockatoo started and ruffled his feathers.

"Be quiet, Pablo," commanded the physician as his nurse entered the room, dressed in a white starched uniform and cap. She stood in the doorway expectantly.

"Yes, Doctor?"

He instructed her to cancel all his appointments for the balance of the day, to set over his next day's patients for the following day and be certain to make his apologies to his evening guests, that he'd call them as soon as time permitted. Before the astonished stiff-lipped nurse could either object or dispute his orders, Dr. Oemolot had removed his white coat, slipped into his Oxford plaid jacket, belted at the waist, removed his bifocals, and slipped them into a case which he thrust into his inner breast jacket pocket. From another pocket, he removed a pair of dark glasses.

"The inexorable hot sun of Texas becomes man's worst enemy at this time of the year," he said, opening the outer door to his office. "*Ondolay, señora.* If you've a long story to tell me, it's best we get started." He nearly shoved her out the door, then stopped abruptly. "You like Mexican food? I sincerely hope so, because I'm taking you to a restaurant I enjoy. *Bueno?*"

"*Beuno, senor el doctor.*"

Five hours later, Madelaina was still telling him about her incredibly adventurous life with Peter, of her own experiences as a *soldadera* and revolutionist. They had left the Mexican eatery where she'd found the food atrocious and told him so. "You call this garbage *comida*—food?" She'd turned up her nose at it in typical *gachupín* fashion. "If I had the time, Doctor, I would cook for you authentic Spanish food that would make of you a true *aficionado* for life."

"That would be a total waste of time, *señora,* since I am already an *aficionado*. Besides, I didn't promise you Spanish food—it was Mexican food I offered. On that I am an expert." His words, however truthful, rankled her.

For a few moments she bridled hotly under his chafing remark, then as he drove maniacally through the streets of San Antonio in his Stutz Bearcat, she, dressed in the duster he insisted she wear, hung on for dear life, giving little thought to his impudence. With her life in the hands of this crazy maniac driving this crazier horseless carriage, she could think of nothing else. *Dios mios!* Even in the thickest of battles she hadn't experienced so many new feelings of fright and apprehension, and she later wondered at her own lack of inner fortitude.

942

"Perhaps I may keep you here in San Atonio long enough to sample your Spanish cooking. Señora Benson," he said, taking a sharp corner off a paved street onto a dirt road leading, it seemed, to nowhere on the vast desert.

"I live very close, another mile or so. I prefer living in the desert, close to nature."

"If you continue to navigate this horseless monster whith such fierce determination, you'll be dead before I leave San Antonio!" she exploded her fright with a frontal attack.

Dr. Oemolot found this terrible amusing. "*I frighten you, señora?*" He laughed with gusto. "A *soldadera* whose has seen front-line fighting? *Chiquita,* you are something very special. I would not think you are capable of being frightened. We both have faced death a thousand times. What can be worse than that?"

"Yes," she agreed. "What could be worse than death? Living—and its thousands of complications and uncertainties."

He turned to her for an instant, taking his eyes off the road, and in that moment, he swerved the car, forcing her to take a tighter grip on the handle bar. She swallowed hard, grimly determined not to register another complaint.

"Look, *señora!* Over there. It's the Alamo! Remember the Alamo? It's quite a landmark. It was close by, so I thought you might enjoy seeing a famous historical structure.

Madelaina's eyes reluctantly assessed the well-preserved building with rancor. "I prefer not remembering such an atrocity, regardless of how much a part of history it's become. I detest what it stands for in these days of racial prejudice. Why, the damned gringos worship it as they would a saint! How barbarous!" She shuddered at the unhappy memories it stoked in her mind.

Thaddeus Oemolot beeped his loud, clangorous horn and made an unexpected 180-degree hairpin turn in the dirt road, carefully avoiding the sand at the shoul-

943

der's edge and retraced his path toward town. He turned off the road onto a deserted trail, and in a few moments he pulled up before an isolated desert dwelling resembling an Indian pueblo, standing stark in the middle of nothing but desert and cactus.

"More historical places?" she asked, still catching her breath over the perilous turn he'd made in the road earlier.

"But of course, Señora Benson. It is the home of Thaddeus Oemolot." He turned off the motor and blew the horn with gusto. In moments a man servant appeared. "José, put a cover over her. I won't need it for the balance of the day. And mind you—don't get carried away with it."

He helped Madelaina down from the auto, took the duster from her and placed it in the seat of the car, as the dark-skinned, toothy servant nodded and replied, "*Muy bueno, señor el doctor.*"

Madelaina sighed with relief when she felt the firmness of earth under her feet. "You are a rugged individualist, doctor," she told him once she entered the unusually decorated house. It was truly a simple pueblo outside, but once inside, you got a vast feeling of space under the domed open-air ceiling of the atrium from which other rooms branched off. It contained the newest innovations, a forerunner of the pace-setting homes that would sweep the western desert states a half-century later.

With a feeling of glowing pride of ownership, he took her on a short tour of the five-room haven which he had designed and helped build in his spare time. It was deceptively large, spacious, and cooler inside by several degrees. The floors throughout were of hand-set terra cotta tiles, buffed to a high sheen. A huge fireplace stood at the center of the living room as a focal point, and the room itself rambled into a dining room and library at the other end. The kitchen and butter rooms were outside in another area adjoining the house, connected by the solarium, containing endless tropical flora and an aviary of exotic and tropical birds

944

of magnificent plumage. The one large master bedroom was upstairs on what appeared to be a cantilevered area overlooking the entire lower level, including fireplace and the hanging gardens of the atrium. It seemed immense, yet Madelaina knew it was a smaller dwelling than Seven Moons. She instantly fell in love with the place. A warmth and loving feeling permeated the entire house, and she felt at home in it from the moment she stepped over the threshold.

"And what do you call this—paradise?" she asked, enthralled by what she saw. Madelaina gave a start at the feeling of something hot and velvety near her hand. She turned and gazed into the glassy black eyes of a sable-colored puma.

"*Dios mios*, you gave me a start," she told the animal, ruffling its neck and patting it affectionately as if seeing one were an everyday occurrence. "How beautiful you are, *gatto mas grande*."

"It has no name, *señora,* until now. I will call it Oemolot's Paradise." He studied her comportment with the puma until the puma moved away from Madelaina and sauntered slowly to his master, stretching its large jaws in a yawn.

"It is strange how Dionysis takes to you," he muttered. "I am delighted that you approve of my taste. I'm not certain why I brought you here, except that I felt certain you'd appreciate it." He petted the animal as he continued to watch his guest through calculating eyes. "Since the death of my wife, I've brought no one here, not even my friends."

"Don't they object? You must be obligated to do much entertaining in your circle of professional friends and acquaintances."

"My circle of friends?" He chuckled ironically. "You know what the friends and acquaintances think of Thaddeus Oemolot? They think he is one crazy man—*muy loco*. It tickles my fancy to observe them as they attempt to analyze me. Especially when I drive through the streets of San Antonio, honking my horn out of the sheer joy of living. They assume that I am some crazy idiot."

Madelaina reflected a moment, wondering at her own sanity for putting her trust and faith in a man deemed ridiculous by his peers. *From this eccentric* viejo *I've come for help for my* marido? Perhaps it was because she too had felt the spur of rejection and ridicule by her peers that she found an affinity with this man. Or was it because of the nature of the man so predisposed to enjoying the real things in life—the flowers, plants, birds, and animals that most people had no feeling for. She wasn't certain. She knew something intangible kept her here in the company of Dr. Thaddeus Oemolot.

They sat on the flower-lined patio of the atrium with the ceaseless singing and chattering of the birds as background music. The puma curled up at his feet. Beyond the perimeter of his property lines, all she could see in the beginning of a golden, coral sunset was desert sand the color of the sky's reflection.

Dr. Oemolot had changed to more casual western attire, and Madelaina had removed the trim navy blue jacket and relaxed in her camisole and skirt, her long hair piled atop her head. He lazily packed his pipe with tobacco from a humidor on a rolling cart brought out by José's wife, Maria Inez, a plump woman with gray hair pulled back tightly into a bun at her neck, dressed in a gaily colored peasant dress. She left a large pitcher of iced tea and retreated quietly.

"Ahhh, this is the life," he said, patting his stomach contentedly. "I keep promising myself to take more time to live, but, alas, each day my patients swell to such proportions that I wonder where I'll find the time to counsel all of them. People who can't cope with their everyday existence in the changing pace of time. God save us if the next fifty years continue at the same rate of speed. We are a growing nation and with growth comes many responsibilities. May I call you Madelaina? You please call me Thaddeus or Tadeo whichever pleases you." He spoke in that same slowed-down, mellow voice which earlier gave her the soothing feeling of being bombarded by cotton puffs.

She nodded and sipped the refreshing iced tea.

"Doctor is so stuffy. It gives man an importance he doesn't deserve. Now then, *chica,* all those tales you related earlier? They were gospel? The truth?"

"I told you it was an incredible story."

"Does your husband know all this—all these experiences of yours?"

"Of course. Perhaps not every precise detail of every moment, but most of it."

"And you, Madelaina, have you ever been unfaithful to your *marido?*"

Madelaina faltered. "That depends on what you mean by unfaithful. In body? Spirit? Mind? What?"

"Oh, come, my dear. Unfaithful is unfaithful. To be more explicit, have you gone to bed with other men?"

Her face burned. "I told you what happened at Madrigal—"

"*Si, por Dios,* you did. What I am speaking of is—willingly."

"No." She paused, averting her eyes. "That is—" A tremor shot through her, a feeling of unsettling guilt. "Tadeo, it's not easy to explain. I will try." She described the seduction of Simon Salomon after he'd arranged to abduct her. Of the drugged condition to which she's been subjected and how she responded. "Do you consider that—willingly?" She had avoided telling him of the outcome, how Salomon had so artfully deceived her. "Do you consider that a willing arrangement?"

"No. Not if it's the truth."

"It's the truth," she retorted hotly. "Why would I lie? You don't know me. I know less of you. I am here only to help my husband. What good are lies?"

"All right, Madelaina. All right. Don't get your Irish up."

"I'm not Irish. I am Mexican—and proudly so. The daughter of a *gachupín.*"

947

He smiled gently. "I didn't mean to infer you were Irish. It's just an American expression—"

"Dr. Towbridge suggested because I was Mexican, Peter might have experienced considerable shame to be marrried to me here in his own land. He indicated it could be a probable cause for his impotency," she blurted out defensively.

He sighed. "In these days it's not an unheard-of situation—not the impotency, but the shame a Texan feels for consortin' with a Mexican. Now hold on, young woman. Don't direct your wrath at me," he said easily, noting her indignation. "Those are not the ideas of Thaddeus Oemolot. I try only to convey to you what might go on in the mind of proud and mighty Texans, especially a self-made man."

Madelaina's astonishment left her totally dazed momentarily. "You know who I am? The identity of my husband? But it was not my intent to reveal this. My husband would die if such information were to be maliciously spread about. You can understand, Tadeo. You must promise me not to speak of it—to no one!" She grew alarmed by the moment.

"I am no gossipmonger, Madelaina, simply a doctor. I received a call from Dr. Towbridge who told me to expect you and felt obligated to run down the case to me. He was only trying to help."

The incredible vast silence of the desert was upon them and it seemed an eternity before she replied. "If my husband were to learn I've betrayed him by even discussing his infirmary with you—*Dios mios!* It would make him more angry, more upset—more impotent. You understand?" Her eyes left his and came to rest on the puma Dionysis. She felt a strange, eerie feeling as she attempted to connect something out of her past. His voice arrested her.

"*Bueno,* Madelaina. *Bueno.* At least you are beginning to understand," he said, nonchalantly puffing his dead pipe. "It is the external things which make a man impotent. At the same time, the more the mind dwells upon those external happenings, the more they transform themselves into internal realities."

"Are you saying that a thought, if permitted to grow in the mind, no matter how foolish, transforms itself into that person's reality? It no longer remains a fleeting wisp of imagination?"

Dr. Oemolot had reached into his pocket for a few seeds which he held in his hands for the few birds that moved in nearer to them. A bright red parrot flew to the table and waddled over to him, cocking its head until Tadeo fed him the seeds. A frustrated mynah bird perched on his shoulder, demanding both attention and affection. Madelaina was fully entranced by it all. She felt as if she were back in Las Marismas, where countless species of birds migrated, and in their presence she felt an inner peace and tranquility.

"Once again I commend you for your quick perception," he said. "We can talk till the end of time, but if I could spend a few hours with your *marido,* it would hasten my work and speed up results."

She shook her head. "Impossible, Tadeo. He'd prefer being caught dead than to confide such a shameful thing to anyone. In truth," she confessed, "I am sure he resents me for knowing. That in a moment of weakness he poured out his heart and soul. He's a proud man. Why, only recently he's told me to go out and find a lover! Imagine? Find a lover!"

"If you'll pardon me for being outspoken, it would serve you well to point out to him, a man can't eat pride and it makes a pretty lousy bed partner, too."

Madelaina smiled, despite herself.

"Now then, let's get back on the track. Have you ever gone to bed with another man willingly?" Finished with the seeds, he stroked the puma's head.

"Back to that again, eh?" She lit a cigarette before he could strike a lucifer and do it for her. If he seemed surprised at her smoking, he said nothing.

Nothing about this unusual woman could shock or surprise Thaddeus Oemolot after the strange and unusual story she'd told him, yet he wondered at her reluctance. Her increased agitation as she mulled over his question earlier and the same hesitation now was answer enough for him. She was troubled by something. What?

If he only knew, she thought. If he only knew. She'd only told him part of the story. Nothing of Tolomeo. How could she speak of that unique experience when it still seemed more like a dream than reality? Yes, she had more than willingly entered into sexual relations with Tolomeo. Had she truly been bewitched? If it had been bewitchment, it wouldn't be construed as willingness on her part.

She toyed with the semantics involved and felt a strong inclination to deny she'd been extramaritally promiscuous with any man. Just as she was about to reply, she thought vividly of William Benson. Her heart sank. After a moment's struggle to collect her thoughts, she realized she had to tell this doctor the entire story. Humiliation and embarrassment flooded her face. What would he think of her?

This was no time for regrets, she told herself, as she gritted her teeth and plunged headlong into the story. She didn't have to wait long to witness the gradual changes reflected in Oemolot's face. Even before she finished the story, she knew the course of his next few questions.

"My dear Madelaina," he began gently. "This is a classic example of how impotence manifests itself in the body of a virile young man. From what you told me, and I assure you my statement isn't purely academic, such abnormal manifestions are common occurrence. You told me Peter left home at an early age, that he and his father, an awesome figure to him, were in constant conflict over his mother. Not only do you—the love of his life—end up marrying William Benson, but you also indulged in sexual relations with the man he loathed. How would you except him to feel?"

Her mortification was complete with the assault of his words. Tears sprang to her eyes. It wasn't enough that the entire episode with Bill Benson had been a degrading, disgraceful experience to her, but now she had to have it flung in her face like month-old garbage. She grew defensive. "It wasn't my fault. It wasn't a willing act. I was abducted, I told you. Forced into the marriage by a man who felt some protective, paternalistic emotion toward me. At the time I didn't know he was Peter's father. They didn't even wear the same names. I swear, Tadeo, he forced sexual relations on me the night the macho Texans celebrated 'Remember the Alamo!' She spat with contempt. "It was a nightmare I'll never forget till my dying day!" She was shaking with rage when she finished.

"*Por favor, señora*. It is not my wish to stir up these painful recollections for you. I am not trying to bully you or make you confess to anything and place the guilt upon you. My only point in discussing such an experience is to explain what it can do to a man when such complications twist his mind. It can fill him with doubt, hate, suspicion, anger, jealousy, and a countless number of destructive emotions. When insurmountable anxieties continue their wrath unchained and unchecked, the manifestation is always a physical one. Subconscious frustrations and negative forces of destruction must be resolved or more violent behavior and tryanny will manifest in your man. Such things can turn inward reaping havoc."

"Peter was impotent before his father married me!" she retorted defensively to cover the fact that she didn't understand his words.

"Physically, you mean? The accident prevented him from copulation. Yes, I understand all that. But tell me. The very next time you met, did he know about his father and you?"

Madelaina set her own frustration aside and stirred her memory. She'd seen Peter the day Antonetta had been killed by the *Rurales*. She nodded slowly. "Yes. He had learned it from—" she paused. "He never did tell me how he knew of the marriage—only that he knew." She explained that his bitterness extended over

951

into his greeting when he bitingly addressed her as "Mother."

Tadeo struck a lucifer on the bricked patio and drew the flame toward his pipe to relight it. The air filled with the aroma of fresh tobacco.

"Don't punish yourself, Madelaina. We have a long, hard pull to go before we can help Peter. First, tell me, do you love him.?"

"*Que va,* do I love him? What question is this? Of course I love him. He has been the only driving force which has helped me keep my sanity all these terrifying years of revolution."

"You really love him? Totally? Unselfishly? Enough to be willing to put up with the pandemonium in hell to make him whole with you?"

"If necessary I'd fight Lucifer and all his *diableros* for him," she said with grim determination. She sat tall in her chair, her hair shoved high off her neck in the hot desert air, with resolve scrawled in her fiery eyes.

"That's just what you'll have to do, my dear woman. And may the Lord watch over you and console you when you find the road precarious and at times utterly hopeless to traverse."

For the next few hours, between wine, a few snacks of fresh fruit and cheese, Dr. Thaddeus Oemolot explained the normal rivalry between father and son over the love of a wife and mother. He called it the Oedipus complex, all of which sounded like some fairy tale of a Greek tragedy to her. She listened to his commentaries seemingly without interest, yet all the while absorbing every word he spoke. And when he explained its counterpart, the Electra complex, which exists between father and daughter, Madelaina's ears perked up even more. On this day, she not only learned much about Peter, but she acquired insight into her own problems with her father.

"Of course, my dear, we are still babes in the field of psychiatric research. Buried in our subconscious minds are untrue records which drive us into weird fields of behavior, and compulsions that cannot be explained.

My greatest wish is to be alive when some brilliant researcher uncovers the key to our emotional conflicts, so we could open the door and dust out the dusty chambers of horrors that some keep locked up for all eternity and never have a momen'ts peace." He rhapsodized eloquently over the possibilities of man's future without the hangups that keep him chained to an abnormal life. "If only man could fully know himself in a lifetime," he despaired. "Unfortunately, most of us remain unenlightened and uncaring until our death."

Madelaina liked him for including himself among the idiots of the world. She also knew that he didn't do this out of kindness, but as a didactic device.

"You're welcome to spend the night here in this paradise, Madelaina, if you wish. Or I shall be happy to drive you back into San Antonio."

"It's best that I return." She glanced at her watch. "Is it bedtime for you?"

"Not at all. I was thinking about you. I know your time is limited."

"It is but this is far more important. What precisely can I do about my husband's condition? If you will explain in detail, I will follow your instructions to the letter."

"If only there was some device by which I could open your husband's head, reprogram him, remove all the insidious thoughts that are rendering him impotent, it would solve your problem. Unfortunately there is no such device."

Madelaina grew reflective. "Tadeo, do you believe in psychic phenomenon?"

He shrugged indifferently.

"Would you believe me if I told you that I saw pictures in my mind telling me that Peter was impotent, long before he told me?"

Tadeo sat forward in his chair and set his pipe down. "What kind of pictures?"

"It's difficult to describe them. They come to me when I am totally relaxed, when my inner dialogue has been silenced and all thoughts are erased from mind."

953

"Do you realize what you're telling me?"

She shook her head. His interest grew more profound. Rising to his feet, he paced the bricked patio thoughtfully, his eyes reflecting unusual lights again.

Madelaina, watching him, felt more strongly that she'd met him before. She was unable to take her eyes from him. Worse, she was unable to explain her quandary to him. From the first there had been a magnetic pull between them, something undefinable. She had unburdened her soul to him as if she'd known him all her life.

They parted on this last note and he drove her back to her hotel.

The following afternoon, shortly after lunch, Madelaina returned to Dr. Oemolot's office. She wrote out a check for a thousand dollars which he protested was too much. She insisted and added that he was to put it to good use in helping her people. "One day, Tadeo, you must come to Seven Moons to visit us. I shall keep you informed of my progress. When I achieve success—"

"You mean when Peter achieves success," he interrupted.

She blushed pleasurably. "Yes, that. When it happens you shall be the first to know. I shall then send you a check for ten thousand dollars, for you to pursue your dream—the clinic you plan for my people in San Antonio. Are you amenable to this?"

Thaddeus Oemolot was astounded. "But how do you know what I've entertained in the back of my mind since my wife's death?"

"Let's just say that I learned you had marrried a Mexican woman and subjected yourself to all the social taboos imposed by the gringos here in Texas, *bueno*? It will be a step in the right direction." She didn't tell him that she'd seen his wedding pictures in the living room of his home and didn't have to be told that Mrs. Oemolot's dark features were those of a *latina*. Nor did she mention that she'd seen an artist's concept of a proposed clinic on the desk of his nurse in the waiting

954

room or that she'd heard the nurse speaking to one of his patients on the phone, concerning the lack of local interest and contributions to so noble a gesture as providing a medical facility to research children's mental diseases for the Mexican population.

He was so excited by her words that he gushed. "We'll name it the Madelaina Clinic!"

"No, Tadeo. Not Madelaina. It shall be called the Clinic of Tolomeo," she said cryptically." You realize that your name spelled backward reads: Tolomeo? In addition, I wish to have one ward named the Lazaro Benson Ward. I promise you, if my husband responds to the treatment you've prescribed, I shall personally assist you in raising far more money than you'll need. My husband has many business interests here in San Antonio. As a matter of fact, we also own land here. But first things first." She rose to her feet, extended her gloved hand to him, and grasped his between two gloved hands. Impulsively she leaned up to kiss him.

He turned to her abruptly. "I'll drive you back. I must ponder a few things by myself this evening. Keep your love for Peter burning brightly in her your heart like a beacon guiding you to the solution. This above all is the important thing. And try to keep yourself detached from the situation," he added.

"Detached? *Si.* How in the hell does a woman remain detached in such a case, Tadeo, when her heart is swollen, ready to burst, because her husband hasn't touched her in over a year? What does a woman do to ease her own needs? How does she command those heavy, pendulous devils poking around her stomach to disappear? How does the heaviness in her heart take flight?"

"How has this woman done it for over a year?" he asked tersely.

She stared into his clear jade eyes, into those mesmerizing, soothing, and tranquil eyes that calmed her and replied, "As you said earlier, we both have faced death a thousand times. What could be worse, eh? So, there's nothing to be lost. I'll try to remain as clear-headed, calm, filled with love and understanding, and by all means as detached as possible." Her lips trembled and her hands shook.

"Madelaina—" he began, moved by her words and her feeling.

"*Si*, Tadeo? At this moment, Madelaina wanted solace, sympathy, and the support of someone stronger than herself, something she needed above all else. What she got was silence, solemnity, and a soft condescending smile.

"It was nothing. For a moment you reminded me of someone I loved greatly." Then he added, "What I am attempting to say is, don't allow your emotions to ride roughshod with you, now that you approach the last legs of the longest journey of your life."

For the next few hours he dealt in specifics, what she must do, how to approach it, and that in everything she must exercise the patience of a saint.

"It makes me nervous when you talk to me with such apprehension in your voice," she told him.

"I'm aware of it. I'm deliberately trying to alert you to the seriousness of the role you must play. It's important that you fulfill the role exactly right. If I stress the dramatic possibilites of the situation, it isn't for effect. I'm simply giving you time to prepare yourself for the necessary adjustments which must be made to your own nature."

"*Muchas gracias*, Tadeo. Thank you for everything. Please pray for us." She fled his office before the tears ran freely, leaving a bewildered, perplexed, and somewhat dazed physician still trying to figure the whole thing out.

"You forgot the books I gave you," he said to an empty room. He picked up the three volumes of Freudian psychology and shrugged. Very well, he'd mail them to her at Seven Moons.

Dr. Oemolot sat down behind the roll-top desk, scribbled a note of instructions to his nurse, and slipped it under the cover of the top book. With pen in hand, he printed his name backward: TOLOMEO.

It was the Spanish spelling of the name Ptolemy. Brother of Cleopatra. Also the name of fifteen Egyptian kings. Also the name of a general in the army of Alexander, King of Macedonia. Also the name of an astronomer, mathematician, and geographer who contributed much to the present-day knowledge of our solar system. What had the name Tolomeo to do with Madelaina Benson?

Why should he care if it meant that his dream of a clinic should be realized. He sat immobile for a long while, trying to sort and sift through the events of the past twenty-four hours. He had mentioned nothing to the *señora* about his wife, yet she seemed to know of her. He wondered what she might have said if she'd learned that his wife's name was also Madelaina?

He felt he was in a state of unusual reality, elicted by the euphoric state brought about by that refreshing, extraordinary, and quite unbelievable young woman, Madelaina Benson.

Outside, she asked herself for what was she crying. She didn't know. A feeling of intense relief shot through her, jolting her into plateau of expectancy where, with hope and faith and downright perserverance in the days to come, Peter would be his old self.

She returned to the Tampico Hotel in downtown San Antonio to find the lobby swarming with cattlemen, cowboys, and uniformed officers, as many as in El Paso and other border towns. She hardly paid them any attention, but instead walked up the circular staircase to the mezzanine floor to make certain she could take the evening train home. She waited fifteen minutes, then asked the clerk to call her room with the necessary information.

She removed her hat inside her room, took off her dove gray jacket, and took two headache powders. She hurriedly packed her bags, then when all was ready, she lay on the bed to rest. She frowned when she saw the time and picked up the phone on the table next to the bed. She called the train clerk. It seemed there was a delay, and she might have to wait until morning.

"What's the problem?" she asked.

"Government troops have requisitioned the train. All civilians are rerouted to morning passage. Would you consider taking a bus, Mrs. Benson?"

Mrs. Benson would not. "Please call me for the first available space out of Dallas," she insisted. "I'll be in my room waiting for your call."

The clerk agreed he'd do his best.

Madelaina hung up. *Government troops requisitioned all trains to El Paso?* What on earth for? She paced the floor, smoking for several moments. Next door to her, the occupants were involved in a heated discussion. If the conversation hadn't been so heated and in Spanish, Madelaina might not have paid attention to it. That, coupled with the fact that one or two voices sounded very familiar, caused her to cock an ear. The tempers abated and she could better understand their words.

"You will please thank President Wilson. Assure him that General Alvaro Obregon will not disappoint him. Our strategy has worked. Whereas I am not in full accord with Señor Carranza's philosophies, he is the lesser evil between the contenders."

Madelaina was glued to the door. Was it possible this was her father in the next room? It was his voice all right. But what on earth was he doing in San Antonio? Why not Corpus Christie or Matamoros, closer to the Mexican border? She leaned in closer to hear.

"You know, General Obregon, what our president really suggests? It's you he feels will be the proper man to govern Mexico. He's quite taken with your ideas and the cooperation you've shown your northern neighbors. Why delay the inevitable? I suggest you take advantage of the good will and cooperation extended to you by the United States. Move to take the helm of your nation and steer it properly."

"I thank you, General Pershing, and you other gentlemen who've been most helpful in assisting me. This will give me considerable experience—all this involvement. I return now to my country and victory.

958

Once the rebels are eradicated, and I've observed more accurately the needs of my people, I'll accept the role your president feels I should play. Meanwhile I'll throw my full support to Carranza and do my level best to cement good relations with America."

"There's one other thing, General Obregon. About Field Marshal Von Klause."

"Forgive me, I know no such man," replied Obregon.

"It is our understanding that Carranza has made a pact with the Germans."

"Not to my knowledge."

"Would he keep you abreast of any negotiations, Obregon? What we mean is, there's no chance Carranza can be double-dealing without your knowledge?"

There was silence.

Another man spoke up. "If the rumors prove to be true, we'll stop all shipment of arms into Mexico and give you no further assistance."

Madelaina sank back against the wall in utter anger. Less than three months ago, these same men had assured Pancho Villa they'd give him their cooperation. What had happened? She'd read the papers—what little they got of accurate reporting from the papers in El Paso—and knew only that Villa had waged several battles victoriously. On the other hand, she'd heard that her father had also been racking up countless victories in and about Mexico City with Zapata's forces. Now this! America's intervention to assist Carranza! No wonder American troops had requisitioned the train. Something was up. If her father was about to engage in the long-awaited battle with Pancho Villa, he couldn't lose—not with American arms and ammunition.

Stop this, she told herself. *Why are you involving yourself? Revolution is in the past. All that matters is your life with Peter and Alejandro. Forget this conversation.* Even as she tried to force a detachment from all she heard, she knew she was fooling herself. Her life was irrevocably bound up in Villa's and Mexico's.

As she mulled over Dr. Oemolot's words about this terrible rivalry between herself and her father, Madelaina became confused. She knew a little, but not enough to carry her through the inner torment of those few moments.

What could she do to help Villa? And if she did, would she bring death and destruction to her father? General Pershing had suggested her father might be president of Mexico! She recalled the Felipe de Cordoba had told her similar things—that her father was indeed someone special. Was she so conditioned to hating him that she couldn't see the merit in his leadership? The qualities others saw?

Dios mios! It was Madelaina who needed to heal her sickness in her head. Why had she turned from her father? Why? She knew deep down in her heart that as a child she had loved him. Why couldn't she love him now? Six years ago? Why did she always have to find the faults in the man and never see the achievements or positive qualities that the American president had seen in him?

She paced back and forth, eaten alive by tormenting thoughts. Only yesterday she'd talked with Thaddeus at length about her father and how she'd rebelled for so long, bringing destruction, agony, and considerable devastation to her own life. His reply turned out to be something quite profound. "Unless the Electra or Oedipus complex is resolved between parent and child early in life, the child's life will be forever affected." In what way? "She'd be seeking her father in every man she met, subconsciously motivated by either her love or hatred of him," had been his reply.

She had scoffed at Thaddeus's explanation until he elaborated. "If you hated him enough, you'd be looking for those qualities in your man quite the opposite to those of your father. If you loved him, you'd naturally try to find those same qualities in a man. If the relationship between father and daughter isn't resolved in its true perspective, you'll be bound up in the shallows of misery and malcontent, because you've never given yourself a chance to attract and be attracted by the man you truly need. All this is predicated, of course, on the facts presented to us by a master psychologist, Sigmund Freud," he added. "It would be best that you read it thoroughly, Madelaina, for yourself, so you understand the specifics involved."

One thing was certain, Madelaina Obregon's life had been very much affected by the poison between father and daughter. But, for the love of God, she lamented, how does one remove this poison? How? It was too complicated for her to understand, much less to resolve such a question.

So, woman, she asked herself, *if it's come to a showdown between Pancho Villa and Alvaro Obregon, which side do you choose? Who will you support? You might as well face up to the situation, the alternatives are measured. Help your papa and—you will inevitably destroy Pancho Villa, all he's worked hard for, and what he stands for. Help Pancho Villa and you'll destroy your father. Which will it be? Why does it have to be either? Why one or the other? Why couldn't she ignore them both?*

Madelaina had turned into a complete nervous and physical wreck. She had smoked all her cigarettes, the butts piled high in an ash tray. She'd give anything for a drink. She needed something. She sat down at the edge of the bed and picked up the phone. The voices next door had quieted down and she could barely make them out.

"Please send a bell man to my suite," she said into the mouthpiece of the phone when a voice answered. Amost as soon as she hung up the bell man appeared. She gave him a fifty-dollar bill and ordered a bottle of wine, cigarettes, and a sandwich, it didn't matter what kind.

"For fifty bucks, lady, I can even bring you Mexicali gold."

Thinking it was a new beverage, she asked, "What is this Mexicali gold of which you speak?"

The thin, scrawny, weasel-faced bell man glanced

cautiously about the room and whispered confidentially. "Marijuana—you ever hear of reefers, lady?"

"*Bueno.* Bring some," she quipped and shut the door after him.

As soon as he returned, Madelaina lost no time in rolling a few reefers. Marijuana always had a calming effect on her. She needed something to calm her down as frustration shot through her, combined with nervous speculation and an all-consuming fear of not knowing what to do in the situation she found herself with Peter and now her father's presence next door. It seemed too much for her to cope with presently.

She lay back on the bed, smoking and inhaling until the calming effect took place. She was fingering the chamois bag she still wore around her neck. There was hardly any powder left, but she was never without it. Peter had asked about the small pouch and why she wore it. Her answers had been vague and ambiguous. She'd told him only it was an amulet to ward off evil spirits. Following the session in Parral when Rosalia Quintera and Lucia and Lola exorcised the evil spirit of Golden Dawn from Madelaina, Peter never suggested the amulet to be hogwash or some foolish nonsense. He simply accepted it. He'd seen too much that day to disbelieve the power of sorcerers.

As Madelaina lay back, she felt much improved, calmer, and able to sort things out in her mind. Even before the pictures began forming, before they gave her insight into what she must do, she knew what course to take. *Detachment and love* were the key words to solve this dilemma. Love and detachment.

Now, if she only had learned the lessons well enough. Madelaina rose from the bed. She stood before the mirror over the dresser and brushed out her long hair. She twisted and turned the long strands and piled them atop her head. She brushed on a small trace of lip rouge and slipped into her jacket.

Picking up the phone, she told the desk clerk she'd be gone for a few moments and to please continue to work on her reservations, She replaced the receiver and walked out the room.

Something mysterious forced her to do what she must.

Madelaina knocked on the door of the adjoining room. After a pause, the door opened a slit. A voice spoke through the crack. "Go away. No one sent fer ya."

"Please, I'm here to speak with General Alvaro Obregon."

"Ya got the wrong place, lady. Ain't no one here by that name.

"You will tell the general that his daughter wishes to speak with him and be fast about it!"

The door closed in her face. Madelaina was certain she had caused considerable commotion inside the room. When it opened again, the door was propelled by a force that nearly shook it on its hinges. General Alvaro Obregon stood face to face with his daughter, his face a mask of marble. His black, fierce eyes looked at her as if he could kill her. His features contorted into a scowl.

It was the look on Madelaina's face, a softness, almost glowing look of love, which arrested him and caught him off guard. Behind him she saw several uniformed men, but more shocking to her was the presence of Armando Cortez. He sat in profile and hadn't seen her yet, since he was engaged in an involved discussion with General Montalvo, another *Carranzista*. Why was he here?

"Can we speak, Father? If it's not convenient here, we can go to my suite. It's next door."

General Obregon closed the door behind him, telling the soldier at the door to lock it. "I'll be next door," he said softly.

In her room, Madelaina asked him to sit down.

"I can hear what you may have to say, standing, if you don't mind."

"May I offer you a glass of wine—cigarettes—marijuana?"

963

"I want nothing. Tell me what you wish—why you've chosen to speak with your father, after the long drought of emotional consideration between us?"

"Can't we end this thing between us? Does it always have to be this way?" she asked quietly. "Please sit. It's easier to talk." She took a chair and indicated the other nearby.

He finally acquiesced and seated himself stiffly on a corner of the chair, moving his gun and holster about so it wouldn't disturb him.

"What brings you to San Antonio?" he asked, filled with suspicion.

"I came to see a medical specialist. I hope to return on the evening's train, but I've been told American troops have requisitioned the entire train for three departures."

"Why are you really here?" he asked, disbelieving her reply.

"I told you. Why do you never believe me?"

"Hah! Coming from you that's got to be a joke. A *Villista* in San Antonio at so appropriate a time, eh, Little Fox?" His bitter laughter was laced with irony.

"I am no longer Little Fox. I've retired from the revolution. Long ago I realized there is nothing that I can do to prevent history from taking its course."

"I wish I could believe you, Madelaina. But I don't," he said harshly. He cocked his head, as if listening to the voices next door. "Is that how you knew I was here? Listening in at keyholes? Or did your spy system apprise you of our arrival and secret rendezvous with the Americans?"

"What's the use? I tell you the truth and you don't believe me. I came here to see a doctor, not as a spy for the revolution—not as a *Villista*—not as Little Fox. It's finished, Father. All behind me. Thank God. Do you have a spare cigarette?" After she accepted it and lit it, she continued.

"It's not important if you don't believe me. We can easily allow things to deteriorate between us if you like. I can return to my home and family and pretend as I have in the past that you no longer exist. But I've grown up these past few years. Yes, I have, Father," she insisted at his disbelieving glance. "I've lived a thousand years in these past few years in a life I never dreamed I'd live. In conditions far more revolting and offensive than most people could cope with." She sat back in the overstuffed chair in a posture of relaxation, one arm draped around the back of it.

General Obregon studied his daughter. She seemed older, more mature, and dressed quite stylishly. He'd lost track of her after Felipe de Cordoba's death in Mexico City, and for a time he didn't care if he ever saw her again. But now, seeing her in the flesh, in so subdued a mood, he had difficulty believing her sincerity. Her presence meant there had to be an angle of some sort, some devilish plot that had to be exacted. He just didn't trust her at all.

"I heard what General Pershing told you about being president of Mexico. Why are you so modest? You know your eyes have been on that choice plum a long time. Felipe mentioned it, a hundred years ago," she sighed wistfully. "Why don't you jump at the chance?"

"You heard that?"

"Yes."

"What else did you hear? Not that you'd tell me—"

"What I heard doesn't interest me any longer. What must I do to prove to you I am no longer a *Villista?*"

Obregon kept his stoic mask without expression. He watched his daughter pour two glasses of wine after breaking the seal. He noticed the rolled reefers on the table and the untouched sandwich.

"Wine, Father?"

He took the bottle from her hand, read the label, and made certain the bottle hadn't been opened or tampered with earlier. He nodded.

Madelaina smiled. "You think your own daughter would plot to annihilate you?" The words were out and she knew what he'd say. He didn't disappoint her.

"Yes. If there's anything under the sun that I can be

certain of, it is the treachery of Madelaina Obregon, especially where her father's concerned."

Her face flushed. "I deserve that. Or shall I say Little Fox deserved that a few months ago. I keep telling you it's all in the past. Please let's not waste our time arguing." She pressed the glass into his hand and took the other for herself. She raised it into the air in a mock toast. "Suppose we drink to Presidente Alvaro Obregon?"

"No. We drink to Presidente Venustano Carranza," he said firmly.

Madelaina put down her glass. "That I won't do."

"Then you're still a *Villista*."

"If you involve Carranza, then, yes, I agree entirely with General Villa."

Sparks flew in her father's eyes and his fists clenched tightly.

"Villa again! Goddamnit! I told you once I didn't want your lips to speak his name in my presence! You still shove his shit in my face and cram him down my throat whenever we meet!" In a burst of violent temper, he threw the filled wine glass across the room. It splattered in a grotesque pattern of bright crimson against the wall and dropped in a myriad of bloody streams.

"It's amazing how much alike you are—you two. You know, Father, you even have the same birth sign. You are Gemini—the twins. No two men that I've met have the same dual natures to their personalities. *Es veridad*. It's true. I must tell you this much, General Villa sent me on a mission to Zacatecas to meet with you under a flag of truce. His greatest desire was to join forces with the man he so admired and defeat Carranza, because he knows Carranza is not the man for the job. Beware, Father, the man is treacherous. Carranza will sell you down the river before the boat docks."

"When did Villa send you to Zacatecas?" he asked, somewhat surprised at this revelation. "He wanted to intrigue with me? Pancho Villa?"

"The week before Villa stormed the fort. Right after he broke with Carranza."

Obregon used his superb memory of recall. "I was nowhere near Zacatecas then. Why didn't Villa's spies inform him properly?"

She told him about Dolores Chavez and her subsequent abduction by Major General Simon Salomon. How the false ruse served to distort the picture—how the interception of the telegrams worked. "The *Huertistas* were after me to use me over your head as a wedge, so you wouldn't defect to Carranza. And now, Father, you insist on supporting a man like Carranza who can be worse than Huerta and Diaz? Why?"

Obregon was on his feet pacing the room, thinking on all his daughter told him. "Villa wanted us to join forces?" He pondered heavily.

"He told me, if he could come to terms with you, his entire Northern Division would have been behind you. You know how sad the *jefe* is because he's thwarted and unable to find the man who should sit on the presidential throne?"

"Sad? Hah! The man lusts for the power himself. Why, that stupid photograph of him seated in the gold chair at the palace made him laughingstock!"

'No one *is* more aware than Villa that he's not the man to occupy the presidency of Mexico," she told him, ignoring his foolish remark.

"I know that to be a gross exaggeration of the truth. Why the *animale* lusts for the power the presidency will bring."

"Is that the fertilizer fed you by your informants? Is that the bull dung Carranza feeds you, Papa? Well, it's always been one of your failings. Your head is buried so deeply in military strategy, you fail to see the fangs of the tigers waiting to devour you the moment you secure victories for them. I never believed it before, but it's all true, the stories I heard about you. You are no politician. But you best damn well learn and *muy pronto! Comprender?* Or you'll be ground down to hog feed the moment you hand Mexico over to Carranza.

967

Listen, there's a game of cards the gringos play called poker. It's best you learn to play such a game so you can practice keeping a poker face when you play politics with men of Carranza's calibre."

Obregon flushed at the display of contempt on his daughter's face. "How dare you? How dare you come into my life again and incite me to anger at a time like this when I am weighed down with heavier things—more important than the life of any one person? You made your choice long ago. Very well, I've conditioned myself to that choice. Nothing you can say, Madelaina, will permit me to believe you. You protest vehemently you're no longer a *Villista*. Bah! You are a *Villista* to the teeth! I know it. You know it. And nothing can convince me differently!"

He had to think as a militarist. He had to prevent her from leaving San Antonio for at least a week. The marijuana. That was it. He could inform the police that she had it in her possession. In the States the gringos strongly enforced the drug laws. He needed time to get the arms and ammunition across the border before she could get word to Pancho Villa. He couldn't trust her, could he?

"Where's your husband?" he asked cagily.

"In El Paso," she lied, not about to tell him Peter was in Washington.

"Liar!" he spat harshly. "You almost had me believing your story—this unplanned meeting of ours. A repentant daughter trying to make up for the lost time with her estranged father. So much for your lies. Your husband, the *gringo gun runner,* is right here in San Antonio, making deals to smuggle arms to Pancho Villa." His voice dripped with sarcasm and resentment.

Madelaina recoiled in bewilderment. "You lie!" she countered, assaulted by the implication of his words. "That was finished long ago. He's no longer involved with General Villa, nor am I. I swear to you, Father, it is the truth I speak to you. We have finished with the revolution—" She stopped suddenly as she thought back to the mysterious comings and goings—the midnight rendezvous with strangers, Peter had involved himself in of late. Her face blanched.

"You know I'll have to detain you, Madelaina. I have no recourse."

"Nothing I can say will ever convince you of my sincerity. I regret having made the attempt at reconciliation," she said in a crestfallen manner. "It's a pity we can't resolve our differences."

"The leopard can't remove his spots," he said pointedly.

"You dare say that to me? All the while Carranza hides his under that long coat he wears to deceive you?"

"Back to Carranza again. You won't stop trying, will you?"

"If I thought I could ever pry open your eyes to what Carranza is, I'd ride into battle at your side— even against Villa, if need be!" Her eyes sparked with brilliant lights and her voice, having risen a notch or two in volume, dropped down to a whisper.

For an instant Obregon faltered. Madelaina had always been brutally honest with him except for the time she'd conspired with Concepción for Pancho Villa. Even then, she'd attempted to tell him about Huerta. Hadn't it proven true? Even Felipe had sided with Madelaina in this. He hadn't believed her then. Now, it was as if history was repeating itself. What if she spoke the truth? How would he feel having her jailed? Now that America had agreed to sponsor Carranza as president, Obregon had little time to learn the answers to his questions. A loud, harried knock at the door brought his head up like an ostrich as he turned in the direction of the sound.

"Who is it?" asked Madelaina.

"Open the door, General Obregon," called his aide.

The general moved across the room and opened the door a slit.

"Your presence is immediately requested inside, *mi Generale*," said the aide.

Obregon turned to his daughter as he removed the

key from the lock. "You'll remain here until I've decided what must be done with you."

Before she could utter a protest, he disappeared out the door. She heard him instruct his aide, "Stand here and don't let a person in or out the room—or I'll have you cut and quartered!"

"*Si, mi Generale*," came the man's reply.

Madelaina was furious. It served her right. She knew better than to bare her soul, divulge her real thoughts, to a man like her father who wasn't complete.

She had never in the past been able to convince her father of the truth in any issue. Not about Huerta or Salomon, not about Villa and now not about Carranza. Why? Why was she so incapable of persuading him? She could never make her father realize the truth. Why, for the love of God, even if his scenting sac was removed, she'd never be done with the smell of that skunk Carranza. Why couldn't General Obregon detect the same stink? Could he be so deluded he is unable to see through the man's double-dealing?

As she paced the floor of her room concerned with her own dilemma, she felt a terrible sinking sensation. He'd told her Peter was here in San Antonio! Impossible. He was in Washington, wasn't he? Her eyes darted about the room to the window. She ran to it and glanced down two stories onto the street below.

Peter wouldn't have lied to her, would he? He would have had no reason to lie. He had a spread outside of San Antonio, but she never learned the exact whereabouts, nor had she asked. Damn! Damn! What a predicament! She opened the window and looked out at the fire escape. She could make it down those iron bar steps. She'd been in far worse predicaments, hadn't she?

Pulling her head back inside the room, she glanced hurriedly about for her bag. She had plenty of cash with her. She could take a bus back to El Paso. Her eyes fell on the phone. What foolishness? Why didn't she use the phone to call the hotel manager? Surely they'd come and rescue her. With a military guard outside her door and two imposing generals next door—who'd be-

970

lieve her in any contest? She could at least call home. Of course! Why hadn't it occurred to her?

In a few moments Madelaina had Pilar on the phone. Did she have *señor el patrón*'s telephone in Washington? "What's wrong, Pilar?" she asked when the hysterical woman made no sense.

Pilar tearfully explained that *señor el patrón* had called and was angry to learn she wasn't at home. She had given him the name of her hotel in San Antonio and asked her forgiveness.

Madelaina thanked her and told her not to worry. She was returning home as soon as possible. She hung up before the woman could respond.

Grabbing her small leather bag, jacket, and hat, Madelaina eased herself out the window and began to descend the ladder. Much to her chagrin, she found her weight insufficient to extend the bottom rungs of the fire ladder to the ground floor. She glanced inside an open window on the floor below her and decided she had to chance being discovered by another hotel guest. Crawling cautiously inside, she expelled a sigh of relief to find the suite empty. Scurrying across the room, she flung open the front door and stopped dead in her tracks.

"Madelaina!"

"Armando!" She'd nearly collided with him as he was about to enter the room.

"What in God's name are you doing here?" he asked, drawing her inside the room. He didn't bother to close the door.

"I might ask the same thing of you, if I were interested. Being a turncoat must be the accepted behavior of society these days," she quipped icily. "And don't bother to deny you've shifted loyalties. What would your father-in-law say to this if he knew you were intriguing with his enemies?"

"You don't know what you're talking about," he said lightly. "Perhaps you might be kind enough to explain—"

"Oh, Armando! Don't be a fool! I know. I know ev-

971

erything! I saw you with my father and the other gringos, upstairs!"

Armando moved in toward her. "I've always loved to see you when you're angry!" He reached for her and drew her close to him and kissed her lustily as she fought him off. She beat her fists against his shoulder and tried with all her strength to put him off.

"So—my beloved wife—this is where I find you?" came a voice behind them.

Instantly Armando released her. Madelaina looked up into the stormy eyes of her husband. Behind him was Tracy Richards. Both men, wearing western garb, carried six-shooters slung low at their hips. They came into the room and closed the door behind them, both studying her disheveled appearance through narrowed eyes.

Peter addressed her. "I'll attend to you later," he said provoked beyond reason. He turned to Armando. "All right, *conquistadore,* suppose ya tell us all about it, eh?"

"What exactly do you wish to know?" asked Armando with a bland expression of innocence on his face.

"We can do it whichevuh way y'all want," said Tracy, fingering his knife with a diabolical gleam in his eye. "When did ya sell out Villa?"

Armando turned to Madelaina. "Is this some form of a joke, *chica?* Who are these men? Are they friends of yours?" he asked with that irksome blue blood coursing through his veins.

Madelaina stiffened. "You have a short memory, Armando. Do you forget my husband, Peter Benson? And this is Captain Richards of General Villa's Gringo Brigade. It's better you do as they request. They are not playing games, *amigo.*"

"So this is the man tamed by Valerie Townsend?" he asked, leveling his icy eyes on Peter. His lips twisted into obvious loathing.

"And you'ah her new plaything. Ah see she's lost all her taste," said Peter nastily. "Now, get cracking. You

972

better tell us about the arms shipment due ta cross the borduh."

"I haven't the slightest idea what you're referring to, *señor*," he said in his heavily accented English. "If you choose to use force on me, believe me when I tell you I will not hesitate to inform the authorities. You see, I am here under diplomatic immunity as a fully authorized representative of the Mexican government. Would you care to see my papers?"

"He was with them, Peter," hissed Madelaina. "With my father, General Pershing, and more gringos from Washington. I saw them."

Peter gazed at his wife blackly. "Stay out of this. Ah can handle the likes of this Spanish *hacendado*," he snapped at her. "Look, Cortez, ya bettuh cooperate with Tracy, heah, and me. If ya don't, weah gonna turn ya other to Villa's butchers, and by God theah'll make a fancy fruit tree outa ya. Ah'm shuah ya heard of Villa's fruit trees. Them *Villistas* ain't nevuh heard o' diplomatic immunity, heah?"

Armando turned to Madelaina. "You'd do this to your own father? How low have you fallen, whore? I heard rumors of your treachery, but had to see for myself that the daughter of Alvaro Obregon is nothing but a common *puta,* a vile and contemptible, lowly pig of a woman who married a whoremaster to keep her enslaved. *Bruta bruja!*" he spat at her, as Tracy Richards moved in and with the butt of his gun caught him from behind and knocked him out.

Madelaina recoiled at the verbal assault. For an instant she was stunned until she understood how Armando would be driven to say such things.

"Take him to the ranch, Tracy. I'll get there as soon as ah can. The whole place is swarming with American troops and turncoats ready ta blow the whistle at us as spies!" He turned to Madelaina. "And y'all bettuh get on back ta El Paso. Ah'll settle with ya as soon as I can!"

She stood firm. "Peter, what are you doing in all

this? I thought we both agreed not to get involved in the revolution," she said when they were alone.

"Ah am involved, don't ya see? Ah can't leave the *jefe* dangling just as his former friends are fixin' ta hack off his balls!" His face reddened at the analogy.

"Supposin' ya tell me what the hell you'ah doing here in San Antone?" His voice blistered her eardrums.

"You wouldn't believe me if I told you," she said unhappily.

"Try me!" he challenged.

Her eyes caught his and held defiantly. "All right." She nodded her head. "All right, I'll tell you. I came here to see a doctor about you."

"Ya what?" His voice echoed through her head painfully.

She winced, then repeated herself.

Peter's anger, his humiliation and degradation was total. He slapped her across the face and sent her reeling backward against the wall.

"Ya hadda tell someone else about me? After ya promised it was ouah secret? Now the whole world will know Peter Benson's no longer a man!" In his raging fury, he struck at her time and again. Suddenly he stopped. His confusion was such that he became bitterly ashamed of his actions. Worse was the fact that Madelaina had hardly reacted to his momentary brutality. She had stood her ground without flinching under the blows, without a whimper.

"That's the truest statement ever to pass your lips! Peter Benson is no longer a man! He's a vile animal. Not because you're impotent, Peter, but because you've lost all sense of reason." She picked up her bag and hat that had flown under the blows. "If you ever come to your senses, I shall be at Seven Moons with our son. You better hear this, Peter Benson. I refuse to live the life William and Jennifer Benson lived with their son, Peter. I'll not permit to happen to Alejandro what happened to both you and your brother Lazaro. When you finish with this gun running and your desire to be a satellite to Pancho Villa, and resume instead command

974

of your own world, then come to me. Perhaps by then I shall have found the answers to this confounding life for both of us." She stormed out the door and left San Antonio more dejected than she'd been on her arrival two days before. Madelaina had finally grown up.

Chapter 37

The contentment Madelaina received as she rode through the vast lands of Seven Moons was inexplicable to her, when she considered the place brought recollections of many unhappy experiences. She rode to Black Mountain on Lorca, the black stallion, son of her own Don Quixote, a magnificent, well-coordinated mass of superb horseflesh.

Lorca scaled the mountain ridge with the fleet-footedness of a winged horse. Madelaina could feel the ripple of his strong muscular body and the skillful ease with which he performed the task of transporting her to the crest of the rugged incline. In these moments she felt as deep a sense of pride in the breeding of horses as she had in the breeding of bulls for which William Benson had made Seven Moons famous. She dismounted at the top of the mountain and allowed Lorca to graze lazily nearby.

It was one of the bright, crackling Texas mornings. No clouds marred the horizon to interrupt the flowing blue velvet sky. It was an inspiring day of breathless beauty in which she found communing with nature an inspiring feat. She sat down on the craggy boulder gazing down at Seven Moons—those crescent-shaped lakes lined by weeping willows and groves of eucalyptus trees.

This morning she was obsessed with thoughts. What a magnanimous gesture for William Benson to have deeded this property to her. Even now, with the reality of Seven Moons staring at her from all sides, she found it difficult to believe it was all hers. With the deed came a letter written in Benson's handwriting. In it he had expressed his most profound regrets and apologies over the despicable behavior he'd forced on her the night Texas celebrated the Alamo. He also expressed personal disappointment in the fates which propel man's life. If he'd met a woman like Madelaina earlier in life, he had written, a woman with the same interests he shared in land, animals, and politics, his entire life might have been different. It was to Madelaina a sad commentary that a man purported to have everything in life should in truth have lived so empty a life.

Madelaina wondered if Peter had read this letter. She could see how intimidated he might have become to feel that the man he'd despised all his life and had gone to such lengths not to emulate had indeed seduced his own wife.

She'd come to know more about Peter's medical problems after she'd read the books sent to her by Dr. Oemolot and the follow-up correspondence in which she asked countless questions of him. The insight she'd acquired into the problems of impotency was well and good as far as theory was concerned. Now, the question arose in her mind, how she could help to resurrect his potency? Could she do it? Would she still have the needed strength and stamina to endure the countless obstacles that were bound to thwart her at every turn? How could she possibly obtain the cooperation of a man who hated her—and hadn't once tried to contact her since they last met in San Antonio?

Madelaina sighed and gazed out at the restful panorama, stirred by the breathless beauty of the place. Perhaps here at Seven Moons, in this somewhat magical land that held her in total fascination each day, she could work the miracle needed to draw them back together.

She was amazed, when she arrived at Seven Moons, at the length to which Peter had gone to make her arrival and stay a welcome one. Nothing astonished Madelaina more on her arrival with Pilar and her son Alejandro than to see the familiar faces of Paco and Lola Jimenez there to greet her. Peter had hired these

977

two bright and cheery people as caretakers in his absence.

It had been a warm, happy reunion, one in which Paco bridged the gap of time since they'd last seen each other with his countless tales of adventure. He'd told Madelaina that on their arrival in Zacatecas, General Obregon was not to be found. Worse, Paco Jimenez, listed among the dead, would have been immediately jailed as a deserter if he made his identity known to certain officers.

So unappealing was the sound of jail to him and Lola, they both decided to travel north again and try to enter El Paso to make a new life for themselves in the U.S.A. They had applied one day for work at the El Paso residence of William Benson, where, to their astonishment, Peter had greeted them and hired them instantly. Later, he encouraged them to travel to Seven Moons to prepare the place for the day Madelaina might appear.

After a while Madelaina found herself speaking of Tolomeo to Paco and Lola. She learned they'd confided to Peter many of their strange and unusual experiences in that fascinating land of Tolomeo and Lago Diablo de Los Muertos.

Peter, naturally interested in what had transpired after witnessing the complications that had beset the man after the infliction of near-fatal wounds to Paco's shoulder, had been clearly baffled when Paco in a moment of boastfulness bared his shoulder to reveal no scars to hint at the diabolical and devastating injury that had kept them in fear for his life.

"One thing led to another, *señora*," Paco had explained. "So it was only the right thing to do, to tell your *marido* the truth about Tolomeo and all that happened. Of the magic performed, of the serenity we felt and most especially of the spectacular Tolomeo who was more of a god than a man to us. Did I do wrong?" he had asked when he saw the deep disturbance on Madelaina's face.

"No, Paco," she had reassured him. "You didn't do

wrong." Yet, Madelaina saw clearly why Peter might have felt even more threatened when he learned of the intimacy between his wife and Tolomeo. She reasoned that his fears of having to compete with such a man for his wife's affection might have been compounded by what Paco and his mestiza wife might have added to what he already had been told—which wasn't enough to allow a clear picture of the situation.

Strange, thought Madelaina, as she lit a cigarette, Peter had never mentioned any of this to her. He had upon occasion asked her the identity of the man whose name she spoke of in her sleep and the source of that special chamois pouch she wore around her neck, and she had answered as best she could.

As part of her legacy at Seven Moons, the private library of William Benson had proved tremendously helpful to her on her arrival. With a cursory glance at the books on her previous visit, she'd never really taken the time to sort and categorize them. She had sufficient time and opportunity to browse and found to her amazement many books delving into the human mind—what the layman might consider a home library on medicine. She was even more astonished to learn that many of these books belonged to Peter, that he'd studied medicine in college, a fact he'd never shared with her.

Now, as Madelaina sat on the boulder, smoking her cigarette, looking down at Seven Moons, she had a sudden and strange thought, similiar to those that come to a person just before they drift off to sleep. It was more than a mere thought, a complete image would be more like it. She saw a montage of pictures of activity taking place below her in the wind-swept fields adjacent to the clear crystal blue lakes. She focused her attention on the seven bodies of water as a plan formulated in her mind. It was as if some mystical power had opened her head and poured into it a set of elaborate blueprints, as if all she had to do was crank an imaginary mechanism and out would come the final result.

Madelaina was so excited by what she saw and felt,

so inspired that she was moved into action. There could be no doubt as to what she must do, no conjecture—no dawdling. She rekindled all of Tolomeo's teachings in her mind and came to the conclusion that his philosophies might be the key to all the answers she needed. In the past she had stubbornly clung to her old ways and refused to take the necessary time to prove his farfetched theories. Now Madelaina had all the time in the world.

She filled with such inspiration that she quickly mounted Lorca and rode swiftly, the wind at her heels, until she reached the ranch house. She knew the way now. She lost no time to begin preparations on what might be termed fanciful plans by most standards. To Madelaina they were real.

That night at dinner she told Paco and his wife, "One day when the revolution ends in our country I shall return to visit the land of Tolomeo."

They both looked at her quizzically, then averted their eyes as an uncomfortable sensation surged through them. Lola, the sensational beauty, nudged her husband. "Tell her, *chico*. Ees better ju tell her now."

Paco shook off her insistent urging and refused to look Madelaina in the eye.

"Tell me what, Paco?" asked Madelaina.

Ten minutes of prodding passed before he'd speak out. Finally, he had no more resistance against these determined females. He scratched his temples and drank from a bottle of *cerveza*. "Very well, *chica*," he said submissively. "Who can deny you anything? It's like this, *señora*. Lola and I, both of us were so affected by what we'd seen in the land of Tolomeo that when we decided to leave all that filth, poverty, and dirt in Zacatecas, we both agreed to return to Tolomeo and live with those wonderful people for the rest of our days. Truly, we gathered what few possessions we owned and headed back over those same roads we'd traveled before. We followed the same trails leading out of Parral, climbed those mountains in the Sierra Madre's belly. We passed the same landmarks, the same trees—even those same man-eating insects that had so viciously attacked us before. Shall I tell you that Lola and I could not find Tolomeo—or his people? *Dios mios!* Word spread from village to village that two *muy locos,* Lola and I, were looking to find some crazy place. 'Phooo!' they tell us. 'Such a place in the interior! You are some crazy burros.' "

"What are you trying to tell me?" demanded Madelaina thunderstruck.

Paco swallowed hard and made an agonized grimace. "Only that there is no such place as the land of Tolomeo. That Lago Diablo de Los Muertos doesn't exist. It never has."

"I know about the lake—" Madelaina stopped. She laughed as if she was the brunt of some silly joke. "Paco, for sure you are *muy loco.* I was there with you. Tolomeo saved your life. Look." She removed the chamois bag from around her neck. "Don't tell me you don't remember this?"

"Ayeiii. For sure *I* remember. It was *my* arm nearly off my body. See?" He opened his shirt to reveal his shoulder. "Even today ees no scar. I tell people I nearly lost an arm and they laugh when they see no scar." His eyes gazed off to view a remote scene in his mind. "All except your *marido*—he didn't laugh," he said solemnly. Then, resuming his earlier mood, he said, "All the other people call me *borrachón,* a crazy drunk who dreams up fanciful stories."

"You must have gotten lost," insisted Madelaina. "You must have made an error in judgment in your travels. It's easy to get lost in those intricate lands. We were there, all three of us. *Dios mios,* my life has never been the same. That's it, Paco, the only explanation. You were lost."

"Me get lost? A scout for the army of General Obregon? *Nunca!* Never! But let us suppose you are right. You forget Lola was with me. Lola, a true Indian, *caramba, chica.* Lola can find the trail of a caterpillar."

Madelaina walked away numb from the conversation. That night and for many long days following she felt as if the very life had been snuffed from her. Had she believed in a myth all this time? What exactly was this strong compelling force that had fed her mind ever since her experience with Tolomeo that had changed the course of her life—her destiny?

She was no longer the angry, resentful, and hostile child of her youth filled with an incomprehensible compulsion to compete with men. The change, however gradual it was, had occurred in her and became irrevocable. It had been an indomitable strength which seemed to rise from her toes and surge through her body like a magic potion of power that pulled her up from the doldrums, from out of the dark helplessness of despair which she had found totally unacceptable. How easy it would have been to adopt the malingering ways of a helpless, clinging female caught in a world threatening to leave her emotionally impotent. Already in the time spent at Seven Moons she had steadfastly refused to submit to the overwhelming feeling of disappointment and discouragement she had felt with regard to Peter.

She wasn't about to spend the rest of her life chasing after a pot of gold at the end of a rainbow, only to find it empty. Not Madelaina Obregon Benson. Not Little Fox. No self-pity for her. None of those negative feelings, which could imprison a soul for all eternity, would find shelter in her mind. She had no time to swoon or succumb to the vapors. She'd learned too much in living and in reading. Why, she'd learned so much about the human mind she hadn't known existed outside the realm of her own reality that she could no longer relate to the small world in which she'd once sought refuge. How much more she could do armed with the knowledge that overflowed in her mind?

The first thing Madelaina did when she came to terms with herself was to impose a rigid schedule upon herself. She rode to Amarillo, recruited an architect whom she paid handsomely and swore to secrecy. For hours she sat with him pouring out her plans. She intended to change everything at Seven Moons to

982

conform to her newfound freedom of expression. Everything about her world would undergo a complete rebirth, with little or none of the past around to remind her or anyone else of the past years. The past was gone—dead and buried—and Madelaina wasn't about to resurrect it.

Back at the ranch she worked feverishly from sunup to sundown, as if there weren't enough hours in each day to meet the schedule she imposed upon herself. Late in the evenings she would retire to her room and study and practice her new way of life.

At first Paco and Lola thought her to be possessed with demons again. They watched her with great apprehension until they began to see the shape of things taking place. Soon, an all-knowing appreciation grew in their eyes and their entire demeanor changed. Then both Paco and his wife threw themselves into the work wholeheartedly. Their cooperation so accelerated their own excitement, Paco could be seen watching the workers with the critical eyes of a self-appointed foreman, making sure the work conformed with the plans.

Not once in the following three months of beaver-like activity at Seven Moons did Madelaina hear from Peter. She had no idea of his whereabouts. She had prayed daily for his safety and knew when the time was right, he would appear at Seven Moons. Meanwhile her responsibility was to prepare herself for the encounter. She no longer concerned herself with the revolution, Pancho Villa, or her father. Long ago, when she first understood things as they were, she'd mentally turned these men over to their own destinies, knowing full well that in the final analysis she would have no influence over the destinies of either of them.

And then one day, having completed her renovations at Seven Moons, she was ready for the final episode in her long-range plans. Her son, Alejandro, was nearly three years old. He not only walked, but he spoke many words. He'd been a precious addition to her life, and she kept him at her side daily for as long as she could before he grew sleepy and took his nap. He looked like a Benson. He had Peter's blue eyes, her own raven hair. The winsome smile and alluring charms of his father were incorporated in every gesture and glance.

Seven Moons had undergone a complete tranformation. Now, finally, she was ready to put all her experiences and knowledge on the line for the man she loved.

Peter Benson had left El Paso on the early morning train hoping to be in Amarillo by evening. He'd called ahead and had his Hayes-Apperson waiting for him. For the past several weeks he'd been unable to concentrate on anything, not business, pleasure, nothing. An inner compulsion, one that wouldn't be assuaged by any will power, drew him to Seven Moons. He consciously argued with himself, citing all the reasons for not going, including the stirring of painful emotions for both Madelaina and himself. But he was helpless to counteract this intense magnetic power that compelled him to go to Seven Moons.

He'd already told himself he couldn't live without Madelaina despite the strength of his determination to do so. He had rationalized that it wasn't fair to her to live with a man who couldn't satisfy her sexually. She was the kind of a woman who needed a man to make her whole. Any red-blooded man could tell that by merely looking at her. Since he was no longer equipped to fulfill such a role, the only decent thing he could do was divorce her, let her go. Months ago he'd taken these measures. All the proper papers were complete, requiring only her signature. Yet he hadn't been able to send them to her. He wasn't prepared to release her and make a free woman of her. He glanced at his briefcase, next to him on the train. He'd packed the divorce papers in it earlier. Now he wondered how he'd open the subject. Straight out was the only way.

Peter hadn't known he could love and hate at the same time, nor was he aware that these same conflicting emotions were at the seat of his sexual problems. He hadn't had time to sort out these feelings because he'd seen to it that each spare moment was occupied, leaving him no time to think. The past year had succeeded only in making him more hostile, more of a driven man than he realized. For whatever reasons his brain had devised, he'd ceased being the easy-going, swashbuckling freedom fighter of the past few years. Of late he drank to excess, became cold and calculating in his business ventures, and entered all involvements with a fierce dedication of a man in perpetual motion.

It never occurred to him that he'd been making an unconscious effort to emulate his late father. Since he'd inherited the bulk of the Benson estate and the formidable political power of the Benson name, he was determined to use both against those double-dealing, political hypocrites in Washington.

Damnit ta hell! What in cotton' picking blue blazes was that idiot in the White House thinking of to back Carranza? It had been enough to make Peter lose confidence in his government. A man who permitted his own personal prejudices to override the recommendations of his own advisers was a fool. It sure in hell was a choice President Wilson would live ta regret, thought Peter. He had increased his efforts to send arms and ammunition to General Villa every chance he had. Recently he'd made a deal with a Belgian arms maker for the largest shipment ever to cross the border. As soon as he returned from Seven Moons, plans to smuggle the arms across the border would fall into place.

Things in that department had been going fairly smooth until he found Madelaina in San Antonio in the arms of her childhood sweetheart, Armando Cortez. He wasn't certain why he felt so betrayed or why it should even matter that Armando had been the rogue who deflowered his wife. All these things never mattered in the past—why should they loom important now, he wondered. He felt such a hatred toward Armando, not only regarding his past relationship to his wife, but also because he ironically had been the one to marry Valerie Townsend. It caused him to color his attitude toward Obregon's spy. Through Peter's and Governor Townsend's efforts, Cortez was still held incommunicado on a series of trumped-up charges and had been incarcerated in a remote Juarez prison cell until the governor was good and ready to release him.

He never forgot that day in San Antonio. The fact that Madelaina had seen her father had increased his suspicions of betrayal. After all, back in Vera Cruz she'd left him with such suspicions no matter how much she explained the situation when they were re-united. Even Pancho Villa concurred that blood was thicker than water. Would she have betrayed Pancho Villa? Had she? Damn! Why Peter continued to enter-tain thoughts of betrayal when he'd never questioned Madelaina's loyalty in the past disturbed him and left him filled with disquiet.

On this train ride, he had time to think, a luxury he'd refused to indulge in before. If anything, Made-laina should be furious with him. He hadn't confided his continuous involvement with the *Villistas*. She had believed his assurance that he'd ceased all activities in this vein. Why had he felt the need to deceive her? Why? After all they'd been through together since their tempestuous marriage, why should he suddenly feel the need for deception and subterfuge? In Peter's distorted mind it began to look that between them, he and Madelaina, there was nothing worthwhile left to sal-vage. Without trust there was nothing. Damnit ta hell! Why ever did she go to San Antonio? It had served only to heighten the breach between them.

He never considered that she'd told him the truth, even though he'd lashed out at her in fury for giving him that convenient story about consulting a specialist over his condition. He wasn't about to listen to such rubbish and closed his mind to it. His insufferable pride and damaged ego led him into a back alley of self-tor-ture, where shame and humiliation superseded all logic and reasoning, turning him into a wild-eyed, frenzied animal. Jealousy possessed him. Violent hatred and burning anger motivated him into shutting out all thoughts of Madelaina's true character. He saw only what he wanted to see regardless of the destruction done to his marriage by such self-inflicted myopia. He anesthetized the pain with indifference.

Peter had managed to keep himself busy these past few months. Immersed in dangerous missions, intriguing with desperados, never knowing if they'd kill you, rob you of your money, and bootleg the arms and ammunition, Peter had in a sense been forced to be alert and on guard. He had had little time to think of Madelaina or their ramshackle marriage.

However, this past month, Peter, in spite of himself, found every waking moment occupied with thoughts of Madelaina, more than he wanted to—when he should have been concentrating on something else. Visions of her sun-kissed face, dazzling smile, and dark, exotic eyes thrust themselves upon his consciousness too often for it to be coincidence. He could feel her soft sensuous body and almost smell the cool, sweet scent of her cologne. It interfered with his work so often that he found himself growing angrier that she should still have such power over him.

He felt certain he had managed to expunge her from his life from that moment in San Antonio when he decided it was the best thing for all concerned. Yet, the recurring thoughts of all those wonderful times they shared in the past, along with the countless times they fought side by side, facing unknown dangers together, possessed him to a point he could no longer voluntarily eject such thoughts from mind. Moved to action, he had to pursue this overwhelming compulsion to see her.

The train was approaching Amarillo when Peter realized most of his own actions had been predicated on the fact that his pride had been terribly injured. That plus the fact that he couldn't possess her as a man should possess a woman had caused him to build a wall of defenses around himself, so he couldn't be hurt any more. Now, as he considered all this, he wondered at the intelligence of his presence at Seven Moons. Why, damnit ta hell, Madelaina hadn't once tried to reach him since the San Antonio escapade. Damn that bitch! She was too damned independent. That's what rankled him and always had, he told himself. With nothing else to take Peter's attention from the situation at hand, he was forced to examine his thoughts more critically, in the manner he once assessed all things. And he came to the conclusion that he himself had contributed to Madelaina's independence. He had only himself to blame for what Madelaina had become. He'd taught her how to be a free thinker, a revolutionist, and hadn't he transformed her into his sex goddess?

Peter detrained in the bustling depot in Amarillo, overrun with cowboys and ranch hands and the overpowering stench of stockyards and dust. Passengers elbowed their way roughly, going and coming in the swarming station. His car was waiting. Tossing in his bags, he dismissed the driver, preferring to drive himself.

It was early twilight when Peter approached the entrance to the place of his birth. Countless old emotions surfaced and a feeling of uneasiness overwhelmed him, constricting his guts more each moment. Peter's growing curiosity at the sights that greeted him instantly neutralized those old feelings as new sensations replaced them. Perplexed, he glanced sharply about the area, wondering if he'd taken the wrong turn off the main road. What in tarnation is that, he asked himself at the sight of the high adobe wall encircling the area of the old ranch house? When he saw the two enormous and brightly lit torches at either side of two gigantic carved oaken doors, he got the distinct feeling he was either plunged forward or backward in time as a visitor in some mysterious land. He forced himself to reread the bronze plaque several times to make certain he was on the right property. *Seven Moons*—that's what the sign read.

What in tarnation had happened, he wondered as he yanked on the pull chain that promptly sounded a melodious series of chimes. The enormous doors opened and Paco Jimenez greeted him warmly.

"Señor Benson, what a pleasure to see you. Please to

988

come in." He took Peter's bags and gestured him ahead with overt politeness.

Peter was totally dazed by the splendor of the lush, tropical gardens that greeted him in the inner atrium. He turned in every direction, pivoting first on one foot, then the other, as he circled his way into the building proper. His open-mouthed amazement was total, his curiosity insatiable. The aviary of magnificently colored birds commanded his attention, and for several moments he paused to stare in fascinated absorption, unable to speak. When he could, he asked, "What happened? Whose idea was this?" As if he didn't know. The question was why? Just as Peter focused his attention on the interior of the house, he came to a sudden and abrupt halt. The adrenaline pumped furiously and his heart stood still. Two sable-colored mountain lions sauntered across his path. Peter remained absolutely still, his eyes alerted to possible danger. Across the room where for years the formidable gun collection of William Benson had occupied an entire wall, there was nothing—nothing for Peter to reach for self-protection.

"What in the name of Jesus is the meanin' of this?" he called cautiously to Paco, indicating the cats.

"It's nothing, *señor el patrón*. They are quite tame— like all the others."

"All the others? Theah's moah?"

"*Si*, ten in all. These two are the friendliest. They are called Tracy and Rosalia." Paco tried to suppress a grin.

Peter smiled despite himself. Once assured of his safety, he entered the enormous room off the atrium. Surprise after surprise exploded before his eyes as Madelaina's triumph, a replica of Dr. Oemolot's desert paradise, blended with some of the magic of Tolomeo's land, came alive before his eyes. He had to admit it wasn't a place he'd ever seen or lived in before, but it was enticing. All those birds! He couldn't be done gazing at the unique beauty all around him.

From the Mexican quarters, Peter heard the soft music of the people played on guitars and muted trumpets. He moved on about the room, noting the obvious painstaking plans that figured prominently in the creation of this spectacular structure.

"Wheah is the *señora?*" he asked Paco when he finally disguised his amazement long enough to speak. Indescribable feelings overwhelmed him.

Paco turned from him to gaze at the top of a cantilevered staircase. Peter's eyes darted in the same direction.

Madelaina stood on the top step, dressed in a simple, flowing, pale yellow caftan, her dark luxurious hair, parted in the center, fell freely to her waist. The only other adornment were the golden seven moon earrings dangling from her lobes. Her dark and vibrant, eyes contained the unmistakable look of love.

Peter stared critically at her as an art critic might view a valuable and priceless painting for the first time, assessing every aspect of her. There was something rather special about her, far different than he'd remembered her. What elegant poise and self-containment she demonstrated, he thought, as she descended the steps that seemed to float toward him from out of nowhere.

Paco left the room at a nod from his mistress.

For a brief moment, Peter felt awkward. He couldn't greet her as they'd greeted each other in the past. Too much strife was between them, creating a formidable barrier.

"Hello, Peter," she said in a deeper, huskier voice than in the one she generally spoke. "How good to see you," she said politely.

"What have ya done ta Seven Moons?" were the only words he could find.

"You like it?" she asked pleasantly.

"Theah was nothing wrong with the old place," he said again for something to say.

For an instant Madelaina was prompted to say, "If there hadn't been anything wrong with the old place, you might not be in the state you're in." Of course she said nothing like that. She turned instead to address the old serving woman who had soundlessly entered the room.

"Pilar, please bring Alejandro to see his father." She turned to Peter. "You can see him and enjoy him until dinner." She withdrew from the main room as Pilar brought the child to be reunited with his father.

She paused at the threshold only to say, "Don't feel awkward. He knows you well even if he hasn't seen you much."

Peter turned his attention to the young child and his heart spilled over with love and endearment. "Hello theah, boy," he said gruffly to hide the moistness in his eyes. He knelt down on one knee and opened his arms to the child.

Alejandro paused a moment, then walked timidly toward him. "Are you my father?"

"Ah'm youah fathuh," said Peter, sweeping him into his arms. He held the child tightly and kissed him affectionately.

Outside in the solarium, Madelaina watched the reunion with joy. God give me the strength to fulfill the rest of my plans, she said, tingling with an excitement which threatened to jar her artful poise. She prepared the drinks for them, and as she did, she opened the chamois pouch on a chain at her neck and sprinkled a few specks of the powder into Peter's drink.

When he finished with Alejandro, Peter joined her in the solarium and accepted the drink from her. "Well, what all do we drink ta?" he asked tightly.

"Why not Seven Moons?"

He nodded. "Seven Moons it is," he replied, downing the drink in one gulp. He smacked his lips. "Mmmm good. Whadda ya call it?"

"Tequila, lime, and passion fruit," she said lightly. "The nectar of Seven Moons—just the thing to drink in this atmosphere of serenity. I hope you brought an excellent appetite. Do you wish to wash up before dinner?"

"Ah can remember when there were times we—" Peter stopped. He was about to recall those days on

991

the deserts in Mexico when there was no food, no conveniences to wash—but sweet Jesus they were happy days. Instead he said, "If y'all will point me in the right direction ta find the proper accommodations. Ah'm lost in this—" he faltered at a loss for the proper word.

"Home." She supplied the word. "Right through that archway to your left."

She watched him loosen the collar of his shirt. His face was flushed as the effect of Tolomeo's dried mushroom powder was taking effect. At least she hoped it was.

When he returned, she promptly led him to the dinner table at the far end of the solarium. "Do you mind dining out of doors? It's so balmy. And look! The stars over Texas are bigger and brighter than I've seen in a long time," she remarked, pouring him another drink, as Peter's eyes searched the sky.

"That's a powerful potion ya fix," he told her. "Ah can't remember when ah've felt mah drinks moah," he said amiably, in a somewhat mellower mood than earlier. "As a mattuh of fact, Madelaina, ah'm not even hungry. Ah thought ah was earlier, but somehow mah appetite has disappeared."

She smiled. "We can always eat later," she said, leading him back to the deeply cushioned sofa before the fireplace. She made every effort at being a marvelous hostess. The fragrant scent of her special cologne drifted to his nostrils. She saw him inhale appreciatively and knew she'd stirred a powerful lot of desire in him.

"Now, then, tell me about yourself. What have you been doing in all this time?" she asked lightly, hoping he wouldn't detect the desperation in her voice. God, how she'd missed him. She'd wanted him from the moment she'd laid eyes on him. He seemed thinner, more tense than she'd ever seen him before. As the drink relaxed him, he seemed less knotted up than he'd been earlier. Her hopes soared. She wanted to fall into his arms and end the charade, but couldn't.

"I've missed you," he said quietly.

She glanced at him swiftly. "I've missed you, too," she said finally.

He caught the desire and urgency in her voice that she tried to conceal. Turning from her, he swallowed hard and muttered, "Don't make it anymoah difficult than it is." He reached into his jacket pocket and pulled out a letter. "This came jus' befoah ah left El Paso. It's from Tracy. Ah saved it so we could read it togethuh. That all right with y'all?"

"I thought we had agreed to forget the past," she said quietly.

"It's about the *jefe's* campaign against youah father—"

Her eyes lit up for a moment. Just as quickly they dimmed.

"Listen, Madelaina, theah's no point in tryin' ta bury the past. It's still too much with us," he said stretching his neck above his collar. "It shuah is pretty warm up heah at Seven Moons."

"Please remove your jacket and tie. You don't have to stand on ceremony in your own home."

"Correction. Youah home. Now, more than ever," he said glancing about.

"Our home," she corrected him. "Our home for as long as you want."

Then she added, "If you want to read the letter, I would like to hear what Tracy has to say."

Peter removed his jacket and tie and sat back down again. He sipped his drink this time, instead of gulping it down as he had the first. He lit two cigarettes and handed her one. Then, his face flushing with color from the effect of the mushroom powder, he propped his feet up on a hassock and stretched contentedly. The change in him was already apparent to her.

It was marvelous to watch his inhibitions melt away as if by magic. Madelaina wished that he wouldn't take too long reading the letter. She had things to do with him, things that would determine their fate. She saw him pat the empty space on the sofa next to him as he used to do. Watching him as a hawk might watch a chicken before she moved in, she finally slipped into the spot he designated with his hand.

Peter opened the letter and began to read: "Mah deah Peter and Little Fox: Hell, it's been a long spell since we visited, ole buddy. Y'all know me. Ah ain't one fer writing. But since it's been a good while an' ah got me this chance ta send a letter off to ya, ah decided ta make up fer lost time. Ah jus' hope this heah lettuh gets ta ya and not inta the wrong hands.

"As ya might've guessed, none of us is as happy as we'd like ta report. But 'sposin' ah begin from the beginning? If we'd of won that first skirmish with Obregon, the whole picture might've been different.

"Y'all know the *jefe* wasn't about ta leave Mexico City to the likes of Carranza, after Obregon marched back inta the capital. As soon as ah left ya, *amigo*, back in El Paso, ah returned to the *Villista*. The *jefe* wired general mobilization orduhs ta all his northern garrisons and, man, ouah power turned southward. Carranza in the meanwhile ordered General Obregon ta vacate Mexico City and proceed to the center of Mexico ta confront General Villa.

"Ah guess the *jefe* approached the battle with Obregon as we Texans might look ta enter inta a personal gun fight. Everything was at stake. And ah suppose that Obregon, now in full command of a Constitutionalist Army equal to the *jefe*'s, grew just as cocky as they come, and decided it was a long overdue showdown between 'em. Obregon was as anxious as Villa to get this confrontation ovuh with. Trouble was, Pete, two of ouah most vital brigades were off on far-flung courses with large portions of the Northern Division at least a full three days' ride from our intended point of impact with Obregon.

"Man, ah tell ya we was all mighty concerned. Even Fierro grew as morbid as they come when Villa kept insistin' ta us he wasn't worried. He felt shuah the other brigades would arrive in the nick of time. They always had in the past, he assured Fierro and the rest of us.

994

"Well, by now y'all must have heard what happened in Celaya. But jus' ta set the record straight, Peter, ya can believe it when ah tell ya it was the bloodiest god-damned battle ah was evuh in. Woooooeeeee.

"We finally got word from the Chihuahua Brigade and General Angeles to wait the three days for the delayed arrival. We heard nothing from Urbina's Juarez brigade. Still the *jefe* remained optimistic as hell. Despite his optimism, ah gotta tell ya ah never saw Villa as unreasonable. He wouldn't wait for Angeles. The only thing on his mind was ta meet Obregon, attack, and crush him instantly. That theah is some burning grudge he holds against the father of Little Fox. Well, since it don't do no good ta be cryin' over spilt milk, ah'll try ta be as sparin' as ah can and describe what all happened.

"Ah don't hafta tell ya that Obregon used every fuckin' military strategy he evuh learned against the *jefe*. God almighty, he dug trenches, strung barbed wire backed by machine guns, then placed his artillery behind high ground an' he waited. An' man, Villa fell right inta it. The *jefe*'s tactics, that overpowering blow that had shattered every enemy he ever had jus' didn't work in this instance.

"Ah tell ya, Pete, it was the meetin' of two distinct minds it was. Obregon, cool, calculating, willin' ta wait forever foah victory. Villa, as usual his impulsive, reckless self, willin' ta wager everything on his daring ability ta shock his enemy. These two opposing forces have some malignancy between em, an' we all feel it. Shoot, man, it's touched every last one of us.

"But heah's the shocker. We just got the word that behind Obregon, supportin' his defenses was a man named Von Klause. Bettuh known as Field Marshal Von Klause of the Imperial German Army. That's right. The fuckin' Germans are backing Carranza! Y'all just get that information back ta youah uppity Mr. Wilson in Washington. . . ."

Peter paused pointedly. He sipped the remains of his drink and stared into space. Madelaina, caught up in

995

the letter, grew annoyed. "That's not so," she insisted. "My father wouldn't sell out to the Germans. He may be many things, but his loyalty to the Americans is well known. I heard General Pershing tell him—" Madelaina stopped, realizing how she'd fallen back into her former role.

"Why would Tracy say such a thing?" said Peter matter-of-factly.

Madelaina shrugged. This wasn't working out as she'd planned. Always the revolution! Always something between them! Damn! With fierce control she made light of it until she rolled the name Von Klause over in her memory. Of course! "Von Klause was the name of the German agent who attempted to coerce Pancho into making a pact with the Kaiser," she told Peter. "You remember?" She recalled her father's words clearly when General Pershing asked him if he knew the German Von Klause. Her father denied it. Had he known of President Carranza's double-dealing all the time? She just didn't want to believe it of her father. "Peter, do you think my father is capable of playing both sides against the middle?"

Peter turned to her. "Isn't that a naïve question ta ask, when ya realize how many times youah father has switched sides? First, he was a *Porfirista* unduh *Diaz,* then he served Madero until Huerta took power. Then he became a *Huertista* until Carranza courted him properly, with added incentives, ah might add. Sugah, theah ain't enough paint in the world ta cover the stripes of so many skunks. Ah speculate that if the *jefe* had played the proper tune for Obregon, he might have come bouncing down the road dancing to 'La Cucaracha.'"

"What you say is that my father still thinks like a *Científico*—a true dyed-in-the-wool militarist?" She flushed with embarrassment. "He can only dance to the tune of another man—not his own?"

"That's about the long and the short of it," replied Peter. "Some men are natural born leaders, others are made. While still others will only be followers all their lives. It ain't no real shame and that ain't ta say that he don't have a brilliant military mind. But there's only so far a *Científico* can go if they don't have a creativity to make themselves leaduhs." Peter reached over and pulled her legs closer to him the way they used to sit close in a posture of love.

Madelaina secretly thrilled to the manner in which he was responding, as if there'd been no breach in their relationship, as if none of the bad things had ever happened. Perhaps reading this letter was a stroke of luck. It drew them closer together. She lay her head on Peter's shoulder and he reached up to stroke her face gently.

He sighed with an inner contentment, fully relaxed, without tension, then commenced reading:

"At Celaya, Villa opened the battle with artillery, followed by a cavalry charge supported by more artillery. Obregon's counter battery fell ta Villa's rear while mines, barbed wire, and machine guns tore us apart. Over and again ouah charges went in and again Obregon's well dug-in infantry, artillery, and sputtering guns littered the hillsides with torn bodies, kicking and dying horses.

"If ya could have seen the *jefe* rage, *amigo,* ya would have thought Pancho Villa was no longer human, but a fiercely raging animal. Ah nevuh saw the fire in his eyes burn with such violent hatred. Then, he came through for a time. Just when it began ta look like the whole Northern Division was kaput, he and Fierro appeared on foaming horses, pistols in hand as Villa's voice, echoing in the desert wind, commanded his *Dorados* to charge.

"Pete, ah never saw anything so magnificent in all mah born days. Why, the whole goddamn lot o' em crazy men thundered up the hill, threw themselves at Obregon's forces, staggering the hell outa 'em. Obregon returned shot for shot an' still one entire squadron was shot out from behind 'em. Villa returned for another charge and another. Each time they staggered Obregon's forces with their spectacular and wild charges. Ah tell ya, Obregon's forces were as solid as the Rock of Gibraltar. Even so, he was on the verge of crumbling, when suddenly from out of nowhere he was saved by a fresh column of 2,000 men arriving at the peak of battle.

"God Almighty, man! Ya nevuh saw Pancho Villa in such a tempest. Ah could heah his voice echoing through the desert. 'Wheah's Tomàs Urbina and the fuckin' Juarez Brigade?' Word came that General Angeles had been intercepted by a *Carranzista* column in the north. But nothin' came from that sidewinder, Urbina. An, lemme tell ya, Peter, from that moment on nothing went right foah us. General Villa knew we done lost Celaya, but he wouldn't admit ta the bitterness of defeat—not by Obregon.

"As time went on, Fierro, wounded three times, was out of action. By the end of April Urbina's disappearance was explained. Damned little weasel! Ovuhcome with battle fatigue, he also came down with a case of itchy fingers. He deserted the brigade and took with him a million-peso payroll belonging ta his troops.

"All this weighed heavy on the *jefe,* still he had the goddamned balls ta disengage, reorganize, and make a thunderous comeback ta strike again at Obregon.

"Well, mah good buddy, then came the final meet. Villa and Obregon met again, their lines strung from Celaya to Leon. Villa's cavalry advanced. Obregon fell back. Villa charged once again. Men fell by the hundreds—then, thousands, littering the hills with bloodied bodies and ruined equipment. Ya should have seen that goddamned, sweet sight, Villa's *Dorados.* Man, if the whole Northern Division had been as sharp and as devastating as them *Dorados,* the government army would have been pulverized. They charged, covered by artillery fire, actually broke over barbed wire, past machine gun nests into the trenches, trampling and killing *Carranzistas,* at pistol range. And when Villa's airplanes flew over their trenches, you would have thought Obregon was finished. And for a time he nearly was.

"Then, Pete, came the mind-boggling mix-ups. Ya know that ammo we got from Juarez was the wrong kind? It was 25-35 calibre, useless for our 30-30 Winchesters and Mausers. Someone had sabotaged the shipments is all ah can say.

"Listen, tell Little Fox we just got word that on June 2, General Obregon, while out on personal reconnaissance of his front lines, got caught in an outburst of gun fire, was flung from his horse, and lost an arm in the skirmish."

There was a break in the letter, a passage of time.

Peter paused once more to glance at his wife. Madelaina flinched at the news, lowered her eyes and shook her head. "He's too proud a man to be able to withstand the shame. Not at the loss of an arm," she added. "For being caught off guard enough for it to have happened to him."

"Ah'm sorry," Peter said softly. "But in war anything can happen. Ya oughta know it moah than anyone."

"Yes, I suppose I do. Isn't it a pity words can offer no solace? Please continue, Peter," she said, fixing him another drink.

"Ah gotta say youah are some iron lady, Madelaina. In the past few yeahs, ya've taken a lot. Still ya take it like it all falls off youah shoulder like tiny rain drops."

"*Si*, I'm some iron lady," she muttered to herself, handing him the drink.

He took another sip to wet his lips and continued:

"Obregon was outa commission. In his place came a sharp-thinking general who made a brilliant decision when he quickly untied five army columns in one desperate attack against us. Foah Obregon's forces it was a stroke of luck. Foah us it proved devastatin'. If Obregon had been conscious, his strategy would have been ta wait, by then we'd have had plenty of time ta replace the faulty ammunition.

"As luck had it, it was the worst sight ah evuh saw from the camp of a *Villista*. We were unable ta defend ouahselves. All around us ah saw men throw away

999

theah empty rifles, retreat into the hills, fully scattered befoah the enemy's cavalry and constant artillery barages.

"By nightfall as we climbed aboard the waiting trains in retreat, Lady Luck shifted foah the *jefe*. Ouah guess was that Obregon's sidekick didn't know how much devastation he'd really done—that further resistance was impossible merely for the lack of ammunition. So, in his hesitation to pursue, he waited too long.

"The *Villista* army had had it. Suddenly we all became *guerrillos* again. We made desperate demonstrations ta confuse ouah enemies by firing sporadically, but without ammunition ouah grand and glorious *Divísíon del Norte* was in full retreat, northward. Listen, ah know y'all read of the broad advances made by Obregon when he regained consciousness a week later. During the month of July he made a complete sweep, recapturing many of Villa's garrisons.

"But all wasn't lost. Rudolfo Fierro pulled some mighty brilliant tactical maneuvers. His arm still in a sling, Fierro detached hisself from Villa's main force and swinging around ta Obregon's rear, that devil went ta town. He began by surprising outposts, sending false wires, tangling troops and supplies, destroying rails and communication lines and routes, and razin' Carranza garrisons to the ground. As Villa's main forces retreated into Chihuahua, Fierro's brigade had retaken Celaya, Leon, Queretaro, San Juan, Tula, and Pachuca. He finally rejoined us at the end of July.

"Now ah come ta the point I've been leading ta. Pete, unless we get help from the U.S. as promised to Villa in El Paso, it may all well be ovuh fer us. Ah'm not shuah what ya'll can do aftuh that San Antonio muddle up, but ah'm keeping mah fingers crossed. Yer good buddy, Tracy Richards. P.S. Ah forgot ta tell ya, me and Rosalia got hitched in May. With luck we may see ya one day."

Normally Peter would have discussed the contents of the letter, taking sides and analyzing both positions like

1000

a former soldier might in replaying the battle. Not this night. His mind refused to attribute any importance to the letter.

Peter let the letter fall to his lap. He lay his head back against the sofa and closed his eyes. There was so much he wanted to say, but his mind refused to concentrate. Nothing mattered it seemed, nothing except for this moment. So many thoughts about Tracy's letter stirred in his mind, but he could find no words to articulate them. Even more unusual was the fact that he didn't seem to care.

For several long moments they were both silent. Their hearts raced with that excitement of new, unexplored love, that made them both quiver internally.

The sounds of laughter and music wafted in through the open-air solarium, and Madelaina rose to her feet and walked to the edge of the floral boughs where the multi-colored birds in the aviary were cooing and chirping contentedly, soothed by the music. She flung open the screened doors and stepped out onto the flagstone patio under the bright illumination of a tangerine moon against a midnight blue sky of luminous, giant stars, the Texas variety. "Not even the stars of Mexico can compare to these in Texas" admitted Madelaina as he moved in quietly to join her.

"Ah gotta admit they don't grow 'em no place like they do in Texas." His attention was taken at a point past the patio where the Mexicans were celebrating a gala. Paco and Lola stood at the center of the activity, dancing their hearts out.

For a time they both watched the excitement. Peter's arm slipped around her shoulder and she leaned in closer to him, wordlessly.

Keeping time to the rousing music, the spectators clapped their hands in a wilder more pointed staccato. Paco with wild abandon whipped his sombrero from his head and with a flourish tossed it on the ground and began to dance in and around the brim, keeping time to the loud clapping of hands. As the tempo increased and the dancing became more frenetic, Lola, a vision in bright yellow, her dark hair whipping around her, whirled and swayed her body sensuously, like dancing serpents. Her turquoise eyes, like fire, flared seductively. The tempo rose to such a crescendo, the clapping so fast that the dance ended abruptly when hand and leg movements could no longer be distinguished.

Rousing waves of laughter and applause followed as the small mariachi band played a more romantic, less feverish rendition of a slowed down "La Cucaracha."

"That little girl is still somethin' special," he lit up in appreciation of Lola's performance. "Ah always had a hankerin' foah her, remembuh, Little Fox?"

Madelaina smiled. "I remember. You were highly susceptible to her."

"Seems like old times, doesn't it, sugah?" said Peter softly. He just couldn't reconcile these new feelings surging through him.

"The old times are gone," she said softly. "It's time to make new memories and plan for a future, *querido*."

"Hmmm." Peter mumbled, meaning nothing in particular because he wasn't thinking. He gave vent to all these mild sensations creeping inside him, pleasurable sensations that removed any feeling of disquiet. Something gave him a particular breathlessness; something provoked him into an effervescent-feeling ebullience that excited him more than the dance he'd just seen. He held on to his wife with more possessiveness than he ever felt the need for in the past.

Madelaina moved with feeling, filling the empty air between them. "You haven't kissed me yet, *querido*. Don't you find me desirable any more?"

For an instant Peter hesitated. In the next moment a soft cry of anguish escaped his lips. He gathered her into his arms and kissed her like a love-starved man. They clung together as waves of passion swept through them. He couldn't stop kissing her, and finally, when Madelaina led him inside and up the cantilevered steps to the open-walled bedroom, he followed like a child, his hand in hers.

Peter stood in open-mouthed amazement, letting his

eyes drink in enchanting atmosphere of tropical splendor, like a dazed neophyte from a far-distant land. A large bed on a cantilevered base gave it the appearance of floating in space. Behind it, one wall was a screened-in hollow containing countless plants and fronds and date palms with love birds of every variety cooing and singing in pairs. Along another wall, an oversized portrait of Peter, done in oils from a photograph, hung in a special gold frame over what appeared to be a small altar in mahogany. Several large candles flickered, casting oblique shadows on the portrait. An emperor's chair stood before it.

Nearly everything in the room was done in white with gold accents. The sheets and silk coverlet were white, trimmed in gold. The furniture was gilded—sparingly. The sweet scent of roses permeated the room and Peter's sense memory was stirred to a spine-tingling, feverish excitation.

"That picture," he asked, when he found his voice. "Wheah did ya get it?" It showed Peter naked from the waist up, his thick drooping moustache and sideburns, longer than usual. His curly and tousled hair and sun-bronzed skin captured superbly by the artist was the perfect setting for those incredibly blue, blue eyes that reached across the room at her. It wasn't the sort of picture an artist would choose to paint, let alone hang in an intimate boudoir, unless one was possessed with the love of that man.

"I stole the picture from Lucia San Miguels. Remember when you were in Moreles with Zapata—before we were united in Parral? It was taken by Miguel Guerra when he interviewed you and Tracy."

"I never posed for such a picture—not without my clothes—without my hat," retorted Peter, recollecting the incident with the reporter very well.

"Of course you didn't, silly idiot. I simply paid the artist to undress you to please myself, so I could see you only as I know you," she temporized. "And perhaps the way a few thousand other *chiquitas* like Lucia have known you, eh?"

Peter flushed with pleasure at the compliment until the memory of his recent travail clouded his sparkling azure eyes to a murky gray. "Why the candles?" he asked, gazing at them under the portrait. Were you sending out prayers for me?"

Madelaina smiled enigmatically. "You ask too many questions, *querido*. Come with me." As she led him into the next room, Madelaina said to herself, If you only knew, querido, how many prayers I sent out to you. Every day for the past two months, when her plans had been nearing completion, she had sat on that throne chair, her eyes fixed to the portrait for a period of an hour a day. She had pictured him in her mind as she knew him, sending mental suggestions to him wherever he was. This part of the procedure taught to her by Thaddeus Oemolot was a sort of mental telepathy. She didn't know the principles behind such an occult teaching only that it worked. Peter was proof of it. Her suggestions, once she was in a state of meditation, were to always speak to him as if he were present. She told him this was his home, where he belonged. That his wife loved him, needed him, and wanted him desperately. Together they could build on their love. She transmitted thoughts of love to him. And these daily procedures, which she at first thought to be quite humorous and ridiculous until she clearly recalled the incident of Golden Dawn in her life. How else could Golden Dawn have hexed her, if not through a negative form of telepathy? If it worked negatively—why not in a positive vein? *Bueno*, she had told herself. She would try it. And *Dios mios!* It had worked!

But this was to be Madelaina's secret, one she wouldn't share with Peter.

Madelaina pulled open the two sliding doors that recessed into the wall at either side, and led Peter into a mirror-walled bathroom far surpassing the one she had marveled at on her initial visit to Seven Moons. At the center of the room was a tiled platform leading to a sunken marble Roman bath, decorously set against a backdrop of green plants and exotic flowers. One entire wall contained a cage of monkeys who were chittering noisily as they swung from vine to vine, branch to branch, or engaged in lovemaking.

"What in the cotton pickin' blue blazes prompted ya ta cage up them theah monkeys?" he sputtered, aghast at such a spectacular innovation. "Ah jus' don't believe mah eyes. How in tarnation did ya manage all this? Wheah did ya find the workmen? Wheah did ya get all these birds and animals?" He bombarded her with a thousand and one questions, as his disbelieving eyes drank in all the remarkable changes done to the place he could no longer relate to as he had as a child.

Peter watched his wife open spigots of bull's horns over the tub and temper the water to the correct warmth. She tossed in perfumes and scented crystals and let the water rush into the tub. She still hadn't answered him.

"Tell me, jus' what do ya intend ta do with all these entrapments?" he asked in a husky, but testy voice.

"What a loving wife would do for her loving, long overdue husband when he decides to come home."

He studied her critically, preparing to barrage her with countless questions, but all he could say was, "Ya still love me aftuh the way ah've treated ya and hurt ya?" he agonized, trying to get his bearing in these new surroundings. His eyes were fixed on a few uninhibited monkeys in the cage as they began to copulate.

"Some of these monkeys were here, left over from your father's hobby. I integrated them with new animals and see how happy they are? It's simply amazing what you can learn from monkeys—"

"Madelaina! Y'all ain't gonna give me the same crap mah father handed ta me when ah was growing up?"

"They don't have to clutter up their minds with imaginary thoughts. They function normally, without inhibitions, without words to get themselves muddled up."

Reluctantly Peter shifted his attention back to the caged animals. He watched them in fascination. "Ya nevuh answered mah question," he said quietly.

"Do I still love you? I've never stopped loving you,

1005

querido. From the moment you taught me how to be a woman—*your* woman, I became yours for all eternity. You put your stamp on me—your brand. 'Do not touch,' it said. 'Property of Peter Duprez Benson.' Since then I've been yours. None other's. Only yours, do you understand?"

"I told you to forget me. I was sure you had after all this time."

"Forget you? Your face—name—kiss—and warm embrace? The love that we once knew, knowing for you there'd be no one else? *Querido,* I've remembered only you, your walk, talk, the sweet tender things you used to say. I've remembered even the cruel, honest things you told me to open my eyes to the world around me. Yes, all those harsh, unacceptable, yet steadfast truths which made me aware of myself and my world. Forget you, eh? Your laugh, your twinkling, yet fiery and seductive blue eyes, that turned on an eternal flame in my heart. I would never forget you, *amado mío,* not when all these things live in the son of our loins. In everything about me that is you."

Madelaina never took her eyes from Peter's. He was growing less and less inhibited, watching two monkeys, two particularly virile and frisky animals in the process of copulation.

"Y'all figure ah can learn from these heah little buggers, is that it?" he said amiably. "Well, mebbe ah can. Mebbe ah can."

Madelaina fixed him a drink from a cabinet of wines and other spirits. She handed it to him and poured another for herself. *Bueno,* she thought, he was beginning to relax to the point where she was ready for him.

He hardly resisted her when she began to remove his shirt and trousers, as if it were a normal ritual between them. When he stood nude before her, she helped him into the tub. He stepped into it and sat down, luxuriating in the relaxing warmth, his mind a complete blank. Only the process of feeling was important to him.

"Relax, my husband. Relax," she cooed softly. "Close your eyes and lay back and let yourself feel the

1006

comfort of the water against your skin. That's better, *querido, mi amore.* Listen and I'll whisper to you the secrets of Tolomeo."

His eyes fluttered open encumbered by invisible weights. "Tolomeo? Who is Tolomeo?"

"A man of great wisdom," she said, leaning over him. She kissed his lips lightly with her hot and moist eager mouth and then began to speak with a rhythmic pacing to her voice. "You remember Parral, Peter, when I couldn't respond to your passionate embraces?"

"Ummmhum," he muttered as the tenseness left his firm and muscular body, and relaxed him into a euphoria of pleasantness and tranquility.

"I put into your drink a calmative powder like the one the doctor in Parral administered to me. No, don't be alarmed. Trust me, beloved. Trust the woman who loves you more than life itself." She rubbed his forehead, the back of his neck and upper shoulders soothingly until he purred like a kitten. Her voice droned on in lulling, hypnotic effect. "You've become a victim of a false reality, Peter. Something you've painted in your own mind through your fears. With your help, we will unlock your mind, permit the untruth to take flight and leave you in peace. Only then will you realize you've been a slave to figments of your distorted imagination.

"We will implant new pictures in your mind, as you were when you were whole, more complete. There is nothing you can't do that you haven't always done except for this period of stagnation when you allowed a false picture in your mind to direct you." Madelaina's eyes watched him—his every reaction critically. His eyes had grown so heavy he could no longer keep them open. His arms hung limply at his sides in the water, his head sagged slightly, his muscles relaxed without tension.

With instant recall, Madelaina continued her ritual as it had been prescribed by Dr. Oemolot and from papers she'd read on the subject of suggestion and hypnosis. What she hoped to do was transfer her thoughts to his mind. What she had going for her, most important

1007

of all, was the strength of her love and a profound faith in what she was doing. It had to suffice.

"Soon you'll see the truth implanted in your mind. You'll only remember the truth—not the distorted counterfeit of truth. You will be whole again, Peter, and feel the power of my love—our love—the most vital bond between man and woman."

Pictures began to form in Peter's mind. He saw himself standing at the top of a mountain with arms upflung like a god, making a sacrifice to the heavens. He stood in this powerful pose, nude under the power of a full erection. The picture dissolved and he saw Madelaina as he first met her in Sanlucar de Barramedas. This picture dissolved into one of their countless intimacies aboard the *Mozambique*. As one picture dissolved, another instantly appeared in a montage of vignettes. Every picture, each scene was crystal clear to him, depicting all the sweet, tender, and savage love they'd shared. Some showed the anguish of their pain-filled separations, others, their joy-filled reunions.

All the time she guided him through their hectic and adventurous life, Madelaina made verbal suggestions bringing into focus in his mind only those positive suggestions that embellished his virility. Finally, her repetitious words and pictures had saturated Peter's consciousness to the point she felt was enough for this first session.

Her strong arms slipped around his waist. She helped him to his feet and wrapped a huge terry towel around him to dry him off. In this semi-dreamy state she led him to the waiting bed. He was like putty in her hands, not a shred of resistance thwarted her in her preparations, not a protest escaped his lips.

Once he was on the bed, Madelaina removed her caftan, and standing nude over him, she removed the chamois pouch from her neck and turned it inside out, using every minute particle of the mushroom powder that was left, she allowed it to fall in the area of Peter's genitals.

Slowly she began to massage the powder into the

area of his groin and about his penis as she chanted in a whispering monotone, "Oh, Tolomeo, pray it's enough to make the magic work." She pressed the area of his solar plexus firmly in a circular motion. "Give him the strength he needs," she continued to chant.

"Focus your attention on nothing except my voice. Clear the pictures in your mind, Peter. Think of nothing. Erase every untrue and false picture in your subconscious mind. Only the truth shall set you free. The truth of my love for you—yours for me. You shall no longer be tricked by vain imaginings into believing falsehoods, even if you attempt to plant such seeds they will be uprooted. I come to you as a pure vestal virgin, my love. Only your love will blow the breath of life into me. There has never been anyone before you, nor shall there be anyone after."

Madelaina paused as she began to feel movement in his loins. Before her very eyes his manhood was throbbing, swelling, trying to come to life. Madelaina traced her fingers lightly over the thick scars of his stomach.

"Unleash the strength girded in his loins," she prayed, tears misting her eyes, and grateful for the miracle.

Peter's eyes snapped open as the most exciting feeling of his life was upon him. He could feel life creeping slowly through his body like a powerful unchained force of manhood growing—growing— swelling into a monolith. Too excited to move, all he wanted to do was feel—feel—feel. Desire mounted inside him to such an electrifying crescendo that Peter found himself at a loss as to what to do first. His hands moved to touch her with incredible disbelief in his eyes, to feel her and explore all those familiar places he'd staked his claim on long ago.

And Madelaina's dark, swimming eyes darted quickly to his face.

"Madelaina, Madelaina," he whispered hoarsely. "Is it for real?" He was afraid to look for fear it was all an illusion.

"It's always been for real. You've been blinded for a time, but now you've been gifted with sight."

He moaned softly and drew her close to him and clung tightly to her. Her arms wound about his strong neck and the sweet, burning pressure of his lips on hers fused them together, blotting out everything except for this moment, suspended in all eternity.

"You've returned to me, my love."

"I've never been away," she told him in truth.

In the next few moments, it took superhuman effort for Madelaina, the talented pupil of Thaddeus Oemolot, to do what she had to do. She slipped out of Peter's arms, turned up the lights, and yawned sleepliy. Peter, more in a daze of total confusion than he'd ever been, sat up and blinked his blue eyes hard several times.

"Wheah are ya going, *querida?*"

"Where else after such a fulfilling display of love, *querido?*" She drifted behind bathroom doors and closed them. She could hear his protestations, his quandary. She stood shaking from the exertion, from the force it took to subdue the desire in her own body. She gulped down a glass of water and quickly looked about for a cigarette. Finding one, she lit it and puffed eagerly until she calmed down a bit.

Madelaina panicked when she thought she had six more such sessions to endure before she would let Peter satisfy himself. Dr. Oemolot had warned her. It's possible that he'll get an erection and become so excited at the prospect of performing that he'll summon up the old fears and grow impotent again.

Dios mios! What of Madelaina? How could she endure the overexcitation of nonperforming, she asked herself, gulping more water to off-set the terrible thirst and scratchy dryness in her parched throat.

Madelaina endured. She managed to make Peter believe he had performed when he hadn't, just to bolster his damaged ego. And on the seventh night, Madelaina, after leading Peter back over the same rocky course, to which he responded without the use of mushrooms, marijuana, peyote, or the other hallucinogens she'd used to prepare Peter for the ordeal they'd both face, was ready for the final test.

Prior to this seventh night, Madelaina had taken the initiative, firmly telling Peter to lie back and feel the sensations. On this night, after a week of growing trust, love, and compassion, she was ready to be a woman. And Peter, unaware that he hadn't already been a man many times over, displayed some of his old control and libertine air. He was more like the soldier of fortune she'd met in Europe than at any other time they shared together. It was a good sign.

After a wonderful day spent together, they dined and had a few drinks and listened to a hand-cranked victrola play some unusual records of an opera sung by a star of the Metropolitan, Enrico Caruso.

All this was merely the prelude, and Madelaina began to feel an electrifying excitement as the expectations of what was to come inflamed her senses.

Peter took her hand at some time during that evening. She didn't remember when and didn't care. All that mattered was the overflowing pot at the end of the rainbow. They bathed together and frolicked like children. It was simply marvelous to see Peter, filled with confidence again, without one single doubt in his mind.

Lord, sweet Lord, she prayed. *Let him be whole tonight and forever.*

Only the glow of two large candles flickered in the Roman bath, their reflection multiplied to hundreds as they bounced off the mirrors on four sides and the ceiling. Madelaina was warm, her damp skin glowed in the candlelight. It was quiet, as if all the sound had been turned off. Moisture clung to the green leaves of the plants like a thousand dewdrops, swelling and glistening like diamond gems in the glimmering lights.

Peter lay next to Madelaina on the thick white bear rug next to the marbled tub on the floor. Their hot feverish bodies clung together cohesively as if they could never be pried apart. Peter kissed her lightly, at first, barely touching her lips, which felt like the fluttering touch of a hummingbird's wings. His strong hands traced lightly the contours of her body.

Madelaina ached for him as she'd never ached for him before. His lips nuzzled her neck in such a feathery touch she hardly felt him, but the shiver of excitement he sent through her body was sheer heaven. It was the anticipation of his touch that made her frenzied and feverish.

So much time had passed that she had almost forgotten just how his passion could arouse her. Madelaina's firm round breasts, no longer virginal, had matured and rounded gracefully and now as they grew unbearably swollen and tender to his touch, she felt as if they'd burst wide open. Every nerve in her body came alive and she felt her stomach doing somersaults. She felt as if she were tied on a whirling zephyr to the moon and couldn't stop. Her hands went out instinctively, reaching for him, but Peter placed them firmly at her side.

"It's gonna be like the first time we were together, *querida*. Remain passive so the sensation will heighten, ya heah?'

Madelaina nodded. If she wanted to speak, she couldn't have, her mouth was parched—her throat was without moisture. His seduction and lovemaking had surpassed anything she'd ever experienced. What was happening between them was incredible. His velvety touch between her legs as he traced the fire that surged through her caused involuntary shudders to course through her. She made little animal noises deep in her throat. He spoke honeyed words to her.

"Ah'll nevuh let youah dark brown eyes turn blue evuh again, mah sweet, sweet love," he purred. "The honey from youah treasure pot is dripping sweet, mah love. Ah've waited a long, long time ta taste its sweet nectars." He took one of her cool slender hands and placed it on his tumescence. "Ah've nevuh been so big in all mah born days, *chiquita*. Ah promise ta be gentle to mah little virgin. Trust me, mah darlin'."

"Yes, yes, I trust you, *amado mio*," she managed to whisper through parched and feverish lips. She felt Peter's hands under her, lifting her. Madelaina raised her body to meet his.

"Not yet, mah love. Not yet," he said.

She felt her passion rising, wanting him as she'd never wanted him before. With an increased surge of madness, she wanted to possess every inch of him and never be done with him. She was ready to burst. It was agony. It was ecstasy. It was delirium as she'd never known it. Feeling, without touching, was a sensation she'd never imagined to be possible, but she was wrong. It served to heighten each of the senses separately.

An involuntary gasp shuddered through her. She opened her eyes and stared at their reflection in the overhead mirror, then at either side of them. As the mirrors converged at one point, she could see the reflections of countless Peters and Madelainas and it heightened everything between them.

"Ya little vixen," he whispered hoarsely. "Ah know what yourah tryin' ta do ta me. Youah've turned Seven Moons into a miniature Madama Tarragona's bordello," he purred with a smile in his voice.

He entered his wife slowly as if he were creating a special artwork, like an artist painting a canvas. Every stroke, every movement nearing perfection. He penetrated her deeper and deeper, making no sharp, hard thrusts. Only slow and sensuous movements, deliberate and perfectly controlled, orchestrated her to his will. They both soared higher and higher and just before that moment of climax, Peter took her moist face between his two hands.

"Look into mah eyes, Madelaina. Right inta mah soul. Ah'm about ta pour mah life and love inta ya foah all time." His fiery blue eyes burned into her mind, body, and soul, and Madelaina screamed like a wild animal. From the very balls of her feet to the top of her head, she felt a series of explosions, one after another. Her body convulsed wildly. She could hold back no longer.

"Look inta my eyes, mah sweet *chiquita*. Love me.

1013

Feel me. Open youah succulent lips ta receive me." He leaned in closer to her, lips over hers, eyes staring into hers until they both went soaring into infinity.

Hours later, as dawn broke over eastern skies, Madelaina's eyes opened. At some time during the night they had both moved to the bed. Now, as she lay back in full contentment with the weight of his body still pressing on her as he lay half-asleep, her hands stroked his body lightly just to get used to having him near her. Her thoughts ran rampant as she focused on those who'd made all this possible.

Thadeus Oemolot, you are a genius, I thank you. Thank you, Sigmund Freud. Thank you, Tolomeo, for all you taught me. I am the luckiest woman in the world to have been singled out for such worthwhile teachings. A shudder passed through her, so involuntary she couldn't control it. The movement awakened Peter.

He lifted himself on one elbow, blinked open his eyes, and straddled her body with one of his lean, powerful legs wrapped around her. His free hand traced the firm, erect nipples on her breasts and traveled upward to her lips and ears, where he paused to toy with her glittering golden earrings.

"Oh Madelaina, mah Madelaina of the Seven Moons, ah love ya so much. My life, mah love, mah heart an' soul," he said in his heavily accented and atrocious Spanish. "Ah'll nevuh leave ya again, heah? We'll nevuh leave each other—nevuh!"

"What about Pancho Villa? What if he sends for you?' she asked guilefully.

"Ah won't go," he said adamantly, then he gazed at her through tilted blue eyes the color of a clear morning. "Besides theah are other ways ta fight than on a battlefield."

"Peter?"

"Yes, *querida*."

"What exactly are you scheming now?"

"Me? Why not a thing, *querida*."

Madelaina sat up in bed, turned on the night light, and looked deeply into his merry, telltale eyes.

"Well, Little Fox, ya caught me redhanded. Ah was

lying ta ya. Ah was scheming something. Truly, ah was. Ah can't lie ta ya."

Madelaina lay back, dismayed.

"What ah was scheming is that we both do something ta increase ouah family. Are we both in accord?"

"Perfectly." She sighed contentedly. Off went the light and she reached for him.

"Mah Little Fox," he purred as he felt her hands teasing his manhood.

"Yes, *querido*," she sighed, ecstatically happy.

"Would ya mind or object strenuously if we raise ouah family inside the governor's mansion in El Paso? Or perhaps in Washington, if I became a senator?"

"Governor's mansion? What are you saying?" She sat up in bed again and turned on the light. She stared at him, her hands on her waist, contemplatively.

"Only that ah've tossed mah hat inta the political ring. Ah'm running foah office in the next election," he said sheepishly. "Ah just can't make up mah mind as ta which ah should do, first."

"Oh, Peter," she sighed despondently. "Whatever for?"

"Someone has ta watch ovuh the *jefe*, wouldn't ya say?" he said softly. "Aftuh all, we owe him something. If it wasn't foah him we might never have seen each other again." He reached up behind him, turned off the lights, and embraced her in a tight passionate grip that fairly took her breath away. His lips crushed hers hungrily.

"Make the world go away, my love," she whispered. "Make it go away, *mi amor*."

"Ah will. Ah will, mah Little Fox," he replied hoarsely.

As he spoke those words, Madelaina knew their future was inextricably bound up in the strange destinies of Pancho Villa and Alvaro Obregon.

She had demanded perfection. It had fallen a little short. But she couldn't have been happier. As long as she and Peter could share the future together—she had everything she ever wanted.

Well, nearly everything. But there was still time—for everything.

Epilogue

Chapter 38

Eight Years Later July 23, 1923

Just as Madelaina had promised, Dr. Thaddeus Oemolot received the ten-thousand-dollar grant. He had long since begun the dream of his lifetime. Now it was his turn to reciprocate.

On this day, he and several colleagues, well-known specialists in the field of psychiatric research, stood in the reception line at the dedication of *Clinica Siete Lunas*. Next to this imposing consortium were a half-dozen state dignitaries, the governor of Texas, congressmen, and senators.

Senator Peter Benson had never been so magnificent—so eloquent and a sheer delight to the attending press. Reporters had come from all over the state and Washington to interview him and his wife. It was a well-known fact that Mrs. Benson had no taste for politics and was quite retiring, despite rumors that she'd descended from a long line of conquerors dating from the time of Queen Isabella of Spain. Curious rumors circulated about this unique woman, most prevalent being she had been a *soldadera* in the Mexican Revolution!

Studying her, standing so regal and dignified next to her husband, the reporters knew these rumors to be unfounded and cruel. Why, the very idea that such a genteel and refined woman would demean herself to trudge in the filth and squalor and live among those desert desperados was idiotic. On this day, her day, at the dedication ceremonies of so special a project as a research center for the cure of children's mental diseases, those rumors were about to be ground to a halt.

You never saw a prouder man than Senator Benson as he stood next to his wife, before the imposing complex built on the spectacular site of seven cresent-shaped lakes in the middle of God's country in Amarillo. The senator, a man who had helped solidify relations with Mexico, had become one of the most dominant figures in present day politics. Why, the man could become governor—even president—if he wanted.

Word was he'd tossed his hat in the political ring for the governor's cap a few years back, but he had changed his mind. No one really knew why, but like those other vicious rumors that infiltrated certain pressure groups from time to time, they threatened to expose some dark sinister secrets concerning Mrs. Benson again. Why, you'd think they leave the poor little woman alone.

Look at the humanity in her. The love she contained in her bosom to even donate such a handsome piece of property to mankind. Half the cost of the building and equipment had been funded by her personal wealth, the other half had been raised through various social functions and charity balls, all of which were spearheaded by Mrs. Peter Benson.

After the dedication ceremony, the reporters and guests were taken on a private tour of the buildings at the *Clinica Siete Lunas*. If they were impressed at the outset, they were elated when many notable of the medical consortium spoke their personal views and praises of Mrs. Benson's dedication to the somewhat intimidating field of psychiatry. No one seemed to know why she was this devoted.

The ceremonies had ended, the ribbons were cut, the power was turned on, and the dream of a lifetime for many dedicated people was about to begin. Reporters were departing, their copy still hot in their hands, with a rash of photo negatives to be developed for press time.

Driving toward the cluster of people, Paco Jimenez gunned the motor of the open touring car, waving his

1017

arms wildly, causing the car to careen back and forth off the road. Riding at his side, hanging on for dear life was the alluring mestiza, Lola, heavy with child for the fifth time. Once Paco stopped that crazy machine, he jumped from the driver's seat calling, "*Senador!* Señora Benson!"

He removed his western hat and swiped at the dust on his pants.

"Telegram, *Senador*." He handed Peter Benson the wire and wiped the perspiration from his somber face. His eyes avoided direct contact with both Peter and Madelaina, and he stared at the tips of his dusty boots.

Peter opened the envelope and stared at the contents for several moments. He handed it to his wife and stared off at the last of the crowd departing in their vehicles. Madelaina searched her husband's face for a telltale sign. Her eyes dropped to the printed paper and she read: *At eight o'clock on this day, Francesco Pancho Villa was brutally assassinated in a political plot by known parties. The Centaur is dead.—Lucita Arango.*

Madelaina glanced at the somber face of her handsome husband. She folded the wire and tucked it into her handbag. Peter took her hand in his, placed it over his arm, and escorted her to the awaiting auto. "It's hard to imagine General Villa no longer with us. After three years of peace in which the *jefe* ended his role as protector of Mexico, he deserved better than assassination," he said.

"Yes, he deserved much better," she replied wistfully. She turned to him, pausing as she did. "Why, Peter? Why wouldn't they leave him alone? Are there still some who considered him a threat to Mexico?"

Peter slipped a hand inside his coat pocket and handed her another wire. "Ah didn't show this ta ya earlier because ah wanted this day ta be youah triumph with *Clinica Siete Lunas*. Since you asked the question, ah'll let ya be the judge, mah deah."

Madelaina hurriedly opened the second. Her eyes fell to the printed words: *In a revolt against the Carranza*

1018

regime, United States fully supports the Obregon regime. Alvaro Obregon is now president of Mexico.

Madalaina gasped. Their eyes met in knowing silence. They walked the few steps to their car and got in the rear seat, their driver waited until Pilar and their three sons, Alejandro, William, and Peter Jr, got into the next car with Paco and Lola Jimenez before starting the motor. He wheeled the auto around in a full circle and drove off toward Seven Moons.

"How long will it be before Obregon is felled by an assassin's bullet?" she asked her husband softly, tearing up the wire. She scattered the bits to the four winds.

"That, mah deah Little Fox, is a question only time will answer."

Another tumultuous romantic novel
by Patricia Matthews,
author of the multi-million
copy national bestseller,
LOVE'S AVENGING HEART

Love's Wildest Promise

P40-047 $1.95

Sarah Moody was a lady's maid in a wealthy London home. But suddenly her quiet sheltered world was turned upside down when she was abducted and smuggled aboard a ship bound for the colonies. Its cargo—whores to satisfy the appetites of King George's soldiers in New York. Was Sarah destined to become one of these women? Or would she find the man she was searching for, the man who would help her to fulfill Love's Wildest Promise.

If you can't find this book at your local bookstore, simply send the cover price, plus 25¢ for postage and handling to:

Pinnacle Books
275 Madison Avenue, New York, New York 1001